PENGUIN BOOKS

FIRE IN BEULAH

Rilla Askew is the author of *Strange Business*, a collection of stories, and *The Mercy Seat*, nominated for the PEN/Faulkner Award and the Mountains and Plains Booksellers Award and winner of the Western Heritage Award and the Oklahoma Book Award. She divides her time between the San Bois Mountains of southeastern Oklahoma and upstate New York.

Praise for *Fire in Beulah*

"A haunting, engrossing portrait of two families—one white, one black— whose lives are woven together and then shattered. . . . Askew's final hundred pages are a cinematic, apocalyptic denouement, as all the characters are swept up in the terrible racial tidal wave."
—*The Washington Post*

"In Rilla Askew's tinderbox of a novel, racial distrust runs deep as marrow in the Oklahoma of the 1920s. Black and white Oklahomans eye one another with deeply embedded trepidation, moving like partners in an uneasy dance where they think they know each other too well, but don't really know each other at all. . . . What clearly compels Askew is that indelible stain on our psyche, the great American dilemma of race that vexes us still. . . . Askew nails as well as any author in recent memory the claustrophobia of racism, the devastation of hate and the way it sucks all the air out of the world."
—*The Boston Globe*

"The novel moves back and forth between the worlds of its two central characters, one white and one black, in order to explore the devastating consequences of the powerful let loose upon the powerless. . . . *Fire in Beulah* recalls and recreates a devastating if largely forgotten historical event in order to explore the awful consequences of human failure."
—*Chicago Tribune*

"Superb . . . with great passion and conviction, Askew has turned the story of the riot into a work of compelling fiction that is nevertheless true to the basic facts of an American tragedy." —*The Baltimore Sun*

W9-BJT-926

"Askew has crafted a gripping drama, infusing this novel with the rich details of human dilemmas. . . . There are no pat machinations here . . . *Fire in Beulah* touches on the substance of morality and the composition of the human spirit, underscoring the fact that our lives transcend perceived boundaries." —*Black Issues Book Review*

"An unflinching, yet redemptive story of America . . . *Fire in Beulah* delves deeply into the troubled history of blacks and whites in America, emerging with scenes so poignant and painfully rendered as to inspire comparisons with the greatest chroniclers of the race line that snakes through our history: Ellison, Baldwin, Morrison." —*The St. Louis Riverfront Times*

"A devastating story of greed, violence, and destruction . . . Askew's novel is riveting and remarkably relevant." —*The Portland Oregonian*

"A fine novel to open our eyes to a history that's more complex than we usually believe . . . many readers may be shocked at the setting, the time, and the violence of feelings, assuming racial hatred was confined to the South." —*The Denver Post*

"In an arresting examination of race and heritage, Askew mixes historical fact with compelling fiction. . . . [Askew's] prose—rich, leisurely, graceful—engages all the senses and encloses the reader in a bell jar of heat, hate, and budding violence." —*Publishers Weekly*

"Askew is skilled at characterization and description, and the reader viscerally feels the anger, evil, fear, anxiety, tension, grief and love of the characters." —*Library Journal*

Fire
in
Beulah

RILLA ASKEW

PENGUIN BOOKS

PENGUIN BOOKS
Published by the Penguin Group
Penguin Group (USA) Inc., 375 Hudson Street, New York, New York 10014, U.S.A.
Penguin Group (Canada), 90 Eglinton Avenue East, Suite 700, Toronto, Ontario,
Canada M4P 2Y3 (a division of Pearson Penguin Canada Inc.)
Penguin Books Ltd, 80 Strand, London WC2R 0RL, England
Penguin Ireland, 25 St Stephen's Green, Dublin 2, Ireland
(a division of Penguin Books Ltd)
Penguin Group (Australia), 250 Camberwell Road, Camberwell, Victoria 3124,
Australia (a division of Pearson Australia Group Pty Ltd)
Penguin Books India Pvt Ltd, 11 Community Centre, Panchsheel Park,
New Delhi – 110 017, India
Penguin Group (NZ), 67 Apollo Drive, Rosedale, North Shore 0632,
New Zealand (a division of Pearson New Zealand Ltd)
Penguin Books (South Africa) (Pty) Ltd, 24 Sturdee Avenue, Rosebank,
Johannesburg 2196, South Africa

Penguin Books Ltd, Registered Offices: 80 Strand, London WC2R 0RL, England

First published in the United States of America by Viking Penguin,
a member of Penguin Group (USA) Inc. 2001
Published in Penguin Books 2002

10 9 8

Copyright © Rilla Askew, 2001
All rights reserved

PUBLISHER'S NOTE
This is a work of fiction. Names, characters, places, and incidents are either the product of the
author's imagination or are used fictitiously, and any resemblance to actual persons, living or dead,
business establishments, events, or locales is entirely coincidental.

THE LIBRARY OF CONGRESS HAS CATALOGED THE HARDCOVER EDITION AS FOLLOWS:
Askew, Rilla.
Fire in Beulah / Rilla Askew.
p. cm.
ISBN 0-670-88843-5 (hc.)
ISBN 978-0-14-200024-3 (pbk.)
I. Title
PS3551.S545 F57 2001
813'.54—dc21   00-043366

Printed in the United States of America
Set in Bulmer MT
Designed by Nancy Resnick

For Travis
and Marlene
and Ebonyrose

Acknowledgments

My gratitude, always, to my husband, Paul Austin, first reader, final critic; and to my sister Ruth, who receives all. Friends and family members have sent articles and clippings about the Tulsa Race Riot through the years, and I appreciate all of them. Warm thanks to my agent, Jane Gelfman, who asks the right questions, and to my editor, Paul Slovak, for all their good work. A special word of gratitude for my friend and teacher, the late Dr. Nancy Vunovich, who in the months of her final illness read these pages with enthusiasm, interest, miraculous patience. For the facts of the riot I've used a number of sources, and have drawn particularly from Scott Ellsworth's seminal work, *Death in a Promised Land: The Tulsa Race Riot of 1921*; Eddie Faye Gates' gathering of oral histories, *They Came Searching: How Blacks Sought the Promised Land in Tulsa*; Hannibal B. Johnson's study of the Greenwood district, *Black Wall Street*; and the contemporary eyewitness account of the riot by Mary E. Jones Parrish, *Race Riot 1921: Events of the Tulsa Disaster*. Finally, a note of sorrowful indebtedness: although the characters here are entirely fictional or, in the case of historical persons, fictionally portrayed, the incidents of racial violence are all real; they took place almost exactly as described, perpetrated by Americans, on Americans, in this promised land.

PART ONE

Wind

Near the Deep Fork River
south of Bristow, I.T.
September
1900

A high, hot wind had been blowing from the south for seven days. It
blew morning and evening and did not lay at night as it should but
cried and fingered at the windows till the sun rose, and then it went on
blowing. A constant wind, an unremitting wind, it did not gust or fall but
blew one monotonous gritty speed. Water could not be kept in the
troughs for the animals but evaporated almost as quickly as it was
pumped and had to be pumped anew each time the cattle started bawling.
Washing on the line did not flap and dance but held a steady northward
angle and dried bone-dry in less than twenty minutes. The older Whiteside girls complained their lips and cheeks were cracking. Their mother
stayed indoors, though it was more miserably hot inside than out, because
she feared the wind would suck the life from her unborn child.

She prowled from windowsill to windowsill in her tiny room, touched
the rolled rags laid end to end across the cracks to hold back the dust, and
pressed them against the openings, tighter. She paused, her hands entwined beneath her belly, stared out the glass at the bluestem grasses
bowed and bending toward her, the stunted blackjacks (those ugly trees)
hunched close to earth like dwarves or gnomes, their gnarled fingers
reaching earthward: dear God, how she despised them! Beyond the jacks
the brooding Deep Fork River crawled west to east, its meandering path
made plain by the paler bark of river trees, the cottonwoods and syca-

mores, within the arc of hickories. Rachel raised her eyes and searched the sky for the moon's pocked face. For a week she'd watched it growing full, swelling as her belly swelled, rising a little later each day to hang above the trees, the blanched sky bleeding through its very features. The daymoon frightened her. For all its grinning, it seemed a malevolent thing: a ragged oval, frayed a little on one side, but soft and permeable, and growing in its porous membrane, like a great ruptured reptile egg, giving forth that cursed wind. Her eyes turned left, and right, straight up above, but the empty sky showed only windspun dust in ruddy light. On the north side of the house the motherless calf was bawling. Lord, couldn't one of the girls go feed that thing, or knock it in the head and leave it for the crows to eat, or something, anything, just shut up, shut up that useless bawling. Rachel eased over to the door and yanked the knotted pull-rag. The door slapped back against the wall. She called down the stairs, "Estaleen! Go feed that thing!" The woman turned, treaded heavily across the roseprint rug toward the southern window.

In the crowded downstairs parlor room, her eldest daughter Estaleen gazed round the room at the frowning faces of her sisters. Each kept a downcast eye upon her embroidery hoop or darning needle or crochet hook, but for the baby Kay playing by herself on the rag-rug floor, and the very middle of the seven girls, Aletha Jean, who stood gazing out the window.

"Lethajean!" the eldest called, though the girl was but five feet away. "Go feed Pet." She turned her face down to the sampler in her lap, but her eyes cut slantwise at her sister's back. Aletha Jean ignored her. Estaleen called again, "Lethajean! Go feed that thing!" Still the girl stood motionless at the window.

"I will!" piped up Winema, the next-to-youngest, a sweet-faced, wiry, amber child of eight, but Estaleen, who was mother to them all, said, "You will not. Letha, go do like Mother said."

Without turning her eyes from the dust-smoked prairie, Aletha said, "Told *you*, not *me*."

"*I'm* telling you," the eldest said, and swept her mothering gaze around the room to see if this rebellion might be joined from another corner. But blond Prudence met her gaze in timid complicity, and pale Dorcas kept her eyes on the embroidery hoop upon her knee, and redheaded Jody, who, at twelve, was hardly a year younger than Aletha Jean and therefore especially resentful of her dreamy, high-and-mighty sister, glared at the dark-haired middle daughter's back with a vehemence outshining Estaleen's own, so that the eldest's pique was in fact enhanced, and she snapped in exact imitation of their mother's former power, "Aletha Jean Whiteside, don't make me have to get up off this chair. Go right this minute and give that calf its ninny."

Aletha continued staring out the window. The calf's bawls came from the corral in a piteous honking wail, the sound so loud it rose above the wind and circled the clapboard house, came in through the shut-tight windows. It had been a fortnight since the old brindle cow tore her bag on a barbed-wire fence, ripped one tit from end to end, and the infection had set in, clabbering her milk right in the bag, the tit so sore, oozing yellow, that she'd kicked the calf away and wouldn't let it suck. The girls' father had tried to turn the calf to another cow, but none would take it, so he'd penned it up and fashioned a teatbag from an old cleaned-out cow stomach and fed the calf one morning before he left the house on his sorrel mare, riding north and east to Bristow. When their father didn't come home the first night and the calf stood in the pen bawling long and weak and pitiful, it had been Estaleen who'd announced that she would save the red calf on her own. She'd gone to the barn at dawn, at noon, and dusk, and nursed the calf for almost a week, and the calf had fallen in love with her and followed her around the pen like a starving pup.

But then the hot southwind had come (though not yet their father), and the days blew dry and full of dust, the burning coin of sun cracked Estaleen's lips, made the buttermilk washes she used on her face to fade the freckles entirely useless, and for the past few days she'd parceled out every one of her outside chores among her younger sisters. In all fairness, if fairness could be had in that household of female wants and needs, it was Aletha's turn to feed the calf, but Aletha was the orneriest of the girls and could be made to do very little on the best of days, and this day was a bad one. She traced the distant trees with her eyes, saying to herself, *Y'all can go to aitch-ee-double-ell.* She had no intention of doing what her sister said. She hated everything there was to hate about that sucking calf. Oh, she'd watched it many times, had stood outside the gate and watched the creature's thick-tongued slobber, the frothing milk trickling out both sides of its mouth while it sucked and pulled at the bag in her sister's arms, its long red tail a-twitching. She hated the way it followed Estaleen from one end of the corral to the other, nudging, bawling, long after the milk was gone, and she cringed to think of its nuzzling snout prying at her private self. The calf bawled and bawled but Aletha's eyes never left the line of river trees; she stood with her jaw clenched and her spine as straight as a hoe handle. *No way on earth,* she thought, *in hell, or under God's blue heaven. I ain't going out there.*

Winema, her heart breaking with the poor calf's distress, begged to be allowed to go feed it, but the older girls told her to hush, and shot their daggered stares at Aletha's back, until she turned at last and faced her sisters. Six pairs of lightbrown eyes, even the baby Kay's by this time, were focused plain upon her. Aletha's thoughts fell self-consciously to her bony arms and washboard chest, but the sisters did not see. She felt it then, as she felt it always: her own worthless invisibility, and with that useless sense came a rush of sorrow for herself. *Ain't one of them can see me,* she thought. *That damn slobbery calf out back gets more attention.* And then, wordless in her mind, she saw her mother prowling the narrow room upstairs, absorbed within her swollen self, and Aletha's self-pity was overswept by anger. Immediately she pushed away from the windowsill and flounced across the room without a glance at her sisters; she stomped through the kitchen to the porch, swiped up the full milk bucket and the disgusting teatbag, and stormed out the back door.

She paused, stricken, on the wooden steps. In the west the sun floated above the lip of earth in a fiery ball; in the east, the moon was rising. Its forehead lifted swollen, full, above the horizon, reflecting the crimson of the setting sun. The sky north and east and west and straight up above was clear of clouds, depthless, wrong in color—saffron, olive, berylline— and exquisite beyond all telling. For an instant she took within herself the strange sky, the reddened synchronous moon and sun, stood trembling on the brink of change: almost, the girl was transformed by the prairie's turning beauty. But Aletha was, in more ways than either understood, her mother's daughter, and in the next instant she frowned against the spitting dust, drew her eyes away from the skies, marched down the steps and out across the pasture.

The barn sat on a northwest rise behind the house, so that Aletha had to angle through the gale to reach it. Flax-colored homespun billowing, brown braids snapping, lifted to her very toes sometimes, Aletha fought and floated through the wind to the small corral beside the barn. She reached between the slats to pull the latch, and then had to fight to keep the gate from being torn from her hands by the wind; in the struggle the bucket tipped and sloshed milk on her skirt, darkened the swirling, manure-spat ground.

She said aloud, "Damn it. See?" as if there were a witness who might, now convinced, agree with her how wronged she'd been. Looking down at the greasy milk streaks on the homespun, thinking she'd have to scrub till her hands were raw with lye to get them out, she squeezed past the gate, shoved it shut with all her strength; she squinted toward the far side of the pen, where the calf stood with its back to the wind. The first trembling hint of fear nudged up within her. The calf's head was lifted and cocked, nostrils flared; it had heard the clang of bucket and creak of gate, and now waited in the wind like a blind thing, all senses homed on one awareness only. Without signal or warning, the red calf turned and, leaning sideways, began to trot toward her.

The little thing was stark-ribbed, knob-kneed, solid red (the ferocious color of the setting sun), and as poor as any calf might be and breathe, but in Aletha's eyes it could as well have been a rutting bull. The urgency of its coming scared her. Pushed northward by the wind, yet hungering east toward its dinner, the calf came loping, dancing, bawling, prancing, sometimes purely cockawhoop sideways, rapidly toward her. The milk pail fell from Aletha's hand, she whirled around to the gate, and couldn't get the gate to open. Nor could she feel the slosh of milk on her skirt and shoes, the sting of windflung dirt upon her face, the lashing whips of her own two braids—but only the rising burn and dark of fear inside her body. The gate's latch was jammed, and though the girl clawed at it and was truly terrified, there was at work a far more compelling force than rusted iron and wind, or the beauty of the prairie sunset sky: in those frantic seconds the girl's soul thrilled to the dark sweet rush of danger.

The calf shoved its snout against her skirt. He smelled the milk; he knew the scent and shape of the teatbag beneath her arm; he knew the smell of young human female and claimed the smell as owed him. He pressed against her with the full weight of his bony flanks, demanding, seeking, pushing, and Aletha, thinking herself in actual danger, thinking her terror a terrible thing and not the delicious, alive sensation that, in truth, it was to her, began to scream.

Inside the house, her sisters' working hands fell still; twelve pale brown eyes stared wide across the parlor. The baby Kay, holding to the hassock, her bouncing stopped by the curdling scream, collapsed her face and began to cry. It was this, not Aletha's screams, that finally roused the mother.

Rachel lay on the bed upstairs in a stuporous, halfwaking dream, numbed by the ceaseless groan of wind, pressed into the muslin sheet by the moist weight of her own body. She heard the bawls of her youngest child and tried to ignore it, as one tries to dismiss a mosquito's whine when it hums into the depths of sleep, but at last she rolled sideways, lifted her terrible weight, and placed her swollen feet upon the floor. She made her way to the door and pulled the knotted rag, started down the steep pine stairs. It wasn't until she came into the parlor, where the toddler girl had fallen to the rug, wailing, and the other five were staring wide-eyed and silent at one another, that she recognized the distant terrified shrieks as something real and not the residue of her own unhappy dreams. The others looked up in fear, for Aletha's screams were horrible to hear, and the older girls, at least, believed she was being murdered. The mother lifted Kay and made a move to put her on her hip, but with her belly so far advanced and wide, there was no hip for the toddler's thighs to clutch, and so she dropped her, still sobbing, into Estaleen's lap and turned, as in a dream, and went rolling side to side through the open doorway, the kitchen, the cooling porch, and didn't pause when she stepped outside and lost her breath for an instant to the sucking wind, never looked right or left to see the full moon rising as the red sun set, but headed straight up across the pasture.

She made a broad target for the wind, but her very bigness anchored her to the earth so that the wind became, in fact, more aid than hindrance, buoying her gently north. The rise, however, held her back. Its slope would have seemed slight enough to a woman who did not bear such weight, whose lungs were not pushed up and crowded against her heart, but to Rachel Whiteside the slant was steep as the pine steps to her upstairs room, and a thousand times as far. She climbed, one loglike leg before the other, her labored breathing drowning, almost, her daughter's screams.

The girl's mind had raced past the first rush of fear, past panic, to pure, unbridled hysteria. She screamed, feeling for the first time the rough post oak beneath her palms, the calf's warm breath through the cotton skirt, the warm, sticky milk upon her legs. She screamed, seeing with quickened eyes the serpentine color of the sky. She saw the moon swimming, pure yolk yellow now, above the dark horizon; and nearer, in a closing circle on the rim of earth, blackjack limbs like gnarled screams against the brightened sky. She smelled manure and dust, the calf's sweet hide, a thousand autumn pollens released like sperm, the pecan trees in the distant grove. She smelled her mother, heard her mother's breath and groans. Aletha began then to scream in earnest. She screamed for all her imagined loss and grief, for having wanted, wanted all her life, and never got; for being her own private self within the world. And then she felt her mother's hands. For a fleeting moment the girl knew gladness; she surrendered to the rough skin of her mother's palms, felt their warmth encase her own, and though the calf still pushed against her hips and bawled, Aletha ceased her struggle.

She sagged, deflated against the gate, felt herself shoved back, her wrists clamped within the cuffs of her mother's hands. The big belly pushed through the opening, and then her mother was inside the pen and the teatbag was on the ground beneath her mother's skirt and the calf was struggling to get at it. Her mother slapped her across the mouth, let go her hands, and Aletha had only the space of a heartbeat to feel the bafflement and pain and, quickly, a righteous flare of rage against this clear injustice, because the red calf then, consumed with its own frustration, turned fully away from mouthing at the mother's hem and whipped its head around, up once, and down, and kicked Rachel with all its hungry might right in her swollen belly.

There came a little sound, like *hoomph,* like sudden air expelled. The mother did not cry out but released that unwilled sound and stood perfectly still on her leaden legs. The calf came at her hem again, grabbed the teatbag in his mouth and tossed it up into the wind, and trotted over to where it landed. The mother stared down at her body. Her whole belly was shoved to the side. Unbelieving, she reached to stroke her stomach where it ought to be, high and huge before her. Her hands fell, lost. The wind pressed her skirt against her so that there appeared, clearly visible though in all ways unreal, the outline of the unborn babe like an overstuffed saddlebag slung at her side, riding low, halfway round toward her kidneys. Beneath her feet a wet spot spread, darkening the red dust.

Late in the night, as the mother lay groaning her terrible labor, the wind changed. Near midnight it fell still, and for some several hours the prairie around the Whiteside homestead waited, stunned with sudden silence. The snarled clutch of blackjacks on the rise, the eerie Deep Fork bottoms, too, were suspended in stillness, and the moon, high and small and very white, cast perfect shadows. The shadows were still. But at three o'clock— the human hour of guilt and the mind's repetition, the hour of human fear—the wind returned. It had shifted shape and become a new entity. It swept down from the north, and in its scent was no salt sea breath but the smell of deep blue, of ice and indigo: the roiling breath of the great northern plain. Not steady now but a spitting, cold, fretful thing, it rose and fell, gusted and died, and gusted again, and pushed before it high, tarry clouds that tumbled between earth and the face of the moon. On the prairie, the moon's shadows chased one another.

Inside the lone clapboard house there were only two whose senses were quick to this change. Aletha Jean knew the moment the wind ceased, and in the hours between the wind's death and resurrection, she suffered. For her, there was a kinship between the dying wind and her mother's travail in the small bedroom at the top of the stairs. She thought this strange, noisome labor had somehow sucked away the wind's life as it tried to suck the life from her mother—and both, she believed, were caused by her own selfish terror.

The other in the Whiteside home whose senses grew alert when the wind stopped, who listened and knew it would come again moments before it roared down from the north, was the Creek woman who'd been fetched from Iron Post to help with the twisted birth.

Wind come like this, come down like something blue and fierce—

Tell me which is it you want then, the wind or the little whitegirl. You the one talking about the wind, I don't concern myself with none of it. All right. Here then.

The little redheaded whitechild come, face pinched up like a fox face and white as that moon yonder, she's so scared. She say, My mama got kicked by a calf and she's dying. It was near on to first dark. I went and told Bluford I was going and he just nod his head, even though I hadn't seen him for two weeks because he'd just got back. He was the best thing. I believe he was the best of the three of them, though they each was good men, but Bluford was the gentlest. Oh, he had a touch. I thought I'd die when he died, but I didn't, I just went on and lived and come down to Boley finally and married Tim—

Well, what you want me in here for? Ain't that like whitefolks, think I got time to drop by and tidy up their story. Think I don't have my own life to tell. You never seen my daddy black as pitch and smarter than any of them allowed, a horse trader deluxe, and they whipped him for that, I know it was mainly on account of that, and that's how come him to carry my mama to this Boley town and quit that Deep Fork country. You never seen my mama no taller than a fencepost and poor as sin and better in her heart than your idea of God, and I don't guess you'd know them if you did see them, much less care. All right, all right, I'm here now, let's go on.

That woman lied. She called me Creek, and I am part Creek, but you look how this colored blood dominate. My daddy was a black man, and my mama was part colored, part Creek, part French, and she was born on the Trail to a slave mother. I'm a Creek freedwoman is what I am. You hear that word? Freed. From slavery. It wasn't my Creek blood got that name. Make up your own mind why that woman lie. But, yes, my husband Bluford Tiger was a Creek-and-Seminole man, and we lived on his allotment up toward Iron Post. I loved them people. It's been many a year since I lived around Indians—and I don't go around whitefolks at all, I stay right here in this good colored town, try to, anyhow, till some ghost woman come around and drag me out to try and make me talk—but I always did claim Indian, married me two of them and loved their families like my own, and not just because of my own mama, not because it come down in me so I got good hair and this pretty mahogany-color skin, but because I known them in my heart and eat with them and went to stomps and danced, and my mother had it in her from her mixed-blood dad. So I was, what? Thirty then. I never had no children, that was the main cross the Lord give me through my life to bear, so in their place, in them unborn children's place, He give me three good husbands and a gift to heal, and that's what I was doing then.

So. The little foxface whitegirl come, and I wrapped my head and went, and yes, we walked through that wind and I don't know what you got on your mind about that. A seven-day wind ain't nothing new in this country, and that quick change ain't nothing new. But I heard when it died along about the middle of the night, and I raised up my head, say to myself, Bluford's ax finally done its work. Quick as he got back from Okmulgee that morning Bluford set that ax in a tree stump with the cutting edge facing south, and I ask him what he do that for and he say it's to cut the wind. So that's what I was thinking in that whitelady's bedroom, I's thinking Bluford's ax finally done its work. But we jumping way ahead. You better let me back up.

I followed the little girl up the stairs and see that mama crouched naked on the floor, holding to the bedspread like she get down and can't get up and got no ambition to try. Bloody water leaking all over that nice roseprint rug. First thing, I got to get on my knees and pray. I never see such a twisted-around kind of mess. Ain't no human help for *that,* I tell myself, and I pray, Lord God have mercy Thy will be done. The whole bunch of whitegirls done trooped up the stairs behind me, I gets up off my knees, turn to shoo them back down. Give my scissor to the little foxface girl, tell her to boil it up good, though I didn't have a hope in the world that baby's going to get down that way. Whitewoman's insides must've looked like stopped-up plumbing, though I guess I hadn't seen plumbing pipes up till then, but in my memory that's how it look. Tell that little fox-face girl, say, 'Fore you bring that scissor back up, y'all send to Bristow for the doctor. Tell him to come quick. I figured we going to have to cut that woman sure. I didn't believe she's going to last till somebody get to Bristow and back, but I sent anyhow, and proceed on with getting that woman up on the bed. She weighed a ton, but I was a big woman myself then, and I just about hoisted her up, say, You git on up here now and lay like this. Propped her sideways on the pillows, that baby raised up like a boil out her side. She one of these women never let scared come on her face. Her belly twisted plumb around to her backside nearly, and her face just look like she's mad. All that come out of her mouth be this low grunting moan.

Lord, that room stink. Any birthroom do, but this one was different and worse, and I lay that onto that stopped-up plumbing and so much blood. There's been just a few times when I seen so much blood. All births is bloody, make no mistake, they completely violent events, and I done see and smelt plenty, cut more than a few babies out their mamas' bellies, and that sure do make some blood, but this one was different, I believe because that woman bleeding way up high somewhere. Time it get down through them twisted pipes, the blood done start to clot and stink. Well, I expect for sure she's going to die and that baby going to die, but there's nothing for it but just work on her and pray that doctor get down from Bristow before she give up the ghost. She don't want to let me touch her. She flat snarl at me any time I get close. I know I got to rub the baby around and down where it belong. Looks to me like she been carrying high anyhow, but you couldn't say a thing for sure, time that calf got done. I spend maybe the first hour moving slow, talking smooth and soft, sneaking in close, same as with a injured animal if you don't want to get bit.

Birth's a slow, tedious thing sometime, unless you talking about an old-timer going lickety split, which she ain't generally going to send for the birthwoman anyhow—but most times you just got to get into that rhythm. You can't be expecting to rush it along, even when you think they going to die. So I was used to moving slow and waiting on God and the baby's time. I was breathing with the woman, I's trying to love her, because you do best to love them, I already known that then, know it better now. But it's hard to love somebody you never laid eyes on till you see her crouched down naked on her roseprint rug, plus which, she's white—though I did not yet have so much bitterness in my heart as come later, because I had not yet seen out of whitefolks what I seen before it was all done, but I finally coax that woman to let me rub her belly. You got to do like this, see: you got to breathe with her while her pains coming, you got to talk to her while you breathing, say like this: Here it come, mama, ride the top of it, ride with it, yes, mama, easy, mama, eeeeasy, eeeeasy, and so. That's the same for any. At midnight the southwind die, and I remembers Bluford's ax, say, Un-huh, ax done its work, and me and the woman just keep on in that time outside of time. I'm praying for the Lord to deliver her safe, plus that doctor to hurry up and get down from Bristow.

Windchange come along way up in the night. Afterwhile I adds another prayer, say please God for Bluford to go out and turn his ax around, because this new wind bringing in something fierce feel like it want to freeze the blood in my bones. That whole house is shaking. Windows rattling, upstairs shuddering, floor just shivering underneath my feet. I look up and see her then, not the little foxface but a darkhaired middling girl, two long brown braids, she's standing on one foot beside the door, got her other foot wrapped behind at the ankle, her hand crammed in her mouth, and that girl is shaking the same way as the house. She's bleeding. I mean, she bleeding just like her mama, out herself all over the rug. Look like she got her monthly but she don't know it. Long bloody streaks down her skirt, little red plops on that roseprint rug. I say, Sister, there's enough blood in this room already take Moses to part it. You best go clean yourself up. Girl look down at herself then, and she do what I certainly do not expect. She pull her fist out her mouth and start to laugh. Laughing like a crazy child. I walk over and tug on the pull-rag, that little door slap back against the wall, and, Lord, the northwind do in that moment rise up and wail. I nudge that girl out the door, but not before I hear the whole rest of them girls downstairs wailing, like to sound near as loud and boiling as the wind, and I thinks to myself, I have never seen such a pitiful house. I turn back to the whitewoman, but she don't know anything about it. She all turned in on herself, like any laboring woman got to do. Everything settle down nice and quiet then, the woman moaning regular, and that is all, because, for her, time and everything stop. The same so for me.

You don't know how it go. Time don't run in a line forward but spiral around and dark and up, till change come, and you don't know because you in it to breathe it and live it, and only outside of birth and dying do you think it's some other way. Woman let me in close now, she in no condition to stop me, and I touch hold of her belly but I can't tell if the baby's living or dead or where its head is, because that belly twisted around so, and I know I got to put my hand inside to feel it, but she ain't about to let me, she still sensible down there, and I think then it's going to be a long time longer, because her pains stay the same, not closer, not spiraling for the change coming, and I just hold on and touch her on the outside when she let me, rub her lightly, rub her and chant real soft and pray that doctor come up the stairs.

Keep on, keep on, and afterwhile I see it's getting close to daylight and that woman's pains don't get no closer together. Then, seem like they getting farther apart. Then for true and certain they coming farther apart, you could piece a quilt-top nearly in between how far they come. And that doctor ain't arrived yet. Window curtains get light. The woman begin to wake out herself, and she look up at me and see me, which scare me plenty, because I don't think she ever before that moment known I was there. That's when I finally see it on her face. She scared. She and me both scared. I pray to Jesus it don't show on my face like it do on hers.

That woman ain't got pain one. You can see it. She's not laboring, she just sweating. She put her lips together, quit groaning, quit with any kind of sound. She way past mad, her eyes just nothing but fear. Well, you know labor don't up and quit like that, not for a loosed-up practiced woman like this one, got children strung like seedcorn all over the house. Labor pains don't quit unless something is mighty bad wrong, guaranteed. I thinks to myself, That child sure enough dead now, and I guess she know it. Maybe it's been dead a long time, maybe that's what stink so.

But I watch the woman's face awhile, and I see stopped pains ain't what put the terror in it. Might be the signal but it ain't the cause. The cause is inside that woman's belly, and that's what make it so bad. You think I don't know? Listen. Me, here, Iola Bloodgood Bullet Tiger Long, I have seen every type of human fear. I seen Laura Nelson and her two children dragged out the Okemah jail in 1911. Yes, ma'am, I will tell it. Again and again I'll tell it. Them whitefolks hanged Laura Nelson and her little boy off a bridge west of town, left that baby crying by the side of the road. I was witness to that, I don't care if folks do lie and say it ain't happened. Stood right there in the alley, me and six other womens from the church, watched them carry her up Main Street, she's screaming—Lord, them screams be in my dreams for eternity—trying to get loose, get hold of her children. She know what's going to happen, we all know, and her fear different from the little boy's fear, different from us churchwomen's, and I seen all three kinds. I seen the kind when you afraid to lift your head, not because somebody's going to do you body-harm but because they going to do you soul-harm, because they going to shame you, make you feel like a worm, and you more scared of that than a licking, so you can't find strength to move. I'm not talking about I felt it, though the Lord do know I have, I'm talking about *seeing* it, how you look at it and see it and know what kind of fear. I have seen children terrified of their fathers, grown men terrified of witches, people terrified of each other in all kind of ways. And I tell you this: that whitewoman's fear been different from any other, and I'll tell you how. She ain't afraid of something coming at her from the outside. Even them that's dying and know they dying without Jesus, they afraid of something outside theirself, which is Satan or Hell or God's Judgment or pure blank empty nothing. But this woman scared of something inside her own skin. My whole life there's been just one other time I see the kind of fear like I seen on that whitewoman, and that was in Wetumka in 1907, time I see Curtis Monday on Main Street, drunk as seven lords, screaming about he got tarantulas crawling out his knees.

The woman is hunched up on her nether side sort of, her right side—she can't lay on her back nor any other way on account of how that baby slung around so—and she's peeking over her great big titty, down around and back, like she's looking for some mess somebody told her been smeared on her. Face so white it's gone to clear nearly, you can see every blue vein in her neck, see little red threads popping underneath the skin. Right then it look like she fixing to go mad—I don't mean mad angry, I mean mad loco insane. She take in to moaning, but not about pain, them moans ain't about body-hurt, they about the lowest sorry you ever believe. Reach back with both hands, touch that swelling like it's not a baby but a blob of something too terrible to talk about that somebody take and smear upon her. Whispering to herself. I can't hear what she say. But something happen to her face, it go from fear to something entirely different, run through madness and sorry right quick, like she got no time to pause with them, they not important enough to tarry, and she lean over with some kind of terrible grunt and spit out the side of her mouth, spit blood and some pieces of teeth off the side of the bed, down on that ruined rug. When she come up, her face covered with the purest—I don't know what you call it—*aim-to-do-it* I ever see. She saying the Lord's name over and over, in all its magnifications.

Well, lady, I taken to praying to Jesus outloud, say, Sweet Jesus, have mercy on this your poor servant and her poor friend a sinner. I was scared,

I don't know what's going to happen, the way that whitewoman blaspheming the Lord. Wind howling around the house, girls wailing downstairs, two of us womens saying the Lord's name outloud. You have to see what happen to know what that whitewoman doing, because she just say like this, like you cuss a dog in the biscuits, she say, *Christ Almighty, you so and so*—she don't say *so and so,* but I don't talk such a way, even in telling—she say, *You so and so, GET on out of there, Jesus Lord God, take it, take it, take me.* She say, *Dear God Holy Christ Almighty God Son of God Son of Man Heavenly Host Lord God Holy Ghost Almighty Father Lord Jesus Christ Almighty Holy Christ Father,* and on and on. Oh, she's sweating, she got her mouth clamped, spitting out Christ' holy name. She touch that swelling with the tips of her fingers, touch it like ten spiderlegs tapping. I look there, I see it: her twisted-around belly start to ripple. Oh, it's huge, you know, big white mound of flesh, purple popped veins running through it, been this huge pale naked mountain in them soaked sheets all this time. But now it look delicate as glass. More so than glass, like a soap bubble, like you could touch it and pop it, like a floatable, frangible, airy thing. And that belly rippling, moving like waves of pondwater pushed by the wind, and I swear to you right now standing before the face of the Lord, you could see inside that pregnant womb. Her skin gone to clear, right there while she praying.

Don't believe me. I don't care. You ask me to tell it, I tell it.

Look now. See that baby's head, huge as a mushmelon. See them big veins. Looky. Looky. It's pressing down. See the butt there, belly stretched so clear you can see the crack between them two little round mounds. Look there, that's a elbow poking out. Baby is living, and, Lord, I don't see how. Baby is swimming. Look at it. Swimming around the side of its mama, wriggling like a great white fat tadpole coming, swimming sideways, wiggling down. Only time in my life I ever see such a thing. That mama don't even appear like she's pushing. You expect a woman going to start to want to push soon as she come up on peaking. Peaking! Shoot. That woman slide right past any notion of peaking, she's going for the whole shooting match right now. And she don't push like a normal woman, like she fixing to pop a vein out her behind. Best I can tell, this woman pushing out of her head. I don't mean she gone out her mind, though she been teetering on that for a long time, I mean she's not pushing with her teeth and jaw and bowels and belly and inside muscles so strong they ought to be laid on a workmule and still yet hid so deep no human eyes ever going to see 'em. Oh, womens will push with they eyeballs, I'm telling you, every particle inch honed to the one purpose of pushing that child out into the world, but this woman do not have her whole entire body set on pushing, but only her mind. I'm telling the truth now. She's laboring with her thoughts, her body don't have nothing to do with it, I don't know how to describe it any better than that. Look like she praying to God and cussing that child at the same time, look like she depending on that child to get its ownself out and God to help if He care to.

I's standing on that bloody rug thinking, Lord, this whitelady's body done gone to pieces, her interior muscles is wore out. Say to myself, This child know its mama ain't helping, this child know it's going to have to get out on its own. I look yonder and see that woman haunched up on her frontside. She done roll over. I don't know how she turned that big old white mountain around on that soft bed and I didn't see, I's looking right at it but never mindfully seen it, but next thing I know, she's crouched up on her knees. Rocking. Got her face in the pillow. Weeping. Weeping like Jesus in the Garden. She's not weeping with pain—this the kind of woman, you could slice her ear off, she'll turn and spit at you. She's weeping with sorrow. I don't know what kind of sorrow, it's no kin of any sorrow I been familiar with. Now I look back I can get mad if I let myself—that poor whitewoman and her poor pitiful sorrow—but I trust all that to Jesus and the Hereafter, let others do what they will.

Sure enough, this is how she going to give birth, up like that, rocking on her knees on that old soft featherbed, big belly hanging to the red sheet, blood just a-pouring. What am I going to do but get myself up behind that woman? Oh, everything, everything all twisted around, it don't pleasure me to be at the hind end in that smell and blood and excrement, but it's how God seen fit to put it, and the baby's head swelling toward me. Ordinarily, baby's crown is going to show and slip back, show and slip back, maybe just twice or three times for a practiced woman—sometime it'll slide back more times than you or the mama either one care to speculate—but this baby ain't going to do nothing like most. That head swell toward me blueblack as my daddy's bald pate, whole mess of hair matted down purple, and Lord God, it is huge, and it never stop, pause for nothing, I think the child fixing to land on its neck and break it, that big old purple head coming so fast. Jesus Lord have mercy, it tear that woman plumb asunder, you can hear it, hear the flesh rip same as you'd tear a old sheet for wrappings. She never let out one scream. Just keep on with *Lord God Almighty Christ Jesus Lord.* You know once any child's head get through, the whole rest going to slip out quick, I got to catch it, so, slippery bigheaded thing, got to try and keep it from dropping, can't get a grip anywhere without I'm afraid I'm going to mark it. I opens my two big palms, slide 'em under. I can't get hold of the child's shoulders, child *got* no shoulders to speak of, skinny, skinny butt, don't amount to nothing, but I catches him, palm the child up toward its mama's belly.

Ease my hands down to the blood sheet. Look here, see what you got. Boychild. No different to what I fully known and expected. Frequently I known the child's sex before I seen its peter if it's a boychild, I don't know why. Girl babies, I'd be guessing right up to the last minute, and I don't really mean guessing, because when you trying to help a child into the world you don't be thinking about boy or girl, you thinking *baby*, that's all. Most boy babies, same way, the majority of them, but when I did know beyond doubting, it's invariably been a male child.

This male child laying faceup beneath his mama's belly. Don't make a sound. But he's wide awake, breathing. Now's when I get me a good look at the child's face, and this here is what it look like: a rutabaga turnip turned blueblack from frostbite. The same. Its neck swoll up the same size as the head, that broad across, plumb even with them skinny shoulders. Eyes like two dried plums set in pudding. Got no nose, can't make out the lips hardly but for where they open and you can see that black tongue. Look like two completely different children joined against each other, top part the color of a overripe mulberry, bottom part white as heavy cream, all except for its little purple privacies swelled up so fat. This is the extent of the damage that calf done.

But I ain't got time to study that neither, because here come the after-birth slithering out, long skinny red thing, look like a slaughtered hog's entrails more than what it supposed to be, laying there midst the blood and all nature of bodily fluids—we all three smeared red, look like that featherbed and rug and my own dress all going to be ruint, because you know blood is one element in nature don't want to come out. Woman give a little grunt—she quit saying the Lord's name, I don't know when she quit it, just notice upon that grunt that she have quit—and she pro-ceed to start 'flating down like she fixing to let all her air out and collapse. I think she's going to lay down upon that baby and smother it like I seen a mare do once when she gived birth to a little mule. I guess a sound must've come out my mouth, because, just in time to keep from killing it, she groan and roll off to the side and lay flat, like a man do when he fin-ish the marriage relations.

Now here come the pause. Here finally come the pause when me and her, and—believe it or don't believe, I don't care—that infant, too, all taken stock. We all three blinking at ourselves. Gray light come in at the curtains, that coal-oil lamp on the table look weak, pee-yellow, how it do in daylight, and I's thinking then it was just past dawn and this all happen in a minute, but later I find out it was almost straight-up noon. We all three blinking, that baby alert as anything, still tied to the mama by the birthcord. The woman look at the child. Look at him. Look at him.

I done back off the bed now, standing, my knees feels like water. Woman look up at me, her face blank like somebody sandpaper every feature off it. Look back at that child. She just taken and roll over, turn her back to it. She don't care about that cord going to jerk its belly or nothing, just roll over and put her face to the wall. She say, Take it. Take it out to the ravine and smash its head in. Her voice completely even. She say, I never in my life wanted to give birth to a monster such as that. Lay still then, big naked whitewoman red from the waist down. Baby lay there breathing, that's all, never cry when that birthcord tug its belly. Never let forth a sound.

But I did hear something then, and at first I put it off to the wind, because that northwind still picking and prying at every window around that little shakeshingle house. But what I heard wasn't no wind. I don't know how it's possible I never felt her. Never sensed her one iota, I don't have any idea how long she been standing there in the doorway. Don't know when she creeped back up the stairs and come watching. Might've been a long time, because, from the look of the bloody streaks all up and down the front of it, she never even yet changed her dress.

PART TWO

Kin

Tulsa, Oklahoma
Wednesday
September 1, 1920

I t began in such a small way.

The girl had been with them three months then. From the beginning there'd been something about her that bothered Althea. On the first day, when the girl had stood quiet in the dining room, tall, big-boned, her high slanted face gazing impassively as Althea gave instructions for polishing the sideboard—even in those first moments she'd felt troubled by the girl. It wasn't just her slow pace, though that was part of it. Althea sometimes watched from the parlor doorway, following the girl's languid movements invisibly, inside her own body, aching to prod her along like a dawdling milk cow. But the girl did her work well, deliberately and thoroughly, and her slowness was really only a vexation. It was something more.

Once, early on, the girl had turned when Althea stood watching behind her. She'd neither smiled nor looked shamed, as so many of them did when they felt themselves watched by a white person, nor changed the indifferent pace of her movement. Her face was serene, and completely unreadable. Althea had smiled quickly, startled at the warm blossom of shame opening inside her, and asked the girl to touch up the flatware when she'd finished. The girl's head tipped forward in a barely perceptible nod, and she'd turned back to the silver coffee urn she was polishing.

After that, Althea hid herself more perfectly when she kept an eye on the girl. Or she would walk abruptly into the room where the girl was cleaning, half hoping, she knew, to catch her at something, though she could never quite lay her mind on what.

The girl's given name was Graceful. That, too, irritated Althea. The aptness of it. The slow elegance of the girl's movements grated on her, and she would find herself gritting her teeth as she watched the girl move placidly from mantel to highboy with her duster, her arm reaching in a slow arc, her hips rolling luxuriously beneath the cotton skirt. Yet, when Franklin began to call the girl Grace or Gracie when he spoke to her, Althea corrected him.

"Her name is Graceful," she would say, outside the girl's hearing. "The least you can do is call the girl by her rightful given name."

Certainly she'd never thought to ask Graceful's surname. Like so much that had never occurred to her, the idea that the girl even had a last name never crossed Althea's mind. If anyone had asked—a neighbor, say, or someone from the Auxiliary, which of course never happened—Althea would have dismissed the question with a shrug of her shoulders. Graceful's family name would be some dead president's, more than likely, Washington or Jackson or Lincoln or Johnson. She'd never thought about the girl's life, or her family, where she'd come from. Never dreamed there was anything more to the girl's existence than her slow, placid movements and the vague stirrings of unease she produced in Althea.

And so when the letter came, delivered by a grinning roundfaced colored boy of about ten, who ducked his head and grinned wider when Althea told him to wipe his feet before stepping onto the porch floor, there was more than a small stab of surprise in Althea's heart.

Graceful had gone to do the shopping, had left an hour before, bareheaded, though a light rain was falling (another source of irritation—other women's housemaids went about with their heads wrapped properly in white cotton rags), the produce basket on her arm. Althea, passing near the pantry, heard the light rapping on the back door.

The boy stood on the steps, reaching up with one hand to swipe at the droplets beading the tight nap of his hair. His other hand was tucked in the fold of his shirt. Behind him, in the side yard, her rose garden was obscured in the grayness. Althea could just make out the spreading boughs of the elm tree in her backyard.

"Yes?" she said, and the boy grinned, hunched his shoulders. A chill passed through Althea, brought on, she thought, by the dampness seeping through the screen, and she turned, crossed the screened-in porch, stepped into the kitchen.

"Well," she said when she turned to close the inner door and saw that the boy still stood outside the screen, "Come in, boy." And then quickly: "Wipe your feet first!"

The boy dug his feet into the soaked doormat, vigorously, over and over, grinning, until Althea said, "That's fine, that will do," and he pulled the screen open, stepped onto the smooth gray-painted planks of the porch floor. He kept one leg behind him, close to the door, as if to make sure he could dart back through it should the situation turn dangerous.

"Yes, what is it?" Althea assumed him to be a neighbor's yardboy sent with a request or an invitation, and she was annoyed at having to answer the door herself—and then was doubly irritated at her own quick irritability. It was with her so often now, she didn't know why.

A flicker of uncertainty passed over the boy's face, and he looked past Althea's shoulders into the kitchen. "Graceful?" he said. His eyes turned to Althea again. "This here where Graceful Whiteside work?"

"What?" Althea said, startled, hearing it and dismissing it within the same heartbeat. "Who?"

"Do a woman name Graceful work here, ma'am? Is what I mean to say." He shifted his weight to his back leg.

"Yes," Althea answered, less sharply. "A girl named Graceful works for me."

"She here, ma'am?"

"She ought to be back in a little while. She's gone for the shopping. I'll give her a message, or—" Althea glanced at the boy's muddy shoes; she went on in a tight voice. "If you want, I guess you can wait."

"I got a letter here I'm suppose to deliver."

The boy removed his hand from the front of his shirt, and as the brown hand pulled free from the threadbare white cotton, a foreboding passed through Althea, a feeling of dread, of something irrevocable begun. The boy held a wrinkled, pale blue envelope toward her. Althea took it from him. The envelope was damp, the inked letters blurred at the edges. But there it was, clearly written in a delicate backhand scrawl:

Miss Graceful Whiteside
Care of Mr. Franklin H. Dedmeyer, Esq.
1600 Block So. Carson
City

"Ma'am?" the boy said. "Ma'am? You could give that letter to Graceful?" He cleared his throat lightly behind his hand. "Ma'am? You could give it to her for me?"

"Yes," Althea said finally. "I'll see that she gets it."

"Thank you much, ma'am." The boy backed through the screen door, turned and jumped down the four steps to the wet ground. He landed on his feet and took off running.

"Boy!" Althea rushed across the porch, and the coiled spring twanged loudly as she shoved open the door. "Boy!" she called.

He stopped halfway across the yard, his shoulders hunched against the mist, or against the sound in Althea's voice then. After a long moment he turned around.

"This name here," Althea called. She held the envelope toward him, though she knew he could scarcely see it for the rain and the distance. "Is this name right? This name Whiteside?"

"Yes'm," the boy called back.

"Whiteside is Graceful's last name? You're sure of that?"

"I guess so, ma'am." The boy grinned, a white flash in the grayness. "That's alla us last name."

Graceful did not seem surprised to find her mistress standing in the middle of the kitchen with an envelope in her hand and the back door open, allowing into the house the sweltering dampness from the screened-in porch. She nodded in the slight, irritating way she had, crossed in front of Althea, and opened her arms to allow the soggy bundles she carried to fall onto the counter next to the sink. Althea watched the long square of the girl's back as she lifted the full produce basket and thunked it onto the counter. She watched the girl's fingers moving among the packages, untying strings and rolling them into small, tight balls, pulling moist tan paper from red slabs of meat.

"A letter came for you," she said finally, and lifted the envelope, creased now in the center from where she'd held it so tightly. Graceful stepped from the counter and took it from her hand. Without a word of thanks or a glance at the inscription she slipped the envelope into a loose pocket of her apron, turned back to the counter.

"You're wet." Althea was beginning to come to herself now. "You'd better get out of those wet things, and then. . . ." Her eyes swept the kitchen, the pantry, the open doorway, landed finally on the brown smears of mud on the gray porch planks by the door. "And then see about cleaning up that mess out there before you start dinner."

Graceful nodded again, the barest gesture of acknowledgment. She walked across the kitchen and disappeared into the back hall, toward the maid's room. Althea stood awhile longer, alone in the kitchen, seeing in her mind's eye—as she'd seen it for the past hour, appearing and disappearing, swimming in some invisible place before her—the image of a flax-colored dress she'd owned once as a girl.

In the evening Althea tried to speak of it to her husband. She sat propped against the feather pillows in the four-poster bed, her dark hair loose upon her shoulders, a new novel loose in her long hands, lying open on the coverlet. Franklin stood before the mirror, his great blond head lifted toward the ceiling as he worked to unclasp the button tight at his collar.

"A boy came today," she began. She fell silent, and the sound of the hard rain in the yard filled the space of the silence.

Franklin glanced over his shoulder, his fingers tugging at the collar. "Well?" he said. "Damn this thing." He turned back to the glass.

"Yes. To bring a letter to Graceful."

"Well," Franklin said. He pulled the button free finally, and his fingers flicked down the shirt front, freeing the others. He went on, seeming to have hardly heard her. "Ran into L.O. Murphy this afternoon. I don't know. He acts like he knows a little too much about that unfortunate business Saturday night." Franklin frowned, shaking his head. "You'd think he'd keep a little tighter lip, the way the papers are talking."

Althea stirred beneath the sheet, irritated; she didn't want to hear any more about that awful lynching. Tulsa had talked of little else for days. It was boring, stupid, ugly. She ran her fingers along an unread page of the novel.

"They tell me the governor's trying to get the names of the ringleaders, though I don't believe it, but they're liable to call in anybody can't keep his mouth shut. That'd be L.O." Franklin glanced at his wife. "He bragged for an hour on that new pool at Bigheart, says they're pumping thirty thousand a day."

His brows came together, frowning, but his eyes were lit bright from the inside. Althea knew this look in her husband, this blend of jealousy and hope warring always in his face at news of the success of another. Delo Petroleum had made creditable strikes, had secured leases for several minor pools, but none of his little company's discovery wells had touched anything like the wealth foretold by the Nellie Johnstone or the Ida Glenn. Still, Franklin never doubted that the next well was going to be the bonanza gusher, that he and his partner were just days or inches, moments or miles away from the big strike, and so news of another's success both confirmed and threatened his faith, for it declared that there was still plenty of the earth's black blood flowing in the hidden sands of Oklahoma, and it whispered secretly, urgently, Hurry, hurry, it will all be gone soon, you'll miss it, fool, hurry, you're going to miss out. "L.O. swears Bigheart's going to be as big as Cushing, bigger than Glenn Pool, but you know what a braggart L.O. Murphy is." The abiding hope and envy did battle in Franklin's face as he shrugged himself out of his linen shirt.

Althea turned her eyes to the window, where water streamed down the glass in dark, trembling sheets. She thought again of the boy and the letter, and Graceful, asleep now, she supposed, in the tiny maid's room downstairs. She tried to think how to bring it up. She told herself it was nothing, there was no reason to tell Franklin. And what would he care? Very little sank into his awareness that did not have to do with oil. She had no reason to tell him. Well, she would mention the thing casually, like a shard of gossip from a neighbor. She thought of several ways to put it and opened her mouth several times to speak it, but in the end Althea could find no casual words for this information that had so stilled her she'd stood for an hour after the boy had disappeared in the grayness. Stood alone in the center of the kitchen, staring at her own family name on an envelope addressed to a colored girl. *It's stupid,* she thought, her eyes tracing the rain's trembling. *There's absolutely no reason to mention it.* Anyway, she knew where darkies got white names; it hardly mattered (and deep in her mind a thought jerked: *What matters anymore? What matters?*), and she shut that away and said nothing. Franklin's trousers fell to the floor, the suspenders clunking softly on the carpet. He reached for his nightshirt.

"Jim's wanting me to come to Bristow tomorrow, says he wants to show me a spot down on the Deep Fork."

A sudden tightening clamped Althea's chest, and her mind closed down as sudden. She sat very still, her face composed, her mind empty.

"Gypsy's got most of the lease land sewed up down there, but . . ." He turned toward her, his blue eyes bright, lit with hunger. "Jim's really hot for me to come down."

Althea stirred almost imperceptibly, thinking perhaps she would get up and go wash her face again; it felt sticky, covered with a light film from the oppressive humidity. Thinking she would go downstairs and make sure the girl had closed all the windows. But she made no move to rise; rather, she lifted her knees beneath the white eyelet coverlet and settled the book upon them. Her eyes glided left to right, following the letters on the page.

"Nobody's 'catting down in that direction lately, but maybe that's a good sign. Might be a good sign. Or not." Franklin's voice was studiedly casual, tight with deception, even against his wife, who paid him no attention. He turned back to the mirror, ran both hands though his thick hair, smoothing it, his fingers sweeping along either side of this head. "I don't put too much credence in it, really," he said. "Those old Deep Fork bottoms don't seem likely, if you ask me, but I'll have a look-see."

A terrible restlessness pushed through Althea, though it showed only in the way her fingers picked at the corners of the book's pages. She sat quite still against the pillows, her eyes steady now, her face a white mask, her fingers stroking the slightly nicked edges of the thin paper. Her husband's gaze was on his own face in the mirror, and he didn't see—nor would he have thought anything of it if he had seen, for in their many years together he'd never come to understand the meaning of his wife's habits. Althea grew outwardly rigid when her heart was in turmoil, her agitation revealed always through small, pettish tics. But Franklin thought of his wife as a serene woman, a transformation of the bold girl he'd married: she'd grown tranquil from grief, he believed, and his eyes never saw anything in her to conflict with this idea.

He went on talking, his voice pitched with excitement, his words guarded, but Althea didn't listen. She turned inward toward the roaring inside her, the rush of blood in her ears. The mention of her husband's partner could sometimes set the outward stillness upon her, but it was not the speaking of Jim Dee Logan's name now that held her. Althea's mind slid over it as over a small stone in silt, and crashed instead against the words *Deep Fork* like a boulder. The name of the brooding river she'd grown up beside caught hold of her and kept her, forcing memories upon her she was unwilling to yield to. Her mind flailed, reaching for something to think of that would push away the images rising, but she could find nothing to seize upon, and she could not will her mind blank. She looked at her husband's slight paunch pressing the inside of his undershirt, his thick neck and golden head turned toward the mirror, and she hated him then, as if he were conspiring with the letter and the flax-colored dress and all that she'd sheltered so long from her memory: as if he knew and were adding with intent to this chasm opening inside her.

She slapped the book shut and placed it on the nightstand, sank down beneath the covers. But she couldn't keep the stillness on her surface now, and she rose up again and threw the coverlet to the side, saying, "Lord, it's hot in here. Don't tell me that idiot boy's lit the furnace already."

Her husband paused, one arm half thrust in the sleeve of his nightshirt. His reflection stared at her from the mirror. "What's the matter with you?"

"Nothing. It's hot. It's suffocating in here. I can't breathe, can't you open a window?"

"That's a blowing rain, Thea. And it's not hot in here—matter of fact, it's damned chilly." He turned fully around and looked at her, hard at first, and then his face softened, his forehead tilted slightly. Althea hated that tilt of forehead that indicated Franklin was concerned and, to her mind, disgustingly sincere. He came toward her, pulling the nightshirt around him. "What's the matter? Are you sick?" He reached to feel her brow for fever, but she shrank back, shaking her head.

"No. No, it's nothing. I'm hot, that's all. Just crack the window a little at the bottom."

He stood over her a moment, and then turned and crossed the rug and pushed the glass up an inch. The sound of pounding rain washed into the room. He finished buttoning his nightshirt as he moved toward the doorway, paused with his hand on the lightswitch, frowning at her. Althea gazed back at him. Her heart was stiller now.

Franklin turned out the light, and she heard the soft shuffle of his feet on the carpet. She felt the mattress sink as he crawled beneath the sheet, and then, soon—too soon, long before she was ready—the tips of his fingers brushing along the silken edge of her gown. She lay rigid on her back, staring up into the black space over her head. Her husband's fingers came at her like some snuffling night-thing, prying, poking, trying to get in. "Franklin," she said aloud in the darkness. His hand stopped, expectant, very still and waiting. Then the weight of the bed shifted as he soundlessly rolled onto his side away from her.

Althea held her eyes open, waiting for the streetlamp in front of the house to balance the sudden extinguishing of the light. Franklin's breathing slowed and grew regular. She was glad. Maybe he would sleep soon and there would not be the silent stiffness between them. She listened to the drumming on the roof, the splashing in the yard below. The day's spitting mist had given way at evening to a rolling thunderstorm driven east by fierce winds across the prairies, and now the great crashes and low rumbles had moved on, leaving behind this gorged, steady drumming.

She waited, waited, she knew not for what. *For the streetlight,* she told herself, though she understood this was not it. Still, she was glad when the thin bluish glow began to give form to the objects in the room, and she looked with relief at the familiar shapes dissolving from the dimness into the lives of themselves: the scrolled wardrobe along the west wall, the mahogany vanity near the window, with the low stool crouched before it and the high oval mirror glinting silverish in the poor light.

Althea had dismissed memory with the sudden closing of the novel, the gesture of placing it on the nightstand; she'd succeeded, with long-practiced skill, in forcing the past into a walled-off place far from her consciousness. And yet the restlessness was here. The monotonous thrumming of the rain drove at her and into her, and she gritted her teeth against it; she tried to force a softening into her limbs, but the easing would not come. She wanted to rise and close the window, wanted to stand at the glass and raise her fists and shout at the glutted heavens, Shut up, shut up, shut up! Convulsively she reached out and touched her husband's back. Immediately he rolled toward her. Immediately his snuffling fingers crept up beneath her gown.

Afterwards, she listened to him sink toward sleep: the ragged intake of breath, the long wait, the plosive exhale. His weight was dense beside her. She moved only slightly, and Franklin roused, grumbled, "For God's sake, Thea." He reached for her and wrapped his arms tightly around her, as if he would muffle her tension, bury it with himself. She held still, and Franklin settled again, his snores at last covering the rain's rhythms. Quietly, hardly breathing, she slipped from his grasp, from beneath the sheets, stood and walked in the blue light's trembling.

The house was silent but for the steady drumming on the rooftop. There was no ticking, no settling of this new house in the coolness of night. In her thin silken gown, her feet bare, she groped toward the bathroom at the end of the hall. She felt the sudden release, the warm clot rolling down, followed by the slow trickle, like blood. Like relief. Like the loss of all possibility. The warmth cooled on the inside of her thigh as she edged forward in the darkness.

Her feet left the smooth surface of wood, touched the tiles of the bathroom. In the darkness she found her facecloth, still damp from the evening's washing, draped on the side of the tub. She wet it with cool water from the lavatory and wiped her face, lifted her heavy hair and washed the back of her neck. Then she raised the front of her gown and washed herself roughly, scrubbing the cloth hard back and forth. Though she almost believed now it would not happen, could not happen, she knew from long experience that sleep wouldn't come until she'd washed away the smell. She rinsed the cloth again, shook it, and folded it neatly over the tub's porcelain lip, and then she turned in the small, dark room, went out into the darker hallway.

Down the stairs, her right hand touching lightly the cherry banister, a moment's pause in the foyer, and then she turned left into the parlor. Laced light crosshatched the carpet through the sheer window curtains. She looked at the pieces she'd placed just so in the room when they'd moved into the house: her small tables and treasures, the silk brocade fainting couch, the high-backed wing chair, the velvet divan. Only a year ago, and the pleasure in it, the newness and luxury that had delighted her for a short time, seemed old now, dried up and sullen. What had she come in here for? She couldn't remember. She turned and went back into the foyer, where colored light streamed from the oval stained-glass window next to the door. *Not here,* she thought. *Nothing here.* In rising agitation she crossed the hallway, stumbled through the dark library into the dining room.

The heavy damask drapes at the French doors smothered the room in darkness. Althea felt her way to the dining table, and began to move slowly in a great circle around it. She paused a moment with her back to the oak breakfront, pressed her palms to the front of her chest; she circled the table again, touching the smooth lip of polished wood with her fingertips, her pelvis bumping the backs of the chairs. Abruptly, she stopped. What did she want here? For an instant she couldn't remember where she was. She stood in swimming black space, with no sense of right or left, up or down. Untethered and terrified in the darkness. Then a pale rectangle of light calmed her from the far side of the room, and she moved toward it. She stepped through the narrow passageway into the kitchen.

There was light here; the white floor grasped the faint glow falling through the uncurtained window and enlarged it, and Althea was relieved a moment, standing in the center, in the same place she'd stood staring at the crumpled envelope for an hour in the afternoon. Such a long time ago. She could hardly remember. It seemed like a dream now. But the sense of that standing—not the mind's memory but the body's recollection— pushed the restlessness on her again. What did she want here? What had she come for? She searched her body with an inward turning of her senses. Was she hungry? No, not hungry. Not hungry on any level.

She stood in the pale box of the kitchen, disoriented, empty. Her mind traced and retraced itself, seeking old comforts: the slow smile and rising gaze of a stranger on the street; a certain woman's arched eyebrow at Althea's entrance into a chandeliered hall, and the immediate stir in that goldenlit room, the turning of a hundred faces toward her. She tried to call up the deep sensuous pleasure, as she'd first known it, at the touch of fox fur, delicate porcelain, sculpted wood, but these failed her, and so she turned to the fail-proof pleasure: the secret dream she'd cherished for years. Jim Dee Logan's name, the thought of his face, a word of him—that, at least, had always been able to raise the small rush of pulse and pleasure. She waited for the sly, familiar warmth at the recollection of his image—but the image itself would not even come. *What now?* the words said. *What shall I want now?*

Quickly she turned and left the kitchen, back through the dark dining room, the library, into the foyer once more. She reached for the polished wood of the banister, but even as her hand lifted, she turned her eyes, unintended, toward the south wall, and at once she stopped.

Street light tumbling through the stained-glass window lit the gilt mirror over the hall table in a trembling chiaroscuro of reds and blues and yellows. Althea's hand fell to her side, and she moved as if bidden to the mirror, stood before it. Reflected in the colored light she saw her own image: the pale oval haloed in darkness, the two elegant curves of her brows, her ivory neck, the angular line of her shoulders beneath the silk gown. But in the trick of light and shadow, the smooth bodice began to coarsen, turn to muslin, darken with glistening streaks; she watched the curve of her face narrow and sharpen, the bone of jaw jutting, teeth gritted, against the sickness inside her mouth. Panicked, she willed herself to escape, but the sense of being ungrounded, without source or direction, trapped her, and she couldn't tell where to run.

She felt the girl's presence first as a square of warmth against her back in the cool hall, and then, in incremental degrees, the dark face took form beside her own in the glass: the luminous eyes first, reflecting light, and soon the planed cheeks, the broad nose and backtilted forehead. The girl's brushed-out hair radiated wildly, without definition against the cavernous foyer, and for a moment longer Althea still could not be sure she wasn't dreaming, for the features were completely immobile, but then the mouth opened, the soft voice said, "Ma'am? You all right?"

Violently, as if jerked awake, Althea whirled around, and from her own mouth there spat forth a sound, profane in its essence, though it had no English meaning. As quickly as the curse erupted, Althea clamped her mouth closed. Graceful stood a few feet from her in a white cotton gown. The expression on the girl's face was as placid, unsurprised, unmoved as ever.

"What the devil's the matter with you?" Althea hissed. "Sneaking around out here in the dark!" Instantly she drew back her shoulders, raised her chin, composed the mask on her face. "Did you close the windows in the library? I'd better not find rain on my carpet in the morning, hear me?"

Graceful's head tilted up only the slightest fraction, but Althea saw it: the soft sheen of light on forehead and cheekbones, the little lift of defiance. It was enough.

"Don't you dare sull up at me! Don't you dare! If you're not the laziest, sneakingest, slowest damn excuse for a housemaid—Shut that sulky mouth! I'll pinch a plug out of it. Get back in the bed this minute. You'd better not ever let me catch you creeping around my house in the dark. Never! Do you hear?"

But the girl had already turned away.

As she watched the ghostly gown disappear down the dark hall, Althea received a new sensation, burning her dulled senses, past the emptiness and the familiar prickling irritation: she hated the girl with a dead white heat.

By morning Althea had managed to do with the previous night's encounter what she did with all uncomfortable recollections: pushed it quite comfortably to a confined corner of her mind, and dismissed it. This was an old trick of memory in her, one she'd developed in the beginning by force and now continued by habit, but on this occasion she'd achieved the separation entirely in her sleep, so that by the time she awakened to the earthy after-rain smell and the sunlight streaming through lace curtains, she had no more sense of her fears of the night before than the vague stirrings of a half-remembered bad dream. This, too, she struggled away from, scrambling from the bedclothes as a cat claws free from water, and she crossed the carpet quickly and reached inside the oak wardrobe for her wrapper.

Franklin, of course, was already up, either downstairs at breakfast or gone now to the office at the Hotel Tulsa or to the Robinson, wherever his leasehound instincts told him to hurry off to downtown. Althea glanced at the window to discover the time, and seeing the full morning light, she moved rapidly, though in a smooth, controlled manner, to the vanity and picked up her hairbrush. Seated sideways, so that she faced not the tall mirror but the nearby window, she brushed her hair with long, brusque strokes and twisted it up and pinned it. She glanced to see that no stray hairs had slipped from her fingers, that the thick brown knot was straight, and then she stood up quickly to dress.

Downstairs she found that Franklin had indeed left. Her place was set at one end of the table. The house was quiet. The clock on the breakfront as she swept past it told her it was already nearly eight-thirty. Relieved at her husband's absence, yet annoyed with him somehow, as if it were his fault she'd slept late, she sat at the table and poured coffee from the steaming china pot. The damask drapes were drawn open, and even with the overhang of the porch roof dulling the panes in shadow, she could see the sun's strength in the side yard. The sudden heat after so much rainfall had coaxed the pink buds to life on her wild-rose bushes near the street. She could see hundreds of small red clusters bursting on her climbers.

A sense of urgency came on her then, a pressing at the day's escape, and Althea's thoughts moved rapidly. She would have the girl do the wash while the sun lasted. Thunderclouds might roll in from the west again, spill a torrent before the washing could be brought in from the line. The season's turning toward September could mean more thunderstorms, the drop of forty degrees in an hour, an unforetold deluge of wind and hail. Althea had grown up with the vagaries of the Territory's weather, and she lived always in expectation of sudden violent change. Of course, this steamy September warmth could stretch well into October; there might be sultry weather for many weeks yet, without a sign of rain. One could count on nothing about the weather in Oklahoma except unpredictability and change—so, yes, the wash this morning, and the girl could do the mending while the wash dried, and then, of course, the ironing. Maybe there would be time before Graceful started dinner to wax the staircase banister and the foyer floor. Althea had observed the dulling of the old wax as she'd come down the stairs and noted it to herself, a task to give the girl. But, no, it wasn't likely Graceful would get to the waxing, the poor creature was so wondrously, exasperatingly slow. It was a good thing she'd insisted on the shopping being finished yesterday, Althea thought then. Otherwise there'd be no telling when the wash would get done.

A small disturbance fluttered in Althea's mind, as if a hand had for a brief moment flicked aside a curtain. She sat very still, staring out at the side yard. Delicately she ran her fingers up the back of her upswept hair, feeling for stray strands, pushing the hairpins in tighter. The curtain swung back in place. She drank her coffee and busied her thoughts with the small details of the day: she would tend to her garden before the heat fell too heavily, and then there was the sorting of clothes to be mended and those to be discarded, and she really must settle the question of whether to give the faded green sateen to Graceful or donate it to the Ladies Auxiliary League.

She heard a faint clink of silver and the rustle of the girl's starched apron coming through the passageway from the kitchen. At once the dread of the afternoon before, the night before, rushed fully formed on Althea. She pushed herself back from the table, touched her fingers to her hair, reached again for the thin china cup, and sipped from it. She calmed her outward face, sat motionless while the girl unburdened the silver tray of covered dishes. Graceful clamped the tray beneath her arm while she poured more coffee, snapped loose the folded napkin and held it out, swung the tray horizontal again to receive the silver tops from the chafing dishes. Her movements were smooth and rhythmic. *Slow as sorghum in winter,* Althea thought. She waited with gritted teeth for the girl to have done with her business.

"You be wanting bacon, ma'am, this morning?" the girl said in her soft, rising inflection.

"Bacon?" Althea was startled at this breach of habit. She always had bacon with her eggs in the morning. But it was a distraction from the dread swimming inside her, and she seized on it. "You mean you haven't cooked the bacon?"

"I didn't yet, ma'am."

"Well," Althea said after a moment, her voice cool and distant, "pray tell, why not?"

"Mr. Dedmeyer say he don't know if you want much breakfast this morning."

"Did Mr. Dedmeyer say why he thought I might not want bacon since I always have bacon?"

"Just that you wasn't feeling good last night."

Althea slowly raised her eyes to the girl's face. Graceful revealed nothing. There was that infuriating, placid stillness, of course, but it was no different from normal. The girl showed no hint of recollection concerning Althea's tirade the night before—except possibly in a certain narrowness in her eyes as she gazed calmly back at her.

"Yes," Althea murmured. "Yes, I . . ." A profound confusion blurred her thoughts. What was it they were trying to settle? And then she remembered. "Oh. Well. Yes. I mean, no. No. Eggs and biscuits are fine this morning." A dull tingling pricked at her face muscles, urging her to motion, and she longed for the girl to leave so she might ease it in some manner. At last Graceful swung the tray under her arm and disappeared through the passageway, her back a high, hard square, like a working-man's, her hips rolling beneath the maid's-uniform skirt.

Althea forced herself to remain at the table. She reached for the serving spoon and scooped scrambled eggs onto her plate. She broke open a biscuit and dabbed it with butter. She closed the biscuit and placed it carefully beside but not touching the soft yellow mass of eggs. Then she wiped her fingers on the linen napkin and folded her hands in her lap. She sat so for a long time, listening to the small thunks and clatters in the kitchen, the sound of the faucet turning, the cold water groan, and then gurgle, and then gush. A muscle trembled along her jawline. Her mind was entirely empty. Abruptly she stood and moved to the French doors, looked past the porch swing, past the shadows, to her rose garden in the side yard. She would work. Yes. That was it. She had much to do to prepare her garden for winter. There was the pruning, the mulching, the cloths to be wrapped at the base of her prize Cimarron Tea Rose—though winter was months away. The first hard freeze might not come before December. But one never knew. It might come sudden. Might come in the night without warning, before she was ready. Althea went back to the table, stirred the eggs around on the plate, smushed them up and scattered them over the delicate blue print in the china. Standing, her pelvis pressed hard into the walnut edge of the table, she took a bite out of the biscuit and laid it back on the plate. The bread was dry, it nearly choked her, and she took a swallow of coffee to force it down her throat.

Steam rose from the soaked ground and drifted in knee-high wisps as Althea walked the footpaths, her pruning shears tight in her fingers. She passed from rosebush to rosebush, from bloom-covered trellis to scraggly low scrambler, from the tall free-standing Cimarron Tea Rose to the new hybrid Pink Ophelia to the climbers sprawling along the white fence in the back. Occasionally she snapped her shears in the open air, or she'd kneel and lift a freshly opened rosebud and cup it in her fingers. The front of her dress was filthy from where she'd knelt in the wet black loam, but she didn't pause to swipe at it. She moved almost as a sleepwalker, as if she hunted in her dreams, unconscious, not knowing what she looked for, and it was only in the occasional pause and kneeling, the sudden snapping of shears from time to time in the muggy sunlight, that she showed any sign of presence in her body.

An automobile passed on the street, sputtering, trailing gasoline fumes, and Althea stopped to watch it disappear north toward downtown. The auto backfired somewhere up around Fifteenth Street, a loud bang like a gunshot, and Althea jumped at the sound of it. She reached a gloved hand to her brow to wipe away the perspiration. The sun beat down, a merciless hellfire. Althea felt it through the wickered straw of her sunhat as if it had just begun its burning: a small, round scalded place on the top of her skull. She turned from the street at once, as though she'd at last found her purpose, and bent to the nearest rosebush and began to snip savagely at the blossoms.

"Althea Dedmeyer, what in the sweet name of Pete do you think you're doing?"

The voice jerked Althea to awareness, a sudden plucking of her nerves like fingers yanking open purse strings. She held still for a long time, her gloves among the thorny branches of a climber, and then she stood up, very calm upon her surface, and slowly turned around.

The woman posed on the stones of the footpath as if the sea surrounded her. A magenta cloche hat hugged her auburn hair; a filmy pink scarf swirled at her throat and drifted to the hem of the pale sheath she wore. The crepe-de-chine skirt was almost vulgarly short, hardly covering the midpoint of her calves. In one hand she held a pair of lace gloves, and she fanned her face with them as if the flimsy material could really move the sodden air. A sly, expectant look touched her features. She smiled at Althea. "Hot, isn't it?" she said.

"Hello, Nona."

"Is this a new idea, to scalp a rose garden like a red war party?"

Nona Murphy laughed, a tripping sound like water. Her small head dipped and turned prettily as she surveyed the rose garden. Althea followed Nona's eyes, her own eyes taking in the destruction. In a ravaged half-moon around her, the remains of a dozen rosebushes clawed the steaming air, scraggly, raw, bleeding sap. Green leaves, twisted green stems, wilted petals, dying rosebuds lay in scattered circles at the bases of the bushes. The prongs of the living branches were cut close to the mother stumps; the stumps were hewed close to the ground.

Lord God have mercy, what on earth have I done?

"Yes," she said aloud. "I . . . I've been pruning my garden." She bent and gathered an armload of wilting green, unheedful of the thorns, and carried the branches to the fence and dropped them. "The blooms are supposed to come back stronger if you prune them back hard in early fall."

"Well, I hope you haven't killed the poor things," Nona said, and her laugh trickled through the air again. "It's not *fall* anyhow, child, on the second day of September." She stood fanning herself with her ridiculous lace gloves as she glanced toward the house. "Might's well be the Fourth of July from the feel of this heat." Now her eyes swept Althea from sunhat to gardening gloves, and the sly smile tipped her features. "Honey, I hate to say it, you look like a fieldhand."

Althea felt on her face the sun's ruthless light, which the straw hat's speckled shade could not soften; she felt the sweat beading her upper lip, sliding down her temples. She saw the ragged hem on her gardening skirt; her muddied shoes, the heels run down to nothing; her gloves blackened with earth, and wet and heavy. She forced a laugh. "Well," she said, "gardening does that." She smiled at Nona with the surface of her skin. "I guess I'll give that murky muck that passes for Tulsa tapwater a chance to show something for itself afterwhile." She bent, gathered another armload of branches, dropped them over the fence.

"You don't look a bit worse than L.O. did when he got home Saturday night. That road was pure mud. Or that's what L.O. *said* anyhow." Nona's voice was buttery with innuendo, slick with implied meaning. "*Some* of us know how to stay out of the mud, though."

Althea ignored her. She had no desire to hear Nona Murphy go on about that lynching. Would people never find something else to talk about? In any case, it had nothing to do with her. Franklin had been home Saturday night, as he was every night when he was in town. They hadn't known a thing about it till the *World* came Sunday morning, and didn't care about it then, Althea didn't, and she didn't want to hear about it now.

"Law, it's muggy, isn't it?" Nona flipped her gloves all around her face as she peered around the garden, scanned the side porch, seemingly looking for something. "I thought the rain'd cool things off some, but I declare it's just made me more miserable."

Althea moved swiftly through the humid air, gathering the cut stems, and Nona followed after her along the stone path, stepping primly in her high patent shoes, prattling on about the weather, the lynching, the Auxiliary League benefit a week from next Friday. Althea would not ask her what she wanted, though she knew she wanted something. Nona Murphy never came without secret purpose hidden in her trickling laughter.

"I said to him, Honey, you're going to spoil me silly, and he said—oh, you know L.O.—he said, What else is it good for? If I can't throw you a little party now and then I might's well pump that oil right back down in the ground. And I said . . ."

Althea closed her mind to Nona's simpering chatter. For a moment she stood looking at the pruned branches, the crushed and fragrant petals gathered on the pile. A grief like the grief of death began to rise in her. She turned and picked up her pruning shears from where she'd dropped them by a fencepost, moved across the garden toward her wild roses near the street.

Nona followed, though more slowly, as she picked her way along the meandering footpath. "Well, I said, October is the absolute soonest if you aim it to be *that* big a shindig, and he said, Sweetheart, I aim it to be the biggest whingding this town's ever seen, and if it takes you a year to get ready, why, you take a year. No, honey, I said, this is a celebration. We've got to celebrate while the news is new, don't we? He just laughed." Nona came up directly behind Althea, where she stood before the ragged hedge of pale pink wild roses. "Two months, going on three, it'll be old news practically as it is."

The new Winton parked at the curb caught Althea's attention, and she lifted her eyes and looked past the roses to the dark leather seats, the brilliant trim reflecting sunlight. Nona Murphy *would* drive over here for whatever sly purpose she held in that mind of hers, would drive though she lived no more than two blocks away. Would drive because her Winton was brand-new and lovely, because she must show off that she *could* drive, that she knew herself to be a scandal in Tulsa because her husband had taught her how to operate an automobile. Althea made up her mind suddenly that, whatever it was Nona wanted, she would not let her have it. Her eyes returned to the rosebush.

"He took me up there last Sunday, my stars, Thea, it looks like a *city*. I mean those derricks march off across those hills like an army or something. You can't even *see* the horizon. You can't see the end of them. It's the most thrilling thing. I said, Honey, it looks like *Glenn* Pool, for heaven's sake, and he said, Sugar, the Ida Glenn was a little duster compared to what's under this spot. Believe it, woman, he said, that's our million-dollar future out there."

Was this what Nona had come for, to brag of L.O.'s strike? Althea glanced up; her fingers paused on a faded bloom before she snipped it. No. She dismissed the notion. Nona never approached a subject directly but always sidled up sideways, tiptoeing around by way of Robin's barn to sneak up on it. And she never came simply to relay information but always—somewhere in her monologues that ran on without pause for answer, some way in a sentence that carried no question mark—always, somehow, finally, to ask. Althea pinched the head off the rose with her fingers. The faded pink petals fluttered to the muddy ground as she reached for another.

"He held me right there by the waist, swept his big old hand across like he was drawing me a picture, and he says, We're going to inaugurate that little ballroom, sugar, quick as you can get ready, and I said, What are you talking about, L.O. Murphy? and he says, I'm talking about a masquerade ball big as this whole country, that's what. I want you to plan us a party the likes of which this little town's never yet seen, and I said, *Bigheart?*, and he got so tickled, I thought he'd never quit laughing. No, now, you know I mean Tulsa, he said. We're going to throw us a party fit to make that town's head swim, and I said, Lord, L.O., that'll have to be going some, and he says, You can believe that, sugar."

Nona prattled on, her voice high and excited, her green eyes darting around Althea's property, looking for something; she turned again toward the house. Her lips never ceased for a moment to talk, but her gaze returned and settled finally on Althea's swiftly moving fingers. Althea felt her. She deadheaded the roses quickly, waiting for Nona's manipulation to complete itself.

"I've been nearly beside myself trying to figure how in heaven's name I'm going to get everything done. That girl of mine's slow as blackstrap. I swear she moves like that three-toed sloth we saw at the Saint Louis Zoo last summer. You could just stand for an hour and watch her lift a duster."

Althea nearly laughed. She'd thought the same thing of Graceful, Lord, how many times.

"Well, of course, we'll bring in a whole crew of niggers for the party and to decorate, whatever, but I'm talking about I don't know how I'm going to get out the invitations and do all the planning and keep up with all my engagements and run a household in the meantime." She sighed with the burdens her sudden wealth had laid upon her, and bent to sniff languidly at a crimson rose near her waist.

God, she's coarse as a stick. Cold contempt rose in Althea, increasing her irritation. She'd long held the secret fantasy that L.O. had found Nona in one of the brothels on First Street and fixed her up like a mended china doll before he paraded her around. Or that he'd come across her in some little hick Southern town and bought her off her parents as quick as she reached puberty. Wherever he'd found her, there wasn't an ounce of breeding in her— The distant flutter sifted in Althea's mind, and she held herself still. She bent to her work again. One thing was certain, poorbred or not, Nona's silly exterior covered a feral mind: slow, sure, full of grace, endlessly stalking its prey with perfect stealth. Althea moved fast along the walk, but Nona followed.

"They're every one slow as sand anyhow, I don't know what I can do about that. L.O. says that whole bunch in Little Africa's just worthless, he says if this state'd ever taught niggers their place in the first place we wouldn't have to have these lynchings, keep people and the papers all stirred up." Althea glanced back, the irritation so prickly and strong she felt that she'd love to just slap her. "Of course," Nona went on airily, flipping her little gloves, casting her eyes about the garden, "that wasn't a nigger the other night, he was white as my foot, but he was sure defiant as a bad nigger, you should have seen him, he lit a cigarette and stared us right in the— Oh!" She opened her eyes wide, touched her fingers to her lips as if she'd let a secret slip out. Then she tipped her vulpine features sideways and tucked her chin, smiling. "Oh my," she said, "guess I let that little kitty out of the bag."

The urge to slap her was so profound Althea feared she might give in to it. She turned away, snapped her shears brutally at the untamed hedge along the fencetop. This, surely, was part of Nona's sly purpose: for Althea to see her as she saw herself, a brave and slightly reckless female, defiantly childless, flaunting her wild acts at the limits of feminine respectability. She wanted Althea to quiz her for details, to be shocked or envious, to react. It was not all Nona wanted from her, but it was part, and Althea would not rise to it. She would not. Her clippers flew at the rambling hedge.

"You should have seen him, Thea. I hate to say it but you practically had to admire the man. He acted like it didn't matter to him one way or the other." She laughed. "But he was guilty as sin, you could see that. I told L.O. on the way home, I said, if ever a man was a coldblooded killer he was. You could see it right in those brazen eyes."

It's no different from her driving over in that Winton, Althea thought. *From how she brags shamelessly about L.O.'s strike.* But it was different. It was odious, vile, monstrous . . . it was . . . what? What was she thinking of? A bitterness crimped at her, an ugly pinched smallness, and she turned despite herself, said, "That's no cat out of the bag, Nona." Her voice was withering with contempt. "Half of Tulsa was out there, from what I hear."

"Oh, well, it was quite a turnout." Nona lowered her voice to a near whisper. "But you won't catch anybody admitting it this week!" Her smile was outright flirtatious. "The police were directing traffic, of all things! Folks were selling pop and little cut-up pieces of rope for keepsakes. Now, of course, butter won't melt in nobody's mouth. I guess it wasn't a soul from *this* town hung that scamp!"

Althea turned away, nearly faint with loathing, and began hacking at the wild roses again. The silence was broken only by the quick snips of the steel shears as she honed the rambling hedge to a tight, domestic neatness. At last the irritation grew so savage within her that she stopped, turned and glared directly in the wide, calculatingly innocent green eyes. "What is it, Nona?"

"What?" The bright eyes opened impossibly wider.

"What do you want? Why'd you drive over here in that ridiculous contraption—" She jerked her head at the Winton, which was not ridiculous at all but beautiful, stunning, and Althea did not even want to see it from the corner of her eyes. She tilted her head so that the sunhat shielded her sight, and she glared a moment longer at Nona. But Nona's soft pink beauty, her of-the-mode dress and stylish cap, her slim ankles and narrow waist and darting, hungry eyes were unbearable to look at, and Althea turned to stare across the garden, but there before her were the mauled and razed rosebushes, and so her gaze fell at last to her own filthy hands, the dark smears on her gardening dress. She saw not black loam but streaked bloody smears down the front of herself. Her vision began to go dark, as if she would faint or fall into a fit in the next instant, and she steadied herself with a hand on the fence beneath the thorny hedge.

"Thea? Are you all right?"

"No, it's nothing. Never mind. I just don't feel . . . The heat. Come back another time," she said. "Tomorrow . . ." Her voice trailed off, and she looked at the shade on the side porch, the swing motionless, the potted begonias and the impatiens brilliant in the shadows. She walked away from Nona without a word of explanation or apology. Without having learned her sly little purpose, without caring. She could hear the light heels tapping along the walk behind her. Althea stopped, said in a low voice, without turning, "Go away, Nona." She could feel the green eyes staring at her back, but that, too, did not matter. She walked on.

"Well. I never. You're going to give yourself a sunstroke, honey!" Nona called after her. "Why'n't you have Frank get you a gardener? Thea?"

Althea stepped up into the porch shade. She sat in the swing and began to rock. She didn't look at Nona again. The Winton's motor started up finally, but she didn't turn to watch Nona drive off. She rocked herself in the porch swing, rocked a long time, and her trembling pulse began to slow. Her clammy palms cooled. Her mind settled, grew calm, grew entirely blank.

Later—Althea couldn't have said how much later: perhaps half an hour, perhaps longer—she stood up and went to the French doors. She didn't wipe the mud from her gardening shoes but entered the house with driven urgency and hurried through the dining room, leaving a trail of ugly smears on the hardwood floor that faded to dull blotches by the time she stepped onto the kitchen's gleaming tiles.

Graceful was not in the kitchen. Althea looked in the pantry, which was likewise empty; she'd started toward the entrance into the back hall when she heard the slow, metallic grinding coming though the open back door. Without breaking stride she shifted course toward the screened-in porch, but stopped short in the doorway, took a stealthy step back.

The girl stood at the wringer washer, running a bedsheet through the rollers into the galvanized tub. The washer was angled so she could look out the screen as she worked, and only half her face was visible. A veiled expression touched her features, so that her almond-shaped eyes slanted more deeply, the lids partly closed. As always, she held her head high, tilted backwards nearly. She wore not her regular maid's uniform but a sleeveless cotton shift, and her clavicle bones showed above the scoop of neckline. The sinews in her arm lengthened, drew taut with each turn of the crank. Her hair had been brushed straight and pomaded, pressed tight to her skull, but the sleek shape of her head was haloed in the sunlight, a radiant haze of black fuzz escaping the pomade's discipline in the heat and the washwater's steam. Althea gazed at the line of perspiration beading the girl's upper lip, the two dark weeping rows that trickled from her temple, ran down the side of her cheek, and disappeared below her ear, where the jagged ends of coarse hair stuck out at the nape of her neck. The after-rain light bounced off the gray porch planks, picked up and illuminated in iridescence each particle and cell. Light played on the curve of her cheek, the broad plane of her nose and forehead; receded beneath the swell of her lower lip; disappeared entirely in the hollow beneath her eye, as if soaked in by the skin. As if the skin might receive light or throw light back as it chose.

Althea became suddenly acutely aware of Graceful's color. Not the classifying tint that declared one of them to be mulatto or black or high yellow or quadroon, not the general darkness that simply said to Althea's mind *colored*—but the precise hue, the very tone Althea's skillful eyes would have scanned and evaluated in matching furniture and draperies. Graceful's skin was a perfect, pure walnut brown: the same deep, rich, true-brown color as Althea's polished dining-room table.

Surprised, vaguely disoriented—and what, after all, had she come to tell the girl? what task had she come to lay out?—Althea watched the two perfect-brown hands reach into the water and pull up one of Franklin's white dress shirts, slowly twist it into a knot, wring it, and begin to feed the shirttail into the rollers' clenched grip. She realized that Graceful was left-handed. The recognition disturbed her, and she tried at once to dismiss it. The fact was irrelevant. A simple, insignificant, inconsequential little actuality—but a fact nevertheless, one she'd failed to note before, one which she could not ever go back to un-knowing, any more than she could un-know the fact that the girl had a last name. Althea's last name. The last name of her father, and her father's father. The dread began to rise in her, and Althea stepped through the doorway onto the porch.

Graceful looked up at her, apparently unsurprised. She did not quit turning the wringer handle. There was a long moment when only the creaking sound of the rollers, the metallic grinding of the iron crank filled the hot, dank air beneath the porch roof. Then the end of the flattened shirtcuff slid between the rollers into Graceful's upturned palm and she bent slightly to lay the shirt among the wet clothes in the tub. She stood straight again, her face in no way expectant.

What? Althea's mind scrambled to remember what she'd come for; her eyes swept the porch, and she spied the wicker basket beside the door, piled high with wet colored clothes. "What's that basket doing sitting there?" she said. Instantly there was a comforting return of order, a grounded sense of things as they should be. "You think those clothes are going to run out and hang themselves on the line?"

The girl made no answer.

"They'll sour in this heat wadded up that way, don't you know that?"

Still the girl was silent. She returned Althea's gaze without expression.

"Don't you know enough to hang one load before you start another?" Althea took in a deep, righteous breath. "Don't tell me you're stupid on top of everything else. That clothesline won't hold all the colored clothes and the sheets at the same time. You haven't got the sense God gave a green goose. What in the world was I thinking of," she said, glaring at the new, brightly galvanized washer, "to have Franklin buy that Eden when I could be sending my laundry out like every other sensible white woman, instead of pretending I've got a girl with enough brains to do a load of wash. Put those clothes on the line this minute. Just stop right now. Stop!"

And Graceful, who'd begun feeding a new sheet into the rollers, stopped turning the handle. The side of her face registered nothing. She dried her hands on her cotton shift, and as she did so, her head lifted slightly; there was the habitual upward tilt of her chin, a barely discernible shifting of weight in her shoulders, but Althea saw it, saw within the gesture what she expected to see: the sullen, resentful look of Negro pride. A clean, terrible rage flared in her.

"I know what you're up to," she spat. "Don't think I don't. It'll be straight up dark night before the laundry's finished, you won't have time for the mending, the waxing, nor much of anything else. You're so afraid you're going to have to do a little work around here. Take the whole day to do a little laundry, maybe you won't have to do anything but cook supper, is that right?"

Without a word the girl sidestepped the washer, walked the length of the porch. She paused at the door a moment before she bent and lifted the clothes basket, hoisted it to her left hip. Still she did not turn to face Althea. The spring twanged loudly as she pushed on the screen, nearly covering her words, spoken in a flat tone just at the range of hearing. "Man come while ago." She pushed through the door, negotiated the steps with the heavy basket resting on her outslung hipbone. Just before starting across the yard she spoke again, the words delivered in the same flat, even voice. "He's sitting in the front room." She turned then, looked up through the fine wire mesh at Althea, her highslanted brown face still without expression, without comment or judgment. "I aks him if he want me to come fetch you," she said, "but he say he rather just wait." She turned away to stride barefoot across the sparsely covered, shaded-out yard.

Man come while ago. Althea's heart raced, and within her chest she felt the rush of blood and heat. She ought to slap that girl, the rude, unmannered thing, saying *Man come,* when the term was *gentleman. White gentleman.* But in fact Althea's flare of anger was already extinguished, replaced by a deep, secret pleasure; she wanted to laugh out loud. It was Jim Dee, of course. Who else would it be? There was no reason for anyone—any gentleman, that is—to come calling to see her rather than Franklin. But, good Lord, didn't he have any better sense than to come in the middle of the day, when the girl or any of the neighbors had to see? Althea's hands flew up to remove the sunhat, the tips of her fingers feeling for stray hairs fallen loose from her chignon as she turned toward the kitchen.

In an instant she became aware of the brown smears on the front of her gardening dress, her run-over-at-the-heels, mud-caked shoes, the sweaty, outdoor smell rising from her whole being. Dear God. Her thoughts were displaced by the sense of urgency, but it was clear, well defined now, voluptuous with pleasure: she tiptoed into the back hall, glanced at the parlor doorway to make sure he wasn't standing there, and, seeing no one, she slipped into the foyer, around the newel, and up the staircase, heading directly for the bathroom, where she turned the thick milky cross on the hot-water faucet hard to the right. A rush of rusty water pounded fullforce into the porcelain tub. Althea didn't wait for it to clear but plugged the stopper into the drain and let the tub fill while she retrieved her wrapper and fresh undergarments from her room.

As she bathed, she called up the image she'd been unable to find the night before: the sunburned face on the far side of the parlor, the unblinking hazel eyes. She hadn't seen him since then, a year ago, at the end of last summer, when he'd come to the house with that rowdy bunch of wildcatters Franklin had invited, drillers, tool pushers, a few strictly lease men, roving about the room with their too-soon-dry shotglasses twirling in their coarse fingers and their loose mouths dropping hints, boasts, joking insults. Althea had smiled as she wandered among them offering tiny ham sandwiches, pouring white mule from the cut-glass decanter, reaching up to light Franklin's stogie, but her eyes were every minute on her husband's partner as he paced the damask confines of the room. The same behavior she loathed in the others seemed in Jim Dee a mark of his tense, masculine nature, and she'd watched carefully to see if he might nod his head toward the side porch to tell her to slip away and meet him. He did not. But once, as she'd stood near the mantel, her hand placed on the cool marble while her husband held her about the waist with one loosely draped paw, Althea had caught Jim's restless glance: he stared at her blankly, refusing to know her; but then his eyes stayed, unblinking, and he'd held her glance, and held it, until she didn't understand what the look meant, and then he'd held it longer, until she could not help but know its meaning: he wanted her, still. As he'd wanted her from the beginning. Seven years nearly. From the first minute he saw her, she told herself, smiling, as she stepped, dribbling rose-scented water, from the clawfoot tub.

For a year she'd nursed the memory of that long gaze; a thousand times and more she'd relived it, burnished it, carried the image beyond remembrance into a dream where she withdrew her waist from her husband's grasp, slipped out of the room and met her lover on the darkened porch: a fantasy revisited so often as to have become firm as memory—more so, for Althea's memory was filled with great blank spaces bordered by fabricated images from her many stories told. She hurried to the bedroom, re-brushed and pinned her hair, put on a simple and elegant gray silk afternoon dress. Only for a moment did she pause to examine herself in the dresser mirror. Flushed with heat and excitement, her cheeks moist and eyes sparkling, her lips red where she'd touched them with rouge—it was only the faintest hint, he'd never know—yes, she looked beautiful. She turned from the glass, pleased, and swept out of the bedroom. Slowly, with tremendous elegance and grace, she descended the stairs, one slender hand lightly touching the cherry banister. At the base of the stairs she paused for a deep, calming breath before she entered the parlor.

The man sitting in the high-backed chair did not bother to stand when she entered the room but merely gazed up at her in silence. In direct contrast to the thick, tawny hair and light hazel eyes she'd expected, this person was dark-headed, sloe-eyed: a stranger, someone unknown to her, although his thin face was uncomfortably familiar. He wore dirty denim pants and a cotton shirt with the sleeves rolled to the elbows, the collar open, and he appeared to be quite young, perhaps no more than eighteen or nineteen, although he slouched against the velvet with a kind of weary contempt unlikely for a young man. The man—or boy—whatever he was (she had to admit the aptness of Graceful's wording: this was no gentleman, even if he was white)—continued to stare at her in insolent silence, until at last Althea said, "Yes? What is it?" She thought she saw him smile slightly.

"You don't know me, I guess."

Her gaze ran down the length of him in a haughty, appraising glance. "No," she said, a clipped word of dismissal. She was ready to order him and his filthy clothes immediately off her beautiful maroon velvet chair, but the strange insolence of the fellow somehow prevented her from speaking.

"Look close," he said.

And she did, taking in the slouching length of him, seeing that the white shirt was in fact clean, as were the lean forearms, the two swarthy hands splayed on the arms of the chair. She saw that the dark blotches on the denim pants were not filth but well-laundered oil stains. He was an oilfield worker, of course: a roustabout, from the looks of him. It wasn't Althea he wished to see, but Franklin. Relieved, she glanced at the face then, but the fellow stared boldly at her, and her relief stopped cold. His gaze swept the room, returned to Althea's face in languid contempt for the parlor, its furnishings, Althea herself. He arose from the chair and came toward her in a slow saunter.

Althea stepped back, ready to shout for Graceful or to rush out the front door if necessary, but the fellow paused a few feet from her, turned with casual deliberateness toward the mirror over the mantel, and looked at himself. Althea followed his gaze, looked first at the young man's reflection, then her own, then caught his eyes where they returned her likeness: sloe-brown eyes beneath arched brows in a mildly masculine, distinctly younger replica of her own thin, beautiful features. His faint smirk widened to a grin. "Good to see you again, Sister."

She stared back without blinking, her expression unnaturally still. Her fingers came up, touched the cameo at her throat; her hand retreated to her side again. The movement of her lips did not disturb the placid surface when she said in a low voice, "I'm afraid you'll have to leave."

The grin dropped from the other's face. He continued to stare at her until Althea herself broke the locked gaze, turned in a whisper of silk to float across the room and seat herself on the divan. She smoothed the skirt beneath her as she tilted slightly sideways on the wine-colored velvet, ankles crossed, her slender calves revealed. It was the very image of the gesture she'd dreamed for Jim Dee as she'd donned the gray silk, though she had no recollection now of the fantasy.

"If you have business with my husband—"

She stopped herself. The last thing she wanted was for this person to speak to Franklin. She could think of nothing then except to repeat the phrase, more harshly this time, with such authority he couldn't possibly disobey: "I'm afraid you'll have to leave."

The young man strolled to the armchair, dropped into it, and crossed his denimed legs almost primly at the knee. "I'm afraid not," he said. There followed a brief silence wherein Althea, furious at her own helplessness, glared at the creature and calculated how much time she might have to get rid of him before Franklin came home, and how she might manipulate Graceful into secrecy without making herself vulnerable to the girl's loathsome, mute opinion.

"Well?" she said at last. "Speak."

"This is sure some warm welcome after— What's it been? Fifteen? Sixteen years? I can't remember. Ma told me, but some things I just can't seem to remember. It's other things," he said slowly, the dark eyes unblinking, "I can't seem to forget."

A highpitched whine sang in Althea's ears. Teeth clamped, chin rigid, one muscle spasming along her jawline, she waited.

"Of course, I was so little, I didn't even remember what you looked like. Now I do, though, sure." The eyes appraised her, then dismissed her, or dismissed something within her, and turned with a kind of lazy derision to survey the room. "You've done well by yourself. Of course, Ma told us that. She harped on that quite a bit." His eyes completed their tour of the parlor, returned to gaze steadily at Althea. "Looks like she was right."

"What . . ." She couldn't get her voice to work properly. "What do you want?" This last was almost a whisper, but the words grated harsh and clear in the airless room.

"Oh, I don't know." He stretched his long arms over his head, clasping them behind his neck, the grin broad now, delighted. "A bite to eat, maybe? That'd be a place to start. The girl offered a cup of coffee, but, now, a man who hasn't eaten in a couple of days, he don't want coffee, he wants meat and bread." He barked a short laugh into the air. "Meat. Bread. You remember those Snake Indians down around Iron Post? Couldn't speak a word of English but they knew them two words. Meat. Bread. Learned how to beg before they learned how to walk." He unclasped his hands from his neck and leaned forward slightly, hunkered toward her. "You remember? Sister?"

And Althea did remember, the image swimming to the surface of her disciplined mind: the two Creek children standing at the back door with their crusted hands out, their mouths chanting in singsong, *meat, bread,* over and over, and then the back door itself, five long rough-cedar slabs tacked together, and the barn behind the house, the manure-dappled feedlot, and behind it the prairie rolling away north and east and west, and the sky arching blue, impenetrable, rising forever. She could see the house then, or feel it, sense its frailness on the breast of prairie: two stories of slapped-together post oak and cedar, and the wind whistling through the whitewashed slats, and at last then, as if everything were conspiring to force the one image and its meaning upon her, she saw again in her mind's eye the flax-colored dress, soiled with blood, lying crumpled in a corner of the barnyard, trampled beneath sharp small hooves. Althea saw her young and naked self, bone thin, arms crossed before her in the cool darkness of the crib's depths, and a voice calling outside, several voices crying the same word again and again, the sound rolling across the prairie with the harsh, spitting wind.

"Letha? Sister? You're not going to faint, are you?"

The voice was amused, artificially concerned. When Althea's sight cleared she saw the person, young man, stranger, whatever he was (her mind would not allow her to say brother), half prepared to rise: boots flat to the carpet, hands stiff on the armchair, the insolence gone now, though not the sardonic amusement. She saw that his hair was not so much dark of its own properties as blackened by hair oil; saw that his swarthy complexion had been burnt so by the sun.

"I told Estaleen you'd faint when you saw me. You going to prove me right?" He watched her a moment, then settled back against the velvet, the white smile flickering in the dark face. "Naw, you're not going to faint. You're too mean and tough for that. That's one thing they always told me: Letha's tough as a hickory stick. I can remember that from before I could crawl."

"Tell me what you want."

"I told you already, a bite to eat. That's the first thing. I'm famished. Stomach feels like an old shriveled up twist of jerky. You're not too mean to feed me, are you? I don't want to have to go back and tell them that."

Without a word or change of expression, Althea stood and left the parlor. Sedately she crossed the foyer into the library, moved through the dining room and kitchen, and on to the back porch. Graceful stood at the washer, turning the wringer handle and gazing out through the screen as if no earth-shattering interval had passed. Althea's voice was quite calm when she said, "Please stop that now and come in and fix the gentleman some dinner. You can finish later." She didn't wait for her instructions to be acknowledged but turned immediately and headed back to the parlor. She stood in the archway and spoke in the same controlled manner. "You may have a seat in the dining room. I've told the girl to prepare dinner. I don't feel well, and if you'll excuse me, I'm going upstairs to lie down." She turned toward the staircase but stopped, frozen, when the voice sang out.

"Letha!"

Loudly. Too loudly. It could be heard on the street probably. Could be heard all the way through the house to the back porch.

"Cut it out now," the voice said. "You can quit the high-and-mighty act, you're not fooling your own flesh and blood. I've come to stay awhile. You might as well have your niggergirl fix me a bed."

O n that muggy Thursday evening, when Cleotha Whiteside stepped out her back door to toss washwater and saw the sun sinking behind the refineries west of town, her sense of another day's passing set a ponderous urgency in her bosom. She slopped the water onto a row of marigolds and zinnias beside the step, turned and went back into the house with the same unhurried determination that marked all her movements, but within her chest a cold weight squeezed her breath. She took off her apron, hung it on a nail beside the door as she passed through the small kitchen into the middle room, where she retrieved her hat from a knob atop the dresser, donning it and pinning it in one motion as she went on into the front room. Her youngest child, William, lay belly-down on the linoleum with his chin on his crossed hands, gazing out through the screen door.

"What's the matter with you, boy?" Cleotha stepped to the mirror beside the door frame and adjusted her hat with all seeming mindfulness on the wavery image inside the glass, though her full attention was on the nine-year-old sprawled, too still and far too quiet, on the floor. She could hear children's voices laughing, hollering, as they played farther up the street.

"Nothin," the boy said. He did not take his chin off his hands to say the word; the top of his head rose and fell with the two syllables.

"If nothing's the matter, I think I know somebody better get his young behind up off the floor."

The boy didn't move, did not raise his eyes to his mother, and in Cleotha's chest there was a further tightening of the stricture that had come on her at sight of the reddening western sky. *Not now, Lord,* she thought, *don't give me trouble with this boy now. I got all I can.* And she began to hum a low, sweet melody, her rhythm of movement slowing as she turned to face her son. "Willie, get up from there now. You know how to act better than that. If you not going to play out, you go see what you can put yourself useful about. Miss Clay give y'all any homework yet?"

The boy dared not be quite sullen with his mother, though still he didn't lift his head, and his voice was barely audible when he pushed himself away from the linoleum and sat up. "Yes, ma'am."

"Time I get home I want to see every bit of it done and you washed up for bed. I want to see your tomorrow-clothes laid out and your today-clothes on the line and a clean glass in the dishpan where you finished your cornbread and sweetmilk and washed up after yourself."

"Where you going?"

"That's for me to know and you to wonder about. Jewell and LaVona going to be here soon. You go on and do like I say." Cleotha turned to the screen door, her chest dense with worry and a familiar sensation, a kind of perpetual heartsickness she felt for this boy, her last child, the one most tender, who took all the world at its ought-to-be, not as it was. As she pushed through the screen she paused, looked over her shoulder, said, "You sure, now, you took that letter to the right house? The lady say it's the right place where Graceful stay?"

The boy shrugged, gazing past his mother to the street. "She say she going to give it to Graceful," he said softly, his mind apparently not on his words but on the children's voices drifting farther north.

Cleotha watched him a moment. "All right, son," she said at last. "That's fine. You mind what I said, now." She turned to go, stopped one last time; without glancing back at him, she said, "Dip you up a bowl of peaches after supper, if you want. Don't forget to wash the bowl out." She went on down the steps.

As she made her way south, the rusty light bled away slowly, turning amber, and yellow, until it had faded to a wan greenish twilight by the time she reached Archer, where tinkling music came from the east, mingled with laughter and soft voices floating on the patinaed air. Cleotha turned toward the candescent lights and gasoline fumes along Greenwood Avenue, though her purpose was not to immerse herself in that rich smoke-and-food-and-music-filled atmosphere but to slip into the redbrick building halfway up the block which housed the *Star* office and speak to a certain young man who operated the linotype machine there. As she moved along the street, her mind taken with her silent worries, she saw the young man in her mind's eye: his skin near as black as the ink on the tiny letters he tapped into place with his long, deft fingers; his broad, white, beauteous grin and infinite politeness. He was a good boy, or he knew himself to be a good boy, and Cleotha did not trust him. Nevertheless, it was to Hedgemon Jackson she'd gone with her request to compose the letter to Graceful, one that would make sure Graceful came home quick but, hopefully, wouldn't frighten her.

Now Cleotha doubted the content of the letter, and with doubt came fear and the old suspicions slipping around her, worn and familiar as an old housedress. He'd written no telling what; she had not dictated, hadn't wanted the boy to know the details of her private trouble, and so she'd left the nature of the emergency unspoken, had not even used that word—*emergency*—by no means, but had only asked could he write a note to Graceful to say someone wanted to see her uptown. A letter had been the best way, surely. A telegram was too dear, and in any case would've scared her, and Cleotha would not even dream of telephoning to a whitelady's house. She'd had to have somebody write that letter. Surely she'd done the right thing.

The lone unsure place in Cleotha Whiteside's front to the world was this old secret sore of not knowing how to read and write. It drove her in a thousand ways: drove her to push her children to work harder, study more, learn plenty, so they might someday be something in the world besides a bootblack and a housemaid on the southside; drove her to use her other gifts to their greatest strengths and beyond, so that she not only sang in the Macedonia First Baptist Church choir in her clear, mellifluous alto but offered that same gift as gospel solo almost weekly, and even led choir practice now and again when Brother Goodlow had to be out of town. Her natural-born skill with numbers had become so practiced she could figure in her head any quantity of the box dinners she sold to the pipeline layers along Dirty Butter Creek and make change in an instant without picking up a pencil or a paper sack to figure on, and without ever making a mistake. From her childhood in the old Chickasaw Nation she'd craved to learn how to read and write, but her mother's death when she was seven, and her father's disappearance a year later (whether by choice or violence or accident, none knew: he'd simply ridden off on a horse one afternoon and never come back), had left her a child orphan with a brother to raise, and she'd given up what hope she might have had for schooling.

For years she'd thought the time would come later, someday, when she would learn to decipher writing, but never had that someday come. At last she'd made up her mind at the age of twenty-seven, exactly during the birth of her fourth child, that she was too old to master such a complex code, and afterwards abandoned all longing in that direction. But Cleotha had stayed vigilant in seeing to it that her offspring attack the written word particularly well. And they *could* write, all five of her living children, beautifully—they each had a beautiful handwrite, every one of their teachers said so—and she had two girls still at home who could write anything you'd want to ask them. But Cleotha hadn't called on Jewell or LaVona because she hadn't wanted to scare them or get their nervous selves stirred up and giddy, how they were apt to do. Now, turning onto Greenwood Avenue, the light and noise coming almost as a blast of air against her face, Cleotha thought she might have made a mistake in judgment (a rare admission, even to the silence of her own opinion): maybe she should have gone down to whitetown and fetched her daughter herself.

Cleotha moved up the block, stopped at the glass window marked with gold scratches, which she knew declared, somewhere within the myriad slashes and humps and crosses and curlicues, the motto and title of Greenwood's renowned Negro weekly, *The Tulsa Star.* No light came from within, but she knew the boy's typesetting duties kept him there late, and she pulled the door open and went in. The sweetish odor of ink and newsprint swelled around her when she entered. She passed through the front office, where the shape of a large desk announced itself among the shadows, and eased toward the back, where she could see a slit of light slicing across the wood floor from beneath a closed door. She knocked once, twice, pulled the door open.

A large brown man stood at the back of the room, where the huge metal presses ground a thunderous, relentless *ka-lack ka-lack ka-lack,* and neither he nor the boy was aware of her. Hedgemon swayed before the linotype machine, a complicated iron monstrosity of wheels and trays and black gears, hitting the keys so rapidly it was hard to believe there was purpose or design to his dancing fingers. His eyes scanned the sheet of scratches tacked to the wall in front of him as his long, quick fingers played the huge keys that snapped the tiny letters into straight lines in the metal tray, to make words, to make meaning, to translate to the whole of the colored community the thoughts and opinions of Mr. A.J. Smitherman, editor, and the news. Cleotha paused a moment in renewed satisfaction as she recalled why she'd chosen Hedgemon Jackson to write that letter to Graceful. His skill with those bits of metal made him a translator, she thought: inside that long-limbed dancing body, the boy was entirely fluent in both languages, gliding effortlessly from written to spoken and back again in the same way Cleotha's father had translated without pause between the white traders and the old fullbloods at Tishomingo when she was a child. Her confidence restored, Cleotha pushed forward into the room to find out just precisely what meaning the boy had translated in his backtilted handwrite onto that blue page.

"Hedgemon," she said flatly.

The boy jumped, looked at her, and his expression was such a wash of guilt and quick, knowledgeable fear, as if he'd been found out about something, followed almost instantly by that wide, beautiful grin as he nodded and reached behind himself to untie his leather apron, that Cleotha instantly remembered why she distrusted him, and her own fears and nameless insecurities rushed back. But the woman was indomitable in any pursuit once she'd set out on it.

"Come out here now," she said over the sound of the clacking presses, "I got a bone to pick with you."

And she turned and went back into the dark hallway and all the way to the front of the building, where she stood at the window. Across the street the show had let out at the Dreamland, and a stream of beautifully dressed men and women emerged from the theater, blinking their eyes, laughing and talking, but it seemed to Cleotha that she could feel the tension through the glass, their laughter a cover-up for their nervous dread: it didn't matter in Greenwood that it was a whiteboy last weekend the people in Tulsa had lynched.

"Anything wrong, Miz Whiteside?" Hedgemon said behind her. "Ma'am?"

"What sort of story you put in that letter? That letter to Graceful?"

"What? Why, just what you told me, ma'am, just could she come home, somebody's waiting to see her. That's all. Just only what you said."

"Whose name did you sign to it?"

"Whose?"

"I'm asking you what name you put on it." She turned to look up at the young man, whose black skin receded to near invisibility in the darkness of the newspaper office, but whose eyes and unwilled smile flashed brightly in the reflected light from the street.

"Why, just . . . I just signed it, you know."

"Sign it what?"

"Uh . . . my name. I just sign Hedgemon T. Jackson, just, you know . . . my name. Is something wrong?"

"What makes you think my daughter going to pay one bit of attention to anything Hedgemon T. Jackson got to say on any subject?" Cleotha said, disgusted, turning back to the window as the stream of folks from the Dreamland bled onto Greenwood Avenue, merged with the grander river of movement on the street. Several automobiles cranked to life. A slow wail from a cornet rose, crescendoed, died away up north somewhere. She wondered if she might still make her way—might dare to make her way—across the Frisco tracks into whitetown this late of an evening.

"I didn't mean to think nothing, ma'am," Hedgemon said, his voice soft. "You requested me to make that letter, I just . . ." The hushed words died away, drowned in the *ka-lack ka-lack* from the back room and the lively, muffled streetsounds seeping through the glass.

"That's all right. It's all right." She didn't mean to make the boy feel low; there was just too much worry in her mind.

"I put it in there you the one say to write it."

"What's that?" She turned to look up at him again. *He must be over six feet tall,* she thought. *I believe he's taller than T.J.*

"I mean, I didn't act like *I* was the one telling her to come home, I put it right there on the page, 'Your mother Mrs. Ernest Whiteside request the honor of your presence'—like that."

"Oh, Lord." Cleotha couldn't feel any satisfaction one way or another. If the boy had made the letter so garbled with his high-toned newspaper talk to where her daughter couldn't make out its meaning, well, that was one problem, and if he'd done the job right and Graceful still hadn't come—and this was Thursday evening, maid's night out; there hadn't ought to be the excuse she couldn't get off from working—why, there was something different, and worse, to worry about. Cleotha's mind was so disturbed now, just filled to the brim and flowing over, that she rejected both possibilities. She simply dropped the issue of the letter altogether and veered onto another track. "What time the cars quit running?"

"Ma'am?" The boy appeared to be fading back into the darkness of the office. "Oh. I don't believe I'd take a streetcar yonder this time of evening."

"I don't believe I would either, if I could help it."

"I don't know. Sure don't. I never took no streetcar this time of night. I never took no streetcar yonder anyhow, not since I was eleven." He was, indeed, moving backward, gliding on agile feet toward the slant of light from the pressroom. "She'll be here tomorrow morning, you watch. Or right now, I bet she's home right now, while you come over to Greenwood."

Cleotha could make out nothing but the tall, gangly shape of the boy, his warm, invisible presence.

"Tell Graceful I said hello when you see her," his voice said. "I didn't make out like it was me looking to see her, I truly didn't, but you could tell her from me I'd be proud . . ." A brief pause. "You didn't say who it was . . ." He hesitated long enough for Cleotha to offer the answer if she was willing, not so long as to seem to be expecting. "I just left it blank, that part, about who it was wanting to see her." The voice was muted, whether from secrecy or shame, she couldn't tell; she could hardly hear him. "But you could let her know Hedgemon Jackson be proud to see her." And he turned, pulled the door open quickly, and disappeared into the brightly lit *ka-lack ka-lack ka-lack.*

Cleotha stood in the dark office a moment longer, pondering the two sounds she'd heard in the boy's voice, understanding two facts about Hedgemon Jackson she'd never dreamed of, any more than she'd imagined his inky, dancing life had anything to do with her or her family: one, that the boy was, and probably had been for a long time, in love with Graceful, and two, that he was a terrible coward.

But Hedgemon Jackson disappeared from Cleotha's reckoning as quickly as she walked out the *Star* office door. She trundled swiftly south along the avenue, weaving among the highly dressed folks making their evening promenade, skirting the clot of youngsters knotted up in front of the confectionery, her senses deluged with the glut of sights and odors and cacophonous voices, and her thoughts circling in their worn, familiar rhythm. As the deep trouble arose, she would receive it and worry it a while before she'd think to speak a word or two to the Lord to take it in His hands. A moment later it would roll to the surface again. In her mind's eye she could see him: T.J.'s thin profile in the kitchen, his face fretted with worry, frowning with that old pettish fretsomeness he'd carried from the womb, but the lines worn deeper, more serious, as he stood in the square of moonlight, saying softly, No, Mama, don't turn on the light. Just spoon me up a bowl of them beans, that's all I want. T.J. home, in her kitchen, three nights ago, and now gone again. *Oh, my Lord, take and keep him,* she prayed in her mind's silence. *Take and keep him, oh, my Lord, help my son.*

Cleotha stopped at the corner of Greenwood and Archer and looked south. She could see electric lights twinkling in the buildings of downtown, twelve and fourteen stories tall, some of them, and dark and silent, unlike the swirl of light and noise behind her on the street. The railroad tracks, too, were silent, hardly visible in the blackness a hundred yards away. She willed her feet to keep walking into that darkness, but they carried her no farther. The darkness was a wall of white, and she could not enter. For a moment she pondered the changes inside herself that had brought her to see in such a manner: the wall stood invisible and solid on the south side of the tracks; she saw it not with her eyes but with a tender, feeling place on the whole front of her, and there was a terrible mystery in how it could look so blank and dark, and yet feel like the heat of fire burning in the distance against her skin. *This belong to Ernest,* she thought. *He pass along plenty things to me besides our children, and one thing he pass is how he grew up to dread whitefolks. Him and the whitefolks both have passed Ernest's way of seeing on to me.*

She gazed south, willing herself forward, thinking of her daughter Graceful and her deep-in-trouble older son. She was a woman of strength, of courage, of unassailable will for herself and her children, but Cleotha Whiteside could not bring herself to leave the light and noise and melodic voices behind her and cross the street, the train tracks, and penetrate that invisible dark border.

I believe that boy's probably right, she said to herself. *Graceful probably sitting in the front room this minute. Let me just go on home and see. If she don't come tonight, I'll go down there myself in the morning. I'll go in the morning.*

And the woman turned heavily and began walking west toward Elgin Avenue, unable to admit to her own mind that the dark wall of white was stronger than her desire on this evening to bring her daughter home.

B oldly, in cunning, he'd hidden himself within the lynch mob. In secret now—although, he considered, with no less cunning—he hid
himself in his sister's house. It was all the same. Fools who searched in the
concealed places might hunt uselessly forever; as for himself, he'd settled
in his mind long ago that the most obvious was the very place the majority of idiots forgot to look. Japheth smiled as he smoothed open the *Tulsa
Daily World,* scanned the headlines, sipped coffee from a fine china cup.

BELTON LYNCHING PROBE CONTINUES
Reward Offered for Arrest of Leaders of Orderly Mob
Witnesses to Be Asked to Tell All They Know

In amused satisfaction he read that hundreds of "witnesses" were being summoned by the grand jury to name the lynch-law leaders. One eyebrow arched delicately as he scanned the paragraph declaring that Belton's
missing partner was still at large, though there were rumors he'd been
spotted in Springfield, Missouri; in El Paso; across the border in Juárez.
Fools, Japheth's mind said. His lips curled.

Among the oft-changing traits of Japheth Whiteside's nature there
abided only two constants: an unshakable certainty in his own immunity

from punishment, and constant, overriding contempt. Five nights ago, when white men stood in the dark at Orcutt Lake, smoking and drinking and cursing, with their hat brims pulled low and their boots propped on Ford fenders, Japheth had stood among them. When one said, Jesus Christ, a man don't have to do nothing to get away with murder in this country, and spat, and wiped the lip of the bottle before swigging and passing the flat flask to the next man, Japheth had said, Ain't it the damn truth, and spat, drank a long swallow, passed the flask in the darkness, wiped his own lips. Later, when they dragged Roy Belton from his cell, jabbing their gun barrels in his ribs and beating and cursing him, Japheth stood at the back of the crowd, watching Belton's eyes to see what fear would do to him, but with his own head bowed, hat brim tugged forward, so that the condemned man's eyes might not meet his.

Within the snaking line of automobiles crawling away from the city, he'd crouched on the running board of the second-to-lead car with his arm thrust through the open window, holding to the armrest with strong, clamped fingers, reveling in the feel of the cool nightwind, thick with a storm coming, gliding over his face. On the black, pitted road east of Red Fork, with the woman beside him and a thousand voices crying for rope (Rope! Rope! Rope! Rope! repeated pondlike in the darkness), his cry had joined the chorus. And when the body was cut down and the mob scrambled for bits of cloth from Roy Belton's death clothes, Japheth had been not first or last but one among many who ripped the soiled cotton from his partner's purpling, cooling body on the dark road. Even as he'd joined the scrabbling mob, he had scorned them in silent derision. No less so now, as he breakfasted in his sister's sun-splashed dining room almost a week later, did he sneer in his soul at the city's mind, turned already, and with great vehemence, against itself. He shook the paper out, reached for a buttered biscuit, devoured half in one bite, placed it carefully on the edge of the saucer before he thumbed to page 37, "In the Oil Fields," to read carefully the day's oil report.

A tall, thick man with coarse blond hair came into the dining room as Japheth was rubbing the last biscuit facedown in molasses. The man stood at the far end of the table and watched him smear the biscuit in the circle of brown syrup flecked with yellow. Japheth glanced up once but made no acknowledgment as he raised the dripping mound to his lips and finished it in two swift bites, wiped his hands and mouth neatly, tossed the linen napkin on top of the swirl of molasses and leftover yolk in his plate.

He pushed back from the table and reached for his coffee, sipped it as he gazed up at Franklin's perplexed, handsome face.

"Have a seat," Japheth said at last, cordially, as if it were his own polished Windsor chair he indicated, his own fine walnut table and steaming china pot of coffee, and Franklin the uninvited guest. "Girl cooks up a good biscuit, don't she?" He took another genteel sip. "Can't say a lot for her coffee, though." He dipped his head for a third small sip, a slight frown darkening his smooth features. "I've drunk better creekwater." Suddenly he smiled broadly, an effect both disarming and chilling. "I'm going to have to guess Sister didn't say a word to you. Is that right?"

Franklin turned without speaking, went out into the library. The smile instantly disappeared from the young man's face. He listened to the dull metallic uncradling of the telephone receiver, the throat being cleared, the authoritative voice say, "Osage six, four nine four," and, in the pause following, the nervous tapping of fingers on the oak desk where the phone stood.

"Miss Greyson," the voice said. A slight curl returned to Japheth's lips.

Another short pause, and then: "Sylvia, listen, ring up Jim Logan and tell him I'll be a little late but I'll be there. Tell him not to get up on his high horse, I'll *be* there, tell him to wait. Now, hurry up on that because he gets out before the damn chickens, and then phone L.O. and Steve Parsens, tell them I'll get in touch with them on Monday. No, no. Just I'll get in touch Monday. I don't have time this morning. I'll ring up from Bristow. Yes. Three or four o'clock, I think, at the latest. All right." There was the thick, muted click as the receiver returned home.

By the time Franklin came back into the dining room, Japheth had transformed his appearance: Where arrogance had cocked the dark head ceilingward as he'd smirked at Franklin from his seat at the table, now he stood diffidently beside the chair with head slightly bowed. Where mockery had crooked the little finger of the long, thin hand holding the china cup, now both hands were clasped humbly before him, and the contempt that had bled through his smile had simply vanished. The young man gaped at Franklin almost stupidly, puplike, as if he cared for nothing more than a kind word, a bone off the table.

"I'm Letha's brother," he said. "I didn't mean to shock you while ago, I thought she would've told you I was here."

"Letha."

"Oh, I mean Sister. We used to call her Letha sometimes. We all had a nickname. Althea, of course I mean. I thought she would've told you."

The young man came forward with his hand stretched out, and Franklin instinctively took the limp fingers in his thick grasp. He looked around the room a moment, as if the answer to his confusion might be found in a corner, or in one of the still-life prints framed on the papered wall. His gaze returned finally to the face before him, which, indeed, bore a troubling resemblance to Althea's, and he said at last, "Well. I guess Gracie took care of you. She does cook up a flaky biscuit, you're right there." And then, vaguely, "You ought to taste her fried pies."

As if her misspoken name were an actor's cue, Graceful entered the dining room through the deep passageway from the kitchen, her arms laden with the silver tray bearing chafing dishes, her features hardened into a carved mask, and yet grinding beneath with a silent, barely controlled fury.

"Ah, here we are!" Franklin boomed, and pulled a chair out at the opposite end of the table from his usual place, where biscuit crumbs and spots of congealed gravy marred the white cloth all around Japheth's plate. It's unlikely he'd have noticed the girl's anger under any circumstance, but in his present state of disturbance he had no ability to see anything except his arriving eggs and meat and gravy, which could as well have been walking through the door of their own volition. He welcomed the familiar forms of silver tray and covered dishes, grateful for the fact they gave him immediate direction. "Thank you, Gracie," he said heartily as the dish of eggs thunked onto the table. "Listen, I wouldn't bother with breakfast for Mrs. Dedmeyer this morning, I don't believe she'll be down. She took one of her sick headaches last night." He glanced at Japheth. "She gets these sick headaches, put her right in the bed."

He waited for a murmur of concern from the one who claimed to be Althea's brother, but when none was forthcoming, he turned his glance back to Graceful as she moved to the sideboard for clean plates and silver. He continued, unseeing, to watch her as she set the place before him, snapped open the napkin, uncovered the lidded dishes with slow, forced violence. Graceful finished her work, turned without letting her eyes pass over either man, and went back into the kitchen.

"Well." Franklin seated himself, scooped a slithery fried egg onto his plate. "It's probably that sick headache. They just flatten her sometimes. They make her so sick." He ate quickly, hardly chewing. "She has to lay in the dark for two and three days." He glanced up at the stranger, who continued to stand, gazing down at him from Franklin's own place at the head of the table. "I know that's why she forgot to mention you'd come to visit." This explanation seemed offered as much to himself as to the stranger, but why his wife had forgotten to tell him, ever, that she had a brother at all, Franklin searched out no excuse for, even for his own mind. "I'll just . . ." And he didn't know what he would do. He filtered his thoughts for his next sure purpose, but, finding none, he went back to eating rapidly. In a moment he said, "I'll let her know you've had your breakfast. You need anything?" The young man was silent. Franklin couldn't see his face clearly for the brilliant slash of orange light coming through the French doors. "Well, if you need anything, just tell the girl. She'll see to it."

"You're in the oil business."

Franklin stared at him. Why wouldn't the fellow sit down, or move some kind of way so that Franklin didn't have to crane his neck so, squint up through the sunlight to see him? "Have a seat. Have a seat," he said at last, in exact unconscious imitation of the other's first words to him.

"Got any openings for an ace tool dresser?"

"Well, I . . ." Franklin chewed a piece of steak, pondering. "It could be. . . ." He reached for the gravy spoon. "Might be possible."

"No!" His wife's voice jumped hard behind him.

Althea stood sheathed in pale blue in the alcove between library and dining room. Light played and refracted on the silk hem of her dressing gown, though her face remained in shadow. She posed, quite motionless, her hair loose on her shoulders. "You know Jim won't have anybody but Ben Koop on his rig," she said. Her voice was strong, certain, only slightly taut. She raised a hand to her face, let it fall to her side once more.

"The lady's right," Franklin said with a forced laugh. "My partner's pretty particular about picking his toolie. Not that they all aren't, but Jim's one driller you can't even discuss it with. . . ." And his words faded, clipped by his wife's judgment and his own ever-present reluctance to share a word about his business. Abruptly he stood, stepped toward the archway. "Here you are, my darling, how's your headache? My goodness, I had no idea. I already told Grace not to fix you any breakfast, but I'll just step to it and have her put the eggs on. Are you better? Do you feel like you could eat a bite of something?"

"Morning, Sister."

Althea leveled her eyes on the stranger a cold instant, then swept her gaze past in apparent unconcern as she floated into the room and seated herself on the east side of the table, between the two men, with her back to the light.

"Is your headache gone?" Franklin asked.

She gave her husband a weak smile.

"Graceful!" Franklin called, and again as if on cue—or as if she'd been waiting just out of sight beyond the passageway—the girl immediately appeared.

"Eggs and grits for Mrs. Dedmeyer. Grits, dear?"

Althea nodded.

"Grits," Franklin repeated. "And bacon?"

The nod again.

"Bacon. Not too crisp," Franklin directed, never taking his frowning gaze from his wife's face. "Guess you'd better whip up another little batch of biscuits if there's none left. Can you eat a biscuit, dear?"

There was an instant's hesitation before Althea nodded.

"All right. Biscuits. No gravy. No gravy, right, dear?"

She nodded again.

"And a little glass of sweetmilk to coat her stomach. You ought to take a glass of sweetmilk before you have your coffee, darling. Dr. Taylor said that."

As if she'd always been of the most agreeable and compliant nature, Althea smiled meekly, nodded yet again.

Had any of the three seated at the table looked up, they would have seen in the sculpted brown face a rage beyond their reckoning, a choked, suppressed fury. But even Althea, who was obsessively aware of Graceful's mien and presence at almost every moment, did not raise her eyes; she continued staring across the table at her husband. While Franklin spoke, Graceful looked at each of the white people in turn, ending with the profile of the one who slouched in the master chair, an amused, careless curl at his lips as he gazed at his sister. Though Graceful's expression remained unchanged, there was a sudden quick flaring of her nostrils, a deepening of the clenched line at her jaw. She turned, even as Franklin continued his instructions, and went back into the kitchen.

" . . . fresh cream for her coffee, and a little dab of that plum jelly," Franklin said. "You'll save room for biscuits and jelly, won't you? You will once you get a taste of this new batch of Grace—" He glanced up then, but seeing Graceful's back disappearing in the passageway, he dropped his gaze seamlessly to Japheth. "She loves wild-plum jelly, the sourer the better."

"Yes," Japheth said. "I know."

Althea's glance swerved to him, snapped back to her husband at once, and remained there. "Darling," she said, and the sound in the word was so natural that even Franklin didn't consider that she hadn't called him by any endearment for many years, "didn't you say that today was the day you were going to take me downtown?"

"She used to climb those scraggly sand plums down at the river, pick off the hard, bitter little fruits before they'd turned orange nearly, eat them till her mouth puckered."

"I really do need to go to Renberg's and pick up a few things."

"Well, to tell you the truth, dear—"

"And I wanted to stop in at Seidenbach's." Althea swept over her husband's words in a rush. "They're having a new fall-suit sale, I could use a good fall suit, I really could."

"Ma used to whip the daylights out of her when she caught her, said her mouth was going to shrivel up like an old lady's."

"And then I wanted to look in at Vandevers. You know, L.O. and Nona are having this silly masquerade ball in honor of that new strike. I guess he told you." Althea's eyes glittered, the long line of her neck arched beautifully as she tilted her head toward her husband. "Nona was here yesterday, she couldn't say a word about much else besides L.O.'s strike and that disgusting lynching—"

"Shrivel up like an old lady's! Isn't that what Ma used to say?"

Althea held her glazed stare on Franklin's face. "The vain thing carried on for an hour, you know how it is when Nona gets wound up about something." She released a brittle laugh.

"Chased her into the middle of Sand Creek with the hickory switch, that's how they used to tell it."

Franklin looked at the two faces across from him, one pale, one darkened nut-brown by the sun, and yet as alike as is possible in two born of the same parents a decade apart and of different sexes. Their kinship was undeniable, though he would have sworn with his dying breath that his wife was the only child of aged parents who'd been killed in a trolley accident at Kansas City when she was fifteen. The abhorrence and fear he'd felt at first sight of this stranger at his table now bled from the stranger to Althea. The thought came to him that in almost sixteen years of marriage he had never, in any way, known his wife. Immediately he stood, came around the table toward her with his voice fixed in a forced tenderness, saying, "Of course I'll take you to town, certainly—but with your headache and all, don't you think we should wait till tomorrow?"

"I'm fine," she said, and smiled up at him.

He reached to feel her brow. "Of course, dear. If that's what you want."

"I thought you had to meet your partner in Bristow this morning," Japheth said.

Althea immediately flinched away from Franklin's hand, darted her eyes across the table, quickly back up to her husband, then to the mirror above the sideboard on the opposite wall.

"Damn," Franklin said. "Damn." He glanced at the mantel clock. "Too late to catch him. Sweetheart," he said, touching her shoulder, "I can't cancel it now, he'll be sitting at that depot till next Tuesday, and red hot to boot. Jim's got something—" He stopped abruptly. Not even to soothe his wife could Franklin bring himself to reveal his business. "I'm sorry, darling." He caressed her shoulder. "Tomorrow. I'll take you right down first thing in the morning."

Althea reached beneath her hair, touched the pulse at the side of her neck, let her hand drop to her lap again; then she folded both hands and placed them before her on the cloth.

"Damn!" Franklin exploded. "Where's that girl with your breakfast? Graceful!" He rushed toward the passageway. "Gracie!" His voice came from the depths of the kitchen. "Grace!"

The one at the end of the table began to chuckle softly. There were only the two of them in the room then, and the unvoiced history. "You don't have any choice, Aletha. I'm here now, I can't help it if you don't like it." He paused, an ear cocked toward the kitchen, leaned over and whispered, "She's gone."

Immediately Franklin came back into the dining room. "She's gone." He turned his perplexed face to Althea. "I don't know where she went. She never even started the biscuits."

"Gone," Althea echoed, her voice hollow. She stood quickly and hurried through the kitchen into the back hall, jerked open the maid's-room door. The rope that stretched across the corner in lieu of a closet showed only two bare wooden coat-hangers. The sheet had been stripped from the narrow cot. The pine shelf below the mirror was empty of brush, comb, blue jar of pomade, though the pomade's spiced scent permeated the tiny cubicle, sweet, petroleum-laden, almost medicinal. Althea swept her gaze again and again around the room, as if she might have overlooked Graceful's solid form in that cramped six-by-eight-foot space. The scent was so strong, it seemed the girl must be somehow present. A weak fury passed over Althea, kin to the inexplicable rages that had ravaged her in recent days, but tempered by fear, muted by recognition of her own helplessness, and the understanding that, in some way she could not comprehend, for reasons unknown to her, she needed the girl.

"Darling." Franklin stood in the dim hallway. Behind him she saw her brother's sylphlike form outlined against the bright kitchen door. "Why don't you go upstairs and lie down. I'll fix you a bite of something, and then let me run down to Bristow and take care of this business. Soon as I get back I'll call Sutphen and see about him sending us a new girl. First thing in the morning. We'll have you some help here in no time. I don't know what got into that girl." He shook his head, looking over Althea's shoulder into the empty cubicle. "I thought we had a pretty fair hand in her. I thought she might stay awhile."

"Don't worry about Sister." Japheth had his arms braced against the jamb, his legs spread slightly, so that the reedy figure formed an X, blocking the door. "I'll make her some breakfast. You wouldn't credit it, but I'm a pretty fair cook myself. I can stir up a flapjack and fry bacon, anyhow." Even with the light behind him, the white smile showed in his dark face. "I learned that in California. You like a good flapjack, Sister?"

"No! No. Really. I wouldn't care for anything, thank you. I'll . . . I think I'll just go upstairs and lie down." She moved quickly along the dark hall to the front of the house, paused a moment in the foyer. "Dearest!" she called back. "Will you come up in a minute?" She didn't wait for an answer but disappeared in a swirl of blue silk up the stairs.

Franklin glanced at the fellow, who remained as yet nameless to him. The other stepped to the side with an elegant gesture, his back pressed to the doorjamb, inviting him into the kitchen. Franklin turned at once and followed his wife. When he entered the bedroom he found her, not lying down, as he'd expected, with the shades drawn and a cool cloth pressed to her eyelids, but pacing dramatically from window to wardrobe to vanity dresser.

"Out!" she said. "I want him out of here!" She turned on her husband as if the presence of the one downstairs were entirely at Franklin's invitation and insistence. "This morning!" she cried, her face twisted. "This instant!"

"Darling—"

"Don't *darling* me!" And then, in a lower register: "Don't you dare . . . one more minute . . . give me that God-blessed fake worried look." She whirled and walked to the window.

Franklin stared at his wife's back a moment, then he turned and left the room.

She waited. A scattering of morning sparrows twittered in the backyard. The sun had eased south with the coming autumn; yellow light burnished the lace curtains at her window, but summer would not release its muggy hold, and already the heat was rising. Her upper lip began to bead with perspiration. Translucent threads of moisture slid slowly at her blanched temples. She was completely motionless, even her eyes were set, unblinking as a deathmask, staring without sight at the bunched pleat of lace curtain. Only the threads and beads of sweat, the slow rise and fall of breast betrayed life in the still figure at the window. But within, hidden from the fixed surface, Althea's mind tumbled with swirling images: a tremendous tongue lolling from a cave of mouth, a thin trickle of red water, and above it a black woman's face swiveling toward her, shocked, and then shouting, and ever returning, relentless, the floating, sinister image of the flax-colored dress, smeared with blood.

She turned to rush out of the bedroom as Franklin came through the door. He was frowning, and it was not the familiar frown of tender concern. Althea stopped short in the middle of the room, her hands clasped at her breast in an unconscious gesture of supplication.

"What the devil's going on in this house?"

"What?"

"You tell me what. What the hell is that fellow doing here? If he's your brother, how is it I never heard about him? And if he's not your brother, who in God's name is he, and where'd he get off to now?"

"I don't know," she whispered. "Franklin. I don't know. He's gone?"

"I looked all through the house, out in the yard. He's gone the same as the girl is. I want to know what the deuce this is all about." His eyes were more demanding than at any time in their married life together, and Althea met them for only an instant before she dropped her glance to the carpet. Immediately she recognized her mistake; she looked up.

"You're the man of this house, aren't you? Whose job is it—"

"Don't pull that," he said. The forcefulness of Franklin's authority with men, with anyone connected to his worklife, settled, for the first time, on Althea. "Sit," he said, indicating with a nod the dressing stool. She did so. "Talk."

Althea opened her mouth, closed it again. His eyes would not turn away from her. She began almost literally to squirm under their demand; she twisted about on the vanity stool, plucked at the silk gown across her knee. "Franklin . . ." she said, and stopped again. "Really . . . I . . ."

She had nothing to say. There was nothing she could say that would not collapse the carefully built structure of lies she'd raised over many years, as a bottom ace pulled from a house of cards will tumble the whole house. She willed her husband gone, prayed he would go on to the office, or just go, completely, leave her alone, disappear from the face of the earth, so that she might not have to deal with his stupid, incessant questions.

"Who is he, Thea?"

"Nobody," she whispered.

"Yes." Franklin walked over and took her by the wrist, not roughly, not threatening violence, but with cold authority. "He's somebody. Talk."

Her mind flew through new lies, a new tale beginning to weave its elaborate intricacies—an old friend? no, not friend, enemy, an old enemy of her brother's—but no! Dear God, there was too much confusion, she needed time, an hour or two alone, to weave a new history. "Franklin, please. My head. I have this blinding headache. I can't . . ." She rubbed her temple with her free hand, her other limp in his grasp. Franklin watched her a moment, and then he released her hand, which dropped heavily to her lap. In silence he turned to leave.

"Where are you going?"

He stopped. Her eyes were wide open, the fear showing plain in them, and for an instant the old tenderness pulled at him. His voice was milder when he said, "Bristow. I told you, I got to go meet Jim. We'll talk when I get home this evening. Or tomorrow. Late as it is, I might have to stay the night." He gave her another piercing look, though there was slightly less demand in it. "We'll finish about this in the morning." And he started toward the door.

"Wait!"

In the very moment before, she'd wished him off the face of the earth, but now Althea understood she would be alone in the house—alone without Graceful, alone with Japheth if, as she suspected, he was only hiding in some rock-slitted, lizardly way—or else just alone entirely, with only herself and her many terrible thoughts and the many cruel mirrors and that restless wanting, wanting, that wanted nothing, that could find nothing to want. Jim! Yes. Jim Dee was in Bristow. She had wanted Jim Dee. For some long time she had.

"Franklin, please."

He turned to look at her. She had not even the strength to wheedle, to manipulate or charm him, as she'd charmed men for many years. She said simply, meeting his eyes, "Take me with you. I'll rest on the train a little and then I'll drink a cup of tea. I'll explain all this, it's very simple really. I'm just too tired right now, my head hurts. Franklin? Let me go with you. Please. I don't want to stay here."

The jitney lurched, and Graceful bumped hard against the large woman beside her. She murmured an apology but the woman stared out the window as if she hadn't heard. Graceful followed the big woman's gaze, staring likewise through the smudged glass at the crowded downtown street. Whitefolks moved along the sidewalk in stiff, henlike struts, nodding to one another, or bobbed ahead to angle across the stream of passersby into a doorway. Across from the Drexel building bootblacks knelt before their wooden boxes, snapping blackened rags over smooth cordovan, or stood at attention, offering their services—Shine, mister? Shine?—to whitemen passing in new worsted autumn suits and gray fedoras. Everywhere along the avenue was a jagged rush of hat brims and angled shoulders. Graceful watched a man in a seersucker suit dart into Renberg's, and her belly cramped. *Some of these whitemen right here on the street was there,* she thought. She couldn't bear to look at them, and she refocused her gaze to the other passengers in Mr. Berry's jitney. The inside of the bus was silent, though the street sounds poured through the open windows. *That lynching's working on them,* Graceful thought. *On me.*

She kept her gaze trained on the nearby women riding with their shopping baskets in their laps, the one lone brightskinned fellow asleep near the front, his naked head bouncing against the seatback. Every few blocks the driver would pause at the corner to receive or discharge another Negro passenger. As she watched the women's faces, the hard sickness in Graceful's chest began to ease. Their features, clothes, sizes were all different, and yet, gazing at the curled and processed hair, the multiple shades of brown and black and coppery skin glistening in the heat, the weary or closed expressions, Graceful had the feeling that the women were every one kin to her, close kin, like aunts. Like near blood to her own mother. She felt safe among them. In another moment she put her head against the seat, closed her eyes, and allowed the wrapped-around feeling to go on and ease her, and presently, rocked by the motion of the motorbus, and in spite of the fumes and noise and sudden pitching starts and stops, she descended toward the wafting images of sleep.

Her mother's face swam forward, and then her brother's face, T.J., whom she hadn't seen in a year and a half. An old longing welled in Graceful, a deep, familiar ache. Within the halfwaking dream, the narrow face of her mistress appeared. The pale jaw opened, and from its depths came the tortured scream of a claw-caught rabbit: the chilling hunt-cry of a redshouldered hawk. Graceful jerked awake, sat forward, gasping. Her vision darkened, and she felt again the whiteman's breath behind her neck, as she'd felt it in the early morning darkness, ripped awake by the smell and feel of him, his breath first, and then the length of him, hard bone and metal, pressing down against her back while she lay facedown upon the cot. She couldn't breathe. She couldn't see. The close depths of the motorbus, which moments before had comforted her, now seemed to suffocate her. In a garbled rush she cried out, "Next block!" and the driver nodded. Graceful reached for the rolled quilt that pressed against her knee. "Let me out, please!" When the jitney paused, the big woman beside her turned sideways to allow Graceful to climb out.

Standing on the hot brick street, she realized she'd not come far enough: she was still in whitetown. On the edge, yes, the northern perimeter, but not yet home. She began to walk toward the tracks a half-mile distant. The small frame houses grew cheaper and shoddier, the whitechildren in the dirt yards blonder and thinner as she hurried north with the awkward bedroll beneath her arm. The morning sun burned the side of her neck and shoulder. Sweat beaded her lip. She felt the sharp pulse in her chest, thrumming in fury, as she tried to justify how she could have mixed biscuits, fried up steaks, stirred gravy, served them, served them on the silver platter, oh Lord. The sickening rage surged again, the revulsion, and she paused, lowered the rolled quilt, kept it clean of street dirt by balancing it on her shoe top while she took off her maid's apron, shoved it beneath her arm. The muffled feel of something inside the starched cotton, the faint, almost inaudible crackle of paper, spoke to her, but she ignored it as she walked on, face lifted, shoulders low. Just as she never knew what showed on her face before Mrs. Dedmeyer, or what the whitewoman thought she saw, Graceful didn't know that her surface presented an image far different from what she felt: her bearing was serene, almost haughtily dignified as she glided evenly along the rough-cobbled street. Whitewomen stared at her from their scraggly yards, but she paid no attention to them or their pale and squawly children, caught as she was in the clamp of fear and rage and the urgent need to get home.

She stepped high over the Frisco tracks like crossing over Jordan and turned with relief toward Elgin, welcoming the familiar square of Booker T. Washington High School, the sights and sounds of the men working in the brickyard, the smells wafting from Mrs. Jenks' laundry and the confectionery. But as she climbed toward her mother's house, she began to walk faster and faster, until she was nearly running. From three blocks away she saw that the front door on the yellow shotgun house was closed. Her mother's door was never closed in warm weather. Graceful understood for the first time that something was wrong. She rushed up the steps, knowing, before she tried the handle, that the door was stayed on the inside by the block of wood turned crossways on its nail. Without pause she dropped her bundle, hurried down the steps and around to the back, where the door was also locked, she knew, by the long metal key her mother used on the rare occasions when she closed up the house: the key her mama always carried away with her, hidden in her bosom on a gray string tied around her neck.

The door rattled in its frame as Graceful twisted the knob, jiggled it, pushed on the wood without hope or expectation. Standing on the cinderblock step, Graceful looked around the narrow yard, past the privy and the smokehouse, toward Standpipe Hill, and she thought of the letter from Hedgemon. She'd dismissed it, of course, hadn't even finished trying to make sense of it, crazy as Hedgemon wrote. Hedgemon. That fool. Even as she'd scanned the swirly script in the maid's room, she had dismissed it as a love letter from the too-black longlegged boy who'd taken to following her home from church a year ago and had not ceased his gangling pursuit of her since. She'd crumpled the page and crammed it back into the blue envelope, jammed the envelope in her apron pocket when Mrs. Dedmeyer shouted at her from the kitchen to come wipe up the muddy porch floor.

Hedgemon Jackson had been the least of her concerns yesterday. Now, though, praying for a sign from somewhere, and the letter having jumped into her mind like an answer, she shook out the apron and pulled the envelope from the pocket, unsheathed the smeared page.

> *To all interested parties, let these presents hereby be made known:*
>
> *Whereas it has been declared and forthwith articulated that upon the First instant of the Ninth part in the area known as Brickyard Hill at a location five blocks north longitude of the Avenue known as Archer there abides on the street called North Elgin an interested party whose express wish is stated to be in a conversant condition with one Miss Graceful Angel Whiteside for the express purpose of which is not revealed to this your humble servant and scribner Hedgemon T. Jackson, Esq., therefore, the honor of said lady's presence is forthwith invited and duly requested to appear at her earliest convenience in the home of Mrs. Ernest Whiteside, her mother.*
>
> *Signed and witnessed this Thirty-First day of August in the Year of Our Lord 1920.*
>
> > *Yours, most truly,*
> > *Hedgemon T. Jackson, Esquire.*

Graceful's eyes traced the backslanted scrawl time and time again. Never could she get the words to make sense to her, but she saw now what she hadn't read on first glance: her mother's name. She could think of nothing except to go talk to him, find out what her mother's name was doing on the page, what foolishness the boy had been up to, and dear Lord let it be some kind of foolishness, let Hedgemon Jackson know where her mama was gone. Within moments Graceful was hurrying toward Deep Greenwood, the crumpled letter bleeding blue into her perspiring palm. Her apron lay forgotten on the cinderblock step with the envelope beneath it, and her bedroll, partially open, spilled its thin contents onto her mother's empty front porch.

Mr. Smitherman leaned against the slats in his oak chair, his forehead wreathed in a green eyeshade, his eyes ringed in dark circles, his smooth amber-colored face frowning as he stared up at her. An uncapped fountain pen rotated in his hand. Graceful stood uncertainly outside the low gate that separated the editor's domain from the rest of the *Star* office.

"Graceful Whiteside," she repeated. "Miz Cleotha's daughter. You remember me, sir?"

"No, miss," Mr. Smitherman said after a moment. "I don't believe I do." He continued looking at her, his expectant expression clearly lined with impatience.

"Hedgemon?" she said finally. "Is he working today, sir?"

Slowly Mr. Smitherman capped the fountain pen and placed it carefully in the center of the page on the desk before him. His voice was clipped when he said, "I'm afraid he's no longer in my employ."

Graceful stared at the editor, waiting for him to say something more, waiting for him to say he was joking, or that he'd misunderstood her, because she couldn't think of the *Tulsa Star* without Hedgemon Jackson any more than she could imagine the newspaper without Mr. Smitherman composing all the articles himself.

"Hedgemon Jackson, I mean, sir."

"Mr. Jackson handed in his notice yesterday."

Graceful stood a moment longer in silence, intimidated by Mr. Smitherman's respectable presence. But it seemed impossible. Hedgemon had been working for Mr. Smitherman since he was big enough to run errands; he lived and breathed that job, everybody said it, and about the only time Hedgemon Jackson couldn't be found hanging around the *Star* office was on Sundays, when the building was locked shut. It was unbelievable that he would just now up and quit. At last Graceful drew her courage around her, and she said softly, "I wonder if you could tell me where I could find him."

"Bigheart," Mr. Smitherman said instantly, and the word might have been a mild curse. "Mr. Jackson has gone to Bigheart, as I understand it, to engage in a business opportunity there." The editor rubbed his forefingers against his eyes beneath the lenses of his glasses. He straightened then, having clearly dismissed her, and picked up his pen, uncapped it, looked several moments at the writing on the paper before him, and then began to add words.

Graceful waited outside the gate. Bigheart. She tried to remember just where was Bigheart. She thought to ask Mr. Smitherman if the interurban ran there, and then instantly dismissed the notion. It didn't matter if it did, Bigheart was too far for her to go track down Hedgemon Jackson, she didn't have time to track down Hedgemon Jackson, because she had to find her mother, her sisters and brother, right away. Something was bad wrong. Still she kept staring at the editor, waiting for him to tell her something, explain something, but Mr. Smitherman scribbled words following words as fast as his pen could dance across the paper, and he didn't look up again, and in another few minutes she turned and wandered back out to the street.

There were only two places her mother regularly went and took all her children with her, and one was to church, which wasn't likely at ten o'clock on a Friday morning, and the other was to her brother Delroy's house, up on Latimer Street. Yes, Uncle Delroy. Of course. She'd go quick and ring Uncle Delroy's garage. She glanced up and down the street, trying to think where she could call from. State law forbade any colored person from talking in a white phone booth, and city law made it illegal for Negroes to operate pay telephones inside the Tulsa city limits; phone booths for colored folks were few and far between, and expensive. Graceful hurried back along the avenue and into the *Star* office again.

Mr. Smitherman nodded toward the phone on the wall opposite the little gate and went on scribbling with hardly a glance at her. She cupped the earpiece tight to her ear, listening to the exchange ring and ring and ring until the operator came on at last and said, "Your party doesn't answer." Graceful rang off and stood facing the wall, telling herself that Uncle Delroy just hadn't opened yet, he'd be at work in a few minutes. But she knew her mother's brother opened the doors to the old livery stable that served as repair center for half the motor machines in Greenwood at seven o'clock every morning. Uncle Delroy was not a man to sleep late, to open late, to change the habits of his workday life, ever. The only time she could remember Uncle Delroy's garage being closed on a weekday was for her father's funeral. The fear in Graceful notched higher. She didn't know what to do. She couldn't think. She stared a long time at the whorls and lines in the oak grain of the telephone inches from her face before she realized Mr. Smitherman was speaking to her.

" . . . something I can do for you, miss, I'll be pleased to render my services, but if not, I'm . . . I'm going to have to ask you to leave."

Graceful turned around then and, seeing the editor as if for the first time, realized that he was a man so weary he looked about ready to weep. A slender, lightskinned man with a high, smooth forehead, Mr. Smitherman seemed to have grown older, thinner, in his big oaken chair. He took his glasses off and set them on the unfinished page on his desk, breathed in deeply once, said, "Miss Whiteside, your Hedgemon Jackson knocked on my door last night and told me he was departing my employ, after almost six years' service—at nearly midnight, Miss Whiteside, and without a minute's notice, this week's paper not even half set, and just now, in the wake of these lynchings requiring our most stringent and calming efforts. I've been up all night trying to teach my pressman to run the linotype. I haven't been to bed, my newspaper has not been put to bed, I haven't written my editorial, which effort I'm in the process of undertaking, and which, if you'll pardon my saying, is the most urgent piece in this publication needed to keep hearts and minds calm in our community before even worse happens. Now, if I can do something to help you, please tell me, and if not, will you be so kind as to leave me in peace so that I can finish my work."

She stared at him.

"Oklahoma shook hands with the state of Georgia last weekend, Miss Whiteside, as you may know." Mr. Smitherman stopped, scritched a few words on the paper. "Two lynchings and a letter from the governor to report, these are not yet common occurrences in the state of Oklahoma, but they're in critical danger of becoming so."

"Two?"

Mr. Smitherman frowned. "Where you been, child?"

"Working," Graceful whispered. "I been working." The dread poured through her. If it was two, one was black; it was always going to be thirty blackfolks for every one whiteman. She waited for Mr. Smitherman to tell her what she already knew.

"Don't you know they lynched a colored man at Oklahoma City last Sunday?"

"Sunday." She could only repeat him.

"Twenty-four hours, Miss Whiteside. Two men lynched within twenty-four hours in our illustrious state: a Saturday-night lynching in Tulsa matched Sunday evening in Oklahoma City. A white lynching matched with a black one quick as they could find a loose nigger. Lest anybody get the notion lynch-law justice is going to be applied equally among the races, observe carefully, Miss Whiteside: they'll find another Negro killed before the week's out. I'd stake my life on it."

Graceful's mind raced. Oklahoma City. What had Oklahoma City to do with her? "Who was it?" she said.

"A colored boy caught in the wrong place at the wrong time. Who else would it be?" His tone softened. "Everett Candler was his name. He was from Arcadia, as I understand it." The editor remained silent a moment, and then he picked up his eyeglasses, twined them around his ears, uncapped his pen. "That's all I can tell you, Miss Whiteside. I'm in receipt of a letter from Governor Robertson on the subject, and am at present composing both response and commentary, which you may read in tomorrow's edition, should you be so gracious as to allow me to get on with my work." He waited for the girl to leave, but Graceful made no move.

The instant she'd heard the name Arcadia, her mind screamed, *T.J.!* She couldn't breathe. Her brother had gone to visit a cousin in that community a year and a half ago, and he hadn't come home since. Sometimes he wrote to his mother, and Graceful or one of her sisters would be asked to read the letter to Cleotha, over and over, until the daughters knew the words by heart and would begin to quote them from memory while their mother stared straight ahead, her face so still with grieving that the girls, seeing her, would look down at the page again, unable to bear her expression. Slowly the name filtered into her mind. Candler? Graceful didn't know any Everett Candler, that was not a name she'd ever seen in one of her brother's letters. She began once again to breathe.

The wooden door at the back of the office opened, releasing into the room the sharp odor of heated newsprint and fresh ink. A huge brown-skinned man poked his head through, said, "Mr. Smitherman, I almost got done with page four. You want me to go back and try and work some on page one?" His glance passed incuriously over Graceful, and then abruptly swept back to her again, and Graceful, looking at the man but seeing in her mind's eye only the face of her older brother, didn't at first realize he was staring at her.

"That's all right, Lawrence," Mr. Smitherman said. "I'll be in in a minute." He frowned down at the paper on his desk. With one hand he kneaded his forehead beneath the visor, and the visor rose and fell in rhythm. It seemed he'd forgotten her, or at least dismissed her. Graceful wanted to ask him more, but she was too intimidated by Mr. Smitherman's frowning concentration, by his exhaustion, his revered place in the community, and in any case she'd suddenly become aware of the man staring at her from the back. She turned and went out of the *Star* office to stand, uncertain, confused, on Greenwood Avenue again.

It was late morning now, and the street was fully alive with activity. A few doors down Mr. Thompson came out to sweep the walk in front of his drugstore. Across the street a boy was changing the letters on the Dreamland Theater marquee. Mr. Berry's jitney passed her, going south now, and all along the street vehicles were passing, belching gasoline fumes and noise, and amidst the Model T's and touring cars were delivery wagons drawn by blindered drays and shining new delivery trucks, and one battered Nash truck careening recklessly down the avenue, which she realized within seconds was her Uncle Delroy's. It seemed like that snubnosed truck had been flying toward her down Greenwood forever, and Graceful stepped to the curb to flag it down.

The truck continued past her, but she saw her baby brother, William, jumping around and waving at her from inside the cab, and the truck, almost to Archer now, suddenly stopped and began to back up against the traffic. Willie waved at her wildly. She darted across Greenwood, dancing between wagons and cars, and before she'd reached the curb, Uncle Delroy stuck his head out the open window and shouted back at her, "'M'on, girl, get in!"

Her little brother scooted over to make room, and the instant she closed the door, Delroy ground into first gear and started down the street. His face was a smooth mask, motionless and intent. William, caught between excitement and his wordless understanding of how serious was the situation, bounced lightly on the seat, turning his head to look up at his uncle, and then his sister, and back to his uncle again.

"Where's Mama?" Graceful said.

Delroy turned onto Archer, squealing the rubber tires around the corner, and, as if continuing a prior conversation, said, "She down there already." He shifted into second and sped up, heading west. Graceful watched the side of her uncle's face. His profile was a leaner, younger replica of her mother's, in which bled through the Anglo features of a forgotten white grandfather, but Delroy was much darker than Mama, almost black, and his very leanness and the tight nap of his hair spoke of Senegal. *He sure do look like T.J.,* Graceful thought, her heart catching on the old comparison that was standard in the family: the two lean, loose-jointed men so alike in their faces, their movements. Unconsciously she glanced down at William to see if he'd yet begun to turn lean; but, no, her baby brother carried his same round face and thick thighs; he would be sturdy-built. His soft features were most like their father's, and Graceful's heart caught on that recognition, too. Ernest Whiteside had been dead seven years, and it might as well have been seventeen for all the presence he still held in the household: a framed studio photograph on the parlor table showing a round, handsome man in a suit and bow tie, with a stern, serious expression. And yet, for Graceful, who remembered him better than the younger children—and maybe for T.J., too, she thought—her father was a smiling man who brought gifts home from his travels as a Pullman porter and tugged the children onto his lap and teased them and sneaked up on Mama when she was cooking in the kitchen and grabbed her in his big arms and hugged her from behind.

"Your mama gone down last night," Delroy said. He stared fiercely through the windscreen and did not offer any further explanation. She wanted him to say he had carried Mama out to the pipeline field with her box lunches early this morning. She wanted him to laugh big once and say, What you doing on the street, girl, ain't you suppose to be working? She wanted a reasonable and lighthearted explanation for her little brother to be fidgeting in the seat beside her; for her mama and sisters being gone from the house on Elgin; for her uncle not being at work in his garage. Graceful waited for the words she knew would never come and watched through the side window as they crossed the trolley tracks and turned west toward Sand Springs. *For sure we not going up by Dirty Butter Creek*, she thought.

"Where's LaVona and Jewell?" she said.

Delroy nodded, as if that told her something.

"Uncle Delroy, what is it? What happened?" Her voice was barely audible above the roaring motor, and yet the sound in it was nearly a scream.

Delroy hunched forward, his hands gripping the steering wheel high and tight. "Nothing to speak of, honey. Just . . . your mama had to go see about some business at Arcadia yesterday evening. She ask me to bring Willie this morning and come on." He glanced down at the boy, met Graceful's eyes, and his face when he turned back to watch the road was so furious and veiled that she would ask nothing further.

She felt her little brother's eyes on her and, looking down, saw him smiling slantwise up at her with the shy grin that could so easily split his face and endear him to any witness to it. "You get that letter?" William said. She saw him trying to be grown-up and sober, but he was just too proud.

"You the one brung that letter?" Graceful said, and the boy nodded, smiling. Her mind flew through adjustments, dropping Hedgemon Jackson as the deliverer of the strange missive and putting her baby brother in his place. *Why?* she thought, and then, suddenly: *What I do with it?* She didn't have the page with her; she carried no pocketbook, had no pockets in her skirt, had left her apron somewhere. *I must of dropped it by Mr. Smitherman*, she thought. *Lord, no telling what he'll think.* Aloud she said, "Come all that way by yourself? My Lord, you going to be grown and gone before I get a chance to turn around."

William ducked his head. The grin spread farther across his face.

"Who give it to you, Willie?"

"Mama," he said, surprised, the grin disappearing, the look on his face asking, Who else would it be? A fleeting confusion passed over his soft brown features, and then the beginnings of fear. His eyes darted swiftly between his uncle and sister once more, trying to decipher how he was supposed to act, how to feel, and Graceful quickly said, "Well, of *course*, Mama give it to you. I just wondered did one of my snoopy sisters write it, didn't look like they handwrite to me."

"I don't know," William said, and the beautiful grin was entirely replaced now with the closed sullenness that was the boy's defense against his impulse to take blame for every trouble. Seeing the change in him, and feeling her own fear rising as her uncle continued west past the shacks at the edge of Sand Springs, Graceful reached down and rubbed the back of her brother's head; she took small, playful handfuls of nap in her fingers and tugged gently, said, "I don't know what to think, you so grown up you taking the trolley all that way by yourself. You're going to be driving a Ford motorcar here in a little bit. Uncle Delroy, you going to teach this boy how to drive?" She touched the round cheek, where the smile was beginning to crack again. "Somebody have to teach him," she said. "Can't me or Mama do it, and I wouldn't trust LaVona to teach him how to fly-swat!" She laughed, and though her voice was edged in fear, the boy laughed with her, and their uncle joined them as they continued west on the rutted road.

E yes closed, head pressed against the seatback, Althea surrendered to the jolting, forward-propelled motion, the railcar's rude lurch and sway. From time to time she would allow her lashes to part slightly, and she'd cast a hidden glance at her husband, or turn slitted eyes to the right, where a golden blur raced past the smeared window. With every mile ratcheting backward, dread and a quavering excitement settled more deeply in her belly. She hadn't been to Creek County since the last morning she'd boarded the train in Bristow in 1904. She hadn't seen Jim Dee in over a year. She tried to conjure the image of him staring at her from the far side of the parlor, the dozen or more men milling about the room between them; she searched for the dream and could not find it. She couldn't even recall in any clear way what her husband's partner looked like.

The train whistle blew a mournful warning as they neared the Kellyville crossing, and the cry filled Althea with sharp, unexpected longing. An unwilled sound, a near whimper, escaped her lips.

"What is it?" Franklin said. She could feel his eyes on her. "Althea?" The tone was without threat, but he never called her by her full name, not since the first weeks of courting. The word frightened her. She would not open her eyes.

"Thea, I want you to sit up now. Talk to me."

She forced herself to breathe slowly, feigning sleep, but he touched her arm, and when she didn't respond he lifted her wrist and shook it.

"Stop!" she snapped, and sat up, frowning. "Lord God, it's hot." She fanned her face with her open hand. Franklin's eyes were steady on her. "What?" she said.

"I believe you're rested now. Talk."

"About what?"

But he only stared at her.

"Oh, that . . . that boy . . . Well. He's . . . Please, Franklin. My head . . ."

"Talk."

Why wouldn't he leave her alone? Her mind was void of creative thought, and this, this grimy railcar was so miserably hot, the leather seat was sticky, the window filthy. . . .

"He's your brother, I know that. I can see that with my own eyes. I want to know how come I never heard of him."

Althea opened her mouth, took a breath, and then just stopped. Not a word came to her, not an image. "Yes," she said at last. "He is."

Her husband remained silent.

"I never told you because . . . Oh, for God's sake, Franklin, I was ashamed! Ashamed of him, them, all of them! What do you think?" She turned to glare out the greasy window. The train gained speed. Jaws clenched, she watched the folds of yellow prairie give way to a snarled clutch of post oak and blackjack, open to rolling grassland again. Had Franklin pressed her then, he could have received not only the answers he was seeking, but much more: an entire history, dark and long secret, and staggeringly different from all he believed he knew about her. But he didn't ask; he simply watched her with cold, unfamiliar precision, as if she were a stranger, and in another moment she put her head back against the seat once more, closed her eyes.

Franklin traced the long curve of his wife's neck, crossed faintly with palely etched lines; he examined the slope of her jaw, the perfectly arched brows, frowning slightly, the tiny whorls of fine black hair at her temples, where the dark tresses began and mounded thickly in a loose chignon toward the crown. As Althea's face slackened toward sleep, the harsh lines softened and her features eased themselves into the appearance of innocence, and he saw her as he'd first seen her in the Raglands' foyer: a young girl stepping away from her cotton wrap, dismissing it to the arms of the housemaid as regally as if it had been fur. She'd glanced at him shyly, her hair clasped to one side with a sprig of mistletoe, her lips and cheeks white with cold. Never had he seen anything like her pale avian beauty, stunning in one so young and frail and unformed. And then she'd come fully around and stared directly into his eyes for an instant, secretly bold, before turning to Joe Ragland to smile and offer her hand. Franklin had fallen in love in that moment. Never in the many difficult years since had that infatuation failed. The old tenderness did battle now with the morning's suspicion and anger; he tried to shrug it away, but the pull was too strong, and he rode swaying with the emotions rolling over him in alternating waves of warmth and cold doubt.

She moaned in her sleep, a low, gritted groaning, and then the little sound came again, clearly now a whimper, animallike in its helplessness and terror. Her hands convulsed in her lap, and her lips moved, trying to form words, though all that escaped was the low moaning. Franklin reached out and brushed the back of his knuckles against her cheekbone. Her hands came up before her throat, clenched, batting the air, and she said distinctly, "No, no, Franklin, get back! There's a snake on me!" She sat forward. "What?" she said. She looked at him, not seeming to see him, then her eyes swept the inside of the railcar, the row of seatbacks in front of her; she twisted to look behind, where a few passengers were beginning to gather their belongings. Her breath cut the air in short, sharp gasps. Franklin could hear it above the rush of iron wheels. "Where is he?" she whispered.

"Who?" Franklin touched her. "It's just a dream, Thea. You were sleeping."

Althea leaned back, allowed him to stroke her, grateful for the fleshy reality of his thick palm on her forehead. Dear God. She tried to retrace the dream, what had terrified her so, but the curtain had dropped, and she was left only with the recollection of a dark, focused terror: fear of someone or something, as if a hidden presence were watching her from inside the car; she couldn't bring herself to turn and look, but shrank further into the seat, tried to make herself small beneath Franklin's hand. The locomotive began very gradually to slow, and the more the train slowed, the more terrible the burn of fear rose in her; she closed her eyes entirely against it.

The whistle sounded, not mournful now but shrieking, a terrified warning. The brakes groaned beneath the car and then began their high-pitched piggish squealing as the locomotive rolled into the station. Althea sat up, shrugged Franklin's palm away. Her eyes were wide as she stared at him, the pupils so swollen her gaze was nearly black. A little boy in a ragged suitcoat raced up the aisle, followed by a woman with a bawling infant in one arm, a battered valise in the other, and two crying toddlers stumbling after. Franklin started to rise, but Althea's hand on his arm stopped him. Still she didn't turn her eyes from his.

"We're here," he said. He pulled away, stood and put his hat on, reached up to retrieve his case from overhead. Althea didn't move. Franklin picked up her cloth purse and blue silk traveling bonnet, extended his palm to her. As though coming fully awake at last, Althea suddenly grasped the hand and scrambled quickly to the aisle, rushed toward the front of the car, and then stopped in the open door at the top of the steps, confounded by the neat redbrick depot trimmed in white. For a moment she forgot where she was. She saw the word BRISTOW etched in bold white letters above the façade; the word seemed to float up from a long-ago dream. A tawny head separated itself from the little clutch of waiting passengers and began to move toward them. Althea's mind cleared then, and she remembered.

He sauntered hatless toward the platform in denim britches and a shortsleeved khaki shirt open at the throat. Even in the relaxed stroll there was an undercurrent of impatience, so that it seemed he kept glancing at a timepiece, though he wore neither fob nor wristwatch. Althea watched him with the same black intensity with which she'd watched her husband, as if she were drowning and the only thing that might save her was the other's face. But, though she expected and longed to feel the old tremble of excitement, she felt only dullness and a kind of empty wonder at how much older he looked. Not some little bit older, not just a year older, but shockingly so, his face more wind and sun scarred, the squint lines at the corners of his eyes etched deeper, the once faint dusting of freckles now distinct and particulate as paint. All she could think of was why in heaven's name didn't he wear a hat.

Jim Dee's eyes lifted and met hers. He didn't blink, smile, offer recognition in any way; his gaze passed on, casually, as he strolled toward them, and it was only by how his pace slowed that she knew he was surprised to see her. He shook Franklin's outstretched hand, nodded at her, turned with hardly a word of greeting and began to walk toward a battered tin lizzie parked at the curb. Althea hurried along, her arm clinging so tightly to Franklin's and the rush in her step so urgent that her husband looked at her in surprise as she pulled him along.

Franklin tried to help her into the front of the open car, but Althea shook her head and climbed into the rumble seat in the back as Jim Dee moved to the front of the old Ford to crank. Hunkered in the narrow space, Althea watched the few remaining passengers milling about the platform. A couple of roustabouts in stained pants lounged in the shadow of the depot wall, smoking handrolled cigarettes. On the wooden bench facing the tracks an old Indian man sat erect and motionless in a tan suit-coat and a broadbrimmed black hat. The woman with the three crying youngsters came to the curb and climbed awkwardly with them into a battered spring-wagon, where a farmer in overalls held the reins to an old dray and did not offer a hand to help. The whistle screamed, the brakes hissed their released steam, the Frisco engine grumbled to a louder pitch. Althea watched the train grind out of the station, gaining speed, until she heard the whistle in the distance, not shrieking now but lonesome, moaning, as the Frisco roared on toward Oklahoma City. Still she couldn't shake the sense of a malevolent presence behind her, and she shrank into the well, pressing her spine against the cracked leather binding.

As they drove south on Main Street, Althea stared at the three-story Laurel Hotel, the new pharmacy, and Stone's Hardware & Furniture lining the brick-paved street that had been, on the November morning she'd last seen it, a mud thoroughfare sentineled by slapped-together wooden falsefronts and plank sidewalks. She tried to listen to what the men were saying, but her mind wasn't calm enough to take in the words, had she even been able to hear them clearly over the popping motor and rhythmic thumps of the rubber tires as they bumped along the brick street. At the edge of town Jim Dee pushed the Ford to its limit, speeding up to nearly thirty miles an hour, so that Franklin had to cram his boater down on his head to keep it from being blown off. The men yelled over the sound of wind and motor, and the wind caught their words and lifted them above the battered turtlehull and blew them north over the prairie. Althea put one hand over her eyes, the other to the top of her head, as the wind beat her chignon to pieces.

Within a mile of town the pavement gave out, and the Ford bucked and jolted so fiercely Althea bit the inside of her jaw. The lizzie backfired once and slowed, grumbling, to a more reasonable gait as the road turned to gritty, wagon-rutted dust. Althea's eyes swept the treeless fields on either side, the salmon-and-ochre-and-olive-colored ditches, where the soft earth, raineaten into pastel furrows, clotted around buffalograss; she raised her gaze to the horizon again. There were no houses, no fences, no manmarks of any kind but for the dirt road itself and, far off on the eastern horizon, a black pumpjack like a rocking horse dipping rhythmically toward the earth to drink, lifting its face skyward again. This was the landscape of her deepest memory, and she couldn't bear to look at it, and could not bear not to look.

After a very long time, what seemed to Althea several hours in the noise and wind and sun, though it was perhaps less than two, the Model T slowed to a near stop, and Jim Dee turned the wheel hard to the right, nursed the front tires over an impossible dirt hump. The chassis shuddered as the back wheels followed and the car thumped to the ground, and Althea bit her jaw again, and the motor, vibrating in union with the chassis, backfired once and died a belching death. Jim Dee cursed and got out to crank. Althea combed her fingers through her snarled tresses, trying to tuck the windblown hairs back inside the hopeless chignon. She could feel the grit in her mouth and the salty irontaste of blood, could feel the oppressively fine dust coating her face and hands and neck. *Lord God,* she said to herself, *I thought I left this damn stuff.* The motor coughed to life, and soon they were driving west on a surface that could not be called road, could hardly be called a blazed trail, and the Ford moved in the salmon dust at a near crawl.

The prairie was thick with blooming milkweed and blackeyed susans and joe-pye, and the track held straight across it, though the way was pitted and rough, nearly invisible in places. But Althea felt somehow protected by the path's absolute uselessness, and she began to relax a little with the Ford's altered rhythm, which was wagon rhythm, which was the slow, creaking rhythm of an ancient stockdrawn cart. She settled back into the seat. The wind no longer struck her but stroked her, so that she could breathe now, she could see, without the windbeat hairs flaying her eyes. She raised her face to the sky—cloudless, crystalline, almost turquoise in its autumn turning—and for an instant her heart lifted. The sun beat on her skin, and she didn't fear its burning. Something old in her tried to awaken, some hard pushed-away memory of space and light, and her chest swelled and she breathed in a sensation very kin to joy. She touched Franklin's arm. "Darling?"

He turned to her, his face showing nothing of surprise at the word.

"Oh, you know, I didn't bring a parasol. I didn't think."

Instantly Franklin turned to his partner. "Jim, can't we put the top up on this thing?"

"No!" Althea couldn't bear the thought of being enclosed in the cramped seat. "No, dear, I just meant . . ." She smiled at him sheepishly, and she could feel how the wind and sun had brought red to her cheeks, and she believed it made her beautiful. She could never have dreamed how badly the dust jaundiced her complexion, how the wild tousle of her hair made her look disheveled and confused, made her look poor. "Oh, this silly thing is just useless." She slapped the small neat blue traveling bonnet in her lap. "It won't do a bit to protect me." She saw something in her husband's face, some new emotion, unrecognizable to her, but since she had no pattern to gauge it by, she dismissed it. "Couldn't I borrow your hat? Just a little something to keep that old sun off me, I'll be burnt crisp in a minute."

Franklin removed his straw boater and handed it to her. She grinned impishly as she put the hat on. In times past, Althea could have snatched a gentleman's hat and placed it on her own head, tilted her face to the side, and flirted from beneath her lashes, and the effect would have been daring, rakish, so that it made that gentleman laugh with pleasure. Now she only looked foolish. Franklin turned away, began to speak in a loud voice to Jim Logan; he didn't glance at his wife again.

Althea listened to the men's voices, lulled by the comforting, deep-throated rumble. Once, she looked behind and believed she saw the dust of an automobile or perhaps a wagon following, but the prairie rose and fell here in great folds, and the dust's source was hidden behind a pleat of land. Even as she watched, the smoking column disappeared, a fading dustdevil, and Althea forgot it as the dirt track began to be closed in on either side by a thick tangle of oak and hickory. The prairie disappeared. The sky receded; there was no breeze at all, only the close swelter of humidity. The darkness was so abrupt it was as if they'd entered a tunnel. The path began to meander, reptilish, undulating, and the Model T kicked and groaned and rattled as the pitted ruts became deeper. Althea thought she could smell riverbank and mud. *It can't be the Deep Fork,* she thought. Surely they hadn't come that far south. Or had they? Her perception of how far they'd come was confused, she had lost all sense of direction, all knowledge of land and distance. She touched Franklin's shoulder. He glanced at her as if a fly had landed on him, some faint distraction; he returned his attention immediately to Jim Dee.

"All right," he said, "let's say the field proves, how do we know you got the right Indian?" he said.

"I'm telling you, I looked it up six ways from Sunday, the courthouse in Sapulpa, went to Okmulgee and checked the rolls myself. She's not Creek anyhow, she's a freedwoman, but the allotment's hers, it ain't her husband's."

"It's unbelievable." Franklin shook his head.

"Believe it," Jim Dee said.

Althea shoved Franklin's shoulder. "What are we doing? We're going to get mired down in here. Franklin, you can't drive down in here!" Her voice was shrill with panic. "These old creekbottoms are quicksand! They sink to the middle of the earth. We'll get stuck to the hub in a minute! The mud goes down, it goes down—" Her throat clamped closed. She looked up at the entwined oaks pressing into the path; the impenetrable tangle would weave closed behind them, they'd never find their way out. "Dear God." She heard the whisper and only dimly realized it came from her own lips. In the front seat both men sat, half turned, staring at her. She realized that the engine no longer coughed and sputtered. A windless silence, dense as cottonbatting, held the earth, the tangled woods. Then, far off, she heard a crow call. As if at a signal, the timbers erupted in a high, urgent din, a thousand million insects crying hard against the coming winter.

"What the devil's the matter with you?" Franklin said. "You are really . . ." But Franklin's voice trailed away. He looked at his wife in silence. Abruptly he reached over the side window and opened his door from the outside. "Come on, Jim, let's go have a look at this thing. I'm afraid Thea's not feeling well, I better get her back to town."

"Where are you going? Franklin, wait!"

But the two men disappeared into the tangled scrub, and she was left alone, surrounded by the clutching tree branches and chirring insects. She couldn't see where they'd gone, so dense was the undergrowth, but she knew the water was off to her left somewhere. She could smell it, the rank mud of the Deep Fork bottoms, and she nearly choked in her terror. She scrambled over the seat, over the shut door, fell sprawling when her skirt caught on the door handle, and got up instantly, rushed toward the thicket of sumac and ivy and ancient blackberry brambles, crying, "Franklin! Franklin! Help me! Dear God, please help!" She heard the low murmur of their voices, but she couldn't see them; she couldn't reach them. The briars snagged her skirt and held her, the low branches of the jackoaks crossed in front of her, black and roughscaled, hard as pig-iron clothed in dry, olivedun leaves; they stabbed earthward like fencespikes, forbidding her, but on she went, driven by her terror, pushing through the tough branches as through a wall of fire, holding her arms before her face.

When she burst through the growth to the slick bank, her face was bleeding in long scratchlike swells; the backs of her hands were lacerated from the clutch of blackjack twigs, the sting of berry thorns. Her husband's face told her at once that she hadn't cried aloud: she could not have made her way screaming, as she'd thought she did, for he was surprised to see her. Both men were surprised. The other thing she understood was the meaning of the look on Franklin's face. This time its substance was unmistakable: he was embarrassed by her. She'd made him ashamed. She saw herself: a ridiculous-looking woman, bedraggled, dirty, foolishly frightened. The image was intolerable to her, beyond endurance. She could not hold it in her mind and live.

"What do you mean," she snapped, "letting me sit and swelter in that blessed car till the mosquitoes carry me off?" She hated her own voice and the words coming from her mouth, hated the hunch in her shoulders and the twisted sneer of her lips. "I could suffocate, I could get eaten by a panther, little you'd care! Either one of you!" She turned her glare to include Jim Logan, fingered her snarled hair in upward combings. "Y'all've got the manners of a pulpwood hauler, leaving me out in the heat and weather like that!" And now she turned her glare entirely on her husband, and the more she hated her own soul and bearing, the more scathing was the loathing she poured out upon him. "You are really beyond belief. I can't dream you'd carry me out into the absolute bojacks and walk off."

"I'm sorry, Thea. We'll be through here in a minute."

"Take me back to town. This instant!"

"In a minute."

She stared at him. Never did Franklin resist her outright demand, she couldn't remember his ever having done so, and yet now he didn't even bother to look at her but turned away, dismissing her, and Althea, more amazed than angered, was thrown off balance. She wanted to whirl on her heel and storm back to the car to sit in wounded silence until he came to her, but her instincts told her that to stumble back into the brambles would make her look not outraged and injured but buffoonish. And she did not want to be alone.

Moving over to stand at the edge of a canebrake, she began to brush the dirt off her dress; she wiped her fingers beneath her eyes, rubbed her cheeks one at a time against her sleeve, pushed and fingered her hair. She longed for a brush or a comb, a mirror to tell her how she looked. She didn't raise her eyes to the men. The same instinct that told her when to leave or enter a room, which tight or sweeping gesture to use, when to blink and smile and when to hold another's glance, told her now that to look at either of them was death. She, who believed masculine regard to be the most telling and perfect mirror, dreaded to see in her husband's eyes, in Jim Dee's eyes, the truth. Turning away, she combed and picked and brushed at herself, silent, absorbed in her grooming as a cat. But her fear was gone now, gone even was the shame that had followed it, all swept into disappearance by the quick and blaming rage, and now even the rage was gone: she wanted only to be still awhile. She wanted a bath, a nice quiet room, a clean dressing gown, perhaps a nap.

"There's no producing field anywhere closer than Depew." Franklin's tone was musing, calculating, though he clearly expected comment. Jim Dee said nothing. Their eyes held steady, very studiedly and frowning, on the water. Althea peered down at the river, murky with washed-in silt, oozing slowly past the bank in olive swirls and eddies. In complete silence, in a dark place within, Althea recognized the clay-contained, viscous waters of the Deep Fork, and in the same instant dismissed it, shut off all recollection. Click. She raised her gaze to the grapevines trailing from the overhanging branches across the river. The insect din rose and fell in the undergrowth. She slapped a mosquito whining at her neck.

"Heard last week Gypsy Oil finally quit drilling on the Yargee lease," Franklin murmured. "That's not a mile from where we're standing. Good anticline, too, not some low, boggy bottom. Twenty dusters, a bunch of teasers, one little nine-barrel-a-day producer." Both men continued to stare at the sluggish place below the cutbank. Althea followed their gaze, the fear trying to snatch at her, until at last she saw what they were seeing: a thin rainbow film upon the water. She saw the exposed roots of a dead cottonwood reaching from the bank. The gnarled wood was covered in a thick greenish ooze. She smelled it now, sweetish, mechanical: the earth-bowel smell of raw crude. Slowly the meaning began to filter clear to her. She looked at Franklin with a sudden surge of hope.

"One thing I know," he said, "it hasn't been this easy in a lot of years." Wonder mingled with the skepticism in his voice. He knelt on the bank and dipped a hand into the water, then raised up, rubbing his thumb and forefinger in an oily circle. "Last time I heard somebody found a seep was back in Fourteen or Fifteen. I thought this whole country'd been gone over with a finetoothed comb." He looked hard at his partner. "You're a hundred percent sure that old freedwoman still holds the claim?"

Jim Dee stared unblinking at the water. His expression was distant, trancelike, his thick brows rising in an odd little frown; his lips, the same tawny color as his skin, pressed together almost primly.

Franklin turned back to the river. "If there is another big strike coming," he said slowly, the wonder and barely kept delight overswelling the doubt in his voice, "another Glenn Pool, another Cushing Field, under this useless prairie, I don't know why this wouldn't be it right here." He knelt and scooped a palm of water, cupped it before him reverentially, let it trickle back to the oily bank. Suddenly he turned his face up and grinned broadly at the late-afternoon sky. "Why the hell wouldn't it!" Franklin got to his feet then and began to pace the clearing. "First thing," he said, "we better get out to that old lady's before somebody else comes nosing around. We've got time for that before dark. I believe we do." He glanced up to gauge the sun's position. "Yes, all right, that's fine. Now . . ." Althea could see his mind flying, calculating, but Jim Dee suddenly came out of his reverie, and without a word turned and walked downstream. "Jim! Where are you going?" Franklin was caught in midstride, mid-sentence.

Jim Dee continued to pick his way through the brambles. He spoke over his shoulder. "Y'all each find another way out of here. Don't go back the way you come. We don't want to leave any sign of a trail." His khaki shoulders disappeared in the tangled growth.

In the back of the roaring, bouncing Ford motoring toward Bristow, Althea struggled to listen to the men talk. The task made her tired. Their words—*paraffin base, asphalt content, bentonite clay*, and on and on— were so much gobbling in her ears, and she could not keep her mind on the sound, much less the words' meaning. There was only one thing she cared to know anyway: was it the big strike? Somehow she knew it was, or she knew that Franklin believed it to be. Never had she seen his face so animated and open, his voice so free of the infernal cautiousness that dogged him. Her husband's belief brought her a new and thrilling excitement. Suddenly the horrors of the past week, her fears and sense of dislocation and the terrible emptiness, were lifted away. Of course. *This* was what she wanted. To be rich as the Murphys were rich, the J. Paul Gettys, the Josh Cosdens, the Gilcreases, the Marlands, the Sinclairs. And it was almost in hand. The first well hadn't been spudded in yet—the lease, in fact, from what she understood, had not been secured—but such details weren't important. Franklin believed, that was what mattered. And Jim Dee did.

Althea watched him through the hairs flying about her eyes. He was no longer scowling, taciturn, but yelling excitedly at Franklin in his near-foreign tongue—*depth of sand, degrees of gravity, syncline, anticline, cavey formation*—words that thrilled her with a sense of his capable nature. She saw that the excitement was as great in him as it was in Franklin, as uncluttered with doubt, and she kept her eyes on him, willing that the old feeling would return, until her senses began to fill at last with the look and scent of him, and she ceased to find his weatherscarred skin distasteful but saw the squint lines and rough texture as masculine, romantic. Her eyes traced the curl of his hair behind his sunburned ear, the skin on his neck rippling in leathery folds as he turned to Franklin, and she surrendered to the old daydreams as if they—or, rather, the man himself—had returned to her from a great distance. But even this she could not hold for long, and soon she turned to her husband, graced him for an instant with a benevolent thought for his caretaking, rushed past him to the new visions that sustained her.

She sat turning the straw boater over and over in her hands, her own silk bonnet forgotten, trampled in the floorboard beneath her feet. Not that she was mindful of her husband's property; she only fiddled with it as one strokes a buckeye thoughtlessly picked up from the ground. Her mind's eye was on herself descending a long staircase in a diaphanous ballgown the color of lit smoke; she saw heads turning toward her in desire, others bending to murmur in awe and envy. Immediately her home on South Carson was shabby in her own eyes, and she built for herself and her husband a mansion as grand as that L.O. Murphy had built for Nona, as grand as any on Black Gold Row, grander, with many more bedrooms, more imported marble, more artworks hung in more galleries, more gold inlay and silk drapery and Italian Renaissance fresco displayed in better taste.

As the Model T picked up speed on the open prairie, Althea's vision of herself transformed. Now she was a gracious philanthropist, broadly renowned in Saint Louis, Kansas City, New Orleans: far beyond Oklahoma's dusty borders. She saw herself moving tenderly along a row of iron beds in a dreary orphanage, and as she passed, the little pinched white faces darkened, became Indian for a time, and then colored, and Althea gently touched the little dark hands reaching through the iron bars, for her largess as patron and benefactor knew no prejudice, just as it knew no bounds.

She was lost in this new vision when the automobile began to slow, the engine popping, and Althea coughed as the boiling dust suddenly caught up with and surrounded the abruptly slowing Ford. Through the coppery haze she could see his lean figure standing in the dirt track with legs akimbo and his two arms stretched laconically overhead, reaching up and outward, a lanky X. The black fear swelled over her. She'd known. Of course she'd known. It was all completely recollected, and yet strange, like the familiar, unplaceable sense of a present moment relived from the past, already seen. He had followed, hidden in the railcar, a wagon, on the bouncing gate of a sputtering truck, and part of the time walking, and all the time she'd felt it; somewhere within herself, she had known.

The two men in the front seat said nothing as Japheth sauntered toward them, smiling as if it were the most normal thing in the world to be found standing on a dirt track at nearly sunset in the middle of nowhere.

"Evening, fellas. Could you give a man a lift?" His smile widened as he reached for the handle on the passenger's side.

Franklin turned to his wife for guidance or explanation, but she only stared back at him, mute. He glanced at his partner then, whose face was baffled, suspicious. Franklin blurted sort of helplessly, "Jim, this is Althea's brother. . . ." He still didn't know the fellow's name.

L ooks to me like I ought to known them. They faces ought to been so burnt in my mind I couldn't help it, or hers ought to been, but I didn't think a thing, only what in the world is that noisy stinking tooloud horseless carriage doing, come boiling up the road and into my yard scaring the daylights out my chickens. But I ought to known, and I can't quit thinking on that, still yet, all these years later, because before ever I heard that rattly old Model T coming, before I seen the dust on the horizon even, Bluford's dogs had already set in to howl.

The yellowhair fellow climbed out the seat first, come walking so nice toward me across the yard. The other dogs kept barking, but old Bone slunk up wagtail at him and try to lick his hand, and see, now, that too caught me off guard, because what I seen in that yellowhair gentleman and what Bone seen might of been the truth on that one day out of his life only, but I do know it for true: that whiteman didn't mean me no harm. I wasn't in the least afraid.

Let me tell you something my daddy used to tell me. He'd always say, One thing Indians got over colored is they don't fear the whiteman. My daddy'd say, An Indian'll go on and die before he let the whiteman make a slave of him, and that is on account of he ain't afraid. My daddy had a powerful respect towards Indians on account of that one issue. You never going to see the KuKlux after the Indian, he'd say, because you can't scare an Indian to make him act like you want to, you can't do nothing but kill him. Well, I have seen Indians scared of whitefolks, but it ain't in the same way. Indians I've known—and I count my two husbands among them—they don't carry the same kind of wicked in their souls, and so they don't have any way to fathom how downright evil whitefolks can be. They don't even have words in their language for how whitefolks act. I'm not saying you won't find a bad Indian, because you sure will—murderous as a rattler if he want to be, and jealous-hearted, Lord God, it's a disgrace how jealous-hearted and wicked some of them can be to each other. But they're not wicked the same way as whitefolks.

All right, I'll tell it to you like this: to me, what I think, at the beginning of the world the whiteman got caught in a stickyball of stuff, just gummed on the material world like he glued to it with pine-tar, and he get greedy, let greed swell up and suck him in till it won't turn him loose, and that's one of the things make him to act so evil. The Holy Word say that, just exactly: The love of money is the root of all evil. You heard that all your life, I guess. What else make somebody want to own all the land on the whole earth if it ain't greed? I know greed ain't the only kind of evil, but it is sure one that do make people act a terrible sneaking lowdown kind of vicious, and I never seen a greedy fullblood in my life, except only some of them greedy for whiskey, and that's howcome them not to be afraid of whitefolks in the same kind of way. I tell you something else, too: the reason they used to have their black slaves to parley with whitefolks in the old days is because blackfolks do understand that particular kind of evil, because they got that same room in their own souls. I can't trouble myself about what you want to hear or you don't want to hear. You ask me to tell the truth, long as I can open my mouth, that's what I'm going to speak. How you think I know it if I'm not telling it on myself?

But look here: if you a person able to know evil, if you been given the means to recognize evil, and it come walking across the yard at you, then, if you got any bit of sense in the world, you better be afraid. And right yonder on that day, I wasn't. I'd seen enough from whitefolks by that time to respect how much harm they can do you, some of them—this was 1920, remember. The nightriders was having a big time in Oklahoma right then. They'd lynched a man at Oklahoma City not a week before, and I sure enough did know about it—we didn't have telephones, no way to get around but a plowmule if we was lucky and our own two feets if we wasn't, which was most of us, but word got around fast back then. We known about the Holdenville lynching—that happened that same year—Sable Merryweather come walking over the field to tell me about it when that man wasn't two hours dead. So you'd think I'd been more cautious when a carload of whitefolks come rumbling up in my yard, even allowing I didn't sense a thing evil in that yellowhair fellow but only just the color of his skin.

But, no, I'm going to stand on my porch and look at him walking crost my yard, I just nod at him, say, How do, mister. Nice evening. Y'all lost?

He say, No, ma'am, I don't believe so.

I only had a whiteman call me ma'am twice in my life, and both times it was nothing but trouble follow after, and that was the first time, and, yes, I got skittish then, finally—but I should of been way more than skittish. I should of been protecting myself. I should of seen them and known them from the first minute they driven up in my yard. Probably I couldn't even tell you when he and she climbed out the car and come over, because I's standing there talking to that Mister Dedmeyer, or I ought to say listening, because he the one do all the talking, and that's what else I mean about being off my guard. He talk all around everything—the weather, which that evening wasn't nothing but average, just hot and humid. He say, Look yonder at that sunset, which was pretty-looking, yes, but just normal for any sunset got clouds building in the west, big bank of thunderheads rising yonder toward Depew. He talk about Bluford's dogs and reach his hand down till they every one hush except Tennie. She slink off out by the privy and snarl and growl from the back side of it till that car finally drive on out the yard, and Bluford, he always did say that's the smartest dog he know anything about, and I ought to taken one look at Tennie and shut my ears clean up to that man.

I don't know howcome me to stand there and listen. You got to act like you listening, sure, but I had learnt the trick long before then how to open my ears just enough to nod at the right place, make them think I's listening, keep my ears shut enough I'm not going to start to believe something I know better, which if you listen hard at them they can sure make you do. I have seen that, more than a few times. You listen much to whitefolks, you'll be believing no telling what. And, see, that's just what happen.

Oh, you think the devil of greed can't get you, but let me tell you something: the devil can shape hisself anyhow he want. If you hadn't steeled yourself with prayer and smoke and right thinking, he's going to jump up and snatch you out before you know what you about. He can make hisself look like a nice yellowhair whiteman don't mean you a bit of harm, and it might be that whiteman don't mean you anything but just to set you in the middle of the road so he can drive over you on his way to getting whatever little bit of something you got. And it weren't a little bit of something, it were a lot of something, which I didn't know, but if I'd been listening to hear only what-all I ought to known and not what-all that man want me to believe, I might could've stopped what was coming right then.

Lord God.

You picture it. Three whitemens and a whitewoman dressed up like sixty and covered in roaddust, stand around in a colored woman's yard saying ma'am and talking so particular and polite, and that colored woman just go right along with them. You think I didn't know they want something out of me? You think I believe they drive fourteen miles from the nearest whitetown to pass the time of day? What make me act like a fool with no better sense than to spill out her business? I been studying the answer to that question a long time.

Afterwhile Mister Dedmeyer start in talking some words I do not comprehend, all letters and numbers, but he say two things I known completely, *Deep Fork* and *allotment*. You put them two together, you know just what he's talking about. My allotment run in a little narrow strip right down to that river, and the rest of it was just nothing but scrub and underbrush, what the U.S. government give me for my portion when they tuck up all the land. Bluford carried me yonder once to see it. I looked at that worthless land, say to myself, They want to give us freedmen what the Indians won't take. They aim us to sit on a piece of land you can't give to nobody but the sorriest old white trash or a fool. I just shake my head, we come on back to our little place at Iron Post, and me and Bluford just go on living just how we was. Probably him and me never thought another word about it, not even when all these mixedbloods from here to Sapulpa been driving around in new motorcars they bought with lease money, because me and Bluford, the two of us together, we known better than that. But he's dead. My Bluford dead, and look like he taken ever lick of sense we had between us right into the grave with him.

Whiteman talking about my allotment, and me there on the porch, I opens my ears to every last word. He say four hundred dollars, I hears four hundred dollars. He say twenty years, I hears twenty years. He say fair percentage, I hears fair. I hears *fair*. You see what I mean? I hears it, and *believes* it, and you tell me when ever on this earth whitefolks intend fair with colored or Indian. Tell me when ever they even know what the word mean. And look at me yonder, I'm going to stand there and say,

Yessuh, oh, yes, massah, where you want me to sign? Which is not the words I told them, but it might as well been. What I said was, Yes, that do sound like my land. And, No, sir, I never leased out the mineral rights. Far as I know, nobody ever come and asked.

You see how the minute I let my ears open, that just shut my eyes blind. Still I didn't recognize her or him either one, not even when he start to talk Indian. Oh, yes, that one. One I ought to seen for a snake if I seen anything, the devil's own progeny, which these own two hands helped birth into the world, Lord forgive me, that very one: he stand there and talk Creek to me. And he ain't going to talk nice like Mister Dedmeyer about sunsets and yard dogs and fair percentage, he set right in to talk about Bluford, am I sure he dead or didn't he maybe just go off and leave me, and how many children we got and was we married 'cording to whitelaw or just Indian, do Bluford have any children from a Creek woman, and things which he got no business to know, and I don't begin to answer but just shut my mouth tight, won't say another word to any of them, Creek or English neither one.

They don't know what he saying, them other two whitemens don't, but they see he's saying something make me start crawfishing, and they both of them step in front of him, and I mean quick, get in between the two of us and talk English hard and fast as they can talk. I bet you that yellowhair say ma'am fifty times if he say it once, and the other one, the frowny lighthair, he tumble his own words out, say, We going to bring you a contract first thing in the morning, cash money on signing, give you half soon as you put your mark on the paper. Say, Tomorrow morning you going to get two hundred dollars right in your hand.

And look at me there, I'm going to stand there and keep listening, let that he-devil and his sister do deals with me right in my yard. Don't matter if it was the other two talking, it was them two behind it, and I should of known it from the beginning. Truth.

Maybe I can't fault myself I didn't know him, but I should of known her, I don't care if it was twenty years nearly since I seen her. She stare at me like she's trying to place me, got a queer, baffledy look on her face, every once in a while she kind of brush the air in front of her, like gnats are flying—but me, I got my greedy mind on what I'm going to do with a little money, and I never pay any attention to that whitewoman, not till they start on off across the yard again and I see her scrawny backside, just how she turn and walk away floating, like she in a trance. My heart give a little jump then, there's a little minute's recognition, and I just wouldn't see it, I wouldn't listen, because I got my mind on how they going to come back tomorrow and bring me two hundred dollars for nothing but just sign a paper, and in my mind all I'm thinking is, I ain't seen two hundred dollars put together in one place my whole life.

They were an odd quartet: the beautifully dressed husband and wife and the two roughnecks seated contrapuntally at the back table, the dark brother and sister opposite one another, the two fair-haired men facing each other across the white cloth, arguing in hushed voices. Their steaks lay nearly untouched in their bloody juices—all but Franklin's, which was now only ravaged bits of meat and fat close to the bone. Their coffee had been served. The Negro waiter, uncertain whether to offer dessert, would start toward the table to remove the plates and, seeing one or another take a desultory bite, would immediately retreat to stand at attention near the kitchen doorway again. But the hunger that radiated from the table was unsated, for the powerful appetites had nothing to do with food.

The brother gazed at his own reflection in the large gilt mirror on the back wall, observing that glee was a hard thing for a man to keep to himself. *Even when a fellow remembers not to smile,* Japheth mused, *it's hard to hide the glow in the eyes and the complexion.* He shifted his gaze to his sister's face. Althea wouldn't meet him but stared, glittery and attentive, at the two partners hunched toward one another.

"I'm telling you we've got to get back out there first thing!" Franklin rasped. He struggled to keep his voice down, although an interested listener could have picked up that the partners had scouted a promising location, as well as the even more attractive fact that they hadn't yet secured the lease. Bristow, of course, was an oil town: interested listeners lurked everywhere. "Drive me out to the old lady's cabin first," he whispered; "then you can go track down Ben Koop."

"He's way the hell and gone up to Osage country, take me a day and a half to get there."

"Can't you reach him by phone?"

Jim Dee didn't bother to dignify that with an answer.

"Take the train, then. I'll drive your old Ford."

"You tend to your business, I'll tend to mine."

"You know damn well we've got nothing until we've got her mark. What do you expect me to do, walk?" Franklin ran his hands through his thick hair, blonder than the partner's, his face ruddier: a beefy, thickened version of the other. He leaned over his plate, spoke slowly. "There's no goddamn train to Iron Post."

He's the more ruthless of the two, Japheth thought. *And the softer.* His gaze drifted to Jim Logan, who sat silent now, sullen and restless, one leg jittering beneath the table as he knifed butter onto a dinner roll so furiously the soft bread turned doughy and mangled. Few pleasures gave Japheth more satisfaction than perusing another's secret nature, and he sipped his coffee as he studied the partner. *This one,* he said to himself, amused, realizing the similarity for the first time, *is very much like the very famous, very late Roy Belton.*

The memory flashed: his own ex-partner standing on the dark road with the hijacked cabdriver on the ground before him, and yes, it'd been Roy Belton's rash anger, his restless, withholding silences, his fidgety nature that had pushed him to fire the pistol twice, stupidly, in Homer Nida's belly—enough to kill the cabbie, not enough to kill him quick. The hack driver had taken four long, stupid days to die, long enough to name his hijackers, so of course they'd caught Belton in Nowata and brought him to the Tulsa jail, from which the good citizens had taken him and carried him out to that same spot on the Red Fork road, and lynched him. *I told him and told him,* Japheth said to himself, *a fellow's got to learn how to hold his temper.*

His attention returned to the two men. Japheth had an unerring sense for the concealed lives of others, a kind of second sight that allowed him to know what people tried to keep hidden, and he saw that the husband was hiding something now. Not ambition; not the merciless depths he'd go to in order to satisfy that craving: those were excellent traits in a good oilman. What Franklin Dedmeyer strove to keep secret was his smallness, the pinched parsimony that derived from that ambition. It wasn't money Franklin was tight with, but information, and that was a characteristic despised among insiders in the business of oil. Even now he was keeping certain facts from his partner, which was part, Japheth saw—although only part—of the other's long resentment. He took another sip of coffee, savoring for a moment his developing knowledge. The smile broadened behind the fragile rim of china cup as his gaze returned to his sister. *And you, my dear, are so filled with secrets as to be a transparency to me. I know your little tawdry wants, and to what lengths you'll go to satisfy them. I know your unpitying nature and where you've come from, which, above everything, you'd like to keep hidden.* As if feeling his eyes on her face, Althea turned to him, and instantly looked away—but not before Japheth saw the fear there, and this gave him the greatest pleasure of all.

"I don't care!" Franklin burst out. "Can't you hear a word I'm saying? It can't wait till Monday!" He glanced at the full dining room behind him, fought to bring his voice under control. "We've got to fix things with the old lady first," he hissed, "take care of the rest next week." He sat back, sawed off a bit of steak. "All right, it's settled, then," he said, though his partner's scowl declared that it was far from settled. "Darling," he said with his mouth full, "I think you'd better take the early train tomorrow. We're going to be driving those old rutty roads again, I don't want to leave you sitting in the car. You won't want to wait around the hotel all day."

"The girl's gone, Franklin. You said you'd get me a new one. I can't stay in that house by myself. You know that."

Franklin turned for the first time and looked directly at his wife.

"Take me home. Please." The light from the chandelier cast a muted radiance that scooped gentle hollows beneath her cheekbones and flattered her pale face. Althea held herself very still.

Japheth watched in grudging admiration as she dipped into a well deep within herself and came up changed. She didn't modify a flicker of her expression, didn't blink or blush or draw herself tall in the chair, but everything transformed about her, and Japheth saw himself vanish from her thoughts, a sheet drawn across him, a curtain.

"Get me a new girl," she said in a flat, firm voice, "then you can come back next week if you have to."

"This can't wait till next week."

"Yes," Althea said. "It can."

She looked boldly, almost seductively at her husband, and then, with equal boldness, cast her dark, glittering eyes on his partner. "Let Jim take care of the lease business," she said. "He can handle that. Jim Dee's capable of handling all kinds of things." She held the driller's gaze. "Aren't you, Jim?" The words were a direct, heated challenge.

Japheth saw the hunger rise over the partner's bronzed, fissured face. *Ah, of course,* he thought. *He's had her, hasn't he?* His irritation at having missed that obvious twist for so many hours was soon overswept by unspeakable delight. *Oh, the fool.*

"Tell him," Althea said. The clink of crystal and the soft murmur of conversation at the nearby tables died away. The attention of the other diners, the waiters, even the mustachioed owner greeting guests near the front, all turned toward the four strangers at the back table. Perhaps it was the abrupt hush of the table's urgent, low conversation, or maybe it was only Althea herself, who'd called forth the vehemence of desire and will that had since her youth made all eyes fly to her. When it flared in her, as now, she was an unsurpassably beautiful woman. The sensation of many eyes watching caused her cheeks to flush with titillation; she lifted her head so that her face might better catch the chandelier's golden light. "Jim?" she said. One eyebrow arched gorgeously.

"Yes. Tell him, Jim," Japheth said. The partner flicked a frown in his direction, and Japheth met it, took a very long, slow sip of water.

"No," Franklin said. "There's nothing for Jim to tell me." His voice was low, controlled. "You take the early train tomorrow and I'll be on directly. Tuesday afternoon maybe, if everything goes well." Franklin's gaze passed from his wife to his partner, back again. "You won't be alone long."

Japheth saw at first only that the man was torn; he couldn't tell what divided him, and he wanted sneeringly to believe it was cowardice that made Franklin turn away. For a moment he was perplexed by the husband's stillness, the slow, calm measure of his voice. It was only when Franklin settled his gaze solely and intently on his partner and went on with his veiled words about the lease that it came clear to Japheth what the stillness meant: in this single day's time Franklin Dedmeyer had passed from a man who kept his marriage and his business obsessions as separate as if they belonged to two distinct lives, to a man troubled by the two worlds' encroachments on one another, to this single moment of division when each weighed in the balance. Franklin's lust for oil had won out. He would rather turn away from the wife than the potential of the big strike.

But Althea drove heedlessly on. She had seen in the driller's unblinking hazel eyes that her desirability still held, and in the rush of that certainty, she interrupted her husband, leaning toward him and touching his arm, speaking in a throaty purr: "If you just have to do it all yourself, then let Jim Dee see me home. He can do that as well as anything, don't you think?"

The look Franklin turned on her was so cold, so entirely unaffected, that she pulled back, abashed. Of the world's many chaotic possibilities, the only one inconceivable to Althea was the loss of her husband's devotion. She could more nearly imagine the prairie around the hotel crumbling and sinking to ashes.

"I need Jim here," he said curtly, and then, as if realizing the presumptuousness of the *I* when they were supposed to be equal partners, he added, "We can't make a move without him. He's got to get the equipment lined up, got to start hauling out to the site."

"Oh, *we* can't, can't we?" Jim Dee's tone was ominously mild. "What time would you like to leave in the morning, ma'am?"

Franklin rolled right over it; he spoke low, forehead tilted. "If that new supply-and-tool here in Bristow won't give you a price on casing, go on over to Conroy's in Sapulpa." He knew very well what would claim the driller's attention. "Conroy played us fair on the Gobeddy hole. And when you find Ben Koop, have him see if he can't lay his hands on a Fort Worth spudder."

"I told you already, that formation's too cavey. We can't machine dig. We're going to have to build a rig."

"It can't be better than six hundred—"

"I said we're going to have to build a rig."

There was a beat of silence before Franklin nodded, letting the tension bleed away. "Of course. You're the driller."

"I am."

"Well. I'll get out to the old lady's cabin at dawn tomorrow—"

"I'm not riding in that low class commuter railcar by myself, Franklin! I absolutely am not!"

Franklin skimmed his wife briefly, and then his glance fell absently on Japheth, who returned it with steady gaze. "Your . . . brother can see you home." The word still hesitated on his tongue, tinged with disbelief. Blood rose instantly in Althea's face and her eyes widened; there was a small flutter of her fingers at her throat, but the gesture was lost on her husband, who turned back, very casually, to press the point about the spudder. "Of course a rig's a lot of time, a lot of money, Jim," he offered gingerly. "We know that's bound to be a shallow sand—"

The partner's frown quickly darkened.

Now! Japheth surged forward, elbows on the table. "I'll be glad to take Sister to Tulsa, if that's the first order of business. I mean, if that's what you want. But I was just thinking: if you're tied up all day on lease business, and if Mr. Logan here is in Sapulpa . . . or wherever . . ." Japheth smiled. "Why then, who's"—his voice dropped low, conspiratorial—"going to stay down on the Deep Fork, protect that seep from some other 'catter nosing around?"

"Hssht!" Jim Dee's voice grated to a whisper. "I've been scouting a week, nobody's seen or heard me. Nobody knows a thing but us right here at this table."

Japheth turned slightly and glanced over his shoulder at the attentive dining room, where dozens of pairs of eyes dropped their gaze quickly to numerous white tablecloths, and the seized-up murmur of conversation coughed a time or two, then purred into a steady low rumble once more. The partners looked at each other.

"I told you. . . ." Franklin's voice trailed away. Of course, it was a good idea to have somebody at the location around the clock until the lease was filed. The sooner the better, before word got out. Franklin shrugged, his thoughts already scrambling toward how he was going to snatch up leases on the land all around the old lady's allotment—not in the name of Delo Petroleum Corporation, but for himself. It was the very bit of secrecy Japheth had detected, though he'd missed its meaning, and he didn't see it now. His attention was on Jim Dee.

"What do you say, Mr. Logan?" Japheth arched one brow in precise, insinuating imitation of his sister. "Unless you'd rather do it yourself?" Something passed between the two, the dark brother and the scowling, sunburned partner, a grudging, instant complicity, made up of equal parts knowledge and loathing.

"Might be a good idea," Jim Dee said finally. "At that."

"Yes, all right," Franklin said. "Better get down there first thing. I'll take you on my way out. We'll haul in some camp supplies tomor—"

"Franklin! Take me home!"

"If you're going to make a fuss, Thea, just stay here at the hotel. We ought to be clear enough I can take you back on the train Monday evening."

"Why, sure, Sister," Japheth said. "You can stay here in Bristow, do a little visiting," and he threw the word away; he might as well have said *a little knitting* or *shopping*. Neither of the men caught the hidden meaning, just as they'd failed to hear the brother in the cramped back seat, whispering as they bumped over the brick streets of the town, *And there's Dorcas's house, that little shack on the corner. That's her oldest boy hanging on the gate. She moved up in Sixteen, right after Jody. You won't see Estaleen, she lives over on Choctaw with Katie. She don't hardly ever come out now since that damn flu took her so bad, but she's dying to see you. She told me so herself.*

Suddenly Althea yearned to escape to the room upstairs, with its beautiful brass fixtures on the sink opposite the bed, its lace canopy and fine rug. She would stay there, she thought, in their room at the Laurel Hotel; she'd simply wait for Franklin each evening. But, no, the thought of sitting in the small room, away from sun and light and air, was impossible to her, she couldn't do it, and in any case, Japheth would be here, always, lurking around corners, skulking along the carpet runners in the hall.

There was only one force on earth that could have convinced Althea to willingly be alone, to travel alone, stay in her large and empty house on South Carson alone, and it was sitting across the linen cloth from her, smirking, sweeping his eyes once around the room to say, *See, Sister? You thought it was all in the past, but, no, it's here in the town of Bristow. If you walk down a sidewalk tomorrow, if you go into one of these nice new brick stores, you can't help but find it. Or it will find you.* She met her brother's eyes for only an instant before she turned away, knowing that in the morning she would take the train to Tulsa, alone.

Althea watched her husband and his partner as they argued; she appeared to be listening, but her eyes were black and vacant. She didn't speak again. After a long time she brought herself to glance across the table. Her brother still sat back, draped languidly in the chair, but his eyes followed the men avidly, ravenously, as a starving cur watches a flock of crows feasting, waiting for its opportunity to rush in among them and snatch away the kill.

T he truck snaked through the low hills on wagon trails gone wash-
boardy from rain, over dozens of swollen creekbeds on rumbling
board bridges, and sometimes straight across the water at rocky fords.
Several times Delroy stopped to add water to the radiator or to pour gasoline into the side tank from the orange can bouncing in the truckbed;
other times he had to climb down from the cab and pull the long timbers
off the pile of tarps in the back and use them to pry the tires free from
mud. At each of those pauses Graceful would stand down to stretch her
legs, and William would scramble out behind her and dance around in
the open land, looking up, or run off chasing after a jackrabbit, until Delroy called them to come, and they'd slam the truck doors and drive on,
along the rutted and muddy roads, along dustbitten cowtracks, past
blackened oilfields steepled with derricks, and green-ripened cornfields,
golden wheatfields, red arroyos cut deep in the earth.

At dusk Delroy did not stop; when daylight came again, they were still
driving. They skirted the boom towns and farm towns—the white
towns—though Delroy bought gasoline at a station near Shamrock, refilled the orange can. In the afternoon they stopped at a little colored store
outside Kendrick and bought sardines and cheese and crackers. They ate
their dinner, washed down with tepid water from a jar, as they continued
west toward the glaring sun, the sky vast with light, brilliant with fuchsia

and orange-vermilion at sunset, fading to mauve, to plum, to purple, and at last blueblack from horizon to horizon, and jeweled with stars.

It was after midnight when they stopped in the yard of a house whose outline was only a darker blackness against the black sky. Wan yellow light shone somewhere in the back. Graceful woke her little brother and walked him, still half asleep, toward the porch. She knew where they were—Uncle Delroy had spoken softly over the sleeping boy's head to tell her—though not yet why. Only that her mama had said come. Bring the boy and some blankets in the truck, and come. Go by the whitelady's house and fetch Graceful, drive as long and hard as it takes, all night if need be, and come, here, to this rickety frame house on the rolling prairie six miles north of Arcadia.

The door opened, and Mama's powerful shape stood outlined in the faint light. Graceful rushed forward, so that William stumbled and nearly fell to the porch floor, and Mama said, "Hush! Hush, now." She grabbed them, pulled them into the house. And then Mama was rasping in the dark at the end of the porch, a harsh sound completely unlike her normal voice, and the edge in it cracked ice in Graceful's bones. William swayed in a groggy stupor beside her. Graceful couldn't make out Mama's words, but in a moment she heard Uncle Delroy's truck start up, too loud in the yard silence, and drive around toward the back, and in another minute her mother's hands came hard around her shoulders, pulling her so tight Graceful's arm was crushed against her brother's bony skull. Mama began to whisper again, not harsh now but murmured, and it took a minute for Graceful to understand that her mother was praying. At last Mama's fierce grip loosened, and she heaved in a long breath. Graceful heard the ragged sob in it, and the fear she'd held away from herself for so many hours flooded over her. But Mama's voice was strong, military, when she said, "Y'all keep quiet, everybody sleeping. Come on back here to the back."

Through the dark room, their footsteps creaking on the raw flooring, the walls sour, and the room filled, Graceful could hear now, with the soft mouthbreathing sounds of people sleeping. She held her brother's hand, felt her way toward the crack of light at the back. Mama's fingers were tight on her shoulder. The sour smell grew stronger as they went into the back room, a kitchen, where a kerosene lantern, trimmed so low as to hardly keep burning, sat on the oilcloth-covered table. The room was hot and close, and the odor was overpowering, familiar, and yet strange, as if it had once been something good that had transformed itself, and degraded as it changed. It made Graceful sick to her stomach. She looked to the stovetop, saw a big skillet and her mama's covered stockpot cooking there, but the sour odor didn't come from that direction. It seemed to seep from the walls of the ratty kitchen, and the floor.

"Sit," Mama said, and then before they'd had time to obey she looked hard at the boy, said, "William, when's the last time you washed them hands? Get up here to the sink. You too, girl. I just brought that water in fresh." And she turned immediately to the cookstove, opened the firebox as if she meant to put in more wood, though the iron stove radiated heat, and the room was sweltering. Graceful thought she'd be sick all over the cracked linoleum if she didn't get some air. She stepped to the door and would have pulled it open if her mother's voice hadn't snapped hard behind her, "No!"

"Mama, it stinks in here!"

"I don't care. You'll get used to it. Get over here and help your brother, we got to eat now. We got to get Delroy some supper and then he got to rest." Cleotha wrung a wet rag into the dishwater, began to slap at the rough board countertop, wiping it down. She glanced over her shoulder, said in a voice that matched the look on her face, "I don't want to have to say it again."

Graceful moved as in a dream to the tin basin at the end of the counter; she picked up a yellowed piece of lye soap, motioned the sleepy William to come over, took her brother's limp hands in hers, and dunked them in the pan. The whole time she watched her mother. The expression, the voice: Graceful had seen it before. Seven years ago. When she was twelve. She'd come home from school one afternoon to find her mother transformed, as now, from a strict, good-humored woman to a harsh disciplinarian who barked orders and had not a smile or a bit of softness about her, and that time, like this, the conversion was sudden and complete, and it marked the end of something, a change in their lives that was irrevocable, permanent, and she'd known on that day by the sign of her mother's behavior, long hours before she was told, that her father was dead.

A welling began to rise in Graceful's throat and chest, and she scrubbed her little brother's hands with the lye soap till he said, "That's good, that's good enough!" The boy was wide awake now, and afraid. She tried to make her voice light when she said, "Rinse off, then. And hurry up so Mama can fix you a plate." She began to rub the harsh soap furiously between her palms.

A tapping came at the back door, and her heart jumped, and she heard her mother release a little jumpy sound—*Oh!*—and Willie shoved himself up against her, silent. *What are we acting so scared for? What is it we afraid of?* And yet she knew, because there was only one thing to cause such silent, quaking fear. She wanted to snuff the lantern, prayed for her trembling baby brother to stay hushed. The tapping came again, a light tick behind the cardboard covering the door window. Her mother started across the kitchen, and Graceful whispered loudly, "Mama! No!"

In the slight moment before her mother reached the door, Graceful passed from fear to resentment that Mama had snapped at her when she'd started to open the door and now was going on and performing that very act herself. Cleotha lifted a corner of the cardboard to peer out, then quickly slid back the iron bolt, turned the wood block, fiddled with the skeleton key in the slot below the knob. Graceful thought, *I never saw any blackfolks' house locked up such a way in my life.*

Her mother cracked the door a bit before pulling it open wide enough to admit Delroy, who slipped in lean and quick. Mama slapped the bolt back in place. "They all right?"

"Hungry." Delroy sat heavily in a cane chair at the table.

"I'll send something out in a minute. Got to get you fed first, you got to have some rest."

"I'm not tired," he said; indeed, his hands were restless at the table, fiddling with the saltcellar and the butter crock, his long ashy fingers touching the tin base of the lantern, now and again reaching out to flick at a speck on the dingy oilcloth. But his shoulders slumped, and his head dipped toward the table as his sister thumped and clanged softly over by the stove.

"You tired all right." Cleotha set a bowl of turnip greens in front of him. "Eat now."

Delroy fished up a chunk of fatback with two fingers (and Graceful thought, *How come she don't tell him to wash his hands?*), wolfed it in one bite, and had nearly finished the bowl before Cleotha put the cornbread and the hoppin'john on the table. "Y'all come eat," she said, and William came and sat obediently, bent his head over the bowl she put in front of him. But Graceful knew she'd vomit if she had to eat anything in that sour, overheated atmosphere, though Mama's hoppin'john was her favorite food on earth. *What she got to lift the lid on that pot of greens for, she going to make us all puke.* Her indignation at being treated as her mother's child swelled, joined with a deep long-ago resentment, and she thought, *This is no way to act. Why she got to act so mean every time somebody die?* Her mind cried out: *T.J.!* The dark welling began, and she saw her brother in the hands of a white mob, white faces hooting with laughter as that one had laughed while he pushed her face into the pillow so she couldn't scream, couldn't breathe. . . . She felt herself begin to descend, the room going dark and turning, and the sour smell smothering her as she went down, but her mother's arms came around her and lifted her.

"Delroy! Clear off that chair!"

Her mother's shout came from a great distance, but the sound was sweet to her, and the strength of her mother's arms around her was firm. The hard ridge of wood came against her legs, and she sank into the spongy cane bottom as the sickness swirled over her, made a great roaring in her ears, and the wretched nausea swelled; she opened her mouth, helpless against it, and vomited fish and putrid cheese all over the table. She heard Willie yelp, heard her sister Jewell cry out, "Mama! Help her!" and she thought, *How did Jewell get here, too?* before she began to sink toward the tabletop, because she needed to lie down, she needed to put her head down. Mama's hands gripped her, held her face, and brushed it with a dry cloth; she could hear the voices going on, many voices talking, but she leaned the weight of her face against her mother, let her heavy, leaden head rest in her mother's hands.

"Ooh, Mama, she making it stink worse!" LaVona's high, prissy voice came from the front-room doorway. She stood barefoot, on tiptoe, her hair springing in a thousand directions, her little slanty eyes big as coins. Beside her, Jewell's legs were long and thin beneath a white cotton gown. Graceful thought, *My Lord, they getting tall.* She tried to sit up, but her head was too heavy, and she leaned against Mama, felt her face wiped again with the dry cloth, and realized it was Mama's apron; then the shame came on her, more sickening than the body sickness. "Oh, Mama, I'm sorry." She pulled away. "I'm sorry, I'm so sorry, Mama." She wanted to stand up and go to the water basin, but her lap was soiled with vomit. She started to cry.

"Hush!" Mama's hands were tender, but her voice was the harsh, exacting voice that stood no argument, no sniveling, no weakness of any kind, and instantly Graceful quit. She pulled away, picked up her maid's skirt in both hands as she stood and walked shakily toward the dishpan on the counter. It was then she first saw the little faces behind her sisters, peeping out of the dark door to the front room.

She couldn't tell how many of them there were, maybe half a dozen, little smudgy faces that blended with the darkness. Their eyes showed round and scared in alternating heights from way-little to pretty-big, and then a bitty one in a dirty gown came toddling out and went to Jewell and put its hands up to be lifted. Graceful couldn't tell if it was a boychild or a girlchild; its unplaited hair was a puff of soft, radiant fuzz all over its head.

The child said, "Hold you! Hold you!" and tugged at Jewell's nightgown, and Jewell bent and picked the child up and lodged it on her skinny hip, and Graceful could see the knobs of breasts on her sister's narrow chest. She felt suddenly that there was a whole world she didn't know, that her family had gone on and had itself, its family life, which was the only life, without her. While she was working at the whitefolks', her sister Jewell had got big enough to have titties and LaVona was more sassy-mouthed than ever and getting tall and Willie was grown up enough to ride the trolley, and Mama had changed again, had gone hard-edged and gruff again, and a whole batch of little children appeared here from nowhere. They all knew what she did not know, and her grief at not knowing was as hard as her fears about T.J., as ferocious, even, as her secret rage and shame, though the grief didn't come in crushing waves, as that other, but held her as fog does, dense and thick. She cleaned herself with the sour dishrag while her mother wiped the table and barked orders. The girls tried to hustle the many strange children back to bed, but the little one on Jewell's hip started bawling, and another one, a boy of maybe four or five, skipped under LaVona's outstretched arm and came on into the kitchen, stood with his hands on his hips, and announced like a big man, "We hungry!"

Before Graceful had finished washing, the whole bunch was in the kitchen, and her mother was allowing what she'd never allowed in her own household, which was a mess of children eating from bowls and cups with their fingers, not at the table with a proper blessing and a clean napkin, but scattered all about the room like a bunch of slave children, eating standing up and squatting on the floor and just anyhow. There were seven of them, five boys and a girl, plus the little one on Jewell's hip. Graceful watched them gobble their food like wormy pups, and her wonder was equally at her mother as at the youngsters, for Mama dipped up the hoppin'john and handed it around and did not say to the children, wash your hands, sit up to the table now, use a napkin, wipe yo nasty mouth. The children's nightshirts were filthy with old dried food, they had blackeyed peas and rice smeared all over their little bug-eyed faces, and Graceful thought, *They not ours, that's why. She don't care how they act.*

"Hurry up," Mama said, and it took a second for Graceful to realize her mother was talking to her. "Take this in yonder and put it on." Mama shoved something at her, and in a minute Graceful found herself in the dark front room, where she could make out an old springy double bed in one corner, three or four pallets spread around. She dropped her smelly uniform on the floor and put on her mother's good white going-to-church dress.

When she stepped back into the kitchen, her mother was setting a small wooden crate by the door.

"Mama!" LaVona's thin voice squeaked from the corner. "You not gone let her th'ow up all over your church dress?" Cleotha ignored her, motioned Graceful to come over, pulled her close, and said, "What make you to get sick like that?"

"This whole place stinks, Mama."

Her mother looked hard at her a minute. "You over it?"

Graceful nodded. Cleotha continued to peer at her in silence, then, finally, she said in a low whisper, "I want you to take this to them yonder in the storm cellar. Listen good at the door once you get outside, you got to make sure there's nobody around. It's out to the side of the barn." Graceful looked down. In the crate were some tin cups, spoons, a cracked blue crockery bowl, her mother's steel stockpot with the lid on, a greasy slab of something wrapped in newspaper.

"What barn, Mama? Storm cellar?"

"Barn's right up behind the house, if you go out the door and walk straight you can't help but go to it. Then feel your way easy around to the side—" Cleotha suddenly turned to the room, said to her brother nodding at the table, "Delroy, go lay down on the bed and sleep. You got to get some rest."

"Mama, that's where me and Jewell sleep—!" LaVona started, but Cleotha looked at her and the girl piped down, went back to feeding a little one with a big spoon. Jewell was trying to edge over to where Graceful stood, but Cleotha gave her a hard look, too, and the girl stopped, bent to wipe the face of the little mannish boy. "Go in and rest," Cleotha said again. Delroy scraped his chair back from the table and went into the dark room.

"Somebody going to be sick all over somebody church dress," LaVona muttered to the child she was feeding. "Somebody's won't have nothing nice to wear to church."

"I wouldn't worry about that, missy. You not going to be there anyhow, you're going to be right in this house minding these children. Hurry up and finish with that mess and get these kids in the bed."

LaVona cut her eyes at her mother, said nothing more.

"Mama, what happen . . ." But Graceful let the words fade away. She shut her lips tight, lifted her head, stood silent while her mother whispered at her to sneak quiet, quiet across that yard, listen hard at the door, because if somebody was outside watching they might follow her and find them.

"Find who, Mama?"

"Hush!" And then, in a barely voiced whisper, "T.J. and them."

"Tee—? You mean T.J.—? Ow! Mama!"

Her mother's pinch was brutal. "When you going to get some sense?" The whisper was fierce with exasperation. She suddenly began pulling Graceful by the arm into the front room. In the dark Cleotha whispered at her eldest daughter, her fingers tight on Graceful's arm, her mouth close to the girl's ear. "If there ever been a time in your life you need to quit asking questions, this black morning right now is it. Hear me? I need you to pay some attention. Keep your mouth quiet and pay attention. T.J. and that trashy girl he got mixed up with and her mama all out in the storm cellar, and now that's the only time I'm going to say it. If the whitefolks find them, they bound to be lynched same as that girl's brother last week." Her whisper went harsher, lower. "They're not the only ones in danger. If that mob come in here and find Delroy, they liable to take him. I don't know but what they'd take you or me. We got to act calm. We got to act like we don't know nothing but just we taking care of these children, we don't know where their mama's gone. Because Delroy got to sleep awhile, we got to let him get some rest. This is the most dangerous time, the most dangerous, and I need you to be your grown self and not some girl going to puke and pass out over smelling a little spilt sourmash. Not some girl going to open her loose lips and say what them in the next room don't need to know. Your sisters too young to keep their face right if whitefolks ask them a question. But you're not." She paused, let her words sink in a moment, and when she continued her voice was softer. "I got to depend on you, Graceful. You my grown girl I got to depend on. How come you didn't come home the minute Willie brung you that letter?"

"Mama, I didn't know—"

"Nevermind. Hush. Listen. You got to carry that food quiet. I wouldn't even send it, but they haven't eat since yesterday, probably won't get another chance till way up tomorrow evening. Now, listen. That cellar door face this way. Knock soft, three quick taps, then wait a little bit, then two more. All right? What I say?"

"Three quick taps, wait, then two more."

"And go quiet."

"Go quiet."

Her mother's mouth drew away, and Graceful felt the coarse palm on her forehead. "You still warm."

"I'm all right, Mama."

"Go on, then. Mind everything I said. And Graceful . . . be careful."

When her mother let out her breath there was again the ragged, dry, unspent sob in it. Graceful, already moving toward the lit kitchen, heard it, and something turned over in her, like a stone plate turned upside down.

Mama's white dress flowed around her, too big and floating, lifting its hem in the nightbreeze. The young moon was hardly a fingernail paring, but the white dress on the crowblack land took the little light and shimmered it back to the night. The crate was heavy in her arms, thumped against her thigh. Twice Graceful paused to listen, but all she heard was the wind soughing, a million night crickets singing, the alien sound of her own breath. Her eyes adjusted to the darkness, and she gazed out across the shadowed land, imagining a white mob hidden in the folds, secreted in the moonshade below the clumps of cedars.

She saw the lump of hill to the side of the barn and made her way toward it, set the crate down. Three soft taps on the tin-and-wood door set into the mound, pause, two more. Silence. She bent over and hoisted the door with both hands, laid it open. The sour smell poured out through the opening, along with the thick odor of mildew, the dank sweet scent of dirt. Graceful waited almost politely, as if at a stranger's front door. "T.J.?" she whispered. "It's me." The adjustment her eyes had made to the moonlight was no good now: the rectangle in the mound of earth was ink black, impenetrable. "T.J.? It's Graceful. I got some food here for y'all but I ain't comin—"

"Where at?" Her brother's voice came from below, and she could have wept for gladness, though the rasp in T.J.'s throat was uglier even than Mama's.

"Here," and she lifted the crate down toward the opening. "Easy, it's heavy." She felt the weight relieved from her.

"In or out, but shut that door!"

She did not want to descend to that hole in the earth, but neither did she want to go back to the reeking kitchen and her mother's hard face and closed mouth. She knew Mama was not going to tell her what she wanted to know. She felt her way onto the top step, stood breathing deeply of the night air.

"Shut the door!"

Graceful reached over for the cumbersome door, pulled it up from the mounded earth in an arc, lowering it over her head as she went down into a dark beyond any darkness. She heard scrabbling sounds below, like rats, a few soft murmured words, the rushed, gulping sounds of eating. Graceful stood as near the top of the ladder as her height would allow, clinging to a dank wooden slat.

"You coming down or you just going to hang there?"

How could he see her in such pitch? And then she realized T.J. was not seeing her but sensing her, as a blind man does.

"Ain't y'all got any light down there?"

"Not at night. Leaks around the door. It's nasty down here, Graceful, why don't you go on back to the house?" She heard more hushed whispering.

"I'm coming down." Slowly she felt her way down the ladder, stood at the foot of it. The dark seemed not an absence but a presence, solid, odoriferous. The rank smell must be sourmash, like Mama said. Her brother's voice came from the back, very low, but distinct. "Delroy get some rest?"

"He's sleeping right now."

T.J. didn't speak again, but she could sense his satisfaction with the answer. Suddenly it clicked into place that Delroy was to carry her brother away from here in the truck; that was the purpose of the tarps in the back, why everybody was so worried about the state of Uncle Delroy's rest. Before she thought, she said, "Where's he going to take you?"

"You don't need to know that. Mama don't need to know."

"Why, T.J.? How come the whitefolks looking for you?"

"Hush!" The small, foul space was quiet a long time. She heard the soft scrabbling sounds come toward her across the dirt floor. T.J. whispered close beside her, "It's better you don't know nothing."

She was silent. After a long while, she said, "You my brother, T.J."

T.J. let out a slow breath of air, and when he spoke his voice was so low she had to strain to hear him. "On account of what I seen."

"What was it?"

"You don't need to know that either. It's for your own good, Graceful. What you don't know, can't nobody make you tell."

"They don't care what a nigger see. It's not something you seen. Why they named you, T.J.? What they name you for?"

"I told you to hush."

"Everybody been telling me to hush. Everybody treating me like I'm four years old, like I ain't got good sense."

"Everybody who?"

"Mama. You and Mama. You're my brother, T.J.! Tell me what it is."

"I didn't do nothing. I tried to save my friend's life. Nothing." He was silent awhile, and then he sighed slightly, as if he were tired of the whole subject. "I didn't set out to kill no whiteman. It just happen."

When Graceful set the crate on the worn linoleum, her mother took one look at her and instantly turned away. *What?* Graceful thought. *What I do now?* But she knew. She had asked questions, and T.J. had told, and now the truth was burned on her, right into her skin, her face, her eyes sharp with fear. Well, maybe she couldn't hide it from Mama, but she could hide it from whitefolks. She knew that she could. Jewell was sitting at the table, bleary-eyed, her chin in one hand. Mama snapped, "All right, Graceful's here now. You happy? Go on in yonder and get yourself some sleep, we got a big day tomorrow."

"Mama?" Jewell said sleepily. "I'll stay with the children. You can let LaVona go to church."

"Take you and LaVona both to mind that many wild children."

"Me and Graceful can do it." Jewell smiled hopefully at her sister.

"We'll see. You go on and get in the bed."

Jewell came and hugged Graceful, hard and quick. *She's the sweetest one,* Graceful thought. *She the best of any of us.* Little Jewell, the peace-maker, who was no longer little but tall and thin, like T.J. As Graceful hugged her sister's long boniness, she thought, *I know one thing, I'm not going back to work for whitefolks. I'm not leaving them no more.* The tail of Jewell's nightgown had hardly disappeared through the doorway when Mama came at her, whispering hard, "What'd I tell you? What did I say? Answer me?" Her mother's face was such a fury that Graceful was afraid to speak. "What you got to go and ask him questions for?" Mama turned, sank into a chair at the table. Graceful watched in terror as her mother sagged, trembling, with her face in her hands.

But when Cleotha looked up, long minutes later, her face was clear of emotion, masklike, stony. She stood, moved purposefully toward the cookstove. "Go wake up Delroy. Quiet, now. I don't want them children getting up again." She turned, held her daughter's eyes a moment, looked away finally, across the kitchen, to some blank and empty space on the wall. "I guess you going to have to go with them." Cleotha snatched the tin percolator off the stovetop and in the same motion went to the bucket, began to dipper water into the pot.

T he sky had begun to lighten in the east by the time Delroy turned his Nash truck out of the yard. Graceful looked back once, but the sight of the black shack in the gray dawn and her mother alone on the bowed porch was too hard, and she quickly turned front, stared through the windscreen. Her uncle seemed to be still half dopey with sleep, though she'd watched him drink down three cups of scalding coffee, standing at the stove blinking and yawning, before he'd gone out to prepare the truck.

Neither of them talked as they drove north across the bucking land. To the right the sky began to glow rose-colored, brightening to coral at the line of the earth. Straight up above arched a teal, gleaming vault, but in the west the heavens stayed indigo, lit here and there with a few winking stars. The toenail moon hung suspended, spurs up, very high in the turquoise sky, and Graceful saw now the shadow above it, the black, dense orb snugged against the gleaming crescent. *Old moon sleeping in the new moon's arms,* she said to herself, repeating Grandma Whiteside's old saying, and suddenly she was overwhelmed with a wash of grief that made her shudder, made her want to weep and wail from some lost place, made her long to cry out. The feeling was new to her and at the same time familiar. She shut her mind against the future. Shut her mind to everything but what was in front of her eyes, beneath her body, what her senses received.

The truck shook and shivered and rumbled over the humped hills.

Again and again they hit bumps hard enough to jar her teeth, make her thrust out her arm and brace herself against the dash. She thought, *My Lord, that must be some terrible ride in the back.* She wanted to turn and look down into the truckbed, see if they were still covered. She wanted to ask Delroy to slow down some, it was too rough for them back yonder, and she wanted to urge him to hurry up, hurry, and she listened to the chugging of the motor, watched the world turning light, said nothing at all.

As the day opened they began to see wagons coming toward them filled to the tailgates with fine-dressed Negroes on their way to Sunday morning worship, and Graceful would gaze at them with that same new-old feeling, while Delroy lifted one hand from the steering wheel in greeting. But when whitefolks passed in their motorcars or wagons, she'd hold herself as still as she could in the bumping truck, hardly breathing, and she would turn her face away. Every white farmer in overalls lumbering along with his family in a spring-wagon, every elegant whitelady with a filmy tied-on hat beside a smirking whiteman speeding by in a roadster filled Graceful with dread and loathing, with the cold beginnings of hatred, and a fierce, driven protectiveness for T.J. and the other two hidden under the mildewed tarps in the back.

It was full morning by the time they reached a town. Delroy still had not spoken, and Graceful asked him nothing, and it was only because she saw the building on the horizon and the sign before it etched with scrolled letters that read LANGSTON UNIVERSITY that she understood where they were. She thought, *Oh, sure, now, this is a good idea—Langston! Six hundred blackfolks going to school in this town. T.J. and them'll disappear here like nothing.* But Delroy drove straight past, and on through the all-black town, or it was supposed to be a black town, but the streets were empty. The fear stirred in Graceful. She stared hard at the frame houses shuttered against the heat, the closed stores on Main Street, the cinderblock church, which was silent on Sunday morning, the big front door shut, and she prayed that any minute Delroy would stop at a good place, a safe place, but Uncle Delroy did not stop. Her tongue tried a dozen times to ask where they were going, where were all the people, but her mother's angry face kept coming to her, saying, You got to keep your mouth quiet and not ask questions, girl. And then her mind's eye saw the silhouette of a colored boy hanging from a tree.

They drove east now, into the brilliant sun, and the only words that passed in the truck cab were when Delroy asked for the water jar or to be handed a piece of cornbread, and once Graceful asked in embarrassment could he stop a minute by that clump of cottonwoods yonder. The tense unbroken silence was not the only way the trip was different from the drive out to Arcadia, as the absence of Willie's smiling face wasn't all, or the fact they were traveling in a different part of the state. For Graceful the journey was a lifetime's worth of different. All that she'd held away from herself before was now fully present. What was known could not be unknown; what had happened could not be pushed away.

Every time they neared a white town, the nausea and fear would come hard on her, and her hands would begin to quiver so that she'd have to jam them against the seat to keep Delroy from seeing. She'd bite her lip, stare at her lap in order to not look at their stores, their houses, their white faces coming from church; she wouldn't lift her head until they were driving in the open land again, so different from what they'd driven through on the way to Arcadia. Every time the truck shuddered to the top of a rise, she could see the red dirt road descending, and rising again in the distance, miles of faded prairie sloping down, and then up, and then down again, in all directions, like ridges in a giant washboard big enough for God. But always they continued east, and at the top of one rise, Graceful suddenly thought with relief, *Why, we going home to Tulsa! Yes. We just going by a different road, that's all. Mama be coming soon. Quick as she get those kids took care of, she'll come.* From that moment, satisfied with the answer she'd made up in her own mind, Graceful felt her fear and sickness begin to ease, and she allowed her unasked questions to float through the open truck window and out across the undulating prairie with the hot wind.

Late in the afternoon, Delroy turned off the dirt track, drove down into a caney creekbottom way back off the road. He set the brake, killed the motor, groaned a little as he climbed down and moved off toward the rear of the truck. Graceful sat gazing discreetly ahead until she heard the thundery sound of the big tarp being pulled off the back; she turned to watch T.J. jump down and stretch, take a sip from the water jar Delroy held out to him. It was the first time Graceful had seen the two women. She stared first at the mother, who grunted when T.J. helped her climb down. The woman was much older than Graceful had expected, considering how young the children in the house were: saggy-bosomed and heavy, her skin ashy as she moved stiff-limbed off into the brush. And then Graceful turned her eyes to T.J.'s girlfriend, and her breath caught. *Lord God, I bet she's not a year older than Jewell.*

The girl stood beside the truck in a sleeveless cotton shift almost the same color as the dirt beneath her bare feet, a sort of soft, washed-out red. Her skin was coppery, her unprocessed hair the dull color of an old penny, and Graceful could see that she was too thin, her arms like a child's arms, her knobby neckbone protruding from the scoop of neckline like a chicken neck, though she had big buttocks that stuck out firm and high beneath the faded cotton. She kept her face turned every minute toward T.J., even when he disappeared into the bushes, and when he came back, his eyes darting about restlessly, his flared nostrils sensing the air, she touched him on the arm as he passed. But T.J. ignored her, as if her touch were no more than the brush of a mothwing. The girl turned once, feeling Graceful's eyes on her, smiled up quickly, and as quickly turned away. She was a little frog-eyed, Graceful thought, but pretty. When her mother came back from the canebrake, the girl darted off the way the woman had come, and Graceful thought, *What is T.J. doing messing with a young switchtail like that?*

At once she was ashamed. The girl's brother had been lynched. That woman's son. Graceful had been hearing about lynchings all her life; she'd never known a family it had happened to. She watched in a kind of humble fascination as the mother leaned against the tailgate, her face deadened, her natty hair matted and sticking up at the back of her head. Looking at the woman's ruined face, Graceful felt the cold nausea welling up again, and the hatred. Again her mind saw the boy hanging, hands tied behind his back, his body slowly turning, but it was T.J.'s face she saw on the lynched body, and despite herself she had to look over to make sure that he was really standing there, alive, on the dirt ground. Yes, it was T.J., her living, breathing brother T.J., bending secretively toward Delroy, speaking low and urgent as their uncle hoisted the orange can. Graceful could tell by how high Delroy held it that the can was almost empty. *We'll have to stop and buy some.* Her belly clenched at the thought of driving into a white filling station. *Maybe we got enough to get to Tulsa.* Her brother and her uncle spoke without expression, first one, a beat of silence, then the other. There'd always been that closeness between them, like Delroy was T.J.'s brother instead of Mama's, though he was fifteen years older than T.J. and had taken care of him since T.J. was a little child. Delroy nodded at something T.J. said—a quick, slight dip of his forehead—and they met eyes an instant, then turned away; in that passing was too much knowledge and a flat, closed understanding, and Graceful craved to know what they were saying. Though she knew they'd hush as soon as she got out of the truck, she shoved the door open, jumped down to the ground.

Uncle Delroy was screwing the cap on the big can as he walked toward the rear of the truck. The moment and its knowledge, whatever it was, had already passed. T.J. looked up impatiently. "Better hurry." He turned to help the mother climb up. Graceful watched as the woman pulled herself onto the tailgate, though there was such bled-out despair in the woman's face that she wanted to turn away, as she'd turned her eyes from her own mother while she read the letters from T.J. This mother was as unlike Mama as it was possible to be, but Graceful felt, watching her, that they shared grief from the same source. The only difference was, in Mama grief turned brittle hard; it made this woman soft as an old shoe. The girl appeared from the undergrowth then, sidled up behind T.J., reached a fluttery hand out to touch him.

"Get in the truck," T.J. told her.

She kept her round eyes on him, watching him in mute, hopeless expectation, though what she expected Graceful couldn't tell.

"Y'all want to eat something?" Graceful said, as if that had been her intention for getting out of the truck, but T.J. spoke before the others could answer. "We'll eat when we get there." He hopped up on the tailgate, reached a hand down. The girl, obedient and shy-acting, took it and climbed into the bed. She hesitated, said softly, "Can't we leave it off now? I can't breathe, T.J., feel like I'm gone choke to death." Her voice was as fluttery and mothlike as her fingers. T.J. didn't answer, but moved front and settled himself on the pile of rags and blankets against the cab as if he'd been traveling this way, hiding this way, his whole life long. The mother, with her despairing face, lay down beside him, and then the girl came and curled up on the other side, and T.J. glanced around, reached above the girl's head and picked up a yard-long piece of blackjack from a hidden fold of blanket, grasped it by one end like a club. He nodded at Delroy and lay back flat, the oak limb cradled across his chest. Graceful watched the girl's face, the still terror on it as the tarp came up and buried her, how she put a hand up over her head to make air space.

Moving on leaden feet toward the cab, Graceful tried to push her own terror down, hold it tight in her gullet, since she could not shove it away. She stood with her hand on the handle, taking big gulping breaths, before she climbed in. Delroy looked hard at her when she banged the door shut. "You all right?" he said.

"Fine."

He shoved the big gearshift into reverse and began to back up.

By the time they drove into the familiar eastern scrub-oak hills, it was almost dark. She worried that they'd run out of fuel, because Delroy didn't stop again. What if they ran out of gas by a sundown town? There were so many towns with green laws, you'd never know if you were in one. Most were marked with signs at the edge: *No Negroes Allowed Within These City Limits Between The Hours of Sunset and Sunrise*—or sometimes just plain NO NIGGERS AFTER DARK—and she knew that Uncle Delroy knew the worst ones, Henryetta and Norman, the towns every colored person had heard of; she knew he'd never drive within miles of those towns at twilight. But there were so many small towns, Delroy might not even know he was by one, and anyhow every Oklahoma town was dangerous after dark, mixed or white, if it was colored people driving. The only safe towns were the black towns. Graceful thought sleepily, *Maybe he fixing to stop at Redbird or someplace, get some more gas.*

The sky was full-dark when they turned north again, and still Delroy drove on. Graceful slept before she knew she'd done so, and it was only by her head bumping against the side glass, knocking her awake, that she realized she'd slept. She worried now that Delroy would fall asleep driving, crash them into a ditch, but her exhaustion was so complete that before she knew it she'd dropped off again. She didn't dream, or if she did, she didn't know it, for the sleep was a velvety black warmth of nothing wrapped around her, and then she'd be thumped awake again, and before she could come fully to consciousness, the fear would be there.

The last time she was knocked awake, she thought for sure she must be dreaming. She blinked at the thousand winking lights rising up out of the darkness, and she thought that all the stars had been shaken down from heaven and landed in stacks on the plains. And then the stink came to her, and the sound, and the great mechanical sense of it, and she saw small figures of men moving about in the lights, but most of all it was the fetid smell that was so familiar, and she knew what she was looking at was not a dream but the lights on a tremendous bank of oil refineries. *Maybe we back in Tulsa,* she thought, trying to wake up, trying to get some sensible thoughts in her head. *That must be the refineries by the river.* But Delroy kept driving toward them, and Graceful didn't see the dotted skyline of Tulsa on the far side, didn't see the Arkansas River or any familiar mark, but just the great stacks of belching, smoking, stinking vats and chimneys amidst the steel girders, and men moving about, working in the brilliant white light spreading out on the dark prairie, miles from any city, miles from any reasonable place on earth.

Delroy turned off the road, and in another moment the truck's head-lamps revealed the tangled growth of another creekbottom, though this one was not caney and willowy, as the last had been, but clotted with scrub oak and sumac, matted with thick vines snaking through the under-growth, looping down from tree limbs, crawling over limestone boulders made distinct and strange in the refineries' glow. When Delroy cut the motor, he sat so long with his head on his arms draped over the steering wheel that Graceful began to get scared; it reminded her too much of Mama at the table, and after a while, her tremored voice rising with the sounds of the nightcreatures scrabbling and chirring all around the truck, she said softly, "Uncle Delroy? We going to sleep here?"

Delroy snapped his head up so fast Graceful jumped back. "No." He looked around, took a long, deep breath. "No, honey." He blew the air out, hard. "We're not there yet. Listen, you going to have to stay here with them. I'll be back quick as I can get here." His voice was hollow, dream-like. He lifted his hand twice before he could get it connected with the door handle, and then he pushed the squeaking door open in slow mo-tion; his movements were thick, lugubrious, like he was dreamwalking, moving underwater. He disappeared slowly into the darkness at the back of the truck. She could hear him talking to T.J., heard the gas can scrape on the metal truckbed, although she didn't hear the tarp being pulled off. She sat very still, listening, her heart beating hard, but Delroy left so qui-etly she never knew when he walked off.

The only sound was her own blood and the ceaseless chorus of crick-ets. The air was ruddy with reflected light from the refineries, hidden be-yond the treetops, though the stink and the low hum told her they were not far away. The moon hadn't risen, or she couldn't see it yet, but the truck was so wrapped around with undergrowth and the pinkish glow was so strange that she couldn't tell if it was getting close to morning. *Maybe they getting some sleep now,* she thought. *At least we not bumping around all over creation.* It didn't come clear to her in words that the one she hoped was sleeping was the whispery too-skinny girl who felt herself buried alive beneath the tarp. Graceful stretched out across the seat to try and sleep, but each time she'd start to drift she would see white faces at the window, white hands reaching to snatch the truck door open, and she'd jerk full awake, her heart pounding. She got up, rolled the windows up tighter, lay back down, sweating. She felt naked. She wished she had a big chunk of blackjack, like T.J., something to protect herself besides her own quaking, shivering silence.

And then, later—how much later she didn't know, though it seemed hours—she thought she heard footfalls, somewhere out in the woods. She held her breath, tried to listen through the din of insects, and then, yes, she was sure of it: someone was coming through the undergrowth, snapping twigs. There was a low whispering sound, though she couldn't make out if it was leaves rustling or murmured voices. She slid off the seat into the dirty floorboard, hating the white dress of her mother because it was so visible, glowing like moonflowers in the dark. Her frenzied hands scrabbled around the truck floor, but there was only the empty water jar to protect her, the sorghum tin of uneaten biscuits and fatback. When the dark head loomed over the window she gripped the glass jar tight in both hands. She couldn't make out the features but she knew it was a black man. It wasn't Delroy. The man's palms came up to cup his face, and he peered into the truck, trying to make out what he was seeing. There was another voice behind him, and she heard the tarp being pulled off the back. The one at the window said something, deep and soft-inflected, muffled through the closed glass, and Graceful's breath released, and she thought she'd weep or shout or something, she didn't know what she might do. Never could she have dreamed she'd be so glad to hear the soft-slurred voice of Hedgemon Jackson saying her name outside in the dark.

PART THREE

Beulah

Arcadia
Sunday
September 5, 1920

That church was too small for such a gathering, just a little slapped-together clapboard country church on a rise of prairie north of town. But on that Sunday morning it was swelled to full and beyond full, people standing in rows at the windows, swatting flies, looking in. There was one white face. A tiny songbird-looking whitewoman with a smile pasted on her face like it had been grown there. She must have arrived early, because she was sitting at the end of a row, halfway to the front. Folks had to step over her to get to the seats in the middle, but she never moved over, never quit smiling. There was little to smile at. You could taste the grief in that room like bad air. What you could taste even more bitter than that was the anger. Maybe she thought smiling would help something.

They'd buried the boy on Tuesday, the day after they cut him down—buried him alongside his father—so it wasn't the funeral that had folks lined up seven deep at the windows and front door. The pastor called it a memorial service, but I believe folks from that community and those of us from around Luther knew pretty well Reverend Shew didn't intend to offer a memorial to that family of moonshiners; he had something else in mind. People rode the train from Taft and Rentiesville, drove down from Langston, came from Boley and Bookertee and Redbird, all the old colored towns. Some of them must have started out the evening before to get there by morning. What they thought that service was going to be I can't tell you.

I heard a few of them milling around in the yard early, before Sunday School, murmuring against the Reverend, why had he called it on a Sunday morning at regular divine worship time, because folks had to miss their own service. But I thought it was shrewd of the Reverend: what other time does it look innocuous for so many colored people to be traveling together except Sunday morning going to church? They came in flatbed wagons and walking and driving new Chandlers and Model T Fords, started before daylight, and they kept coming on late into the morning. Folks quit murmuring afterwhile, because every time there came a new wagon, muleheels kicking up dust, we could feel it, every person in that church and outside it could: we knew something powerful was taking place.

I will tell you something. That wasn't the last time colored folks from all over Oklahoma came together in the wake of such trouble, but to my mind, as far as I know, that was the first. And I will tell you something else: Reverend Shew was one of the cleverest men I've ever witnessed. He was a small-church country preacher, but he had an extremely subtle mind. I admired him sufficiently that, had it not been for the fact that the drive from Luther was twelve miles, which, in those days, took several hours in bad weather on the kinds of roads we had to drive, and had I not belonged to our AME church from a child, I would have joined his little Mount Zion Baptist congregation. He had my respect to that degree.

He began the service in a completely ordinary manner, sitting very simply in his chair behind the pulpit with his fingertips together, his head bowed. If a person didn't happen to see the dignitaries in dark suits seated on the front pews, he could almost imagine this was a regular Baptist Sunday-morning worship service, or the last service of a revival, maybe, to account for all the people standing along the walls and the back and outside. The choir came from the rear of the sanctuary in customary processional, moving up the aisles in their white robes, clapping and singing "Marching Up to Zion." They were small— no more than a half dozen women on each side, and three men—but as they climbed the podium the congregation joined voice, and there began some clapping, a little shouting, but the Reverend was not ready to rouse us yet, and he stood and came forward, and everybody drew quiet while he offered a prayer to the Holy Spirit to pour out His mighty presence on our service here this morning, and then he went back very simply, sat down again, and bowed his head.

Here, now, I'll offer evidence of the subtlety of that pastor's mind, for I've no doubt that he selected the hymns just as he selected the passage of Scripture for his text and the hour of gathering and the very list of men seated in the front pews. A woman in the choir stood and sang alone, without accompaniment. She had on a worn housedress, which was strange there among us, white gloves, a little white lace cap on her head. She started out slow, singing the shaped notes, and in such glorious voice that the bosom of the entire congregation swelled: "I Been 'Buked, Lord, I Been Scorned." She moved from that old spiritual right into "Beulah Land" like it was an extension of the same song. When she came to the chorus the choir joined in, and in another beat the whole of that congregation, from youngest to eldest, was singing, "Ain't going to stop till I get there, I got a home in Beulah Land," and there was much shouting and clapping, because it is, you know, our story. But the Reverend Shew was not done with us yet.

At a sign from him, the soloist bowed her head, went silent a moment, and the clapping dropped away. When she lifted her face and began again, her voice had slid from the joy of Beulah to a great lowbelly sorrow, and she sang "Were You There When They Crucified My Lord?" so slow and sacred no one thought to join voice with her, and when she came to the part that sings, "Were you there when they hung him to the tree? Oh, sometimes it causes me to tremble," we were all, I believe, every one, trembling. The woman—I never did know her name, she was not from around here, but, my Lord, she had a glorious voice— she swung from sorrow right on into "Victory In Jesus," and the whole of the congregation once more lifted voice and sang till we about raised the shingles off that little church, and it was the whole story, wasn't it? In that precise and telling order. The Reverend had reminded us of the whole story, and still no one had mentioned the word lynching. It was the loudest word in that sanctuary, not a soul had whispered it with their lips.

Now he stepped to the pulpit himself, and very slowly he began to sing, "Lord, sometimes there is trouble in my life." The man had such a power that none joined him for several moments, until the sound began to roll in through the open windows. The preacher sang out, "Trouble in my life," and the response, "Some-t-i-i-ime," came from without like the echo of thunder, low and deep, from the throats of the men standing outside. How many there were I had no idea then, but the sound was a great rumbling, a great power, and in a moment the women's voices joined in. Think of it. Oh, I see it in my mind's eye to this day, I hear it, I remember: that small clapboard church on the rolling prairie, and the day sweltering, burning as this land burns in early September, the earth so hot the colors are bled from it, switchgrass fading to beige, and the sky white with heat, the red dirt itself fading, gone sifting coral and salmon, flour-soft, and around this little country church the sound is rising, swelling in waves like the heat rising toward heaven. Men and women in rows at the windows, women in blue and red and yellow dresses, in silk hats, and the men in straw dress-hats, white suitcoats, cream-colored jackets, brown faces bleeding sweat, and their mouths open, the sound rising, and the yard trampled, wagons and buggies and motorcars lining that red-dust road, and our voices within the sanctuary joined with them outside, joined as one voice. And the Reverend led us on. "Jesus, He will fix it," he sang, and the voices answered, "After whi-i-ile," and a great shout went up from that place, the seat of the Lord, the Lord's house: "Jesus, He will fix it, afterwhile," a shout not of anger but of faith, and that is the gift the Great God of Zion did give us.

From the corner of my eye I could see the little whitewoman trembling, smiling and trembling. An usher came forward and gave her a hymnal, and you would have thought that poor woman's face could not crack any wider, but it did. She smiled up at the usher and opened the book just anywhere and looked at it, still smiling, but she didn't sing. I'd seen her mouthing the words to "Victory In Jesus," which showed her to be a Christian, or at least somebody who went to church, but she did not sing this hymn with us.

We sang a good long time, long enough for the Spirit to begin its work, to still our thoughts and our anger and even the old grief finally, and that of course is what the Reverend intended, because he knew we could not hear him till our minds were still and the Spirit moving among us. He meant us to be receptive before the Lord. It took a long time. When he led us down to quiet finally and began to pray, we were ready.

"Blessed Father, look down on Your children here this morning. We hurting, Lord, our hearts are broken, and You know that, Lord."

Throughout the congregation the people murmured, "Yes, Jesus. Yes, Lord."

"Your word tells us there's a balm in Gilead, Lord."

"Oh, yes, Lord."

"We just ask You to pour Your balm out upon us this morning."

"Thank you, Jesus."

"We ask You to heal our hearts, Lord, lead us in Your path of righteousness."

"Yes, God."

"That we might do Your will, Lord. In the name of Your Son Jesus we pray. Amen."

He opened The Book then. "Would y'all turn with me this morning to the sixty-first chapter of Isaiah." There was the sifting, shuffling sound as Bibles were opened and leafed through. "Isaiah sixty-one, the first verse." Very calm, very slow he started. "'The Spirit of the Lord God is upon me,'" he read, "'because the Lord hath anointed me to preach good tidings unto the meek; he hath sent me to bind up the brokenhearted, to proclaim liberty to the captives, and the opening of the prison to them that are bound.'" He paused, looked up at us. "Y'all hear the Word of the Lord this morning?" he said. "'Bind up the brokenhearted.' Are we brokenhearted here this morning?"

And from the whole of the congregation went up a mighty "Amen!"

"What do the Lord say He's going to do for the brokenhearted? Bind us up, amen?"

The people answered, "Amen."

"Do the Lord say He's going to proclaim liberty to the captives?"

"Yes, Lord!"

"Do the Lord say He's going to open the prison to them that are bound?"

"Praise Jesus!"

He looked at us very quiet for a minute, and then he read on. "'To proclaim the acceptable year of the Lord, and the day of vengeance of our God, to comfort all that mourn.'" He repeated very slowly: "'The day . . . of vengeance . . . of . . . our . . . God.'" Looked up at us. "Whose vengeance He going to proclaim?"

"God's vengeance!"

"Do He say He's going to proclaim the people's vengeance?"

"No, Lord."

"Say He's going to proclaim *God's* vengeance, amen?"

"Amen!"

"And here in the third verse: 'To appoint unto them that mourn in Zion'— Lord, listen to it—'them that mourn in Zion'! Are we mourning in Zion?"

"Yes, Lord!"

"Is the Lord going to comfort us?"

"Amen! Praise God. Thank you, Jesus. Yes, Lord."

"'To give unto them beauty for ashes'—y'all hear it?—'beauty for ashes'— amen?—'the oil of joy for mourning, the garment of praise for the spirit of heaviness.' The Lord is not going to leave us alone in our mourning. He is not going to abandon us in our grief. He's going to exchange the oil of joy for our mourning, don't He say that? Going to give us a garment of praise for our low-down spirit of heaviness, amen?"

"Amen!"

"Now, why is He going to do that? Because He loves us, yes. Because He don't want to see His children eating their hearts out in grief and rage."

"Yes, Lord!"

"But you look here at the third verse. He is going to give us beauty for ashes. Why? 'That they might be called trees of righteousness, the planting of the Lord.' The planting of the *Lord*, do you hear it? 'That he might be glorified.' Let us pray. Lord Jesus, make us Your planting here this morning. You promise to bind up our broken hearts, Lord, we trust You on that."

"Yes, Lord."

"You going to ease our hearts with that oil of joy, Lord."

"Oh, yes, Lord."

"We know You are able."

"Thank you, Jesus."

"But, Lord, we asking You now, Lord, to show us how to be a planting for You, Lord. Show us how we going to be trees of righteousness for You, Lord, that Your will going to be done through our right doing, Lord, our right doing and our faith, Lord. Amen."

"Amen."

And then the Reverend Shew stood quiet with his head bowed for so long that the congregation inside and outside began to get restless. All over the sanctuary people had their cardboard fans going, moving the hot air. We all were perspiring, we all were waiting, and though the Spirit had just a minute ago been moving among us, now people began to shift in the pews, stirring, because the heat seemed to rise in Brother Shew's silence.

It was in that uncomfortable quiet that I realized that the family of Everett Candler was not among us. I looked all around. No passel of children, no widowed grieving mother. I craned my neck to look behind, though they wouldn't, of course, have been seated in the rear of the sanctuary; they'd have been on the front pew, right directly before the altar. Rather, the first three pews across the front of the church were filled with dignitaries in dark suits; they were not craning their necks, as the rest of us were, looking around; they sat very still, facing forward. But the family of the lynched boy was not there.

The Reverend raised his head after a long time, he laid his eyes on us, stood behind the pulpit in his white robe with the two gold crosses embroidered on each breast, stood so very still, his face that high, clean, copper color, so perfectly still you could see the peace on it, you could see what surrender he'd done made with his Lord. He said, "I want y'all to open your Bibles one more time to Isaiah, the sixty-second chapter, the fourth verse. Isaiah sixty-two, four. Y'all got it?" For the first time he turned and acknowledged the faces crowded at the windows. "Y'all got it out there? Isaiah sixty-two, four. All right now, I want you to read it with me."

And the sound went up in a low rumbling.

"'Thou shalt no more be termed Forsaken; neither shall thy land any more be termed Desolate: but thou shalt be called Hephzibah, and thy land Beulah: for the Lord delighteth in thee, and thy land shall be married.'"

The Reverend closed his Bible, and all over the sanctuary you could hear little thuds as many Bibles shut. "We all know what happen last Sunday. Not a soul here don't know that one more time one of our sons been taken out by a white mob and lynched."

The hard murmur began to rise among us, and you could feel that house ready to be exhorted to rage. We wanted to be. I believe that's what most of us had come for, whether we knew it or not. But the Reverend put his hand up, he eased us down again; he had something different on his mind.

"Now, there's lots of rumors been flying all around our communities, too many rumors. Here in a little bit I'm going to ask Mr. Roscoe Dunjee to come up and relate the truth to us, tell us all the facts he knows as a newspaperman and a member of the governor's Race Relations Committee, and as one colored citizen that have the acquaintanceship and the ear of Governor Robertson. Mr. Dunjee going to tell us what did happen, what's going to happen, and all of that. We going to settle some of these wild rumors."

A murmur of approval went up, a few scattered amens.

"But I want us to listen to the Word of the Lord here a minute longer. The Word say our land is going to be called Beulah, isn't that right? That's what we read here this morning. And God knows we've been dreaming about the Promised Land a long time, amen? And what do the Lord tell us? Again and again He says, I'm going to deliver My people. He says, I'm going to lead My people to a land of milk and honey, amen? Are we the Lord's people here this morning? Amen. Amen. And if we the Lord's people because we are faithful to Him, will He not do as He promised? Amen. And now there are some among us, I'm going to say maybe even most among us, who came right here to this Territory believing we getting to the Promised Land at last, amen? And what do we find when we get here? Find out things in Oklahoma aren't much different from Memphis and Mississippi, from Arkansas and Texas and all those other places we come from, am I right? I hear some mighty amens. So what are we going to think now? Do we suppose to think the Lord been fooling us? Why would the Lord want to fool His people? Well, what are y'all thinking? Maybe it wasn't the Lord fooling us, but just us fooling ourselves. Maybe we the fools."

He paused a minute. That little church got so quiet. All the amens and the Yes, Jesuses just disappeared from the air. The Reverend looked down at them on the front pews and said softly, "Brethren? Would y'all stand?"

They stood as one man. Then, in the next beat, they turned around and looked at us. The Reverend said, "You look here among us. Do we have a bunch of fools gathered here this morning?"

The Reverend gave us a long time to look at them. In the center stood Mr. Roscoe Dunjee, editor of the *Black Dispatch* out of Oklahoma City, and on one side of him stood Mr. Smitherman from the *Tulsa Star*, and on the other Mayor D.J. Turner of Boley. I recognized the mayors of Taft and Rentiesville, several ministers, a number of doctors, our grand master of the Knights of Pythias, Dr.

Wickham, a half-dozen editors of colored newspapers from all over the state. At the end of one row stood attorney I.H. Spears, and next to him, in great dignity, President Marquess of Langston University. They stood there, men in their prime mostly, and of every color known to the Negro race, looking out at us, and we knew they were lawyers and educators, business leaders, writers, doctors of philosophy and medicine and the Word. They were our leaders, the very cream of our colored leaders. The Reverend waited for us to comprehend.

I cannot speak for others, but as for myself, that moment settled something deep in me. I understood we were gathered for a purpose not like any gathering of our people before. We had come together not to memorialize, not to grieve, or to give vent to that old powerless wrath. We had come to *do* something, come to make something, create a new way among us: there was change coming. I did not know what kind of change, but something powerful. Something unspoken before in this land.

"The Lord don't lie," the Reverend said softly. "If we come here believing, then we got to go on believing." He held his peace yet a while, and the deep understanding ran through the sanctuary. "Thank you, brethren," he said finally. "Y'all can be seated."

And the men sat down again.

Reverend Shew stepped out from behind the pulpit, came front and stood at the very lip of the podium. "From the time our people came in chains to this America," he began quietly, "we been waiting. The Lord promised He was going to lead us, and He did lead us. Right here to Beulah. Right here to the Promised Land, and we making something here, amen? In Tulsa and Oklahoma City, in Langston and Boley, in that old Creek town Muskogee and that good colored town of Taft and all over this state, we are making something, can I get a witness? Amen. Amen. We come here, we say we going to build us a home Over in Beulah, like the old spiritual says. Did we build us our home? Amen. Built us some strong black towns, some fine businesses, a powerful Negro university, and come to find out, what? The whiteman's no different in this land. No different in this land. They going to make laws to have us to live separate from them—that's going to be the first laws they make soon as they become a state. They don't want to allow us to ride in the same railcar with them, they don't want us to use their same telephone booths. Well, that's all right, isn't it? We going to go on and live our own lives. But here now, come to find out they going to write up a grandfather clause like they got all over the South, say we can't vote unless our slave grandfathers voted. But we just going to put our good lawyers on that one—amen, Brother Spears?—going to get the U.S. Supreme Court to turn over that one, we going to go on and live our own lives.

"But now, here, come to find out, they going to lynch this young man Everett Candler Sunday evening, like they lynching black men in Georgia and Alabama and Chicago, Illinois. Whoa now. Whoa, now. We can't go on and live our own lives in the light of that, can we? What kind of land is this? This the land of milk and honey? How we going to believe that when they come in the night and snatch up our sons and take them out on a dark road and murder them? They lynched Everett on Sunday, but what do we find out they did on Saturday night in Tulsa? The very night before, at·the other end of the state, they gone and lynched one of their own."

We began to murmur amongst ourselves.

"Is this the land thè good Lord promised us?"

The murmured fury was rising.

"Listen here, now. I'm here to tell you something: yes, it is."

We all got quiet again.

"What is it the Word tell us? 'Thou shalt no more be termed Forsaken.' Hear it? We going to be called Forsaken no longer. Praise God. Our land is going to be called Beulah. Why? Because the Lord delighteth in us, the Word says. And what does that name mean, Beulah? We talk about Way Over in Beulah like it's the heavenly hereafter, but I'm here to tell you Beulah is a real place, it is right here on this earth we going to quit being called Forsaken. It is here our land is going to be called Beulah, the Book says that, and what does Beulah mean, brothers and sisters? It means *married*. What do the Lord mean to tell us, *married*? Just this: we married to the whiteman. Oh, no, now, I don't want to hear y'all grumbling. What else is it? They were our captors to start with, yes, now they our doctors and lawyers and newspaper writers, they the opposite to us and the same as us, and we are *married* to them. But let me tell you something else, brothers and sisters. The whiteman is married to the Negro just as well. Y'all know it? Amen. And there's no place the whiteman knows it like he know it in Beulah. That's why they make Jim Crow laws hard and fast as they can make them. That's why the Klan rising up so bad in this state. They know it in the truth of their hearts, and those that don't know it yet, we're here to teach them. Amen?"

"Amen!"

"Whiteman might think he'd sho like to get a divorce from us. We might think we sho like to do the same. Lots of blackfolk saying they don't want nothing to do with the whiteman, and Lord knows we feel like that. We'd like to not ever have to deal with him anymore. We come here to this land, we think maybe we going to be allowed to do that, but we find out last Sunday night that's not going to be the case. We got to deal with the whiteman. We got to *deal* with the whiteman here in Beulah. Amen?"

"Amen!"

"We don't know what the Lord's after, but let me tell you this: He is after something, and He aim it to be right here in *this* America. He aim *us* to be right here in this America. Brother Garvey up in New York, he saying we all got to go back to Africa together, but I mean to tell you something this morning: what God hath joined together, can't *no* man put asunder. Oh, yes, I hear you: Preacher, that weren't God put our people in them slave ships. The whiteman done that. You right. You right. But listen here. The Lord God is a mighty God, y'all believe it? He can bring ten plagues on top of Pharaoh, am I right? He can part the Red Sea waters, lead His children safe over on dry land. Great God of Zion can do anything He want. He can allow anything He want. He can *stop* anything He want. How come He don't stop the hand of these whitemens lynching our children? Last year in Chicago, how come He didn't stop them going yonder to the South Side and burning down our houses and killing us like lambs to the slaughter? This very year, fifty-three black men already been lynched in America. That's the truth in this country. That's the truth. I want to ask you something: could the Lord stop these whitemen's hands if He wanted? What? Y'all mighty silent out there. Any believers here this morning? Can I get some amens from some believers here this morning?"

"Amen!"

"Is the Lord God a mighty God?"

"Amen."

"Then could the Lord *stop* them if He wanted?"

"Amen."

"Amen. Amen. Now, I don't believe the Lord *want* these things to happen, but He sure do *allow* them to happen, and we here to ask ourselves this morning: why?"

The Reverend got quiet then, looking out at us, letting us ask that question of ourselves. Like we hadn't asked it a thousand times, a hundred thousand times over, and never come up with any answer but the pure mystery of evil, the plain old wickedness in whitemen's souls. And still the Reverend was silent, so that we went from asking it of ourselves, to asking God. Like we hadn't asked it of Him, too, a hundred thousand times for every black man and woman and child dead.

Very softly the Reverend said, "What do He want from us? What does the Book say: 'that they might be called trees of righteousness': that they might be *the planting of the Lord*. Would y'all bow your heads.

"Almighty Father, we gathered here this morning to look and see how we might be a planting for You. This is Your Word, Lord, and Your promise. You know what's in our hearts, Lord, like You know what's in the hearts of them that have done this terrible thing. Like You know the hearts and minds of all Christians and all non-Christians alike, Lord, white and black, red and yellow, all over this world, Lord, just like You know the instant any little sparrow fall. You have not turned Your face away from it. You know what have happened and what is going to happen, Lord, and we know You going to see us through. We know You are able.

"But now, Father, we asking You to send Your Holy Ghost Spirit here among us. You promised to send us a Comforter, and we need to be comforted here this morning. We asking Your Presence among us, because, Lord, we got to face some hard things. In a minute Brother Dunjee is going to stand up and relate some terrible things to us, some hard truths we going to hurt to hear, some facts going to fill us up with hatred, make us wrathful in Your sight, Lord, and we know if we angry we can't be Your tree of righteousness. If our hearts are full of hatred we can't be Your planting. But, Lord, we can't save our own selves from anger. It's too hard, Father. It is too hard. They killing our sons, Lord."

"Yes, Jesus."

"They killing our daughters."

"Oh, help us."

"We in the sieve of Satan, Lord, he is testing us mightily, and like Job we want to know why. We asking ourselves that question. We asking You, Lord. Why? How long You going to suffer them to do like this here in this country? How long? Almighty Father, we need You to come here among us to save us from anger. Hold back our hearts from hatred, Lord, that we may be Thy planting. That Thy will might be done, Lord, on earth as it is in heaven. In Jesus' holy name we pray. Amen."

The Reverend raised his head and looked down at the front pews, said, "Mr. Dunjee?"

Now, Mr. Roscoe Dunjee was a very handsome, very dignified man, slender in his physique, but he had a mighty power in his presence, and he came and stood to the side of the pulpit, put his hand out to touch it as if it might keep him steady. That church grew completely silent, and all out in the churchyard and beyond—how far distant, I do not know: perhaps far across the prairie—there was silence: no murmuring or shuffles, no sound even of the dense air being stirred by cardboard fans. I have never heard such a silence. It was as if a glass bell had been placed over us by a great hand, and inside that bell the absence of sound was complete.

Mr. Dunjee cleared his throat, said, "Folks, we all know what happened, in its essence. We know young Everett Candler, nineteen years old, was taken from the Oklahoma County jail by several whitemen posing as officers. We know he was given up by the jailer without a struggle, and that he was driven to a dirt road ten miles southwest of the city and strung up by the neck. We know that when the young man's body was located the next day it was found to be desecrated by two gunshot wounds to the forehead as well. He'd been hung to a tree. His right eye was wide open. The pupil, a dull, unnatural color, seemed to gaze upon the world. His left eye was closed. One shot had been placed in the center, the other in the right center of his forehead." The editor paused a moment. The church held its breath, waiting. "The gunshots were perhaps a final *coup de grâce*," Mr. Dunjee said, "for the young man died by hanging. His tongue protruded from his mouth and hung over his lower lip. His hands and feet were tied. He wore a filthy suit of white ducking made red with his own blood. Those are the facts of the lynching."

Brother Dunjee seemed to sink a little then, grow smaller, as if he felt sick. His formal manner changed. "We tried to stop them," he said. He took a white handkerchief from his breast pocket, dabbed it on his forehead. "When word came that the boy had been taken, the whole of the Oklahoma City Negro community joined together to prevent that lynching. We gathered on East Second Street. Many of you here this morning were there. We had a caravan of automobiles ready to head out in any direction, had we only known what direction to go." He paused, looking out at us, and he spoke so low we had to strain to hear him. "When we found the lynching site the next day, that grass was hardly trampled. There could not have been more than a half-dozen of them at the killing. We were almost a thousand. And, citizens, I want you to know, we were powerless to stop it. Powerless. Probably by the time we started to gather on Second Street the boy was dead. I don't need to tell you, ladies and gentlemen, that the time to stop a lynching is before the Negro man is taken, not hours later!"

I heard a kind of low rumbling from without, and I thought at first it was far-off heat lightning, the way it will sometimes send its murmurs across the prairie, and then I knew it to be crowd sound, murmured words in men's voices passed back from the open windows to the farthest edges of the gathering. I thought, All our kept anger will burst forth now.

"Now, ladies and gentlemen." Brother Dunjee raised his voice. "One of the many rumors that have gone round this terrible week is that the mother and sister of Everett Candler were also arrested and taken to the county jail at Oklahoma City. The Reverend has asked me to dispel that rumor, and I can and will. Last Monday evening, I must tell you, the Negro community in Oklahoma City, stirred up as it was and filled with wrath, came near to unleashing its own mob violence because of that tale. We'd heard that those two innocent women were incarcerated in the very cell from which the boy had been taken. We heard that another white mob was gathering to storm the jail and lynch mother and sister, to 'finish the job,' as it was said. Remembering, as we all do, the lynching of Marie Scott in Wagoner six years ago, we had no doubt that the women, too, would be lynched if they could be found. We'd been too late for the Candler boy, but we would not be too late for the women, we were determined—*determined*, ladies and gentlemen, on that! Many hundreds of us gathered, fully prepared if need be to march on the Oklahoma County jail. We sent a delegation to Sheriff Johnson to ask entrance, that we might see for ourselves if the women were there. It took the personal intervention of Governor Robertson, but we were at last allowed to enter and look around the jail, and we were able to satisfy ourselves that the Candler women were not there, so let me lay that particular rumor to rest."

I thought the editor would tell us then what had become of the Candler family, why they were not here at the declared memorial service for their son, but he did not. "We are gathered today for several reasons," he went on. "We're here to mourn Everett Candler, another of our black sons dead at the hands of a white mob. But we are here to do more than that. We must this day speak the unspeakable. We got to tell not just what happened to Everett Candler but what happened to a whiteboy in Tulsa Saturday evening. We got to tell what is happening not only in Oklahoma but in our neighbor Texas almost weekly, what is happening daily in Georgia and Alabama and Illinois and Missouri and Mississippi, throughout this nation. We are here to tell it, and to shout, as God is our witness: No more! No more!"

"No more!" came a cry from the crowd. "No more! Amen! That's right!"

"We don't want to go to that dark place, brothers and sisters. We don't want to tell again how our sons are taken from jail cells, how they are pulled from railcars and automobiles and their own beds, how they are chased by bloodhounds through canebrakes and swamps. We don't want to describe how they're tortured and hung, how their bodies are wrapped in chains and dragged behind cars through our communities. How they are literally butchered alive, or riddled with a thousand bullets, or slowly roasted to death, crying out to their Maker and their torturers to deliver them. How their bodies are mutilated, their fingers and toes snipped off, lips and ears sliced from their heads while they are yet living, their parts severed and forced in their mouths, or kept as souvenirs in jars of alcohol on white storekeepers' counters—"

Mr. Dunjee stopped then. The complete and utter silence had returned. He passed his handkerchief over his face.

"Yes," he said, after a long time. "It is unspeakable. What they do is unspeakable. Too horrible for us to remember. Too horrifying to forget. We don't want to say the words. As a newspaperman, as an informed Negro citizen, I know what they do, what they have done, as you all know it. My soul is outraged, folks, as your souls are outraged. My heart is cold, knifed through, it is sick. I can't stand here before you and describe it any longer, the words are too terrible to say out loud. But I will declare to you this: the only way to stop the cataclysm of lynchings in this nation, this apocalypse that has fallen on our people, is to bring these white mobs to justice!"

"Amen!" said the people. "That's right! Yes, Lord."

I glanced at the little whitewoman then, unconsciously. It was not that I thought of her but that she seemed merely to appear in my line of sight. My inner eye was in a place of horror, and it took a moment to realize I was seeing the woman's face. The smile had at last been wiped from it. Her skin was a sickly yellow, her lips were thin and clamped, though whether in disbelief or judgment or nausea it was impossible to say. Her chest was heaving. She seemed to have shrunk into herself even smaller, as if she'd soon sink away into the pew.

"You cannot stop a mob's fury in the midst of it," Mr. Dunjee continued. "They rage with impunity. They seize battering rams and break down jail walls. Once they've made up their minds to lynch a Negro, there is no human force that can stop them. Their own people cannot stop them—and, yes, there are decent whitemen who try, men of conscience who will stand against them, but I tell you, brothers and sisters, decent whitefolks are not a force powerful enough to stop the bloodlust of a raging mob. One year ago, just last September, the very mayor of Omaha, Nebraska, died at the hands of a lynch mob when he tried to hold them back from taking a Negro prisoner—their own elected mayor! There have been others who died trying to stop them, and we thank God for the ones who will stand against them, but they can't do no good.

"That was a throng of two thousand men, women, and children in Tulsa last Saturday night, and it is told that the Tulsa police directed traffic at the site! That's the kind of crowd gathered in Tulsa to watch the life wrung from the neck of one of their own! If they will gather by the thousands to lynch one of their own race, if they will bring their wives and children to watch the festivities and scramble like hounds for snippets of the rope that choked the life from a whiteman, fight like snarling curs for little shreds of that whiteman's clothes, tell me, ladies and gentlemen, what can we hope for? What can the black man expect in this Oklahoma? Governor Robertson has called for full investigations on both these lynchings, he's calling aloud to bring the mobsters to justice, but I want to ask you, can we get redress from the law in Oklahoma? Who do you think is going to convene a grand jury to investigate the lynching of Everett Candler? Why, none other than Oklahoma County Attorney Cargill—the very man who had that boy brought from Arcadia to his own jurisdiction, where the sheriff was in sympathy with his views—in sympathy, folks! Yes, I will say it! And for what reason? For the *crime of being a black man in the vicinity of the killing of a white man!* For such 'crime' that young man was lynched!"

The low, angry hum began to swell out toward the windows.

"Now, I can make a prediction, ladies and gentlemen, I can tell you just as well as a gypsy what's going to come of that investigation: the conclusion is going to be brought forth and declared to the world that Everett Candler met his death 'at the hands of parties unknown'!"

The rumbling gave rise to angry voices, saying, "Yes, Lord. That's how they do!"

"Always it is declared following another outrage that none of the participants was recognized; always it is the same old story: 'death at the hands of parties unknown.' I tell you, ladies and gentlemen, these parties are known!"

"They known! That's right, brother! Amen!"

"And we may begin with the sheriff of Oklahoma County, for who else is responsible for the safekeeping of a prisoner in the county jail? Now, one of our purposes here this morning is to form a second delegation, one made up of our most learned and articulate men, gleaned from the Negro communities all over Oklahoma. We are going to go directly to the governor's office tomorrow morning—"

Brother Dunjee stopped then, as did all the low, rumbling words of anger rising throughout the congregation, for the little whitewoman had stood up from her place at the end of the pew, and she opened her mouth and held it open as an ugly, featherless baby bird does.

"People," she managed at last. Her voice was faint, screaky. "People, I . . . I . . ."

We were silent. We waited. She was perhaps sixty, though she may have been younger, a frail, pale, gray-headed lady with eyeglasses and bony arms protruding from silk sleeves. Her dress was stylish in an old-fashioned manner, and she had a cameo pin at her throat. No trace of the embarrassed smile remained. Her face was twisted with pain. She looked as though she might faint. At last she found her voice again. "I just wanted to say to you, that . . . I feel . . . terribly . . . sorry. I'm just so . . . so sorry. . . ." Her thin voice trailed away. She looked baffled, helpless, and it came to me that she had practiced over and over what she would say to us, and then, at the moment's unfolding, she'd gone blind, gone mute and mindless. At last she turned and made her way back along the aisle toward the door. An elderly Negro in a chauffeur's uniform slipped out of the pew behind her and followed. The people parted, watched in silence as the whitewoman walked out the open sanctuary door, the old man limping to catch up with her. After some time we heard an automobile motor start up in the distance.

Brother Dunjee did not speak again. None spoke, and yet there was not the silence as before. There was sound among us, coming from us, and yet it was not whispers and murmurs, not the hum of anger or the low, bitter rumbling. It was a kind of rustling, almost like the sough of wind. I'm not certain I can say what it was, but I do know this: the swell of our wrath was halted in its rise by that whitelady standing up to speak. Not her few useless words. The most well-spoken words of regret from a whiteperson could not have assuaged our fury that morning, and it was not, by any means, a fact that our anger had bled away. Quite the opposite. There were many of us whose ire was made worse by her presence, by her very presumption to speak. There were some who hated that whitewoman and her garbled "I'm sorry" with a horrible hatred, and I could feel that around me, too.

But there were others whose anger was tempered by embarrassment for the lady's clotted tongue; some, perhaps, who grudgingly admired her courage to come among us. There were yet others, I believe, who felt compassion for her pathetic cry, or thought her sorrow genuine, if thin, innocent of the hard sources of true grief. No doubt there were even a few who were thrilled at the woman's coming, as there will always be some among us who suck up to white-folks and curry their favor and believe that a whiteperson's good attention is better than God's. As for Brother Dunjee himself, I believe he was simply thrown off stride. The climax, the crescendo of his speechmaking had been ripped from him, and he had to regather himself.

We were thrown out of unity. Yes. That is what it was. We had been, as a crowd sometimes is, of one mind, one heart rising, as we listened to Mr. Dunjee's furious, articulate, truthful words—and that whitelady threw us wide from each other. She scattered us from one mind to many hundreds, made us pause to ponder or feel or think, and what had been building was in this way dispersed.

I was not angry then—I cannot say to this day what was within me, other than my curiosity at that strange soughing sound—but now, when I think back to all that happened afterward, I get angry. Because she may indeed have felt sorry, but regret is not repentance, and that is what we have not seen in Beulah, repentance that owns its part—that is, like the Word tells us, at once sorrow and self-knowledge and a changing of the mind. I saw no mind changed that morning. And yet, if that whitewoman, whom I had never seen before and have never seen since, had not come among us with her few choked words that came from sentiment and meant nothing, stopped nothing, but altered everything—if she had not appeared, the thing that was building among us would have come to its full power.

Many times I have asked myself what would have happened if she had not come, if we had remained, as we were that morning, of one mind. But we'd been scattered, and the oppression of the day's heat began to press upon us, for it was almost noon now, and still no one spoke. Mr. Dunjee stood mopping his brow with his handkerchief as that strange sound, that disjointed murmur, like the fitful whispers of a dry wind in tall grass, passed among us, and then, after a long time, the big woman in the faded housedress stood up in the choirbox and began to sing "There Is a Balm in Gilead."

In a few moments Reverend Shew joined his voice with hers as he got slowly to his feet and came front; he stood just a little behind Roscoe Dunjee, and I saw him reach out and place a hand on the editor's shoulder. In another few moments Brother Dunjee also began to sing, and then we all began, and as the other hymn had swelled from the outside of that little church inward, now the sound arose from the front of the sanctuary and undulated slowly backward and out the windows and beyond, and it was way long out on the prairie, I'm certain, before it stopped its swell.

F or two nights Althea prowled the rooms of her house in darkness, her terror growing more horrible with each tick of the mantel clock in the dining room, each hour chimed by the grandfather clock in the front hall. She napped fitfully Sunday afternoon on the fainting couch in the parlor, only to waken at dusk with the fright unabated, tindered now with a vague guilt and the sight of her face in the hall mirror: puffy, creased, with queer paisley lines swirled on her cheek from the imprint of the silk brocade. Monday dawn found her sitting sideways on her still-made bed as gray light swelled through the lace curtains to reveal the image in the mahogany mirror. The puffiness was gone now; the woman in the mirror looked simply haggard, aged, hawklike and bony. She was nearly mad with fear.

Abruptly she stood in the sullen light and went to the dresser. She sat down to brush her hair, savagely twisted it into a tight knot, arose and crossed the room, flung open the door to the wardrobe. Within moments she was dressed, had locked the door behind her, and was moving swiftly and with great purpose down the front walk. Carefully she trained her eyes front, that she might not by accident catch a glimpse of the ravaged rose garden in the side yard. She'd reached Fifteenth Street before she realized that she didn't know how to get to Little Africa. The recognition gave her only an instant's pause. It was north, wasn't it? That's how they called it: Little Africa, niggertown, North Tulsa. That was all she had to know. She stepped off the curb, crossed Fifteenth Street, walking north.

The obvious solution, of course, would have been to go right to Bill Sutphen's office, order up a new girl, and tell him to make certain she arrived by early dark. But Althea didn't want another girl; she wanted Graceful. It was her sudden recognition of that fact which had driven her up from the bed, out into the silent, dawn streets. She could not have, under direct questioning, said why. She might have answered, Why, the girl knows how to cook bacon just how I like it, or some such pointless answer. The truth was hidden from Althea's conscious mind: that she felt her soul bound to the girl who bore her own birth name—the one who'd seen her terror and rage in the dark foyer, who had witnessed and turned away in silence, and so had become watcher and knower and silent, secret judge. Althea understood only that the urgency she felt to have Graceful back in the house on South Carson was as compelling as any of her many little driven hungers, and as easily remedied. Never did it enter her mind that the girl might refuse.

She walked so fast that in less than half an hour she'd reached the edge of downtown. The city of Tulsa seemed to rise up and close behind her as she entered. Though there'd been milk trucks and delivery wagons stirring in the residential area when she'd left it, not a vehicle, not a pedestrian broke the silence of downtown. The sun had risen in the east, but the many-storied buildings held her in shadow, the brick walls on either side echoed her footfalls. Once, she glimpsed herself in a department store window, and the image, so ghostlike and faded, made her breath catch, her already tense jaw clench harder. She rushed forward, cursing silently her kid leather shoes with their too-high heels, the impractical, narrow-at-the-knee hobble skirt that limited her stride.

When she emerged at last from downtown, stood panting and sweating on the street, looking north toward the community on the far side of the tracks, she didn't realize she was looking at Little Africa. Never had she formed an image of the place clear enough for her mind to give shape to it, any more than she'd given thought to a last name for Graceful, a family, a house. The sunlit buildings gleamed like a distant city across a river. She'd heard stories of sporting houses and pool halls, choc joints and gambling holes in North Tulsa, of course, though she believed those places would be closed this time of morning and she could walk quickly through the shacks and shanties till she found the girl. The business district coming awake before her was too well appointed and prosperous for

Althea to imagine that such a place could be Tulsa's niggertown, and, staring at it, she thought only, with an inward groan and another silent curse for her shoes, of how much farther she still had to go. With gritted teeth, and limping slightly from the blisters coming on both heels, she walked toward the tracks.

She stopped just south of the crossing. Across the iron rails dozens of brick and stone and wooden buildings lined the streets, with printed signs overhead that declared them to be pharmacies and rooming houses, cafés and grocery stores, but the groceryman in his white apron sweeping the walk in front of the green awning was a colored man. The woman setting out a sandwich board in front of the café was colored. The men driving the delivery wagons were, and a man in a straw boater and bow tie driving an elegant roadster, and the bunches of young people, male and female, teasing one another and joking loudly at the trolley stop. The several women walking fast, holding tight to their children's hands, were colored, and the children were colored, and the ones in motorcars and strolling along the sidewalk and opening doors to barbershops and drugstores and newsstands and moving everywhere as far as her eyes could see.

Althea felt faint. Her disoriented sense returned in full measure: this world was unbehaved, unreal, without proper order. She would have turned and fled, had she been able to move. But Althea's feet were burning fire, not only the blistered heels now but the very soles burning, as if the brick street beneath scorched up through the leather; she could smell the scent of her own perspiration, could feel it trickling between her breasts, down her sides beneath the charmeuse middy she was wearing. A girl in a maid's uniform came toward her, paused almost imperceptibly on the far side of the tracks, and then crossed them, stepping carefully over the wooden planks raised in the roadway to meet the rails. The girl moved decorously to the other side of the street, her head tucked properly, so that she might not stare at the strange whitewoman standing on the street in an ostrich-feathered hat and silk dress clothes, sweating and glaring.

Althea followed the girl with her eyes, took a step as if to go after her, and winced as pain shot from her blistered feet. She stood a moment longer, tears coursing down her face from the shock, though she made no sound, and her features did not scrunch with the look of crying. She seemed as unaware of the tears as she would have been of a stray eyelash on her cheek or a flick of lipstick on a tooth: she needed a mirror, or another human, to tell her that her face was marked by them. She stared north across the Frisco tracks once again.

Several of the Negroes moving along the avenue had become aware of her. She felt their scrutiny pass over her, taking in everything about her and registering nothing in that invisible manner they had, and the heat of resentment rushed over her, followed instantly by a deep, instinctive swelling of pride. Althea in that moment claimed inheritance to her mother's defiance of pain. She squared her shoulders, lifted her chin, began to walk toward the railroad tracks again. She did not limp. She didn't wince. She glided over the tracks effortlessly, unaware, even as she traversed it, that she was passing an invisible, inviolable boundary. A woman as self-absorbed as Althea held freedoms others might never win. By the time she reached the intersection she could hear the trolley bell clanging as the car crested the hill, coming south, carrying bootblacks and porters to their jobs on the southside, and motorcars were spewing fumes in all directions, and the bustle and movement had risen to full morning peak.

She walked on, and she would not look in the faces of the Negro people as she passed them; nor did they appear to look at her, but went on about their business of opening shop for the day or walking to work or standing on a street corner awaiting the jitney, but she felt eyes following her, could feel their stares burning into her back, and she moved forward briskly, with great purpose, as if she knew exactly where she was going, what she intended to do. The more swiftly she walked, the more a sense of panic began to push her, drive her, and though it was she who was moving, to her sleep-deprived and fearsick brain it seemed that the hundreds of dark faces were sweeping past her, rolling over her like a black sea tumbling and cresting in waves, and she rushed north, deep into the heart of Greenwood, because she felt herself drowning and knew only to keep moving, keep moving, before the sea swept her under.

"Ma'am?" a voice called out behind her.

Althea stopped, caught by something soft in the voice; she turned to find a black woman in a flowered dress, her hair pressed and fingerwaved tight to her skull, standing, broom in hand, beside an open door, above which ran a brightly lettered marquee that said BRYANT'S DRUG STORE. "You want a bandage or anything, ma'am," the woman said, "we got everything right here." Her glance dropped, and Althea's eyes followed, and she saw for the first time the spots of blood that had begun to seep through the bone-colored leather of her shoes. "You welcome to come in and rest you feets awhile," the woman said.

Althea stared blankly at her feet as if they were foreign objects entirely unrelated to her, then she turned vaguely and continued up the street, slower now, the sense of aimless panic still upon her, but subdued. She saw a glass-fronted brick building ahead, neat and square, the gold lettering on the window declaring in bold, crisp letters that the building was occupied by THE TULSA STAR, Fearless Exponent of Right and Justice, Oklahoma's Largest Circulation Weekly, and though she'd never heard of the newspaper, she thought with a great shudder of relief that she was safe: she'd passed through the raging sea to the far and sacred shore. Nearly running now, she rushed toward the glass door, pulled it open, stepped in.

She was met by a sweetish, clean metallic odor, and complete silence.

She stood very still, listening, but all she heard were the harsh little barks of her own breath. Her knees were trembling; her throat was dry as ashes. The desk area to her left was empty, and the door at the back of the room was shut tight, but a telephone on the wall just outside the gate gave her a renewed burst of relief. As soon as she'd found a sip of water and had retrieved her breath and voice, she would phone Franklin to come get her. A surge of secret gladness swelled in her: this, surely, was reason enough to call him back from Bristow. Her mind was instantly fuming with words of blame for her husband, the damned selfish fool, forcing her to stay alone, making her live that nightmare in niggertown. The pain in her feet sprang awake, burning, searing, so excruciating she thought she would faint.

"Help?" she called thinly. "Can somebody help me? Please?"

In the silence she heard automobiles rumbling on the street, the sounds of voices muffled through the glass, a fruit seller calling out "A-a-a-apples! Pe-e-eaches!" as he drove his wagon slowly past, fading away north. She would not turn to look out the window but made her way gingerly to the low gate, pushed it open, limped to the chair behind the desk and lowered herself to it. She pulled the hatpin from its nest of ostrich feathers, removed the hat, and set it carefully to the side, then lowered her head to her hands on the desk.

"Might I be of some assistance, madam?" The voice was clipped, harshly intoned.

Althea jerked her head up from her hands. She hadn't heard him come in. Had she fallen asleep? The light was behind him where he stood on the far side of the desk, and she couldn't make out his features. She saw only that he was a thin dapper-looking gentleman, wearing a brown derby and a chocolate-brown suit. A vaguely familiar scent of cologne wafted over her, clashing with the rich smell of coffee and warm bread from the paper sack he carried, and Althea's mouth, previously dry enough to spit cotton, suddenly filled with horrid-tasting water, and she recalled that she hadn't eaten since she'd breakfasted alone at the hotel in Bristow two days before. She could have nearly snatched the sack out of the man's hand.

"Oh," she said, "oh," and she blinked up at the man, tried to smile. She thought of how dreadful she must look, and she reached to straighten her chignon; but the knot was as tight and neat as she'd pinned it earlier. She smiled beautifully at the gentleman, glancing up from beneath her lashes. "Oh, thank God you've come! You've no idea what I've just been through!"

The man was silent.

Althea waited a beat longer than her instincts wanted for the man to begin his solicitous murmuring, but finally, when no sounds of concern were forthcoming, she leaned back against the oak slats and smiled again, wearily. "If I could trouble you for a tiny sip of water, sir? Just a cool drop to wet my throat?" She spoke in tight, short syllables, hardly exhaled, for the taste in her mouth was wicked as old pig-iron, and she did not want to push the gentleman away with her breath. "I . . . I . . ." And she cleared her throat lightly behind her hand, looked with such tender longing at the paper sack the fellow held that she couldn't imagine him denying her an instant longer. Still the man stood over her, silent.

She sat forward, and her tense fingers moved unconsciously to her throat. How dare he stand there like a nincompoop, staring at her, when she was obviously in such distress. "I've been chased, sir!" she burst out at last, forgetting her coquetry, her rank breath, hair, sweat.

"Indeed," the man said, slowly.

"Yes. Indeed!" she said, and her fingers moved to the back of her head, swept upward, swept upward again, pressed the snug hairpins in tighter. Who was this rude fellow? Why, she'd have Franklin on him in a whip-stitch. "A sea of them, sir! A big bunch of niggers chased me up the street, I thought I'd never escape! I saw your open door, your sign," and she waved her hand at the backward gold lettering on the plate glass. "I thought, Oh, thank God, thank God, and I . . . I . . . came in . . . to . . ." What the devil was the matter with the man? He ought to go to the telephone this instant, call the sheriff, call *some*one, for God's sake.

Mindless anger flashed though her, and Althea started to rise, ready to come around the desk, though whether to slap him or to leave she could not have said, but instantly she shrieked in pain. Quickly the man stepped away from her. Althea, collapsing into the chair, gasping , staring down at her feet, did not see the man's eyes dart swiftly about the office, out to the street—nor could she have recognized the fear and fury in that racing glance had she seen it; for never could she have known how meticulously this man had worked for fifteen years to defeat just this sort of situation. Althea wept, and her tears were conscious and fullflowing, her face was twisted, mounting toward hysteria as she stared at the puffy white flesh, engorged now with fluid, swelling out over the tops of her kid shoes, the iron-red blood at her heels drying in blotches on the outside of the leather.

Had Albert Smitherman been anywhere but the womb of his own office in the heart of Deep Greenwood, probably he would have, despite his long habit of controlled dignity, turned to run. No Negro knew any better than he the dangers of a whitewoman's screams. But Tulsa's Greenwood was the last safe place, the haven he'd searched for since leaving the South as a younger man: a world separate from the white world, a prosperous and autonomous place entirely of blackfolks' making. If he could not be safe here, there was no safe place anywhere. He watched the weeping woman in a kind of raging despair, for, as his thoughts said to him, the troubles with whitefolks must reach to the ends of the earth: if you won't go among them, they will come to you. What good would it do to run?

"Help me," the woman whimpered, and she looked up at him, her face ugly with weeping. She was hunched forward in the desk chair, her skirt pulled up, revealing the pale flesh of her thighs. She held the beige silk off her knees, as if that were where the pain hurt her, though he could see the bloody swellings of her feet now, lightly touching the wood floor. Smitherman looked at her a moment. In silence he set the sack on the desk and turned and exited the little gate; he walked toward the door at the back of the office, went inside, and closed the door behind him.

Althea sobbed and sobbed. After the man left she didn't try to stop, for there was no need of vanity now, and she gave herself up to it, wailing as she bent to pull the leather away from her blistered heels. She sobbed harder as she peeled off the kid shoes, seeing the misshapen feet, the swollen flesh, the opened wounds oozing blood; she surrendered to a great wash of self-pity, for of course it was Franklin's fault that she'd come away in a stupor at dawn without stockings. The weeping was delicious, a great release, like the hysteria that had swept the girl in the pen with the red calf twenty years before. But as Althea wept, something began to change in her. The bottoms of her feet were lacerated, the fragile skin burning as if it had been held against hot coals, and something in that searing pain in the most tender place seemed to lay her open, cut her and make her raw and new with pain; the hurt radiated on flaming nerves upward through her flesh to her life's soul: burning it clean, leaving her with no core, nothing true of herself but these bleeding strips of her own mortal flesh. In terror Althea tried to pull back, control the surrender, but it was too late.

The editor returned from the back room to find the woman prostrate across his desk, her shoulders rising and falling in great shudders, the feathered hat clutched and crumpled in one hand, as she beat her forehead rhythmically against the bare wood. His sack of bread and coffee lay on the floor, leaking a dark pool.

He stood without moving, only watching, and the cup of water he'd brought for her trembled in his hand as his mind whirled with a thousand riotous thoughts, all of them leading directly to danger. Was it possible she'd really been chased? He thought of the rising outrage here, the anger kindled by the back-to-back lynchings. Yesterday's gathering at Arcadia had been calm enough, had reinforced the resolve of Oklahoma's black communities to meet the malignity with law and intelligence; still, there was a lawless element in the colored population of Tulsa, just as there was in the white; there were dope-runners and bootleggers and gamblers, and any number of Negro soldiers who'd come home from Europe bold and fearless, unwilling to submit to the old lynch law's reign of fear—and if a reckless and stupid whitewoman had made a liaison, had come north to meet her lover within days of these lynchings, and instead, having met a loose, half-lit gathering . . . ? No, it was impossible. Impossible. But . . . what could explain such a paroxysm of pain and hysteria in the woman? How to account for her bloody feet? With sudden relief, he thought, *Maybe she isn't white.* Certainly he'd known colored women as fairskinned as this one. But no, he thought, looking at her shaking shoulders. This was a whitewoman. His instincts told him unerringly she was white.

When the pressman Lawrence came in a half-hour later, Smitherman still stood outside the gate, staring at the woman, the cup of lukewarm water yet in his hand. The woman no longer sobbed, no longer beat her head; she lay quiet across the desk. She might nearly have been dead, so still was she, and Lawrence turned his eyes from the woman to his boss and back again, trying to see what this strange scene might mean. He couldn't see yet that the woman was white.

Smitherman didn't change expression or glance up, seemed in fact not to have noticed the other come in, but, as if arrested in mid-motion and suddenly released by this new presence, he went on to the gate and swung it open, stepped in, and set the cup on the filing cabinet behind the desk. He picked up the coffee-soaked sack and held it away from himself. "Lawrence," he said, his eyes on the woman's back, "go over to Frankfort and get Dr. Blanchard. Tell him to come as soon as he can."

The woman moaned slightly, rolled her head to the side, and Lawrence, seeing her race then, backed out the door as fast as he could move and turned to run down the street.

She couldn't imagine where she was, or who were these men standing around. She lay on her back, blinking up at the three masculine faces. The brown one she dismissed instantly, as completely as if it were a dog's face, for it was colored and therefore not truly a man's face, and so she allowed her gaze to pass between the other two as she tried to remember where she was. The man in the brown derby seemed familiar, though she couldn't place him, and who the other might be, she had no idea. The men did not speak but continued staring at her. She made a move to sit up. No hand reached to help her. Surprised, she pushed herself upright and sat dizzily on the edge of the desk, and as she did so the three moved away from her in a ragged half-moon, the colored man farthest, halfway out the gate, and she thought bizarrely she must have come down with a contagious disease. The pain in her bandaged feet began to throb then, and she remembered.

She looked at the white gauze taped around her heels, glanced up at the sallow man in the derby, whom she recognized now as the one who'd come in earlier, then she cast her eye to the tall, handsome fellow who stood beside him in a vested herringbone suit and silk tie. She tried to smile. Still the men looked at her in silence. The sallow man stepped forward and handed her a cup of water, and as he did so, the familiar scent wafted over her once more; this time she recognized it. It wasn't cologne she smelled on him but the faint odor of pomade: the same blue pomade that permeated her maid's room on South Carson. She understood in a slow dawning that the man was colored.

"I'd recommend having those dressings changed tomorrow, or the day after," said the other. "They're going to suppurate rather severely." Her gaze turned to him. He was indeed handsome, dark-eyed and delicately mustached, his tawny cheeks shaved smooth and his black hair slicked straight at the sides, trimmed precisely to meet the immaculate white collar at his neck. He, too, was a Negro. The shock came to Althea first as a seeping, like the slow swell of floodwater beneath a doorsill, followed by the deluge.

"Is there . . . ?" The man hesitated. "Would there be somebody you'd like us to telephone?"

Althea hardly heard him. Her senses buzzed, every instinct in chaos. She dropped her gaze to the floor. Not that light-complected blacks were an uncommon sight: Nona Murphy's yardboy was redheaded as a new penny, with queer green eyes and dark freckles on his coppery skin—though the boy's features were thickly Negroid, his rust-colored hair appropriately nappy; a person had no embarrassing trouble knowing he was colored. But it wasn't the humiliation of having mistaken these two for white; it was the fact that they looked and spoke so much like—well, there was no other word, was there?—like gentlemen. She'd never in her life been at a loss for how to behave in the presence of gentlemen, and yet . . . these were colored men. Weren't they? She couldn't look up. The very sight of them tossed her instincts into turmoil, tilted her mind and her will completely askew.

"Madam?"

She resisted the impulse to reach up and fix her hair. After a moment she shifted her gaze to the men's shoes a few yards away. The handsome man in the herringbone suit wore brown-and-white oxfords, polished to a high sheen. The silence grew longer. She could hear the darky by the gate breathing, and she ached to glance up at him; she'd know how to feel looking at him—imperious, superior, slightly fearful if she'd been alone with him, for he certainly qualified as a big buck nigger—but she couldn't bring herself to raise her eyes. Why didn't one of them say something, for pity's sake?

The gulf that separated Althea from the three men was so deep, so wide, that none of them could see it. The men shared one desire: to get this whitewoman out of the newspaper office, out of Greenwood, and back to wherever she belonged quickly and quietly, without bringing the wrath of white Tulsa—the wrath of the whole of American race history—down on their community. Oklahoma was dry as touchwood in the wake of the two lynchings. A whitewoman's fear, malice, hysteria could ignite it in an instant. The editor was the only one who gave even vague credence to her claim that she'd been chased; he told himself it was because he'd seen the depth of her nervous frenzy, but in truth his credulity belonged to the kind of rage he'd witnessed following other lynchings. The other two knew she lied, knew it mattered not that she lied, because a lie was the same as the truth from a whitewoman.

Althea herself—shaken and confused, stripped of her most familiar presumptions, and yet inescapably, irredeemably white—couldn't imagine that the silence in the room was born of fear; she believed it must be the silence of judgment. *Nigger judgment*, she said to herself, and a weak swelling of outrage pushed through her, followed by deflation. She was too sick, too tired. Aching and flayed raw as she was, she longed for a mirror.

"Do you have—?" She stopped herself. Dear God, she couldn't ask these colored men for the powder room.

"Yes? Madam?" It was the sallow man who spoke.

No, not sallow, Althea thought. *High yellow.* "Nothing," she mumbled. Lost, she simply sipped the warm, acrid water, kept her eyes unseeing in the middle distance at the level of the men's neatly pressed and creased trouser knees.

At length a peculiar sigh escaped from the editor, and he said softly to the man beside him, "I wonder if we might send her back in your car?" But the doctor shook his head fiercely. Immediately Smitherman understood. The only permissible way a Negro could be seen driving a whitewoman would be as chauffeur: Dr. Blanchard would have to borrow a chauffeur's uniform, seat the woman in the rear of his new Maxwell touring car and himself in front as liveried driver. Even lightskinned as he was, it was the only safe way. Not even the doctor's desire to get the woman out of Greenwood could make him humiliate himself in this manner.

The silence stretched longer, stretched beyond confusion and discomfort to a kind of absurdity. Althea had a terrible impulse to laugh, but she bit the inside corners of her lips and managed to choke it off. Still she did not raise her head.

"Madam?" Again it was the voice of the sallow man. "May I ask for what purpose you've come to our community? Perhaps we can be of service. Are you . . . were you looking for someone?"

"Oh—" Althea looked up. "Why, yes. I am." Like spinning cylinders suddenly locked into place, the proper positionings in the world returned to her. Of course. She'd come to fetch Graceful. That was all. Her face lifted. "My maid, Graceful," she said calmly, and she smoothed the front of her skirt. "The goose ran off last Friday, God knows why. I'd simply dismiss her, except I need . . . I expect her to stay the month, at least. Till the end of September. Or October. She's already been paid." She reached up to smooth her hair as the lie slipped serenely off her tongue. "Would you know where I could find her?" she asked, as if the more than eight thousand souls in Greenwood ought, by the simple fact of their shared race, to know one another.

"What did you say her name was?" This from the handsome man, and Althea stifled the impulse to smile at him the same way she'd choked off the urge to laugh, by biting down on the inside corners of her mouth. The effect gave her an odd look, a kind of flirtatious primness that pursed her unrouged lips.

"Graceful," she said. "I don't—I don't know her last name."

"Whiteside?" The sallow man's voice was thin, the inflection rising.

"What?"

"It isn't Graceful Whiteside you're looking for?"

The brown man beside the gate released a low, wondering sound, "Unhuh," very softly.

"Well, yes. I guess. Graceful. Graceful isn't common, is it? The name?"

"By coincidence, she was just here." The editor's voice was tinged with a kind of irritated curiosity. He seemed to be speaking exclusively to the doctor now, as if Althea were an uninterested party, or a child. "Last week. When was that, Lawrence? That girl asking for Hedgemon?"

"Next day after Hedgemon quit, Mr. Smitherman. She come that next morning."

"That'd be Friday."

"Friday. Yes, sir."

"Do you know the family, where the girl stays?"

"No, sir. I wouldn't know." The pressman glanced at the whitewoman, and quickly away.

Smitherman took a step toward the desk where Althea still sat, but almost at once he stopped. "There was a letter," he said vaguely. Then, as if coming to himself, "If you'll permit me, madam, that drawer there," and he motioned toward the desk drawer partially covered by her skirt. "Miss Whiteside left a letter behind. I found it on the floor some while after she'd gone, and put it in the drawer for safekeeping. Perhaps there's an address?"

A renewed hope surged in him, a sense that this jeopardous circumstance would be rendered harmless more quickly and easily than he'd thought. But the woman made no move to clear the way for him, and he would not come within such intimate distance of her—the drawer was just below her thigh—and so the editor stood awkwardly, an old fury rising, certain that the whitewoman was purposely trying to confound him. Althea, for her part, was numbed by the very mention of the letter, for it seemed that it was that blasted letter—oh, she had no doubt it was the same one, brought by the little colored boy less than a week ago—that was the cause of all her disturbance and turmoil and grief: the same letter that had been the beginning of chaos, Japheth coming, the old memories and recognitions. She remained motionless on the desk, staring straight ahead.

The doctor saw Smitherman's hesitation and at once stepped forward. Blanchard had passed as white when he was a young man in Milwaukee, and this secret of his own history, assiduously kept, had left him thoroughly unintimidated by white skin, though acutely distrustful. "Madam?" he said and gestured at the long drawer, and Althea rather automatically turned to the side so that he might open it. Dr. Blanchard shuffled through the many papers and clippings and pencil stubs and envelopes; he glanced up once, but the editor didn't come forward to guide him. At last he picked out the crumpled thin sheet smeared with ink, opened it, and read through it quickly. Lawrence edged forward a few steps from his post by the gate. The doctor handed the page to Althea. She didn't open it but merely clutched it, creasing the center, as she had the pale blue envelope the boy brought. Her curiosity was strong, but her fear was stronger, and she was made still by her terror that the letter held some secret which would open the abyss so wide and inescapable she could not help falling in. In another moment Dr. Blanchard discreetly took the page from her hand and read it aloud in his crisp voice:

"'To all interested parties, let these presents hereby be made known:

"'Whereas it has been declared and forthwith articulated that upon the First instant of the Ninth part in the area known as Brickyard Hill at a location five blocks north longitude of the Avenue known as Archer there abides on the street called North Elgin—'"

Althea began laughing.

"'—an interested party whose express wish is stated to be in a conversant condition with one Miss Graceful Angel Whiteside for the express purpose of which is not revealed—'"

The peals of laughter made it impossible to continue. The men stared at her, and she tried to say something but collapsed back into laughter, her shoulders and chest shaking, her face twisted, the peals pitched toward hysteria. The editor and pressman began to grow angry, for Lawrence believed she was laughing at his friend, Smitherman believed she was laughing at his race. The doctor frowned as he watched the rising hysteria, and he tried to think how he might calm the woman without touching her; his mind quickly inventoried his black bag for a sedative.

"No, it's nothing! Nothing!" Althea managed at last, squeezing the words through her chopped breaths that were like sobs, and in fact tears were streaming down her face and she didn't quite know if she was crying now or laughing; her belly ached, the muscles cramped along her sides and her jawline, and she couldn't catch her breath. The laughter was kin to the earlier weeping, it came from the same place inside her, and yet it was different, filled with relief as it was, and a strange, ineffable joy. Oh, see, it was nothing. Just a stupid letter to a stupid colored girl, it had nothing to do with her. Nothing. Althea reached up to wipe the wetness from her cheeks, sighing deeply, shuddering. She felt herself seared clean once more, and she forgot what she wanted. "Ohhh," she said, and sighed heavily again.

"If you like, madam," said Smitherman, his voice taut with dignity, "we can send Lawrence over to Elgin to see if we can locate this Miss Whiteside and let her know you'd like to speak with her. We can telephone someone for you, someone to come see you home. We'll ask Miss Whiteside to contact you, as soon as we find her. Would that be all right?"

Althea gazed at him. A small sound escaped her, a little voiced exhalation that was almost a whimper. "Oh, I'd better go."

Immediately the editor went to the telephone and lifted the ear cup as he turned the crank in a brisk black whir; he looked back with lifted brows. "The number, madam?"

"No. My God. No. There's no one to telephone. He's out in the bojacks, they both are." Her eyes cast about the office, seeking. "They're down at . . . No, don't you see? There's nobody home!" She looked at the editor, hardly seeming to see him. "That's what I mean. Graceful. I really need to find Graceful. I can't go home without her. Where is she? You'll . . . you'll have to take me over there. To Graceful's . . . To that house."

The party in the Maxwell was a peculiar vision never before seen in Greenwood: the two well-dressed and dignified businessmen in the front seat, the pallid whitewoman in silk and ostrich feathers in the back, and the big-shouldered workingman walking swiftly beside the open touring car as it moved slowly west along Archer, turned north, climbing the hill at hardly two miles an hour, past the shoemaker's and the photographer's and Williams Confectionery, continuing on past the high school and the brickyard and a row of shotgun houses to the area, five blocks north, where the smaller frame houses gave way to brick homes of the stout Craftsman design. Dr. Blanchard eased the car to the side of the street and parked it. Althea stared at the fine brick houses and the several small Negro children in the yards who'd paused in their play to stare back at her. Lawrence stood gazing across to the west side of the street, at a certain narrow yellow-painted house nestled between the larger, porched homes on either side. The front door of the house was closed. A lump of quilt lay on the wooden porch, beside the door.

Smitherman saw the look on the pressman's face and instantly grasped, not through a succession of deductive thoughts but in an instant's revelation, that this was the Whiteside girl's house; he saw, too, that Lawrence had known it all along, just as he knew more than he'd told about the girl's appearance in the *Star* office on Friday, and that any further information was to be gleaned from the big man through great difficulty, or not at all. The editor followed his gaze. The house was empty—not abandoned, as if someone had moved out, but vacant of human souls. Something more than the shut door in the bright morning made him know it, something blank and distant in its affect. Like the face of a blind man, he thought. Or, no, not like the blind, for there'd be active listening and sensing there: more like the emptiness in the face of the dead. The half-drawn shades were like the drooping lids of the recently departed.

Still, there was nothing to do but continue. Reluctantly he got out of the Maxwell and started across the street. He glanced back once at Blanchard, but the doctor sat stiffly behind the steering wheel, hands gripped as if the car were yet moving, his eyes straight ahead, his immaculate boater cocked at a precise angle, his head high, neck stiff above the starched collar. Smitherman's eyes fell on the whitewoman in the back seat, and the urgency he felt to get her out of Greenwood rushed upon him, and he turned away, continued at a brisker pace over the worn path across the yard and up onto the porch. He picked up the bedroll and held it fastidiously away from himself as, without hope, he rapped on the wooden door. He didn't knock long, for he knew there'd be no answer, but turned and motioned Lawrence to come up on the porch. The pressman ambled slowly across the road, obviously disinclined. Smitherman gestured for him to hurry up, and at last came down off the porch and met him halfway across the yard, told him to go around and try the back, and could he move a little faster, please, they had work to get back to, a newspaper to get out.

And then the editor stood alone in the yard, holding the rolled-up quilt away from his clean suit. He gazed south at the buildings of downtown Tulsa, thinking that this was a broad view here at the top of Brickyard Hill. People spoke of Standpipe as being the dominant hill in the area, and it was, of course, and white people owned it. But one could stand here and see most of Greenwood, could see all of that other city, Tulsa, the one they called the Magic City, across the Frisco tracks. His gaze swept the horizon, turning in a slow circle, across the tops of the buildings in Greenwood, taking in the delicate spires of the white churches downtown, the erect peaks of the brick skyscrapers, the stolid squares of the grand hotels, all the buildings oil had built; he allowed his gaze to drift to the right, pass over the smoking, stinking refineries on the banks of the Arkansas River, and settle at last on the low humping hills beyond. The hills seemed almost a gentle barricade between Tulsa and the western rolling prairies, and the editor pondered a moment how whitemen had succeeded in taking the riches from beneath the earth, secreted yonder, without bringing the soil and muck of it to their glistening city. The imagery worked on him, and his thoughts began to form the cadences of written language: an editorial was shaping itself in his mind, perhaps an essay.

"Mr. Smitherman, they's nobody back at the back."

The editor was startled, lost as he was in his reverie, though Lawrence had spoken softly, his head tucked low, one arm held diffidently behind him. Smitherman looked at him for such a long time without speaking that at last Lawrence brought his hand front and said, "I found this," and held out the white apron, the crumpled blue envelope pressed against it with his thumb. Smitherman took them and started across the street, ignoring the several neighbor women who'd emerged from kitchens and parlors and bedrooms to the nearby front porches, as he ignored the questioning look on Blanchard's face, as he ignored above all, most studiously, the ashen face of the whitewoman in the back seat of the car, though, had he looked at Althea, the expression he'd have seen there would have been unfathomable to him. Perhaps no one could have named that expression, or the truth it told of what was inside her.

Fear, yes, but fear had been with her all her life. She had tried to make it an ally, or at least she'd learned long ago to court danger so that the thrill of fright might titillate her senses, make them acutely present, and so subsume that greater fear: the dark one, unnamed and unnameable, that threatened always to engulf her. In some ways her face was like that of a combatant in defeat, yielding without humility, in hopeless, angry surrender—and yet that wasn't all. What made the woman's expression such a puzzle was the absolute, accepting wonder there. In the same way that the mind, witnessing something intolerable—the earth exploding, a head severed from its body—will at first deny and then at last make its adjustment and close around what an instant before had been unthinkable, so Althea's mind had opened to accept a reality as unimaginable to her as one where men walk on water. She sat in the Maxwell with her feet seared, her soles burning, and watched the black man who looked like a white man moving swiftly and irritatedly across the street, holding in one hand the thin quilt Graceful had carried into Althea's kitchen, wrapped tightly around her small cache of toiletries and clothes, the first morning she'd come to work, three months before. The man's other hand pressed the blue envelope against Graceful's apron, as the big Negro's brown hand had pressed it so when he'd brought it forth from behind his back, as the little colored boy's hand had pulled that same smeared blue envelope from his threadbare shirtfront, and Althea had known, in ways far beyond her small and selfish comprehension, that something irrevocable had begun.

Trancelike, she watched Smitherman open the car door, toss the bedroll and apron and the fluttering envelope onto the leather upholstery before seating himself quickly. "Madam, if you'd care to leave a note, I'll see that Miss Whiteside gets it." Althea nodded. But she didn't reach out to take the small leatherbound notebook and stub of pencil he tried to hand back to her. She got out of the Maxwell and limped on her bandaged feet across the road. The several women on the neighboring porches stared in silence at the shoeless, footbandaged whitewoman who mounted Cleotha Whiteside's front steps, went right up to the house, and did not even pretend to knock, but turned the knob and hobbled in through the unlocked door.

"Graceful?" Althea called out. The parlor was dim, the two front windows darkened by the half-drawn shades. She could see straight through to the closed back door. The smell in the house was the odor of a house well lived in and well cooked in, shut up for days. Slowly she crept forward, and as her eyes adjusted to the lowered light, the character of the room revealed itself, and she looked closely at the objects as if they were displays in a museum.

There was about the room an immaculate, almost painful neatness. A braided rug lay in a precise circle in the center, and the linoleum surrounding it was shining with wax, its mottled green-and-white surface patterned with large red flowered swirls, and the curtains at the windows and front door, too, were spattered with flowers. Against the far wall stood a horsehair divan, the back and arms draped with large white crocheted doilies, like threaded snowflakes, and next to the divan was a polished table, also dotted with doilies, starched to lacy, intricate coils, each cradling a framed photograph from which stared one or several Negro faces. Beside the little gas heater a leather hassock crouched before a green armchair, and on the wall above hung a framed print of The Last Supper. Althea's eyes passed over the picture. Jesus leaned on one arm in the middle of the long row of disciples, looking sorrowfully at Judas, the Betrayer, as he sneaked guiltily out the door. *It could've been any of them,* she thought oddly. *Any one of them could have betrayed him.*

But Althea's gaze did not linger with the colorless faces at the Last Supper but kept returning again and again to the photographs with dark faces; then she raised her eyes to the corner above the divan, where the walls met. A darkwood treasure shelf was wedged there, holding on its various shelves a china teacup and saucer, a porcelain cat, the figurine of a blond angel with folded hands and wings, its pale painted face bowed in prayer, and a large, elegant, gold-embossed frame, from which gazed the broad, smiling face of a black man. Within Althea a kind of dull queasiness began to arise, a nauseous sense of familiarity conjoined with otherness, as if something ordinary were suddenly wedded before one's eyes to another thing very foreign and strange. She heard footsteps on the porch but didn't answer the voice that called to her, "Madam?"

On she went, into the middle room, where a trundle bed huddled against one wall, an iron bedstead against the other; she hurried past the dressing table, into the kitchen, brighter than the front of the house, with its bright yellow curtains and yellow walls. Upon the counter sat a basin of soured dishwater, floating with scum, as though someone had washed up swiftly and neglected to finish the task of emptying the pan.

"Graceful?" she said again, softly, almost in a whisper. She stepped to the door and turned the knob, but the door was locked. She jiggled it absentmindedly a moment before turning back to the room, her eyes sweeping over the pump at the sink, the icebox standing in a little pool of meltwater from the overflowing reservoir, the dried-out dishrag draped on the back of a chair, the several plates and cups turned upside down on a dishtowel spread open on the counter. Looking up, she saw at the other end of the house the sallow man on the porch at the front door. He held his face to the screen, his hands cupped on either side to see into the dim interior. In one of his hands the blue envelope stuck out, clamped between two fingers. She believed that he saw her, but he would not come in.

"Madam?" he called. And when she didn't move or answer, he held up the envelope and the letter with it, wagged them in the air. "This letter is from my linotype operator! I know the boy's handwriting!" He paused for response. "My pressman knows where he's staying. Madam? We'll send a telegram to Hedgemon Jackson at Bigheart, he'll know where your Miss Whiteside is."

"Yes," Althea said, or she believed that she said, though the man still stood with his hands cupped around his eyes, peering in the door. She moved toward him. In the next room she paused. The narrow room was cramped with the two small bedsteads, a cheap wood-veneer vanity dresser, a painted chifforobe standing by the window, its door gapped open to reveal two limp cotton dresses on wooden hangers. Against the lamp on top of the chifforobe was propped a cardboard-framed photograph of a little bunch of colored children lined up in front of a log country school. It was winter in the picture, for the branches of the trees in the background were bare, although the children were in shirtsleeves. They stared straight out of the picture, unsmiling. Graceful stood at the end of one row, tall and gangly, and yet her highboned face was soft with the softness of late childhood, her hair radiating in a dozen ribboned braids. She, too, stared soberly out of the cardboard frame, as self-consciously serious as the other little darky children. Little darky children. The strange pressure began to rise in Althea's chest.

On the vanity stood another elaborately framed studio photograph, like those in the front room. Where did they go to have such photographs made? What studio made such elegant, formal portraits of colored people? How could they afford them? The vision of Negroes arranging themselves so formally, with such dignity and presumption, in a photographer's studio dug at Althea's chest. In this picture the broadfaced man posed in a Pullman uniform, standing with his hand on the shoulder of a beautifully dressed colored woman seated with a white-gowned colored baby on her lap. At her side stood a thin, solemn boy of perhaps seven, and a little gap-toothed pickaninny, the only smiling face in the picture, beaming out at the camera from behind her mother's voluminous skirt. Though the child was round-cheeked, grinning through missing front milkteeth, Althea recognized Graceful. In gold lettering at the bottom of the frame were the words:

MR. & MRS. ERNEST WHITESIDE & FAMILY

J. H. Hooker Photographers,
Tulsa, Oklahoma, 1907.

The feeling in Althea's chest as she stared at the words was not a pressure now but a dark rush, a burning that surged from her core through her face muscles to the top of her head. She had no words for it. The closest she could have named it would have been to cry out that she'd been left out of everything: something huge, significant, of infinite importance had been going on in the world, and no one had told her. How could this child be here in this picture? This impish round-cheeked colored child with black slanted eyes that were Graceful's eyes, who had had a life, a history, a family. They had lived out in the country, Graceful had gone to school, she had plaited her hair, her mother had plaited her hair in those many tight corkscrew braids, she had worn gingham, she had worn muslin, she had worn floursack dresses. Within Althea a new impulse was rising, a kind of secret maternal swelling she believed she had long ago cut away from herself, and the recognition was too terrible to receive, a betrayal, and she turned away from the picture.

On her surface Althea moved as she'd always moved. She could not let the thing opening inside her show. Not even to coloreds. Especially not to coloreds. She hobbled toward the front of the house. The man at the door stepped back to allow her to come out, but Althea stopped in the center of the front room, stood quite still, closed her eyes and smelled for a moment the smell of the house, the familiar, ancient odors of old food and floorwax, and dust.

"Madam?"

Would the man never shut up? She opened her eyes. He stood back from the screen, leaning forward from the waist, peering inside, as if he dared not contaminate himself.

"Are you . . . ? Will you come out now?"

His amber face frowned with worry, and something else, some other emotion she didn't identify. Without speaking, she moved toward the screen, and he retreated farther, to the end of the porch. The pain in her feet was horribly awake now, and she limped out of the house, down the front steps, feeling the eyes of the colored women on the nearby porches, and the eyes of the big brown man beside the car, and the light-skinned handsome man behind the wheel of the Maxwell, and she made her way across the street without looking at any of them, got into the back seat, and said, with implacable authority, "Take me home."

F our miles east of Bigheart the patched and dingy U.S. Army tent stood, flaps closed, seemingly abandoned, beside a nameless feeder creek. There were few signs around the tentsite, hardly any footscuffs on the creekbank, but at certain hours smoke could be seen rising from a crude pipe at the rear of the shelter. On the days that it rained, the smoke stood in the air above the tent, motionless, making the scene look like a photogravure. If you kept watch at dawn, you could see a tall Negro slip out of the tent and make for the nearby footpath, or, again, on a bright morning, you might see a young girl, delicate as red gossamer, lift her face as she emerged from the closed tent, look up toward the sun, and dart quickly toward the bushes behind the tent.

Of the five people living cramped together inside the tent, only two ever went into town. Hedgemon Jackson walked to work before daylight, came home after dark. The uncle, Delroy, had been gone for over a month, so it was T.J., the fugitive, who determined that his sister Graceful should be the one sent to buy supplies in Bigheart, just as it was T.J. who bossed, directed, allowed or disallowed everything the three females did.

Her brother's bullying was something Graceful had never seen before; it seemed to have appeared all at once, in the moment of his emergence from beneath the mildewed tarp. As the women sneaked from the back of the truck into the shelter, T.J. had stood in the tent doorway, holding the flap open, looking at the Nash truck nosed to the creek like a spent horse caked in mud and red road dust. Delroy had been standing on the bank beside it, staring dazedly over the hood toward the water, when T.J. said with quick, sure authority, "After you get rested, go fetch Mama, carry her and the girls home. I don't want them riding that dirty Jim Crow car again." And Delroy had nodded without protest, as if T.J. were the uncle and himself the young pup, although he'd slept a full day first, his loud snores scraping the very tree limbs above the tent, before he got back in the truck and headed out again.

To Graceful it seemed that the hours her brother spent in the black smelly cellar, and later, beneath the tarp, had completed the metamorphosis that had been coming his whole life. He'd always been tense, fretsome, a little too serious, but now he was transfigured into a new form of himself, harder, with no trace left of his old humor, no tenderness, or at least none that showed through the new impenetrable shell. *Everything done happen*, she said to herself. *What he been fretting about all these years already come to pass, he don't need to fret anymore.*

Still, she'd find her back rising when he told her to come inside now, somebody liable to see her, each time he caught her standing at the tent door. He ordered his poor fluttery girlfriend and her mother around with such rough thoughtlessness that Graceful found herself defending them, at least in her own mind if not to T.J.'s face. The girl, Elberta, kept her eyes on T.J. every minute, watching him with that hopeless expectancy, but it was Mrs. Candler who most touched Graceful's heart. The woman sat day after day on the army cot, her breasts heaving slowly beneath the dirty bodice of her dress, the great crescent sweatstains beneath her arms getting larger, her face blind. The only time she moved off the cot was when T.J. told her to do something; then she'd obediently get up and go do what he said. It wasn't only the woman's son who was dead but her husband, too, killed in a shootout, not lynched, but it was still whitefolks that killed him. *T.J. act like he's the only one know about trouble*, Graceful thought. *He ought to ask that woman right there.* She would glare at her brother when he told her to wash this or clean that. Though she knew that he bullied them, in part, because there was no man-work to do, she would lift her chin at him and say, "Wash it your own self." T.J. didn't argue with her but would instantly turn and snap at one of the other two to do it. Sometimes, he'd fly into a wordless rage, pace up and down the dirt floor from tent-wall to tent-wall, but there was no place for him to go.

He don't like nobody to give him any sass, she thought as she picked her way along the main street in Bigheart, trying to keep the mud off her mother's white dress. *That's how come him to send me to do the shopping, just to get me out his face.* An automobile beeped its nasal horn behind her, and Graceful jumped up onto the board sidewalk, but a little white-boy came barreling along the planks, and she stepped down into the road-way again. Bigheart was a boomtown, sprawling, filthy, wild as Kiefer or Whizbang, composed of hundreds of tents and makeshift shelters, slap-dash stores rigged together from tin and wood and canvas, haphazard rows of clapboard buildings fingering outward for miles from the old trading center. In the middle of Main Street an oilwell pumped midst the perpetual din of honking horns and rumbling timber wagons. The place had been a quiet Osage settlement before Josh Cosden opened his re-fineries here in 1909 and produced the first boom, then took his operation to Tulsa and created the first bust. But the town was exploding again with a new boom from the fast-growing Barnsdall refineries that had replaced Cosden's, and now—as if to make sure the old Osage village erased all memory of its former self—from L.O. Murphy's tremendous strike a few miles north of town. The muck and noise and sheer man-ness of the streets had at first frightened Graceful, but it had all grown so familiar that today she moved calmly along the unpaved street, sidestepping the mudholes, skirting the muledroppings, as deftly as if she'd been doing it all her life.

Her reaction to the white faces was not so easy to get used to. There were a few colored folks and quite a few Indians on the streets, but the town was mostly white, mostly men, mostly all in their high young prime, and they didn't frighten her so much as fill her with that familiar nauseous loathing. Primarily it was the shouting roustabouts and the muleteam drivers who set the bad feeling on her, although she felt nearly as ill watch-ing the whitelady in the mercantile measure out her little purchases of beans and saltmeat. She couldn't look white people in the face, so sick did they make her with cramped, useless rage. She kept her gaze lowered as she hurried along the board sidewalk, and when she sensed one of them coming toward her she gave such a wide berth that she spent more time in the muddy streets than on the wooden planks.

"That pretty dress of yours about ruined," a soft, deep voice said. "You better quit jumping around in mudholes like that."

Looking up, she found Hedgemon Jackson in his blue cap and blue uniform walking backward, away from her, on the plank walk. He had a big leather satchel at his side, and he smiled, walking slower, his eyes skat-ing over her head to glance up the street, then back down to Graceful standing on tiptoe in the mud. He looked so tall and familiar, with his wide white smile, and his eyelashes long as a girl's, curling up, and his awkwardly long, endlessly moving legs, that she smiled back against her will. Hedgemon's retreating steps went even slower, until he stopped completely, though his restless legs shifted weight side to side as he shoved the satchel on its long strap around to his back, then front, then back again.

"Where you going?"

"Nowhere," Graceful said. "Just yonder." She nodded toward the wooden falsefront of the mercantile a few doors down. "Thought I might buy us some very delicious beefsteak and Irish potatoes for our supper, get us some storebought cake for dessert."

"How about you get a nice angelcake?" Hedgemon's smile widened. "Hadn't had any angelcake in years."

She looked to see if he was making a joke about her middle name, but his grin was innocent. "I guess I could," she said. "Serve it up with some good fatback."

"Mmm-mmm, hadn't had good fatback in years either." He had pretty teeth, big white straight teeth, and when he smiled like that his lips couldn't close around them.

"You welcome to come eat with us, we going to have plenty brown beans to go with that fatback and angelcake."

"Oh, I might. If somebody don't give me a better invitation." He glanced around the street again, back down to Graceful. "You going to be here long?"

"No longer than I can help it."

Already he was moving away. "I got to go deliver these, quick," Hedgemon said, "but I'll be right back. I'll walk you home a ways." His gaze flicked up the street. "Past the bawdy tent, anyhow." He looked down at her, not smiling now. "Just wait here when you finish? I'll walk you back?" It was almost a pleading, and he was suddenly the too-eager black boy who'd followed her home from church so many Sundays. Graceful shrugged, her own smile fading. But Hedgemon's grin flashed again, and he turned and ran.

She watched him go around the poor-looking whitemen crowded in front of an oil company office, past several women in hats and hobble skirts making their way along the board walk, and though it was nobody but just Hedgemon Jackson leaving her standing on the street, Graceful felt bereft. Slowly she stepped up onto the planks, turned toward the mercantile again, but she'd forgotten to protect herself and immediately she bumped into a whiteman coming out of the tool supply. "Whoa there, little heifer!" The man grabbed her around the waist, laughing, and the smell in his mouth was the same as the pit of the cellar, the same as the rank walls of the kitchen from which Everett Candler had been taken and hung.

She twisted free and ran into the alley beside the store, leaned back against the tarpapered wall, gulping air, heaving. She heard the man laughing in the street, as the whiteman had laughed when he pushed himself down on her spine in the tiny maid's room, laughed as he held her head down while he rubbed his skinny hard thing on her, rutted against her nightgown, rutted against her backside, pushing her face into the pillow so she couldn't scream, couldn't breathe, pushed her down harder, until she thought she would die, until the whiteman quit laughing and only rutted against her in silence, pushed himself, pushed himself, and Graceful convulsed at the memory of the devil whiteman brother groaning against her head while his nasty seed came in a hot and then cool and then cold mucousy blob, and in the alley beside the supply store Graceful bent at the waist and vomited in the dirt, over and over, until she could heave no more.

It took a long time for the shaking to slow enough that she could lift the front of her skirt to wipe her face, longer still before she could force herself to go back out to the street. But when she stood in the mercantile a few moments later, holding herself motionless in the center of the sawdust-covered floor, keeping her hands in plain sight so that the whitelady behind the counter, with her thin pressed lips and her lank hair and her washed-out squinty suspicious eyes, might have no cause to accuse her, the sickness came on Graceful again. The whitelady weighed out the cornmeal, the brown beans and pale, hard kernels of hominy, in pursed silence, and Graceful saw the woman's thumb on the scale, but she could say nothing, she was allowed to say nothing, and suddenly she turned in fury and walked out of the store. *I'll come back tomorrow,* she told herself, *Berta soaking the beans already, we got enough for one more night. We don't need coffee. T.J. can do without his coffee one more morning.* Though she dreaded her brother's wordless snapping rage, she dreaded whitefolks more, and Graceful turned east and hurried as fast as she could through the street, past the tents and clapboard buildings, heedless of the mud splashing her mother's dress, because it was ruined now anyhow, had been ruined a long time ago, she didn't know why she bothered to try to keep the mud off. She heard him calling behind her.

"Graceful? Graceful!"

And she was glad, just glad, to turn and see Hedgemon Jackson trotting up, breathing hard, the satchel bouncing at his side. Hedgemon's wide smile was gone, and his dancing nervousness; he stood panting in his blue messenger-boy uniform, staring hard at her.

"Where's your beefsteaks and angelcake?" he said at last between breaths, trying to renew the joke, but his face was serious. Graceful didn't answer. "Graceful? Something happen?"

She shook her head.

"You run out of money? I got money. Here, I can give you some money." But Graceful turned her face away. "Is it . . . T.J.'s trouble?" Again she shook her head. "What?"

She didn't even shake her head this time. She wouldn't look at him. The terrible taste in her mouth made her ashamed. They turned and walked in silence, on the plank walk now, where Hedgemon led her, and he took her arm as they passed the brothel tent, the saloon that operated openly in spite of the law, and walked on to the edge of town, where the planks surrendered entirely to the muddy roadbed. Still they didn't speak. As they drew near the stinking vats and smokestacks of the refineries lining Bird Creek, Hedgemon stopped. "I can't go all the way out there," he said. "I got to get back to the telegraph office."

Graceful looked at him from behind a stone mask.

He grinned. "I sure didn't expect to be no messenger boy when I moved up here from Greenwood. They told me I could learn the telegraph machine easy as I learned the linotype, but when I got here they had a whiteman on the key. They said I could run the wires around town, out to the refineries and camps." He was silent a moment. "Think that might have been a mistake, I think I should have stayed working for Mr. Smitherman." He waited for her to say something. "Well," he said, "a man can't go back, can he?" There was another beat of silence. "Graceful, what is it?"

She didn't want to look at Hedgemon's asking face. She turned her gaze to the ground. There were spatters on the toes of her worn shoes, her muddy maid's shoes, which looked so stupid with Mama's dress. There were spatters on the hem of the dress, too—new, ugly spatters from where she'd been sick, mixed in with the splatters of mud. Shame burned in her at the sight. There was no way to wash herself clean, no way to wash Mama's dress, nothing to wear while she washed it, and no place private to wash. Suddenly she missed her mother with a pain that was all-engulfing, too huge and agonizing to allow room for anything but itself.

They hadn't heard from Mama, and T.J. said they couldn't send word to her, they'd just have to wait for Delroy. Uncle Delroy would soon come in his truck to bring news from Mama. Maybe he'd bring Mama herself. The thought gave Graceful sudden hope, and she lifted her face. "You know when Delroy's coming?" But Hedgemon shook his head. She thought then of something she'd been meaning to ask first chance she got to talk to Hedgemon out from under T.J.'s frown. "Hedgemon? How did Delroy find you that night? That first night we come here in the truck?"

His shining black eyes darted up the road toward the creek, back again toward town. "I don't know if I'm supposed to say."

She waited.

"He knew before y'all come," Hedgemon said finally. "Delroy the one give me that cot. He didn't tell you that?"

"Neither one of them tell me nothing."

"It was Delroy come by with T.J.—"

"T.J.? In Tulsa?"

Hedgemon looked pained, as if he knew he was telling what he knew better than to tell. But he kept talking, his bright gaze tracing every inch of roadway and refinery smokestack and tacked-together shack within seeing distance. "The two of them came by late, pretty late. Well, it was Delroy knocked at the window, but T.J. was in the truck. They picked me up and we went driving, they didn't tell me anything except T.J. need a place to hide. I didn't ask questions. That was right after. . . ." He glanced down at her. "The lynchings. Just a few days after. I didn't ask." His gaze went back to tracing the roadway. "It was my idea to come to Bigheart, on account of my cousin Terence live here, he's the one told me about that telegraph job. That suppose-to-be job. Delroy carried me up here. He help me to set the tent. They didn't tell you?" And then, vaguely, when she didn't answer, "I don't know why it matters. It don't matter."

"If T.J. was already in Tulsa, how come we had to drive all that way to get him? How come Mama to go to that nasty house way out in the middle of nowhere?"

"I don't know about your mama." Hedgemon shrugged. "T.J. went back to get the girl."

Graceful made a little sound, half recognition, half contempt. *He sure don't act much glad to have her now he got her.*

"What?"

"Nothing."

"Graceful? Listen, I got to get back."

Graceful lowered her head, made no move to go. Laughter spilled down the street from the saloon; grumbling wagons and oilfield trucks rolled by; a pumpjack across the road hissed and squeaked its grinding, monotonous complaint; but between the two of them there was silence. At last Hedgemon said, as if it were the most normal thing to think about, the most logical next subject, "You hear anything from Carl Little?"

She looked up, surprised. "What make you to ask that?"

"Oh, nothing. I was seeing him around a lot, and then next thing I know I hadn't seen him in a while."

"Last I heard he's living in Memphis. I don't know. I ain't seen him since he got out of the army."

"Oh." His smile was starting to creep back. "I thought y'all . . . I thought maybe you'd know . . . Oh, well. Yeah." The smile was broadly back on Hedgemon's face now. "I got to go but I'll . . . I'll see you tonight. Okay? Okay?" Though she didn't answer he grinned anyway, and turned and began to run fast toward town.

Graceful stood a long time before she could make herself walk on, across the timbered bridge over Bird Creek, over brown water slick with crude, reeking with refinery runoff, and on east toward the camp. Carl Little's name woke up the old ache in her, not because of who he was—she hadn't seen or thought of him since before she went to work at the Dedmeyers'—but because the sound of his name, the soft, ticking syllables, called up a whole lifetime in Greenwood, a world where she and her family fit smooth as dovetail joints, and she'd had a sweetheart and lived in a nice yellow house and walked to Booker T. Washington High School in the mornings with her friends, and white people were a distant, unfathomable power, like fickle gods—unappeasable maybe, but far enough off to be forgotten most of the time. It was too hard to think about the past, and there was no perceivable future to swing her thoughts to, only the dull, cloistered present, the closed tent and the two sad women and her testy, bullying brother.

A dozen times she'd opened her mouth to ask him what they were going to do, where they were going to go, but that hard crust on him and her mother's warnings about asking questions wouldn't let her speak. Her biggest fear, the one barely whispered in her own mind, was that T.J. didn't have a plan. That they were just going to stay in the dank U.S. Army tent till the clothes rotted off their shoulders and T.J.'s little cache of money ran out, till Hedgemon Jackson got tired of having his salary go to buy beans and saltmeat for four people not even kin to him and kicked them all out, and then what? She'd tried to tell herself that they would soon go to live in one of the colored towns, Taft or Boley, Redbird maybe. Go live as they had lived when she was little, far out in the country, among their own. But if that's where they were going, why didn't they do it in the first place, instead of coming to this stinking, roiling whitefolks boomtown? It made no sense. *T.J. got a plan,* she tried to tell herself. *Sure he do.*

In a few moments Graceful turned off the road and began to wade through Indiangrass and big bluestem tall as her waist. The amber seedheads nodded in the morning sunlight; the air flicked with flying grasshoppers, black-and-yellow wings buzzing as they sailed over the plumed heads. Here the land was not yet blackened and fouled with the mess of taking oil from the earth, the air wasn't rank with the stench of alchemy but sweet with goldenrod and compass plant, and in the open grassland Graceful walked fast toward the line of trees scrawling off on the horizon to the north. She dreaded that khaki square of tent worse than a prison, but there was nothing else to do but go back. *He going to be mad enough anyhow, might as well get it over.*

Inside the tent the kerosene lantern smoked and stank on the crate, its wick needing to be trimmed, globe needing to be cleaned, and the feeble light threw shadows on the three sitting so still, Mrs. Candler in her usual blankfaced dream on the army cot, her daughter useless and listless beside her. T.J. crouched in his same place against the back wall with that stupid chunk of blackjack in his hand, and yet he didn't even glance up when she came in. It was as if they were waiting—for what? Someone to come, some outside occurrence to change things. *They act like they still hiding in the dark in that cellar,* Graceful thought. *In their minds they still laying down underneath Delroy's tarp.* The only variation she could detect since she'd left was that the tent's odor of mildewed canvas and unwashed bodies, of kerosene and cooked pinto beans and dirt had swelled in the morning sun, and the stink and the despair swept her as bad as the sick feeling from whitefolks, and suddenly she was just so mad.

"How long y'all aim to sit around here in the dark?"

All three pairs of eyes looked up at her.

"Somebody come along and see this tent," she said, "if they looking for you, they going to find you." She glared directly at her brother, her chin lifted. "Crouching in here in the dark ain't going to stop them. Keeping these tentsides rolled down ain't going to stop them. Holding on to that little switch of blackjack ain't."

T.J. looked at her in silence. He didn't make a move to get up.

"What are we going to do, T.J.? We can't sit here in the dark till we rot like last year's sweet potatoes."

"Hush."

"Don't tell me to hush. Tell me what we going to do."

"I'll tell you when I know it myself."

"I tell you what I'm going to do," she said, and she came on into the center of the dim square, stood looking down at all of them. "I'm going back to Tulsa."

"No, you're not."

"I am, T.J., I am! I can't stand this."

"What are you going to tell them when they come around Mama's yard looking for me?"

"How you know they looking for you? Maybe they're not. I haven't heard anything about they're looking for a colored boy. You know they always blare that all over the white papers, and I've never seen it. I would of seen it, T.J. I'm the one goes into town."

"Hush your mouth."

"I won't."

"You don't know a thing about it."

"Tell me, then. I want to know how come I got to live like a mole in a hole without a way to wash or eat nice or fix my hair, no way to see that pretty day outside without you going to stand behind me and tell me to get back in here in the dark. Tell me!"

"Keep on, girl. Didn't get yourself in enough mess asking what you got no business knowing."

"Then let me go. Let me take the train to Tulsa."

"You're not a prisoner here."

"Oh, sure I'm not, only every time I go to the bushes you like to have a fit till I get back, you so scared somebody going to see me, and we way out in the middle of nowhere!"

"You don't know when whitefolks going to show up, they're hunting oil over every inch of this country."

"What did we come here for, then? This was stupid, it's a stupid place to hide from whitefolks, in the big middle of their faces!"

"We're not going to stay here, we going on soon as Delroy get back from Tulsa."

"When's that going to be? When!"

"Hush your loose mouth!" T.J. made a move as if to rise from the damp earth, and Graceful felt herself flinch and pull back, afraid of his anger, and she thought in despair, *We like dogs in a pen, we going to tear each other up.* But her brother settled back on his haunches, said softly, "You get that coffee?"

"No." Her face lifted. "I didn't get no coffee. I didn't get none of they filthy whitefolks' nothing." She waited for his anger, but it didn't come. He remained silent in his coiled crouch. She glanced over at the Candlers. The mother stared at the dirt floor, unblinking, as if she were deaf to them. The girl had one hand on her mother's knee; the fingers of her other hand tugged restlessly at the ratty quilt on the cot, pulled and twisted a bit of leaking batting into a little corkscrew mound. She'd plaited her hair since the morning. Already Graceful's anger was bleeding away. "Whitefolks make me want to puke," she said. And then, softer, "I'll get your coffee in the morning, T.J. I'm sorry. I'll go back tomorrow." And she turned and went out of the tent.

She heard the girl scrabbling out behind her. Immediately Graceful headed toward the path beside the water. She wanted Berta to think she was going off to do her personal business and not follow. She didn't feel like dealing with the faint mothy creature in any way. Graceful went at a steady pace, pushing the vines and sumac out of her way, but the girl came along, and Graceful went a little faster, but the girl would not be discouraged. So Graceful stopped. She waited in the tangled growth for Berta to catch up.

"Where you goin?"

"Where do it look like?"

"I wanted to talk to you a minute."

"You talking."

"I just wanted to tell you, he don't mean to be mean, he just . . ." Her breathy voice fluttered off into the air, soft and trembly as her gestures. She gazed up at Graceful from sienna eyes round as marbles, not froggy enough to be ugly, only enough to make her look scared every minute. "He don't normally act like that."

"You don't got to tell me about my own brother."

"No, I didn't mean . . . There's somethin else. Can't we sit someplace and talk?" Berta looked back along the path, and Graceful, torn by the same tug of sorry she'd felt at the girl's terror when the tarp came up over her head, now felt her resistance go, draining away as her anger had done. *She just a child,* Graceful thought. Her old mantle of calmness returned to her; the stillness rose up into her face, slowed and gentled her gestures. "Down there." She nodded at an uprooted cottonwood on its side on the bank; it was grown up with ivy and brambles, but the trunk lay bare above the tangles, skinned free of bark by years of weather, and the two made their way to it, sat down looking at the water. The creek was so high from the recent rains it pulled at the tangle of sumac and riverwillows on the bank.

"I'm listening," Graceful said. The girl met her gaze for only an instant before she turned her face away. Her copper features began to twist and purse and bend themselves, and she started to cry.

Graceful watched in silence. Every few moments the girl seemed to descend to a new circle of grief, spiraling deeper, so that her weeping became progressively more ragged, more wrenching, more uncontrollable. After a long while, Graceful put her arm across the girl's shoulder. Berta covered her face and collapsed into long voiced sobs, close to wails, not hysterical but horrible, and from a place so deep and ancient it didn't seem possible they could belong to her young self but must be wrenched up through her body from the soil beneath her feet. She began to blubber between the sobs, the words mauled and broken.

"I— don't—know—what I'm going to do! I can't—" And she put her head down in her lap until the sobs quieted enough that she could squeeze more words out. "They was running around the house, like that, outside, outside, man shot him through the back, my daddy just fell down in the yard and they was so much bl— bl— bl— bloood." She pulled her shift up to wipe her face. "They couldn't even get his tongue back in his mouth! Graceful, they bury my brother with his tongue hanging out and my mama gone and lost her mind, they say whitefolks fixing to come take us to jail, me and Mama, we had to go down in the cellar, but I think she lost her mind on account of the children, she's afraid we never going to see the children, and T.J.—" And now the sobs returned fully, and Graceful just let her bawl.

"He act so *mean*! And, oh, Graceful, Graceful, he don't want me no more! I can't even get him to look at me, we was going to get married, he said we'd get married, he say he'll carry me to Tulsa, we going to get us a house, and he, he promise he'll quit running liquor, because that's what killed my daddy, but he don't want me, and I—I—" She held her hand cupped over her nose and mouth, stared at Graceful with those huge eyes, gulping air, trying to control herself. Finally, she managed to calm the sobs enough to say, "Will you tell him for me?"

"Tell him what?"

But the girl started crying again, and Graceful knew. She was swept with anger at her brother, and it seemed to go such a long way back, to him leaving home even, going off from the family and staying gone and getting himself into no telling what kind of business, and then he'd come sneaking back in the middle of the night to get Delroy to risk his neck for him, get Hedgemon to fix a place for him, get Mama to come clean up his mess, just barrel on getting everybody in trouble, most of all his own self— most of all this girl. Graceful couldn't keep the anger from her voice when she said, "How old are you?"

Between sobs Berta said, "Fifteen."

"How far gone?"

"I don't know," she said, hiccuping.

"Then how you know it?"

"On account of—I keep getting sick, that's how my mama do. Any time she going to have another baby, we all know it 'cause she be so sick in the morning she have to lay in the bed. I don't eat, but sometime I be sick anyhow. I'm scared to tell T.J., on account of how he act. He didn't use to act so." She lifted her face, pleading with Graceful to believe her. "He treat me good. He so sweet. T.J. sweeter to me than any boy ever been. Now he act like I got poison or something. . . ." And her breathy voice faded away; she turned to gaze out over the water. When she went on, her voice was dull, the words shaken from time to time with a jagged sob, as if she were retelling a bad dream. "I didn't think I'd see him again. T.J. run away the minute it happen. It happen so fast. We all just sitting down to break-fast when the whitemen come, they talk so quiet and normal, we didn't know nothing, I didn't, I didn't even know they was sheriffs till way after, but it was just in a minute everybody start shooting and T.J. come running from the barn, I seen him running, my daddy and that whiteman chasing each other around the house, around and around outside the house, they come by the back door three times. They kilt my daddy right at the cor-ner of the house, whiteman shoot him, and T.J. shoot the whiteman, but them others already got hold of Everett and start to beat him, and me and Mama run upstairs with the children."

Graceful's stomach pitched. She didn't want to hear those words. *T.J. shoot the whiteman.* She didn't want to think of the terrible truth she'd closed her mind to since the night in the storm cellar at Arcadia: the unspo-ken reason they all had to live in a cramped tent outside Bigheart, the reason her brother had changed into a gaunt, harsh, bullying man who crouched in a corner with a chunk of blackjack. Hiding from whitefolks. T.J. had to hide; they all had to hide. Whitefolks would lynch him if they caught him, because whitefolks would do anything. Anything. Graceful was knifed through with hurt for her brother, pitying, fearful; the pain was followed, as she stared at the swollen-eyed, hiccuping girl, by an impossible dawning.

"I didn't see where T.J. went," Berta said. "Time I go to look for him, he was just gone." She repeated with a kind of low wonder, "I didn't think I was ever going to see him again. But he come back for me. He come back, and now he act so mad." She paused, gazing at the roiling creek. "I say to myself he's going to be glad when I tell him, he'll quit being mad. But how am I going to tell him if he won't look at me?" She drew quiet again. Somewhere in the open land behind them a flock of crows cawed. When Berta went on, her tone was oddly reasonable, explanatory, like a child imitating its mama. "T.J. wasn't mean when he first come back, though. He didn't start to be mean till we gone down in the cellar, it was all them nights in the cellar, they 'bout make us all crazy." And then, as if to correct herself: "He's not *mean.*" She looked up. "He's just rough."

Graceful kept staring at the girl as if she were listening, but she only half heard. Her mind had turned away from her brother, turned in on herself, her own body, the floating sense of fullness and the cold nausea she had thought to be hatred, which was not hatred only. She blinked when Elberta repeated her name, and she realized the girl had said it several times.

"Graceful? Could you?"

"What?"

"Tell him. You the only one can talk to him. He won't even answer me, he won't look at me, but you're his sister." And the girl went on in her whispery voice, absorbed in her own woes, so that she could not recognize the look on the other's face. "I'm not going to tell my mama, not ever going to tell my mama. She don't need more trouble. She'll kill me anyhow, she been warning me my whole life." Berta began to cry again, not the deep sobs of grief as earlier, but the self-pitying, frightened tears of a young girl in trouble, and she reached over and took Graceful's hand, held it tight between her own. "I been wanting and wanting to aks you. You a sweet lady. Please? I'll do whatever you want. You want me to fix your hair? I can fix hair good, everybody in Arcadia come to me to fix they hair for them, sometime."

"Yes." Graceful said. "Go on back, now. Leave me be awhile. I'll talk to him." Without speaking the girl leaned over and hugged her hard; she was thin and bony as Jewell or LaVona, a wisp of a child with hard, swelling breasts beneath her shift of brick-colored cotton, and when she pulled back she swiped her forearm across her face to wipe the tears. She smiled as if her troubles were all over, jumped up from the old tree and darted lightly up to the footpath.

For a long time Graceful sat without moving; she couldn't see anything. She couldn't think. The unfolding knowledge blocked out the external world of afternoon light and humming air, blocked her inner world as well, the mind's round of thought and plan. She sat motionless, feeling her body, knowing that it was true. After a while she got up from the cottonwood and made her way to the water's edge. She could hear the crows in the distant field. Trembling, she stepped to the little roaring creek.

The water ran fast near the banks, but out in the middle the current was slower, a thick, powerful flow pulling branches and broken sticks downstream. She had no thoughts; there was no past or future, only the demanding *now* of the body, and so she received with her body, slowly, in a rising swell, the full knowledge of her condition. The thing was inside her. She could no more resist it than those sticks in the water could resist being carried downstream. Dizzy, afraid she might fall, she lowered herself to the bank, sat on the muddy ground in her mother's dress. She sat for a long time, without tears, without thinking, her face buried in her hands, letting the truth enter: she carried a white child, a half white child, from that devil. *What am I going to do?*

No answer came. In another moment she got to her knees, palmed creekwater into her mouth, spit it back, again and again. The water tasted of earth, dank and darkly sweet, and she swallowed a little before she splashed her face with it. She stood and began to undo the buttons down the front of her dress; she took off the dress and knelt again in her thin chemise to wash it. With both hands she scrubbed the white cotton against a rock, rubbed without soap the spots of mud and vomit, taking big handfuls of skirt and rubbing one against the other, wringing the material out again and again, the dirty water raining down onto the bank. When she shook the dress out she saw that the material was no longer white but a light tannic color. But the soiled spots were gone. Gathering the sopping dress in her arms she climbed toward the path; she didn't turn onto it but kept on straight through the undergrowth, clutching her mother's dress tight in her hands. She made her way from the tangled creekbottom straight out to the open land.

The dress made a billowy tea-colored tent on the tops of the big bluestem when she spread it to dry, and she sat down beside it, the tall grasses coming up over her head, sheltering her, hiding her, and she sat so for a long time, trying to think. Once, she reached inside the scooped neck of her chemise, touched her changed breasts, felt the heat and the swollen tenderness, felt again the floating sense of fullness in her, as if the air were displaced each moment by the turning of her head. How could she not have known? *On account of T.J.*, she thought, *so much trouble.* And then, *Lord, help me. What am I going to do?* She had to get home to Greenwood, that was all. She had to go to Mama. Immediately the cold nausea swept her. Mama would take one look and she would know. Mama would see what that devil did, how he did it; she would suffer the scent and grunt and feel, she would know all of it, and Graceful could not bear to think of looking in her mother's eyes and seeing the knowledge there. *After*, she thought. *When it's gone. Then I'll go home.* She wouldn't let her mind say what she meant by the word *gone*.

Elberta was outside the tent, pacing up and down in the clearing. As soon as she saw Graceful she came running, breathless, saying, "Where you been, where you been? We been looking everywhere! T.J. about to have a fit! Hedgemon, he, Hedgemon—" And she stopped, out of breath, her excitement and fear choking off the words.

"What? Something happen to Hedgemon?"

"He come in over an hour ago! We been looking for you! They gone back to the creek, they both about to decide you was drownded but I knew you wasn't because you promised you'd tell him, oh, Graceful, you won't forget, will you? You ain't going to back out?"

"An hour?" She glanced at the sky. "What's Hedgemon doing back so early?"

"He come to tell you! Whiteman looking for you! Right in town, he say a whiteman come right to his office, aks for you by name!" And Berta's big eyes grew even bigger as T.J. and Hedgemon appeared from the brush, walking fast toward them. "Where you been?" T.J.'s fury was not cold and fretsome now, but hot, focused entirely on his sister.

"Nowhere. I washed my dress." Graceful's chin lifted. "I couldn't be sitting around here in my underdrawers while I'm waiting for it to dry."

T.J. strode past her toward the tent, where Mrs. Candler's face was framed in the V of the entrance; as T.J. got nearer, the woman shrank back, and in another instant the despairing face in the entryway disappeared. T.J. ducked inside, and Elberta followed him. Graceful didn't look at Hedgemon.

"What kind of whiteman?" she said.

"I don't know. Just a whiteman."

"What do he look like?" She stood with her back to him, facing the water. "What color hair?"

"I don't know. Just look like a whiteman. I don't remember what color hair. He had a hat on."

After a moment Graceful said, "Did he say what he want?"

"He just ask for you."

"Me personal?"

"You personal. Except he didn't say your last name, but it couldn't be nobody else, could it? Man was sitting at the telegraph office when I got back. Mr. Belcannon say, Gentleman in yonder want to see you. He'd asked for me by name. Both names. First and last. Mr. Belcannon told me that."

"He didn't say nothing about T.J.?"

"He only ask me if I know you. Or, no, he say"—Hedgemon twined his voice up into his nose—"'I understand you're acquainted with a young woman named Graceful. I understand you might possibly acquaint me with her whereabouts.'" Hedgemon mimicked whitefolks' talk perfectly, but Graceful was too sick to laugh. She walked away.

"Graceful, what is it? I thought all this time . . ."

But she was already across the clearing, standing in front of the tent, breathing deeply, the nausea rising as she faced the closed flaps. Hedgemon came up behind her. "You going to go?" he said.

"I got to ask T.J." She couldn't force herself to enter that dark interior.

"Man say he'll give me twenty dollars if I can tell him how to find you. Said he'll be at the Gusher Hotel, if I come tell him where you're at, he'll give me twenty dollars cash."

When Graceful shot him a glance, Hedgemon said quickly, "I don't aim to take it, that's not what I meant! I'm just telling you how bad he want to find you!"

"T.J.!" she yelled. "Come out! I got to talk to you!"

Immediately T.J. ducked out of the doorway, the piece of blackjack in his hand, and here came the mothgirl fluttering after him. Graceful's heart ripped with how bad her brother was changed, his face thin as a flint, and murderous hard. *They killing us,* she thought, *every way they can.*

"What do you want me to do?" she said.

"How come a whiteman looking for you?"

"I don't know, T.J. I don't even know who it is."

"You going to go see?"

"That's what I'm asking. Tell me what to do."

But her brother turned his gaunt face to the water, staring in silence, staring hard, as if he saw something there too terrible to allow him to speak; his face was grim, ashy, like an old man's face, but it was rigid with fury, stupefied with fear. Graceful couldn't bear it. "Say something!" she cried. "You been bossing my every living breath for weeks now! Tell me what to do!"

"I don't know!" he exploded. But the spell was broken, the vision, whatever it was he'd seen. "If you don't go," he said in a moment, staring at her, "they're liable to come out here looking for Hedgemon." T.J.'s gaze was steady on her. "If you go yonder, you fixing to tell them? You going to show it in your face?"

"I ain't going to tell nobody nothing."

He stared at her a minute longer. "You better go, then. Find out what it is. Maybe—maybe Mama sent word." But neither he nor any of them believed it. Graceful stood silent a moment. She looked around the campsite vaguely, but there was nothing to gather; she had no handbag, no apron. "Come on," she told Hedgemon. "You might's well get your twenty dollars." When he started to protest, she walked out of the clearing, calling back over her shoulder, "Take it, Hedgemon. Buy a nice angelcake, bring it back for supper."

She heard quick, light footsteps behind her, and she kept going, but the girl's fingers brushed her elbow, and the breathy voice pleaded behind her, "Graceful? Graceful, you won't forget?"

She turned to snap at the girl to go back. The pouchy lids of Berta's round eyes were swollen with crying; her whole face was swollen. "Shhhh," Graceful said. "Go on, now. Quit your worrying. I'll be back before dark."

"You going to tell him tonight?"

"Sure."

"You promise?"

Looking over the girl's shoulder, Graceful saw her brother's bent back disappearing into the tent. Her gaze returned to Berta's face. "I promise," she said.

They walked fast toward the hotel, and Hedgemon held her by the elbow and wouldn't let her step down in the mud; he guided her between the whitefolks crowding the plank walks so deftly that nobody could have accused them of being uppity. The town was even more swarming because it was just four o'clock and the refinery shifts were changing. With every step Graceful grew more sickened, more frightened, but Hedgemon Jackson negotiated the crowds as if he'd been doing it all his life. When they stood in front of the brick façade of the Gusher Hotel, he put both hands on Graceful's shoulders and deposited her by the front window, next to a reeking brown-spattered spittoon, saying, "Keep your face down, don't look up at anybody, if they ask you anything wag your head, don't look up and don't talk."

Graceful watched through the window as Hedgemon entered the lobby in his messenger-boy uniform and spoke deferentially to the man at the desk, ducking his head, one of his hands on his leather satchel as if he had a wire to deliver. *He sure learnt quick how to shuffle his feet in front of whitefolks,* she thought miserably, *considering he been working for Mr. Smitherman his whole life.*

The man at the desk nodded toward the lobby, and Hedgemon started toward the big leather chairs facing one another around a low polished table. Graceful saw him then, Mr. Dedmeyer, sitting in one of the chairs with his gray fedora propped on one crossed knee, a newspaper before him, held wide in both hands. Her heart bucked up, gagged her, as if it would be the very thing she'd finally vomit out from herself, and her pulse beat hard in her throat, deep in her chest. Every muscle in her legs tensed to run. But it was already too late. Mr. Dedmeyer was lowering the newspaper, raising his gaze to the window as if he felt her eyes on him; immediately he bounded from the chair and started toward the door. Graceful began to walk away very fast, but she didn't run, and when she heard him calling after her, she slowed down.

"Gracie! There you are! Graceful!"

Whitefolks in the street were staring at her. She stopped, turned around. Mr. Dedmeyer hurried toward her, and Hedgemon was behind him, both of them rushing up to her. Mr. Dedmeyer's face was burnt red from the sun, how whitefolks get, and he was beaming at her, happy to see her, obviously relieved. She couldn't understand this at all. She looked down at the roughcut planks below her feet. The sickness was rising. The world had gone crazy.

"Thank goodness! We've been hunting all over! I was about to give up."

She was so confounded she could only stare at her feet while Mr. Dedmeyer went on about he was sorry if they'd insulted her some way, he wouldn't for the world want to do that, he knew Mrs. Dedmeyer acted a little nervous sometimes, a little flighty, but really she'd never for the world want to offend Graceful, she appreciated Graceful, she really did; in fact, she'd be tickled to learn he'd finally tracked her down. *How?* Graceful looked up. *Do he know about T.J.?* But she could tell nothing from Mr. Dedmeyer's expression.

He paused to clear his throat, and when he went on, his voice was hesitant, almost secretive. "I know Mrs. Dedmeyer acts a little vexed sometimes. It's those sick headaches, they just torture her, but really, you know . . . uh . . . we . . . I was hoping . . ." He stood with his hat in his hands, his blond head cocked to the side; he seemed to look up at her from beneath his eyebrows like a shamed dog, and Graceful was so bewildered she dropped her gaze again. Everything was too unnatural, too strange to comprehend.

"You could take the early train in the morning. I'll leave a ticket for you at the window. I've got to go back this evening, but you can take the colored car tomorrow morning. You'll come?"

Slowly she realized what Mr. Dedmeyer was saying. "You want me to come back to work?"

"Yes. Didn't I say that? If it's about money, we could, I'm sure we could make a better arrangement, say . . . twenty-five a week?"

Graceful stared at him. Twenty-five dollars a week? Nobody paid their live-in servants that much money, not even the richest oil people. *Blackfolks be lined up six deep every morning,* she thought, staring at him, *jumping to go to work in whitefolks' kitchens. Dedmeyers don't need my particular self to scrub their floors.* She tried to read in the man's face if this was a trick to get to T.J. But Mr. Dedmeyer's face was blank and open, though he did frown a little as he stood watching her. Graceful's mind swirled; she wanted to walk away, but there were white people everywhere, in the streets, all up and down the sidewalks.

"Mr. Dedmeyer, I can't come to work for y'all."

"But . . . but . . ." Then his eyes narrowed with suspicion. "I don't know what you're thinking," he said, although she could tell he believed he knew just exactly what she was thinking. "But twenty-five is my absolute top offer. That's as good a dollar as any Nigra servant's going to bring anywhere in Oklahoma. What's the matter with you?"

She hadn't even the will to be angry at that slithery word whitefolks used when they were too ignorant to recognize their own scorn. Graceful's mind was fully consumed by two facts warring within her: one, she knew she had to go back to work for whitefolks—she had to, because there was nowhere else to work, and she was not going to go home to Greenwood, not yet. The Dedmeyers wanted her. Mr. Dedmeyer was here looking for her, they would pay her, pay her good, and she would not have to stay in the dark tent with Hedgemon's eyes watching, T.J.'s eyes watching, while her belly got big. The other thing she knew was that as long as she lived and breathed she would never go back to the house where that man was. That devil whiteman brother.

"I can't stand here all night." Mr. Dedmeyer's voice was exasperated, a little frantic. "Are you coming or not? I need to know so I can tell Mrs. Dedmeyer. She's most . . . anxious to have you back."

"How many folks I got to be cooking for?"

"Why, two, of course." The man looked at her, puzzled at first, and then relieved. "Why, you thought— No, no, it's just the two of us. I'm surprised at you, Gracie. Trying to hold me up for more money, thinking you're going to have to do a little more work. At twenty-five a week you shouldn't care if it's two or two hundred. Now, come, tell me you'll take the train in the morning. I'll leave your fare at the station, all right?" His impatience was showing. "All right?"

Graceful nodded.

"First train out with a colored car. Go check at the station this evening to find out the time. You'll do that?"

Hedgemon stood behind him, a head taller, his face so serious.

"Yes?" Mr. Dedmeyer said.

"Yes." Her voice was barely audible, but Mr. Dedmeyer turned immediately and started back to the hotel. Graceful pulled her gaze away from Hedgemon, called out, "Mr. Dedmeyer!" The man paused, frowning as if his patience were at last stretched too thin. "Hedgemon brung me." Mr. Dedmeyer's frown deepened. But Graceful would not be swayed. She said, "Hedgemon the one come got me. Like you wanted." Her face lifted, lips tight around her teeth. Without a word, Dedmeyer took a money clip from his pocket, released a folding bill from its clasp, held it out to Hedgemon, who looked to Graceful for direction. Her tone was harsh, exacting, when she answered in a voice that was like the changed voice of her mother: "Take it."

M oney got such a power, even if a person don't have it but only think it, that invisible force going to change them, the way hunger do. But money power is not what I'm talking about. I'm speaking of the earth's own black blood, and that power don't come because oil turn into money. Listen. Oil got its own power. That power come from under the earth.

Bluford's mother told me. Way back when whitemens first come into this country with these pounding machines, boom, boom, boom, pounding holes in the world to go deep and open up a shaft for that power to get loose, she told me, You pray, daughter, pray plenty. A terrible time coming. These whitemens don't know what they doing. The earth's bleeding now, a terrible time is going to come. Bluford's mother passed over before the worst happen, but many a day she smoked us with cedar, prayed over us, me and Bluford and Cunsah and Joy. She told us, not for a warning to try and stop it, because you can't stop it once it let loose—I tell you, there are forces we can't even begin to dream—but Bluford's mother want us to prepare ourselves for what's coming, because she have the power to see.

You think I prepare myself like she ask me? Well, I tried. I did try. But somehow the Lord didn't give me the eyes to see then. Or maybe it's because I'm too much colored and not enough Indian, I don't know. But let me tell you, unless you been witness to it, you can't imagine what oil will do to people. You can't picture how a man will sell his soul to get timbers to make a hole because he believe he smell oil flowing under the earth. How it will turn a town mean as seven devils in a heartbeat. Yes. The very minute oil spouts up near a town, in that very instant that town's heart going to corrupt. Oil have the power to bloom a new Sodom overnight on the prairie, same place yesterday nothing but switchgrass stood. It'll turn a man so wicked he'll kill little children to get hold of they lease rights. I tell you, honey, God have made plenty mysteries under the sun, but the single biggest mystification I ever see is what I seen unleashed yonder from my own native dirt. But it took me too long to know what it was.

First time I gone down to the Deep Fork I stared right at it, but I couldn't see. I can tell you very well what put the mud on my eyes: nothing but old plain greed. Now, that's money-power mixed up with oil-power, Lord, Lord, it's a terrible force. It'll snatch you out quick as Satan, you never even feel it because you got a mind telling you lies right inside your own head. Them whitemens never did bring me my two hundred dollars, never brung me no paper to sign, so I took a notion they change they mind, and what I say to myself is, I'll just go down yonder to that allotment, see if I can't find out what make them to come around so interested one evening and then never darken my dooryard again. But what I really wanted, I want to see if I can find where that oil's at so I'll know where to show some other whiteman so *he* can bring me two hundred dollars.

I get Bluford's nephew Istidji to carry me down there. Istidji just a boy then but he's a good driver, and he come in the wagon, we start out from Iron Post way up in the morning. What I got on my mind, I'm going to look over every acre of that useless scrubland, see if I can't find me a medicine weep—that's what they used to call it. Indians used oil for all kind of medicine on account of its power, a lot of us did, and they known from a long time back about these places oil seep out the ground. I couldn't figure how I's going to be able to look over that whole allotment, but the way it turned out wasn't any need to worry over that, because before we reached halfway to the river we could hear it. Istidji's little horses like to had a fit, he couldn't hold them, finally had to get down and talk Indian to them, grab their faces and make them settle down. Sound like the most terrible popping, but loud and completely regular, like this: *Bang. Bang. Bang. Bang. Bang.* Like a heartbeat, like God's thunder heartbeat—or, no, not God's: it's something else, something else—making a hole in the world.

We drived down toward the water, and you talk about power—we seen power that day, yes, Lord! They have built this big wheel, like a

wagon wheel, only that wheel ten feet tall maybe, and it have a belt going around it, run around and around in this huge whipping circle like a
rolling snake, and I seen that! I seen it but I couldn't see. That belt turning so
fast you know if you get close it's going to snatch your arm off like snapping
a twig, and it is whipping around that wheel, running from the big wheel
over to a little wheel, and this wheel in a wheel is what's giving the power to
the big wooden machine, tall as a hickory tree, pounding a hole straight
down into the Lord's earth. But you think I know what it is I'm seeing?

Listen. Right there before me is these two signs: Big Snake show itself
in that belt looping, Ezekiel's prophecy show itself in the wheel in the
wheel. No, you wouldn't know anything 'bout the Big Snake. I ain't going
to talk about that. They don't like us to talk about it. But surely you know
God's Holy Word? You don't know that old verse? Where Ezekiel tell
God's children he seen a wheel in a wheel by the river Chebar? Ezekiel
seen the heavens open, God's terrible messenger come down, and he tell
us right then the spirit of the living creature is in that wheel in a wheel by
the river Chebar—but me and Istidji, we on the Deep Fork, and I ain't
looking for God's sign because I got my mind on two hundred dollars,
make me blind as a cob. Or, no, I do see, but all I recognize in it is plain
old whiteman's power, the same as these big steam engines on railroad
trains, same as motorcars and aeroplanes, whatever they want to make,
because whitefolks got a strain in them make them have to get hold of
natural power and hook it up short, bend it to they will. I don't believe
whitefolks is the only ones God made to be that way, but around here
they the only ones act like it. And these two whitemens here, they sure
enough got hold of some power, and they working it, yes Lord.

The redhair is one whiteman I never laid eyes on, but you can tell by
how hardknotted his arms is, how he jump and scramble, he's one of
these little rooster men works without pause from kin to can't, no matter
what. The lighthair one I don't know yet, I don't recognize him, he's in the
grip of that power, make him look changed, and he is working like crazy,
same as the redhair, dodging in and out around that stick beating a hole
in the earth, they both keeping out the way of that rocking arm on the
hickory tree and that belt whipping, them wheels turning, and even if it's
just two men working, they making as much stir as a beehive. Act like
they believe God's fixing to strike them dead if they stop or slow down,
they don't have time to talk to a old colored woman and a Indian boy in
a wagon—and I think maybeso they haven't seen us yet. That power scare

me, scare Istidji's horses, scare the boy himself, and we all know this is not a good place. But still yet I do not have the sense to tell the boy to turn his wagon around and carry us home.

The pounding stop. The two mens don't stop, only the pounding, and they go to clinking and clanking with big tools, and that's when I finally see who that lighthair one is. Mister Logan. The very one stand in my yard and tell me he's going to bring me two hundred dollars. But here is how oil got such a power: it make this whiteman's whole face to change. He don't look a bit like that man in my yard two weeks past. That man was fidgety maybe, but he talked polite. This man look like he'll snatch the veins out your throat with his teeth if you cross him. The redhair walk off for something, and Mister Logan take over beating that steel bar at the forge. Lord God, he beat it, beat it with that sledgehammer big as a stone.

He lift his head one time, he got the hammer raised up and he look right in my eyes, and believe it, he don't see me. Not that he don't remember me—I mean, he don't see. You know how a earthworm got no eyes for anything but the very soil it crawl in and out of? This man's the same: he got eyes only for the earth, except his eyes are not for the earth-skin, how a farmer see, but for the blood and bones under it: he sees down to the rocks and water and that power in its deepest part. Because nature call to nature. Fire speak to fire, earth to earth, iron to iron. That's so. And oil been calling a long time to something in the spirit of this lighthair man Logan—but what I don't know is: oil taint me, too. There's never been no deep-earth nature in me, my nature is for the two crossovers, the coming-in and the going-out, but this is how I'm telling you the degree of oil's power. It's going to call out to a person and claim them, even if that one never had a nature for it before. Mister Logan put his head down and go back to pounding with the big hammer, but this been enough to make me get down from the wagon. You see how it work on me? That invisible, that fast. Same as money's power: the *idea* have power in your mind.

Here in a minute the redhair man come back carrying a long metal pole, and him and Mister Logan put the steel mouth back on, and here go the rocking arm, the wheel in a wheel, the whole force winding up again, starting, *bang, bang, bang, bang,* and in a bit the redhair notice me standing by the wagon, he shout something to the lighthair, and Logan look up then, he see me now. First thing he do is swivel his head and look hard at the dark one yonder by the little wood shack.

Yes. That one. He been back there the whole time. You see how greed make me blind? I never seen him before that moment, nor yet did I know him, except to know he's the one talked Creek to me and asked me questions in my yard. He push off from the shack wall and slink over to talk to Logan and right away they having words. But the lighthair Logan, he's the bossman, and he's so busy arguing with the dark one that the little redhair rooster man can't keep up with the rocking arm, and pretty soon they all three shouting, but you can't hear what they saying because that machine going *Bang. Bang. Bang. Bang.* But I know they talking about me. I know.

Well, it is not long till the redhair walk back and turn off the engine, and everything grind down so quiet it is like you gone deaf. We all of us looking at each other, three whitemens and me and Istidji and his little horses and the two mules they got hobbled yonder by that shack. The dark one start toward us, but Mister Logan say something to him and he stop. Then Logan himself come over, and he is not saying ma'am nor anything like it, just stop maybe twenty footpaces in front of me, say, What do you want?

Two hundred dollars, I say. Lord, Lordy, them words just pop out my mouth.

Next month. Didn't he tell you next month?

Who tell me?

But he don't answer, he just turn and glare at the dark one again. Sure enough, now, that one is going to come over. My blood feel like it want to turn solid inside me, to watch him gliding toward the wagon, and still I don't know him. I smell the water in the river behind him, yonder where the trees mark its path, and it come to me right then to remember everything Bluford's mother told me about the Big Snake, how it will part the Deep Fork waters, rise up huge, and if you look at it, just look upon it once, it will capture you, carry you down, hold you forever like a soul thief. Maybe Istidji thinking about the Big Snake, too, because he whisper to me in Creek language, Let's go!, because Creeks and Seminoles, Euchees, all the Indians around here know about the Big Snake, they respect it, they won't mess with it, because it is a terrible force, but listen: this new force being unleashed from under the earth is way more powerful than that. I seen it. I witnessed it, I watch it come up and spew its power and rain down destruction. Not that day, later, but it have started that day, and I took my own part, Lord help me, I did.

One thing I know now, if we going to unleash it, we going to be the ones receive its sorrow. And we have done. We still receiving. You look at what happen since it get loose, look at Tulsa, look at the whole earth gone to war with itself, not once but twice, three times, we *all* warring each other, who set that to work? God? You think God do it? Or Satan? Or man? I'll answer you: none of them. That force do it. That power is what make humans capable to do it. How is the whole earth going to war itself without oil? God the one create the power, yes, but He bury that force deep where we can't get to it. Don't that make you think we not supposed to get to it? God didn't open up them holes in the world and unleash that power for a hundred years. Man done that, and it is not Satan's power he unleash, though some will tell you so. It's not human evil, either, though it is surely enlarged by man's sin, nursed with sin till it get to be so powerful it want to tear the world asunder. The name of one sin that gorge that force like a baby: greed.

The dark one slink toward me, he don't stop twenty foot back like the lighthair, he got to come right up in my face, say, Next month. I told you next month already, what's the matter with you?

When you told me that?

You must be sick. You sick? He lean in so close to me I can feel his breath on me, but the breath got no smell. Oh, that make me shrink back. You losing your memory? he say.

I got my memory. My memory say this man here— I lift my chin at the lighthair. He tell me he's going to bring me two hundred dollars next morning, that's the last I hear or see any of you peoples.

Mister Logan come close then, but he ain't studying me, he's mad at the dark one, and they take in to arguing. I go back and climb up in the wagon. Istidji getting more and more scared. He don't know what they're saying, he don't speak good English, but he knows we in the presence of danger, and he's looking at me, wanting me to tell him to turn the horses and go. Me, I'm scared too, but not scared enough. I speak good English. I know what they're saying. They trying to talk around it, but I know. Mister Logan say, I thought you said you fixed it, and the dark one say, I did, I'm telling you I did, can I help it if a old crazy niggerlady can't remember from one day to the next? And Logan say, Don't be lying to me, it's one thing I can't stand is a liar. And the dark one say, You ain't been lied to and you ain't going to be. And Logan say, What's she doing here, then? And the dark one say, I told you, she's crazy. And Logan say, Crazy, my foot, did you fix it or not? And the dark one turn and glare at me, say, I fixed it all right, but looks like I'm going to have to fix it again.

What I see is, they two have made a bargain together—not like they joined up to be partners, but more the way Judas and the Pharisees made their deal together. And I see another thing: these two don't neither one trust the other. They both thinking the other one fixing to cut him in the back any minute. And I see that this bargain is about me—or not me, but about that allotment I drawed for being the daughter of a freedwoman on the Muskogee Creek Indian rolls. You not going to believe what come out my mouth. I don't know where it come from unless the devil slip his fork-tongue in my mouth, because I jumps up and hollers, You whitemens, listen! Listen to me here! I am Iola Bloodgood Bullet Tiger, and this is my allotment! You hear me? This is my land! Y'all got no right upon it.

That sure quiet they mouths. They both turn eyes to me now, black eyes on the dark one, greenbrown eyes on the lighthair, a thousand thoughts flitting between them, and every one of those thoughts a danger, a murderous danger. I see it, but the greed devil got hold of me, and I just keep on. You got no right to be drilling holes here, I tells them, without you pay me my money. Two hundred down, two hundred when the oil come. You don't give me my two hundred dollars, I'm not going to sign that piece of paper you asking!

Oh, Mister Logan shoot eyes at the dark one when I say that.

I'm going right up to Bristow this evening, I hollers, tell the sheriff I got trespassers on my allotment cutting up my land with they oil-drilling machine!

Them two whitemens stand yonder and stare at me, and for that minute they fearful, I can see it, and I feel the power, what it is to have hold over somebody. Oh, Lord. I ought to been praying like I never pray in my life, but I can't think to pray any more than I can think to get away from that place, let them keep what-all they aim to unleash from under the earth. I stay in the presence of that power while it get loose, get big enough, while it roll up and come catch me, make me to stand there in the wagon bold as anything, say, You whitemens hear me? I'm going up and get the Bristow sheriff to come run y'all off.

We hear you, the dark one whisper. But you hear us, old woman. If you got a lick of sense in that woolly head of yours, you ain't going to do that.

He start to walk toward the wagon, but Istidji slap up his little horses then, he ain't going to wait on me to tell him, and he drive that wagon out of that clearing, fast. I don't try to stop him, because my mind so full of greed. That power already own me. You don't think so? Look here:

I wake up next morning at Iron Post, and I forgets to pray. You understand? I *forget* the Lord.

I don't feed the dogs, don't do anything but sit on the porch thinking. Old Bone laying under my chair, I can hear his tail lift off the wood, come down again, thump. Afterwhile, thump. The other dogs scratching around in the yard, whining, they hungry, except that Tennie dog, I think she's gone off somewhere, but I ain't studying no yard dogs, I got my mind on what I'm fixing to do about this situation. You think I don't know better? Bluford's mother teach me. I ought to been smoking my house with cedar and sage and tobacco, I ought to prayed unceasing for the Holy Spirit to come breathe on me. No, sir, I'm going to sit on my porch without any sign of protection, sit there waiting, until that dark one come driving up in my yard. I'm not a bit surprised to see him. I known one of them would come.

He climb out that old car and come stand with a foot on my porch step. It's pretty late in the morning, the sun's already high. He got a piece of paper. Just a white piece of paper with writing on it. Ain't it strange how much power whitemens put in a piece of paper? Someplace there's a paper say that worthless swatch of Deep Fork bottom belong to me, another piece somewhere say all this land in Oklahoma belongs to Indian people as long as the waters run. Just depends on which piece of paper you paying attention to—or which piece they intend you to pay attention to: which one they want you to sign. Who give power to that white piece of paper? Nobody but the whitemens themselves. But this dark one act different than yesterday by the river. Look different, too, he duck his head, talk nice, talk polite. He say, I believe we had us a little misunderstanding yesterday. I come to fix it with you.

I wait on him. I hear Tennie now, growling; she's right here under the porch.

He smile up real big at me, say, I come to settle.

You got my two hundred dollars? I ask him.

That's what I come to tell you. We had to use that for drilling equipment, but soon as my brother-in-law gets back from Tulsa, we'll bring you your money.

He make a move like he's fixing to come up the steps, and I can hear thumping and scrambling then, Tennie wiggle out from under the porch, growling like she mean business, and the dark one stop. Smile up at me so polite, say, You can call your dog off. I'm just looking to conduct a little friendly business.

I ain't signing nothing, I say, till I get my money. Take me for a fool if you want to, I got better sense than that.

Everything on his face change then. He can't hide it, no matter how much he smile and duck his head. He start in talking low, say, If you're not a fool or crazy, maybe you remember what happened to Mary Big Pond and her family.

I don't answer.

What was it happened to Moses Wolf? he say. You remember Ada Harjo and them six children?

Of course I remember. We all hear about it, same as we hear about a lynching, every time they put dynamite under somebody's house and blow it to smidgins. That's one of they favorite tricks. Ada Harjo was the worst, every one of her little childrens was killed. Most times they'll give a warning, because they don't so much want to kill somebody as threaten them, make a freedman or a Indian sign that white piece of paper. A lot of times they'll get somebody drunk, get the mark that way. Some other time they just kill us, sign the lease paper theyself. But listen, I know all this, and I look at the dark whiteman, and I am not afraid. Greed got no fear but fear of losing what it crave. I look at the dark one, stare straight at him, say, I'm not Ada Harjo. I'm Iola Bloodgood Bullet Tiger.

You can see what pass over him: he just mad at first, for me to sass him, that's how he think, I got a big gall to sass him. Then he get madder, because he see I'm not fixing to lay down and do what he tell me. Whatever he have writ up on that paper for me to sign is going to have to wait a little longer. Then I see a flick of fear pass over, because he see something in me. What it is I can't tell you, but it's inside me, he's not just mad now for how I cross him. I'm still sitting in my chair. I never did stand up. Tennie growling steady now behind him, she's getting louder and louder, got her lips pulled back, showing her teeth.

The dark one step down off the step, slow and easy, start easing himself backwards across the yard. I'll be back in the morning, he whisper. We'll talk.

PART FOUR

Oil

Tulsa
Saturday
October 30, 1920

The orchestra began to play at seven-thirty, long before the invitational hour etched in gold baroque letters on silver paper and sent a month earlier by Nona Murphy to all the best homes in Tulsa. It was L.O. himself, rushing through the ballroom in white tie and tails as he attended to several last-minute calamities, who motioned the maestro to the edge of the stage, shouting, "Good Lord, man, I didn't bring y'all down from Kansas City to sit around and drink coffee! Play something, for chrissake!" before he hurried off to his quarters to don a magnificent floorlength Sioux headdress for the party. The seventy-five borrowed Negro servants finished their preparations to the sounds of "Hungarian Fantasie" and "I'll Build a World in the Heart of a Rose." Relieved of the gentleman's bullying direction, many of them allowed themselves to nod and move in time to the orchestra's rhythms, although the nine regular mansion employees didn't so much as pause to tap a foot as they rushed about trying to get everything done.

When L.O. came back downstairs at half past eight, the first thing he did was to fling open the solarium doors and dash through the salon into the great chandeliered ballroom, tux tails and eagle feathers flying, shouting, "Crank it up, boys, I want 'em to hear you clean up to Skiatook!" Again and again he exhorted the bandleader to crank it up, so that by the time the earliest guests began to arrive the piercing tones of clarinet and trumpet could be heard a mile away above the continuous rumble of automobile engines. Each time the twin carved oak doors with their twin brass lion's-head knockers opened to receive a new party of masqueraders, the sweetish strains of harp and violin, undergirded by tympani, swelled out of the Murphy mansion and drifted along the five-acre lawn of imported Kentucky bluegrass sod, to float west into the darkness over the Arkansas River.

It had been the talk of the town for a month, this upcoming masquerade ball at the Murphy mansion, and it wasn't only Tulsa oil society that had made moves to wrangle an invitation: the famous baron of Ponca City, E.W. Marland, had made certain he was on the list, as had the relatively unsociable Mr. and Mrs. Frank Phillips from the little city of Bartlesville, fifty miles north. But of the several city-states oil had spawned in eastern Oklahoma, none was more self-created, self-defined, self-obsessed than Tulsa—the Magic City, it called itself—and the Murphy masquerade was the premier event of the Tulsa season. Everyone who was anyone, and many nobodies, had donned elegant costumes and headed out in their Pierce-Arrows and Rolls-Royces to make an appearance at the newest and grandest (if perhaps not the most tasteful) mansion on Black Gold Row.

For a state as young as this one—hardly thirteen years old in 1920— Oklahoma had an extraordinarily mythic sense of its own character, and its many exotic selves could be recognized each time the liveried doormen swung wide the oaken doors. In pairs and little clutches, and sometimes singly, the mix of aviators and ballerinas, rodeo stars and bandit queens, pioneers, divas, dance-hall girls, baseball players, an inordinate number of outlaws, and too many cowboys and Indians to count entered bowing and gasping, laughing, depositing their mink wraps and silk capes in the arms of the several Negro servants who stood at attention in the front hall.

By ten o'clock the ballroom was aswirl with caped men and masked women, and the crowd was forced to spill from the terrazzo dance floor onto the open terrace at the rear of the ballroom, into the salon to the north, the formal dining room to the south, the large entry hall facing west. It would have taken a discerning eye to pick out from the crowd the lone Southern belle in the pink ballgown standing in the salon archway, gazing intently from behind her silver mask at the front doors. She stood as close to the marble wall as the wire hoops beneath her skirt would allow, an open fan before her lips, her beautifully coifed head slightly bowed. Each time the doors opened, her face would lift and she'd watch L.O. dash forward to kiss a can-can girl or slap a lawman on the back, his bulky head dwarfed by the huge war bonnet of black-tipped white eagle feathers that swept from his brow all the way to the tiled floor. When at last she'd discovered the identities of the newly arriving masqueraders— or at least determined to her satisfaction who they were not—her head would again bow, up would come the silk fan, and the belle would retreat from the swirling crowd once more. It's likely that none but her closest intimates would have recognized her, for Althea Dedmeyer was very changed. She stood motionless in the archway, and from a distance it appeared to be diffidence that bowed the dark head, modesty that lifted the silk fan. If one were to draw nearer, though, look closely, pierce the shadows behind the silver mask, one would discover a glazed stare not so much of fear but of a woman who, beyond all reasonableness and expectation, found herself trapped.

Shrinking from the press of revelers, Althea turned her caged stare to the many Negro servants passing busily through the ballroom, or allowed it to wander past the sea of masked faces on the dance floor, through the open French doors, to the terrace, where her husband stood outside smoking with several other men in the torchlight. She could just see the puffy silk edge of his white sleeve. But, no, it was not Franklin she hunted. Her gaze wandered toward the front hall just as Josh Cosden entered with his new wife. Cosden was the man who'd clinched Tulsa's place as oil capital when he'd moved his refineries down from Bigheart, but this wasn't the only reason Tulsa called him the Prince of Petroleum: he was an extraordinarily fetching man, blond, debonair, movie-star handsome. Tonight he was costumed as a flamenco dancer. Althea watched him sweep into the ballroom with his hand on the bare arm of his new wife. The wife, too, was dressed as a Spanish dancer, a black lace mantilla crowning her head, a red rose in one hand, and in the other a small jeweled mask on a stick, which now and again she held up to her face. Althea stepped back to the wall as they passed. The hooped skirt belled out in front of her in a ridiculous manner, and she had to step away again. She opened her painted silk fan in front of her lips, forced her gaze past the Cosdens to the foyer, where the wildcatter Tom Slick suddenly rushed in looking as tousled as a roustabout in the field; he hadn't a sign of a costume about him. Behind Slick sauntered a thickset pair in matching Harlequin outfits, and then another couple, their heads poised beneath tremendously large white powdered wigs, their faces hidden behind gold-trimmed masks, he in a tailed waistcoat, she in a wide, magnificently hooped skirt. Althea turned away. Near the dining-room doorway a man in blackface suddenly dropped to one knee, strummed his banjo, and burst into song, and the little party in front of him laughed and applauded.

"You'll never guess who that is." Althea, startled, turned to find Nona Murphy in a fringed white buckskin dress and feathered headdress smiling up at her. Nona was barefoot—a shocking, bold stroke—and thus half a head shorter than Althea. She wore no mask. Her ordinarily pale skin was stained a deep copper color; her green eyes were lined in kohl. Two perfectly drawn brows arched teasingly beneath the intricately beaded headband. "So? Who do you guess?"

Althea glanced across the floor at the plinking minstrel, but Nona laughed, "No, silly!" She flitted her smile over the crowded ballroom, allowed it to settle on the couple laboring toward the dance floor beneath the huge powdered wigs. "That's none other than E. W. Marland and his adopted *daughter,* who is also, by the way, his wife's niece, but *his* constant companion. The girl never leaves his side, but the wife, eh? Where is she?" The sly face tilted up at Althea.

"I wouldn't know," Althea murmured, though she was hardly aware of what she was saying; she passed her eyes over the crowd in search of a different face: the brown, closed mask that revealed nothing.

"I declare." Nona clicked her tongue. "Tom and Belle Gilcrease look like they're having a nasty fight. Is she supposed to be Carrie Nation, you reckon? Oh. No. Silly me. She's trying to be a suffragette. In honor of the vote Tuesday. That'll be something, won't it? Voting for a president? Of course, L.O. said he'd spank me if I tried to register, but"—her voice dropped to a whisper—"what L.O. don't know could fill a liberry. Oh, but, now, who's that bank robber coming in?"

Althea blinked, tried to concentrate. She couldn't see who Nona was talking about, only the polyglot mix of disguises, some masked, some not, several who could hardly be considered to be in costume at all. It occurred to her that Nona had intentionally led some to dress one way, some another, for the perverse satisfactions of her own twisted mind.

"Oh, look." Nona grasped Althea's arm. "Yonder's Chief Bacon Rind." The Indian man entering did not pause beside the liveried servants in the foyer but passed immediately through the arch into the ballroom: erect, heavyset, dignified to the point of austerity, he wore a suitcoat and a beaded amulet, gold looped earrings, a headdress not of feathers but of some kind of sleek fur shaped like a brimless top-hat perched on the crown of his head; he was followed by a short, roundfaced woman in a blanket. "That Indian's rich as Croesus," Nona whispered. "He's got a Pierce-Arrow for every day of the week and two for Sunday. L.O. had to invite him. Oh, watch this, watch this!" And she pulled Althea's arm in excitement as L.O. strode toward the Osage man with both hands outstretched, the feathered war bonnet sweeping behind him like duckwings, and his big voice booming, "There you are, Chief! Welcome. Welcome!"

The image of the white man masquerading as Indian rushing up to the Indian dressed as Indian—who wasn't in costume but, like the wildcatter Tom Slick, simply dressed as himself—was so odd that Althea opened her mouth to say something. But Nona was already gliding away from her, tripping delicately on her baré feet across the room to join her husband. The fringed skirt hardly covered her calves, and her legs, too, had been stained chestnut. She was not wearing stockings. Althea watched them, the whitebuckskinned white hosts chatting with the two Osages, who even still did not seem very Indian to Althea, because to her Indian meant poor, meant dirty, meant two blackhaired blackeyed children holding out crusted hands at the back door, chanting, "Meat. Bread. Meat. Bread." The recollection made her dizzy, made her afraid she might swoon. She stepped out into the center of the ballroom, rushed toward the terrace, the hoopskirt belling and swaying awkwardly, her callused feet spooned into tiny lace-up shoes.

She stopped just inside the French doors, put a hand down to still the bobbing skirt, held herself near the wall as she tried to catch her husband's eye. Franklin stood in the center of a dozen or so men, all of them hatless and coatless in the crisp air, their fingers clutching fat cigars, their shotglasses in the torchlight glowing with bootleg bourbon. Franklin was holding forth loudly, good-naturedly, and the others were listening. His silk shirt was open at the throat, a black one-eyed mask pushed up and riding his forehead. Franklin said something, and the others laughed, and Franklin laughed loudest of all. Althea longed to step out into that cold torchlit darkness, but the terrace was a gentlemen's domain, a woman could not simply walk out there. She turned toward the ballroom as if that had been her intention all along—to view the masquerade from this vantage point—and it was then, finally, that she saw Graceful, in a black maid's uniform and white apron, carrying a tray of hors d'oeuvres across the room. The sight of Graceful's face instantly calmed her. She had an impulse to move toward her, though she didn't give in to it but merely folded her fan and slipped it into a secret pocket of her dress. Graceful had been here since yesterday, as had the majority of the best servants from the best homes in Tulsa, installed at Nona's clever behest inside the immense buffbrick mansion to prepare for the Murphys' party. Althea watched the solid black-and-white form moving through the costumed dancers: the brown face backtilted, more perfectly concealing than any of the gilded masks on the white people in the room. The girl's visage was hard, and yet Althea thought her features seemed somehow softened. How was it possible that Graceful's face was at once softer and harder? Had it been like that when she came back from Bigheart? Althea couldn't remember. An image began to push in on her—the girl standing on the porch in a cotton shift, turning the crank of the Eden washing machine— and then another picture, not of Graceful but of herself—sitting up in the bed in the gray light of early morning, the sheet pulled over her knees as she stared with swollen eyes at her own image in the mahogany mirror. The long-submerged source trembled close to the surface. She turned blindly and started toward the hallway that led to the powder room.

"Ah, here you are, my darling!" Franklin's big paw came around her waist and stopped her; she could feel his warmth through the boned corset. He bent to deposit a kiss on her forehead. "You look so beautiful," he nearly shouted, though his words were barely distinguishable above the orchestra. For an instant she leaned against him.

"Dance with me," she said. Her voice was flat, loud. Her voice had nothing to do with the pleading inside her: the words sounded like a command.

But Franklin was flushed with bourbon and the heady rush of his own happy secrets. He grinned down at his wife, his forehead tilted. "And why wouldn't I want to dance with the most beautiful woman in the room?" he shouted. "Madame?" He bowed at the waist, took his wife's hand, and escorted her to the dance floor.

Althea allowed her arms, ribcage, cinched waist to go limp as he led her in a waltz; she followed her husband's feet as if bound to them, glad for the music and the motion as Franklin whirled her around the floor. For a time her thoughts were hushed; her mind filled only with the music's three-four rhythm, the swirling crescendo of harp and violin, the sweeping movements of her own body. But then the orchestra swung into a foxtrot, the clarinets chortling, the snare drum rattling a complicated tempo, and Althea tried to perform the alternating gaits in her tiny lace-up shoes, but her mind was distracted, she couldn't rely on her body's memory, and she suddenly dropped her hand from her husband's shoulder, turned and walked off the floor.

"Thea! What's the matter? Darling—" Franklin trailed after her, but Althea hurried across the ballroom, weaving through the crush of quick-stepping guests; she made her way swiftly into the formal dining room, which served now as libation room for the boldly flowing illegal liquor, where dozens of men stood about talking business in deep-pitched, urgent clutches of threes and fours as they sipped champagne punch from crystal goblets. At one end of the room an elderly Negro stood at attention behind the long table, where a gold-rimmed crystal punchbowl sat squarely on a French-lace tablecloth.

The room shut silent the instant she entered. Althea ignored the men who glanced up as she passed, and the men in turn, seeing the husband rushing along behind the woman, quickly looked away. The room began to thicken again with the low rumbling of male voices. Althea made her way to the table, the great bell of her skirt bumping against masculine knees; she barked at the servant, "Two, please." No tremor of expression flickered over the dark face. The old man ladled champagne punch into two gold-rimmed goblets, handed them to her as if it were the most common thing in the world for a lady to demand liquor. Althea turned to Franklin rushing up behind her, stared at him as she held out one of the goblets, put her lips to the rim of the other, and drank. "We're celebrating, aren't we?" she said quickly, as Franklin started to speak. "One ought to have champagne to celebrate, I thought. Don't you think?"

"Are you all right?" He tilted his head toward her, frowning, and she suppressed the impulse to click her tongue, turn away. Her face felt brittle, but she smiled at him.

"I'm fine. Why wouldn't I be fine? It's a party, after all. Besides, this masquerade is nothing." She swept her hand airily over the crowded room, and in the same glance and gesture indicated the glittering ballroom beyond the arch. "Nothing! It's a little pale tea party compared to the ball we're going to give when the Tiger well comes in!" She took another sip from the goblet. "Nothing!" she said again. Her voice was faint, a bare whisper, but she smiled ravishingly at her husband. As she turned to have the glass refilled she caught sight of her own image in the mirror above the mantel: it was not the horror from her upstairs bedroom that gazed back at her, but an exquisite silver-masked creature in a diaphanous pink ballgown, surrounded by sleek anonymous masculine faces.

Whether it was the effect of that image or only the rapid soothing of the champagne, Althea felt herself suffused with warmth, her limbs relaxing with a slow, delicious ease, her thoughts focused and calm. She returned her smile to her husband, but Franklin had already turned his attention to the many magnates in the room. She watched him sip his drink as he eyed the other oilmen. He'd lost weight in the past month camped out on the Deep Fork; he was less fleshy than he'd been in years, less soft-looking, and for an instant she admired the rakish tilt of his head, the newly revealed line in the thrust of his jaw. Franklin's lean face, his tanned skin, the unruly golden hair springing out around the black line of the silk eyepatch riding his forehead all made it seem that this was not the man she'd lived with for nearly sixteen years, but a new man, mysterious, hard-edged, perhaps even a little dangerous.

"I'm damned," he said.

"What?"

"That's Harry Sinclair right there, talking to Bill Skelly. That's him. Damn."

She followed his gaze to the two tuxedoed men standing near the mantel, and it took her an instant to realize that the two stood out precisely because they were not in costume. Casting about the room, she saw that several of the men were in black tie and tails.

"You believe it? Here comes J. Paul." Franklin nodded at a hawk-nosed man coming through the door in a white silk tuxedo. "Son of a gun lives in London, don't tell me he's come back to Tulsa for L.O.'s stinking party. I don't think so. Something's up." He pulled the one-eyed mask off, tucked it in his waist sash. He drank deeply of the champagne punch and murmured something else, but Althea, sipping her own drink, did not listen. Her inner eye turned to imagining the party they'd give a year from now, the mansion she'd have Franklin build. She tipped her head, gazed up at the vaulted, frescoed ceiling, inlaid with platinum and gold, the magnificent Waterford chandelier pendulous in the center. She skimmed her eyes over the displays of Italian art on the walls—beatific blond angels; pale, big-bosomed women lying prone in filmy gowns within fantastically ornate frames—trying to imagine for herself and her future mansion a new style, a singular identity, when the Tiger well should come in. But Althea had passed a threshold. She couldn't call up an imagined future, couldn't see anything with her mind's eye; she saw only the very real crush of masqueraders around her, the Sheffield silver-plated sconces on the oak-paneled walls, the gilt mirrors, the dozens of fainting half-clad women reclining in rococo frames. Her dreams failed. Perspiration slicked the buckram on the mask against her face. She felt closed in, claustrophobic. Abruptly she turned to have her goblet refilled just as Graceful came through the service doorway.

The girl's shoulders were slightly bowed under the weight of the tremendous silver tray she carried, filled with dozens of the heavy crystal goblets. Althea, standing by the table with the empty chalice held out in midair, felt her hand lift slightly when the old Negro took the goblet away. She stared at Graceful from behind her mask, a secret, attentive, trapped stare, while the girl thunked the goblets one at a time onto the table, slowly, methodically, as if it were the most significant task in the world and she had the rest of her life in which to do it.

An image came to Althea suddenly, not in mirrored reflection or daydream but in clear recollection: a vision of herself sobbing, shrieking, prostrate across the desk in the newspaper office in Greenwood. Other images followed unbidden, inescapable, one tumbling upon another: the big pressman, buttoned tightly into a too-small chauffeur's uniform, steering the Maxwell through downtown Tulsa in silence in the late afternoon, his thick profile sullen, furious, and she'd known he was furious, could feel it like spitting rain from her position in the back seat, and he would not help her into the house but sat in the car staring straight ahead like a man who did not understand English when she'd begged him, begged him, to carry her up onto the porch; he wouldn't answer, would not speak, but stared at the windscreen, mute and angry, as the two light-skinned Negroes had been angry when she'd demanded they take her home, and how dared they? How dared they be angry? In her mind's eye she saw the two men on the street in front of the yellow shotgun house, in front of Graceful's house, their faces like the faces of gentlemen, their expressions hateful and closed.

"Another!" she barked at the champagne server. Shame flared into anger, for there was no other escape, and she shook her outstretched hand impatiently, frowned at the old man. Graceful stood four feet away, working steadily as if she did not recognize her mistress. The thick curve of the girl's mouth pressed tightly over her teeth as she picked up the used goblets, stacked them on the tray. Althea was struck once again by the impression that Graceful's face was suffused with tenderness, a kind of softness, beneath the hard, sculpted lines. "I'll have to come back for them others," the girl said. 'Want me to bring anything else up from downstairs?" A secret communication seemed to pass between them, some unspoken knowledge that Althea would never be privy to, and her fury rose higher, and she longed to say something, to give an order, but she couldn't speak. Graceful turned in her slow, placid manner and left the room, thickset, solid, her breasts swelling against the white starched cotton apron, her face still as stone.

"Getty's here after something," Franklin whispered against Althea's ear. "Bound to be. There's a new field opening—a mighty big one's my guess."

Althea caught sight of Nona Murphy slipping across the room toward them. At once her fury whipped away from Graceful, snapped onto the gliding Nona; she suddenly understood how it was that Nona seemed to materialize at her elbow when Althea least anticipated her: she was intentionally trying to sneak up on her. But then Nona paused beside a group of men, lifted her banded head as she said something to make them all chuckle, her figure slender, delicate, vaguely brazen in the soft buckskin. She never glanced in Althea's direction, and yet Althea felt her attention. An impulse slid over her to hide herself behind a statue, behind one of the giant fronds, or out on the terrace in the dark. She watched Nona tip her face at each of the gentlemen, trill her laugh. "Y'all are so *bad!*" Nona wagged a finger side to side, and the men laughed, and Nona laughed again as she sauntered away from them, aiming directly for Althea and Franklin near the punch table. Althea gripped the crystal stem of the goblet, pulled a brittle smile to her lips.

"Althea Dedmeyer, aren't you a caution? Go and dress up like the ladiest lady, come in heah and drink this naughty champagne! I declare!" Nona leaned toward Franklin, the honey in her drawl thick as mead. "Your wife is so *bad!*"

"Looks like we're all bad!" Franklin said. "If the law gets a good whiff of this party we might all be spending the night in jail."

"I wouldn't worry about *that,* sir. Sheriff's right out yonder on the terrace, imbibing some good bonded bourbon right alongside L.O. and a bunch of others, including none other than Josh Cosden himself! They're all waiting on you to come back. I heard L.O. say those very words: 'Where's Franklin Dedmeyer, where's our new Baron of Deep Fork!'" She blinked her kohl-rimmed eyes and dimpled a sweet smile up at him. Franklin tipped his head toward her.

"The dull conversation of those oilmen, Miss Murphy, tempts me from present company about as much as an invitation to dine on a mess of swamp rabbit could tempt me away from a feast of pheasant under glass."

"Don't be an ass," Althea muttered. She retrieved her silk fan from her pocket, whipped it furiously in front of her face. *What does she want?* She waited for Nona's little asides and glances, the insinuating smiles and drawled-out inanities to declare her purpose. But Nona went on simpering at Franklin, flattering him even as she mentioned the name of every tycoon at the party. Not that Althea had ever understood what Nona wanted: even after she'd figured out the surface motive, what it was Nona was most immediately after, she still never quite felt that she knew the reason behind it, what Nòna *wanted*. It was as if Nona's mind, her hungers, were hidden behind a sealed wall, beyond Althea's powers to comprehend.

Nona suddenly purred up at Franklin, "Guess who just came through the front door!" She swept her wide green gaze to include Althea. "None other than that handsome partner of yours!"

Althea stepped toward the ballroom, but instantly stopped herself. Nona's eyes were riveted on her.

"I know I'm not a bit mistaken, because that scamp don't have a sign of a costume on!" She shook her feathered headdress, pouted up at Franklin. "Some folks, I don't care what you say to 'em, they're gonna dress just any old how. You'd about like to not even invite 'em, except. . . ." Her face was still tipped toward Franklin, but now her gaze was on the tuxedoed oilmen, Skelly, Getty, Sinclair, gathered in an elegant black-and-white triad near the mantel; she went on in a seductive whisper: "Some of the biggest fish got the toughest mouths." She cut her eyes at Althea. "Isn't that right, Thea?"

Althea saw instantly that her notion had been right: Nona had tricked the partygoers so that the wealthiest, the absolute oil elite, for the most part, were not in costume—and yet the pattern was unclear. Wasn't Josh Cosden in costume? And Waite Phillips and Tom Gilcrease, and the famous Marland, who'd just opened the Burbank field? No oil gambler was more successful than these. Nona's reasoning was indecipherable, just as it had been that afternoon in the rose garden when she'd come to borrow Graceful. Althea had only finally understood what she'd wanted some three weeks later, when Nona again came sauntering up the walk in a sequined silk afternoon dress to beguile that commitment from her, as she'd gone around "borrowing" all the decent houseservants from all the best families in Tulsa—and why? There was unfathomable purpose working in that feral mind of hers, Althea sensed it, just as in the rose garden she'd known by how her eyes darted everywhere that there was one other thing Nona wanted.

"I'll tell you what, though." Nona straightened, toyed with a bit of fringed buckskin dangling from her sleeve. "Your Mr. Logan's got somebody with him dressed up to beat anything I ever saw. You ought to see people turn and stare."

Althea glanced through the doorway. She couldn't see Jim Dee anywhere.

"I guess whoever it is might just walk away with that little prize L.O.'s gonna give out at midnight. That's what *I* think. If somebody don't have a fit and faint. That whole ballroom went dead quiet the minute they walked in. I mean, they shut that room like a *door!* Only I guess y'all couldn't tell it"—she smiled sweetly at Althea—"on account of all the noisy men in here!" She trilled her little laugh. Franklin was already halfway across the floor, making his way toward the ballroom.

"Franklin!" Althea called out to him. He stopped instantly, turned, and hurried back with his elbow extended. He dipped his head in a little cursory bow. "Ladies?" he said, and held his other arm to Nona. "Shall we?" Althea took her husband's arm in a kind of stupor, a muted dream, and she walked with him, Franklin's big thighs bumping her hoopskirt, making it sway and bounce, while Nona squeezed up close against his other side.

"Franklin Dedmeyer, you are the long-leggedest thing!" Nona laughed. "I'm gonna have to stand on my tiptoes and *run* to keep up with you!" Franklin slowed his rush, gathered a new and avuncular dignity as they passed into the ballroom.

The orchestra continued to play and a few people were dancing, but the center of the great hall was empty, the masqueraders pressed back near the walls, as a low, excited buzz hummed just at the level of hearing. Althea tried to understand the sound's meaning, but it was as unintelligible to her ears as the rhythmic whine of cicadas in summer, a lyric, undulating *whyyyyyy*. She saw Jim Dee standing just inside the entrance talking with L.O. Murphy. He was wearing work khakis and a knotted red kerchief, his tawny head bare; he looked as rough and unkempt as Tom Slick, and Althea's heartbeat quickened at sight of him, but she had only an instant to notice him, because the creature beside him, the cause for all the stir and buzz in the ballroom, drew her eyes immediately, as it drew to itself all attention in the room. Looselimbed, scarecrowish, it slouched near the wall as if it did not intend to insert itself too deeply into the gathering, or as if it could not stand on its own. Its head was cocked sideways, hands tied behind its back, a thick flaxen rope around its neck. But what made the thing so hideous was not the sheer vulgarity of portraying a lynched man, or the purple tongue swelling from the thick lips, but the fact that the creature had painted its face, had drawn a line down the center from scalp to throat and smeared one half white as alabaster, the other half black as soot.

The buzzing sound in the room rose louder, and at once hushed again, like wind dying, as Chief Bacon Rind appeared from somewhere, walked past the bizarre tableau without looking, without speaking to L.O., and continued on to the entrance hall with the short woman in the blanket behind him. They had no wraps to retrieve and so walked straight through the carved doors left standing open and out into the cool October night. But then, as other guests—a few couples, a foursome—began to edge forward with downcast eyes to make their awkward excuses, their too-early farewells to their host, the situation gradually came clear: the servants had all disappeared. There was no one to retrieve the guests' wraps from the cloakroom. No one to serve up more illicit champagne or bootleg whiskey to distract the guests from the room's sudden chill. No Negroes passed through the ballroom balancing canapé-laden trays; no colored servants stood behind the linen-covered tables, no brown hands carved thick slabs from the haunches of barbecued buffalo and beef.

The realization seemed to pass in a wave from the front hall, through the ballroom, all the way to the dance floor near the terrace at the back. There was confusion, indignation, a few titters of scandalized amusement. The orchestra ceased to play. Althea had the sense that the room's legs had been knocked from underneath it, and it had gone down—whump—on its back, the wind knocked out of its chest. She glanced over at Nona, who stood on the other side of Franklin with her wide eyes flicking this way and that, as if she'd never seen such an appalling turn of events. Althea might not know the secrets that drove Nona Murphy, but she recognized the lie in the bronzed face: Nona wasn't appalled. She was not even surprised. She was, more than anything, tickled at the shock to Tulsa society. Nona suddenly detached herself from Franklin's side and started across the room, the down of the white feathers in her headdress waving airily, fanning the currents like cottonwood silk, as she glided over the empty floor in her supple buckskin, her feet buttersoft, silent on the marble in the near-silent hall. Her laugh trilled, echoed toward the vaulted ceiling, as she took the apparition by the bound arm, said in her drawl, "Law, child, you liked to scared all the niggers to death, comin in here lookin like that. They're gonna think we're gettin ready for another little Tulsa necktie party, you scamp!" The lynched man didn't lift his head from his shoulder, didn't blink or flinch, or seem even to breathe.

Now Franklin stepped away from Althea and strode across the room as the murmurs began to rise again, the low whispers and grumbles, for this was a subject unfit for the season's premier *bal masqué*. This was appalling, unheard of, intolerable; it could not be borne. Nobody looked at the lynched man. One could have almost thought the thing was invisible, an apparition that only one's own eyes could see—except for the fact that the room's gaze was trained very studiously away from the halfwhite/half-black corpse. Althea watched her husband join his partner, the two of them dipping their fair heads toward each other in a kind of swanlike gesture as they met. Instantly she swept her gaze to the ballroom, searching for the brown face that had become somehow the only sight that could ground her. But there were only two dark visages in the room: the costumed minstrel, whoever he was—a white man in blackface standing in front of a huge sepia-toned tapestry of a foxhunt—and the half of the lynched man's face that was folded down toward its shoulder. As she watched, the monstrosity raised its head, stared directly at her. The creature's eyes were open, unblinking, locked on hers across the vast swirling distance; both halves of the split complexion were squared in alignment, and Althea at last recognized her brother. The abyss opened in front of her.

She closed her eyes, willed everything away. Everything. This moment, that miscreated freak across the room. Jim Dee. Franklin. The loathsome Nona. Tulsa. The past. All. All. But when she opened her eyes, Franklin was listening as Jim Dee talked in hushed urgency. L.O. Murphy stood off to the side, an unlit cigar in his mouth, the war bonnet cocked at an absurd angle, a baffled, angry expression on his face. Nona's little hand was wrapped around the sleeve of the lynched man, while she simpered up at him. The world was here, in all its grotesquerie, without escape—though Althea longed for it, yes, not merely to run away, but to disappear. Vanish. *I want to die,* she thought calmly. And then, *No!* No. She did not want to die. She wanted . . . something. She gazed across the room, slowly lifted a hand to her forehead, touched a stiff curl, dropped the hand to her side again.

Nona stood very close to Japheth, as if they were the warmest intimates, but how was that possible? Where could they have met? Glancing up with the sly, secret smile on her lips, she motioned Althea to come over. All at once Althea knew what Nona had wanted that day in the rose garden, or, rather, who: she'd been looking for Japheth. The knowledge seeped in as a kind of surprised aftertaste, as when one learns the name of a certain spice in a recipe and the mind says, Yes, I should have recognized that, but the tongue has known from the first savor. Her brother's eyes held on her, clear and shining, obsidian even across that great distance. She started toward him. She was aware with some part of herself that her husband and Jim Logan were arguing furiously in hushed voices off to the side near the doorway. She sensed L.O. talking behind his hand to a cowboy in a big hat and leather chaps, sensed the cowboy hurrying off in the direction of the terrace, even as she felt the several gentlemen behind her watching from the arch of the libation room: every eye in the chandeliered hall followed her as she walked across the floor. If she'd had capacity for irony or humor or self-reflection she might have almost laughed, for her fondest vision of herself had always been that of a beautiful girl in an exquisite gown entering a softly lit ballroom with all eyes upon her. But the submerged source was fully present; it left no room for anything but itself. Her revulsion was powerful, the compulsion stronger. From the corner of her eye she saw her husband and Jim Dee break from the doorway, but she didn't pause; she glided serenely over the floor, the bell of her skirt swaying, her feet burning inside the antique shoes.

"Holy Christ, man!" Franklin said, as the three reached Japheth simultaneously. "What the devil's the matter with you? Good God, Thea!"

Althea paid him no attention. Her brother seemed to be grinning, seemed to be whispering, though she couldn't hear him; she could not quite see his lips move. Her blood coursed furiously. Her ribs could nearly burst with loathing. She longed to do something, *do* something, she could take both her hands and . . . Memory swelled, images swept over her. A sound started within her, a low tremulous vibration. She pushed it down, clamped the unvoiced scream tightly behind her jaw, held it within the boned cage of her breast.

"Hello, Sister." The lynched man's lips still did not seem to move, or perhaps it was only the illusion of light and shadow on the painted face. Abruptly he flopped his head to his shoulder again, shut his eyes, pushed the purple-stained tongue out from his lips. Nona whispered, "Oh, watch this, watch this!" She called across the ballroom, "Evening, Sheriff!"

The sheriff, wearing his khaki uniform, strode nonchalantly toward them. The cowboy in chaps and a big blond man dressed as Teddy Roosevelt trailed after him. At the back of the hall, several men emerged from the terrace darkness, shotglasses and lit cigars in hand, to see what all the quiet was about. Japheth held his same neck-snapped slouch, but a little quiver passed over the painted face. The purple tongue disappeared inside the thick lips. Nona didn't let go her grasp on him, even when the sheriff and L.O. moved in close.

"Oh, come on, now," Nona drawled, "where's y'all's sense of humor? What a bunch of old party poopers. L.O.?"

"Excuse me, Sheriff." Franklin stepped forward as if to take the lawman to the side and talk privately, his earnestly tilted forehead saying surely they could settle this uncomfortable little breach of manners in a discreet fashion.

But Japheth suddenly lifted his face, grinned broadly. "Why, hello, Sheriff Woolley. How nice to see you again." He slipped away from Nona's grip, slouched back against the wall, hands behind him, his demeanor more nonchalant than the sheriff's own. "Hadn't seen you in a month of Sundays, or a month anyhow. Hadn't it been about that? Or no, no, it was still summer, I guess. With all that rain that night a man couldn't much tell."

The sheriff's expression was chary, a little bewildered, but he rocked back on his heels, thumbs hooked in his gunbelt, waiting.

Japheth chuckled softly, rolled his neck around as if he had a crick in it, said, "Oh, I guess you don't remember me, sir. I can understand that. There was such a crowd. Such a crowd." Nona laughed. Japheth turned his painted eyes to her. "Mrs. Murphy, you've been so kind, such a fabulous hostess, I wonder if you couldn't untie me here." Their shared glee was obvious; no one could mistake it, or their collusion. Casually, Japheth turned his back toward her, and Nona fumbled with the rope at his wrists while he talked on, addressing first L.O., then the others. "I know y'all wanted us to stay in costume till midnight, but you can't imagine how crippled a man feels with his hands tied. It was some trick, tying them. You might not credit it, Sheriff, but that's a feat I pulled by myself. I asked Mr. Logan to give a hand. But I'm afraid he's on the taciturn side, just wouldn't help out a bit. He's a fine driller—the best in the business, they say—but I don't know, sometimes he does get his tail over a crack."

There was a beat of murderous silence as Japheth stared at Jim Dee while he rubbed his freed wrists; his hands had been painted, too—one black, the other white—along with wrist and forearm. He grinned at the semicircle of men's faces. "Of course, I didn't have any trouble with this." And he tapped the hangman's noose about his neck. It was strange how clean and new it looked, pure flaxen-yellow, the dangling end cut neatly across. "We got practice with these type of knots, right, Mr. Murphy? Right, Cletus?" And he looked intently at the one dressed as Teddy Roosevelt, who in turn dropped his pince-nez, stepped back. "This criminal element don't watch out, we're going to get plenty more practice, isn't that right? You know, Sheriff, that very evening out on the Red Fork road, I said to myself, See here, Tulsa's going to show them. The criminal element better keep its head down in this town." No one present, not even Nona, could have understood the sweet pleasure within Japheth, to face down the sheriff who'd hunted him, to say baldly: I was there, sir. Right in front of your noses. You've been looking for me all over the country. I was there. I am here.

"Not to mention the niggers," Japheth said. "Niggers got to quit showing out, don't they? I been hearing good things about this new Klan, any of y'all been hearing about it?" He perused the nearby faces, the distant crowd of masqueraders who were by now creeping forward, straining to hear what was being said. "They tell me folks are joining to the tune of a thousand a week down in Texas. Of course, it's not the highest element in society, not like present company, but I'll make a prediction right now, I'll predict that before two years are out we'll have a Klan member right in the governor's office, right here in Oklahoma. I'd bet on it. Would anybody care to bet?"

Silence came from the nearby circle; the revealed faces were frowning, including the sheriff's, but there was fascination as well, a kind of wondrous anticipation to find out what would come next. Nona's face was rapt, her green eyes glittering, wide and innocent. Only Althea seemed not to be listening. She stared out from her silver mask, not at the lynched man but at a blank space on the wall to the side of his head. On the fringes of the ballroom the murmuring had renewed, the hanged man's words whispered in undulating waves back to the terrace. Slowly the gathering moved toward him, seemingly outside its own will.

It was curiosity that kept them from dispatching the one who'd slipped in to hold up a mirror, make them recall what their minds had comfortably shut away. No one talked about the Belton lynching anymore. The papers still mentioned the grand-jury investigation from time to time, but since no one expected, or certainly wanted, anything to come of it, the probe was not a topic for town talk. Lynching had, by joint silent agreement, become a taboo subject for social discourse, but here was this creature among them, declaring it for some unfathomable reason, and the masqueraders waited to find out what it meant. All looked for signs. They gazed round the room, eyed one another, glanced in the direction of the lynched man, trying to discover the secret symbols—for there were always signs, weren't there? If the face had been all black, the message would have been clear—as the message had been clear in a recent ad placed by a local store in the *Tulsa World*, neatly bordered and highlighted: *K!K!K!*, the ad said, *Just say "KKK" to the grocer. Kellogg's roasted KORN KRISP. You and your children deserve KKK.* If the face had been all white, it would have clearly been a direct reference to Roy Belton, and they'd have grasped the warning to all such hijacking hooligans, as well as the naughty slap that the spectacle was to Tulsa's sense of decorum. But it was the half-colored, half-white face that confused the gathering, made the meaning less discernible, more mysterious.

"Of course," Japheth said, smiling, "that new Invisible Empire's got nothing to do with present company. Far as I hear, it's all just a bunch of small-town do-gooders. So far." His eyes lifted to take in the garish grandeur of the mansion. "Mrs. Murphy." He nodded very formally, bowed to Nona, turned to L.O., and did the same. "Mr. Murphy. Allow me to compliment you on the taste and elegance of your lovely home." The weirdly divided face was made stranger by Japheth's sudden clean diction and formality of manner: one of his favorite chameleon tricks was to be crude as a hayrick one moment, suave and polished as a debonaire the next. "I was saying to Mr. Logan as we were motoring up from Bristow—"

"See here! Who are you?" L.O.'s eagle feathers were trembling. "Who let this fellow in?" He wheeled around to vent his rage on the Negro doormen, but, seeing no dark face anywhere, he turned in fury on the two partners. "Logan, did you bring this abomination? Dedmeyer, what are you trying to pull? I'll have the lot of you tossed out. Sheriff?" But L.O. couldn't wait for the laconic sheriff to make a move; he whipped his war-bonneted head at Franklin again. "You're up to something, you son of a bitch, I know that. I been knowing it. Laying out for weeks, and when you do come in, you strut around the lobbies tight as a tick, or else I hear you telling crap to any fool you can get to listen, spreading that conniving pile of lies and mystification."

"I think you'd better calm down, L.O." Franklin's voice was tolerant, a little patronizing: it was the voice he'd evolved years ago to try and quiet Althea's rages.

L.O. turned to the audience. "One minute he's acting like he's got the biggest strike since Spindletop, next he's crying poor, crying duster, crying broke like a lying son of a bitch."

"Listen here, friend," Franklin's soothing voice began, "let's take a deep breath. . . ."

"Listen here, fella," Japheth said in unctuous, pitch-perfect imitation, "let's not say anything that'll make us sorry."

L.O. whipped on Japheth now, both fists raised like a boxer, like the feisty street-fighter he'd one time been. A crone's shriek rose into the great goldenlit space, and the room was stunned once more into silence. None could tell the scream's source, but as it echoed, Althea suddenly leapt at her brother with her hands clawed, reaching for his face. Franklin stepped in front of her, gripped her hands, as Nona gasped and rushed forward, and L.O. shouted to the sheriff, who quickly moved in, as did the cowboy and Jim Dee and several others. The men grabbed hold of Japheth's arms, detached Nona's hand from his sleeve. There followed an almost balletic, inverted *danse macabre*, as the handful of men mimed the movements of a lynch mob; they surrounded the noosed man in silent slow motion, hoisted him, struggling, cursing horribly, spitting from his purple-stained mouth, his black and white hands twisted behind his back and held tight. The only voiced sound in the room was Japheth's cascade of curses as the men half dragged, half carried him out of the hall. The room's gaze passed over them, though without pause, pretending not to register what it was seeing.

The silence extended itself a beat longer. The masqueraders' eyes returned to the empty wall, where the phantasm had appeared. There stood now only the two women, the belle and the buckskinned hostess, both staring out the open doors, and the silkshirted pirate with his arm around his wife. A clarinet tootled a few aborted notes, the piano joined it, and then the orchestra swung into a tinkling ragtime, as the masqueraders turned back to themselves. Gradually, in the tiniest increments, they began to move, to breathe, to pretend that all was natural, all was normal. Men turned to one another and spoke business or politics. Ladies excused themselves to the powder room, disappeared in rustling taffeta and satin whispers.

In the same manner that the city's mind had sealed over the swinging, stripped, beaten body of Roy Belton on the Red Fork road two months before—had opened, received the horror, knit itself quickly, like a scab—just so, the gathering in the Murphys' ballroom now sealed its mind over the vulgar invasion that had pierced the room. The floor filled again with masqueraders, moiled with sound and color, the loud and rowdy laughter of the inebriated guests underlaced with a kind of glittery hysteria, a scandalized excitement, now that the horror had been removed from their sight. No one noticed when the belle in the pink ballgown pulled away from her husband and hurried across the room, disappeared down an empty hall. A mulatto man with a penciled mustache and shining, straight black hair stepped to the front of the bandstand and began to sing into the microphone, his voice at once tinny and smooth, nasal as the muted moan of a trumpet. One by one the Negroes began to reappear.

A lthea ran into the powder room, slammed the door shut behind her. Two women in red net dance-hall dresses bent over a low ebony vanity, leaning into the mirror, applying rouge. A velvet fainting couch reposed in one corner, a teardrop chandelier dangling over it. Gold-embossed fixtures adorned the basins; a naked cupid stood on tip-toe opposite the ebony vanity, peeing into its own little seashell. One whole wall was a mirror. A colored girl, innocent of all that had transpired in the ballroom, stood beside the basin with a stack of small white linen towels she was supposed to hand to the ladies to dry their little fingers. Althea kept her eyes trained away from the mirrored wall as she snapped at the attendant to come help her with her underthings—quickly! Quickly! The attendant set her towels on the lip of the basin and pro-ceeded to amble toward where Althea stood just inside the doorway.

"Ma'am?" the girl said. She was round and light brown, her brownish hair fuzzy beneath the white cap, and she moved slow as syrup, and Althea could have knocked her in the head.

"Help me!" The words echoed back in her memory, to the day in Greenwood when she'd cried out in the newspaper office, and she bit the inside of her jaw till the taste of salt made her stop. She hissed at the girl, "Can't you see I need help?" She snatched up the filmy skirt of the ball-gown to reveal the layers of petticoats in white complicated strata over the hoop-slip and bloomers and lower rib of the corset, an hourglass vise of bone at her waist.

The girl looked at her blankly. She put a tentative hand out and tugged ineffectually at a dangling corset lace. "What you want me to do, ma'am?" she said. *Fool! Help me. Help me. It's your job to help me, what else are you here for?* The dance-hall women were staring at them from the vanity mirror. "Oh, for God's sake!" Althea whispered. She pulled a mass of petticoats up to her chin, turned around, bunched the mass in one hand, waved the other behind herself: "Untie me!" She felt the girl's fingers fumbling at the small of her back, where the hoop-slip was tied beneath the petticoats. "Hurry!" she spat. "You idiot, just untie the lace!" At last the hoops fell to her feet in collapsing rings, and Althea stepped out of the slip, rushed past the two staring women into the next room.

The pink-tiled inner room was mercifully mirrorless. Althea reached up and untied her mask, laid it in her lap. Still she did not weep, though it was what she wanted. But her old habit was gone, self-pity swamped by the source which held capacity only for grief, absolute sorrow, hate, pity. The source, in turn, was blocked cold with fear. She shuddered deeply, rubbed the indentations around her eyes. She sat staring, unseeing, for a long time.

When she emerged from the toilet she saw that the two white women were gone. Her hoop-slip lay collapsed in the same place near the door, a small pointy-toed footprint exiting in plain outline on the circle of white. The attendant was bent over, peering at herself in the vanity, her lips pursed, frowning, as she plucked with plump fingers at her hair. Suddenly, inexplicably, Althea was swept in a tide of roiling fury, and she shrieked at the attendant, "What's the matter with you? Pick it up! Pick it up!"

The girl jumped, her eyes huge as she jerked her face to Althea, and then she turned and ran toward the fallen slip as Althea also rushed forward—to do what? Beat the girl, slap the girl, as she'd wanted to do from the minute she saw her. The girl snatched up the slip and held it in front of herself like a flaccid shield as the door opened and a dark-haired ballerina and a blond cowgirl sashayed in, followed by a sober-faced woman in a gray dress carrying a placard that said ONE WOMAN, ONE VOTE. Althea stopped. Unprotected, having forgotten to defend herself against it, she caught sight of her own image in the wall of mirror, and what she saw bled the rage from her as quickly as it had come. Yes, her hand was raised to strike the girl. She allowed the hand to drop to her side. The three women sidled into the crowded room, and Althea stepped back to allow them to pass, but her eyes were on the strange woman in the mirror, whose pink dress, without the buoyant hoops to support it, sagged forlornly; whose hair was wilted, whose lace bodice was limp. The lip rouge applied hours earlier now lingered on the rims of empty champagne goblets somewhere in the mansion's basement, and the lips in the mirror were bloodless and thin. The cut lines from the face mask appeared as scarlet slashes along the upper ridges of both cheekbones, like stripes of paint, or scars. But it was the eyes staring back at her that so completely stilled Althea: they were stark, big, dark, and glittery, and they had in them the same look that had glared at her across the ballroom from her brother's contemptuous, raging, hate-filled eyes.

Her soul screamed, a mute howl that could not make its way to the surface. She saw the attendant, big-eyed and scared, clutching the white hoop-slip to her breast; she heard the women's voices behind her, but the sound came from a great distance, like the sounds of the many voices calling outside the corncrib. The frightened girl stared at her from the other side of the abyss, the gulf of black terror: the girl stared at her from across the ravine of cut red earth and sandstone where the water trickled in the bottom the color of new blood, and the voices called, *Le-e-e-etha! Le-e-e-etha!*, coming nearer. Her throat made choked, garbled, near-silent drowning sounds. Mouth working, the soundless scream clawing her breastbone, Althea reached out a cold hand and jerked the attendant away from the doorway; she stepped into the massive hallway, where at one end chandeliered light glowed and there was the tinkle of piano, the wail of clarinet and trumpet, the sound of laughter, and she turned the other direction, ran down the vast, empty, echoing hall.

In the ballroom the masquerade went on at an exhilarated pace, fueled by the free flow of liquor and the titillation of the scandalous event taking place, not in secret rooms or on hidden roadsides, but right out directly in Tulsa society's glittering presence. The euphoria was fed by the sense of mystery in the room, the ravenous curiosity, the questions that were whispered behind hands and fans: What did it mean? Who'd dare do such a thing? What was the message? Most significant of all to the masquerade's mind: Who among the party guests was in on the secret? Several of the masqueraders behaved as if they knew very well the meaning of the lynched man; they raised their brows significantly, nodded sagely, closed-lipped, in response to the whispered questions; others gaped their own ignorance, for they wanted no one to suppose they'd had anything to do with it. The mystery was of the grandest, most delicious character, and the gaiety in the great hall rose in proportion to the wildness of the rumors flying from one end to the other as the orchestra played "Pickaninny Sleep Song."

L.O. Murphy had made a great show of dusting himself off when he came puffing back in ahead of the others, his white tuxedo smudged and dusty, his white war bonnet askew; he'd called out for the guests to partake of the feast of quail and prairie chicken, buffalo and beef and wild turkey, he'd had prepared and spread for his honored guests' delectation: Eat up now, folks, y'all come on and eat! With tremendous restraint, it seemed to him, L.O. ignored the sullen glares of the Negro servants (though privately he thought he'd fire the uppity lot of them if they'd belonged to him), and with great joviality he grabbed a passing porter, held him by the arm, and called out, "More wine, Sam! More wine! Fetch up some bottles of that French stuff! We're sparing no expense here this evening!" He went around one by one to the most important guests to reassure them that the intruder had been effectively dispatched, no need for the little ladies to worry, until finally it became clear, even to L.O. Murphy's dull perception, that the spectacle, far from dampening the gathering, had in fact enhanced his party's cachet. L.O.'s deprecations changed swiftly from apologetic to prideful, the words coated in false chagrin. So full of himself and his success was he that he didn't notice his wife gliding on her silent feet into the foyer, didn't see when she slipped out the front door.

As for Franklin Dedmeyer, he'd assumed his own wife was merely rushing off to powder her nose while the turmoil died down, and so he'd allowed his concerns about her to slide to the back of his mind while his full attention keyed in on business, for it was trouble at the drilling site Jim Logan had come in such agitation to tell him. They went on arguing in hushed voices, and only once did Franklin's words digress: "Why in God's name'd you let him come in here looking like that?" he grumbled, partly to shift the subject away from the thick bentonite clay they'd drilled into, partly because he couldn't understand why neither his brother-in-law nor his partner had any better sense.

"Me let him? I don't let that loco do nothing." Jim Dee wiped a little nick of blood from his lip. There was blood on his shirtfront; his red neckerchief was twisted to the side. He spread the fingers of his right hand, examining the swelling knuckles. "Son of a gun does just what he wants, which is mostly set around and let me and Ben do all the damn work."

"Well, he won't be sitting much longer. If you see his face within a mile of the location, you've got my permission to lay some birdshot in it. Looks to God like you could've reined him."

"Hell, man, I didn't know he was going to do that. Nobody knows what's in that weird head—a sane man couldn't dream it." Jim Dee brushed at his shirtfront. "He must've had that noose in his pocket or something. All I knew, when he came to the car he had his face painted up, said it was for the party. I didn't spend a whole lot of time worrying about it. We got bigger troubles than that lunatic brother-in-law of yours. That hole's swoll up like biscuit dough. I told you that formation's too damn cavey—"

"All right! I heard you," Franklin said. "Go on and pull it! You'll get your damn rig!" He caught himself, seeing how his outburst made nearby heads turn. But the delay was going to cost on too many levels to count, and Franklin's rancor was increased by the fact that he knew he should have let Jim build a rig from the outset, like he'd wanted, instead of trying to save a few dollars. Franklin went on, his tone slightly more subdued: "Send Koop to Bristow Tool first thing Monday morning. Or, no, maybe you'd better go in yourself and make the order. I'll be down in a day or two."

"I didn't come to ask your *permission*, Your Lordship." Jim leveled a dangerously mild gaze at Franklin. "I already been to Bristow, I was there yesterday morning. They cut us off. Zeke won't turn loose of a screw or a timber unless you come in there yourself and give him something on the note."

"All right, all right," Franklin said, frowning, "I'll come Monday." He had no cash, no collateral left; he'd sunk everything into tying up the nearby leases, but never mind; he would figure something out. He cocked his head toward the hallway. Althea had been gone an awfully long time. "Have you seen Thea?"

Jim's hazel eyes held on him in a cold, appraising look. "I haven't seen your wife," he said finally. "I'm trying to tell you something, don't you hear me? The old lady's gone."

There was a beat of silence, and then Franklin shrugged, his eyes skimming the crowd for his wife's pink ballgown. Why'd Logan keep harping on that? Colored folks and Indians disappeared all the time; hadn't their own Gracie run off without a word? "She'll turn up, I tell you. Quit your worrying. Those people go off to visit relatives or something, they don't have sense enough to leave a note on the door saying when they'll be back."

"You don't hear a goddamn word I'm saying, do you?" Jim Dee's voice dropped to a harsh whisper. "That fool brother-in-law of yours never got the old lady's mark!" Immediately he began to backpedal. "Or he did, maybe. He said he did, I don't know."

"What do you mean, *he* never got it?"

"I had other things to worry about. That's your blame job."

"Not when I leave it with you, it's not. You said you'd get right back out there."

"I had to get that well spudded in! You don't like it, you can just take care of your own damn end." Jim Dee's voice suddenly turned mild again, disinterested-sounding. "Hell, you can't tell anything about what he says. That lunatic's a full-out liar. Anyhow"—he shrugged—"you better get to Sapulpa and check on it. He said the paper's gone."

"What paper's gone?" Franklin said. "You don't mean the lease?"

"Told some cock-and-bull story about he got my lizzie stuck on the way to Sapulpa, said the courthouse was closed when he got there and he had to get a room to wait till morning, said when he went in to file and reached in his bag the paper with the old lady's mark was missing. I don't know what to make of it. He's your damn kin. Listen here, I knew good and well that hole wasn't going to stand up." Quickly Jim Dee returned to the subject of the wrongheadedness of commencing the well with a spudder, for on that issue he'd clearly been right, Franklin wrong.

But Franklin couldn't hear his partner's blaming words for the roaring in his own ears. He understood fully the meaning of what Jim had come to tell him: it was all going to be ripped away. Before the dream was in his hand, it was going to be filched from him. If the Tiger lease had never been filed in the name of Delo Petroleum, any wildcatter could come along and steal the field out from under them. Franklin cursed himself silently. How could he have failed to perform that one most critical act himself? It was a blank spot in him, he couldn't imagine what had been in his mind, that he'd left that most vital task to someone else. He nodded cordially at Tom Slick, who appeared to be eyeing him from over by the meat table, and at once a great suspicion seized Franklin: what if the appearance here tonight of Sinclair and Getty, Cosden and Slick and the others was somehow connected to this calamity? Jim Dee was saying something, but Franklin, consumed with dread, could only think how all his leasehound work—the weeks of sneaking around Creek County, on down into Okfuskee, leaving small deposits here, larger ones there, securing dozens of leases—all that work was for naught, because he knew what his partner didn't: Gypsy Oil already held claim to the land most directly abutting the old lady's allotment. It was only a miracle or an oversight, or, as his fear now told him, an act of dreadful cunning, that Gypsy hadn't yet drilled an offset well on the line. Franklin's discovery well, the Iola Tiger No. 1, was a phantom. The lease had never been filed.

Unconsciously Franklin's eyes searched for Althea. If his wife in her secret apocalypse sought grounding in the brown face that revealed nothing, for Franklin there was and had only ever been Althea. Not seeing her anywhere, he felt the old worries rising, and it came to him why he hadn't been there to take care of that crucial filing. Of course. When he'd tried to telephone Althea from the hotel in Bristow, the exchange rang and rang and rang. He'd had to go home to see about her, and it was a good thing he'd done so, for how had he found her but lying sick in bed with her feet wrapped in bloody rags? He'd tried to call in Dr. Taylor, but she wouldn't hear of it. He could get no explanation from her except that she'd gone for a walk by the river and had wandered too far, that's how she'd got such terrible blisters. But, Franklin, she'd cried, listen! She'd clutched his hand, staring up at him. Listen! I know where Graceful is! The flighty thing ran off to Bigheart, of all things. Mr. Sutphen said so. Franklin? Darling? No doctor, please. Just bring Graceful home. He'd gone to Sutphen's and hired a new maid, Althea wouldn't have her; she wouldn't let up: oh, she had to have Graceful to tend her, Graceful surely would make her feel better. And so Franklin had agreed finally to take the train to Bigheart. But really it had not helped much, having the girl back. There was something changed in Althea, something he couldn't put his finger on. Where was she? She'd been gone half an hour.

"Excuse me a minute," Franklin said, and he bowed slightly, as if Jim were a stranger, and began to make his way across the noisy floor toward the libation room. His partner stared after him, took a step to follow, but then he checked himself. Jim Dee's gaze swept the room as if he, too, were looking for someone; the hazel eyes were deeply skewed, his lips pursed. Turning, he walked swiftly to the foyer, paused for one last glance around the ballroom before he strode outside.

Althea fled along the hallway, past the open door to L.O. Murphy's trophy room with its many stuffed heads of bighorn sheep and bison and grizzly, all bought from a seller in Fort Worth, Texas; past the library with its thousand leatherbound volumes, purchased *en masse* and shipped by rail from a dealer in New York; to the very end of the south wing, where she came upon a great walnut staircase leading up to living quarters or guest rooms, and a more cramped set of tiled stairs leading down. She didn't hesitate before selecting the tiled steps, and she ran down into the labyrinthine lower level, designed with great craft by the Chicago architect to allow for the greatest invisibility of the many servants needed to run such a grand home. Althea wandered along a dim, cramped passageway until she saw light ahead, and she hurried toward it. Then, for the first time, she faltered.

The light poured from the service kitchen, candescent, yellowish, teeming with Negroes moving about in the brightness. Althea shrank back into the dark corridor. She watched the servants' faces as they worked, some loading food onto trays, some unburdening trays of dirty dishes, some cooking, some washing pots, others drying crystal glasses; it seemed to her they all bore Graceful's expression, that same enigmatic closed look. But as she peered directly at the faces, Althea grew more and more frightened: she was seeing in too much detail. In the brilliant yellow light it seemed she saw the very pores of their skin, every nuance of texture and color; she saw their big or small eyes, their nappy black hair, their pomaded brown smooth hair, their noses, their lips, the shapes of their heads. It was the same as how she'd seen Graceful, acutely, on the back porch that morning, long ago, it seemed years ago, before the abyss cleaved the world. The sounds of the orchestra drifted down a service stairwell on the far side of the room, and the music swelled each time the door at the top of the stairs opened to receive another servant toting a tray piled with the leavings of the partygoers upstairs.

At every new entrance Althea looked to see if it was Graceful, but the girl's face was not among them. The returning servant, male or female, would hand off to a pair of waiting hands in silence, and in their faces was that terrible, closed mystery, that furious constraint, like Graceful's, as they passed trays of half-eaten slabs of meat and crusts of toasts and mauled canapés from hand to hand. Their silence frightened her. What had she thought? That they'd all be happy darkies singing and clapping in the kitchen? Althea's fear disgorged itself into resentment, into the same dull rancor she'd felt inside the girl's house in Greenwood, and it had the same source: her slighted sense that these people had something or knew something she did not know, and would never understand.

The elderly champagne-server appeared from somewhere, coming directly toward where she stood in the dark passage. Althea made a convulsive movement, almost cried out. The man stopped dead; a surprised bleat erupted from him, and all movement in the kitchen behind him instantly ceased. Upstairs the orchestra swung into a jazzy upbeat tempo, but the servants stood watching in the lighted kitchen, trying to peer into the passageway; they did not resume their work.

"Ma'am," the server said at last, "I got to go in that door there behind you. Ma'am? Mr. Murphy want me to carry up some more wine."

"What? Oh, yes, of course." And she stepped aside. As he emerged from the wine cellar with laden arms, she caught him by the sleeve. "Where's Graceful?" The old man didn't answer. "Please. Tell me. I know you know her. She's my— I'm Mrs. Dedmeyer. Graceful works for me."

"I don't know. I'm sorry, ma'am." Very deftly, without seeming to do so, he pulled away and started back toward the kitchen. Althea rushed forward and caught him again. "Where is she?"

He didn't look directly at her, but neither did he lower his head. "I'm sorry, ma'am," he repeated. "I don't know who you talking about." The old man gazed straight ahead; his features were in profile and she couldn't make out his expression. She released the sleeve finally, and he stepped away in a kind of agile, respectful two-step, walked swiftly through the silent kitchen, disappeared up the far set of service stairs. Suddenly Althea was furious, and she ran after him, but he'd already gone. She was caught in the center of the too-bright kitchen with the many faces watching her. Drawing herself up, she looked at them all imperiously, her eyes sweeping the room, and it was a lie, it was not even old habit now but sheer bluff, and had she known how unkempt and shameful she appeared to them she'd have been a hundred times more mortified: they thought she was drunk.

"Where is she!" Althea demanded.

It was a long time before a woman in a white headrag standing beside the huge oven said, "We don't know, ma'am."

And another said, very politely, "Who is it you want, ma'am?"

"My maid. My maid, Graceful. It's time to go."

"Who she, ma'am?"

"Graceful!" The idiots. "Graceful Whiteside!" There. She'd said it. The name had slipped out smooth as cream.

The headwrapped woman said, "We ain't know any Graceful Whiteside. None of us." And she folded her arms and glared a challenge to the rest of them.

But the polite voice came back: "Maybe she gone, ma'am. A bunch of us . . . some folks . . . left while ago."

"Left? Why?"

Here was the gulf fixed. The people stared at her across the expanse of gleaming kitchen, which was in fact a chasm, a great cleft in the world. Althea couldn't conceive that her brother's appearance in the upstairs ballroom had any larger significance than the personal horror it was to her own soul: the questioning whine had been a mystery to her, its source unfathomable. Furthest of all from her imagining was the living, breathing memory of the men and women before her, who, for their part, couldn't dream of the ignorance of the disheveled whitewoman standing in the middle of the kitchen floor. They disbelieved her, they suspected her, they lowered their heads in fear, or glared at her in rage from their unfractured, unsuppressed, long night's memory of lynchings, beatings, tortures, black bodies burning. They knew well that the lynched man was a sign for blackfolks' eyes, saying, Hearken, niggers, this shall be your sons, look here, bow your heads, niggers, we do not need a nigger in hand to warn you uppity Greenwood niggers: get down off your high horse, do not think you can be like whitefolks, do not dare to think you can be equal, self-sufficient, rich.

Althea looked at them a moment, and some returned her gaze and some did not, and the woman in the white headrag eyed her with such formidable defiance that Althea, baffled and intimidated, turned away, retreated into the dim corridor, fled once again up the back stairs.

Out, out into the darkness at the side of the Murphy mansion, down the long sweep of sodded lawn, soft beneath her feet. The full moon made the open spaces day-bright, but dying leaves clung to the trees at the edge of the lawn, cast trembling shadows, and the shadows shuffled and whispered. She turned only once to look back. Lights glowed in every room in the ugly rambling yellowbrick aggregation. Long black motorcars drove up the circle drive, disgorged or received passengers. A pair of liveried doormen stood at attention on either side of the carved doors; voices and laughter floated in an aural mist along the surface of the damp lawn. The orchestra music was muted now, perhaps by the constant drone of laughter and engines, or because of the thundering pulse in her own ears. Althea started to run again, not toward, not away from, but simply to be running, to disappear.

Graceful walked fast in the cold moonlight, almost running, except that her gait was too controlled. The night was frosty and she wore neither sweater nor jacket, but the heat inside her and the swiftness of her stride allowed that she was sweating by the time she reached South Carson, and still she didn't know what she would do. She'd be fired, of course, for walking off without permission from the job the Dedmeyers had hired her out to do. No matter. She was not going to stay in this place anyway, where that white devil would come around. If it had taken a moment for Althea to recognize her own blood-kin, Graceful had known him instantly. Her body had known, in fact, before her mind fully owned it: hatred swept her at sight of him, a hot, wretched, flaming surge, like a flashfire in her chest, searing her instantly from cheek to groin. She'd whirled away, not in fear, but to give vent to the horrific might of her own hate, her scalding rage, her helplessness before all that she felt, seeing that painted, choked, harlequinesque mask.

When she turned off the rustling, oak-canopied street, she fancied she saw him lurking in the dark on a neighbor's side porch. She hurried over the flagstones at the side of the garden, her breath pinched tight, and she was gasping by the time she slammed the bolt shut inside the house; she moved through the dark house and slipped into the tiny maid's room, where, without reaching up to pull the light cord, she sat down on the bed, panting, and tried to think.

Again and again her mind returned to the painted corpse with the noose around its neck, as one revisits in horror and fascination an old nightmare. It was now, for the first time, that she thought clearly of T.J., and she understood finally what the workers in the kitchen had known at once. Whites had lynched a whiteman in this town, they would a hundred times rather lynch a Negro, as they'd lynched Everett Candler, as they would lynch T.J. if they could ever get hold of him. She had to try to send word to T.J., she ought to warn T.J.!

Although she was already sweating, Graceful went warmer, flushed with an old, familiar shame. She had abandoned her brother in the filth and dark inside the army tent. Hedgemon Jackson, too, had left him, had followed Graceful to Tulsa, and so that was also her fault. Half the evenings of the world Hedgemon Jackson would be standing in the alley behind the Dedmeyers' house, waiting to talk to her, and sometimes she'd go meet him, just to have someone to talk with, someone to tell her how things were in Greenwood. Didn't Hedgemon say T.J. was going to come back to Greenwood? And if Graceful asked, When? Hedgemon would say, I don't know, soon as that lynch talk die down. But the lynch talk would not die down. Hadn't the white devil declared that to the world?

And anyhow, what would T.J. do in Greenwood? He couldn't go home to Mama's. He'd better not go to Mama's. *I'll go up to Greenwood in the morning, tell Mama to tell Delroy to tell T.J.: don't come home.* At once she was ripped with longing for the yellow house on North Elgin, for her sisters' complaining voices and Willie's broad grin, and for her Mama, just to see Mama, to be with Mama, just to go home. Her hand touched her belly. The old feeling of powerlessness came on her, caught by the forces inside and outside herself that had so little to do with her own will. *In the morning,* she said, but she knew she would not go.

A muted sound, the scrape of chair wood on tile in the kitchen, stopped her round of thoughts, stopped her heart. She sat breathless, listening for the intruder, but then she heard another sound: human, wounded, like whimpering, although it was not quite that. She got up and went to see.

The woman sat at the little wooden table in the dim light of the kitchen, the tulle-and-lace ballgown foaming around her as she pressed her face into her open hands. If the whimpering sound had been coming from her, she was quiet now, though her back and shoulders shuddered with spasms. Graceful didn't speak, for she was sure to receive the long spew of complaint and blame, and she knew she would not bear it, not one more time, not another ugly word; she turned to go back to her room, but the woman jumped up, crying out, "Oh, there you are! Thank God!"

Graceful turned to stare down the expected tirade, but what she found was an expression as mystifying as Mr. Dedmeyer's face through the hotel window: a look of gladness on the woman's face, of gratitude almost, and the look stopped Graceful completely, turned her still and cold with suspicion.

Althea rushed on as if nothing had happened, no lynched man, no rebellion on Graceful's part by having walked off the job; as if it were perfectly normal for the two of them to be standing facing one another at midnight in the lightless kitchen. "I was looking all over, my God, I looked everywhere, how'd you get here so fast? I practically ran. Well? Come, come, come upstairs and help me get out of these things, Lord, what a time I had getting into this garb, it takes a strong hand to cinch a corset properly, naturally a lady can't do it by herself, that's why in the old days they had— Oh, well . . ." And she began laughing. "You should have seen Mr. Dedmeyer, God, he's no help, the man is all thumbs, completely, just a nincompoop when it comes to ladies' unmentionables, as any man is, or should be, but I lost something, I dropped my— God, I was so mad at Nona Murphy. At myself, really, I never should have let her have you."

She paused, breathing hard, staring at Graceful in the wan light reflecting off the white floor, so that Graceful understood that the look on the woman's face wasn't because she was glad to see her, but because she was wrought up, crazy, madwoman crazy, and for Graceful the whole complexity of her feelings about the woman gave way to pity and fear.

"Maybe you better go on to bed, ma'am."

"I need you to help me."

Graceful returned her stare, silent. If Mrs. Dedmeyer could get herself dressed for the party while she, Graceful, waxed banisters and lugged goblets and food trays and polished tile floors on her hands and knees at the Murphy mansion, the woman could get her own self undressed. "I'm not no lady's maid, ma'am," she said. She looked steadily at Althea. "I'm a domestic who work in the kitchen and keep the house clean. I'm not no slave to loan out to the neighbors. I was going to tell you in the morning, but I might's well say it now. I'm giving my notice. I'll stay till Mr. Sutphen send you somebody if you want, but this here is my notice."

"No," Althea said. Her voice was as controlled as Graceful's, as firm. They looked at each other a moment, and then Graceful turned to go. Althea followed her to the maid's room, stood in the doorway while Graceful sat on the bed in the dark.

"You can't leave." It was a simple declaration. "I forbid it."

"I'm not no slave."

"No, no, I don't mean that . . . I'm sorry. It's— Graceful, I can't—"

Althea looked at the figure sitting on the bed in the small square of moonlight from the high, small window. The girl's cheekbones were distinct; her narrowed eyes were almost closed. Althea's memory arrived fully born: the afternoon she'd come home from Little Africa, when she'd collapsed in the foyer and wept till she could weep no longer, and then slept on the hall floor, only to waken hours later, alone, with the street light streaming through the stained-glass window, too frightened to cry, or to cry out; the memory of how she'd crawled up the stairs on her hands and knees, grunting, panting, clawed her way up onto the bed, under the covers, to stay there for days, not eating, not bathing, lying curled beneath the sour sheet while her feet wept bloody water, and she'd dared not sleep, for when she slept she was tormented with nightmares, and it was on the last night that the old memory came, the first memory, the ancient one, and after that it wouldn't leave her, nor could she wall it off, make a curtain, because she could not cut away the image of herself, her own real self, the Whiteside girl, holding the small ivory legs, the tiny white feet in her hands to better swing the misshapen sloe-colored head, the blueblack mass attached to the scrawny, pale buttocks. . . . Who was it who'd stopped her? Who knew of her murder and her sin? And who would absolve her? The one who witnessed. Only the one who bore witness had the power to release her. Althea had no words for what she'd understood then: that it was the girl who knew the truth in her, the girl who would somehow save her, or judge her— or, no, not judge her. Forgive her. Know her and forgive.

"No. Please listen. I need you," she whispered.

Graceful's narrowed eyes became slits in the darkness. "What for?"

"I . . . can't . . . explain. Did you know . . . you know something?" Althea voice lilted into a peculiar, hollow friendliness. She took a step into the room, and then stopped. It was such a tiny space. It was so dark there, so airless. "My name when I was a girl growing up—my family name is Whiteside. Isn't that funny?"

Graceful was silent.

"I mean, I thought it was odd when the little boy came with that note—"

Willie! Graceful thought, and her heart twisted.

"—had that name on it, I thought, why, there must be some mistake. But you, well, it didn't surprise you, so I thought, well, my stars, what an odd coincidence. I mean, I thought it was odd. It's not so common a name, really. I mean, I . . . it just sort of seemed . . . Not that I think we're . . ." Althea's voice drifted into silence, and the silence grew long in the cramped room. The grandfather clock ticked in the front hall. Outside, a balmy southwind had blown up, and the ground leaves skittered at the basement window and the oak leaves yet on the trees rustled along the drive. Inside the room, there was only the sound of their breathing. When Althea's voice came again, there was simple truth in it. "Graceful, I'm asking you. Please stay." Still the girl didn't answer. After a while a thought occurred to Althea. "Is it because I sent you to the Murphys'? I won't again. That was a mistake. That was stupid, really, I don't even know why I let Nona talk me into it, she is such a sly fox. I don't know what I was thinking. That won't happen again." She waited for Graceful to say something; she expected a sullen acquiescence, for Graceful to say, All right, ma'am, that'll be fine, ma'am, in her soft, infuriatingly slow voice, but the girl remained silent, and despite herself Althea's voice rose in desperation. "Whyyy?"

The silence went on a beat longer, and then: "I'm not going to stay and work anywhere that man come around."

"What man?" Althea was mystified. "Not Mr. Dedmeyer?" Graceful's head moved in a barely perceptible shake, a faint no. "What are you talking about?" And the girl looked up at her, and in the slanted eyes and hard face was pure revulsion.

"Him," Graceful said. "Your brother."

"Oh." There began to rise in Althea a kind of strange, satisfied hope. Why, yes, the girl loathed Japheth as she loathed him, and Althea didn't question why such a thing should be so, she thought only that here at last was both explanation and answer, something concrete she could control. "Oh, you don't have to worry about him. He won't be here. I promise you. He'll never darken my door again."

"He's your brother." The meaning in the flat voice was, He will have to.

"He is not. He isn't. Not really. He's just . . . some person. . . ." Althea's voice faded. There were no words to explain such things, not this mystery, this trouble, this old, hard past. She changed the subject. "Mr. Dedmeyer's going to be gone a lot for the next couple of months. Won't you just stay until he comes home? Just that long. I'll see if we can afford a bonus or something." Desperately she reached for the old concerns, a kind of vacant normalcy. "I mean, I'm not promising anything, but I'll ask him. You're already making a very good salary, I mean, it's not the money, surely? No. No. Of course not. How about this: how about you'll stay until after the first of the year? Just through Christmas, and then if you still want to go, well, that will be fine. It'll be too hard to find somebody here right before the holidays. Won't it?" She reached up to smooth her hair.

"How you know he won't come?"

"He won't, that's all." The odor of pomade, familiar, medicinal, infused the room with its oily scent of petrolatum masked with spice. "I promise you," Althea said. "He won't." There was silence. "Just two months." It was not a question but a statement.

Graceful stared straight ahead. "I can't stay two months and then go."

"Why? What is it? For God's sake, what more can I do?"

"Nothing, ma'am. You fine. Y'all been fine." Which was not true. Oh, the man had been fine, Mr. Dedmeyer, he'd treated Graceful with nothing but the nicest condescension, whenever he was around. And the woman had spewed out only two tirades since Graceful had come back, though she followed her everywhere, sneaking into rooms behind her back; she was worse now than in the beginning, last summer, when Graceful had first come to work here and realized Mrs. Dedmeyer was following her around room to room, spying on her. Graceful looked up at the white face in the doorway, and the image struck, as it had struck on Mr. Berry's jitney when she'd fled this very house, this very room, where that white devil laid down on her, and Graceful made a jerky move to rise, to escape the nightmarish vision of the mouth opening, and the hawk's hunt-cry shrieking out from the blackness, but the woman stood in the doorway, blocking her, too close, choking her back, and she couldn't touch the lady, make her move. "Please, ma'am!" she whispered.

"Hssssht!" Althea grabbed Graceful's arm, held it tight, digging her fingers in, listening as the front door snicked shut. There was the muted click of a man's shoe on the tile, one cautious step. They listened, their breaths stopped, hearts pounding. Neither of them thought then how they were joined together, but in those few seconds the gulf receded the tiniest increment, shrunk by the force of what they mutually dreaded. The footsteps left the hall and started up the stairs, and Althea recognized the tread and weight of her husband's step, and the knowledge passed silently to Graceful, without word or signal, so that the two breathed again, in union. Althea eased her clutch on Graceful's arm, and in the small room they stepped away from each other, even before Franklin's muffled voice wafted down the stairwell, calling out softly, fearfully, hopefully his wife's name.

"The fools," Nona hissed into Japheth's ear, though there was no need to whisper. They were far from the buff mansion, far from champagne, lights, harp, voices, far from hungry eyes and attentive ears. She'd found him at the end of the lawn, where the men had thrown him, the white half of his face glistening with black swells where the dark blood streamed. Carefully she'd pulled the buckskin skirt above her knees to keep it pure of grass stains and knelt beside him. With a small, delicate hand, avoiding the blood, she'd shaken his shoulder, again, yet again. It had taken some ten minutes to rouse him.

He blinked at her. The moon's light turned night to blue day on the sweep of lawn above them, but for a very long time he seemed not to see her. "I never dreamed for a minute they'd act like that!" Nona pouted. The white half of his face grimaced as he twisted to sit up; she couldn't make out the black half at all. "You'd think most of them wasn't right out there on the Red Fork road with us. Now they're gonna act like butter won't melt in their mouths." He struggled to his feet, began to walk away. "Where are you going? Wait!" Nona jumped up and ran after him

She tried to keep up with him as he left the damp lawn, walking fast, making his way down the hill toward the Arkansas River. In the moonlight, in the distance, she saw him plunge into the undergrowth near the bank, and she hurried after him, but the ground was harsh beneath her naked feet, and she had to cull her way through the scrub like a berry-picker. By the time she reached him he'd already washed the blood away, washed most of the black cork and white clay from his face and hands. He crouched on the bank, staring intently, slit-eyed, at the glowing refineries across the river.

"You all right?" He didn't answer. Nona stood preening a moment, smoothing her hair, brushing imagined dirt off the buckskin. "D'ja ever see such a bunch of hypocrites?" Her laugh trilled, and then her voice dropped an octave. "'Dedmeyer! Did you bring this abomination?'" she imitated her husband's bombast, then her voice silvered into oily tenderness: "'Now, listen here, friend, let's just calm down a minute.'" She laughed again. "Tell you what, this town's going to talk of nothing else for a month! Nothing!" She was so taken with her triumph that she didn't notice the silence of the one crouched beside her. "We sure stirred up a little storm for the old sanctimonious frauds, didn't we? Like Cletus Floyd-Jones wasn't out there in the big middle of it, shouting orders like an old army sergeant, 'Y'all fetch that rope over here!' And now he's gonna act so shocked. Did you see his face? 'My word, Sheriff!'" she tsked. "'What're we going to do about this fellow barging in here reminding us of our nasty little selves? Why, we better beat the hell out of him like we done Roy Belton!'"

She caught herself, reached down and caressed Japheth's shoulder, a little breathless, aroused by the scent of violence, though the evidence had been washed clean, all but that which could not be bathed away: the cut above his left eye, the bruised swelling along the bridge of his nose, which she could see even in the cold moonlight. "Well, you know good and well why the sheriff got so mad," she cooed. "He's fixing to lose the 'lection over that lynching and he knows it! Don't tell anybody, but he'd've lost if he *hadn't* let them take that scamp out his jail. He's bound to lose either way." She laughed again, looking up at the swollen moon.

Nona was too excited to perceive the force rising from the sand earth. Her mind was filled with images of the last Saturday night in August, a sultry night so different from this one, hot, dank, the sky thick with storm scud and the bass rumble of distant thunder, black clouds racing across the moon's half-face so that it had appeared to be the moon itself running madly across the dark heavens. They'd brushed against each other by accident at first, or perhaps it was accident, but she hadn't moved away. L.O. was over with Cletus Floyd-Jones and some reporter interrogating the prisoner, and Nona stayed just exactly where her husband put her, gazing straight ahead at Roy Belton smoking a cigarette and mumbling answers to their questions, while the side of a strange man's thigh pressed against hers. She knew he was a roughneck, or she believed he was, though she didn't look at him, and she'd have been content with just that, would have liked it, in fact, preferred it: to stand side by side with a stranger, touching the side of a man's thigh with her hip for half an hour, and then walk off and never see his face, never look at him. But just before they put the noose around Belton's neck, the stranger leaned toward her, breathing scentless breath on her cheek, said, "He's doped."

"No," she said.

"Sure. Look at him. Look how glassy his eyes is. Somebody doped him." She looked at the condemned man, uncertain if the whisperer was right, but then Belton swayed a little as the rope thunked thickly around his neck, and she decided the stranger was telling the truth. "How'd you know that?" she whispered.

"I ought to know if the fool's doped. He's my partner."

Nona looked up at last, titillated, shocked, pleased. The newspapers kept saying Belton had a partner who'd escaped. She saw his face then, shadowed beneath a soft hat-brim, flickering in the torchlight, slender-featured, sensuous, distinct. He winked at her. "Just kidding. You ought to see your face. Name's Charley Ware. You?" And she told him, not just her name, but many things, while the prisoner choked and kicked and fell silent, while the body dropped to earth when they cut him down and the people rushed forward to snatch bits of rope and cloth and skin. Told him her husband's name and how to get in touch with her once he'd settled in at his sister's, and she told him where his sister lived. He spoke Letha's married name, and she described for him precisely the house on South Carson, all the while scanning the crowd of a thousand, passing again and again over the highest and the lowest, the young and the old, male and female, wealthy and working class and rock-sucking poor, all strata of Oklahoma converged on the Red Fork road for one purpose—except they weren't mixed black and white and red, as the whole population was, but white only. That was the very night she'd come up with her idea for the lynched man's exhibition at her masquerade.

Even now the brilliance of the idea electrified her. Nona's mind skated again to the hushed ballroom, the shocked faces, vanished servants. She laughed. "Oh, I got to get back, L.O.'ll have my hide!" In fact, it was the chaos, the consternation and turmoil she'd created, that she wanted to return to. Again she touched his shoulder. "You gonna be all right?" He kept silent. "Ring me up Monday," she whispered, though there was still no need to whisper: they were far, far from anyone. "Regular time. I'll tell you when I can come. Charley? All right?" She was confused, unprepared, more astonished than her own astonished ballroom had been a half-hour past, when the slim, dark form leapt up at her from the bank of the river.

He couldn't stay longer, exposed on this sandbar beside the meandering water gliding slowly south, too wide, in its vulnerable crawl. Japheth found a sandstone boulder, stripped off his bloody shirt, used it to bind the stone to the body's belly, and with uncanny strength he dragged the lifeless weight over the sand. He kicked off his boots, hurled them one at a time into the water, waded out. The body tried to sink before he'd got it well into the current, but he put his arm around its neck, the way one rescues a drowning victim, and swam out to the heart of the river, and then he let it go. The white buckskin gleamed only an instant in the moonlight before it disappeared. Japheth kept swimming, across the dirty Arkansas, thick with sand, slick with oil washed down from the Cleveland field, rank with the spewings of Josh Cosden's refineries on the other side. He moved in a slow, leisurely breaststroke, his dark head gliding on the surface.

If the river was cold he didn't feel it, any more than he felt heat or strain or fear. He was aware only of the viscous flow buoying him downstream, the scent of deepearth dregs merged with the water, floating on the surface, foul, gummy, ignitable. About the woman whose life he'd squeezed from the copper-stained throat he felt nothing. One moment she was the cause of his ignominy, his outrage and defeat, and the next she was a passing danger, for she knew too much, but neither of these truths caused him to kill her; he'd killed her simply, coldly, without feeling, in surrender to the force rising inside him.

After a time he stopped stroking, allowed the current to move him, his gaze on the small licks of fire darting up from smokestacks on the far bank, where the foul odor belched. When the river had carried him well south of the refineries, Japheth began to swim again, but lazily, without purpose. His first impulse to escape was eased now, and he drifted in a kind of pleasurable dream. The polluted waters swelled the darkness in him, enlarging that absolute to which he'd surrendered long ago, as the lynching of Roy Belton had swelled it, as the killing of Nona Murphy made it grow, as each breath and thought and stroke increased it. The odor of alchemy wafted downwind from the receding smokestacks, where the earth's blackblood was being distilled into gasoline, into casinghead gas, fuel oil, kerosene—into power of force—and he inhaled it as he glided down the wide khaki river.

He walked out of the water naked from the waist up, though in the moon's glow he appeared to be wearing a white shirt, for his skin was dark where the sun had touched, fishwhite in the covered places. The pale chest and back and arms were bruised all over, and greasy with oil. For a long time he stood on the bank, shivering, chillbumps mottling his flesh as he peered through swollen eyes across the river at the lights of the Magic City; the malice in him widened before he turned and moved quickly over the sand beneath the cold eye of the moon, ducked into the tangled undergrowth.

There was the freezing all-night walk to Sapulpa, where he garroted a drunken pipecat for his boots and dry clothes and a pistol, shot a line rider at dawn for his Ford motorcar. Afterwards he drove directly to Iron Post, but the old lady's cabin was still empty. He spent the next several days in Bristow (hadn't he learned long ago that fools never hunt in the obvious places?), loitering around the speaks on the eastside, buying drinks with the dead men's money, trying to find out something. He scanned the papers, listened to oil talk and gossip, but never did he hear word of the Tiger woman. No word of his first murder either, though the second and third duly received their two inches of space in the Bristow and Sapulpa papers, along with several other notices of hijackings and killings in the oilboom towns. He'd thought it would make a tremendous scandal; he was disappointed to find no mention of Nona Murphy at all.

But soon Japheth dismissed her as his mind turned fully to his next purpose. He loaded commodities into the stolen Ford secreted in the brush along Sand Creek: a month's worth of dried beans, cornmeal, tinned meat, blankets filched from a clothesline, a checkered coat and new tan derby he'd taken off a drunk drummer passed out in the alley behind the dry-goods store. Once, he met Jim Logan coming out of Bristow Tool, and Japheth stepped into a nearby doorway. The driller continued along the street, got into his own battered Model T. Japheth smiled, fingered the faint babyhair mustache he'd started to grow. On his list of those he would obliterate, Jim Dee Logan ranked near the top.

That sweet enmity, in fact, almost made him incautious: he drove out to the location in bald daylight, seeing the driller's scowling face before him. As the stolen Ford topped a rise, he spied the X of a crown block above the snarl of oak. Japheth stomped the footfeed harder, thumping in the rutted road. But sense and stealth returned to him before he rounded the last curve, and he cut the motor, coasted to a silent stop. Quietly he set the brake and pushed open the door, moved along the rutted road until he stood just in the curve's bow, looking up. Gorge rose in him.

In the litter-fouled clearing, where a week ago there'd been only a clogged spudder, some broken casing, and a pond of mud, now, on this gray November morning, some fifty yards from the old hole, a fully outfitted cable-tool rig stood. The perfectly crosshatched grid towered eighty feet above the trees. Two roughnecks hustled around the derrick floor, a third balanced himself on a girt forty feet above the earth, holding on to one of the sway braces. The belt and engine houses weren't closed in, the floor remained exposed on sills, but the rigging-up had begun; he could see the derrick man setting the rig irons. Ben Koop was bent over in the engine house tying the boiler in to the engine. Jim Logan was striding the length of the platform, shouting orders at the roughnecks in a spume of oath-laden urgency.

Crouched on the leaf-strewn earth, Japheth watched the crew prepare to spud in the new well, and idly he wondered at how they'd got a rig built so fast, where Dedmeyer had scrounged up the money, but mostly, watching Logan through slitted eyes, he relived the beating he'd received from the half-dozen pompous oilmen, and from this one, Jim Dee Logan, high-and-mighty driller. At length the boiler roared to life and the bandwheel began to turn, and as the heavy spudding bit started to rise, Logan straddled the hole in the derrick floor; he steadied the cable with one hand and with the other he guided the thousand-pound bit as it plummeted. It met the soft earth with a thud. Japheth heard the sound of fists on his own giving flesh. The bit raised and dropped, raised and dropped, and the hidden earth beneath the floor opened, the subterranean water gurgled in, and the rocks below the world's surface were pulverized with a rhythmic *poundpoundpoundpound*. In that great disguise of sound Japheth returned to the stolen car, cranked the motor. He backed up along the track, dreaming sabotage, dreaming night destruction and ruin, dreaming murder.

Bareheaded, barehanded, Jim Dee revolved the spudding bit each time it came up out of the hole, turned it with ungloved hands, daring the half ton of metal to crush his flesh, take off his head. By the time they'd made enough hole to switch to regular tools, his callused palms were fissured with tiny cracks, his lips and cheeks chapped with cold. He didn't pause but stamped over to check the loose brake on the bull wheel, hollering at Ben Koop to slap a tong on that screw, hurry up, dammit, they had a goddamn well to drill.

Within minutes he was lowering the two-ton string into the hole. He worked the tool string with one hand on the drilling line, reading the mud and rock below, while Koop hurried from engine house to forge to temper screw on his short legs, his red turkey-neck stretched heavenward, the sinews in his arms tight with knots. They worked rapidly, wordlessly, driller and tool dresser meshed in the mute rhythm they'd synchronized at Drumright seven years before. Neither man had any use for the rites and rituals of religion, but the two shared, sacredly, the sacrament of work. Once a well was spudded in, they hardly ate, seldom slept until the hole had proved or been abandoned. Koop and Logan had made better than five hundred holes together, and they shared a union that was like a marriage, more compatible than most marriages; they didn't need to talk, because work was the sacrament, and work was not about words; it was about the feel.

Within days they'd drilled through the treacherous bentonite into shale, into sandstone, were passing a thousand feet, and the drilling went on, unceasing, but there was something about this hole that did not feel right to Ben Koop, or, more accurately, there was something about his boss. Never had he seen the driller distracted, but twice now he'd had to remind him to watch that slipping brake on the bull wheel, and once he saw him drilling a loose line, so that Koop feared what he'd never seen from the hands of Jim Logan: a crooked hole. That time he'd called out and caught him, but mostly the toolie said nothing, just kept his eyes open and went to pull the tools before Logan hardly seemed to know it was time to dress them, and in general found ways to make up for the driller's puzzling and dangerous distraction.

If Jim Dee was distracted, he was no less relentless: he worked like a man hounded by demons, born to pound holes in the planet, a natural-born driller, which he was, though he'd lived aimlessly for a quarter of a century before finding it out. It seemed now like fate that he'd been passing through Indian Territory in those first days of the oil boom, though at the time he'd thought it just a run of bad luck: I.T. was the very place he'd avoided since he walked out of his father's house at the age of eleven, changed his last name, and headed west. For years he'd wandered through California, Texas, Utah, Arizona Territory, driven by an itch to roam coupled with a lust for work received from his father, from the long line of men before his father, who worked because work was the salt and meat of living, because work was the one salvation they could believe in. He had tried his hand at cowboying, coal mining, panning for gold, but no job of work could assuage the restless burn in him.

He'd been on his way from Denton, Texas, to a rail job in Kansas City when, sitting on a siding in Sapulpa one noon in 1906, he heard that the toolie on an oil rig near Kiefer had been blown to bits when the nitro wagon hit a bad bump. Shredded like wheat, the fellow said, right along with the shooter, you couldn't tell whose parts was which. Takes a fool to hitch a ride on the nitro wagon anyhow, but they were sure looking to hire another, and damn quick, though a man needn't apply unless he could sling a sixteen-pound sledge one-handed and wanted to travel from rig to rig to rig. Jim Dee thought the job might suit him, and he'd gone to Kiefer that evening and hired on.

Before the next day was ended—June 7, 1906—Jim Dee Logan, born Lodi, had found his life's work. He saw right off that it wasn't worth beans to dress tools, because the driller was the force on the rig: the driller was blacksmith, steamfitter, plumber, carpenter, mechanic; the one who gouged a hole in the world with a ton of steel and never paused any longer than it took to sink a well or plug a dry hole, strip the rig, load up, and move on. He hired on as toolie in the Glenn Pool, but six months later Jim Dee had made driller, and he'd been drilling ever since, never stopping as long as there was hole to make and light to see by. He'd partnered with Franklin Dedmeyer during the mad Cushing glut with the understanding that he'd be the sole driller on every one of their wildcat wells.

Now, though, when the crude-saturated Deep Fork Sand was only a few hundred feet down, Jim Dee couldn't keep his mind on his work. He barely glanced at the cuttings in the bailer, would log them carelessly, haphazardly, or dump them in the slushpit without bothering to record them at all, while his mind circled in resentment and doubt. Almost seven years he and Dedmeyer had been together, and that, too, was like a marriage, a bad one, but Jim Dee knew his partner very well. And one thing he knew was that Franklin Dedmeyer never willingly surrendered a sliver of control. Other oilmen might trade and barter endlessly, might sell off shares on a proven lease to develop promising new ones, but Delo Petroleum's meager history could be directly traced to that closed-fistedness on Franklin's part: if they ran out of capital he'd call a halt to drilling until he had the money coming in from elsewhere; he simply wouldn't trade lease shares for more operating funds—or he never had. It was a peculiar trait in a wildcatter, not a very good one, but Jim Dee had never tried to persuade him otherwise, because if it weren't for Franklin he'd still be a hired-out driller jobbing around, and because, secretly, he had that same greedy streak in himself. Always he'd believed that when they finally made the big strike the wealth would be split fifty-fifty between them.

And now Franklin had let L.O. Murphy in on the lease. He hadn't consulted Jim Dee about it, had just showed up in a hired buggy the next Monday after Murphy's party and told him Delo's credit at Bristow Tool was good, go order what he needed, hire in a crew quick, and get that rig built. Zeke Loveless at the tool supply was the one who told him who was signing the checks, and Jim Dee had been furious, but his blood could smell the earth's blood flowing in the Deep Fork bottoms, and he'd had to go on. He'd made out the order, hired the crew, built the rig. Now, though, the closer they got to the source, and the more the oil called out to him, the more he loathed the idea that somebody else was going to have a piece of it. This strike was going to pass Cushing, he knew it, beat Cleveland and Burbank, rival even the legendary old Spindletop. Greed turned to suspicion as he mulled over the fact he'd seen nothing to prove Franklin's claim that he'd tracked down the old colored woman, got her *X* on the wildcat lease, had it all legally signed and notarized and filed in the Creek County Courthouse in the name of Delo Petroleum Corporation. Franklin hemmed and hawed when Jim Dee asked to see his lease copies, had promised to bring them, but he never had. Inside Jim Dee the suspicion swelled like the waterlogged bentonite clay, became thick certainty, clogging not just his mind but his capabilities.

By the bright Tuesday morning before Thanksgiving, when Franklin rode out in L.O. Murphy's new Pierce-Arrow, with L.O. himself behind the wheel, puffing a fat cigar, that certainty in Jim Dee had turned to viscous, numbing rage. It was powerful enough that he did what for fourteen years he'd done only to pull tools or lower casing or fish the swallowed-up tool string out of the hole: he shouted for Koop to disconnect the piston arm, and the ceaseless rocking of the walking beam ended, and the pounding at the earth's core went suddenly still.

From his position on the derrick floor Jim Dee could see a woman in the back seat, sitting sideways in a veiled tulle hat and a man's duster. His brain tried to dismiss her as Murphy's little trollop of a wife. But one does not fail to recognize an icon carried in the mind so many years. Jim Dee squinted skyward. The sun was wasting. He turned and glowered at Franklin, at L.O. Murphy, but his scowl was for Althea, and though her face was hidden behind the gauzy veil, he knew she saw. He watched her open the car door, open a parasol, lift it over her shrouded head; he kept his eyes on the men, but his awareness was on Althea as she picked her way through the mud, her arm on Franklin's arm.

Of the several reckless acts Jim Dee Logan had performed in his life, sleeping with his partner's wife had been the most lasting—though it hadn't been anything nearly so intimate as sleep, but a hard, awkward coupling on the sweaty dufold in the rented house on Olympia, with the cicadas whining in the yard trees, the sticky August light filtering through the venetian blinds, both of them listening every minute for Franklin's step on the porch. There'd been no pleasure in it. She was bristly as a currycomb, all teeth, nails, bones, tension, and it had happened just once, three years ago last August. But for Jim Dee, who was used to taking his relief from deft if bored professionals, it had not been about that anyway. It had been about . . . what? Not her beauty, which was harsher each time he saw her, and in any case was completely obscured now by the veiled hat. She paused, lifted her head as if to peer up at the towering derrick, and he surrendered to the old wordless connection that had little to do with carnality. Her will was part of it, that gritty hunger in her, which his desire responded to, and there was the fact that he knew, or he believed that he knew, every minute, what she was thinking.

Franklin called up to him, "How's it going, buddy?" The power was still roaring in the engine house but the shout carried well; it was that condescending "buddy," as if the driller were another hired hand, no more skilled than a boll weevil, that caused Jim Dee not to answer. L.O. Murphy strutted along in front, reached the belthouse before Franklin and Althea were halfway across the clearing. He stepped up onto the walkway as if he owned the rig, and probably he did, probably his assets had paid for every cable, brace, tool, and timber. A grunt escaped him as he climbed onto the derrick floor; he swept past Jim Dee, went immediately for the logbook, calling out, "How many feet now, you reckon?"

Jim Dee didn't answer. He stood with arms folded, leaning on the Samson post, staring down at Franklin guiding his wife onto the planks. "What the hell'd you bring her for?" he called, but he couldn't keep the calm in his voice over the sound of the steam engine, and so he hollered for Koop to cut it off. The toolie shot him a look, but he went and cut the boiler. Jim Dee's voice was mild, detached, when he said to the cold air, "Ain't you heard it's bad luck to bring a woman on a rig?"

Franklin laughed. "Aye, Cap'n. See, darling, I told you he'd give us a hard time. Watch your hem there. I'm afraid there's no place to sit. Jim won't build a lazy bench, I told you. He doesn't care much for an audience."

"Waste of wood." The tone was bland as pudding, but the hazel eyes skewed down as he watched Althea step up before her husband onto the derrick floor; he tried to pierce the netting that spilled from the wide hat-brim, covering her face, her neck, foaming into a great filmy bow beneath her chin.

"You don't have to stop for us, buddy!" Franklin was in a magnanimous mood, his head thrown back, voice booming. "We're glad for the noise. Stand right there, darling." He positioned Althea beside the bull wheel as if she were a mannequin. "We were talking on the way out." His excited gaze swept from his wife, to L.O. Murphy poring over the logbook, back to Althea again. "We're glad to put up with a little grease for the privilege of seeing it, isn't that right, darling? Crank her up, Benny!" he yelled. "Thea's never watched a well blow in!"

But Ben Koop took his orders from the driller, and since Logan remained leaning on the Samson post, Koop continued pumping the forge bellows as though he hadn't heard.

"Let's have a look at that log." Franklin started toward L.O. "I'll tell you what, if you can make sense of this driller's shorthand you're an abler man than I am." He glanced at the greasy, graphite-blackened book, frowning, and set it back in the cubbyhole; he took a couple of steps toward the belthouse. "Say, we'll go down and try to get a look at that seep in a minute. The water's half over the bank and all muddied to Jesus, I don't know that we'll see anything this time of year, but we can try."

"I'm in on your bragging, Dedmeyer." L.O. reached for the drilling log again. "If it's a dry hole it's coming out of your hide." The tone was jovial, his florid face wreathed in cigar smoke, but the threat underneath was perceptible enough.

"I got a thick hide, friend. I believe another slice or two out of it won't take me to the bone yet! L.O.'s been anxious to have a look at his big investment," he muttered to Jim Dee, then he turned grandly back to L.O. "No better time to come have a look than the day she's drilled in, right, partner?"

Jim Dee heard how he himself had been transformed in Franklin's loud munificence from "partner" to "buddy," L.O. Murphy converted from "that chiseling s.o.b. Murphy" to "partner," and the viscid rage swelled in him. He stepped away from the post. "I want to know what the hell you're up to."

"Up to?" Franklin tried to laugh. A baffled look crossed his face.

"You know what I'm talking about."

"What?"

"My blame lease copies, for one thing."

Franklin's face darkened. "Is that what you called us out here about?"

"Called you? I ain't called you for nothing, but I'm getting ready to call you on something. You told me six times you were going to bring them, I ain't seen 'em yet."

"I'd like to know what's got your nose so out of joint. When did you ever want paperwork brought out to a location? Place for that's the safe-deposit box at the bank. What are you going to do with them out here but get the blame things lost?"

"That'd be my lookout, wouldn't it?" Jim Dee turned suddenly to Althea. "What have you got on that ugly widow's hat for?"

"Why, to protect myself," she said vaguely from behind the veil. "My complexion. The wind . . ."

"You look like you're ready for a funeral."

"We scrounged up that duster to protect her pretty dress, too, didn't we sweetheart?" Franklin said, as if it weren't a strange comment, weirdly intimate from one man to another man's wife. "Darling, don't you want to go sit in the car? It'll be warmer." Smoothly, Franklin stepped across the platform, took Althea's arm. "When that gusher blows she'll rain crude from here to Christmas."

"What makes you so all-fired sure she's coming in?" Jim Dee scowled at Franklin. "Did I say a goddamn word about any goddamn show?"

"Watch your language in front of my wife. You're treading dangerous water, buddy."

"You call me *buddy* one more time, you're going to be wearing this tong for a hat."

"What's got into you? I never saw you act like this."

"Listen!" Althea hissed, the word released like steam in the cold air. She had untied the netted veil and rolled it up to the hat's wide brim; she was staring at the muddy curve where the track turned out of the clearing. The bright, still air, hushed with the absence of machine sound, rang crystalline with silence, so that the vibration in the distance spiraled through the bare arms of the blackjacks: the low signature grumbling of a tin lizzie motor coming along the built road.

The Model T chugged into the clearing, stopped nose-to-rear behind the Pierce-Arrow, snubbed up incongruously against it, like a plowmule cinched to a racehorse. When her brother stepped from the mudcaked car, there was a faint huff from Althea, a sudden expulsion of breath. He was thin as a knife blade, pale, famished-looking, wearing a dirty tan derby and a shiny check-vested suit, his chin and upper lip graced with fine, sparse dark hair.

"Good morning, people," Japheth said. "Sister." He tipped the derby. "What good luck to find y'all here. I didn't expect to find you all here together." And the insouciant smile he lifted toward them told Franklin it had been Japheth, not Jim Dee, who'd left word at the Hotel Tulsa that Delo Corp was wanted out at the location; told Althea it had been her brother's hand which had penned the scrap of paper she'd found in the mail box: *Come with them. J.D.*

"What the hell do you want?" Jim Dee gave voice to the unvoiced question ricocheting in the clearing.

"Why is it folks always think I want something? Just thought I'd drive out and have a look."

"You been banned from this location," Franklin said.

"How's that?"

"You damn well know what I'm saying."

Ben Koop began to edge toward the engine house to lay his hands on the twelve-gauge shotgun propped in a corner. L.O. Murphy relit his cigar. He was irritated at how close Japheth had parked behind his Pierce-Arrow, could see clearly that the fellow was up to something, but he hadn't yet recognized the piebald lynched man who'd ruined his masquerade: the very man L.O. believed his wife had run off with. Within a day of her disappearance L.O. had hired an ex-Pinkerton detective to track Nona down, and in the meantime he'd had it noised about that his wife was in Georgia visiting relatives. It wasn't the first time she'd disappeared: he'd found her once in Dallas with a cattleman, once in a Colorado silver-mining town. If any of the masquerade guests had noticed that he was alone as he wished them good night when the ball was over, none had commented on it to him, and L.O. had pushed that night's turmoil to the back of his mind. But there was something about this fellow that didn't sit right, and as L.O. puffed on the Cubano to get it lit, he watched the man closely.

"Speaking of location." Japheth stroked the down on his upper lip, smiling faintly. "This well's just about six miles from where Letha and me grew up. Isn't that strange? Life has a peculiar way of looping back on a person." He looked steadily at Althea. "No matter how desperately that person tries to go in a line straight ahead." His gaze passed to the curve of trees by the water. "About like the path of that Deep Fork yonder. That's how that crazy river does, you know it? Acts like it's going one direction, but if you try to walk it, you'll find yourself looping back where you came from, like a nightcrawler. You ever done that? Hold a nightcrawler in the middle, watch it twist and curl back on itself?" It was hard to tell whom he was asking. "I have. A snake'll do that, too."

Koop had retrieved the shotgun, was coming along the walkway with it, not aimed, but cradled loosely in his arms. Japheth smiled, shook his head. "You intend to use that, you'd better be ready to shoot Sister, too. She's a witness." He held his hands up, fingers spread. "I'm unarmed."

"Trespassing is grounds to shoot a man in this state," Franklin said. "You're on my land."

"Whose land?"

Franklin felt both Jim Dee and L.O. turn and look at him. "What's that sign say?" he snapped, after an instant's hesitation.

Japheth stepped backward, feigning surprise. He read aloud the painted board nailed to a tree: "'The Delo #2, Drilled by Delo Petroleum Corporation.' Ought to say the Iola Tiger #2, hadn't it?"

"Sign says it's Delo's well," Franklin said. "You are no part of Delo Petroleum, so I suggest you remount that automobile, turn it around and head back to town."

"Whose well?" Japheth's voice was smooth, unguent. "Whose well, Mr. Logan?" He tipped his head. "Mr. Murphy? Your partner here wouldn't be hiding anything from you, would he?" Something in Japheth's sneer, the cocked turn of his head, suddenly made L.O. recognize him.

"It's that son of a bitch!"

"What?" Japheth's smile vanished.

"Where's my wife, you bastard?"

Japheth began to back toward the automobiles. "I don't know anything about your wife, Murphy! I'm here on oil business! Dedmeyer's lying to you! Both of you!"

L.O. had already started toward him. "I'll wring your goddamn neck."

"Wait!" Jim Dee stepped in front of Murphy. "Let's hear him."

"Don't you all know when you've been taken by a liar?" Japheth paused near Murphy's Pierce-Arrow. The smile he turned up to the driller was pure venom. "I guess you know your partner's jacking you over with Murphy here. The minute the field proves, you're going to find out just how tight they got the noose around your neck, and I'll tell you why: Mr. L.O. Murphy wouldn't come in for any less than half." His voice rose over L.O.'s threatening rumble. "Or that's what he *said*. But just to let you in on a secret, I happen to know he was desperate to get in on this deal. So desperate he couldn't be bothered to go look for his missing wife— Oh, sir, this is a swell automobile." Japheth's head swiveled as if he'd just noticed the Pierce-Arrow. "Beautiful. You know," he offered confidentially, "from what I hear, you might try Saint Louie when you get around to it, heard she ran off with a cornet player. Of course," he addressed the others, holding them with the purity of his audacity, "Mr.

Murphy's desperation was matched by Delo Corp's, no doubt about it. But he's a skillful old poker player and he put on a good bluff, didn't you, sir? Got in for half, like you wanted."

Japheth crept slowly forward in the sudden silence. "Now, we all know Franklin Dedmeyer's not about to split half in half again and take only that. Not Franklin Dedmeyer, wildcatter deluxe. After all, he's the one had to go track down the old freedwoman, get her mark on the papers, on account of me and the driller messed that deal up. You had to get the lease filed properly, didn't you, Brother? Isn't that what you said? Of course you've got to squeeze out your old driller friend, you can't take a measly little quarter-share. Oh, don't feel too bad about jacking over a seven-year partner, son of a bitch's been doing it right back to you. That's something you didn't know, isn't it? Logan cut me in months ago. But then he tried to renege on the deal." Japheth cocked his head toward the driller. "A full third partner, yessir, just for me driving out to Iron Post to get the old lady's *X*. Reckon why he'd want to do that? Wouldn't pay her a nickel, though. Hell, I didn't have nothing to negotiate with but a stick of dynamite, no wonder I couldn't get the job done." He smiled at Franklin. "What do you suppose went with that two hundred you gave him? He didn't hand it over to the old nigger, I can testify to that. Now, that's one lie from Logan, but it's not lie number one. Lie number one would be how he's been screwing your wife. I always figured he cut me in—"

"He's a liar!" Althea shrieked. "He's lying!"

The cry echoed away, and in its absence the roar of the forge fire behind the engine house huffed like distant wind.

"Somehow I knew you were going to say that, Sister. But how's a body to believe it when a liar calls a man a liar? Say, that's some sour faces y'all are pulling. What have you people got to be sour about? I'm the one's been lied to. That's all right, though. I can deal with liars, I got no special prejudice against them. Everybody's liars. Take Letha there, for instance, her whole life's a lie. Or maybe she just neglects to mention a few facts. Like how she's got five living sisters. You wouldn't think a little thing like that could slip a person's mind, would you? Used to be seven girls altogether, but Winema's dead. Did I tell you we lost Nema, dear? Same damn flu that took Mama, back in '18, that blame epidemic flu. I guess I forgot to tell you. Must be a family trait, this absentmindedness. It's really something, isn't it, Brother?" Japheth lifted the derby, swiped the back of his forearm against his brow as if to wipe sweat, though it was cold in the clearing, cold and stunned and silent. "Looks like there's just no end to what you don't know about your wife."

"Shut up," Althea said.

Japheth turned his slitted gaze on her. "She came back to see us one time," he said. "Wagging a sack of horehound candy. Lord, we scrambled and fought over that junk. I was just a little bitty thing, but I remember." He seemed to be addressing an invisible audience, but his eyes never left Althea's face. "I guess she was already on her way to being a *fine* lady. You ought to see how she lives now. Got a big fancy white house in Tulsa, got her own personal nigger. That's true. She's got a pretty nigger maid'll do just whatever you order her to do. Man, if I had one of them, I'd eat breakfast in bed every morning. I surely would. I used to dream about that, somebody to do all my work for me. We worked hard, all us kids. We had to. Daddy took off and left before I was born, or that's what they tell me, I don't remember. Sure remember how we worked, though. Except Letha, of course. She was already gone."

He paused, scanned the men's faces. "She tried to kill me before she left," he said matter-of-factly. "I didn't know that for a long time. It's funny, I used to think there was something special about her because she was gone and nobody'd talk about her, and then she showed up that time with a sack of candy, looking so pretty to my four-year-old eyes, I guess, in that goosefeather hat. I thought she was my dream mama. I didn't know she'd tried to beat my head in. I don't guess anybody ever would have told me, I just heard it by accident. Learned right then it pays to keep your ears open. I come in from the barn one morning, Jody and Mama were in the kitchen screaming at each other. I was six then, maybe. Yeah, six. Mama's yelling, You're going to end up like your sister, and Jody's shouting back, I ain't like Letha! I never tried to kill a hours-old baby, for one thing! Well, of course, I didn't know they were talking about me. Jody's screaming, You did it, Mama, you put her up to it! and Mama's hissing, If you don't shut that smart mouth of yours I'm going to come over there with this skillet, and Jody yells, You know the reason Japheth ain't right in the head is because she dropped him on it the day he was born!"

His voice dropped to a suave whisper. "You know, that was a real revelation to me, all that news at once. I never knew they thought I wasn't right in the head. Mama wasn't yelling at all then, she was hardly whispering, I had to lean my ear close to the door—Mama's hissing, Shut up! She never dropped him!" Now Japheth's voice oscillated between a young girl's high-pitched whine and the rasp of an old crone: *"She did, Mama, she did!* Shut your mouth, girl! *She was going to beat his brains out! I saw her!* Get out of my sight before I snatch you baldheaded! *She had that ugly baby slung up over her head right over the rocks.* I'll shut it for you! *If that old Creek woman hadn't stopped her she was going to smash him like a gourd!* Shut up! Shut up! *I won't shut up! I saw it! She's wicked bad and good riddance to her, but I ain't like that, don't you dare say I am!*

"Hunh!" Japheth spat. "Saved by an Indian on the day I was born. That's funny, isn't it? Ugh. Meat. Bread." He gazed at his sister; his finely arched eyebrows, the feature that most declared his kinship to her, lifted in elegant contempt. "You remember them kids?"

"What do you want?" Althea rasped

"There's that blame question again. Well, I'll tell you. I want my share, that's all. Just my fair share. Now, a few weeks ago I was in for a third. Of course, that was before your husband here ran out of money and got in such a greedy big hurry, had to bring Murphy in to get hold of some capital." Japheth crooked his neck to peer up the eighty-foot derrick. "But Murphy's built us a pretty little rig here, hadn't he, Dedmeyer? I'm a reasonable man." His gaze passed slowly from one to another. "I'm willing to talk."

He started toward the Ford, but stopped abruptly, snapped his fingers. "Oh, you know, Brother, I been thinking. Hadn't you better let them know you never found that old niggerwoman? It's a shame to put all this money into a lease that's never been filed." His emollient voice rose in the clearing as he grinned up at Logan and Murphy. "Y'all don't believe me, go to the courthouse like I did and check." He clanged the car door shut, stuck his head out the open window. "Now, y'all please don't kill yourselves trying to sort out this mess of lies. I got some business to go see about." He tipped the filthy derby, started the motor; his eyes were on his sister when he called out over the noise of the motor, "After that, I'll be back."

J apheth drove away exulting, his insides raw with glee. He'd triumphed for an instant, and he suffered a kind of gnawing joy, but the winning wasn't complete. Its pleasures only whetted his hunger. The day was bright and cold, and he couldn't abide the thought of sitting alone in the thicket of brambles and riverwillows at his campsite. He drove on to Bristow, to a gin mill on the eastside, ordered a shot of white mule, stood at the bar eyeing the other drinkers as he savored the memory of the stunned, frightened faces on the derrick. He longed to have someone see how he'd beat them, his victory craved an audience, but the strangers at the bar couldn't bear witness; they didn't know what he'd been through. Japheth's mind turned to the final vanquishment. A dozen ways he dreamed it, and in every vision it was his own sly machinations that destroyed his enemies. He left his drink on the splintered wood, walked out blinking into the sunlight, got back into the murdered line-rider's Model T.

For the fourth time since September, he followed the rutted wagon road to Iron Post. The old woman was the last piece. As soon as he found her, he would have them all bested, completely. All of them.

The triumph was so real to him that he expected to see smoke rising from the rock chimney when he rounded the last bend. He was furious to find the old woman's cabin still empty. He sat in the car, thinking of the ways he would make her pay when he found her. She'd messed up his plans from the beginning, and his first plan had been so artful, so easy, because the driller had played right into it. Logan had blown the lease money almost as soon as Dedmeyer gave it to him, spent the whole two hundred on casing like an old sot on whiskey, and Japheth had been able to jump in, offer to fix it with the old woman. The plan, of course, was to claim the lease himself, but he'd been willing to bide his time, wait for the drilling to progress, because Japheth was no idiot: he was glad to let Delo foot the bill. For over a week he'd had Logan in his palm, would have had that horse's ass Dedmeyer, and so, finally, Sister herself, just exactly where he wanted, but the old niggerwoman showed up in a wagon with a dirty Indian, so that Logan started asking questions. Japheth had had to come out with the damn Delo lease, try to get her to sign it, in order to make the driller shut up—and the old woman had sat in her chair and stared at him, her nigger face closed; there'd been cunning in her, he thought, and stubbornness—but no submission, no fear. He was livid, he could have killed her right then, but he was too smart.

Instead, he came back the next night with a few sticks of dynamite for persuasion. When the bitch cur started toward him, growling and snapping, he blew a gratifying hole in her belly with Koop's twelve-gauge, and the other dogs yelped and took off. He crawled under the cabin and set the dynamite charges, and then went to hide in a nearby oak thicket till the old nigger should come home. It had poured rain all night, but he'd kept waiting, until dawn, until noon, until he knew she wasn't coming, and the hunger and fury and wet misery had driven him out of the timber, back to the Deep Fork, and as he bumped and slogged along the muddy road in Logan's tin lizzie, he'd promised himself that, when she did come, he would kill her.

The third time had been the day after he strangled Nona. The bitch dog's carcass, rotted and half eaten in the yard, spoke to him before he got out of the car. He could see the old redbone on the porch, lying flat, its ribs showing. The hound whined a little, thumped its tail once when Japheth climbed the steps, but the dog was too weak with starvation to stand up. Japheth shot the redbone, not to put it out of its misery but out of spitting frustration, and he tore up the inside of the cabin for a warning, though his heart wasn't in it. Even then he'd had a feeling she wouldn't be back.

Now he sat in the stolen Ford and glared at the cabin, its very presence an affront to him. The bones of the bitch cur gleamed in the yard, white in the afternoon sun, scattered, the skull dragged off somewhere. Beneath the shade of the porch roof he could see matted red hide flattened against the porch slats, as if the redbone's liquefied flesh had melted into the wood. No, the old niggerwoman had not been here. She defied him, still. He climbed the cabin steps; the stench of animal decay, the odors of disintegration were like musk to him as he pushed open the door. The one dark room was in chaos, chairs broken, crockery smashed, how he'd left it, only covered now in cobwebs. The thought flitted that she might in fact be dead, as Dedmeyer was gambling on. No. Japheth wouldn't allow that Iola Tiger could be dead. It didn't fit his plans. He seized a coal-oil lantern from the mantel, broke the globe, sprinkled the kerosene, but there were only a few drops left in the reservoir, and so he went back outside and fetched the gasoline can from the turtlehull, and when he sloshed the fuel on the puncheon floor the scent of petroleum mixed with the other smells and rose up in a kind of intoxicating fume of power inside the cabin. He paused in the doorway, inhaled deeply, tossed a lit match, and ran.

He was standing in the yard, watching fire lick the log walls through the broken window, when the explosion came. The concussion thrust him back, a satisfying blow against his chest, surprising—he'd forgotten the dynamite charge under the house—and though the log cabin was too strong to be blown apart by such a small blast, the force of it opened holes in the floor and ceiling, and the wind rushed in and fed the fire. Japheth watched, arms folded, leaning against the Model T at a safe, thrilling distance, as the logs went up like tinder; he wished he'd set more than three sticks of dynamite under the cabin. He wished the old woman was still inside.

After a few minutes he took a pistol from under the front seat and hid in the blackjacks east of the burning cabin with a mind to pick off a few nigger neighbors when they showed up to put out the fire. But no one came, even though the smoke billowed black in the November sky, signaling over the treetops. Nothing happened. The flames roared a while, and then the fuel was used up, and the fire began to wane. Japheth grew bored, grew empty. There weren't even any dogs to kill. He got in the Model T, drove back to his campsite.

But something had changed. No longer could he bear to conceal himself in the brush, weaving plans. Sons of bitches didn't do what his mind dreamed they'd do anyhow. He tried to keep his thoughts focused, but inside Japheth two forces pulled against each other: one called him to his old pleasures of sly, scornful scheming; the other, birthed by the beating on the Murphys' moonlit lawn, rushing into him from the oilsoaked sands of the river, swelling as he'd squeezed the life from Nona's slim neck, called him to pure destruction.

The next morning he drove to Sapulpa, to the Creek County Courthouse, and found that Dedmeyer had already filed a forged lease. His mind boiled with outrage. A damn forged lease, of course it was forged, and Japheth would prove it to them, prove it to the courts—as soon as he'd tracked down the old freedwoman, got her to sign over to him every last lying drop. He would need her alive for that. He'd have to put his mind on where to find her. As he perused the record of filed leases, Japheth realized for the first time that Gypsy Oil, not Delo Petroleum, owned the leases on the abutting allotments. How had Dedmeyer let a thing like that slip past? Japheth smiled. A new plan began to unwind itself.

On the way back to Bristow he stopped at a juke joint near Kellyville, and throughout the afternoon he leaned on the bar, sipping choc beer, plotting, but he couldn't keep his mind on his plans. The more he drank of the thick, milky liquor, the more he kept seeing his sister's features, her black, scornful eyes and haughty sneer, or, in his mind's eye, he'd watch the driller's scowling face turn away from him, dismissing him in contempt. Japheth drank in silence, glaring now and then at some white man or Indian whose glance caught his attention; he dreamed a dark, unfocused vengeance, on the old niggerwoman who'd defied him, the toolie who'd held a shotgun on him, the two pompous husbands who'd tried to bully him. But the sweetest depths of his hatred centered on the one who'd beaten him bloody on the moonlit lawn, and on the other, the sister who had tried to smash his head in before a time he could remember.

By nightfall Japheth was back at the Deep Fork, hiding in the brush, watching. They were all still here, except Sister. The men stood in a small circle, warming themselves by a campfire. At first Japheth felt a kind of dull, half-drunken pleasure, seeing that Dedmeyer hadn't gone home with Aletha, but then he realized that his brother-in-law stayed, not because of Japheth's triumphant accusations, but because he expected the well to drill-in any moment. They all expected it. No one was willing to leave the rig, even to sleep.

Just after daylight, Japheth watched in impotent fury as Logan and Koop screwed on the control head, fit the Christmas tree. When the rumbling started in the earth's bowels and a spray of gas and oil began to siz-

zle around the drilling line, there was only hushed excitement on the derrick floor. The control head vibrated mightily, and the driller opened a
valve, slowly, and a stream of oil shot into the tank. Carefully, excruciat-
ingly slowly, Logan opened all the valves on the Christmas tree, but within
minutes he was shouting at Koop, "Shut her in! Shut her in!" The five-
hundred-barrel tank had filled in less than twenty minutes.

On the rig the men were weirdly quiet, eyeing one another, eyeing the
woods, as if they expected the very blackjacks to betray them, proclaim
their unprotected strike to the world.

They shut the well in till they got hold of more tankage, turned the oil
into the line so fast an outsider could believe nothing had happened—but
it was already too late. Within an hour of the strike Japheth was sitting in
Gypsy Oil's front office in Bristow, suggesting they might want to send a
scout to the Delo location at Section 35-T, 16-N, R8E, on the Deep Fork.
The next morning Gypsy recommenced drilling on the Yargee lease, a
half-mile west of the Delo location; this time they were making hole right
on the line.

Logan and his crew had to pull tools and rush over to where the two
Creek allotments joined one another; they had to start drilling offset wells
immediately, fifty yards across the line, because the law of capture said oil
belonged to whichever company pulled it up from the ground. Gypsy Oil
could siphon every drop from under Iola Tiger's allotment if Delo didn't
match each hole Gypsy drilled, rig for rig.

By week's end, Gypsy was spudding in their fifth well, and Dedmeyer
and Murphy had hired four new crews, and the drilling went on furiously
along the line, day and night.

Japheth hated to lose that amount of oil to Gypsy, but it was worth it,
his mind told him, to get Delo away from the original location. Fools
might hunt uselessly in the hidden places forever, but Japheth knew—had
known as he watched the first greenish-black spewings around the
drilling line—where the old niggerwoman would finally show up.

An old hen will steal her nest out, won't she? Lay her eggs in the hay meadow, way up in the barn rafters, anywhere she think that farmer can't find them. Her mind say, Them's *my* eggs, I'm going to hide my eggs till my little chicks come. Un huh. That is just what I done. I couldn't steal the Lord's earth out from under them whitemens, so what am I going to do but steal out myself? For a long time after the dark one leave that morning, I just sit on my porch, thinking. Afterwhile I gets up and walks off from that house where I lived with Bluford in all our time together, my own Bluford, leave the dogs whining in the yard, just step off the porch and walk away. I wasn't afraid. I know how whitemens will set dynamite, knock a person in the head, do whatever they want to get hold of lease rights, but fear is not how come me to leave. The greed-devil got hold of me, that's what.

I come down to Boley and stay awhile with my daddy, but you think I tell my own daddy what I'm about? No sir. I don't tell a breathing soul. I do not tell God. That's how the spirit will do when it's been corrupted, and here is the full power of corruption: you don't have to have them little eggs in your hand, you only got to dream them, your mind say, *They mine.* Seven times seven days I lived in that narrow twisted greed place, look like this in my soul: burnt up, hungry, twisty pig trails going around and around in they same tracks, saying *Mine*, saying *Now*, saying, *Give me,* saying, *They, They, They,* saying *Hate* and *More* and *Too Late.* I quit doing the work the Lord have set for me. How am I going to help a child come in the world when my whole brain is eat up with lies? My mind telling me like this, say, That's *my* land, allotted to me by the U.S. federal government, what's in it and on it and under it supposed to be *mine.* Mind say, They haven't got my mark on the white piece of paper, let's just wait now. We going to bide our time, hide out in Boley and wait on them. When that oil come spouting out the ground they going to wish they did bring me my money, because we fixing to go right back there with our own piece of paper, see what kind of smile these whitemens got for theyself. Who's this *we* I'm talking about? Me and the greed-devil, I believe.

Weather turn cold finally, and my mind say, They bound to have got it by now, and I prepares myself to go. How? By right doing and right thinking and right praying? No ma'am. By calling on the Lord's power, how He have given it in medicine, in tobacco and cedar smoke and prayer? Never cross my mind to think about purification. All I'm thinking is how to get me a lawyer. A *lawyer,* child, that is what I got my crazy mind on. Quick as I get a good look at that oil, I'm going to go up to Tulsa, find me a colored lawyer knows just how to work whiteman's law. My mind whispering, Hurry. Go yonder and see what they doing. Hurry. Catch them stealing your oil out from your native earth.

So. I proceed on back to the Deep Fork, and this time everything change. I come alone, come walking. I taken the train up from Boley, because nobody going to notice a lone colored woman riding in the colored car, and I thinks at Bristow I'll hire a buggy to carry me out to that place on the river. But when I climb down off the train I see that Bristow town is just wild with the greed-hunger, whitemens everywhere, noisy, rushing, they all in a fearsome hurry, seem like any direction I look is a danger. Seem like every person I see, colored, white, or Indian, is scheming to steal my oil money. You see how the greed-devil got me? I ought to been afraid of so many things, all I'm scared of is somebody going to take from me. I never once question how I get to thinking so strange. That day's a cold, gray day, look like it's fixing to sleet or spit rain or something, and I don't know what I'm going to do when I get yonder, but I don't want to join up with nobody. Nobody. My mind say, All right, we going to walk.

Trucks and wagons pass me, carrying pipes and lumber and big machine tools, they all going the same way I'm going, headed south. My mind say, See now, they carrying these things yonder to steal what rightfully belong to you, and I walk faster, choking in the cold dust from them trucks. Way down past the Little Deep, I come off the road, set out across the prairie. I don't aim to go by Iron Post, just go quiet around it, like you'd sneak past a sleeping yard dog. My mind won't let me think on Bluford, won't let me think on my house. Rain come finally, a cold fretsome rain, spitting needles at my face, I go in a empty barn shack, stay there all night listening to that freezing rain peck the tin roof. I am cold, I'm wet, hungry, miserable, miserable—but you look at the power of that force: next morning I go right back to that frozen mud-rutted road, set my face toward the Deep Fork again.

Late next day is when I come to the place where the road divide. Me and Istidji never seen no fork such as that one; these whitemens have cut a new road, and the many stumps are still raw where the trees have been hacked down. Off somewhere at the end of it is that terrible *bang bang bang bang*, and not one but many, yes, Lord, many, many, layered over each other like a great thunder. The old fork is the one that twist down to the river, where Istidji carry me that long time back. That's the road I take. Night is coming, and I am far from my peoples, far from home, far, far from my Lord. Let me tell you something, God have made no more haunted place on His earth than the Deep Fork bottoms at nightfall, but I keep walking on.

By the time I reach the water, the sky is darkening purple, the woods are turning black, but I can see a timber ladder rising like it want to climb up to heaven. It is no Jacob's ladder, though, I know that for true. The wheel-in-a-wheel is gone. That pounding sound still booming soft through the treetops, way off west, but the clearing is quiet—not ordinary cold winter quiet, but more like something have gone out of the world. I stand back, just looking. Nobody around. Whitemens can't find it. That's what my mind say. They have quit pounding here because there's no oil under my earth. And, oh, the grief come on me, a terrible, unnatural grief.

Low and rushing then, finally, I hears it, a steady humming. The clearing is quiet, but it is not silent. Listen. Hear it? *Hmmmmmmmm.* The earth's pulse. *Hmmmmmmmm.* That's the sound of the world's blood pumping, pumping, up from the core through steel tubes into pipes into them huge round tanks hulked off in the distance. No kind of machine is pumping it: that oil is coming up through the power of its own force. Oh, they have found it all right, tapped the earth's bones, un-huh, and that black blood spewed forth, and now they siphoning it into pipes, into tanks, they going to try and hold it, but that force is not tamed.

Well, well, a voice say, look who's here. He step out from behind the sky ladder. You sure saving me a lot of trouble, old woman.

He look different, eaten away, the bones in his face sharp, his skin lighter, like a man locked away from the sun, like a jailed man. But the eaten-away look is not the whole change. He stand back, peer all around the clearing, up the road behind me, eyes squinched down to slits nearly, he say, How'd you get here? The light is drained away, but I can see his face floating like a ghost face. He keep studying the road behind me. You came out here by yourself, didn't you? he say, and then he start toward me.

I feel that hunger force, the greed rising, and something else, but I can't name it, swelling in that clearing.

They take me for a fool, he say. He talk soft, coming toward me. You ever heard of fool's gold, old woman? They got a million dollars' worth of fool's black gold. He stop sudden, listening. You hear that? he whisper.

I think he's talking about the low earthpulse under that sky ladder, but, no, he look off behind the trees, where the pounding is coming from, over west.

Know what that is? he say. Night drilling. Guess where.

He stare past me at the empty road. A smile slice his face then, a cold, white thing in the darkness. He turn and look at me. Tell me something, old woman. What would it take to get that driller to walk off from a hole, come down here where I want him?

An owl start up hooting then, way off in the shadows by the water, and my soul is frightened, it sense something so terrible, so awful, it want to shrink down.

He keep looking at me, say, They're sure going to be surprised to see you. His smile look like a pale glowing fishbelly in the dark. In my mind I see a half-blueblack half-fishwhite baby. I see a great mound of white flesh, moving, crawling, I see blood and water, red dust swirling in high wind. Everything fall together inside me, and I see that misshapen infant I taken out his sister's hands. That same one.

Now—now, when it is too late—I'm going to know him.

My mind full of every picture, the little foxface girl running, shrieking, so I got to turn back, go quick to the ravine behind that house, see the darkhair middling girl raising up that blighted baby, she holding him over her head, to smash him, smash that infant down to the earth. In my mind I cry out, how I cried in Creek language that gray noontime twenty years ago, No!

His long white fishhand come from behind him, where he been hiding it, he's holding a coiled rope. See, old woman? he whisper. I knew you'd come.

I try to turn, try to get away from that place, but he flip the rope around me so fast I can't run. He cinch my arms down, pull the rope tight, and take to shoving me up the road, to the place where the road curve, push me against a post oak at the edge, wrap that rope around, tying me to the tree. All while he's wrapping, he talk soft and steady, not to me, though. He's talking like he got people listening inside his head. He's saying about it would of been so easy, he wasn't in no hurry, he had them fools right in his hand, and on and on. In my mind I see that dressed-up whitewoman in my dooryard, see her scrawny backside, how she turn and walk away. I see blood up and down the front of that little muslin dress. The same one. They both two the same. My whole self is shaking. I can feel that power-force swelling. I don't know what it is.

He knot the rope, step back. It's full dark now, I can't hardly see him. When his voice come it is like the night talking, and the sound is flat, no rise or fall to it, he say, You're going to sign this. I can see a white flutter, he's holding out a piece of paper. Right in front of those fools, he say, in your own ignorant nigger-hand. He lean toward me, breathe on me his breath that have no smell. I know then he don't know me, or he don't know me for the birthwoman who saved him. He only know me for a freedwoman been allotted this cursed piece of Deep Fork-bottom land. He whisper, You and me's fixing to drive up to Bristow this evening. You're going to tell the law just exactly what I tell you to say.

Then he turn and walk off.

I am caught in a deep place, trying to know what my soul is feeling. I am trembling now, oh Lord, in my soul. It's not death I'm afraid of—death is so close it breathe on me, too, but death going to carry me to my Saviour, I'm not afraid to die. What make me so scared is what I feel rising in the clearing, swelling, I don't know what it is—not evil, my mind say. Evil born of the spirit, it's a spirit force. This force here come from the material world. There under the sky ladder, that hole yonder: that is where the force pour into the world.

Over in the dark by the river I hears a little boom, and then a great whoosh, and one of them big tanks lights afire. That whole clearing turn bright as noon—I sees him walking back toward me, slow in the road, swinging his arms like he got all the time in the world. He have a knife in his hand, I can see the light glint on it. He stop in front of me.

We got us a little wait, he say.

Off west I can hear motorcars coming, and when they get near, he cut the rope, fast as anything, go to push me out to the road. Here come a long black car roaring around the curve, and behind it two trucks, coming fast. They all got to stop sudden, squealing, because us two standing in the middle of the road. That yellowhair man, Mister Dedmeyer, he jump out, come running up fast, and behind him is the lighthair Logan, and the little redhair banty man, they all running, other whitemens jump off the two trucks, everybody cussing, shouting.

The dark one stand still, smiling, he got that knife point stuck against me. Now the yellowhair man get close enough to see me. He stop cold. The others stop behind him. Everybody get quiet. I hear the fire now, like a roaring, feel the heat on my back.

Much obliged y'all come to help me, the dark one say.

Move out of the way, Mister Dedmeyer say.

The dark one start in to talk about me like I'm a stump, say, Ain't you even going to mention what I got here? Found her right here at the location, ain't that strange?

Mister Dedmeyer won't look at me. He shout about they got to get in there, that separator's fixing to go. The lighthair man, Logan, take a step forward, but the dark one lift up the knife, say, Naw, now, I wouldn't. And Mister Logan stand still.

The dark one keep talking, like he can't stop hisself, like he been sitting out here in the haunted bottoms so long his mouth want to boil over with words. He talking 'bout it's a dirty shame this poor old nigger ain't seen a drop of lease money. Yonder's her well, he say, you people can't find it in your hearts to pay her a red cent.

He put the knife to me, right up against my belly. I can feel the point of it touching. That's all right, though, he say. She's done signed this lease here. And he wave that piece of paper in his other hand, like a weapon, like it have its own power, like I already put my mark on it. But that piece of paper is not the power. The dark one sneer at the whitemens, say, Ain't I told you people Dedmeyer's a liar? That lease at the courthouse is a fake. It ain't got Iola Tiger's mark on it. Am I right, old woman? Right? And he push the knife against me, slip it like a silver flash against me. But that knife is not what cause me to tremble.

Mister Dedmeyer say, Somebody shoot that son of a so and so, we got to get in there.

But the others don't move.

See, now, the dark one say, that's how it is. Folks aren't usually just jumping to risk their lives on a fire ain't theirs.

That lease is worthless, Mister Dedmeyer call out. And then he start talking all about how I can't make no such decision on account of I'm crazy and I'm ignorant and I ain't got good sense. He say he already got me declared, he's my guardian, I can't sign a thing without his say-so.

But I hold my peace, trembling. It don't matter what that yellowhair say. Don't matter if I put my mark on that paper or don't put it, don't matter if any one of us standing in that road lives or dies. Because I know now what my soul feel pouring through that clearing: it is two forces joined together—the spirit force of evil and that power from under the earth, joined together. I feels them, united, pulsing up from below, unleashing a terrible destruction into the world.

They's another little boom sound then, and another tank lights up, *whoosh*, and the other whitemens all take off running back to the trucks, motors start, they're yelling, shouting, and the front three, Logan and Dedmeyer and the redhair, they stand still one second, and then they too turn and run. The dark one let me loose. He have forgot all about me. I feels that knife point just fall away. He's jumping up and down in the road, cursing, shouting, waving that white piece of paper. Them trucks fixing to drive over him, look like, trying to get to where that oil is burning. I just turn and walk away. Go into the brush like maybe I can hide there. But I can't hide. Can't nobody hide anymore.

T he winter stretched before her, interminable, hopeless, moving toward a spring she neither expected nor desired. She thought it would last forever: endless ugly gray days strung together with jeweled afternoons of brilliant sun and sudden warmth. On the bright days in particular, Althea took to her bed. She ordered new heavy damask drapes to replace the lace curtains at the window. Perhaps once a week she roused sufficiently to put on the veiled hat and take a cab to the Exchange National Bank to draw funds; she portioned out the money to Graceful for the shopping. From time to time she'd appear at the bottom of the stairs and bark a few orders, tell Graceful to polish the teakwood and silver, or she'd slip into the library and stand with one hand draped along the ebony curve of the telephone, her eyes gazing in the middle distance as she tried to think of whom she wanted to call.

But a life lived on a lie, once the lie is extracted, becomes remarkably flaccid, limp of purpose, soft and tenebrous around the hole where the lie stood. Mostly Althea read in her bedroom, sensational novels that held no threat of edification or truth. She'd draped the mahogany mirror. That trick had come about by accident one evening when she flung her silk robe against the wall and it inadvertently landed on the vanity, but the relief was so enormous that she'd left the robe across the mirror's face for three days before replacing it with a triple-folded swatch of the lace curtain that had once filtered light at the window.

Downstairs, Graceful went about her duties in a kind of leaden remoteness. She was grateful that the woman stayed in her room, but with the husband gone there was too little to do. Mrs. Dedmeyer hardly ate enough to justify heating the stove; the woman wore the same dressing gown for days on end, so there was almost no laundry to put through the Eden, and she no longer tracked in mud from the garden, so that the kitchen floor stayed clean for a week after Graceful mopped and waxed it. Often Graceful would find herself standing at the back door, staring out, unseeing, as her mind explored the interior of her body. One noon in the third week of December, she felt the child move. A faint flutter, like mothwings, like delicately batting lashes, but it was inside her: inside her, and separate from her, and one with her. Living. Her soul tore.

Christmas came and went, a day of hurtful sun and church bells pealing in the distance, along Boston Avenue downtown. Mrs. Dedmeyer didn't seem to notice its passing, but Graceful was aware every minute of the day's meaning. She prepared the woman's breakfast (which would be left entirely untouched on the tray outside the bedroom door: the only sign Althea was aware of the date), seeing in her mind pictures of her mama and sisters and brothers in the house on North Elgin, the rush and secrets and cooking and Willie hanging at the table, saying, How much longer, Mama, how long? Graceful hadn't cried since the afternoon by the creek near Bigheart, but on Christmas Day her insides cramped and raged and trembled, and she thought if grief could kill the unwanted thing inside her this day's hurt would kill it, and she surrendered to the ferocity of the pain, guiltily, in that awful hope. But the next morning, when she got up to light the stove, the eyelash heartbeat flutter yet quivered in her belly, the living life. It was then that Graceful sat down at the little table against the wall inside the kitchen and wept.

She was sitting just there, again, many days later—how much later? Two weeks? A month? After the year turned, the days flowed one into another without definition. But she was sitting just the same way, her hand on her womb, touching the swelling mound as she stared out at the gray, cold porch, when she sensed Mrs. Dedmeyer standing in the passage. Graceful didn't flinch; for some minutes she didn't even bother to glance up. The woman's silent, sneaking approaches had always been the condition of working in this house. Graceful expected a feeble carping: Mrs. Dedmeyer's tirades now were faded, toothless; they barely irritated.

Woman need to eat more, Graceful thought indifferently. *She 'bout to dry up.* But Mrs. Dedmeyer didn't speak, and at last Graceful looked up. The woman was staring quizzically at her, a sort of half-distracted, half-interested gaze.

Slowly Graceful rose from the chair, stood waiting beside the little table. The black skirt of the maid's uniform rode up toward her breasts, and she reached to smooth it down. "Ma'am?" she said at last.

But the woman remained silent, staring at her as if she only half perceived her, as if in the back of her mind she calculated something. "My word," she said at last, faintly, the sound drawn out in a kind of distant wonder.

Don't tell me she don't know, Graceful thought. Each morning when she delivered the linen-covered tray upstairs, she waited for the woman to say something, but Mrs. Dedmeyer only asked about the mail, any telephone calls; often she didn't speak at all but merely motioned impatiently for Graceful to set the tray down and leave. *Take a blind woman not to know.*

Blind was the choice word. On some level Althea had known, yes—she'd perceived it even as far back as the Murphys' party, when she'd seen the softening in Graceful's face—but she had no willingness to receive it. Now, sunk since November in the blue misery that desired neither light nor air nor food nor future, she was blind to all the world, including, perhaps most especially, Graceful herself. But the accident of coming upon her in that classic gesture, hand touching swollen belly, a sign she'd seen her own mother make so many times, forced the unwanted knowledge into Althea's cobwebby brain. She narrowed her eyes. "Graceful?" she said at last. "When's that baby due?"

Graceful gazed ahead, mouth closed.

"Have you made arrangements?" At the girl's continuing silence Althea swept into the kitchen, crossed the gleaming white floor. She stopped a few feet away, eyeing Graceful's skirt. "Looks fairly soon to me."

"Not soon." Graceful had never reckoned the exact time, because reckoning would force her back to the night of the seed's planting; she refused it. All she carried were the vague words: *when warm weather come.* It was not warm now but a day of sleety rain changing to all-rain changing back to sleet, a slate day that had seemed all day to grow darker. *She going to make me go, on a spitty day of cold rain. That's how she do.* "You be wanting supper, ma'am?" she said dully. The woman's appetite was so fitful that Graceful had quit trying to predict it, just prepared what she wanted for herself, dished up a small amount on a fine china plate and carried it upstairs. Sometimes the woman ate; sometimes she didn't.

"Why . . . yes." Althea's voice was surprised. "Yes. I believe I will have a little something. Just a bite. Graceful?" Her tone softened, became hollow, less true, but infinitely nicer. "Is the fa— Do you have somebody to take the baby? I guess you've taken care of things?" She'd almost said *father*, but she didn't want to shut the girl's face even tighter; she didn't want to acknowledge anything of the girl's separate life. She wanted only to hear that arrangements had been made, that this bump in the monotony of her own existence would quickly be rolled over, smoothed down. Well, that was how other people's live-in help did, wasn't it? Left their offspring with relatives or . . . somebody . . . and stayed through the week in the servants' quarters over the garage or in the maid's room, returned to Little Africa on Thursdays and Sundays to tend to their own. Some did. Most did. "Are you—" She couldn't bring herself to finish the sentence: *going to leave me?*

"I got a fryer cut up in the icebox," Graceful said. "Do chicken sound good to you?"

"Chicken'll be fine. Not fried, though, chicken and dumplings, how you used to make them for Mr. Dedmeyer." Althea frowned; a shadow passed behind her eyes. She put a hand to her temple, stood quite still, breathing deeply through her nostrils. When she spoke again her voice was low, well modulated; she didn't look at Graceful, but her tone was direct. "I don't know if Mr. Dedmeyer . . . I don't know what's going to happen. What I mean is, where, or, that is . . . how are you going to . . . have the baby? I mean, are you going to go . . . Do you people . . . have midwives or . . . ? What I'm trying to say, if you . . . Will you have to go back to colored town?" She was pained, embarrassed.

But there the question was in the damp air of the kitchen: the very question that Graceful herself had skeered away from, dreaded, lain awake nights asking without ever reaching an answer.

"I don't know, ma'am."

"What do you mean, you don't know? What do colored girls usually do?"

Graceful continued to stand with her face lifted, nostrils flared; her eyes canted toward Althea for an instant. What did the woman think, having babies was different for colored women? At last she muttered, "Some have a midwife. Some go to the doctor. Some just . . . have they child."

Another moment of silence passed. The freezing rain ticked at the porch roof. Althea shivered, drew her wrapper around herself. She looked out the window. In this cold rain Franklin would be . . . What would he be doing now? There'd been no word since his telegram saying there'd been some trouble in the field, a rig fire; he'd arranged for her to draw an allowance at the Exchange National Bank. The wire mentioned nothing about him coming home. Althea's gaze remained on the fogged glass as she asked vaguely, "What about you?"

"I haven't made up my mind. Just deal with it . . . when it come along. That's all."

Althea's full attention returned to Graceful. "You can't do that. You have to plan for it. I mean, doesn't a doctor have to see you or something? You can't just call them up out of the clear blue . . . ?" But her thoughts trailed away. Perhaps they could. Perhaps that was the way colored people did things. "Well," she said, and crossed the floor briskly to the sink, trying to dismiss from her mind the declarative fact that her own mother never made plans for childbirth; for Rachel Whiteside, in the four pregnancies that Aletha Jean as middle child could remember, the birthwoman had come only once.

Althea jerked the spigot on fullforce, and the rusty water gushed. She held her hands under the stream, spoke loudly over her shoulder. "You have to give me some notice. You know you can't just go off and leave me." She splashed her face with the cold water, elbowed the spigot closed, stood with her hands and face dripping. Her teeth were chattering. She wore only the thin silk gown and wrapper. Suddenly she looked down at the dark splotches where the water streaked the blue silk. When had she last dressed herself? Washed her hair? What if Franklin should come home and see her like this? Oh, she'd have to draw a bath; she would put on the rosepink tea dress. She would have Graceful come up right away, freshen the bedroom—dear God, when was the last time that girl changed the sheets?

Rousing herself to start snapping orders, Althea turned, and was surprised to see Graceful still standing in the too-tight maid's uniform, still staring at the floor in silence, her face closed in the old manner. The girl's hand was on her distended belly; it was not a tender gesture but more a tentative prying, the way one's fingers return again and again to a half-healed sore. Graceful's face lifted; she met her gaze.

Without words, facial tic, gesture, the knowledge passed between them: not the full truth, not the abhorred name of the father, but even to Althea's self-absorbed mind Graceful's dread and wretchedness were plain, and she understood that there was no husband, no boyfriend. "Graceful? You don't have to go back to Greenwood." She tried to make her voice sound efficient, empathetic, though it feathered out almost wistful. "Wouldn't a colored doctor come here? I mean, it could be here, as far as I'm concerned. You could have it here."

The girl didn't answer. After a moment she dropped her hand away from her womb, crossed the floor to the icebox. "You want your supper upstairs?"

"No. No. The dining room will be fine," Althea said. She stayed in the kitchen, watched Graceful moving slowly, methodically, mixing flour, rolling dumplings between her palms, and in the back of Althea's throat there was a tense, relieved satisfaction.

From the cocoon of her darkened room Althea emerged, if not transformed, at least focused on the world in a new way. In the few seconds of wordless exchange, when she'd recognized not just the girl's pain but their mutual isolation, their dependence on each other, Althea received a new purpose. She told herself that she would, magnanimously, allow the girl to stay here and have her bastard child. She would, in fact, help her. The next morning, she went to the Ladies Auxiliary League and procured several lying-in dresses, a bit faded and threadbare perhaps, but perfectly serviceable. She bought a new feathertick to put on Graceful's cot, that the girl might sleep more comfortably, and she told Graceful to order an extra quart of milk from the milkman every other day—And drink it, if you please, you'll lose a tooth. Althea's old vision of herself as a patroness of benevolence and grace returned, but this, too, was changed, tempered by the puzzling sadness that would well up from time to time, surprising her, flooding her chest as she watched the girl work.

More than once Graceful wished the woman would take to her bed again and shut the door. Althea no longer appeared out of nowhere in little catsneak creepings; she openly followed Graceful around, not issuing orders as before, but solicitously directing her in how to do things, getting in the way. She didn't lessen Graceful's load—in fact, her emergence from the bedroom caused more work than Graceful'd had to do through all the late autumn and winter—but she often trailed behind her saying, "Here, let me get that." When Graceful hoisted a heavy laundry basket to her hip,

Althea would grasp one handle awkwardly, bump Graceful's hips or belly, nearly force her out the door backward, or she'd walk ahead of her and limply hold open the screen. Yet in some ways Graceful was glad for the whitewoman's company. At least she, Graceful, no longer had to sit alone in the kitchen for hours, thinking, or trying not to think. And when she lay down at night she was too exhausted from the day's work and the demands of the growing baby to lie staring into the darkness. Her most immediate dread had been assuaged: for a little while longer she would not have to find another place. She could stay at the Dedmeyers' until it came.

And then there was that: the indefinite pronoun shared. In the same way that siblings in a family with a violent father might never put a name to the force that rules every breath but refer only in low tones, without need of explanation, to "he," just so "it" dominated the lives of the two women. Each took the oblique pronoun to mean, equally, the unborn child in the womb, the newborn when it should finally get here, and the event of the birth itself: an unseeable and unknowable future fated "it." They seldom spoke the word aloud, but it was the shared unspoken knowledge of an unnamed force, and it silently joined them.

Spring came early and hard, not stealing slowly, fitfully awake, but bursting fullblown out of the southwest, ferocious with nightstorms, blustery with daywinds, and by the second week in March the redbud trees had bloomed all over the city, and by the third week the beautiful blossoms were gone, ripped from the trees by the violent wind, skittering in tiny magenta flutters along the paved and unpaved streets, bleeding in matted wavelike piles soaked by the plunging rains. Graceful seemed with each passing day to grow slower in her movements, more calm, or perhaps she was merely in a stupor: she seemed to move as through a swamp, her very center of gravity settling deeper and deeper, sucked down toward the earth. But Althea grew more restless. Daily she paced the house, unable to settle on something to do, and as the weather warmed she grew increasingly frightened. The sun had returned, but her husband had not. Still she had no word from him; she had tried calling the Laurel Hotel in Bristow, but they said there was no Mr. Dedmeyer registered there. She pored over the oil reports in the newspapers; she knew the Deep Fork field had been fully defined, that it was producing fifteen thousand barrels a day for Delo and Gypsy, a good strike, though it was no Burbank or Glenn Pool: it wasn't the big one. Why wouldn't he come home? The only way she knew he was still alive was by how the bills were always paid, and when she went to the bank on Mondays to draw her household funds for the week, that precise amount, and no more, was in the account, along with a terse note signed in Franklin's hand for her to be allowed to withdraw it.

At first Althea kept her fears fused in her mute bones, and only at night, in her room alone, did she give in to them. Then she would stand at the undraped window and shake her fists at the passing storms, or pace up and down, cursing under her breath. But she did not take to her bed again. In the daytime she'd sit in the swing on the side porch, gazing at the clustered dandelions and tender poke shoots erupting all over her rose garden, telling herself she was to begin weeding today, this very afternoon, but always she would end by going into the house and calling out some mindless chore for Graceful. Their lives were so unvaried, so mired in the routine of meals neither cared to eat and a too-big house shined and mopped and waxed which no guest ever entered, and their turgid conversations were so mutually understood, so internally referential and plain, that the two women were like an old married couple. "That do?" Graceful would say, meaning, *Is this sideboard polished to suit you?* or *Is that all the laundry you want done?* or *You want toast with your eggs this morning? I don't aim to mix biscuits*, and Althea would nod or murmur "Fine," or perhaps "No," or "Once more, if you don't mind." Althea might say, "It's going to be too late for Easter, I think," or "Weather's going to be hot as sin by the time it gets here," meaning the child and the impending birth, and Graceful would not even bother to nod but would simply acquiesce or deny with her dense, torpid silence. Eventually Althea began to speak about Franklin.

Her words were cryptic at first, as elliptical as their other exchanges, though more nervously rendered; she would say things like, "You'd think he'd have finished by now. Wouldn't you think he'd be tired of hanging around that trashy town?" or "I'll bet he'd give anything for one of your fried pies. Doesn't it look like he could come home on Sundays? At least?" and, later, "There were some things I shouldn't have done," and, finally, "He won't forgive me. I'm afraid he's not ever going to come back. He . . . might not come back. Oh, Graceful, what am I going to do?"

Graceful never answered, never commented, but received, unruffled, in that placid pool of her seeming equanimity, what Althea told her. She had her own troubling thoughts, and they paralleled Althea's and contrasted them, thoughts that said she ought to phone the *Star* office this morning, just speak to Hedgemon a minute or two, see if he'd heard anything from T.J. Maybe she could ask him to go by Mama, go see the children a little while, so he could tell her how they looked, how they were. Then she'd catch a glimpse of her ever larger and larger self in the library mirror, and the impulse to telephone Hedgemon would vanish. If she called, he would ask to see her. If she called, he might refuse to keep picking up her letters from the post box and carrying them to Mama. Often she'd gaze down at herself, saying silently, *After it come*, meaning in an inverted way, *after it's gone*, as if the act of birth would wipe out all her troubles.

The sixteenth day of May was sweltering, with a gauzy haze of sunlight that shimmered all around the house, veiled the street, hid the full length of the garden. Althea had gone so far as to don her gardening dress and dig her sunhat out of the hall closet, but at ten o'clock in the morning she still sat in the porch swing, fanning herself with it. Inside the house she could hear Graceful moving slowly through the dining room with the dustmop, *thump* and, feebly, *thump*, and after a long while a faint little *tump*. Then she heard the dustmop handle crack against the wood floor at the same instant Graceful cried out.

Althea cursed herself as she hurried through the French doors, for of course she knew what it was, as she'd known all along that this moment would come, and never, damn her for a thoughtless fool, had she prepared for it, really. Her mind flew through all the possibilities she'd dreamed up and never settled on, and she stopped on the opposite side of the walnut table. The girl's back rose and fell in shuddery breaths as she leaned on the breakfront, resting her full weight on the polished wood. After a long while Graceful straightened, stood up tall, but she didn't turn. The two looked at each other in the mirror.

"Well," Althea said, the word at once a flat comment, a question, and a kind of chagrined shrug. Graceful answered only with her steady gaze, but between them passed the wordless acknowledgment that, yes, her time had come, and then she was cramped with a fresh pain. She tried to hold the sound inside, but the sound and the pain were one, and, gasping, she let the sound loose, a sharp high cry, as if that would spew out the pain, but the pain went on stretching and closing and clamping, and she cried out even louder, a near scream; she heard the sound as if it did not belong to her mouth. The pains had been coming since before dawn, low, grasping her insides, like her monthly gone mad, or like she needed to empty herself, and she'd entered the little bathroom a dozen times, but that couldn't help. She'd tried to keep on working through them, because motion helped, or it seemed to help, and she'd been able, through the morning, to hold in the sound, but the pains had moved around to her backside now, and they were worse, twisting, cramping, stabbing her spine; she wanted to bend over with them, but she was too big to bend. She leaned on the breakfront again. From a great distance she heard the whitewoman's voice.

"What do you want me to do? Do you want me to call a doctor? What doctor? Give me a name!"

The pain ebbed, fell away, was gone finally. Graceful stood once more on her own weight, panting slightly.

"I told you we had to make some arrangements," Althea snapped. She came around the table. Graceful was nudging the head of the fallen dust-mop out from under the breakfront with her foot; grunting a little, she leaned over as if to reach down and pick it up. "What are you doing? Give me that! Jesus." Althea snatched up the dustmop, leaned it against the wall. "Well?" she said. "Here we are. What did I tell you?"

She was furious that she had not made a plan—or that was not quite true, she'd made several plans, she'd simply not settled on any. She'd toyed with the idea of calling Dr. Taylor, but she was almost certain he would not treat a colored girl, and what if there should be a problem? No colored person could be admitted to Hillcrest or to any other white hospital in town. A white doctor was no good. She'd thought of bringing in the handsome light-skinned doctor who had bandaged her feet; she didn't know where he was, but she could find her way to the newspaper office and the editor would tell her. Good God, no, what was she thinking? She was not going to go traipsing into Little Africa again, that was out of the question. Sometimes, though, she found herself imagining the yellow shotgun house, seeing herself on the front porch at the door, the dark woman from the photograph, wearing the same elegant white turn-of-the-century dress, standing inside the screen, and Althea speaking to her, warmly, urgently, saying, Your daughter's in my home; she needs you. But no. If Graceful wanted her mother, she would have gone to her. Althea understood very well that the girl did not want her mother. She'd questioned her several times about a colored midwife who might be willing to come, but the brown face would instantly close down, and Graceful would murmur something like, I got to aks around.

Well, it was only a baby, good Lord, women had been having babies since the beginning of time. This colored girl did not need a doctor; she probably didn't even need a birthwoman. But what if something went wrong? What if the baby got stuck? What if—? Thoughts of the actual labor would erupt, always, into memories of the one terrible birth Althea had witnessed, and immediately she had to reduce everything to that vague future "it": she would turn her mind to the weedy garden, the cherry banister that needed oil, something, anything, in order not to see. And so they'd never decided on anything, never made the proper arrangements, and now here the goose was trying to have her baby in Althea's immaculate dining room, and the old returning visions of fluid and blood roared through her, and she said, "Get in the bed! This minute. You can't have it standing up like an old milk cow."

The girl groaned and leaned on the breakfront again, and the groan grew louder, grew high-pitched and shrill; it frightened Althea. The cry became a howl, a gaping, wordless wail that rose in union with the pain, and Althea said, "Come on!" Terrified lest water and blood pour down on her beautiful polished hardwood floor, as it had poured down on her mother's roseprint rug, as it had poured from between her mother's legs, darkening the red earth beneath her mother's feet, Althea shouted again, "Come!" She tried to take the girl's hand pressed to the breakfront, and Graceful instantly grabbed her fingers, gripping like the clamp of teeth, squeezing until Althea herself yelped with pain, and still Graceful held on—gradually, slowly easing her clench as the wave passed.

She let go of the whitewoman's hand, embarrassed. Lord, she had never thought it would be this bad, why they never told her it was this bad? She was sweating; the shapeless shift she wore was soaked under the arms, all down her front. The woman was griping again, what she say? Would the whitewoman in her awful ways never shut up?

"Come on, here, I'll help you."

They had to stop again as they crossed the kitchen, once more in the back hall for the pain to pass, before they reached the maid's room. Graceful did not want to lie down, but she couldn't stand up, and so she sat on the edge of the narrow cot, leaning into the pain, groaning, until the groan became the released sound, and it was so bad in her spine, so bad; she tried to reach behind herself to press against her own lower back, but the pain came too hard, and all she could do to ease it was yell. She was still sitting so, spraddlelegged, arms braced on the feathertick, riding into the beginning of another pain while the woman's distant voice carped around her, when her water broke. It poured from her like a flood that would never stop, like she was wetting herself without control, and she batted the woman's hand away, but the woman's hand was firm, insistent, and Graceful let her pull the soaked shift up over her head, but she stayed inside the pain, and when it began to recede she felt a piece of cloth come around her, a clean, soapsmelling sheet.

"Lay down," the woman said. "Aren't you supposed to lay down?"

Graceful shook her head, not so much to say no, but in confusion, exhaustion; she didn't know what she was supposed to do. She allowed the woman to help her to lie down on her side as another wave began to cramp and twist. "My back," she grunted. "Push my back." It took Althea a minute to understand what the girl wanted, but when she reached over the huge body and put her palms on the girl's naked lower back, Graceful gritted out through clenched teeth, "Harder. Ma'am. Harder," and then surrendered to the groan that turned to cry and then to howl. When the long wave of pain had passed, she said, panting, "That help. Some."

"Well," Althea said, and then, uselessly, "here," and she pulled the sheet up to cover the girl, though it was so hot in the little room she herself was pouring sweat, and the smell, dear God, it was enough to make a person retch. "I've got to go put some water on," she said, although she didn't know what for, but she'd always heard that: first you boiled the water. She wanted to get out of that room. Graceful lay very still on her side, eyes shut, and Althea, thinking she hadn't heard, started to repeat herself, but the girl moaned and reached out for her hand, said, "Here it come." She squeezed Althea's hand so hard she pinched the bones, and she began that strange, strained huffing as she reached with her other hand, snatched off the sheet, pleading, "My back. Ma'am. Please." She gripped Althea's fingers tight, and Althea tried to pull away, she tried not to look down at such a swelling of brown skin, such a living mass of brown womanflesh; she didn't want to see Graceful's navel pushed out, tumescent, like a man-thing on the great brown swollen globe, she didn't want to see Graceful's breasts, the excruciating intimacy of Graceful's belly and thighs, and her mind said stupidly, That brand new feathertick is going to be ruined. "Ohhhh," Graceful groaned, "push on my back. Push my back. Ma'am!"

There was nothing else to do. Althea twisted free of the girl's grip and reached across her, put her fingers on the girl's spine, and pressed hard with the slim strength of her slight arms, but the angle was awkward, there was no room, she was actually pulling the girl toward her rather than pushing, and she could feel the heat of the girl's body beneath her, felt the great soft flesh and the drumhard belly rise and fall with the girl's yell. When the wave had passed, Althea straightened up immediately and took a step back; she said officiously, "You're going to have to turn over, Graceful. I can't get a good grip from here."

Again Graceful lay motionless with her eyes closed, as if in a deep sleep, but when Althea prodded her shoulder, she mumbled, "Yes, all right." With a low groan she allowed Althea to help her turn to her other side, allowed her to spread the sheet across her once more, but the instant the next pain came she threw it off. Althea didn't need to ask this time. She pushed at the girl's lower back with all her weight. She could feel the hard muscles radiating from Graceful's spine, could feel the incredible strength of the girl's body, like the strength of the whole world converged, homed on the one task of laboring forth this baby. She pressed harder and harder as each pain welled, and Graceful rode with the pain, yelled with the pain, not in fear or hurt but for the release of its sound, so that the two women, joined in near silence through the cold months into spring, were married now in a loud, wordless, voiced rhythm as the birthpains came closer and closer together, multiplying in intensity, purpose, strength, and for Graceful the whitewoman was a only pair of hands kneading their feeble relief into the torment in her back, and for Althea the laboring girl was only an extension of her own barren, fading self, but it was the pulse of the labor that dictated their actions, as it dictated their union, as it dictated the moment Graceful had to roll over, and Althea had to help her to sit halfway up, head against the wall, and Graceful did not yell any longer but grunted deep in her diaphragm, an ancient sound, as she bore down.

What had been too flesh-real and private to be looked at an hour ago was now no more separate from Althea than her own skin. "Lean back," she barked. "Brace yourself. Here," and she tried to soften the wall with a pillow as Graceful pushed. "Oh, it's coming," Althea said. "It's coming!" The top of the child's head, wet and matted, showed in a round mottled patch, and for the slenderest part of an instant the old memory welled in Althea, but the dark head receded, sank back inside its mother's flesh, and every pore in Althea's being hummed, unmindful of self; she forgot everything but getting the baby free of the womb, the dark tunnel, out into the world. Graceful wasn't sounding the pain now, but Althea was, or she was talking loud, chanting, "Here it comes, it's coming, good, honey, you're doing good, oh, oh, here it is now, Graceful, push!" But the patch of head, having swelled forward, receded once more. "Almost," Althea puffed, and then her chant rose again, "It's close now, here it is, one push, now, here it comes, we're so close now, come on, come, baby, push, mama, push—"

And when the baby's head emerged, facing up, Althea reached forward and turned one tiny shoulder as naturally as if she'd been told what to do, and the other shoulder came, the whole slender slick body slipped out, and Althea held him, gasping. Or no. She was crying. "A boy!" she said, as if Graceful couldn't see with her own eyes. Breathing hard, sobbing, half laughing, half crying, Althea held the living child in her two hands, unable to think what to do with him. She was exhilarated beyond anything she'd ever known. The baby blinked at Althea, silent, slick as salve, his fists and legs moving, his belly still corded to Graceful, his mouth open wide, nose clotted, round face shiny with mucus. You were supposed to spank them, Althea thought. Weren't you supposed to spank them? She gave the child a faint, trembling little shake, and he gulped for air, began to cry. Althea laid him on the bloodsoaked sheet between his mother's knees, took the hem of her gardening dress and began to wipe his face.

It was only then that she looked up and saw that Graceful, too, had been crying. Graceful was still crying, but her tears were not like Althea's tears, nothing like. In the brown, twisted face Althea saw an agony that was beyond her ken, unknowable to her: a sorrow that went to the heights and depths of the world and had nothing to do with her, and everything to do with her. The sadness that had hinted itself from time to time in the past months now rushed through Althea, multiplied a hundredfold, unfathomable, its source and meaning nameless, boundless. She watched, understanding nothing, as Graceful reached down between her legs and picked up her child.

PART FIVE

———

Fire

Greenwood
Tuesday
May 31, 1921

T he call came in to Mr. Smitherman's office a little after four-thirty in
the afternoon. The new sheriff didn't stay on the line long; he said
only, "We got this boy up here and I think we can keep him, but there's a
lot of talk going round, a lot of talk. I don't know if you've seen the evening
paper, but looks like there's going to be trouble. You might want to come
down."

Smitherman clicked the earpiece in its cradle, stood for a long time
staring at the oak casing on the wall before him. In his mind he saw the
hard-burned image of limp, hanging bodies, the evil fruit of Southern live
oak and elm, and a powerful dread was on him, and anger, and a furious
fixed coldness. *No more!* his mind said.

On the top floor of the county courthouse at Fifth and Boulder, a
young black man named Dick Rowland stood at the rear of a jail cell, his
pulse pounding too loud in his ears for him to be able to pick out specific
words from the angry murmur he heard rising from the street below. He
was being held for assault on a white woman, though he and the elevator
girl both knew that the car had jarred and he'd stepped on her foot—
that's all, he'd stepped on a whitegirl's foot—but he knew, too, that the
truth had no more power than that old deceitful word *justice* in the face of
a mob's will to murder, and so Dick Rowland's thoughts were little different from the silent, bloodracing thoughts of Roy Belton as he sat in this

same Tulsa jail cell on a stormy Saturday evening last August, or of Everett Candler in the Oklahoma County jail the following afternoon. No different from those of seventeen-year-old Marie Scott (Negro) in the predawn hours of a March morning six years ago, just before she was dragged screaming from the Wagoner County jail and lynched a block away; or of Oscar Martin (Negro) before he was hanged from the second-story balcony of the courthouse at Idabel; or the four horse thieves (White) left twirling silently in a barn near Ada; or the unnamed drifter, an anonymous black man, strung up from a light pole and shot on the main street of Holdenville last December: of any prisoner anywhere who ever waited in a jail cell sweating, praying, crying to believe, right up until the final writhing moment, that something would happen to stop men's killing hands.

At half past four, in the house on South Carson, Graceful was cutting lard into a pie crust on the kitchen counter; her baby slept, its lips nursing air, inside a pillowed basket on the tile floor at her feet. Outside, in the muddy garden, Althea knelt beside her riotously blooming Cimarron Tea Rose, mulching the roots. Her husband sat alone in a great leather chair in the lobby of the Hotel Tulsa. He had returned home just over a week ago to find his wife quiet and careful, a new little mulatto baby in the maid's room. He spent very little time at the house. Franklin took out his gold watch to check the time; frowning, he snapped the watch shut, tapped the ashes of his glowing cigar into the brass tray standing at his elbow.

On the north side of the city's invisible border, inside the printing plant in back of the *Star* office, Hedgemon Jackson worked with Lawrence at the great presses, darting forward to lay down sheets of fresh newsprint, jumping back out of the way. Out front, on Greenwood Avenue, a certain Creek freedwoman emerged from attorney I. H. Spears' law office, paused a moment, looked around. A faint shudder passed over her. She turned, made her way toward the Woods Building on the corner. Farther north, in the shotgun house on North Elgin, Cleotha Whiteside stirred her cavernous kettle of fresh-picked poke salat, while her daughter LaVona desultorily squeezed suds from the clothes in the tin washtub beside the back door. Willie played in a yard across the street with some other children. Jewell was down on Archer helping to decorate the hall for the high-school senior prom. Cleotha's new daughter-in-law lay hugely pregnant and useless on the bed in the middle bedroom. Over on Latimer Street her brother Delroy lay on his back on the garage floor beneath the

Nash truck. And in a dim and odoriferous choc joint near the Frisco tracks her eldest son was playing pool.

T.J. moved around the felt square noiselessly, on thin cardboard soles; his cuestick danced in the air, came down, slipped silently between kneeling fingers, stabbed suddenly. The balls snapped apart with a sound like cracked bones. Whether he missed a shot or ran the table, T.J. didn't speak. The big brownskinned war veteran he played against was also silent: Carl Little kept an eye on the game from his position against the bar, where he leaned on the roughcut slab in a cream-colored suit, sipping choctaw beer. Reports of the boy's arrest had spread quickly through Greenwood, and at the other end of the room angry voices rose in the smoky light.

"Dick Rowland ain't touched a whitegirl, he got better sense than that—"

"That don't matter, fool, they'll lynch a man for breathing the same air as a whitewoman—"

"I'm just saying—"

"You know they fixing to do that boy like they done the whiteboy last summer. . . ."

Downtown, on the white side of the divide, the crowd in front of the court-house was getting larger. Day laborers coming off shift were joining the scores of out-of-work oilfield men and half-grown schoolboys milling on the corner near the newsboy hawking the bulldog edition with the cry, "Nigger nabbed for assault on white woman!" There were several here who'd been in this same location nine months before, on the last Saturday night in August, when the young man on the top floor who dreaded them and hated them and prayed for deliverance from them had been white. Across the street, leaning against a brick building, was one who'd hidden himself in that Belton lynch mob; he held back now, a shapeless hat pulled down over his eyes. The sun was still too high, too hot and bright, ruthless in its telling glare.

Japheth listened to the mob voices, but the men were spewing only the same boring maledictions, cursing the same unimaginative oaths, sucking from the same tin flasks secreted in the same mudcaked workboots. A wave of profound emptiness passed over him. This lynching would be tiresome, dull, ordinary; it would prove nothing new. Squinting against the westering sun, he peered from beneath his mashed hat-brim at the barred windows on the third floor. His lips lit suddenly in mockery of the old insouciant smile. Well, yes. He might as well wander on uptown, to the good choc joints in Little Africa, drink a beer, see how the niggers were taking this bit of news. Covertly, gracefully—at the precise moment one of the men in the crowd spat and asked in indignation, "Are we gone let these niggers rut all over our wimmin?" and the other men answered back, "Hell no!," Japheth slipped away from the corner of Fifth and Boulder, began walking north.

He stopped only once, to buy a copy of the evening *Tulsa Tribune* from a newsboy near the Frisco station, before he sauntered across the tracks in bright daylight, as other white men did after dark when they made their frequent, secret forays to the gambling houses and brothels, the juke joints and speakeasies on the north side of the tracks.

No stir occurred as he passed from the bright yellowgreen afternoon light into the sawdust-floored cavern nearest the station: Japheth's entrance was sleek, glabrous, like a grass snake gliding over a doorsill.

The only light in the joint came from a high, barred window at the rear of the room, two kerosene lanterns in sconces behind the bar, and the lone, bare incandescent bulb hanging over the pool table. Japheth ordered a choc beer, moved into the dim light at the end of the bar, spread his paper out on the roughcut slab, and silently sipped the thick milk-colored liquor as he read. The owner kept an eye on him, not so much because of his skin color, which was so blackened with weeks of sun and dirt as to be indeterminable—he could have been Indian, maybe, or Mexican, or Gypsy—but because Japheth was a stranger. The uneasiness and anger were running high in the room, and any surly newcomer might set off a brawl.

A couple of hod carriers rushed in, brick-dusted, mortar-smeared, sweaty; they'd walked off their jobs downtown and hurried home to Greenwood to bring the latest lynch-talk news, and one of them, seeing Japheth's newspaper spread on the bar, said, "There it is. That's the paper right there!"

Subtly, so subtly one could hardly distinguish the motion, Japheth lifted the paper so that the bold black letters of the headline were illuminated in the lamplight. The headline read: TO LYNCH NEGRO TONIGHT.

"See!" the first hod carrier declared. "They aim to do it tonight!" And the other one shouted, "They won't wait till night, they're not afraid to be seen. No law's going to come after them. We got to arm ourselves and get back downtown, quick!"

Voices were raised in agreement, but a muffled voice said, "They say tonight right here in the paper, don't they? Y'all don't want to go off half-cocked." Only the two pool players and the owner, who were nearest him, realized that the words came from the slouch-hat-shaded figure at the end of the bar. Worried that a fight might break out, the owner moved nearer, swiping at the rough slab with his rag. The big man in the cream suit stood to one side with his pool cue balanced loosely in his hand. The service insignia and war medals gleamed on Carl Little's vest. His white silk derby, brushed to a high, buff sheen, was pushed to the back of his head. Without taking his eyes off the stranger, he said to T.J., "Your shot."

But T.J. did not step forward; his eyes were fixed on the newsprint. TO LYNCH NEGRO TONIGHT. Before T.J.'s eyes swam not symbols on a page but the clear image of his friend's face as the nine whitemen dragged him from the back seat and wrestled him to the elm tree. Midst the angry voices raised in the beer joint, he heard Everett Candler's polite, terrified voice on a dusty road at sunset, calling the whitemen *sir* and *mister,* showing his teeth.

"I been renting from Dad Rowland since I first come to Greenwood. We can't let them lynch his boy."

"We're not. We not about to!"

"This ain't about Dick Rowland, this about every black man in this country."

"You got that right!"

"You going to shoot pool," the big vet snapped at him, "or stand there gawking?"

T.J. bent over the cue, lined up his shot. In his mind the memories tumbled, the white lawmen outside the house and Everett's daddy firing from the window, the rusty six-gauge in his own hands, how easy the whiteman fell. It had happened so fast. He'd thrown the gun down the cistern, he would run, they'd never know, they would never find him, but they took Everett. They took Everett instead, and T.J. had to follow.

"They gathering already. There's a hundred or better at the courthouse right now."

Had to stand outside the jail and watch the whitemen bring him out, put him in the front car. Had to go after them, catch up with them, only to hide cowering, unarmed, unmanned, in the rustling corn.

"They fixing to take him, you watch!"

T.J. jabbed at the cueball, seeing again the stunning competency of those colorless hands, as efficient as if they'd whipped such a knotted loop around a hundred black necks, and Everett, with his own hands tied behind him, swearing hopefully, politely, that he'd had nothing to do with shooting no whiteman. They had been silent, the nine whitemen, except for the one who told Everett one time to shut the hell up.

"When we going to stand up and make 'em quit?"

"Right now! Who-all's got a gun?"

"My army pistol's right here in my pocket, loaded and shined—"

Everett's narrow, scuffed, useless shoes jerked in the air, dancing upon nothing; then the gunshots, and those same twitching shoes were instantly still, and the blood on the duck suit so brilliant in the dying sunlight, carmine red on white cotton, and the nine men turned and walked back to their cars, their weasel faces—unmasked, grim weasel faces that would burn in T.J.'s memory forever—showing only a mild satisfaction, as if they were glad to have done with a nasty but necessary little job. Inside his mind, T.J. watched again as the three cars drove away in crimson dust; again he turned to the elm tree, to know again, in the same sinking bloodrush, why they'd hung Everett as well as shot him. Because the image of the hanging black man was part of the terror. Because Everett's body had to hang there for black men to find, for a sign, for a warning.

"I got a shotgun home and a couple of pistols, Luther Adair's got some fine carbines—"

"A bunch of us got service revolvers, ain't we?"

"Oh, yeah, we good enough to get killed in their goddamn war, but we not good enough to try on clothes in their goddamn stores—"

Feet poised, toes down, in graceful silent pointe, silhouetted on the horizon, through the brilliant sunset, through the purpling dusk, going darker and darker with the loss of light, until the limp form was only a blacker black against the night sky while T.J. crouched in the corn, wanting to go to him and cut him down. Wanting to run. But fear whispered that the whitemen were waiting just beyond the curve of road in the distance, murmured that they would come roaring back in their automobiles, that T.J. would be caught in their headlamps, unarmed and helpless and terrified, as he was terrified now, in the dim light of a choc joint in Greenwood. But not helpless. Never would he be caught helpless again. T.J. reached beneath his shirt to touch the butt of the Colt tucked between belt and skin.

"Who's got shells? We're going to need plenty ammunition—"

"Sook, run up yonder to the Dreamland, see who-all's up there, tell 'em to meet us at Archer and Greenwood in half an hour—"

"I'd wait for first dark, fellas." Japheth folded the paper, laid it face-down on the bar. "They're not going to move before night."

The vet in the cream suit called out, "You don't sit around till they strong! You got to strike like a thief in the night!" And then, more softly: "Ain't y'all learned nothing? We got to go down now, while they still con-·· gregating, before they expect anything. And we can't go aiming to shake our fists and threaten somebody, we got to go ready to shoot to kill."

"You right, Carl!"

"Let me run home and get my Winchester."

"I'm ready this minute. Let's go!"

"You people better be ready to kill a bunch of them peckerwoods," Japheth said, "or they're going to come burn you out. Don't you know that?"

"Where you think you at? This is Greenwood, mister."

"We going to *defend* ourselves. We'll defend our homes."

The men began to move in a ragged wave from the far corners of the room to the lighter area around the pool table, and for the first time they looked hard at the stranger. Japheth's features were shadowed and blunted, but he had no mastery over the ravenous hatred in his hooded eyes, and it was this the men recognized. Someone in the back of the room said, "Shit, that's a whiteman."

T.J.'s hand clamped tight on the cuestick.

"You all ready to kill white men?" Japheth asked.

"If I have to." The vet gazed steadily at him from beneath the clean buff brim of his hat.

"Tell you what, sons, *I'm* ready." Japheth tapped the folded newspaper. "This is as much my fight as it is yours."

"How's that?"

The darkness in Japheth's mind raged with a thousand answers, how his enemies had insulted him, tricked him, beat him, banished him; in the months since the tank fires at the Deep Fork, he could not go among them without a fight. They had joined forces against him; they would beat him mercilessly. In Japheth's mind the loathing swelled large, but his cunning homed to the one answer that could be heard by the men facing him.

"That was my partner they took out the jail last August and lynched on the Red Fork road."

"Like hell it was."

"He's a liar!"

"What you want here, whiteman?"

Japheth put his back to the bar, held his beer glass in front of him. "I'd like to go burn the sonsabitches out," he said. "I'd like to wipe the street with their sniveling faces."

T.J. reached again to touch the gun beneath his shirt, as the voices in the room lifted in a deep, threatening chorus, and the stranger's nasal tones whined among them, an eerie, angry call-and-response.

"If it was up to me, I'd take a torch to white town this minute!" Japheth said.

"You here to stir up trouble, mister, you're about to find more trouble than you ever dreamed."

"Kill every goddamn one of them."

"You best get on out of here, sucko."

"I'm telling you it's my fight, too!"

"Fixing to be your fight sure enough!"

T.J. watched the whiteman's face, and it was to him the same as the nine weasel faces on the dirt road at sunset, and the whiteman's hands tight on the beer glass were the same as the bloodless hands holding the rope; his gut twisted with hatred and the old pointless, empty longing to go back and undance Everett's feet, to erase the hours of terror in the rustling cornstalks, the nights cringing in the storm cellar. To remember it a different way: that he had not slipped away at dawn and left his friend silhouetted on the graying horizon, motionless, silent, hanging from a tree. Quietly T.J. leaned his cue against the pool table, slipped his hand under his shirt.

"You think they only lynch niggers?" the voice whined.

"Shut your mouth, whiteman!"

"I stood by and watched them lynch my friend!"

T.J.'s hand stopped. The chorus of threats stopped.

"What else could I do?" the voice whispered. "I stood there and watched it!" As if the voice came through him and not of him, Japheth went on in a kind of chanting singsong: "They acted like it was a party. The cops kept the crowd back, but it was just to give them a clear space to lynch him. He was my partner. He was just a kid. He was too damn stupid, I told him so, I told him when he shot that cabbie, and I told him later, when he blabbed about it. He wouldn't keep his stupid mouth shut. They gave him a cigarette, but he never finished it. He didn't die right off, he jerked a long time. A long damn time." Japheth's gaze swept across the men in front of him. "What could I do, one man alone? That was a thousand men, women, and children on the Red Fork road. Once that mob had aholt of him, I couldn't do nothing. The time to do something is *be-fore*! We got to go downtown and stop them!"

"We're *going* to stop them!"

"You got that right."

"We going down there this minute!"

The chorus lifted again, not in threat to the stranger but in unity with him, and the men turned, moving toward the chartreuse light slanting through the open door. The big veteran in the cream suit led them, and T.J. was with them, not at the front of the crowd, not hanging back in the rear, but slipped in with the others, unobtrusive.

"We ought to go set some of their damn homes afire!" Japheth's voice twisted higher as the men spilled together out the door. "We got to go on the offensive, burn 'em out before they come up here like that mob in Chicago done!"

But it wasn't Japheth Whiteside who lit the fire. For all his malevolence and hatred, he hadn't the power to bring into materiality the paroxysm to come. Japheth was in service, as others were in service; his voice one among many, as the gathering in the choc joint was only one of hundreds taking place in those hours throughout the city, on street corners and courthouse steps, in cafés and billiard parlors and law offices, on both sides of the divide.

Downtown, scores of white men balanced themselves on car hoods or stood up on crate boxes, spewing bloodlust and hatred, while others gathered in closed rooms to discuss how to calm this lynch-mob fever. In the lobby of the Hotel Tulsa, Franklin joined a group of oilmen gathered with anxious faces near the front desk. Inside the courthouse, in his office, Sheriff McCullough hung up the telephone; he stood a moment in silence, one hand scratching his brushy mustache, before he turned to a deputy and said, "Kelly, go get Brill and Duncan and y'all take the elevator upstairs. Prop a chair in the door so they can't call it down."

In North Tulsa, as the knot of angry black men, with Japheth in the midst of them, spilled out onto Archer and began walking east, several community leaders were gathered around Smitherman's desk in the *Star* office, composing an urgently worded telegram. They had tried, without success, to place calls to the mayor, the governor, the police chief and commissioner. This telegram was to be sent directly to Governor Robertson's home, with similar wires fired off immediately to Congressman

L. C. Dyer and to that most eloquent decrier of lynchings, Mr. W.E.B. Du Bois himself, who'd visited Greenwood just two months past and declared it the finest example of Negro self-sufficiency in the United States. The men in Smitherman's office believed that the combined forces of articulate Negro voices and powerful white men of good will could prevent this lynching. Standing at the file cabinet, Hedgemon Jackson took down their dictation in his elegant backtilted script.

On both sides of the Frisco tracks, knots of edgy men, black and white, mirrored each other, excepting in this: On the white side of the divide, the gatherings as yet had multiple purposes—some came together to foment mob violence, others to avert it; some gathered out of curiosity, or hatred, or to taste sanctioned murder; some had missed out on the Belton lynching and did not want to miss this event. On the north side of the divide, the people of Greenwood, although not in agreement on method, were of one mind in their resolve—they were going to prevent the lynching of Dick Rowland. In Smitherman's office, as in the furious minds of the men marching in phalanx toward Greenwood Avenue, as within the myriad gatherings all over North Tulsa in those hours, there was but one unified purpose: whiteman's lynch law was not going to rule this promised land.

I t was one of those weird yellagreen twilights like we're apt to get of an evening in early summer. All off toward the river and looking back to the east, both directions, the sky appeared like it was lit up with sulfur from horizon to horizon, that kind of bright weird yellagreen. You ever seen it? Looks like it just never will get dark. Not that we were waiting for dark—no, sir, I don't mean that. To tell you the truth, I can't say exactly what we were waiting for. Just milling around, how folks will do. It wasn't to lynch that boy. The colored and the Commies are the ones who keep saying that, but we weren't aiming to lynch nobody, we were just milling around. Me and Stinson had come off shift at six-thirty, and I mean that whole town was buzzing. You could feel it clean up on Second Street—the ironworks was right there by niggertown—and a couple of fellas had already run in and told us a nigger'd raped a white girl and so forth, but that wasn't so much what we were het up about. We'd just come downtown to see what was going on.

Well, sure, we wandered on over to the courthouse, that's where the crowd was. Not that it was that big a crowd, I mean, not so big as folks are saying. There weren't two thousand white men on the streets, not then there wasn't, maybe later, along about daybreak, when we had to go in and clean that nest out. But right then I bet you there wasn't over a couple hundred—well, maybe a few more than that, but we weren't doing anything, just messing around.

Naturally folks aren't just jumping to talk about it. None of us expected it to get so out of hand to that degree. But, listen, the coloreds brought it on themselves. They did. Look at the papers, they'll tell you. Right there in the *Tribune* the next evening it told it: that whole mess started on account of a bad element in the colored population, just a handful of bad niggers stirred up by the reds. These Bolsheviks have been trying to come in here for the longest, agitating, telling the coloreds they ought to expect "social equality" and all that nonsense, and I guess those poor folks in Little Africa didn't have any better sense than to listen. But I'll tell you what, you let the coloreds get their minds wrapped around that kind of notion, first thing they're going to do is look for a white woman. Ain't it? You know it and I know it. So you've got to watch them. You've got to come down hard on 'em, you can't be letting them get away with what that boy in the jail tried to get away with. But, no, I don't believe anybody was trying to lynch that boy.

Oh, there were some, sure, had some pretty foul mouths, saying all about what they'd do to any nigger they caught with a white woman, which I'm not going to repeat. It don't bear repeating. There's always going to be a bad egg or two. But most of us, we were just looking for a little something to do. It was a nice evening out, warm, but the weather hadn't turned hot yet, and that yellagreen twilight just lingering for hours. Maybe one or two of us had a little something stashed in a boot, or somebody'd slip down a alley and take him a nip. It was just a kind of little social gathering. I heard that a couple of men tried to get in at the courthouse and the sheriff run them back out, but I didn't see that. But listen here, if that bunch of colored boys hadn't marched downtown, nothing would've happened. I believe that for a fact.

It'd finally got dark—that twilight drained off sometime when I wasn't looking—and it was pretty well dim on the side streets, but the courthouse was lit up, and the streetlamps, and somebody'd scrounged up some pineknot torches from somewhere, so there was light enough right there where we were. We'd swelled up a little bigger, our bunch there on the street. Fellas kept coming. Sometimes, a situation like that, it'll peter out after-while if it looks like nothing's going to show. Folks said Sheriff McCullough'd jammed the elevator on the third floor so nobody could call it down, and then set his men around at the top of the stairs with shotguns so they could take a potshot at anybody trying to get up to where that white boy was—I don't know if they would've really shot a white man, but they might—anyways, it looked like the sheriff meant to put up a show. So who's to say but what folks would've just gone on about their business after-while if the niggers hadn't rushed us?

Along about ten-thirty or eleven, maybe, everybody standing by me hushed, just all at once. I seen everybody looking north, so I turned to look, and here they come out of the darkness, this whole wall of black faces materializing out of that black. They weren't coming fast, they weren't running. Just walking, and it was spooky, now. It was weird. Walking right down Boulder Avenue toward us, dead silent, maybe fifty or a hundred of them abreast, and I mean to tell you they were armed. And they didn't try to hide it neither. You see what I'm saying? Arm them up and send them out to war in a white man's army, let them get these "social equality" notions running in their blame knuckleheads, that's how they'll act. Well, you've got to put a stop to it, don't you? You got to nip that kind of crazy malarkey in the bud.

Just to give you an example: this bunch of colored boys came right directly at us, and when they got to where our bunch was knotted up there on the steps they didn't even flinch but just kept coming, straight up to the door. I'm surprised it didn't start that minute, I'm surprised somebody didn't haul off and start shooting right then, and I don't know why somebody didn't. I reckon we were too dadgum surprised. And then these Negroes had the gall to offer their services to the sheriff! You believe that? It's the devil's own truth. They'd come up to see if the sheriff needed their help to protect that colored boy up yonder on the top floor!

But I'll tell you what, that sheriff could've done a whole lot better job calming things down if he'd acted right. He never took a gun off a single nigger. He never acted like they were out of line in any way. He'd ought to arrested every last one of them, but I heard him stand there and talk to them reasonable as any- thing. He had his pistols out, but all he said was, Y'all go on home, boys, we got everything under control.

Well, naturally, with a sheriff as mealymouthed as that, the niggers just kept standing around like they owned the place. They had I bet you thirty shotguns, a whole bunch of army-issue .45s, I don't know what—all. You see what I'm saying? You can't be soft on 'em. Nobody wanted to hurt anybody, but those colored boys are the ones that brought it on themselves. Give them an inch, they're going to take over the whole damn country, that's what they're aiming at, most of them. Now, a few of them turned and started back down the steps, acted like they'd got some sense finally and would go on home and settle down. I seen a cou- ple boys I recognized, that shoeshine boy that works at Louie's and Mr. Stedham's chauffeur, I think, and a couple others, and, really, up till that evening I believe the majority of our col- oreds here in Tulsa knew how to act. Most of them were pretty good niggers, or they used to be, but niggers are just like any- body, there's good ones and bad ones, and there's not a creature on this earth lower than a bad nigger, and that night at the court- house there were sure some bad ones in that bunch. I couldn't be- gin to tell you where they'd come from. Folks were saying a nigger mob was headed over from Muskogee with some dynamite, but I don't know if that was some of the Muskogee niggers or not. Might've been some of these agitators and wobblies you're al- ways hearing about. What I do know, that was about the arrogant- est crowd of niggers you'd ever want to look at. Black as the ace of spades, some of 'em, and some near about as white as you or me, and every damn one of them had their noses stuck up in the air. And they had all them goddamn guns. That kind of behavior makes a fellow plain mad.

Well, somebody got mad. Wasn't me. I'm not saying who, if I knew, which I don't. No, I'm not saying. But look here, what do you expect? Here's this one big buck nigger on the steps, he don't act like he's going nowhere. Had him on a pretty white suit and a pretty white derby hat, and, oh my, didn't he think he was fine? Had a big old revolver about the size of my mama's skillet laid across his arm, like this, just this kind of cradled sideways like a baby, and he wasn't waving it or anything, but you could tell he thought him and his white suit and his big gun was just about the cat's meow. So somebody says, What're you doing with that gun, nigger? And this nigger comes back in a slow voice like fleas are going to drop off him, he says, I'm going to use it if I need to. And this other fellow, I ain't saying who, just some white fellow, he tells the nigger. Naw, you ain't, you better let me have it. That nigger looks at him a minute, comes back with, Like hell I will. Well, what are you going to do? You can't let them act like that. The white fella had to go to take that gun off him, didn't he? He had to. I don't know who shot first, don't know if it came from that nigger's gun, but I don't think so, because it sounded to me like a .22. All I know, there was one shot, and then there was a hundred, and I seen about a dozen men drop, black and white both, right in those first few seconds, and, man, I dived for cover, and them niggers took off. They ran a gun battle all the way up Boulder and some of our bunch took off after them, but I stayed there at the courthouse for a while. A doctor showed up from somewhere and tried to help one of the niggers that was dy- ing yonder on the sidewalk, but some of our fellas wouldn't let him, they said to let the nigger lay there and writhe, which maybe that wasn't right, but the way the fellas seen it, it wasn't right for a white doctor to give aid to the enemy, because the way the fellas seen it, right then, we had us a war on.

W hen the telephone in the library began to ring sometime after midnight, both women were still awake. Graceful lay on her side in the maid's room with the baby asleep in the curve of her arm, her body fatigued and trembling on the narrow cot as she stared into the darkness. At the shrill cry of the black gnome on the library table, her heart contracted. She knew the call was for her. Never had she received a telephone call in this house, such a thing was unheard of, but her heart knew at once that the insistent ringing in the library, that bell-cry of trouble, was for her.

Althea was sitting up in the fringed and shaded lamplight of her bedroom, propped against the feather pillows with a gardening book in her hands, though she wasn't reading, but listening, to the ticking house, the ticking hall clock, the ticking of her own heartbeat, waiting for something, though she would not admit to herself that what she was listening for was Franklin's tread on the stairs. Since the night of his return more than a week ago, when he'd stood several minutes in the bedroom doorway, staring at her in silence, she'd waited for him. Each afternoon, bathed and dressed for dinner, her hair arranged, she sat waiting in the parlor, sewing, and though their dinners passed in that same bloated silence, and though he retired each night to the guest bedroom across the hall, Althea's fears were eased. Her husband was home. But he was so late this evening, far too late, and she'd heard no word; she was afraid he'd gone away again, that he wouldn't come back. And so when the phone rang she was swept with relief, an easement followed instantly by greater fear.

They met in the front hall. The phone shrilled and shrilled in the library. They hesitated before each other, unsure for an instant. Of course it was Graceful's charge to answer the telephone, as Althea had taught her, greeting the caller with a pleasant "Good afternoon, Dedmeyer's residence," or "Good morning," or "Good evening"—but what of a call in the middle of the night? There was no etiquette for catastrophe. Althea rushed into the library and jerked the phone from its cradle.

"Hello!"

"Graceful?" a soft Negro voice said.

Althea was so surprised that she simply handed the receiver to Graceful, stepped back. She watched the girl's face in the reflected light from the streetlamp, heard her dull greeting, and then, after a long time, heard her ask, "Where they at?" Graceful listened to the lengthy answer in silence, without a murmured yeah or un-huh or any of the verbal courtesies that told a speaker his listener was attending to his words. After some time she said, "Where's Delroy?" And then, "Did anybody go by Mama?" Althea could hear the low hum of the man's voice rising and falling through the receiver, but Graceful's face revealed nothing, as ever, though there must surely be a death in her family, or a near death, somebody dying, to account for the boldness of a Negro man calling up in the middle of the night. "I'll be there in a little bit," Graceful said. And after a beat, "I *am*, Hedgemon." The insect voice rose louder in the black scoop, but Graceful's mask remained unchanged. Later she said, "All right," and put the phone down without saying goodbye. But she didn't turn to leave the library, not even when her baby began to cry in the maid's room. Althea could see her chest rising and falling in long, slow, deeply drawn breaths.

"What is it?" Althea tried to give her voice a kind of friendly, concerned kindness, though it echoed back to her own ears sounding false.

Graceful didn't look at her. "Nothing, ma'am." The baby was crying hard now. "I got to go."

"Go where?"

"Home."

"Is something wrong?"

"They having trouble, ma'am. I got to go." And she disappeared into the dark hall.

Althea followed, flicking on lights as she went; she stood at the door and watched Graceful in the square of light falling from the hallway as she picked up the wailing newborn and put him to her shoulder, patted his back.

"What kind of trouble?"

In evidence of the profound change between them, Graceful sat down on the bed without apology or permission, opened her gown to nurse the baby. "He say it's a war."

Althea wasn't sure she'd heard correctly over the baby's cries.

"A what?"

But Graceful didn't answer.

"Who told you that? That's ridiculous!" The idea was absurd. How could they have got into another war so soon? The papers had mentioned nothing about it. Why, the Great War was the last war, the one to end all others—surely they weren't already having trouble with another country? "War with who?"

Graceful looked at her in silence. After a moment she turned her gaze down to her baby. "Whitefolks," she said, without looking up.

Her meaning began to seep into Althea's understanding. "Oh," she said after a long time. The baby was quiet now, nursing. "Oh," she said again, her mind flying through a dozen scenarios. Almost as quickly as she'd received the word, put the word *race* in front of it, she dismissed the idea. Negroes were always exaggerating those things. *War* was such an extreme word, it implied armed conflict, engagement—*combat,* for heaven's sake. Maybe there was some unrest over that colored boy raping a white girl, which the papers were so stirred up about, but surely *war* was not the right word. Althea had an impulse to ask for details so she could patiently reject the notion, calm the girl's fears. But something in Graceful's face made her too timid to ask.

"Well," she said at last, dismissing the whole issue, returning to her first thought, that a death in Graceful's family had been the reason for the late-night call. "I'll have Franklin take you in the car tomorrow morning." Again she tried to find the proper placement for her voice, the correct tone of solicitous concern joined with serene certainty that Franklin would in fact be here in the morning. "Who was that on the phone?"

Graceful stood, put the baby on the bed, placed the pillow beside him, stepped over to the wall and pulled one of her plain dresses off the hanger, tossed it on the foot of the cot.

"Graceful! Answer me!"

But the girl went on getting dressed in the dark as if Althea were not present, and the telephone began shrieking at the front of the house, and Althea whirled, certain it was the same caller, and went to answer it herself. She would get to the bottom of this. So prepared was she to grill the soft-spoken colored caller that she was stunned to hear her husband's voice.

"Darling, I'm sorry to wake you. You were sleeping?" Franklin's voice was agitated, breathless. "I wanted to tell you not to wait up for me. There's some serious trouble downtown. Darling? Are you there?"

Darling. He had called her *darling.* After a beat she answered: "What kind of trouble?"

"Oh, it's a— Some Negroes— Never mind, I'll tell you when I get home, but listen, Thea, I wanted to tell you: don't let Graceful come up here. Maybe you'd better make her— I don't know. There's some talk. You might want to put her and the baby in the basement. Just to be safe."

"The basement!"

"Or . . . I don't know. It sounds crazy, but it is crazy, the whole town is mad, I've never seen anything like it. There's a thousand or two thousand in the streets, I don't know how many, they tried to break into the armory—"

"The Negroes broke into the armory?"

"No, no, some of these rabblerousers. I can't tell you now, just, she might hear about it, and want to—"

"She heard. Somebody called. She's on her way."

"No, run catch her! Or, no, no, don't you come outside. Let her go if she's gone."

"She's getting dressed."

"Well, go talk some sense into her. Tell her they're shooting every Nigra on sight."

"What?"

"Dear God, can't you understand me? It's a race war! The coloreds are shooting white men, whites are breaking into pawnshops, they're arming themselves like it's Armageddon. She can't come up here, it's a battlefield all over downtown!"

"Come home!"

"I can't, somebody's got to—" He broke off in silence, and in the interval she heard for the first time the faint popping of gunfire through the receiver.

"Got to do what? Franklin, come home." Now it was the whine of sirens, which she heard simultaneously through the telephone and through the library windows, off in the distance, to the north, downtown. "Oh, my God," she said, "Franklin! Come home this minute!"

But her husband's voice was tinny, far away, distracted. "If you want that girl to stay alive, you'd better stop her. I've got to go. I'll be home as soon as I can." And the line was dead before Althea could say his name again.

The light was on in the maid's room. Graceful was dressed, shoes on, her hair pulled back tight into a stiff, brushy tail at the nape of her neck. She was bent over the cot, changing the baby's diaper, her hands folding the tiny white square in deft, quick strokes, sliding the open pins through her hair to grease them before stabbing them into the cotton; she jerked the baby's gown down, pulled the drawstrings around his feet like he was a sack of potatoes, and almost in the same motion turned, without acknowledging Althea, and snatched up a burlap sack from beside the bureau, began to stuff it with diapers.

"What do you think you're doing? You can't go up there!"

But Graceful kept on snatching items off the bureau, and Althea cried, "Graceful! Listen to me! That was Franklin. They're shooting people on the streets! You can't take that baby up there!" For the first time the girl seemed aware of her, not that she turned to look at her, but the swiftly moving hands suddenly slowed. "They're shooting Negroes on sight, do you hear me? You can't!"

The sounds of many sirens snaked through the walls into the tiny room at the core of the house. Graceful's hands stopped moving, and in a moment the burlap sack thunked to the floor. She sat down on the cot, staring straight ahead. For an instant the mask held, and then the smooth features crumpled, and Graceful began to sob. She sat with her shoulders back and her head raised and the whole of her chest moving in deep, ragged sobs, tearless, shuddery. Her face was twisted. The baby lay blinking in the light, staring up at his mother.

Althea stood uncertainly in the doorway. If Graceful had collapsed, buried her face in her hands, if there'd been tears, Althea would have probably reached down to pat her back, for that awkward impulse burgeoned in her at once. But Graceful's stiff, erect figure, her contorted features as unreadable in their extremity as ever they'd been in their masklike stillness, cut off the impulse, made Althea clumsy, unsure of herself. The baby began to hiccup, the tiniest little normal sounds, incongruous against his mother's dry sobs and the distant wailing of sirens. At last Althea announced matter-of-factly, "Mr. Dedmeyer will be home soon. He'll know what to do."

Graceful didn't look at her, but the sobs began to ebb, the silences between the ragged huffs growing longer, punctuated by the baby's tiny rhyth-

mic hiccups. After a long time she spoke softly, dreamily, without explanation, as if she were recalling a long-ago experience. "He say they trying to
hold Greenwood, but they keep falling back. Whites be taunting them from
the train station, shouting about they going to come in and shoot everybody
in their beds. Going to catch them kneeling at prayers and shoot them in the
head." She paused. "He thinks they might have got T.J. He's not sure." After a moment she said, "They been trying to kill T.J. the longest time."

"Who? Who was that on the phone?"

"Nobody. Hedgemon. I got to go home," she finished dully. Graceful
stood and moved to the bureau as if she were fatigued beyond telling. She
ignored the hiccuping infant, ignored Althea, began once again to stuff
the burlap bag with bits of clothing she pulled out of the drawer.

"You can't take that baby."

"I can't leave him," Graceful answered simply. Her hands did not stop.

"What are you going to do up there? You can't do anything."

"Somebody got to tell Mama."

"You can't." It was almost a whisper. "Didn't you hear what I said?"

"I got to go home."

For the first time since the birth, Althea touched her, but it was hardly
the rhythmic intimacy of that event: she stepped into the room and
grabbed Graceful's moving arm, clutched it so fiercely she could feel the
soft give in the little layer of flesh over the hard muscle beneath the cotton
sleeve. "You can't get through downtown! Didn't he tell you that?"

Graceful stood as a statue facing the blank wall, her features hard and
empty, nostrils flared, and yet expectant, as if she were waiting for the fullness of the event—not this old back-and-forth tug of power between them
but what was taking place in the city in that hour between all blacks and
all whites—to seep through to this whitewoman.

In fact, Althea understood the peril of what was happening downtown
far more realistically than Graceful. She'd heard the staccato gunfire
through the telephone wire; more than that, she'd heard Franklin's voice,
and the sound of it, strung at the far-tether of fear and excitement, echoed
back to her. Unconsciously she aped him: "They're shooting every Nigra
on sight, you fool! What do you aim to do, wag that baby through it?" She
let go the girl's arm. Graceful continued to stand motionless, staring at the
wall. The baby was quiet now.

"All right," Althea said. "Tell me what you want done. I'll go."

At last Graceful turned to face her, and the half-lidded stare she leveled
at her was cool with challenge. "They shooting whitefolks, too," she said.

Althea took a step back. She hesitated, trying to adjust her thinking, but quickly she rejected the outrageous notion. Her sense of white immunity was too ingrained, her assumptions of feminine privilege too deeply set. If there was danger downtown, she, as a white woman, was exempt from it. "That's ridiculous," she said. "Is it your mother you want?" Suddenly she saw the solution. "I'll go find Mr. Dedmeyer, he's right downtown somewhere." Her chest relaxed with the notion. "He can come home and get the Winton and we'll go fetch your mother, bring her here in the car. Would that satisfy you?"

But Graceful was bent over the sleeping baby now. She hardly heard what the woman was saying. A new recognition had begun to open inside her: Mrs. Dedmeyer was right. She couldn't take him. Not just for the reasons the woman said, but for her own reasons. She studied the baby's face, her feelings alternating in the familiar seesaw of tenderness and ice. He was light as a tan eggshell, but not white. Not wholly white. When he was asleep, as now, his little pink tongue bulged from his mouth like he hadn't grown into it yet. The boy had her lips and flat nose, her almond-shaped eyes. Chinaman eyes, the other children used to call them. The same narrow eyes as T.J. and Jewell. But the baby's eyes were closed now.

"You could keep him," she said. She raised up, the fatigue like an iron press on her belly and shoulders. "He could stay here with you."

"My God, no! How would I feed him?"

"He won't be hungry for a while." But even as she glanced down at the baby she knew he'd awaken in a few hours, and if she were beside him he'd drowse and nuzzle her breast and nurse awhile, go back to sleep. And if she were not there he'd cry until he'd worked himself into the trembling, leg-jerking, hiccuping hysteria from which he could not be calmed.

"I have to go," she said.

"Well. You can't. I forbid it."

In the silence that followed, a lone siren sounded, seemed to grow louder as if it were coming toward them, and then it turned northward, drew away. Still the siren wailed, thin and eerie in its isolation. Faintly, very far to the north, there was a continuous peppery knocking, like a mad woodpecker deep in a far woods who couldn't stop. Inside the maid's room there was only the sound of their breathing, the aloof, distinct ticks of the grandfather clock in the hall. Looking at the stubborn face before her, smooth and brown and stony as a buckeye, Althea understood that she could forbid the girl nothing: she could not make Graceful do anything that was outside her own will.

"We'll go together," Althea sighed, as if this had been at the back of her mind all along. "You'll be safe with me. We'll go find Mr. Dedmeyer. He'll take you and the baby home." Immediately her hand went to her hair, loose and uncombed on her shoulders; she glanced down at her night-gown. "Let me get dressed." As she turned to go, a new thought occurred to her. She looked back at Graceful's thin, shortsleeved dress of bright print cotton, unmistakably a colored girl's dress. "You too. Come up-stairs. We've got to find something to cover you up."

Althea flung clothes from the wardrobe onto the carpet, pawing through hobble skirts and shirtwaists, looking for an outfit loose enough to fit over Graceful's solid shoulders and hips. At last she pulled out a floorlength green evening dress, loose-fitted and flowing, somewhat faded, and hardly of the latest style, but far too good to put on a colored girl. How-ever, it couldn't be helped. "Put that on," she said, and hurled the dress at her. Graceful backed into the hall with the dress in her arms. "Hurry up!" Althea called. With a satisfied sense of purpose, she turned to put on a light housedress; she jerked the hairbrush through her thick mane a few times and twisted it into a knot, shoving the hairpins in as she crossed the room, knelt on the rug to dig her gardening shoes out from under the bed-skirt. She wouldn't make the mistake a second time of walking to town in dress shoes.

Graceful returned and stood waiting quietly at the door. Althea, glanc-ing up to bark another order, felt a slicing pain in her chest. Framed in the doorway, with the bed lamp's light on her sculpted face, the dim hall be-hind muting the silhouette of the green sateen dress flowing around her, the girl looked regal. In spite of her darkness, or because of it, she looked majestic, like a forest queen. How was it possible, Althea wondered, that for all the unwilling attention she'd paid, she'd never realized that Grace-ful was beautiful.

"Well, don't stand there like an idiot," she snapped. "Go get the baby and meet me in the front hall. No. Here. Wait. Come here a minute." And she went to the wardrobe once more, reached overhead for her hatboxes, pulled down a stack of them, and spread them on the carpet, opening lids and tossing them to the side until she'd found the one she wanted. "Come on," she said, and snicked her tongue against her teeth in impatience. Graceful came slowly into the room, her heavy brown maid's shoes peek-ing out from beneath the hem at each step. Althea merely glanced down at them in silence. There was no point in even thinking about that; there was no way any of her tiny shoes would fit those big feet. Graceful stopped, caught by her own image in the mirror, but Althea pulled the girl around by the arm and set a veiled hat squarely on her head, though the clever feathered concoction had been designed to tilt cunningly to the side. She tugged the veil down to cover the girl's face, stepped back to look at her, frowning. "Well," she said. "It's dark out."

They made their way along the front walk in silence. The beautiful new Winton Six gleamed dully in the driveway. Franklin had driven it home and parked it, and left it sitting each morning while he took a private car downtown. None of the wealthiest oilmen drove themselves. Althea thought as they passed it that she was going to make Franklin teach her how to operate that automobile, and people's notions of ladylikeness could just be damned. If the scandalously absent Nona Murphy could learn how to operate the thing before she took off with that ragtime player or wherever she went, Althea could most certainly learn how to drive. It was absurd, having to walk all the way downtown, for of course no streetcars were running this time of night, no cabs.

In silence the two turned north, an incongruous pair hurrying along beneath the streetlights; or, rather, it was Graceful whose appearance was most strange: a tall, elegant, overdressed lady in hat and veil walking fast in the mild darkness with an infant slung over her shoulder. The baby was swathed head to foot in a blanket. They no longer heard the ratchety gunfire, and Althea's mind relaxed in a sort of relieved exhalation. Thank God, the disturbance was finished. Now it was only a matter of finding Franklin. But as they crested the little rise above Fifteenth Street, they both saw at once the first faint ruddy glow in the distance, lighting the sky behind downtown, and immediately their swift pace quickened, led by Graceful, who, unhindered by the yards of material in the voluminous skirt, took such long, free strides that Althea had to double-step to keep up with her. Soon they were nearly running.

They were not the only ones hurrying toward the center of Tulsa in that hour. Throughout the city, north and south, telephones jangled in dark houses. Telegraph wires were singing. Footsteps thudded on brick and stone and hardpan; fists pounded on doorposts; automobiles roared to life in garages and carriage houses, rumbled toward that line of steel rail slicing east to west across the midpoint of Tulsa: the visible line marking the invisible partition that separated north from south, black from white.

Like parallel magnetic bars, the silent, inert Frisco tracks seemed now to draw to themselves the life of the whole city.

In the lobby of the Hotel Tulsa, Franklin Dedmeyer lit his fifth cigar of the evening. The gunfire had become sporadic, scattered, and it came from well north. Hearing the lull, he contemplated going outside to see if the worst had passed. But through the plate-glass window he could still see armed men running in the street, and he thought maybe he should wait a while longer. No matter. He'd been waiting all evening, had started out in the late afternoon impatiently awaiting the driller's arrival on the three-twenty from Bristow, his anger growing with each passing half-hour, because it seemed that Jim kept him waiting far too often these days. But then the trouble had started, and Franklin had dismissed Jim Logan from his mind, as he was later to drop all thoughts of his wife the instant he'd hung up the desk telephone after speaking with her. His mind was too saturated with all that he'd witnessed: The young dead man's oozing neck, for instance. The odd, strained faces of the businessmen coming in from the streets. The gun battle he'd watched moving slowly north after the first eruption—Negroes in slow, organized retreat, taking cover behind automobiles and building corners as they fell back, firing constantly at the disorganized batches of white men in pursuit.

It was during that running gun battle that the hotel manager had lugged the young man's body into the lobby. All the porters and bellhops had disappeared, and there'd been no one to help him, and so Franklin and a couple of other oilmen had gone to offer their aid, but there was nothing to be done. The young man, a white boy, was dead, though he continued to bleed profusely all over the carpet. Someone said he'd stuck his nose out the side door into the alley a moment ago to see the action, had instantly fallen backward, shot in the neck.

Franklin had taken a seat then at a small round table, well back from the window, at the east end of the lobby, near enough to see out but far enough back to be out of the way of flying bullets. From time to time he'd get up and go stand near the front, close enough to hear the news as it dribbled in excitedly from the street, but at a great enough distance to not attract others' attentions; he waited at the fringes, listening to what others were saying while denying any connection, and though he had clearly wanted Althea to think he was doing something to stop this horrid business, in fact, he had done nothing. In fact, it was just as he was speaking with his wife that he'd first seen the roadster race by with the shouting white boys hanging all over it, perched on the running boards, clinging to the hood, waving their guns from the turtlehull above the back fender. Connected to the bumper by a taut, vibrating rope, a dead Negro man bounced on the pavement behind them like a loose sack of grain. Franklin had hung up on his wife, returned to the little table, lit a cigar. Now he watched the car pass again, going north this time. It had passed by several times. The dead Negro was so mauled that if he'd not seen them go by the first time Franklin would have had to guess what kind of bloody thing the car was dragging. Other automobiles filled with armed men continued to race past the window, and still more men on foot, and boys, a lot of young boys, some of them hardly out of kneepants, most of them carrying pistols, walking fast, running, all headed north, toward the Frisco.

From her position at the window in her front room, Cleotha Whiteside, too, saw armed men running. The porchlights were on at many of the other houses on Elgin, and in their muted glow she saw shadowy figures of men hurrying south along the avenue, but, unlike the flow in white Tulsa, which moved only in one direction, the traffic in North Tulsa flowed two ways. Already women were carrying their children away from the gunfire, north beyond the section line, to stay with friends or family until the inconceivable fighting should end. Cleotha's gaze seldom stayed long with the people hurrying past in the dark street, but returned again and again to the ruddy glow on the horizon. She was trying to guess where the burning was. It looked to be somewhere along Boston, but she couldn't tell which side of the tracks it was on.

She had a powerful urge to go see, but she did not want to leave the sleeping children again. She'd left them once already, early in the evening, before the shooting started, and she'd worried the whole time, and not just because she'd feared that Elberta's baby, so long overdue, would finally make up its mind to come while she was gone. She'd told Jewell to go fetch the birthwoman immediately if the pains started again, as they'd been starting and stopping for days now. "You go straight to Miz Tiger's," she'd told Jewell, "and bring her back the minute Berta start, if she start again. Hear? Don't come looking for me. I'll be home soon enough."

"I want to come with you, Mama. Bessie and Louise are still down there." Jewell was the one who'd first come panting into the house with word of the trouble, holding her hand to her side, gulping air, telling how Mr. Ferguson had rushed into the hall where they were decorating and told everybody to go home because there was going to be race trouble. Before Jewell finished gasping her excited words, Cleotha had turned and gone into the bedroom for her hat, because of course she had to go right down to Deep Greenwood and get T.J., because race trouble was the very trouble he didn't need to be anywhere near.

"Annmarie still down there," Jewell pleaded. "Everybody down there. Mama, let me come with you. Please?"

Cleotha had turned a hard look on her best-behaved daughter. "You got no business in that mess on Greenwood. You hear me?"

Jewell nodded slowly, with her head down, cutting her eyes up at her mother. But even as Cleotha hurried away in the eerie twilight, she'd been nagged by the thought that Jewell would sneak out and follow her. She'd stayed half an hour on Greenwood, her eyes searching the crowd for T.J., growing more and more terrified by the race talk, men ranting on the corner like preachers, others grumbling and shouting their approval, but the whole time she couldn't get her mind easy about Jewell. The notion had so pricked at her that finally, despite having seen no sign of her son, she'd turned and hurried home, only to find Jewell standing at the window, with the curtain lifted, trying to see south, almost exactly as Cleotha herself now stood. Of course Jewell had stayed home and done like her mother told her; she was a good girl. She'd always been a good girl. Cleotha knew she should have turned right around and gone back to look for T.J. But she hadn't. And then the distant shooting had started, and she wouldn't—not out of fear for herself but because she wouldn't leave the children alone.

Standing at the window in the dark house, Cleotha allowed her mind to touch each of her children: the three youngest asleep in the middle room, along with her son's young wife, whom she could hear moaning faintly from time to time; her mind reached for the silent, angry eldest son, whose troubles had so seized her thoughts and attentions for almost a year. And Graceful. Cleotha's chest constricted. She hadn't seen Graceful since the night she'd sent her out with T.J. and Delroy from that stinking shack in Arcadia. Seldom did Cleotha Whiteside doubt any of her decisions concerning her children, but she grieved that one. What she'd feared had never happened—whitefolks had never come around looking for T.J.—but, as a result of her acting on that fear, the one thing she'd never imagined had come to pass: her daughter had gone away from home. From that night, almost as if Graceful had traded places with her brother, she'd quit the family entirely. At first T.J. swore he didn't know where she was, but finally Cleotha got it out of him that she was working for a white family in Oklahoma City, and not long after that, Graceful had started to write. In every letter she promised to come home soon, but she never came. *Well,* Cleotha thought, watching the beautiful orange semicircle lighting the southern sky, *at least she safe with her white family down in Oklahoma City.* But where was T.J.? Cleotha noticed then, with a little lifting of the tightness across her breast, that the gunfire had stopped. People were still going by on the street in the front of the house, but, she thought with relief and a little prayer of thanksgiving, the trouble must be over.

Berta moaned again from the inner room, louder this time, and Cleotha thought she heard the girl whimper. Then there was a terrified scream, and LaVona's voice squealed, "Mama!" The screaming continued, one long, high, hysterical yodel, and Cleotha rushed into the middle room to find her two daughters standing scared-looking beside the cot, where Berta sat up, wild-eyed, staring at the wet bedclothes beneath her, yelling at the top of her lungs.

"Oh, hush!" Cleotha pulled the girl around by the shoulders and shook her. "You hush up this minute! What's the matter with you? Ain't nothing but your water broke! Jewell! Get your shoes on and— No. No. Nevermind. Just . . ." Cleotha couldn't think. She prayed that this was another false alarm, even as she tugged at the soaked sheets, told Jewell, "Bring me some towels. And go put the kettle on." Her youngest daughter started to whimper. William was pressed up against the wall with his hand in front of his mouth, grinning broadly in his confusion and fear. "LaVona, you hush too, I'm going to give you something to cry about. Take Willie and y'all go in the front room. Keep an eye out the window for your brother, he's going to be home any minute. Hush, girl!" She turned on Elberta. "T.J. going to be here in a minute, can't you hear? That ain't nothing but water! Now hush!" But the girl wouldn't hush. Her hands were on her huge belly, and she screamed now with the pain coming, and Cleotha knew this wasn't any of those practice pains her young body had flirted with for days. Berta's water had broken. The baby was going to come this time, sure.

In a moment Jewell was standing beside her with her arms full of towels and her dress on and her shoes on and a very grown-up expression on her face. "I'll go quick, Mama," she said.

"You're not going nowhere." Cleotha took the towels from her, bent over the cot.

"But, Mama, how we going to get Miz Tiger?"

"We're not."

Jewell sucked in her breath. Cleotha did not even glance up but went on shoving the clean towels under the thighs of the shrieking girl. "You put the water on like I told you?"

"Yes'm."

"Go in the front room, then, you don't need to be looking at this." But Jewell didn't budge, and Cleotha didn't say it again, as she realized, not for the first time, that the swollbellied girl on the cot bawling and carrying on was no older than Jewell anyway. "Stand around and gawk, then," Cleotha murmured. "See what happen to a girl who don't keep herself to herself. Quit that screaming, missy!" She poked Berta. "I'm going to put you out on the porch!" But her words had no effect on the terrified Berta, and Cleotha went on shoving towels pointlessly under the girl's legs as she tried to think what to do next. Cleotha had never attended a birth. She'd given birth to seven babies herself, yes, and lost two, but she'd never witnessed another's, and all she remembered of her own labors was the sweet time afterwards; all she knew about birthing was how to lean into the pain, how to push. *Can't be that much to it,* she tried to tell herself. *Just hold your hands out, tie the cord and cut it when the child come.*

But Berta would not quit screaming, and Cleotha couldn't tell if the pains were coming that close together, neverending, so fast, or if it was just the girl's fear and hysteria, or if, as Cleotha herself feared, there was something wrong. She couldn't tell anything. She didn't know anything. She turned finally to Jewell, dressed so neat in her pink school dress, with her hair freshly plaited—when had she had time to do that?—and her almond eyes gazing directly at her mother in confident expectation. Cleotha turned her ear toward the south and listened with her whole soul to all that was happening outside the walls of her house. Silence. Nothing. No, there was a siren, wasn't there? Down toward the tracks? Well, yes. That would be the firewagon. The firewagon come to put out that orange glow on the horizon. There was no sound of gunfire. The crazy trouble was over now. Surely it was. Cleotha looked back at her waiting daughter. "All right," she sighed. "Go quick. Go straight there, straight! And come right back. Tell Miz Tiger she been—"

But Jewell was already gone.

Inside the *Star* office, Hedgemon Jackson was alone. He, too, heard the lull in the gunfire. From his position at the window he could see armed men in the upstairs windows of the building on the corner, taking aim toward the south, but nobody was shooting. There was no movement on the street; the shouts, the thudding footsteps had ceased. The fire in the distance was getting bigger, the night sky dancing yellow, but Hedgemon couldn't see what was burning. Greenwood Avenue was dark, no street-lamps lit anywhere, the businesses all shut tight, but the fireglow showed up the brick buildings across the street as plain as a drawing; he could see other faces watching from other windows and doorways; he could see gun barrels poking out between venetian blinds. Sometimes he heard whitemen's voices coming from the train station, shouting taunts and curses; sometimes he heard scattered shooting, but the gunshots, when they came, were lusterless, drowsy-sounding, like the growl of a sleeping dog roused just enough to give warning. He looked at his watch again. It was after three o'clock. His glance returned to the telephone on the wall, as it had done a hundred times in the past hour.

He was supposed to be waiting for calls from the governor and Mr. Du Bois. Or else it was the mayor and Mr. Du Bois. Somebody and Mr. Du Bois, the Du Bois part he was sure of. It didn't matter. If a call came in from anybody he'd dart out the door and up the street to Mr. Smitherman's house so fast they'd think he was a jackrabbit. The only men with guns he'd seen were colored, but Hedgemon trusted nothing. Since Mr. Smitherman rushed in looking wild and frenzied, saying that Tulsa had exploded like a firebomb and the city was in the middle of a race war, Hedgemon understood that anything could happen. Mr. Smitherman had gone right to the telephone and placed several calls. As soon as he rang off, he'd started back out the door, calling over his shoulder to Hedgemon that he had to go home and see about his family, but if Mr. Du Bois or the governor (or the mayor or some white somebody) returned his call, Hedgemon should come get him. *Wait here, son, these are important calls, very, very important, wait here where you'll be safe.*

And Hedgemon had waited. He'd heard the battle coming nearer, until finally he could see men running in the street, armed men, darting in and out of doorways. He looked for T.J., who'd been in the crowd headed downtown, but he never saw him. He did see Carl Little trot past, a pale moving target in a cream-colored suit. A flush of jealousy surged through Hedgemon at sight of Graceful's old boyfriend, but the feeling was soon swept away in the strange excitement and fear. After a while there weren't so many running; there was only the sound of riflefire from hidden places on either side of the tracks. The shooting slowed to peppery sniping, and yet Hedgemon waited. He was a good boy, a good employee, and Mr. Smitherman had said to wait for the call from Mr. W.E.B. Du Bois, and Hedgemon waited, though he no more believed that call would come than anything. It had been two hours since he'd got up the nerve to phone the whitepeople's house and speak to Graceful, for which he was both sorry and not sorry, because she'd said she was going to come. He'd told her to stay with the whitefolks until he called to say it was over, but she had not really said that she would.

Hedgemon stared at the dark, quiet street, trying to decide if it was safe to phone Graceful, safe for her to come on now. He wanted to see her. He wanted to talk to her. At last he left his post at the window, telling himself he ought to just call and make sure she was all right. But when he cranked the telephone, no operator came on. He whirred the handle harder and harder, jammed the bar down a dozen times, but the deadness in the black cup was like an ocean pressed to his ear. The wires were cut. He returned to the window. No movement on the street. Silence. He pressed his face to the glass, trying to see south. But Graceful wouldn't come to Deep Greenwood anyway. If she came north again, she would go home. He turned to look up the street, past the business district, toward Mr. Smitherman's house. If the phone was dead, Hedgemon thought, he didn't have to wait anymore, right? Whether the callers tried or did not try, it didn't matter, because no calls could get through. Right?

He reached for the door handle, but a burst of gunfire from the west made him jump back, a ratchety nonstop barrage, like a hundred guns firing one after another. The chattering fire was followed by silence, but Hedgemon knew what had caused the sound. Colored folks didn't own machine guns. Only whitemen. They'd cut the telephone wires coming out of Greenwood, they had set fire to some of the buildings, now the whites had mounted a machine-gun on the hill by the granary. Anything was possible. His eye was caught by a movement in the street, and he turned to glimpse a man running north, and then a slim figure in a pink dress, darting across the avenue toward the Woods Building, a delicate lightfooted girl, running. He had only an instant to recognize Graceful's skinny little sister before the girl suddenly whirled, a lithesome half-turn in midair, like a dancer, and fell down in the middle of the street. She lay still, unmoving.

For what seemed like an eternity Hedgemon watched the dark flower blooming across the pink material, irregularly etched, blossoming from her collarbone, spreading toward her breast. He thought maybe it wasn't Jewell, maybe he'd been mistaken. The girl's face was turned away from him. But in himself he knew the tiny form on the street was Graceful's sister. If Graceful ever dreamed that he'd watched her sister fall and done nothing, she would hate him with a hatred from which there'd be no pardon, ever. Hedgemon opened the door and ran into the street. There was another scattering of gunfire from the tracks, and an answering volley from the top of the Woods Building, but Hedgemon kept running, and when he got close he saw a big woman kneeling in the street beside the pink figure. He bent to scoop the girl in his arms, but the limp body was heavy, and he was thankful when the woman took the girl's legs and hoisted them around her waist. Together they carried Jewell into the *Star* office and laid her on the floor.

They stood each on either side, looking down. The flower on the pink cotton did not appear black now; this close, in the reflected firelight, the blood was dark red. Jewell's eyes were half open, her mouth was slack. Hedgemon had never seen a dead girl before, but he knew Jewell was dead. Slowly, very slowly, he began to realize the truth of the thing that was happening. The truth that he could have died just now, running out in the street. You did not have to be caught in the wrong place at the wrong time. You did not have to sass or rob a whiteman or look at a white-woman; you didn't have to lift your eyes the wrong way. You could be a young girl in a pink dress running, or an old woman in the street bent over to help her, you could be anybody. If they saw you they would kill you.

"What in the world this child doing out on the street?" the woman said. And then, "Must be the baby come, un-huh." She bent over Jewell, straightened the girl's crooked head, touched a finger to each eyelid, and rolled it down. She muttered something else, which Hedgemon couldn't make out at first, and then he knew she was saying prayers. After a while the woman raised up again. Her hair was plaited in a thick braid down her back, her face was smooth, thick-featured, mahogany red. She looked at Hedgemon, looked hard at him. "What you going to do, son?"

"Do?" Hedgemon felt his heart jump. "What do you mean, do?"

"You going to help me carry this girl home? Or am I fixing to have to go to that house alone, tell her mama where she's at?" The woman's gaze returned to Jewell. "She a sweet child, too. I hate to leave her, but I can't carry her myself." She paused, and Hedgemon could hear gunfire again, faint, off to the west. "Lord, Lord," the woman said, "what was that mama thinking, to send this child out on such a night?" She exhaled a long breath. "Baby don't wait for a peaceful night, anyway. Don't wait on good weather. Child have its own time. Its own time is God's time." She met Hedgemon's eyes again. "So?"

Hedgemon didn't know what the woman was talking about, or why she spoke of Graceful's sister as if she knew her, but he understood that she wanted him to carry Jewell home. Home through the firelit streets where whitemen had mounted machine guns to kill Negroes, through a world where anything could happen. He stared at Jewell's face, peaceful now, with the eyes shut: she'd been living, running, a tall, agile, strong girl moments ago, and now she was dead. His mind whirled as he realized that he couldn't be sitting here with a dead girl when Mr. Smitherman came in to-morrow morning. But he couldn't go back out there. And yet maybe Graceful would love him, finally, if he did such a thing, carried her dead sister home. The longing in him was terrible; the longing was as bad as the fear. He thought, Delroy! Sure, he could telephone Delroy and tell him to come in the truck to get his niece, and then he thought: No. White-men cut the phone lines, didn't they? Cut the wires to keep Negroes from talking to each other, to keep them knifed off from the outside world, and he thought, *They shooting any black face they see. They will shoot me.* The woman was watching him, but he couldn't meet her eyes or speak. His mind whispered, *Maybe she's there already. Maybe Graceful gone home to her mama's house.* Hedgemon felt rather than heard the woman start toward the front door.

"No! Wait! Not that way!" Before he understood what he was doing, he'd pulled her away from the glass. "Go out the back," he said. The woman was nearly as tall as he was. Her skin in the fireglow was a deep, ruddy color. She waited, watching him. "Go up the alley toward the section line," he said finally. "We can cut over from there."

He squatted beside Graceful's sister, folded each of the girl's limp arms across her belly, and then he wrapped his arms around her and pressed her to his chest, lifted her—she was heavy, so heavy for such a slight girl— and carried her over his shoulder toward the back of the office. The woman went before him, opened the door leading to the big room, where the presses were silent. The alley was silent when they emerged from the back of the building. All of Greenwood, it seemed, was silent, but for the roar and crackle of the fires farther west. For a moment, as he hurried north with the old woman beside him and the weight of the girl across his back, Hedgemon had the feeble hope that it was finished, that the whitemen were done with them.

Franklin stepped into the street with his head lifted, feeling the air. Men were everywhere, and little boys, running. He followed the flow of foot traffic until he came upon a crowd in front of McGee's Hardware, where the big window was smashed and a man in a police captain's uniform stood inside, handing out guns and ammunition as fast as his hands could deal them. A man on the corner called out, "Did you get deputized yet?" When Franklin looked at him blankly, the fellow said, "Hell, man, jump up there and tell him to deputize you! They're deputizing every two-legged white man that's got a weapon. If you ain't got one they'll give you one. They need all the help they can get. There's a nigger army coming from Muskogee, hadn't you heard?"

Franklin shook his head, turned away; he withdrew immediately to the safe surroundings of leather and brass and cigar smoke inside the hotel, where oilmen and business magnates stood about in little concerned clutches of threes and fours. He did not join them, only lingered close enough to hear snatches of conversation: . . . ought to go in and clean out that nest of vipers . . . turn that hellhole into an industrial-and-wholesale district . . . nothing but a red-light district full of choc joints and whorehouses . . . place for a new train station . . . crying shame, all those colored shanties sitting on that prime real estate.

A young man in white seersucker and a straw boater came rushing in, shouting, "They're taking the depot! Come on!" and some of the businessmen followed the young man into the street, but Franklin stepped into a recessed alcove at the end of the lobby, behind a brass spittoon. From here he could see most of Third Street through the window and, on Cincinnati, a river of men, streaming north. The voices inside and the muted yelling voices outside swelled and echoed each other, a garble of voices rising and falling, half-understood phrases: . . . secure the Frisco! . . . damn buildings across the tracks . . . wait for daylight anyhow, the niggers got . . .

Where the hell was Logan? Franklin was convinced that he was still waiting for his partner, though it was almost four in the morning and there was a small war raging between First and Archer, the heart of the battle centered at the Frisco station, where Jim Dee should have arrived hours ago if he was coming. Still, for the hundredth time Franklin consulted his watch. In a great show of impatience he snapped it shut, turned again to the window, where the glow on the northern horizon had grown brighter. The crowd had set fire to some Negro shacks, he'd heard, but the colored snipers had driven them back, and so, when the firetrucks arrived, the crowd of whites surrounded them, wouldn't let them through, and the firemen had returned to the station, let the fires burn.

"They ought to set fire to the whole mess," a familiar voice said behind him. Franklin turned to find L. O. Murphy clipping the end of a cigar with gold nippers. "They're trying to, we're damn sure going to, but that goddamn police inspector Dayley's perched in front of the depot, threatening to shoot the first white man who goes across." L.O. examined the leaf carefully, put the nipped end in his mouth. "He won't be inspector much longer, pulling a stunt like that. We've got to get in there and clean out that cesspool."

"I was wondering where you were. Logan stood me up again."

"When are you going to get rid of that insolent son of a bitch?"

"When I find a man half as good."

"Never mind about that. Listen, go home and get that Winton I sold you and bring it around. We're going to need it come daylight."

"For what?"

"I told you. We've got to clean up that cesspool of a niggertown. Should've done it a long time ago. If you own a weapon you'd better bring it. The whistle's set to blow at daylight, that's the signal."

"What are you talking about?"

"There's only one way to stop typhoid, set a torch to every goddamn thing that's contaminated, and these Tulsa niggers are sure as hell contaminated. Haven't I been saying that, just exactly? We've got a dozen planes sitting at Arbon Field this minute, gassed up and ready to take off, but they'll have to wait till it gets light enough to fly. Then, by God, we're going to run the niggers out of Tulsa."

"What's the matter with you, Murphy? This is none of our business."

L.O. blinked at him. "It's every white man's business. Go get the car and meet me at the Frisco station in an hour. We're finally going to put that part of town to good use." He turned, made his way across the lobby to join the other businessmen. Franklin lowered his head and peered through the plate-glass window, patted his vest pockets for a cigar.

Althea had never seen so many men in one place in her life—so many humans, if they could be called humans. To her mind they were little better than animals panting through the streets with their guns and tongues hanging out. She kept just back from the edge of the building, watching the stream of men pass. Oh, would they never all get to where they were going and get out of the street? In irritation she turned to see if Graceful was still sitting where she'd put her. The dark form in the dark dress blended with the dark alley, but the baby was wrapped in a light blanket, and she could see that it was still lying loosely, unattended, in Graceful's lap. The nitwit had run out in the street chasing after a roaring man-and-gun-loaded roadster, and Althea had had to grab her and pull her into the alley, make her sit down on the store's back step. The girl had been slumped like a ragdoll ever since, barely keeping hold of the swaddled baby in her lap.

Now what were they going to do? It was another five or six blocks to the Hotel Tulsa, which was the logical place to look for Franklin. Althea's agitation eased a little as she thought of her husband. Franklin would know how to negotiate this mess. But how was she going to get Graceful through that mob of trotting white men? She'd like to just let her wait in the alley, but some of them might find her, and then no telling what would happen. Althea glanced at the road again, but the flood of men, rather than lessening, seemed actually to be swelling, as if it flowed from an inexhaustible source. On the far side a tawny head glided smoothly in the crowd. Her heart stopped. What was he doing in Tulsa? On such a night?

In the midst of a trashy, filthy, vulgar mob of poorborn white men? Althea stood on her toes to see better, but already the dark-blond head had vanished in the river. Instantly she convinced herself it wasn't Jim Dee, only someone who looked like him, and she turned and started back into the alley as the baby began to cry.

Graceful stared straight ahead. She seemed to hardly know the child was there. Althea picked up the wailing baby, put him to her shoulder and patted his thickly padded bottom, but his cries didn't lessen. "Here," she said, and laid him back in Graceful's lap. "Feed him." Graceful gazed down at the sateen bodice stretched tight across her chest. Dark spots welled in two places, where her breasts were leaking milk. Althea said impatiently, "Oh, good God, here," and pulled the girl forward by the shoulder; she reached behind and unbuttoned the back. Graceful put the baby to her breast mechanically. Her naked torso was revealed in the dim light of the alley, for a ballgown was hardly a nursing dress, but Althea barely noticed; her mind was elsewhere. She turned an ear toward the men's voices, the old restless impatience coursing in her, as she tried to think what to do next. Probably she should just turn around and take the girl home. It was going to be too hard to reach the hotel in the first place, and Franklin would never be able to get the Winton through that mass of men running in the streets anyway.

"When you finish, put your hat on and we'll go." She narrowed her eyes then, glanced around, but she didn't see the feathered hat anywhere. She hadn't even noticed when Graceful took it off. The dress was ruined, greasy milk spots down the front and filthy all over the back, no doubt, from the alley floor, but Althea had known she was discarding the dress by the very act of giving it to a colored girl to put on her body. For some reason, however, she'd thought to salvage the hat. "Where is it?" she snapped. She couldn't take the girl through those wild streets bareheaded. "What did you do with my hat?" She didn't wait for Graceful to answer. "Hurry up now and finish. We can't take all night. What's the matter with you?" She reached to tug the bodice up but was stopped by the sound of the girl's flat, listless voice.

"They finally done what he say they going to do. All that time he know it, and now it's done."

"What's done?"

"He know all along they were going to. Now they done it." Graceful inhaled so slowly, so deep in her lungs that the baby's head rose and fell several inches with the strength of the breath. "I shouldn't have treated him so. Sass and talk back. I should have stayed. If I stayed, maybe he wouldn't have come back to Tulsa. He wouldn't be dead now. Look what they done to him." She raised her eyes to Althea. "You see what they done."

"What?"

"Lynch T.J."

"Who's T.J.?"

Graceful stared straight ahead, said dully, "My brother."

"Nobody's been lynched. That's not your brother raped that white girl? Is it?" In her mind's eye Althea saw the solemn little colored boy in the studio photograph on the dresser inside the yellow house. "Listen," she said, her voice very businesslike, authoritative, "I want you to understand that nobody's been lynched." She took the baby in one arm, reached awkwardly to tug the bodice up over Graceful's breasts. "Nobody," she repeated, though she was in no way certain that a lynching wasn't just exactly what that mob of men was running toward. A lynching and a bonfire as well, it appeared, for the whole of the northern sky was glowing. "Come on, now. Let's go."

"They lynched T.J.," Graceful repeated dully. "Tie him up to a car, drag the flesh off him, drag the skin off my brother till he don't even look like himself."

"That wasn't your brother. Don't be ridiculous. Graceful, that was not your brother!"

Graceful suddenly got to her feet and started toward the front of the alley.

"Stop!" Althea screamed. But Graceful had stopped anyway, standing in the breach with her shoulders heaving horribly. Althea snatched up the hat from the alley floor and reached her in an instant; she said again, "That was not your brother! Hear me?" Because she was unwilling that it be so. Because if they were going to drag niggers behind cars it should be nameless niggers, bad niggers, dangerous ones who raped white women and carried knives in their boots, not little boys who stared solemnly from photographs, and Althea said it again, hissed the words, "That wasn't him!"

Graceful said, "Don't you think I know my own brother?"

"No. You do not. You're—you're distraught, that's all. It's sad. It's terrible, but it doesn't have anything to do with you."

Graceful stared at her a moment. She turned to look again at the men running in the street. The baby was crying. She held him so carelessly, so loosely, that his big head lolled back on the fragile neck.

"You're going to break that child's neck!" Althea took the baby from her. "Cover yourself," she ordered, and Graceful pulled the sleeve up. "Turn around." Althea put the bawling infant to her shoulder and tucked the hat beneath her arm as she tried to fasten the dozens of tiny mother-of-pearl buttons, but it was entirely too awkward. "Take this baby," she said, and handed him back to Graceful. "Hold his head! Here." She plopped the hat on Graceful's head, twirled her like a seamstress's mannequin, and now Althea's fingers flew as she buttoned the ballgown. "All right, now, we are going to go back to the house. I'll carry the baby. Walk straight. Don't look at them. Keep your hands down, hide them in the skirt. Like this. Don't talk. We'll walk home, and in the morning Franklin will carry you to your mother's house in the car. Do you hear?"

"I got to go home."

"We can't get through that mess."

"I got to go home."

"All right," Althea sighed, but her heart was racing. "We'll go around. Do you know how to go around?"

Graceful was silent a moment, staring at the roiling street. "Can't go around," she said. "There's no way to go around."

"Yes there is. You'll have to show me. Wait!" Althea cried as Graceful started into the street. She pulled the girl to her and reached up to straighten the hat; she tugged on the black veil, smoothing it, trying to tuck it into the high collar. "Here, let me have him." Althea held the baby in one arm as she draped Graceful's hands inside the folds of the skirt again, wondering why it hadn't occurred to her to put gloves on those dark hands. She covered the baby's head with the blanket and grasped a firm hold on Graceful's arm, but when they emerged from the alley they were taken up like drift in the rushing current. Without willing it, completely powerless against it, they merged with the river of white men sweeping north. Along First Street the river swelled outward, became a sea of armed, hatted men pressing forward and yet held back by some massive obstacle blocking the flow. Althea couldn't see what held them back.

"You ladies better get off the street," a voice said behind her. "Them niggers are armed, ma'am, hadn't you heard?"

Another voice cursed and spat. "I'd whip my wife if she come out here."

"This sure as hell ain't no place for a lady."

"You sure it's a lady?"

A burst of low, ugly laughter made Althea clamp Graceful's arm harder, pulling her toward the west. The baby was bawling, bawling, and Althea wanted to shake him to make him stop. The crush of men, chests and elbows and foul breaths and curses, began to thin around her, seemed to part and allow her to go through; in a moment she understood that it was the wailing baby that made the men separate and make way for them. "Let the nurse through," she heard someone say, "Let 'em through!"

"Lady, you better get on home, away from this business, you don't want to see what we're going to have to do—" The man was talking to Graceful.

"Ma'am, hadn't you better take that baby someplace safe?"

Slowly it began to filter into Althea's perception that the men thought Graceful, in her sateen ballgown and black-feathered veiled hat, was the lady and Althea the nursemaid to the squalling child. Mortified, drenched in shame and fury, she tried to stop in the street, but she was shoved from behind, forced forward in a world turned upside down by men's eyes, for she'd put her own clothes on the back of a colored girl, had come away from her house in her filthy gardening shoes and plain housedress, without a sign of a parasol or a decent hat, and what the men saw was what she most dreaded in the world: her own lowborn, ugly self. Where was Graceful? She'd lost hold of her, and she could not stop the force that propelled her. Althea was swept around a brick corner, and the press of men at her back lessened a little, spreading out on either side as the street opened onto the railyard, where a crowd was gathered around something on the ground. Fire licked up in the blank eyes of a building on the far side of the tracks. The odor of gasoline was strong, as was the odor of whiskey, the smell of roasting meat.

Between khaki pantslegs she saw the thing on its back among the cinders, its legs bent at the knees, stumps of arms reaching up. At first she couldn't tell what it was, because the hands had been burned off, or chopped off, and the skin was charred black, but it was the mouth, finally, the gaping, white, lipless smile, that made her understand it was a dead Negro; its lips had been burned away, or cut away, so that it seemed to grin up at the ring of laughing firelit faces. Not all of the white faces were laughing. Some seemed to hardly notice the corpse in the cinders; others looked greedy, as if they'd like to burn and kill again what was already dead and burned. Some were drinking from tin flasks, or squinting overhead at the great slash of leaden sky swathed in red, or looking hungrily northward, like jackals, like wolves, she thought, and suddenly a burning claw of rage and loathing came up in her throat: she saw her brother in the distance among them, or she believed it was her brother. But she was shoved from the back again, and she lost sight of the swarthy face; for an instant she watched the nearby faces, shadowed, flickering in the firelight. On the other side of the circle was a familiar face, though she couldn't quite place it: ruddy, sunworn, eyes narrowed against the smoke from the smoldering tar as he peered down at the blackened corpse, and she thought then that this was her brother. No. NO! Dear God, what was she thinking? *He is kin to me*, her mind said. *They're all kin to me.* The baby was crying, and she smothered his face against her shoulder.

Graceful! If these men saw Graceful, if they realized she was colored, they'd do the same to her. Althea tried to turn around, but the bodies were pressing at her back, jostling, pushing, the baby was crying, and men's voices were shouting, the sounds were so loud, and the crackling fires roared. Suddenly the wind turned, blew the thick smoke from the building across the tracks toward them, mingled it with the stinking creosote beneath the dead Negro; the wind whirled up glowing cinders, floated red-limned black ashes through the stinging air, made some of the men cough and choke, and the crowd opened a little, enough for Althea to catch sight of the tall figure in the black veil standing, swaying, at the edge of the track. How had she got all the way over there? Althea started toward her. But in the next heartbeat she realized that if the men saw her with a colored girl they'd believe she was a nigger lover. She hesitated. Oh, *would* this baby never shut up its bawling!

A darker thought touched her, and she stopped completely now, paralyzed, for she understood that if the men saw her carrying a colored baby they would think it was hers. The newborn's eggshell skin wouldn't save her: he was too clearly a colored baby. He was a child born of both races, and she had to get rid of him, had to give him back to his mother, but the press of bodies was too close around her, she couldn't see Graceful, and now two recognitions came to her at once, mute, but fully alive and understood. Graceful's skin would betray her. No matter how well disguised she was, how dark the veil hiding her face, Graceful was not safe anywhere on this night inside her brown skin. The other thought, more terrifying than the first, and entirely inconceivable before this moment, was the understanding that Althea's white skin wouldn't save her. If they thought she'd lain with a black man—

Oh, the men's bodies were so close together, the stench was wretched, rising all around her. A voice at her shoulder said, "Sweet Jesus, what'd you bring a baby out in this for?" And another said, "Daylight's coming!" Desperately Althea looked around for a place to stash the baby, somewhere hidden, that the men might not see.

In the east a thin line of red made a slit in the gray at the horizon. A metal silo loomed out of the smoke, and Althea started toward it, holding the baby so tight to her breast its cries were muffled, like a kitten mewing under the house. Some men were running, and as she came up on a little rise by a tin storage-shack she saw hundreds of people, thousands, moiling in the railyard. A dozen uniformed white men stood on the tracks with guns drawn, facing the crowd, but it was the Frisco rails themselves that seemed to hold the mob back, dammed the flood, forcing the crowds to swell east and west along the tracks. Men and little boys and a good number of women stirred restlessly along the rails as far as she could see, all facing north, as if for a road race, as if they were chafing at the line before a land run. Althea pressed herself against the corrugated wall of the tin shack, trying to hide herself and the baby.

A nightmarish whistle sounded, a piercing shriek that split the universe, followed by a breath of stunning silence. Then the people moved in a wave across the railyard, overrunning the men in uniform; heads bobbing, knees jacked high, voices hollering, they crossed the rails, running. Automobiles and oilfield trucks crammed with armed men roared among the racers, and past them, into Little Africa, shooting, shouting, as the mad woodpecker waked in the silo overhead with its ratchety endless roar of knocking, which was not knocking but machine-gun fire from the high, square window of the granary.

In the same way it had taken time to see the human form in the charred corpse in the cinders, now it was a minute before Althea understood what was happening. She saw men breaking windows in the stores across the tracks, splashing kerosene, shouting orders; she saw a woman, a perfectly well-dressed white woman, lug a bolt of cloth out through a shattered door; the woman dropped the bolt in the street, disappeared back inside the store. Althea's mind didn't want to receive what her senses were telling her. A dozen or more buildings were burning already in Greenwood. The sound of breaking glass reached her again, and again, and again. Dear God. They were going to wipe them out.

The memory flashed of the morning she'd stood on the little rise above the tracks in her kid-leather shoes, looking across at colored town gleaming in the sun like a distant city across a river. Now black smoke billowed, bowed low, darkening the coming daylight, but she could see the hundreds of white men and women looting those same stores, breaking windows. The heat from the flames radiated toward her; the very tin of the shack behind her seemed afire with heat. Over to the west a pair of armed men herded a family of Negroes out the door of a little woodframe house. The Negroes, a man and a woman and three children, were in nightclothes. They walked down the porch steps with their hands in the air, even the children. Althea could think of nothing except to hide herself. The smoke was horrific, but it wouldn't cover her. Where was Franklin? And Graceful? What had they done with Graceful? Althea peered through the smoke, but she saw only white faces now, and the baby wouldn't stop crying; he was hungry again, or wet, probably, or burning up in that smothering blanket, or simply terrified by the noise and smoke, as Althea was terrified, and furious, and despairing. She held the baby to her chest, patted his back, but there was nothing she could do for him. There was nothing she could do for any of them, for Graceful either. She'd tried. Hadn't she tried?

"Shhhhhh, baby," she whispered. "Shhhhhh. Hush, little baby," she crooned, "don't say a word." Her voice cracked. She hunted for a cleft, a crevice in the tin in which to hide; seeing a door in the side of the shed, she quickly went to it and pushed on it, but the door was locked. Althea turned to face the riot again. Well, it was not a riot anyway, was it? Not a war, as Graceful had called it. It was—what? She had no word for what she witnessed, the thunder and rattle of gunfire, smashed glass shattering, the hiss and snap of flames, and everywhere the rolling, choking smoke. Shifting the baby to the crook of her arm, she peeled back the blanket to give him some air. He was such a limp little thing, so tiny and boneless. His cry was weakening, growing bumpy; he arched his back, opened his mouth, turned his face toward her. She placed the knuckle of her forefinger between his lips, and the baby quieted, sucking hard. He stared at her a moment from almond-shaped eyes the color of granite. Slowly his lids drooped, and then closed, but he continued sucking. Althea surrendered to the sensuous pleasure of the soft gums on her finger, knowing he would not stay contented very long. Maybe she could just carry him back to her house on South Carson, maybe the rioters in the streets wouldn't know he was colored. His hair was black and curly, yes, but not frizzy, not nappy; it lay in little sweat-matted swirls on his crown. And his skin was so light, the color of age-faded beige silk, nearly transparent in places, like the finest membrane. Gazing at him, she thought that perhaps his nose wasn't so broad after all. There was something almost feminine in his face, his lips like an open rose, and his eyebrows distinct for such a tiny one, finely arched, naturally arched, like her own. Althea lifted her head. *Like my own.*

The knowledge settled in her with a terrible force. She tried to dismiss it, wall it off, deny. But Althea's powers of deception had been stripped from her long months ago, on the banks of the Deep Fork, when she'd stood listening to her brother's bitter voice speak truths she'd kept hidden a lifetime. There was no need to filter and calculate, to review the signs that had passed to show her. *Kin to me,* her mind said. She raised her gaze to the fires burning in Greenwood, the fury and chaos, the feast of destruction. Graceful was even now making her way through that devastation to the shotgun house on North Elgin. Or she was dead somewhere, or dying. A drone hummed high in the sky. Althea squinted against the smoke, saw an airplane coming from the northeast, flying low. The meaning didn't register. There was but one obsessive thought in her mind: she had to carry this baby at once to his mother, give him back quickly, before it was too late.

T J. peered over the edge of the roof at the whites pouring across the tracks. His hand was on the butt of a carbine rifle he'd picked up from a fallen soldier, but the rifle was useless. He had no more cartridges. The pistol tucked in his waistband was also useless; he'd fired all the shells. He eyed the assault for a few minutes; then he turned over and lay on his back on the tarpaper, gazing at the sky lifting pale bird's-egg blue above him. Automobile motors rumbled in the streets below, blended with the pop-pop-popping of many pistols, the crack of riflefire, the sounds of tinkling glass. Above him the light blue sky swirled with pink and yellow, a gorgeous pastel dawn, a fine early-summer morning, June 1, his father's birthday. T.J. marveled at how tranquil he felt.

A high distant hum came from the north, grew to a buzzing, and then a loud roaring overhead, as a shiny new biplane, wings gleaming, flew in low, banked away from the smoke; it was followed by another, and another. T.J. could see a whiteman leaning from the open seat of the first plane, firing a rifle over the side, down on the streets of Greenwood. A canister plummeted from the second plane, trailing fire, and where it landed there was an explosion, and a roof somewhere on Frankfort or Easton burst into flames. Quickly T.J. rolled over, crawled on his belly to the rear of the building and heaved himself over the side; his dangling legs searched for the open window from which he'd hoisted himself to the roof in the darkness, hours ago.

When he swung himself into the dawnlit room, he was relieved to see that the woman and her little girl were gone. Good. She'd done what he said. He didn't know her name, had never seen her before he knocked at her room at midnight and asked to use the window, but when she'd begged him for news of what was happening on the streets, he'd told her, Take your little girl and go north, past the section line. Whites coming at daylight, he'd told her; won't be no place down here safe. She'd looked at him helplessly, unbelieving, and turned back to her little girl asleep on the dufold. T.J. hadn't had time to mess with her; he'd set the chair in front of the window, looped the carbine over his shoulder, crawled out. All night he had sniped from the rooftop, as long as he'd had ammunition. Twice he was certain he'd got one, a dark head falling back, and it was nothing like shooting the whiteman who chased Everett's daddy. That had been accident, the shotgun in his hand by instinct, not to *kill* the whiteman, but to stop him. Now he knew there was only one way to stop whitemen. T.J. carried in his mind the image of white weasel faces, Everett's silhouette on the horizon, fallen black men around him as the line retreated toward Greenwood. He was going to kill every white face he could see, but he had to find more shells.

He took the stairs four at a time, was almost to the ground floor when a voice caught him. "Son! Son!" A tiny elderly woman was hunched in a doorway on the second floor. She was dressed up like Sunday in a fine navy dress, a string of red beads at her throat. Her hair was white; her fingers, gnarled as willow roots, were wrapped around the knob of a cane she grasped in both hands. "Help me! I can't run!"

"You safer here than on the streets," T.J. said.

"They're burning everything. They'll burn the hotel down over my head."

There was a crash of shattered glass at the front of the building, followed by a splintering sound, and T.J. stepped over to the woman and picked her up piggyback. The cane clattered to the floor, her old lungs grunted as he hoisted her, but she weighed no more than one of his little sisters, and he ran with her toward the back hallway, away from the sound of the breaking glass.

Out the back of the building and into the alley and through it till they reached the Midland Valley railyard. In the distance he could see people running north along the rails, women dragging their children by the hands, old people in nightclothes tottering in the center of the tracks, and men, too, young prime men, running, his people running. T.J.'s soul rebelled. No! He'd not come down to the streets to run but to fight. The gunfire behind him was constant, wild, unconnected, issuing from a hundred directions. Smoke billowed, dipped low; the old lady started to cough. He ran with her out into the open space of the railyard. What had he done with the rifle? He'd left the carbine on the rooftop; he must have, because he didn't have it. But his Colt was tucked in his belt, he could feel its smooth, bloodwarmed barrel against his skin; he'd find more shells, find someplace to stand and fight, he thought, as he jogged along the side of the tracks, running north with the others, running with the old lady on his back. He heard her faint wheezy lungs. Then she grunted hard and slammed against him, shoving him forward, and the stick-thin arms around his neck went slack; she began to slide backward. T.J. crouched low, hunkered forward so that the old lady's body might not fall off, and on he went, running.

Graceful, too, was moving north. She wasn't running but gliding serenely among the white rioters on Elgin Avenue. If any had paused in their frenzy to notice, they'd have been struck by her purposefulness and composure, but the rioters were looking for loot and for niggers, and the tall, veiled lady in old-fashioned evening dress met neither description. She passed Johnson's Shoes and the confectionery, where whitepeople streamed through the shattered doors in antlike relays, carting vats of cherries and chocolate syrup to add to the pile of round black tables and brass chairs; carrying leather workboots and children's oxfords to toss onto the great, tumbled, multicolored mountain of shoes. Already small fires were flickering inside the stores. Hours earlier, when she'd seen the mauled black body being dragged in the street and believed it was T.J., Graceful had entered a deep, listless mourning. Her brother's fear in the tent at Bigheart instantly became prophecy, she herself the unheedful sinner, and for those few hours in the alley, she'd been lost.

But the sight of the blackened corpse in the cinders had wrenched her from grief to purposeful fury: it might be T.J. on his back in the railyard, might not be; might be Delroy, or Hedgemon, might be a woman, even, because there were no clothes or genitals to show who it was. With the odor of burned flesh in her nostrils, Graceful had crossed the tracks. The masses of whitepeople breaking and pouring north made her struggle easier, that was all. She held no conscious thought of Mrs. Dedmeyer, or the baby, though the tingling gut-deep pull went on coursing from her breasts to her parched throat, her belly, her privates, because her body would not so easily relinquish the child. By the time she started up the hill, her milk had let down again. A baby was crying somewhere. She stopped, turned to look behind.

The whole of Archer was in flames now; smoke blackened the daylight sky. Graceful pulled the veiled hat off in order to see better. The cross streets were afire as far north as Brady. Open carloads of whitemen with shotguns and rifles, men with badges and hats and guns, patrolled the roads, but they were not trying to stop the white looters. They were gathering up Negroes. In the distance she saw a young woman with a crying baby in her arms being pushed along the avenue by a whitewoman. Two men in stocking feet, with their arms raised over their heads, were being marched south by three young whiteboys with guns. The front line of looters had passed the stores now; they were starting in on the homes a few blocks below where Graceful stood. The sound of breaking glass was everywhere. She watched a half-dozen whitemen trying to wrestle an upright piano through the doorway of a two-story brick house. A whitewoman stepped out the shattered front window with her arms full of silverware; she dashed down the porch steps and hurried south, dropping spoons and forks as she ran. Graceful walked on, her breasts weeping, her breath labored, her step calm and deliberate, but quickened. She had to get home.

Throughout the city all living creatures were moving, the rats and cats and stray dogs fleeing the fire, as the black population fled, and the white rioters swelled north and east and west from the train tracks, burning, looting, or taking Negroes into custody and marching them to the newly spawned prison camps at the fairgrounds and the convention hall. Near the Frisco station hundreds of National Guardsmen, sent by the governor, were disembarking from a train just arrived from Oklahoma City, and those already on the ground were moving, too—not north, to stop the riot or to put out the raging fires, but south, toward City Hall, to prepare and eat breakfast. The sheriff was driving east in a closed car, with two deputies guarding the prisoner, as they spirited Dick Rowland out of town. Franklin Dedmeyer hurried south on Carson Avenue in the bright morning sun, his palm at his forehead in a salute, for he'd misplaced his hat somewhere. Miles away, Althea walked north, with the child in her arms. Mr. Smitherman, having watched the *Star* office surrender to the fire, was in that moment crossing Dirty Butter Creek with his wife and children and another family in a Ford motorcar, as Hedgemon Jackson, for the fourth time since daylight, climbed the front steps of the yellow shotgun house, where, inside, in the cramped middle room, Elberta's baby moved through the moist tunnel, in the darkness, the violence, the crushing waves, without light. Even the blackened corpse in the railyard was moving, as it was hoisted by disinterested hands and tossed onto the flatbed of an oilfield truck, to join the other black bodies stacked like cordwood near the cab.

Behind a car shed near the train tracks, T.J. eased the old lady to the ground. He stood pondering her a moment while he caught his breath: a tiny slackmouthed brown woman, a stranger in a navy dress, dead. Still panting, he stepped to the corner of the shed and peered south, where the smoke covered everything; he turned and squinted west. The whites had mounted another machine gun inside Greenwood; it was raining fire now from the top of Standpipe Hill. Another glance at the dead woman. Nothing to do for her. Nothing he could do, same as there'd been nothing to do for Everett Candler, except kill whitemen. He had to get hold of some ammunition somewhere. T.J. slipped from the protection of the car shed, walked fast along Latimer Street, and then he was trotting, and finally running toward his uncle's garage. Behind him the dead woman lay like a thin shadow in the alley, curled around itself.

The old stable that Delroy used for a garage was empty, a few tools and engine parts scattered on the dirt floor, the Nash truck yawning, its hood raised, front wheels on blocks. T.J. ran next door, but the house, too, was empty, Lucille and the kids gone, the beds unmade. He hurried to the closet in the front room, tossed clothes and hats on the floor, but he knew Delroy didn't own a gun; there'd be no bullets here. Pulling his pistol from his waistband, T.J. went to the window, pushed aside the curtain; he could see two whitemen coming along Rosedale, and the fury in him was terrible, to have a gun and no ammunition. He could kill them so easily from here. T.J. shoved the empty gun back in his belt and rushed to the kitchen, slung drawers open, grabbed a butcher knife and a paring knife, and ran out the back door, hunkered over, crossed the yard to the garage. A voice down the street hollered, "There's one!" and guns popped below him, but T.J. ducked in the stable door.

When they came in, he was up in the old hayloft, pressed against the back wall. He was hiding from whitemen, yes, but it was not the same as cowering in the cornstalks: if they tried to climb the ladder, he was ready. Both kitchen blades raised.

"Watch out, them sonsabitches'll snipe ya," one whispered.

"Burn this dump down," the other answered. "He'll show his coon ass quick enough." There was the muted sound of boots scrabbling on the dirt floor, the clank of metal on metal. "Me and Skinner torched a whore-house on Archer, Christ, you ought to seen the monkeys run!" Both men laughed. T.J. could smell gasoline.

"Shit, it's livelier'n shooting ducks at the fair," the first one hissed, and then there was the whoosh of flames. "Let's get out of here!"

T.J. didn't let himself think; he stepped to the edge of the loft and leapt down, and where the blade entered there was no resistance, the butcher knife slipped slickly in the soft side, like cutting lard. He twisted the blade as the whiteman gasped, tried to holler, but T.J. already had the man's gun, and he shot the other one as he turned his surprised weasel face toward him, and then this one in the head, and then was sorry to have wasted the bullet. Whitemen died easy. He felt their pockets for car-tridges, took the rifle and the two revolvers, let the fire have the two men.

Inside the yellow shotgun house Iola Bloodgood Tiger took the child in her two hands and laid it on the mother's belly. The shriveled cord pulsed feebly; the baby's skin was withered, ancient-looking, as if she'd already begun to die in the womb, but the child breathed, and her cry lifted to join the sounds coming from the front room. Iola turned to tell Hedgemon Jackson, All right, we can go now, get them in the front room ready. The young man had been at the door a dozen times in the last hour, saying, They're burning Greenwood, we got to take these children and go! Behind him, always, she could hear the old mother weeping in the front room—

—sometimes wailing, sometimes sobbing, sometime little low whim-pers like a child. Sometime no sound at all but the old mother walking back and forth across the floor. That sound of weeping been accompani-ment for the little mother's birth groans all night, and I heard them like a song, right up till that child come into the world dying. For true. Birthcord flat and twisted. Baby look like an old woman, skin wrinkled, frizzly hair sticking out all over, little fingernails long enough to scratch. I have seen such things, more than a few times, because sometime a little soul don't want to come out. Sometimes it stay in the womb so long the child have to be born dead, because life will go right out if the child won't breathe this world's air, and sometimes it kill that mama, too. I would not blame any child coming into such a world as we showing that morning if it take one look and go right back to God, but this child do not go back, she lay slick on her mama's belly, crying like a cat.

I don't know how that little mother is going to travel, but she is going to, because we are all going to, because we do not have a choice. This is what I tell myself when I turn to speak to that tall boy. But he's not standing at the door now, how he been so many times through the labor, and when I go in the front room I don't see him there either, only the old mother on the divan with her dead daughter, touching the girl's face in her lap like the child is sleeping, and her other two young ones ringed on both sides. All night, whatever way the old mother is crying, that's the same way her two childrens cry—if she sob they sob, if she cry silent that's how they do, the little boy and his sister. Right now Mrs. Whiteside is facing straight ahead, making a slow shuddery sound deep in her chest, and the children match her, breath for breath. But the tall black boy is not here. He's not dancing fidgety at the window like he done all night, watching. I say to the old mother, Child born, and she nod, but she don't look at me. Girl child, I tell her, and I ease myself to the window, look south. The whole world have disappeared into smoke. I got to step outside to see how far the fire is.

Everything looks different in bright morning to how it looked in the dark when we carried the dead girl up on the front porch, when I stopped and looked south, seen the lone pillar of fire burning way off in the distance and little lights winking everywhere. Now the world have come to full daylight, but the light is turning dark from a hundred clouds of smoke rolling toward heaven, and when those many clouds gets up high they join together, make one huge gray boiling cloudbank to rise up over the world. Behind me, before me, all around me I hear the guns rattling, because death is coming from all directions, we are fully surrounded. What have I tell you about such force? That power's been unleashed, and there's no might on this earth going to turn it back under, no return till the story finish, and we a long way from finished. This hour of destruction is no more than a eyeblink to God.

I stand on the porch and look toward where the fire's crawling, and I see whitefolks running, blackfolks running, or walking slow with they hands in the air, I see men in cars rumbling everywhichway. Then I spy the tall black boy in a yard just down a ways, and I holler, Boy! We ready now! The child come! But he's turned away, looking south into the smoke.

All at once he start running away from me. I thinks to myself, Well, son, you been wanting to run all night, haven't you? Now you going to take off just the minute I could use you. I was so pure disgusted I turned and went back in the house.

The dead girl lay by herself on the divan, so peaceful looking, so pretty, except for the dark dried blood spread out on her chest. I hear the old mama in the middle room, barking at her two childrens, fetch this, do that, and when I go in I see she is wiping the infant clean with a wet rag. She have covered the little mother with a fresh sheet. The girl's face is swollen, her eyes look terrible, the afterbirth laying on the floor beside the cot, and the old mother ignore it, just step over it to carry the baby to the other bed. She look straight down at the little mother, say, Missy, you going to have to walk. I say, Miz Whiteside, you carry the baby, I'll help her. But that woman ignore me, turn to the chifforobe, jerk a dress off a hanger, say, LaVona, take Willie's hand, don't you let him go, I don't care what happen. Here, girl, sit up. And she go to help that little mother lean forward so she can slip the dress on over her head. The girl groan, say, Where's my baby? Mama? Is the baby all right?

I say, Your baby just fine, honey. Hear her? And, sure enough, that baby is crying strong now. I go to pick her up, she jerk her arms and legs good, the skinny wizened thing, little naked ancient child, hard as blackjack sticks, face like a bone; she's wailing loud, demanding, she ready to nurse this minute, but we got no time to wait for that. The two younguns standing in the doorway, the girl holding to the boy like she'll die if she let go of him, the old mother's putting a shift on the little mother, what am I going to do but wrap that baby up? I wrap her snug in a piece of blanket while Mrs. Whiteside help the little mother to stand, she wobble a minute on shaky legs, sit back down on the bed. Mrs. Whiteside lift her up again, hold her under the armpits to make her stay standing. She look over at me. Seem to me like it's the first time she have truly seen me since we come in the door, me and the tall boy, carrying her dead girl. But now she look directly at me, she say, Mrs.Tiger, where's Hedgemon?

I shake my head. He's gone, I tell her. He run off.

The woman stare past the two children to the front room. I can see her thinking, Who's going to carry my daughter? And I wonder the same. Mrs. Whiteside and me together could carry the dead girl, maybe, and the two childrens could take turns with the baby, but who's going to help the little mother? She can't walk. I don't believe she's going to walk a block without her womb fall out in the street. The woman keep looking at the front door, but her soul's eye is on the dead girl in her pink dress laying on the divan.

I say, Miz Whiteside? We got to go now. They coming. Fire's coming. We got to take these children and go north.

The old mother turn to me. She stare at me for a long time, silent. In a bit she turn to the two younguns, say, LaVona, you going to have to go with Mrs. Tiger. Y'all got to mind her now, hear me? Willie? You hear? The children nod. She come take the baby from me and put her in the little mother's arms, push that little mother away from the cot toward the front door. But when that little mother get to the front room and see the dead girl, she start to wilt down. Like a tallow wick on a hot stove she melt toward the linoleum, and when she get to the floor she let out a long whimpery wail.

Hush! That old mama's voice so fierce, the girl quiet at once; even that just-born babe in arms hush up her mouth. Outside folks are shouting, motorcars roaring, guns chattering, but inside is so quiet. The old mother whisper, My child come back to me dead, but your child is living. You going to take her. Take Willie and LaVona, because they are your flesh now. You got to help them. There's nobody else to help them. Daughter! You hear me? The little mother nod her head. Mrs. Whiteside turn to me, her eyes dry as breath, not even shiny now with wet. She say, Wait for us somewhere by Turley, if you can find a good place to wait.

They're burning everything, I say. They'll burn this house down with you and your child in it.

I got to stay with Jewell. That's all she answer. She disappear in the middle room, come back with a knotted handkerchief, hold it out to me, say, We thank you for your help. I don't put my hand out to take it. Very soft, in that dry feather-whisper, she say, I have lost enough children this night, Mrs. Tiger. Take my children someplace safe. Then in a loud voice she say, TeeJay going to be here in a minute. Him and Delroy coming soon. She keep talking in that loud everyday voice, like the world's not on fire, like the whites not swarming like an army into Greenwood to kill colored folks, like blackfolks not shooting whitefolks either, and her daughter's just having a little nap on the divan. She say, Y'all wait for us at Turley, or Bird Creek, or Dirty Butter, whichever look best. We'll find you. Soon as Delroy get here with the truck, we going to come. LaVona! What did I tell you? The girl grab her brother's hand, quick. The woman look steady at me when she put that knotted hanky in my hand. I can feel the little stack of coins tied so smooth in it. Her eyes never blink. We just going to be a little while, she tell me. We'll soon come. She turn and hold the screen open. I pick up the baby, put my hand under the arm of the little mother, help her up from the floor.

On the porch Mrs. Whiteside bend down and hug those two young ones, and they both take in to crying, but she say, Hush! And instantly they hush. The smoke is rolling thick now, the little boy start coughing. The old mother don't look at us anymore; she pull open the screen and go back in the house, sit down on the divan, take the dead girl's head in her lap.

Japheth moved openly among the rioters—not unobtrusively as he'd slipped among the lynchers when they hanged his partner, but brazenly, at the center, the coreheart of violence. In the first moments of eruption, when the armed black men, firing, began their retreat toward Greenwood, Japheth, seeing who was winning, turned immediately and joined the white mobs. It was Japheth, yes, whom Althea had seen at the burning of the corpse in the railyard, as it was Japheth who'd found the gasoline can in the first place, doused fuel on the dying body, shouted, Let's burn the nigger! Japheth's hand that struck the match. Japheth's voice crying from the steps of Mount Zion Baptist, The niggers got an arsenal in here, burn down the church!

It was Japheth who sauntered forward now among some white men in the yard of a fine brick home on Detroit Avenue, where a Negro doctor in a houserobe and slippers walked down his front steps with his hands clasped on top of his head. Japheth whispered to a teenaged white boy with a pistol, That nigger raped a white woman, or The nigger's got a gun, or That uppity nigger's got better things than you'll ever have, or some words, Japheth said some words, and the boy pulled the trigger, shot Dr. Blanchard pointblank in the chest. The others nearby whooped or shouted, What the hell are you doing? Japheth turned, made his way to the next block.

In a strip of dirt yard he paused, looking north. The street was filled with Home Guard, hundreds of white men waving their guns, bellowing, as they rounded up Negro prisoners, set fire to Negro homes. A familiar dark-blond head moved among the others, hatless, the frowning face unmistakable. Japheth started toward it; then he stopped, his eyes narrowed, his cunning returned. He watched as the driller and several others separated a group of black men from some women and children, searched them, took whatever money they had in their pockets, and herded them into two silent clutches. In Japheth's mind the images rolled: thudding fists on the Murphys' lawn in the cold moonlight; the scowling, scornful face in the clearing. He retreated into the narrow space between two houses, crouched low to the earth to gather himself.

Some of the Home Guard began to march the black men down the middle of the street, four abreast, arms high in the air. They were coming directly toward him. The driller was in the midst of them, anonymous in oil-stained khakis, looking like any white man, but Japheth knew him. He raised the barrel of his gun. In a moment they'd be beside him. He would call out softly, Logan! and no one but the driller would hear. A delicate squeeze, and the sound of the discharge would be lost in the sounds of other bullets, in the roar of fire and voices, but Japheth would call out his name, and the driller, dying, would look up and know by whose hand. As Japheth waited, anticipating that delicious moment, a faint pop came from somewhere, and Jim Logan fell. There was a staccato burst as the Home Guard shot three of the unarmed Negroes, another shot from the sniper, and a second white man dropped, and Japheth sucked himself back into the crevice, the great ravenous place in him exploding in fury. The sweet moment had been stolen. Ripped from him by niggers! Japheth slipped back farther, hid himself deep in the cleft between the two Negro houses. In the crevice, in the dark, he tended his rage.

When he emerged from the narrow space a half-hour later, he was starving. Dark skin was the marker. Dark skin was the sign and permission. He found a black man hiding in a basement across the way, and he shot him, but the man wasn't destroyed. Japheth doused the man with gasoline, lit him, watched the body burn a few minutes before he climbed out the basement window. His gluttony, whipped by fire, enhanced by the earth's blackblood refined to the incendiary liquid he carried, was aimless, insatiable. He walked to the next street, found an old couple praying on their knees in their bedroom, shot them each in the back of the head, piled their curtains and bedclothes on the mattress, sprinkled gasoline on the pile, lit the sheets. But even before the flames licked up, Japheth walked out of the house, hungry. At each death the craving within him swelled larger; at each fire the great ravenous place increased. By the time he emerged from a gasoline-soaked house onto a porch on Elgin Avenue and saw the tall, graceful figure walking out of the smoke toward him, the gluttony in his soul was as large as the world.

N orth was the direction she'd begun, north she continued, striding fast in her gardening shoes, until she came to a place where a church was burning, a massive church of brick and stained glass, but the flames licked up tall through the broken windows and men swarmed around it, shouting, and Althea turned aside, went west a ways before she turned north again, climbing now as the land climbed. She held her brother's child tight to her breast, secret from the world, owned within herself, as she moved through the morning light, the hot light of early morning. The yellow light of September. It had been early September, yes, and she'd walked such a long way, through a sea of black faces, faster, the swells rushing over her, faster, until she was running in this same place, this same street—or, no, not this street, another, where a brown-skinned grocer swept the plank sidewalk, where a café owner was setting out a sandwich board, and somewhere, at the end of the block, a black woman in a flowered dress stood in a glass doorway, saying, You welcome to come in and rest your feets awhile.

Althea stopped, looked around, but there were no colored people readying for work, no shopkeepers, schoolchildren, mothers tugging their youngsters along; only burning houses, and Negroes walking in the center of the road with their hands in the air, shoeless, hatless in the smoky light, and the hatted and booted men behind them, around them, holding rifles and shotguns, men in open cars roaring in the dirt street, churning dust to rise up and mingle with smoke. She walked on, holding her baby brother carefully; she was sweating in the heat, coughing, and the baby was crying, its face muffled against her. In the distance she saw the back of her green sateen dress moving away, growing smaller, disappearing, as if she were watching herself draw away from herself in a dream. No. She'd given that dress to Graceful. It was the flax-colored dress she wanted, not that old green one. She put the baby to her shoulder, hurried to catch up, but the green dress was gone.

Just ahead a handsome man in a maroon bathrobe and slippers was coming down his porch steps, his amber-colored hands clasped on top of his head. Althea's heart jerked with recognition at sight of the doctor's shining black hair and thin mustache. She started forward to ask how to get to Graceful's mother's house, for of course he would know. He'd driven her there in his touring car. But the doctor was surrounded by white men, and she hesitated. There was one among them, a familiar sylphlike figure, whispering in the ear of a young white boy, but his face was shaded, concealed by the dirty brim of a slouch hat, and she couldn't quite see. Then the sound popped and the doctor fell, and she heard the shouts, saw that one slinking away. Althea recognized her brother. She turned at once and followed him, followed in the grip of blood-recognition, without thought of what she'd do if she caught up with him, without any effort to catch up, but only to keep him in sight. He slipped into a crevice between two houses, and she stopped, waited in the street for him to come out again, but a new burst of gunfire made her run for protection. She sank down beside a frame house, crouched low, patted the baby's shuddery back.

The guns peppered the air for a moment, and then there was silence, only for an instant, but she heard them calling, the voices faint in the distance, Leeeetha, Leeeeeeetha. It was dark in the shadow of the house. The baby was crying. She lifted his tiny scrunched face close to her face. The velvety forehead was warm, emollient, bathed in the spiced scent of his mother's pomade. "Shhhh, baby," she whispered. It was dark where she was hiding. She couldn't run because she had torn her dress off. She was naked. It was dark in the slatted light of the corncrib. She remembered the plump milkwhite legs in her hands, the surprising heft when she lifted him, the rubbery weight. The birthwoman shouted a Creek word, something she couldn't understand, but Aletha saw fear in the brown face, saw shock and judgment. The abyss opened before her. In the bottom of the ravine she saw the red water trickling. She'd thrown the baby down, run away. Run to the corral. No. What was she thinking? Yes, she'd called the red calf, and when he came trotting she'd raised the chopping ax, hit him in the head, the blood spurted, and she hit him again, and again, but it was nothing; it was only how they slaughtered hogs in winter, it wasn't why she hid the bloody flaxen dress beneath a stone, hid herself naked in the slatted dark while they called and called, because she'd killed her brother.

But the baby wasn't dead. He was here. He was alive, in her arms, shuddering. She touched her lips to his forehead, his warm temple. He smelled of milk and urine, petrolatum, newborn skin. Somewhere a siren wailed. More gunshots. The baby coughed in tiny little spasms as the smoke rolled into the sheltered place, dipping low. Althea sat motionless. Something welled up from deep within her breast. She put her fingers to the baby's face. His skin was so fragile, soft. She brushed her face against him, his soft eyelash-flutter cheek against her cheek. "It's all right," she whispered. The feeling kept rising, spreading honeylike through her. She was weeping, and she didn't know why. Out in the street the gasoline engines roared, the voices went on shouting. But they weren't calling her. She kissed the baby's soft crown.

Dear God, the world was burning. One could not mourn private sin when all the world was burning. Althea leaned against the house, forced deep shuddery breaths into her lungs, bit down on the inside of her jaw. Slowly the shudders began to ebb, the honeyed feeling seeped away. She tugged the blanket up around her nephew's face. He was quiet now. In another few moments she got up from the soft early-summer grass, settled the baby against her arm, walked out to the street.

There were bodies in the road, colored men and white men lying dead beside each other. Althea turned her eyes away. She peered south, but the world was a wall of fire to the Frisco line. She couldn't take the baby there. She saw no way to turn back, no way to go around; she had to move forward, that was all. Keeping to the near side of the road, she hurried past the dead men; she wouldn't allow her gaze to settle on the lightsoled bare brown feet, the shattered limbs in cotton shirts and filthy seersucker suits, the oil-stained khakis dark with blood.

Before Graceful cleared the crest of Brickyard Hill, she saw Hedgemon Jackson bounding down the slope toward her. She hadn't seen him in many months, but all she could think was that he shouldn't be here, on Elgin Avenue, on Mama's street, just a few blocks down from Mama's house. "What is it?" she called, but already her heart was caught. Hedgemon's face was stark, the muscles jiggling beneath the skin as he ran toward her. Graceful walked faster. They met in the middle of the block, and Hedgemon stood in front of her, panting; he raised his hand as if to touch her, let it fall.

"What they do to him?" Graceful said. "Where is he?"

Hedgemon bent from the waist a little, put his long hands on his knees. "Not T.J.," he puffed.

"Who, then?"

He shook his head, raised up, looking over her shoulder, past her, to the fires in Greenwood. His face had filled out; he looked mannish now. "Hurry. We got to go." He was breathing hard, but already his feet were edging backward as he reached for her hand.

Graceful slapped his palm away. "Tell me!"

"Last night. Berta." He was still trying to catch his breath. "Berta's baby start to come. Your mama. She send—" His beautiful longlashed eyes flicked sideways, guilty. "Send Jewell. Down to Greenwood— Graceful! Wait!"

She was past him, moving in strong strides toward Mama's house. She could see the edge of the porch now. Was that Willie in the yard? She started to run.

"Graceful!" Hedgemon was trotting after her. "Wait!

There was the screech of automobile tires, voices yelling, whitemen's voices. "Stop right there, nigger! Put your goddamn hands in the air!"

"Wha'chu running for, nigger?"

"Somebody grab that gal!"

Rough hands grabbed her from behind, and it was the same as the first whiteman's hands, the brother's hands, and the cold rage swelled up as other hands clutched at her; she tried to keep running, but they had her by the arms, the skirt. "Where'd you steal this dress, nigger?" She struggled to get free, she had to go, her mama needed her, Jewell might need a doctor, they couldn't keep her, she had to get home.

"You been looting white ladies' bedrooms, gal?"

"Keep those hands up, nigger! I'll shoot 'em off!"

Hedgemon was in a yard a little ways away, his hands high over his head, palms toward her, his face frozen in fear. Graceful felt a wash of unforgiving fury, and then the white hands were shoving her, turning her in a circle. Somebody said, "Get that white woman's dress off that nigger!"

and the voices laughed. White hands plucked at the yards of material, jerking it, pulling at it. Somebody grasped the lace collar, yanked it away from her throat. The flimsy material ripped like rotted cotton.

"Whoooeee! Looka there, they're going to strip the bitch."

With a mighty flailing heave, she twisted away, and the sateen at her waist shrieked in one long tear as she broke free. "Get her!" She ran, but something hit her in the back, a fist or a rock, knocked her to the ground, knocked the wind out of her, and her face smashed against the earth. They were at her back, and it was the same as in the maid's room, the same, they would do the same thing to her, and Graceful rolled over, she fought them with a strength beyond her strength, she lashed out in terror and fury, but she couldn't stop them; they were everywhere, tugging, whooping, laughing, clawing. She felt the sateen bodice tear, heard it rip down the back as the tiny buttons gave, and then she felt the hot, blank air upon her chest. Graceful folded up, crouched in the grass, shrinking away from their white weasel faces, their spotted faces, colorless laughing faces, ringed around her naked on the ground.

Naw, now, that gal tore her own dress off. I don't know where you're getting your information, but, what I seen, that colored gal went to hollering when we tried to arrest her, and then she just laid down and wallowed in the grass, screaming and carrying on like she'd got a scorpion in her britches. Next thing I know, she's naked. That's all. Who knows what those people get in their crazy heads. We were just doing our job. The governor'd declared martial law, see, and our orders were to disarm the coloreds and march 'em down to Brady, to the convention center on Brady, and that's just what we were doing, rounding up loose niggers like we been deputized to do. Well, some of them cooperated and some didn't. That black buck she was with put his hands up right off, so we didn't have to shoot him, but I'll tell you one thing, I's about ready to shoot that white woman. Dear God, what a witch— and you can drop that w and put a b in front of it, you'll hear a word closer to the damn truth. She come swarming up there, wagging that baby, hollering, "What do you think you're doing? Take your hands off!" and on and on. Lord, you could hear her a mile. We tried to tell her she could have her niggers back if she wanted them but she was going to have to come down to Conven-

tion Hall and sign them out, same as anybody else. They were going to issue tags for the coloreds, see, once we'd got them all
gathered up, and then they'd let white folks come vouch for the
good ones. That way we'd know which ones was good niggers and
which wasn't. Any upstanding white person could sign for their
chauffeur or housemaid or what-have-you, there was no problem,
but you were going to have to do it proper, do it right, go down
yonder to the holding pen and make it legal, according to how the
mayor and them had figured it out.

Well, we tried to tell that to the woman, but you couldn't tell
that banshee nothing. We were about ready to arrest her too,
make her stand yonder with that sullen colored boy. Tell you
what, if you could've shot them for looks, that boy would have
been dead on that count, for sure, but he stood quiet enough, kept
his hands over his head, and anyhow we were busy trying to get
that wench to stand up. A couple fellows prodded her with their
boot toes or the barrel of their gun, but she was hunkered down
like a bobcat, you didn't want to wade in too close. Naked as a
jaybird from the waist up. It was funny, but then again it wasn't
funny. I thought Stinson was going to shoot her in the head and
be done with it, he was that mad, but you felt kind of sorry for
her, too. Somebody'd ought to give her something to cover herself up with, that's what I thought. But we had us a job to do, and
that colored gal wouldn't cooperate, and here come this white
woman, making matters worse, screeching around—

"Stop! This instant! You fools! You absolute idiots. Give me that!" Althea
tried to grab the barrel of a rifle poking Graceful's buttocks. The man
jerked it away, stepped back with the gun turned on her, and then he spat,
lowered the muzzle, said, "Lady, hadn't you better go home?"

"What in God's name do you think you're doing?"

"We been deputized to round up niggers. What is it? This gal steal
your dress? Get up from there, gal. Stand up!"

"Watch him, now, watch him."

"He's all right. You all right, nigger? He's fine. He's a good nigger. You
a good nigger, boy?"

"Look out, Tim, don't get too close. That wench's liable to bite your
pecker off."

"Leave her alone!" Althea screamed. "Leave her!"

"Lady, you better stand back and let us do our job."

"I'll have every one of you arrested! Do you hear me? Sheriff McCullough's a personal friend of my husband."

"Somebody shut that woman up."

"This girl works for me. Stop! Stop that!" She turned on a snickering boy using the barrel of his pistol to try to pry up one of Graceful's clamped arms. The boy was laughing. "Let's see her titties, I never seen nigger titties! She's nekked! It's a nekked nigger! Let's see!" A carload of men squealed to a stop on Elgin Avenue, and the same impulse that had caused Althea to run shouting when she crested the hill and saw Graceful on the ground, now caused her to wheel and turn on the newcomers as a she-bear rears up to swipe at a pack of dogs, but she had no weapons, no claws or strength, only her impotent shrieks and her sex and her white skin to fight them with. A half-dozen men poured from the automobile, joined by others swarming up the hill on foot. The men swaggered into the yard. "You fellas need a hand? My, my, my, what have we got here."

Althea recognized a clerk from the shoe department at Renberg's, and she called out to him, "Make these idiots stop!" The clerk, so obsequious and flattering when he knelt to help her try on shoes, shoved past her as if she were nobody, as if he'd never seen her before, waving his gun in the air. "Y'all step aside! We'll get that nigger on her feet!"

"Take your hands off her!"

But the clerk and a second man were already hoisting Graceful by the arms, holding her up to stand exposed in the midst of them. The baby was wailing. Graceful stared straight ahead. Althea kept repeating, shrilly, pointlessly, "Leave that girl alone! She works for me!" as she rocked the shrieking baby, patted his back. Behind the shoe clerk she spied another familiar face, an oil acquaintance of Franklin's, she couldn't think of his name but she recognized him from the dining room at the Hotel Tulsa. The oilman stood off to the side, armed with a little pistol and a cardboard star pinned on his chest, big-bellied, puffed up in a fine summer suit, his graying hair neatly coifed, like Franklin's. For an instant she was flustered by thoughts of her husband. Was Franklin running around bullying people with a gun and a paper star, like these men? And Jim Dee, hadn't she seen Jim Dee running in the street with the others? No. Jim Dee was in Bristow. That had been her overwrought imagination, hours ago, a lifetime ago, in the alley downtown, before—

Japheth. She had forgotten about Japheth, almost from the moment she'd seen him slip between the houses. But, no, that wasn't him either. That had just been her wild imagining, like thinking she'd seen Jim Dee. She searched the dozens of white faces. Men in battered felt hats and porkpies and summer boaters jostled one another, bullying, bellowing, bloated with their own lawless authority, but Japheth wasn't here. Of course he wasn't here. Her brother was dead. "Hush, baby," Althea whispered. Graceful's lips were drawn tight over her teeth. Still she didn't meet Althea's eyes. The baby was crying so hard, his face covered by the blanket. It was murderously hot, hellish hot, the fires like a furnace at her back, and the ceaseless voices kept barking.

"Stinson, you and Lambert haul these two down, we'll meet you at the section line."

Althea peeled the blanket back from the baby's face.

"Eskew, take your bunch and fan out west."

The baby's face was wrinkled, sweaty, dark with rage.

"Me and Cletus'll go back downtown and see if we can't scrounge up some more ammunition."

Althea lifted her gaze to the deep indentations in Graceful's arms, the brown smooth upper arms clamped tight in chalky fingers, the marbled marks on her breasts, her belly swelling above the sagging half-chemise. The cotton slip was ripped and dirt-smeared, its limp drawstring dangling. With no thought but to cover up what she did not want to see, Althea unwrapped the child, held the blanket out to Graceful. It stank of urine. The baby's gown was sopping wet. Althea stood holding the little strip of blanket, foolishly shaking it up and down as if to say, Take it!

When Graceful turned at last and looked at her, the fixed expression on the smooth, slanted face startled Althea, and then swept her with fear and pain. Graceful stared at her from hooded eyes as if it were Althea who pinned her arms, Althea who cursed and shamed her, who lit the fires, burned the blackened corpse beside the tracks. The girl hated her. How could that be? Hadn't she tried to save her? Hadn't she put her own dress on the girl's back, set her own hat on the pomaded head? Hadn't she done everything for her, for months now, since the very day the girl had come to work in her house—

"It's not me!" Althea hissed. "I didn't do any of this!"

Graceful turned away. She stood with her face lifted, shoulders down, unclothed and dignified in the white fingers' grasp.

From the back of the crowd a voice piped, "For God's sake, somebody cover that wench up, y'all are going to start a riot."

"Hah!"

"Gimme that!" The shoe clerk jerked the blanket from Althea's hand, flung it over one of Graceful's shoulders. As if the gesture had opened their collective eyes, they all turned to stare at the white woman's colored baby.

"Wouldja look at that!"

"Yella as my daddy's toenail, ain't it?"

"No wonder she's th'owing such a fit!"

"She's a nigger?"

"Naw, she ain't a nigger, she's been screwing niggers."

"That's a mulatter baby, sure enough."

A disgusted voice said, "Take her into custody. We'll bring her in with the rest."

"Dear God, no!" Althea held him away from her. "He's not mine! Look. Look at her, she's the mother. Graceful, take your son!" She thrust the baby out, her hands circling his little hiccupy chest; the baby's head lolled, his legs kicked inside the gown. The girl stood across from her, without moving.

"Take him!"

The girl stood across the abyss of cut red earth, the slashed crater in the world where the water rolled in the bottom the color of new blood.

"Step over yonder," a voice said. "Move."

She had to drop him. Yes. She would simply open her hands and let the shrieking newborn fall to the earth. Drop him! she told herself.

"We can't take in a white woman, Jack."

"We can if she's got a nigger baby."

Althea felt suddenly that she held in her hands the power to undo sin. Her own sin, the past. She pulled her arms in, put the baby over her shoulder, muffling his cries; gently she patted his back. In a clear, calm voice she said, "This baby's starving. He's got to nurse." Graceful met her gaze, and the whole history passed between them, separate, skewed, held in common: the single narrative of their bound-together lives. "I can't feed him," Althea said. "You know he'll die." There was a beat of silence, punctuated by the baby's wails. Graceful didn't speak, but Althea saw the slow exhalation through her flared nostrils, the little surrender, before the girl flicked her eyes to the tall black boy, who stood with his hands in the air, lightish palms open, staring from confused, scared eyes. Althea took a step forward. Several men made abortive half-moves, but no one stopped her.

"Which one's the mama?" someone whispered.

"Hell if I can tell."

"Lady, is that your maid?"

"Let her go," Althea directed the shoe clerk in the same calm voice, and the clerk and the other man released Graceful's arms. Cradling the baby horizontally in her arms, she held him out.

From the porch across the street, Japheth watched. The sweet scent of gasoline radiated from his hands, clothes, shoes, the wooden pillar before him, the shingles of the house. He inhaled deeply, breathed the fumes like source as he watched his sister raise the tiny figure, lift the baby crosswise, an offering, and in his mind's eye he saw two girlish hands rising over the fishwhite line down the center of her dark head, the relentless repetition of a life's litany recalling what he could not possibly remember: the blood-smeared girl in dark pigtails raising the bloody newborn over her head to kill it, kill it, kill him. Japheth was cold now, deepearth cold, though the fires burned all around him. It didn't matter: he could feel how it didn't matter. Hatred for the sister was no more personal than for the black ones; it was all the same, it had nothing to do with them, or with him; it was only the need now to satisfy the deadening hunger. Hate, transformed from rage into lust for slaughter, had become only this dull, cold will to annihilate the world. He walked out of his hiding place as Graceful reached for her son.

He was a shadow flying from her side-vision but Althea knew him, even before she let go the child, spun to face him, thinking to fight him, to hold him, embrace him, thinking she had to protect herself. She struck at the air as one flails at a fluttering night moth's wings; there was no flesh to strike, only the warmth of delicately splashing liquid, the sharpness of the smell.

"Holy Christ!"

"Get back!"

Japheth dropped the can, stood back away from her, fumbled with the box of matches, and in the eternity which was no more than the slivered part of her next heartbeat, she knew what he'd done. She felt the force in the gasoline darkening her gardening dress, knew there was no power on earth to combat the death he'd drenched her in. Somewhere there was a great shout. Her brother came toward her with the tiny flame lit, and she reached for him. There was a white searing flash, Graceful screamed a name, but it was not her name. A body was on top of her then, rolling her on the ground.

Sound like one loud shout to crack heaven. I was already moving, hurrying them young ones away from that hellplace. I done seen the world collapsing, flames licking, when I step off the porch of that yellow house. I'm not going to stand in some yard looking behind like Lot's wife, I gathers them children, put my arm around that little mother, she holding her baby, we halfway up the street time that shout come.

The little boy, he give a shout, too, twist loose, take off running back yonder, and before I can understand anything, I got to turn, I got to see them two flags in the street—oh, yes, that dark one and his sister. They tiny small, way down the hill, but I sees 'em, Lord, I knows them at once, and I say to myself, Yes, this hour won't pass without them. I see the dark one is nothing now but that destruction force walking: empty hands, eyes, feets, evil walking. In my soul there's a great eruption, and I wishes him dead off the earth. I sees it plain in my mind, same as I see that whitewoman move, and in that same heartbeat the brother go up in flames.

Whooosh! He light up like a pineknot, just *whooosh!*

Stand straight up burning an instant before he run; run just an instant before he fall. Then they all running, all them whitemens running, shouting, and the little boy is running, little girl screaming, Willie!, she take off down the hill after him, and I see that tall black boy then, way down there among them, the tall boy helped me carry the dead girl, the one I thought run away, he's sprawled on top of that whitewoman on the ground.

You couldn't hardly tell what was happening. You had your pistols trained on them, you were trying to keep order, see, but you didn't know which ones to shoot. That son of a gun just appeared out of nowhere, out of absolute thin air, seemed like, but you didn't know what he was doing till he'd already throwed the gas on her, and then it was too late. Who'd dream it, anyhow? She was a white woman. We didn't get deputized to burn up white women, I don't care what she'd been doing. It happened so damn fast. Somebody shouted at her, but her dress had already caught. I don't know how come that colored boy didn't get his head blowed off when he jumped on her, except that white fella had caught fire, too, and our eyes were all on that. Lord have mercy. His clothes must have been just soaked in fuel oil, because he went up like a gas rag, he only run a few steps before he dropped. You'd think he'd have been screaming, that white woman was sure enough screaming, we all were shouting, but that fella run silent, burning, absolutely silent. By the time you could get your mind wrapped around what was happening, he'd fell to the ground. He was still flaming, but you knew inside them burning clothes he wasn't nothing but a crisp. I tried to think to do something. Stinson's standing yonder going, Christ, oh, Christ. They'd got the fire put out on the white woman, and it looked like she wasn't dead yet, she wasn't screaming, but I could kindly hear her moaning, that colored gal was bent down over her, kneeling over her, and she had that little yella baby on her, suckling greedy, like it's about to starve to death. I tried to think what we were going to do with the white woman. We couldn't take her to the internment center in that condition. Somebody'd already told me the white hospitals was full. I couldn't think clear. I turned and told Stinson to shut the hell up, but he kept standing there, repeating himself, saying, Jesus, would you look at that, Jesus. Christ Almighty. Lord God.

W ith the child in her arms Graceful knelt beside the woman. Mrs. Dedmeyer's eyes were closed. Her face was bright red, scalded-looking. The charred housedress curled away from her in black, flaking strips, and beneath it her throat, her upper chest were seared pink. She was moaning. Her eyelashes and eyebrows were gone. A great feeling of pity welled up in Graceful and she reached a hand out, drew it back quickly, afraid to touch her. *I tried to warn her,* she said to herself.

But Graceful knew that the sound exploding from her throat had not been for the whitewoman. *NO!* she'd screamed in a rush of terror and hatred when she saw him running with the gasoline can in his hand, *NO!* her soul screamed, her mouth screamed, and it was with joy and relief and loathing she'd realized it was the woman he was running toward, not her, not Graceful, and in that same breath she was glad. *Look out!* she shouted when she saw the matches, because then Hedgemon was running, and when the fire went up between them, the whitewoman and her brother, it was Hedgemon's name Graceful screamed. She saw him burning alive, the hated father to her son, burning alive, running, but she felt nothing when she saw it, not even relief.

The other whitemen were everywhere, shouting; some were near the fiery body, circling it, holding their arms out like scarecrows to keep each other back. Hedgemon was on the ground on the other side of the woman. A deep moan rose from the woman's throat, and when Graceful looked in the peeled, scalded face she could see two hugely dilated pupils staring up at her from narrow slits, like shining black berries inside the puffed lids. Mrs. Dedmeyer lifted one of her hands, seemed to be trying to say something, but one of the whitemen shoved Graceful aside and she had to catch herself to keep from tumbling over, she had to clasp the baby, and whatever the woman meant to say was lost in the shoving hands, shouting voices, the whitemen swarming all around.

"Graceful!" a high, child's voice called. She looked up to see Willie pounding down the hill, and behind him LaVona running. Graceful scrambled to her feet, covered herself and the nursing baby with the blanket, looking north to see where Mama was coming; she saw instead, from the corner of her eye, a whiteman raising the butt of his rifle. She wheeled around as the man clubbed Hedgemon in the side of the head. Hedgemon fell over, put his arms up to protect himself, and the whiteman turned away, and then, as if in afterthought, turned back, raised the rifle stock, clubbed Hedgemon again. "Hedgemon!" She took a step toward him, but Willie raced into the yard then, his thick legs pumping, his eyes terrified, round face shiny with sweat, and yet beaming with his wide beautiful grin. He threw himself on her, hugged her waist, and she could feel his wet face on her skin. LaVona came after him, sobbing hard as she grabbed Graceful around the neck, and within Graceful was such a storm of love and shame and fury. The humiliation she'd refused when the whitemen stripped her, when she'd stood defiant before them, saying to herself, *They dogs anyhow, it's no shame to be naked in front of dogs,* now overcame her as she tried to hold the blanket up with one hand, keep her bared torso covered, hide the nursing child. "Where's Mama?" She had no free arm with which to hug them. "Where's Jewell and T.J.? LaVona!" And LaVona stared at the baby's blanket, but she was crying too hard to answer, and Willie was crying, holding on to her, and beneath the scrap of blanket, the baby nursed as if he'd never get his fill. An oilfield truck crammed with colored prisoners roared down Elgin Avenue, ground to a stop beside them; a voice shouted, "We got room for a couple more, how many y'all got?"

"Two nits, two lice!"

There was laughter, more shouting, and she felt Willie being jerked away, felt the blanket pull loose as he tried to cling to her, and there was no time for shame or questions, because a gun barrel gouged her lower back, dug deeply into the skin above her hip, pushing her toward the truck, and everything moved so fast; she was afraid they would shoot Hedgemon where he lay groaning on the ground, and she cried out, "Hedgemon! Hedgemon! Come!" He rolled to the side as if to rise, and Graceful scanned the street then, looking north toward home, thinking she might still see Mama and Jewell and T.J., she might be able to warn them as she had not been able to shout in time for the children, Run, Mama! Hide! Don't come down here! The edge of Mama's porch was obscured now, but in the distance she thought she saw the slender outline of Elberta, though that made no sense. Elberta wouldn't be out alone, and the truck would have stopped and got her anyway, it had come right down Elgin Avenue. They were picking up all Negroes, they wouldn't have passed Elberta by.

But Graceful had no time to think, for she was being manhandled onto the back of the truck. The flatbed was jammed tight with bodies, some of them lying down, wounded, but most crouching or sitting, crushed together like livestock. Whitemen with guns were standing on the running boards, or on the bed up front, leaning against the cab, where two men with rifles perched on top. There was no room, but Graceful and the children were shoved from the ground, forced to climb up, and she struggled to hold the baby; a brown hand reached down for her, and some women squeezed aside, made a place for them. The baby was wailing again, furious to have been pulled away from the breast. Willie and LaVona were with her, but she couldn't see Hedgemon. "Hedgemon!" she called as the truck ground its gears.

"Hey, gal! Catch!" A whiteman on the ground threw something at her; it landed across her face, began to slide back, and when she grabbed it up, she found it was the voluminous sateen skirt from the green dress. "It's ruirnt now," the man called. "You might as well have it." She wouldn't look at the whiteman, but she did draw the skirt around her shoulders, covered herself. A voice hollered from the street, "They're plumb full at Convention Hall, can't cram another nigger in there without it's a midget! Take this load on to the fairgrounds!"

"All the way out there?"

"Hell, yes, even the ballpark's full, we're liable to be hauling 'em to Claremore before it's all over!"

She was wedged in tight, facing the back of the bed, and yet there was nothing to hold on to, and when the truck lurched, Graceful grabbed for Willie. Her eyes searched the street as the truck began to roll. Mrs. Dedmeyer lay very still on the grass, her arms flung out to the side, her thin chest, from this distance, looking childish, flat, pale. The men were moiling in every direction. Farther back in the yard, the dark brother's body was still burning. A half-grown whiteboy darted forward, stomped at the fading fire a second, jumped back. Desperately Graceful searched, but she couldn't see Hedgemon, and then the mob parted a little, and he was there, standing in the road, under guard, his hands on top of his head. A thick trail of blood eased down the side of his face. Hedgemon's eyes were on her. Willie was wedged next to her, completely silent, and she only knew he was crying by how his shoulders shuddered. LaVona was behind her, penned inside the too-many bodies pressing at Graceful's back. She put an arm around her little brother, and he shoved his face against her, his head under her chin, hard against her collarbone. As the truck lumbered away, she stared at Hedgemon Jackson over the top of Willie's head, trying to understand what his eyes were saying, until she lost sight of him in the sea of white faces.

Cleotha hadn't heard the back door open, but when the thunks and crashes started in the bedroom, she knew instantly who it was. Gently she eased Jewell's head off her lap, went to stand in the archway. At sight of her eldest son's thin form hunched over the dresser, her throat emitted a little chirp, like a bird's. T.J. whirled, slamming the drawer shut; he stood panting in front of the mirror. "Mama! You still here! Where's my shells?" Cleotha didn't answer, and T.J. turned and rushed into the kitchen. The spoon drawer clattered. The pantry door opened and slammed shut. T.J. reappeared in the kitchen doorway. "Those boxes of cartridges I had hid, what y'all do with them?" His eyes were wild as a mare's.

"I don't guess you wondering what went with your wife."

"I had two full boxes, Mama. Twenty-two shells. Where they at?"

"Your sister is dead."

He stared as if he couldn't comprehend her meaning. Then he went to the chifforobe and jerked it open, began pawing through his mother's and sisters' dresses.

"You got a new baby daughter." She waited a moment. "Your wife and your child just gone with Mrs. Tiger. They're on their way to Turley."

T.J. backed away from the chifforobe with a small paper box in his hand. "Where's the rest of them? This isn't all of them. You ain't let Willie get hold of them!" He rushed toward her, forcing her against the door frame as he pushed past her into the front room, hurried to the south window, brushed the curtain aside to see out.

"Your sister is dead," Cleotha repeated. T.J. ripped open the box, pulled the pistol from his waistband and started loading the chambers.

"Son! Look at me!"

His eyes flicked toward her, turned to the open front door as he finished loading. "You got to get out of here, Mama. Go up by Skiatook. Quick."

"Look at your sister."

His gaze roved the room, paused hardly an instant on the divan, returned to the screen door. "I see her. You aim to join her?" He started back across the linoleum, and would have pushed past her again had Cleotha not reached out and seized his arm.

"T.J., what's the matter with you?"

"They're killing every nigger in this country, you want to sit here in this house till they come—"

"I can't carry Jewell by myself."

"Leave her." They stood silent a minute, staring at each other. His eyes were half slitted now, not wild and rolling. Cleotha took into herself the fullness of the change in him, how the hate and fear had eaten out the tender place in her firstborn. In the hard bones of his arm, his panting breath, she felt the force with which the newmade cavity was filled. After a moment T.J. looked away.

"You go on ahead, son," Cleotha said, watching him. "Go find your wife and daughter." She waited for him to say something. Beneath her closed hand, his arm shook.

"Go quick, Mama. Whitemen's just down the street. You might have time."

"Willie and LaVona are with them, somewhere around Turley. Mrs. Tiger going to carry them someplace safe."

"There's no place safe! Good Lord, Mama. They're going to burn this house down." He glanced at the girl on the divan. "Burn her up with it."

"We'll come just as soon as Delroy get here."

"You ain't coming with Delroy!" He turned on her now, glared at her as if he hated her as much as he hated the thing roaring and chattering and burning outside the door. "Your brother is dead!" he yelled in her face. "Jewell's dead! We all going to be dead, they're going to kill all of us, but I'm going to kill every goddamn one of them I can—"

"NO!"

The shout was so great it seemed all the world was silenced. When Cleotha went on, her voice was quiet. "No more," she said. "Hear me?

Been death enough already." T.J. was still trembling. She let go his arm, waiting. He didn't look at her as he made himself slim to get past her, went into the dark middle room, on into the lighter kitchen. Cleotha's eyes were dry when she watched him go out the back door.

That shout sound like the last trumpet, the last denial and fury, the last time the world going to say No! To this day I tries to understand to myself what I seen. I can't explain it. Sometimes I think she do it, that whitewoman, his sister: she turn and throw fire on him to finish what she start twenty years back. Some other times I believe he do it himself, set his own body afire, because that force for destruction don't care what it burn. Or else me. All this life, these many years since, I been thinking sometimes that maybe it was my own mind that do it, jump up and cause a spark to set fire to him, that same one, the boychild I kept her from killing on the day he was born. Maybe in that hour of destruction I tried to repent myself.

Me and the little mother stand on the hilltop, watch the little Willie boy and his sister run right into the arms of them whitemens. The little mother cry out, but her and me both know there is nothing we can do. Them two young ones are gone. We got to save her little baby, save ourselves. We turn and go, fast, fast, through the fiery furnace. I will tell you something, that little mother way more stronger than I thought. She have a young strong body, yes, but what give her the most strength is that new baby; she running to save the life of her child. All around, on every side, peoples are running. We all trying to flee that destruction, but the little mother can't go so fast. In a minute we got to stop again, let her rest. I turn around, see the world collapsing, bowels of the earth opening to suck that place in. Flames licking. Black smoke rising. Then is when I seen what the truth is: we only going to save ourselves for a little while. That force is not finished. We can't hide from it. We can't get away.

To this day I been studying in my mind why the Creator set me in it, to bear witness to the end and the beginning—or his, anyway, that dark one—because he dead in his flesh, maybe, but that force is not dead. Evil can't be destroyed. You try and destroy it, evil just change its shape, become something look different on the outside. Inside, it always act the same. I don't know why the Lord let me get caught by the greed-devil, or why He cause me to have to stand on a hilltop and watch them fires raging before I get free. I don't know why it is, I can't see yet, but I know one thing: we peoples have joined them two forces together, turned that power loose in the world, and I done my own part. Oh, yes. Listen. Evil is spirit force, yes, but it have to manifest in the material world. That deep-earth power belong to the material world, but it is capable to manifest in the spirit. And we have let it. We have loosed our own destruction.

Whose hand set them houses afire? Not God's hand. God don't make that gun on the hill to spit and chatter, He haven't created machines to fly in the air above smoke and drop fire in jars and bottles, to make fire on God's people, by God's people, to kill God's people, Lord, Lord. How do He say the world going to be destroyed? Not by water but by fire next time, the Book tell us that, but it is not going to be God who do it, we do it, you and me do it, because that power come into the world by human hand, and it is going to live in the world through human hand, and we can't none of us turn it back until the whole story done.

Cleotha was standing in front of the divan, bending over it, when she heard their boots on the porch. The glass in the front window shattered, and a voice called, "Anybody in there?" She pulled the pink dress back up to Jewell's throat, dropped the washrag into the red water in the basin on the floor.

"Come in," she said, straightening, turning. "Door's open."

But the men smashed the screen anyway, butted through the wire with a rifle stock, splintered the wood frame, broke the rest of the glass out of the window beside it, before they stamped into Cleotha's front room. There were only three of them, but they made as much noise as an army.

"Come on out now, Auntie, we got orders to take everybody in."

Cleotha turned back to the divan, reached across Jewell to smooth the skirt of the girl's white Sunday-best dress lying like a buoyant lace antimacassar across the back.

"Oh, Jesus, what're we going to do with that?"

"I don't know. Go see if there's any more of them in yonder."

She had waited too long to begin to wash her daughter. The long, limber body was already rigid. The pink school dress, tucked up modestly around her throat again, was stiff with blood. It would be hard to take off. Cleotha listened to the sounds of drawers being jerked open in the next room, things smashing against the wall. In the kitchen she could hear glass breaking. She knew these sounds' meaning as clearly as she'd known her son was hunting bullets when she heard him in the middle room a short while before. She seated herself on the divan, lifted Jewell's head into her lap, stroked the glassy cheekbones, the smooth, firm eyelids. Her daughter's beautiful brown skin was cold, despite the searing heat.

"Get up from there, Auntie. We don't want to have to shoot you."

She looked up at the man. His gun was pointed toward the floor. He wore sooty overalls and a checkered shirt, and beneath his shapeless, sweat-stained hat, his eyes were flitty, blue, uneasy-looking. "Don't make it hard on yourself," he said. His attention was taken by one of the other men returning from the back of the house. "Anything in yonder?"

"Naw, just some nigger trinkets." The new man went to the front window, jerked the flower-spattered curtain down, tossed it onto the braided rug in the middle of the floor. "Tubbs is getting whatever's to be got. What're you going to do with her?" He nodded toward the divan but didn't wait for an answer as he went to the south window and pulled that curtain down, too. The windowshade fell with it, clattered on the linoleum as he tossed the curtain on the rug. "Tubbs!" he shouted. "Bring that coal oil in here!" He went to the armchair and snatched the crocheted doilies off it, swept the framed photographs off the end table and plucked up those doilies, dropped them all on the curtains. He reached behind Cleotha to take Jewell's burial dress off the back of the divan, tossed the white dress on the rug.

The third man appeared in the archway. In one hand he held Cleotha's half-full kerosene jar, in the other the ornate gilt frame with the family photograph from off her dresser. "There's nothing here. Where's your jewels, old woman? You got your silverware hid?"

"Fetch that jar over here. You sprinkle the back room down good?"

"Waste of kerosene, but I did it. Let's go. Silas and them are plumb the hell up to the section line by now."

"Stand up, old woman. We got orders to burn this place."

"Who?" Cleotha said softly. "Who give you orders to do this?"

But the men did not answer.

"Light that and come on," one of them said, and two of the whitemen went out the door. The man in overalls went to the corner and jerked Cleotha's whatnot shelf off the wall. The delicate china cup Ernest had brought her from Boston tumbled and shattered, the porcelain cat he'd found in New Orleans, the blond angel with folded wings from Pittsburgh, the frame with Ernest's picture, all fell when the shelf came down. The man picked up the gold-embossed frame, ripped Ernest's broad smiling face from it, and tucked the frame in his bib pocket; he tossed the photograph on the pile. He broke the wooden shelf in two and tossed the pieces on the curtains and starched doilies, picked up the kerosene jar and began to shake it around.

"You know you going to have to burn me with it," Cleotha said.

The man straightened up, looked at her. His pale, uneasy gaze dropped to Jewell's face an instant, slipped around the walls of the room, past the pictures and the old lamp sconce and the place where the Last Supper was framed on the wall. Then the man turned and walked out the broken door. Cleotha expected him to come back, or for there to be others. She heard yelling in the street, but a few minutes passed and there was no sound of boots on the porch; she reached into the basin at her feet, squeezed the rag out, began once again to bathe her daughter.

The fires were raging on both sides of the road as the oilfield truck drove down Elgin Avenue, or Graceful believed they were still on Elgin, but she couldn't recognize anything. The streets of Greenwood had been transformed to an alien, dreamlike world; she couldn't tell where she was. The baby had begun to nurse again. Graceful was tortured with thirst. She thought she wanted nothing in this world but a drink of water, she was dying for water. The notion came to her that maybe she was already dead, on a truck, driving through hell. But, no, she could smell odors, soap and sweat and pressing oil, her brother's unwashed hair in front of her, and behind her the iron scent of blood, and smoke, everywhere the black choking smoke, becoming thicker as they drove. Her eyes teared; she began coughing. She needed water. A sip of water to drink. Willie sat up, coughing, too, now, and behind her in the truck other children were coughing, whining, crying, and women's whispers rose, harsh, frightened: Be quiet, honey, shhhh. In the street Graceful could see small groups of colored men being marched south, four abreast, surrounded on all sides by armed whites; there were whitemen everywhere, Lord, she had not known there were so many whitemen in the world. It occurred to her to wonder who was running their city if they were all here.

The truck passed a standing brick building, unburned. *That's the high school,* she thought. *That's Booker T.!* For an instant she knew where she was, but the truck made a turn, and once more she was lost. They were passing through an unearthly landscape, no longer lit with huge raging fires but flattened, black, ghostly. In every direction sprawled piles of burning rubble; small licks of flames flickered here and there. A few iron bedsteads, some blackened cookstoves jutted skyward, attended only by smoke tendrils rising in wisps.

The people in the truck were silent; even the children did not whimper. Off to the right was an area of hollow brick shells, low to the earth, the blackened centers burned away. Graceful saw several huge squarish shapes hulking in the rubble, and her throat tightened as she realized she was looking at Mr. Smitherman's presses. Near them, Hedgemon's old linotype machine lay on its side. They were passing Greenwood Avenue. Deep Greenwood. She couldn't tell which piles of bricks had been the Dreamland Theater, which the confectionery or Bryant's Drug Store, only the building that had housed the newspaper office, because the steel presses would not burn. She heard sobbing behind her in the hushed truckbed, muted beneath the grinding motor. *Fire take everything,* she thought. *Everything.* Then she thought, *They going to kill us all.*

But the white driver kept going, beyond the ruined landscape, beyond the steel border of what had been Greenwood, and soon they were driving through the white section. On the streets, in the front yards of houses, behind windows, and on shaded porches, she could see white faces— women, children, a few men—and some were laughing, some looking on in seeming sympathy, some staring as if gaping at a circus sideshow. Her eye was caught by one woman, standing in a yard beside a whitehaired old man. The old man stared steadily up at them, shaking his head. The woman's face was squinched tight, eyes red and swollen; she had a toddler child on her hip, and the little boy was teething a biscuit. Graceful turned away. She was so thirsty. Another truck was coming behind them, the back crowded with colored prisoners. Where the bed stuck out on either side of the cab, she could see women clinging on, grasping the oil-stained boards beneath them to keep from falling off. She bent toward her little brother.

"We going where it's safe," she said softly in his ear, and then raised up to speak over her shoulder to LaVona. "You all right back there, honey?" She tried to make her voice airy, but it came out sounding like a frog's croak, her throat was so dry.

"What are we doing?" LaVona whined.

"Won't be long now," Graceful said. "These whitefolks taking us where it's safe." She shifted her baby to her other arm. With her free hand she stroked Willie's neck, rubbed a light sweaty circle with her thumb. "They going to give us a drink of water. Real soon." She squinted skyward.

Smoke lay over everything, but she could see the sun, high in the sky now, a bright, ferocious coin burning in the haze.

During the night one primary force had held sway, one rhythm building to a crescendo—pounding human feet, rumbling gasoline motors rushing toward the Frisco—but now, as the day opened, disparate rhythms made themselves known. The National Guard had begun, at last, to stop the white looters and burners, but they were moving north very slowly, disarming white men, dispersing the Home Guard, telling them to go on home. Some white citizens, in the safety of daylight, emerged from their houses and motored north to gape at the devastation, watch the police bring in Negro prisoners, and take photographs if they were so fortunate as to own a personal family camera. Others worked to organize the relief operation, to get food and water to the internment centers. Several reporters, having rushed to their rented rooms at dawn to dash off news articles, now stood in line at the telegraph office to send their revised dispatches out on the wire. A few men put themselves to the task of gathering the dead. Black bodies were stacked in front of Convention Hall, on the open beds of oilfield trucks, in piles at Newblock Park near the river, and still dozens of burned bodies lay about in the dirt streets. Most of the white dead had been taken to the city morgue or the white hospitals, although some of them, too, were burned, and the gatherers could not always tell black dead from white. An urgent call went out for gravediggers. But Tulsa's gravediggers were under guard at McNulty Baseball Park, Convention Hall, the fairgrounds, penned up inside the detention camps. There was as yet great general confusion, but it was becoming clear to the city fathers that one of the first orders of business was to issue release tags to the colored gravediggers, to get this mess cleaned up.

Franklin Dedmeyer sat bareheaded in the open Winton, sick to his stomach, sweating, trying to maneuver the car through the clotted streets. He told himself that the nausea came from too many cigars smoked, lack of food, lack of sleep. A flatbed truck filled with Negro prisoners lumbered past him, and he looked away, his chest so constricted he could hardly breathe. It had taken such a long time to get through downtown. There'd been broken glass from the pawnshops to drive around, police wagons parked everywhere, hundreds of men in the streets. Now he was at the edge of the tracks, and he could see the razed buildings of colored town, but he couldn't get through. Automobiles angled in every direction, horns tootling; firetrucks and police wagons blocked the roads, sirens wailing. The urgency ripped at him. He slammed the heel of his hand against the steering wheel, tried not to think.

He'd gone home at daylight, climbed the stairs to her room—their room—the bedroom he hadn't set foot in for over six months—not knowing what he meant to say or do, thinking only that he wanted to see her, to see that she was all right. He'd stopped short in the doorway, confused by the empty bed, the scattered hatboxes and dresses strewn about on the carpet. Then he thought of Jim Logan, and his confusion vanished, swallowed in sickening jealousy. He understood suddenly why his partner had failed to meet him: he'd stood him up so that Franklin would sit like a fool all night in the lobby of the Hotel Tulsa while the driller sneaked around to Franklin's own house and ran off with his wife. The illogic of the idea, the insanity, didn't occur to him.

He rushed immediately downstairs to interrogate Graceful, but the girl was not at the stove preparing breakfast; she wasn't on the back porch or in the pantry or the maid's room. The tiny maid's cubicle was tossed about in hurried confusion, like the upstairs bedroom, and her little baby was gone. Franklin went outside to the cellar door and opened it, called down into the dark, Graceful's name, his wife's name, descended finally into the damp darkness, feeling overhead for the lightcord, but the bulb showed only the empty basement, and he stood on the dirt floor, staring at the stone walls, knowing beyond sense, reason, calculation that Graceful and her baby had gone to Little Africa, and that Althea had gone with them. In an instant he was standing in the back hall, calling his wife's name, shouting it to the empty house. Then he was running out the front door, climbing into the Winton.

Franklin sounded the Winton's horn at a Model T stalled out in front of him. He scanned the road as far as he could see, but there was nothing to look at except Guardsmen, prisoners, burned-out buildings, fires on the horizon. He could feel nausea joining grief joining fear, threatening to boil up and explode from him, and he took his foot off the clutch, the motor shuddered and died, and Franklin got out of the car. Glass crunched beneath his shoes. He struggled to think rationally, but the world had gone mad around him; there could be no logic in the midst of madness. He had no idea how to find her. He began walking north.

For a time, as he moved deeper into the riot area, he peered into the faces of the people passing, but the dark and light faces threatened to disrupt his purpose, and soon he quit looking. He was drawing near where the fires were still raging, and the panic in his chest, the heat and smoke and nausea made him faint. He paused at the side of the road, but there was nothing to lean against. People were coming toward him down the center of the street. He hadn't eaten since yesterday. Hadn't slept since . . . when? He couldn't remember. Most nights he lay awake in the guest room, angry, silent, listening to his wife's silence in the bedroom across the hall. Oh, why hadn't they stayed quiet, the Nigras, everything would have been fine if they'd just stayed in their own part of town. He'd told her, he'd called and warned her. Hadn't he told her to put Graceful in the basement? Surely no sane woman would come out in such danger. No sane white woman. It was her damned peculiar softness for that hired girl. He'd never understood it. Gracie was a good hand, but Althea was entirely too tenderhearted about her, and now look—

Franklin raised his eyes. Walking toward him were twenty or so Negro men under guard. None looked directly at him. His eyes searched their faces, seeking something to justify the frenzy of destruction all around him, but in their set, dark features he saw only caution, fear, immutable anger. They marched past in silent formation, followed by uniformed white men with guns.

"Dedmeyer! There you are!" The voice bellowed from the passenger seat of a closed touring car in the street, pointed north. Franklin had to bend to see the face beneath the visor, flushed, excited, a fat cigar clenched between yellow teeth. There were pale, puffy bags under L.O.'s eyes, like little thumbs. He took the cigar out of his mouth. "Where the hell you been! Get in!"

Franklin stood staring an instant, confused, and then the thought came to him that L.O. Murphy had been out in this all night, that he knew where Althea was and had come to take him to her. Quickly he reached for the door handle, had hardly climbed in the back seat before the driver started off.

"You damn near missed it." L.O. craned his head over his shoulder. "They're scattering like chickens, heading for the damn hills." The interior of the car was sweetish, sour, choking with cigar smoke. "Spreading all up towards Skiatook, Owasso, who the hell knows, right, Tom?" The driver nodded. "Chapman's been up in his plane," L.O. said. "Told us you can see 'em for miles, just streams of 'em, runnin like ants. They'll be hid out in the creekbottoms if we don't act quick."

"Where—?" Franklin started to ask about Althea, but was struck silent. In the floorboard were three rifles, a shotgun, several boxes of shells. He must be the mad one. She wouldn't be out in this, she wouldn't.

"Hell, man," L.O. answered, "I just told you. The niggers're runnin off."

"Seems to me," the driver said dryly, "that about this time yesterday you were the one bellyaching about we got to run the niggers out of Tulsa."

L.O. leaned forward. "You can't let 'em off scot-free after this awful business; besides, who'll do the nigger work if we let 'em all get away?"

They were passing a group of prisoners, men in overalls, women in headrags, being marched south. L.O. twisted in the seat to follow them with his eyes.

"What are they doing with them?" Franklin's throat was parched, his belly burning.

"Arresting their black asses, 'cept I don't know where they're going to put 'em," L.O. said thickly. "Convention Hall's crammed to the damn ceiling, God Almighty, does that place stink." He ashed his cigar out the window. "Tell you what, if they let 'em get down in them canebrakes we'll have to use dogs to flush'm out."

"What are they doing with them?" Franklin said again.

L.O. glanced round at him. "Who?" His face was swollen, his eyes bloodshot. For the first time Franklin realized he was drunk. "Teachin'm their goddamn place," L.O. said. "For one thing. I don't know. Ask Tom. What're y'all doin with 'em?"

"I don't know. I think they're carrying some of them to the ballpark."

"Stop," Franklin said. There was no response from the front seat. They hadn't seemed to hear him. "I said stop!" The driver stopped the car as Franklin shoved the door open, climbed out.

"Dedmeyer! What the hell's the matter with you?"

Franklin reached in through the open window, smashed L.O. in the side of the face with his fist. Then he turned and started walking back. He would find Graceful. He'd go wherever they were holding the coloreds and track down Graceful, and she would tell him where Althea had gone.

But he'd taken only a few steps before he stopped, confused again, uncertain. Overhead a great black cloud boiled over the entire city. Down the street several corpses were being loaded into a wagon. In every direction the fires were burning. He stood paralyzed. How had such a thing happened? This was Tulsa, Oklahoma; this was America. It made no sense. Why hadn't somebody stopped it? All that he'd witnessed the night before, the cold, cut-off feeling he'd steeped himself in, his silence, guilt, terror, everything wrapped around him, and he stood at the side of the road, gazing down at his new well-shined cordovan shoes, covered in ashes, fine as sifted dust.

In the back of a farm wagon Althea lay on a stretcher. Her eyes were closed, the seared eyelids fluttering; behind the tender reddened skin, memory joined dream. The mule-drawn wagon, pressed into service as an ambulance, began to move slowly south. It would be many hours before she would come to consciousness in a crowded hallway at Hillcrest Hospital, and then her mind and body would be entirely consumed with living pain. It would be days before she'd remember the flash that killed her brother, longer still before she would recall her own hand reaching toward him the instant before the fire went up.

Japheth's blackened body lay atop other charred bodies in a truckbed designated *For Colored Only;* the truck was heading toward Newblock Park, where the bodies would be stacked in piles to be consumed by a different fire, neat, controlled, kindled by strict ordinance to prevent, it was said, the spread of disease. The white dead were laid out at the Tulsa morgue, waiting to be claimed by grieving loved ones, among them an unidentified dark-blond oilfield worker in stained khaki workclothes.

Beneath the baking sun on the open fairgrounds, Graceful held the sateen skirt out to shade her baby while she stood in line for a cup of water. She'd set Willie and LaVona to wait in the thin shade of the judges' booth. The livestock sheds were already full. On every side of her, spread out over the open space of the fairgrounds, blackfolks stood or sat without protection. They were mostly women and children, and very few of them had on hats, though several women had fashioned makeshift coverings for their little ones by piecing together sycamore leaves. Graceful glanced around, thinking she might try that for Willie and LaVona after she got them some water, though where the women had found the leaves she had no idea. There wasn't a tree of any sort in sight.

The Red Cross people had set up a tent; they were handing out sand-wiches. She almost believed now that the whites weren't going to slaugh-ter them—why would they bring sandwiches?—but she couldn't fathom what they meant to do with them. The line moved so slowly. Everyone was acting polite. Especially the whitefolks. Some of them were walking along the line taking down the names of white employers, saying that would help the people get out sooner. There were armed guards posted around the perimeter, to keep, she supposed, these dangerous half-starved colored women and children inside Exposition Park. Graceful looked up and down the line, across the fairgrounds, scanning the brown and black and copper faces, hoping for a glimpse of Mama and Jewell—and yet half hoping not to see them. Maybe they'd got away. The Negro men had been taken to Convention Hall, someone said, and the ball-park—the ones who'd been captured, that is. The ones who hadn't es-caped, or been shot. That would include T.J., maybe. And Hedgemon. Her mind kept returning to the image: Hedgemon standing in the street as the truck carried her away, his hands on top of his head, his face bleeding, eyes saying something. What? *Wait for me. Meet me . . .* where? How would she find him? Find any of them? She realized that the women in line on both sides of her were looking around in the same way, frowning against the sun, turning their heads to search the hundreds of dark faces inside the fairgrounds. *We all been separated,* Graceful thought. *Every family in Greenwood been cut off from each other.*

"Who do you work for, dear?" A roundish whitewoman with powdery skin and small worried eyes stood in front of her holding a pad of paper, a poised fountain pen.

Graceful didn't answer. *We're hunting loved ones,* she thought; *we all looking for our family. Woman only want to know the name of our white-folks.*

The woman tried to smile, but peering into Graceful's face, she hesi-tated a moment, uncertain; suddenly she dropped her gaze, frowned down at her pad, made a few superfluous checkmarks beside some names. Without looking up she said, "If you tell me the name of your em-ployer we'll try to get word to them that you're here. They can come sign for you."

Still Graceful didn't answer. The whitewoman turned to the next per-son. "Who do you work for, dear?"

Then, with a little rift of pain, Graceful saw the thin, burnt form on the grass, the pale arms flung out to the side. Mrs. Dedmeyer. "Mrs. Dedmeyer," she said aloud. The round whitewoman looked back. "Mr. and Mrs. Franklin Dedmeyer," Graceful said softly, and the woman scribbled on her pad. "Sixteen twelve South Carson. Osage six, three seven six." The whitewoman moved on.

Behind Graceful someone's baby was crying. Babies were crying all over the fairgrounds, and yet her milk had not let down; she thought maybe it was because she was so dry; there was no liquid in her body to make milk with. The sateen was hot, draped around her as it was, like a shawl. Her baby was quiet. She held the skirt out, looked down at him. He was sleeping, his tiny pink tongue showing between tawny lips. One thing was certain. Whatever the whitefolks meant to do with them, her fate and the baby's fate were the same. By blood he was hers. By whitefolks' beliefs he would always be more colored than white. The baby yawned, smiled in his sleep. She put her finger to his cheek, traced the line of it, thinking, as she'd thought so many times, that very soon she was going to have to give him a name.

September
1921

On the last morning in September, Althea awakened before daylight from a dream of such grief and loss that before she'd come fully awake she knew she'd been weeping. The gaslight on the street had lost its power to the coming dawn, but in the bedroom the light was yet gray, shadowy. She lay still a moment, staring at the ceiling, trying to escape the dream's sorrow, and finally, unable to shed its residue, she rolled over, slipped from between the starched white eyelet sheets carefully, so as not to waken Franklin. His snores continued undisturbed as Althea left the room. She drew her silk wrapper around herself as she eased down the stairs.

Graceful stood at the enameled kitchen counter stirring up biscuits; she wore a cotton print shirtwaist with tiny yellow flowers embedded in a blue background, protected by an embroidered butterfly-bodice apron. Her hair was combed smooth. She didn't glance up when Althea came in but immediately turned from the mixing bowl to the coffeepot, saying, "I didn't expect you to be up so early."

The kitchen was hot already with stove heat, and Althea could smell a pie in the oven. A chicken was cut up and floured in a tin dish, ready for frying, and a big pot of something, stew perhaps, simmered on a gas burner. Graceful must have been up cooking since three or four o'clock. Althea watched her scoop ground coffee into the basket, light another burner, and put the pot on to percolate. Graceful turned back to the counter, sprinkled flour on the enamel, plunked down the biscuit dough, and began to roll it out.

"What time are you leaving?" Althea said finally. She went to sit at the little table against the wall, drew the wrapper more tightly around herself, as if she were cold. In fact she was perspiring; she ran her fingers along the nape of her neck, tugged at a few strands of her bobbed hair.

"Hedgemon say he'll be here about nine."

"No, I mean Tulsa. When are you—? Are you going today?"

Graceful went on cutting perfect neat circles with the biscuit cutter. "Tomorrow. I got things to do up home."

Althea nodded, watched the deft brown hands cut the raw biscuits so fast, so close together. "I don't guess you'll change your mind," she said. It wasn't really a question. In the silence she gazed out at the screened-in back porch; the day was drawing lighter now, though the sun was not quite yet risen.

"What's wrong, ma'am?"

"Wrong?"

Graceful stood with the biscuit cutter cocked in the air, looking at her. Almost as an echo, Althea realized she'd released a great plosive breath into the hot kitchen, a tremendous sigh. "Oh. Nothing," she said. "I was just thinking. . . ." She stood as if to go upstairs to dress, at once sat back down, and watched Graceful plop the biscuits in a pan, turn to open the oven door. A rich apple-pie cinnamon scent breathed into the room. Graceful put the biscuits in the oven, turned the flame down beneath the perking coffee.

"You want me to start your bacon now?"

"I'll wait till Mr. Dedmeyer gets up."

Graceful lit the burner under a large cast-iron skillet, and the odor of heating bacon grease joined the sweet pie scent, the homey smell of baking biscuits, all soon dominated by the scent of frying chicken. The familiar, clashing smells filled Althea with a wave of inexplicable sorrow.

"How long will it take you to get there?" she said.

"I don't know. Half a day maybe. It's just down by Okemah."

Althea nodded, watching Graceful turn the browning pieces. She couldn't seem to shake the dregs of her dream, though she couldn't remember it either, only the one image of the nursing child, and not just the image, the sensation, for it was her own withered left breast the child suckled. "Is that coffee ready yet?" she said irritably. Graceful poured out a scalding cup, brought it to her at the little table, poured one for herself, set it on the counter near the stovetop, went on frying chicken. Althea frowned. "How many chickens did you cut up?" she said. She thought to get up and go look, but she felt too tired.

"Four."

"My goodness. We can't eat that much in three days. The new girl will be here Monday." There was a pause. The grease popped and hissed as Graceful put in several new heavily floured pieces. "Take some with you," Althea said. "You can eat it on the train."

"Thank you, ma'am." Graceful glanced at her. "I already meant to." She dropped two more pieces in. Without changing her tone, she said, "I didn't think you'd mind I cooked the two frying hens I bought myself while I was cooking up you all's food for the weekend." It was neither challenge nor explanation.

"Oh," Althea said. She sighed again. They'd been over it many times in the past month; she had asked, promised, tried to bargain, but Graceful wouldn't bargain. Her mind was made up; she was going to go live with her new husband in one of the all-black towns, and there was nothing Althea could say to dissuade her. She was taking the baby, of course, her whole family was going, and really, Althea tried to tell herself, who could blame them. The city had made it so hard for the Negroes to rebuild; the city fathers had created those impossible fire codes, had turned back the donations that poured in from around the country to help the Negroes get started. All over North Tulsa, apparently, colored people were still living in tents, on mud streets, without heat or facilities or sanitation. It would be winter before long. Althea had not been up there to see, but Franklin said it was terrible. Graceful's family was not living in a tent, but there were fifteen or sixteen of them crowded together inside her mother's house. Althea tried to visualize how that many people could fit, eat, sit, much less sleep in the tiny shotgun house she had visited. Once, she'd asked Graceful how her mother's house was left unburned, but a cold, sealed, unreadable look passed over Graceful's face, and she'd turned away, her lips clamped in silence. Althea hadn't asked a second time.

"You know," Althea said, "if you could just wait a little longer, we could put in servants' quarters over the garage. You and . . . your husband— We could perhaps find . . . something. . . ." Her voice trailed away. Well, of course, that had been one of her first suggestions. Graceful had answered, Yes'm, me and Hedgemon and the baby and Mama and LaVona and Willie and Uncle Delroy and Lucille and their four children and Miss Campbell from Latimer Street and Mr. and Mrs. Douglas from next door and . . . Althea had let the notion drop. No point in bringing it up again. It was as if Graceful had had no family before the disaster, and now all of a sudden she had more than a dozen people to take care of, and she was so stubbornly attached to them, she no longer slept in the maid's room but went home every night.

The first evening after Althea was discharged from the hospital she'd asked Franklin to send Graceful up with some hot tea, and that was the first she'd learned that Graceful was walking home after work. There was no longer a colored jitney, of course, no streetcar service, and so Graceful walked seven miles each evening, Franklin said, through downtown Tulsa and the devastated colored section, through several checkpoints, with her green pass openly displayed so the patrols wouldn't arrest her—home to her mother's house. The following morning, Althea had greeted Graceful at the back door with, "You know, there's no problem with you bringing the baby to live here," and Graceful had answered, "We doing fine, ma'am, just how we are." Althea had had to pry it out of her, how many there were, where they were living. The new husband was listed as a kind of afterthought. It infuriated her, Graceful's stubbornness to go home every night, the new husband, all of it, but there was nothing she could do—no more than there was anything she could do now to make Graceful stay.

"Well," Althea said, and set her coffee cup down on the little table. "I'll go get dressed." But she didn't move. It seemed that beneath the popping grease she could hear the relentless tick of the grandfather clock in the front hall. "What time did you say they're going to be here?" she asked after a moment.

"About nine."

"Well." Althea sighed again. She felt Graceful's eyes on her, and she stood up briskly, saying, "You might as well start the bacon. He'll be awake any minute," and left the kitchen quickly, went upstairs to draw a bath.

Inside the little bathroom, as the water pounded into the tub, Althea stood at the window. The emerald leaves of the magnolia tree in the side yard gleamed in the sunlight, blurry. She turned again to the mirror, to the strange woman in the mirror, an unknown face, browless, the skin pink and strangely smooth beneath short wavy hair: a youngish face, if one did not look too closely and discover that the smoothness came with a seared, masklike tightness. The tight skin across Althea's nose and cheekbones burned with the contortions of her weeping.

She heard their voices in the kitchen as she came down the stairs, Franklin's baritone, followed by a low, vibrating, rounded bass. Althea stood in the foyer, listening, her back to the hall mirror. The voices were muffled—a soft mumble from Graceful, and then the bass Negro voice, and then Franklin's. She tried to make herself go on into the library, but she couldn't. The stained-glass window beside the door threw the sun's brilliance in a dazzling iridescent oval onto the polished hardwood floor.

"Sweetheart." Franklin stood in his new fall suit in the library doorway. "I was just coming up to see about you. Graceful's got your breakfast ready."

"Aren't you going to eat?"

"You were so long with your bath I went ahead and ate a bite. I've got to get on to the hotel, there's rumor about a new field opening around Tonkawa. Got to keep my ear to the ground."

Althea nodded. "I forgot my hat." She touched her bare neck. "I thought I might sit out in the swing awhile. I was just going back up for it. Would you mind?" She tried to smile at him, but the drawn skin surrendered no more to smiles than it did to weeping.

"I think some fresh air would be just the thing for you this morning. It's a beautiful day!" And Franklin took the stairs two at a time, like a young man.

She continued to stand, waiting for Franklin to return. Beneath the two low alternating voices in the kitchen she heard the contented gurgling of a baby.

"Here you are, sweetheart. This one? It was on the bed. Not much brim to it." Franklin handed her a soft purple cloche hat designed to wrap close to her head; it offered almost no protection from the sun but the flaps could be pulled low over the ears and brow.

"That will be fine." She took the hat, turned to the mirror. Franklin came up behind her, put his hands on her shoulders. "You look beautiful!" he said with that loud heartiness that had become a permanent part of his tone. "I'll be home early for dinner. Looks like Gracie has cooked us up some tasty leftovers in there! Or would you rather eat out?" His brows lifted in a question as he tilted his head toward her. "No, no, of course not. Well . . ." He leaned down and kissed her on the back of the neck. "You'll be all right?" he said against her. She reached up and placed her right hand on top of his.

"I'm fine. Thank you, dear," she said.

Franklin retrieved his new fedora from the rack beside the door, glanced at her with a question, and this time Althea did smile, though it came out almost a grimace, a twisted little tugging at her lips, but Franklin smiled back at her, broadly, blew her a kiss. When he'd gone, Althea gathered herself and went on down the hall to the back of the house. She entered the kitchen through the rear hall door by the maid's room rather than through the dining room. This had become her habit. At the little table against the wall, a Negro man sat holding the baby. Graceful was not in the kitchen. The Negro stood up. He was very tall, very black. The baby looked so light, so very small in his arms, though Althea realized he'd grown a great deal since the night of the disaster. His face was rounded, alert. The Negro man held him about the waist, facing toward her, and the boy waved his arms, kicked his legs, gurgling. His eyes were brown, very bright in his light face, and he was drooling from teething gums. He smiled at her. He was, if anything, more beautiful.

"How do you do, ma'am?" the Negro said. "We just— Graceful setting the table—"

Althea looked up at the man's face, and her heart gave a little kick. She'd only seen him once clearly, and that was in the moment a white man lifted a rifle to club him, but she understood, in the great interlocking of pieces, that this was the Negro who had jumped on her, rolled on her, put out the fire that would surely have consumed her as it had consumed her brother, and she was at once filled with gratitude and fury. He stepped toward the dining-room passageway, called softly, "Graceful? Honey?"

Althea took a slow step into the room. It was something she'd never dreamed of, that Graceful had married the man who'd saved her. Why hadn't Graceful told her? And then Althea thought: Why would she? Never once had Althea mentioned the person who'd put out the fire; she had not, in fact, thought of that moment for more than a fluttery, frightened instant in daylight since she regained consciousness, a hundred and twenty days ago, in the hospital hallway, because to do so made her see her brother's hand reaching toward her with the lit match, her own swiftly moving hand flying toward his, grabbing his wrist. To see was to make herself ask the question she'd lain awake asking a thousand times in the long, tortured nights since; to ask was to ponder the unknown, unknowable answer: had she been reaching toward Japheth to hold him, draw him to her, or to turn the flame back on him?

"Miz Dedmeyer, this is Hedgemon." Graceful held the silver serving tray at her side; her face was as expressionless as ever.

"How do you do, ma'am?" the young man said again.

They stood facing one another, Graceful and her husband holding the baby just to the side of the dining-room passage, Althea across the gleaming white tiles from them near the pantry door. The young man bowed slightly, very formal, and it suddenly seemed to Althea that this was a moment of great import, great dignity, and if they had not been colored she would have invited them into the parlor, to sit stiffly on the edges of the silk and velvet chairs, receive tea perhaps; she would have created some kind of ritual, a formal thank you, a parting, a farewell. But of course she could not do that. They were Negroes.

"How do you do, Mr. . . . ?" Althea glanced at Graceful.

"Jackson," the young man said.

"How do you do, Mr. Jackson."

"Well," Graceful said. There was in her face a kind of softening. "Here he is." She took the baby from the man's arms, came across the floor. She stopped a couple of feet away, held the baby up to show him. "He getting big, isn't he?" She nuzzled her brown face against his tea-colored one. "Already trying to cut a tooth, too." The baby was gnawing at her closed fingers, a long string of spittle dangling off her wrist. "That's how come he drool so bad."

Althea reached out her arms.

"He'll get your dress wet, ma'am."

"That's all right," Althea said, and after another instant's hesitation Graceful gave him to her. The baby immediately fit himself against her; he didn't feel like the fragile newborn she'd last held. He was so strong, bobbing one hand in the air, as if conducting an orchestra, and with his other hand he held on to Althea's sleeve. He was making babbling noises, looking up at her as if he had something to say.

"He's going to be a real talker," Graceful said. She took the edge of her apron and wiped his chin. "Aren't you, Theodore?" she said, and smiled at the baby. Althea realized that it was the first time she'd ever seen Graceful smile.

"Theodore? Is that what you named him?"

"Hedgemon Theodore Jackson, Junior," Graceful said. She looked in Althea's eyes. "After his daddy." Her face showed nothing, but in her tone, in the very lack of expression, was that specific truth neither could speak, and not just the one truth, but many truths, passing back and forth between them, so powerful, so full of hurt and love and sorrow, that Althea, feeling the skin tighten across her face, the great welling in her chest, turned and began to pace the kitchen, patting the baby's back as if he were fussy, though he was still making little repetitive cooing sounds.

"What's the name of that town again?" she asked sharply over her shoulder.

"Boley," Graceful said.

"Boley." Althea stopped near the back door. She looked out past the screen. The leaves on the great elm were already turning yellow. "Down by Okemah," she said softly.

"Yes, ma'am. Twelve miles west."

It might as well be twelve thousand, Althea thought. She could no more go to Boley, Oklahoma, to see her nephew than she could fly to the moon. That was one of the truths which had passed between them. When Graceful left this morning, they would not see each other again.

"Are there a lot of folks from . . . here . . . moving to Boley?"

"Some," Graceful said. It was quiet in the kitchen, and Althea turned around. Graceful and her husband were not looking at each other, but something was being communicated between them. "Your breakfast is on the table, ma'am." Graceful busied herself at the sink. "You don't want your eggs to get cold." Now she glanced at her husband, and he edged away from the dining-room doorway, as if to give Althea clear passage.

"Well, I mean, do you have people there? Do you know people?"

"Hedgemon know a few folks. Honey, take Theodore so Miz Dedmeyer can eat her breakfast." He took a tentative step in Althea's direction, but stopped when she made no corresponding move. Graceful sprinkled soap flakes in the dishpan. "I put the chicken in the icebox. There's some potato salad in there, and I cut up some of the pears Mr. Franklin brought." She stirred the sudsy water. "I left the soup on the stove for y'all's supper."

"Who are you going to work for?" The question was meant for Graceful; it was something Althea had wondered, though she'd never thought to ask her: if there were no white people in Boley, whom would Graceful cook and clean and wash for? How could she get a job? But Graceful mistook her meaning.

"Hedgemon know how to run the linotype, the presses, he can do about anything around a printing press wants doing. They got a nice paper in Boley. We're going to see about that first. Elberta wrote Mama there's plenty of jobs."

"Who's Elberta?"

After a beat Graceful said, "My brother's wife."

"Your brother's down there?"

Again the silence, and this time it seemed to extend beyond the boundaries of the kitchen, to join, in great soundless waves, the silence that covered the whole city: the unspoken names of the dead, the disappeared. There were so many who could not be found in the chaotic days after the disaster, and the papers said that the missing Negroes had fled to avoid prosecution, though at first there were whispers about dead blacks buried in mass graves, or dumped by the truckload in the Arkansas River, or burned in gigantic pyres. Then, within days, the silence had descended, and names were no longer mentioned, not even the names of missing white men, the drifters and itinerant oilfield workers: aimless unclaimed men with no family to ask after them. Althea's brother's name was among the unspoken. Graceful's brother was perhaps also among them, but Althea wouldn't press further. There was one other secret she carried: the image of a tawny head moving in a river of white men. Jim Dee Logan had vanished from the Deep Fork, had not been seen or heard from in the oilfields anywhere in Oklahoma, since that violent night.

"Well. Goodness." The baby was starting to fret. Althea put her cheek to the top of his smooth head, began to pace the kitchen again, patting him.

"I left the cover on," Graceful said, "but them eggs already been cooked awhile."

"Yes. Thank you. I'll just— How near ready are you?"

"Just got to finish washing up. My things are all packed. Honey," she said quietly, "take him." This time Althea surrendered the baby, and when Graceful's husband held him he instantly settled down. "He behave better for Hedgemon than he do for me. Of course, Hedgemon's the one take the most care of him. Mama don't feel much like . . ." Graceful's voice faded as she turned to the sink. "I got to get cracking." And she plucked a handful of silverware up from the bottom of the pan.

Her husband went outside to sit on the back-porch step. Althea could see him balancing the laughing baby on his knees jacked up high on the bottom step. She went into the dining room and sat at the walnut table, removed the lids from the chafing dishes and served herself, listened to the pots and pans clanging in the kitchen as she pretended to eat. When Graceful came in to remove the dirty plates and serving dishes and the lone delicate gold-rimmed china cup, she'd already taken her apron off; she held the serving tray away from her chest as she disappeared through the passageway.

Althea followed, watched in silence as Graceful hurriedly washed up the last of the breakfast things, dried them swiftly, put them away. A small bundle wrapped in a brightly colored scarf sat on the floor beside the door. Graceful folded the damp tea towel over the rack at the end of the counter, turned for one last quick look around the sparkling kitchen, and, seeming satisfied, went to pick up her bundle. In Althea now there was a great urgency just to have it over. She came on into the kitchen, saying, "Here, let me get the screen," as if Graceful might need help wrestling the small bundle of worldly goods out the door.

Then they were on the footpath in the side yard, and Graceful's husband was holding the baby. Then they were out the gate, moving along the walk beside the fence, and Graceful turned back once. She stood for a moment, and it was too far for Althea to make out her expression, but it didn't matter; she knew that Graceful's smooth brown features were completely still, completely unreadable. Althea lifted a hand to say goodbye, and Graceful raised her hand briefly, palm outward. Then she took her son from Hedgemon, and the two of them walked on. Althea went to the porch swing and watched them, both of them tall, the baby hidden from her sight in Graceful's arms, until they'd crossed Fifteenth Street.

Long after they'd disappeared from her vision, Althea sat in the swing, motionless, her mind restless, unable to stay on any one thought for more than a few seconds. She had so much work to do, her garden was an absolute disgrace. The roses were blooming, of course, but the weeds were abominable. When was the last time she'd worked in it? Where in the world would she start? If she ever did want to try to get in touch with Graceful she wouldn't know how, because she didn't know her married name. Well, yes, of course she did. It was Jackson. Graceful Jackson. Well. That was the one thing she'd never asked, wasn't it, where Graceful's people had come from that had caused her name to be Whiteside. The baby's name was Theodore Jackson. Teddy. Perhaps they would call him Teddy. No, probably not. Come to think of it, there must be others. She surely had other nephews, and nieces. It wouldn't be too hard to find them. They were all living in Bristow. She wouldn't know her sisters' last names, of course, but Bristow was not a large town. Well. If she meant to get a lick of work done this morning she was going to have to go upstairs and change in a minute. Lord, it was hot for the end of September. Althea took her hat off, laid it in her lap, and with one hand smoothed down the skirt of her silk mourning dress.

ABOUT THE SERIES

From the nineteenth century until the outbreak of World War II, American interest in Russia followed an erratic course. Americans joined the rest of the world in admiration for the great Russian novelists, but despite several instances of direct involvements in Russian affairs, as in the Treaty of Portsmouth and the civil war intervention, we were content for the most part to follow the headlines. Even the violent transformation of Russian society in the twenties and thirties provoked little interest. In 1940, the United States had only a handful of Soviet specialists—three universities had departments of Slavic languages and literature and only nineteen colleges and universities taught Russian. World War II, the alliance, and the Cold War changed everything. We are now more preoccupied with Russia than with any other country. This is reflected not only in our foreign policy but in the massive expansion of curricula on every aspect of Russian culture.

Unfortunately, many of the most informative and significant volumes on Russia were written and published before the postwar interest developed and have long been out of print. Many volumes of memoirs, historical studies, novels, analyses of Soviet power and policies, and untranslated works by Russians which could provide significant information and understanding are not now available, or can be purchased only in expensive editions.

Classics in Russian Studies is designed to make available inexpensive but high quality paperback reprints of some of these interesting and important books. The Series is designed for students of all ages, within and outside organized educational institutions, in the hope that it will increase our knowledge and understanding of a country and a culture which will always be significant and fascinating.

ROBERT F. BYRNES
SERIES EDITOR

The Strange Alliance

THE STORY OF OUR EFFORTS AT WARTIME CO-OPERATION WITH RUSSIA

by John R. Deane

Indiana University Press

BLOOMINGTON / LONDON

TO MY WIFE

This edition is published in 1973 by Indiana University Press
by arrangement with The Viking Press, Inc.

Published in Canada by Fitzhenry & Whiteside Limited, Don Mills, Ontario
Library of Congress catalog card number: 72-88915
ISBN: 0-253-18520-3

Manufactured in the United States of America

Foreword

Major General John R. Deane arrived in Moscow on October 18, 1943, to attend the Moscow Conference of the British, American, and Soviet Foreign Ministers as a military observer and to begin duty as head of the United States Military Mission to the U.S.S.R. His responsibility was to help coordinate Soviet and American military efforts and to direct the Russian end of the massive lend-lease program, which provided the Soviet Union $11,000,000,000 worth of munitions, equipment, and food. General Deane, who joined the regular army in 1917, had served three years in Panama and two in China, and had been named a brigadier general and Secretary of the War Department General Staff shortly after Japan attacked at Pearl Harbor. In September, 1942, he was named United States Secretary of the Combined Chiefs of Staff. In short, he had had excellent experience abroad and at the very center of combined Anglo-American staff operations before General Marshall advised him to remain absolutely frank and open in his new post in Moscow. On the other hand, General Deane had little knowledge of the Soviet Union and no experience in dealing with Russians. Moreover, he reflected perfectly the contemporary attitude of most American political and military leaders, and of the American public—we should concentrate on winning the war, because defeating the Germans and the Japanese and destroying their capacity to make war was central. Political issues and decisions could safely be left until after the war.

The Strange Alliance is a remarkably candid and fair chronicle of General Deane's attempt to work with the Russians. Eager to support an ally fighting under the most heavy pressure and anxious to cooperate with the Russians in the Grand Alliance, General Deane, like his Commander-in-Chief, displayed a generosity which historians have long considered extraordinary. In fact, he urged our policy of appeasement end only late in the war, when he was exhausted by continued Russian failure to honor commitments which would have advanced the interests of the alliance as a whole, while demanding—and obtaining—prompt and efficient American technical aid and the steady flow of lend-lease supplies. As he says, we were providing all possible assistance to the Soviet Union without recognition and without Soviet consideration for our needs, such as in obtaining quick access to American prisoners captured from the Germans

v

or an opportunity to build air bases in Siberia for use against Japan. As General Deane shows, in our negotiations we failed to identify our national interests clearly and to work effectively for them. We were baffled by Soviet resolution with regard to long-term Soviet interests and by Soviet negotiation tactics. At the same time, as General Deane points out, we realized that the Soviets ruled a country often invaded. Inexperienced in joint operations or close cooperation, suspicious of all foreigners as Russians generally are, and doubly suspicious because of their conspiratorial history, the Soviet leaders concentrated not only on driving their enemy from Russian soil, but also upon acquiring control beyond Soviet boundaries after the war. Soviet determination to extend Soviet power was so sustained and vigorous that General Deane by the spring of 1945 began to fear that the ally he sought so much to aid had become a threat to all its neighbors and to hopes for a stable and peaceful world.

The Strange Alliance is a description of General Deane's efforts to work with the Russians and of his reaction to the rebuffs and deceits which he experienced. It pays tribute to the great courage of the Russian people and to the constancy with which they bore the sacrifices forced on them by the Germans—and by their own government. It provides clear insights into the national feeling which united the Russians, and into the divisions of rank and class which divided them even in war. Above all, it indicates how the Soviet leaders turned their most eager allies against them. While not so well-informed or so reflective as his colleague in the American embassy, George Kennan, General Deane reached the same conclusions as Kennan concerning the nature of the Soviet system and its ambitions. His book, widely read in 1946 and 1947, translated into French; and also published in part in *Life*, was favorably reviewed by newspapers and journals. It contributed significantly to the shift in American attitude and policy, which Soviet policy in Eastern Europe, the February 1948 coup in Czechoslovakia, and the Berlin Blockade helped to turn into the confrontation which has bedeviled the world since.

The book thus gains remarkable insight into the origins of a tragic, but inevitable disagreement, inevitable at least so long as Stalin and his successors remained single-minded in their ambitions. At the same time, it shows that we were both loyal and generous during the war and that our ignorance and even stupidity were only the obverse side of other noble qualities. At least, we began the confrontation convinced that we had done even more than we should have to demonstrate our commitment to the common cause.

Indiana University   ROBERT F. BYRNES

Table of Contents

First Steps toward
Soviet-American Collaboration

I. Arrival

I WAS eager, hopeful, confident, and happy as we circled the Moscow airdrome late in the afternoon of October 18, 1943. Eager, because there was so much to be done in uniting the allied war effort; hopeful and confident, because I was empowered to make a frank and generous approach which I thought could not fail to produce a similar Soviet reaction; happy, for many reasons—I had cut loose from Washington, I was to have a command of my own, and most of all I was to work with a man for whom I had and have the greatest admiration, respect, and devotion, the newly appointed Ambassador, W. Averell Harriman.

From the window of my plane I could see the domes of the Kremlin blackened with war paint, the sparkling waters of the Moscow River, Red Square, St. Basil's Church, and the glistening bayonets of a guard of honor waiting in the field below to salute for the Soviet Union our great Secretary of State, Cordell Hull.

Our caravan of transports landed and taxied to a spot where the Foreign Office team of Molotov, Vishinsky, Maisky, and Litvinov were waiting to greet Secretary Hull and the new Ambassador. Ours were the first of the then new C-54 transport planes to arrive in Russia. They represented the very epitome of effete Capitalism, and the eyes of the Russians plainly evidenced their amazement. Thereafter their efforts to obtain a fleet of C-54's through lend-lease were as persistent as they were futile.

The reception was identical with the many that I was destined to witness in the ensuing two years. The weather was freezing, and the

Russians, having come an hour ahead of time in the fear that they might be late, were blue with cold that had penetrated to the marrow. Smiles were set and greetings exchanged in Russian and English, with or without benefit of interpreters. The principal greeters and the principal guests led a hodgepodge procession past the guard of honor. It was my first glimpse of soldiers of the Red Army and I was much impressed. Uniforms were well tailored, helmets shone, gloves were snow white, and postures rigid. As we approached the right of the line we were stopped by a rendition of the "Internationale," followed by an excellent though slightly unfamiliar version of the "Star-Spangled Banner." Both gave me a thrill and for the moment at least I felt that we were among Allies.

At a command the soldiers turned their heads and eyes to the right and rotated them individually and successively to the left as we passed in front of them. I thought this a sensible procedure as it satisfied the soldiers' curiosity to see the celebrity in whose honor they had left the warmth of the barracks. It was new to me but I understand we have since adopted it in our Army.

When the troops had been inspected by Secretary Hull the reviewing party lined up in two ranks with the principals in front and the lesser lights in the rear. I had to crane my neck to see. The guard of honor then marched past in review. The music was rhythmic with the downbeat so explosive that the troops had no choice but to keep step—and what a step! It closely resembled the goose-step, with arms rigid and legs kicked stiffly to the front. Feet slapped the pavement with a jar that shook the soldiers' jowls and induced a sympathetic quiver in those of the spectators. The marching struck me as being not so sensible as the procedure described above. It pointed plainly to a discipline oriented toward German methods, which tends to destroy individual initiative in the battle pay-off. The American swinging gait which emphasizes marching as a means of getting from here to there is preferable. So far, one for the Russians on the head and eyes business, and one to the Americans on marching—I shall try to remain objective.

Following the review of the guard of honor, Mr. Molotov made a few welcoming remarks into a microphone. Mr. Hull responded. During my stay in Russia I always wondered if these microphones were connected with anything. I never saw movies or heard broadcasts of the words of wisdom uttered into them. With the ceremony thus concluded, the Americans were bustled into automobiles, while the quartet of Molotov, Vishinsky, Maisky, and Litvinov, together with helpers, remained behind to repeat the performance for Anthony Eden and his crowd who were scheduled to follow us in a half hour.

I was led to my car, a new shiny two-toned cream-colored Buick of 1942 vintage. It was quite the most glamorous motor car in Moscow, and the British Ambassador, Sir Archibald Clark-Kerr, always referred to it as Greta Garbo. My chauffeur was Naum Maronovitch, and except for the fact that his foot was always heavy on the accelerator, I learned to love him as I would a brother. Like all employees of foreigners, he was probably used by the Secret Police of the N.K.V.D. to report on my activities. If so, he did his observing unobtrusively, and for all I could tell his desire to serve me motivated his every act. Above all, he wanted me to learn Russian, and when he introduced a new word into my vocabulary he illustrated its meaning with his hands and feet regardless of the speed at which we were traveling. It was most frightening when he looked around to see whether or not his instruction was taking.

The Moscow airdrome is about five miles west of the city. During the drive to my apartment I gained impressions which did not change much during my entire stay. I saw factories, with people swarming in and out of gates in the high fences which surrounded them—war industries working around the clock in the utmost secrecy. The buildings were dilapidated; windows, pavements, railroad stations, trolley lines—everywhere paint and repairs were needed. New construction was half finished; steel girders were exposed and rusting; every effort toward better living had been stopped in favor of the war effort. As we went east on Gorky Street toward the Kremlin, we saw block after block of closed stores—there were no consumer goods to sell. The people were either in uniforms of fairly good quality or in shabby civilian clothes. Most able-bodied men and women were in uniform; the civilians were preponderantly those who were very young or very old. Faces were neither happy nor depressed, but rather intent and determined. On the whole, the people impressed me as being lean, hard, and well nourished but not overfed. Malnutrition was apparent in some of the children and in many of the aged. Women were repairing trolleys, sweeping streets, driving trucks, and in general were doing all sorts of jobs which I had always thought of as being reserved for men.

My flat was in the Embassy building on Mokhavaya Street next door to the National Hotel, which houses most transient foreigners while they are in Moscow. It overlooked a tremendous square the size of three or four of our city blocks. Directly across the square was the west wall of the Kremlin. Above it one could see the Byzantine domes and cupolas that characterize the Kremlin architecture. The Kremlin itself is a walled city about six city blocks square. It includes the Palace, several churches, a museum, and a few buildings now used for offices of the highest Soviet officials.

My flat was completely furnished in the careless style that might be expected from a succession of bachelor occupants. It had been the home of our military attachés since 1933, and the accumulations of each incumbent were sold to his successor. Major General Sidney P. Spalding, who had come to head the Lend-Lease Division of the Military Mission, agreed to live with me, and that was my outstanding stroke of good fortune on the first afternoon.

The flat was staffed with two servants. One was Proskovia Palna, a woman in her sixties who was to be our cook; the other was Ganya Palna, a very pretty woman in her middle thirties, who was to be our housemaid. Neither spoke a word of English, but both knew their duties so well that conversation was unnecessary and was not attempted for the first few days. Proskovia proved to be an excellent cook who could work wonders with meager Russian rations supplemented by a generous supply of American canned goods. She was not the tidiest individual in the world, and I shudder to think what my wife would have thought and done had she seen our kitchen. Ganya was the exact opposite. The house, except for the kitchen, was her bailiwick, and she kept it and herself immaculate. Her husband had gone off to war in 1941 and that was the last she had heard of him. I think she had given up hope of his return and devoted her life to bringing up a daughter of twelve whose greatest need was the sturdy hand of a father applied in the right place. So far I had met three Russians whom I was to know quite well—Naum, Proskovia, and Ganya. I shall always remember them with the deepest affection. I cannot but feel that they were representative of the mass of the Russian people. Their faults and virtues, joys and sorrows, were human ones, with the good far outweighing the bad. They had the normal Russian fear of discussing government, politics, and ideologies with foreigners, but also I received the impression that they were not much interested. They did their jobs well and their aspirations were identical with those of the rank and file the world over. I am certain that a great hope for world peace lies in breaking through the wall of Soviet officialdom and reaching the Russian people.

I had not been in my new home for more than half an hour when I was called to the Kremlin. I did not realize at the time that this was establishing some sort of record. The Kremlin is not a place one drops into at will, but I did not yet know how well its gates were guarded. The delegates to the Moscow Conference, of whom I was one, were to have their first preliminary meeting.

"What was my chauffeur's name?" and "What was the number of my car?" I know now that I made considerable "face" with Naum when my interpreter directed him to the Kremlin. There was at least a platoon of guards at the gate and the leader was expecting me. After questioning Naum, he designated a soldier to ride on the running board and guide us to the building in which Molotov's office was situated. Soldiers were spaced every few feet in the luxurious red-carpeted hall leading from the entrance to Molotov's office. They were members of the secret police, dressed as soldiers and distinguished by deep blue caps. Their salutes were smartly executed, and I was quite exhausted from returning them by the time I reached Molotov's office.

Secretary Hull, Ambassador Harriman, Green Hackworth, the Secretary's legal adviser, Charles E. (Chip) Bohlen, the State Department's Russian expert, and I assembled in an anteroom. There we met Anthony Eden, William Strang, Sir Archibald Clark-Kerr, and General Sir Hastings Ismay, who represented the British. In a moment Molotov, Vishinsky,. and Maisky came in with an interpreter, V. N. Pavlov. We then went through a handshaking procedure that was typical of all British-American-Soviet relations. The British and Americans paid no attention to each other beyond a casual nod or "Howdjdo," but both Anglo-Saxon delegations shook hands with every Russian in the room. This process was repeated every time we met or departed from a group of Russians. It was indicative of the casual and informal relationship we had with our British ally as contrasted with the formality and reserve which attended our relations with the Russians.

The meeting was for the purpose of making conference arrangements. It was agreed that there were to be no press releases until the Conference was concluded. Molotov was reluctant to accept the chairmanship which the Anglo-American delegations insisted he should have as the principal representative of the host nation. We discovered that the Soviet delegation had only one subject for the agenda, but they insisted that it be the first subject considered—"Ways and Means of Hastening the Conclusion of the War." This meant that General Ismay and I, as the British and American military advisers, were going to have to satisfy the Russian apprehensions about a second front or there would be no more agenda. The British and Americans shook hands again with the Russians and we adjourned until the following day.

After the meeting Averell Harriman asked me to come and see his quarters, and I had my first introduction to the famous Spasso House. It had been built by a wealthy merchant before the revolution and had been taken over as the American Ambassador's residence by Wil-

liam Bullitt when we established relations with the Soviet Union in
1933. It has about the same shabby grandeur as Grand Central Station
and impressed me as being almost as large. During his tour of duty in
Moscow, Averell made it a real American center, and its thirteen bedrooms were usually bulging with visiting Americans, among them
Harry Hopkins, Ed Stettinius, Don Nelson, Brigadier General Patrick
J. Hurley, Senator Claude Pepper, Lillian Hellman, Lieutenant General Ira Eaker, and General Dwight D. Eisenhower. American gatherings on the Fourth of July, Thanksgiving, Christmas, and New Year's
were memorable occasions for all of us who were there.

When I returned to my flat that first night I found that Sid Spalding
had arranged for us to be at the airport at seven o'clock the following
morning to bid farewell to our old friend Donald Nelson, who had
been in Russia as the guest of Commissar of Foreign Trade Mikoyan.
Seven o'clock seemed rather early, and I am sure I would never have
gone had I known what was in store for me. Sid and I were included in
a farewell breakfast for Don which consisted of vodka, cognac, and
champagne, with the usual *zakouskas* that are always present at a Russian party regardless of the hour of the day. All toasts were bottoms
up—Sid and I could cheat on some of them but Don Nelson had no
chance. He left Moscow in his aircraft figuratively higher than a kite—
figuratively only, because airplanes do not fly that high in Russia.

I had had my first inkling that I was to go to Russia early in September 1943. I was then the United States Secretary of the Combined
Chiefs of Staff and had a very close working arrangement with my
British colleague whereby I obtained much information from British
sources concerning the subjects of communications between President
Roosevelt and Prime Minister Churchill. For some reason our President often kept our Chiefs of Staff in the dark on these matters until
the die was cast, and, at times, the advance information that I could
obtain was invaluable.

The first Quebec Conference had just been concluded and Churchill
was visiting Roosevelt in Washington. The British Secretary showed

me a telegram the Prime Minister had sent to the British War Cabinet discussing the forthcoming Moscow Conference. In it he said, "The President is sending General Deane as Mr. Hull's military adviser and I propose to send General Ismay." A week or so later Averell Harriman invited me to lunch with him and, after disclosing that he was to be the new American Ambassador in Moscow, he proposed that I should go with him as the head of a Military Mission which would include all Army, Navy, Air, and lend-lease activities.

During the early stages of the war the United States had been represented in the Soviet Union by its Ambassador, the usual Military and Naval Attachés, and by an agency known as the United States Supply Mission which had the function of facilitating the lend-lease supply program.

There can be no criticism of the manner in which these agencies performed their respective duties. Each was an entity, however, and each had a different objective. As a result there was no unanimity of purpose among the United States representatives. Their divergent aims led to internal friction that soon became common gossip in Moscow. In addition, Ambassador Standley had never been kept advised of the strategic directives and operational plans of the United States Armed Forces. This was a natural condition but a particularly unfortunate one in Soviet Russia, where the head of state is at the same time the active head of its armed forces. Since the Ambassador was the only American who had ready access to Stalin, it was imperative that he be kept advised of American operational plans if military liaison on the highest level was to be accomplished.

The choice of Harriman as Ambassador was particularly fortunate. Aside from his outstanding attributes of character, his war experience made him ideally suited for the assignment. He had long been one of the President's intimate and confidential advisers. He had attended the military and political conferences that had been held between the President and the Prime Minister and their combined Chiefs of Staff. He had been the President's representative at the first military discussions between Churchill and Stalin in August of 1942. Moreover, he had played a leading part in the lend-lease program. Together with Lord Beaverbrook, he had negotiated the initial lend-lease agreement with Russia in 1941. He had served for two and one half years as the President's personal representative in England in connection with the British lend-lease program and with regard to shipping and production matters. His appointment to the Soviet Union was warmly received by the Soviet Government and the Russian people, who appreciated the part he had played in starting the flow of American supplies to Russia.

Harriman discussed his plans with General Marshall and proposed the establishment of a Military Mission which would act under his general direction and thus weld the whole United States political and military representation in Russia into a co-ordinated team with a unified purpose. As a result I received a directive from General Marshall designating me as the head of a Military Mission to the Union of Soviet Socialist Republics and ordering me to report to the United States Ambassador at Moscow immediately upon completion of the Tripartite Conference to which I was to go as a military observer. The directive informed me that the Military Mission would include Brigadier Generals Sidney P. Spalding and Hoyt S. Vandenberg, the latter of whom was to return to his station in Washington not later than six weeks following establishment of the mission. General Spalding was given the responsibility of handling lend-lease matters in the U.S.S.R.

The objective of the Military Mission, the directive stated, was "to promote the closest possible co-ordination of the military efforts of the United States and the U.S.S.R." I was authorized to discuss with Soviet authorities all information concerning United States military strategy, plans, and operations, which, in my judgment, it was appropriate to discuss, but to "make no commitments which cause an increased deployment of U.S. Army supplies or troops without War Department approval."

The United States Supply Mission, together with personnel remaining in the United States Military Attaché Office, was to be absorbed by my Military Mission, which was to work directly under the United States Ambassador, its activities subject to his direction and approval.

This directive was later amended to include a Naval Division in the Mission and thereafter I was to report to the Joint Chiefs of Staff rather than to the War Department as indicated in my original instructions.

II. The Moscow Conference

LIKE every other project during the war in which Russia was a participant, the Moscow Conference progressed at the Russian tempo. The first meeting was scheduled for three o'clock on the afternoon of October 19, but it was preceded by a luncheon given by Molotov which was apparently designed not only to delay the start of the Conference but to render all participants unconscious.

We assembled for the luncheon at the Soviet guest house at 17 Spiridonevskaia Street at one o'clock. The house is a relic of Czarist days. It is huge and ornate with spacious halls and rooms, gold ceilings, and brocaded walls hung with oil paintings in heavy gold frames. Floors are highly polished and covered with exquisite oriental rugs. The care with which the art treasures have been preserved in this and many other buildings gives ample evidence that the Soviet leaders have no hatred for luxury per se. While such surroundings are reserved for the official use of a very few, they probably provide an incentive to improve the condition of the masses in that they point to the glories of the past and the hopes of the future.

We sat down to a table laid for about thirty. The delegates to the Conference and some leaders from other Commissariats of the Soviet Government were there. For the most part they were those who had either had or would have official dealings with the British and Americans—but none of the party leaders who lurk behind the scenes and never come into contact with foreigners. They included A. I. Mikoyan, head of the Commissariat of Foreign Trade, A. D. Krutikov and V. A. Sergeev, his principal assistants, and a few General Staff officers. Of course Marshal Klementy Voroshilov, then Vice Commissar of Defense, and Lieutenant General A. A. Gryzlov of the General Staff, both delegates to the Conference, were there.

I had never before seen such an elaborate table service. The centerpieces were huge silver bowls containing fresh fruit specially procured from the Caucasus. It was only at such functions that one saw fresh fruit in Moscow. Beautiful cut glass ran the gamut from tall thin champagne glasses, through those for light and heavy red and white wines, to the inevitable vodka glass, midway in size between our liqueur and cocktail glasses, without which no Russian table is set. There were bottles the entire length of the table from which the glasses could be and were filled many times. Interspersed among the bottles were silver platters of Russian *zakouska*, including fresh large-grained dark gray caviar, very black pressed caviar of the consistency of tar, huge cucumber pickles, raw salmon and sturgeon, slices of not very well cooked ham, salami, chocolates in bright-colored tinfoil, and innumerable other delicacies that the Russians must have in order to work up an appetite for the meal to come. Knives, forks, and spoons were of gold, and service plates of the finest china heavily encrusted with gold. The whole spectacle was amazing and called to mind the banquet scene in Charles Laughton's movie *Henry VIII*.

Luncheon was an endless succession of courses, starting with a heavy borsch, progressing through a delicious fish in hollandaise sauce, a roast, and a salad, and ending with a huge architectural monstrosity made of ice cream which presented a series of interesting and different problems as it was attacked successively by the guests on its way around the table.

Molotov had scarcely seated himself when he was on his feet, vodka glass in hand. On his initiative there followed a succession of toasts on the general subject of friendship but which were adjusted to meet the special case presented by each person at the table and some who were not. It started with a series to British-Soviet-American friendship which, including British and American responses, accounted for three drinks. Toasts were then given to Churchill, Stalin, and Roosevelt, which made three more; then the Foreign Secretaries toasted one another. This went on and on. Finally through the haze I heard my name and knew a toast was being aimed at me. To my consternation I was expected to drink bottoms up to myself and, even worse, I was expected to respond.

On the whole I was having a beautiful time and, on this my second day, was seeing the Soviet Union through rose-colored glasses. Had I returned to the United States that night or even a week or so later, I would no doubt have had sentiments similar to those of all "vodka visitors."

Prior to my departure for Russia an old friend, Colonel W. McC. Chapman, who had been in Russia with General Graves in 1920, taught me a few Russian phrases. Among them was *Ya vas lebleu,* meaning "I love you," which I never had occasion to use. Another was *Oo Boornya Yest?* which he said meant "Is there a toilet?" I had occasion to use this upon the conclusion of Molotov's luncheon but was rather afraid to do so since Chapman is known as a practical joker. However, the need was urgent; fortified by the vodka, I asked the question in a loud voice. It worked. I was hustled to the correct department—just in time, else I never would have made the first formal session of the Conference which was to start at four o'clock.

The conference room was across the hall from the dining-room; upon assembling there the British and Americans again shook hands with the Russians. We gathered round a huge circular table which had a little stand in the middle holding Soviet, British, and American flags—my but we were allies!

Molotov called the meeting to order. On his left was Marshal Voroshilov. Well along in his sixties, he is one of the very few of the original members of the Communist party who have survived the vicissitudes, reorganizations, and purges that have been the lot of the party leaders in the evolution of the present regime. At that time he was Vice Commissar of Defense and deputy to Stalin. Since then his standing has waned and at the time of this writing he is Chairman of the Allied Control Commission in Hungary.

On Molotov's right was Andrei Vishinsky about whom everyone whispers, "He was the prosecutor in the purge trials." It was not difficult to imagine him obtaining the confessions which characterized these trials. One look at his cold pale blue eyes convinced me that I did not want to be in his buggy while he was in the driver's seat. On Vishinsky's right was Maxim Litvinov, erstwhile Foreign Minister and Ambassador to the United States. I gained the impression at the Conference that although Litvinov was present he had been definitely relegated to the background. As time went on this impression was strengthened by the fact that his principal duties seemed to consist of greeting visiting dignitaries upon their arrival in Moscow. The only other Soviet delegate at the table was Lieutenant General Gryzlov, a representative of the Red Army General Staff, who was completely overshadowed by Voroshilov's marshal's star and who participated very little in the proceedings.

The British representatives were Anthony Eden, Sir Archibald Clark-Kerr, General Sir Hastings Ismay, and William Strang. In the United States corner were Secretary Hull and his delegation—Averell Harriman, Green Hackworth, James Dunn, and I. Behind each delegation were interpreters and advisers, Chip Bohlen acting in both capacities for us.

Molotov at once took up the first item on the agenda—a Soviet proposal that the three nations should make immediate preparations in 1943 to insure an invasion of northern France. He also wished to discuss the possibility of inducing Turkey to enter the war immediately and of persuading Sweden to permit Allied use of her air bases.

The phrase "the three nations" in the principal proposal was included only through courtesy. What was actually meant was "What in hell are the British and Americans doing about establishing a second front?" The Russians had some reason to question the sincerity of our intentions in this matter. We had at one time decided on a small-scale invasion to establish a bridgehead on the Continent in the fall of 1942. This was to be followed up by exploitation of the bridgehead in the spring of 1943. When the African operations were undertaken in the fall of 1942 the invasion had to be postponed until the fall of 1943. When it was decided to exploit the African successes by invading Sicily and Sardinia, Overlord receded into 1944. After each big conference of the President and the Prime Minister and their Combined Chiefs of Staff the last item of business was to prepare a message to Stalin telling him of the decisions that had been reached. They were in terms which perhaps gave the Russians more hope of a second front than was justified. Invariably there would be a follow-up message a few months later indicating further postponement. In August 1942 after the decision was made to invade Africa at the expense of further delay to cross-channel operations, Prime Minister Churchill made a special trip to Moscow to break the news to Stalin. The interview was stormy, to say the least. It was against this background of suspicion that General Ismay and I were given the task of convincing the Russians that our plans at last were firm and that this time they would be carried out.

Looking back in the light of succeeding and present events, one can realize the Russians' interest in the establishment of a second front was more than that of the immediate military value involved. It was vital to Russian national policy, adopted long before the war and carried on aggressively since its conclusion. In the early days of the Bolshevik regime the Soviet leaders believed that the final conflict between Capitalism and Communism would emerge through dissensions among the capitalistic powers which would lead to world revolution, the death of Capitalism, and the triumphant emergence of Communism. They attempted to further this end through the activities of Communist agencies abroad. The program of world revolution was unsuccessful, and Stalin was the first to realize it. It was on this issue that he broke with Trotsky. The nationalistic build-up which grew out of this realization was fostered by a propaganda for home consumption that stressed the perils of capitalistic encirclements. This fear became real with Hitler's ascendance to power, which made Germany an actual rather than a fancied threat to the Bolshevik program. Russia then turned to the western powers to save her from Germany. She joined the League of Nations and became an outstanding proponent of collective security. However, the apathy of the western powers in the face of each new Hitlerian conquest convinced Russia that she was leaning on a broken reed. Her hopes then turned to the development of her own military strength and a policy of territorial expansion designed to give security in depth which would protect her from the encroachment of imperialist powers until such time as she had accumulated sufficient power to resume the offensive. The Munich incident destroyed Russia's hopes of western assistance, and she was ripe for the German approach which resulted in the nonaggression treaty of 1939. What Russia, together with the rest of the world, failed to foresee was the rapidity of the collapse of Western Europe and the short duration of her ill-gotten gains.

It is not surprising that when Germany turned on Russia in 1941 Russia again looked to the western powers for help; nor is it surprising that the western powers responded. Victory was a possibility if Germany could be squeezed from both directions. I said in the opening paragraph of this book that I was "confident and hopeful because I had been empowered to make a frank and generous approach which I thought could not fail to bring a similar Soviet reaction"— how naïve!

In describing the plans for the invasion of Europe, Ismay and I pointed out that at every British and American conference from Casablanca through Quebec the necessity to assist Russia had been a paramount consideration in reaching all strategic decisions. We emphasized the part expected of the combined bomber offensive and displayed photographs of the results being obtained. We went into detail concerning the build-up for the cross-channel operations, including the requirements for landing craft, floating piers, transportation, and all classes of supply. Finally, we reaffirmed the decision of the Washington and Quebec Conferences that the invasion would be undertaken in the spring of 1944 subject to the existence of the following conditions: 1) that there must be a substantial reduction of the German fighter aircraft strength between then and the date of the invasion; 2) that the German reserves in France and the Low Countries on the day of the assault must not be more than about twelve full strength, first quality mobile divisions, exclusive of coastal, training, and airborne divisions; and 3) that it must not be possible for the Germans to transfer more than fifteen first quality divisions during the first two months of operations.

We informed the Russians that we confidently expected to create these conditions by the softening effects of the bomber offensive, maintenance of pressure in Italy, secondary landings in Southern France, guerrilla activities in the Balkans, and last but not least, by relying on continued Soviet pressure on the eastern front.

Our presentation lasted perhaps an hour and at its conclusion we were questioned by Voroshilov and Gryzlov. They were particularly concerned about the conditions necessary for the attack. Voroshilov wanted to know if the presence of thirteen German reserve divisions would delay the invasion. We assured him that our figure of twelve divisions was only approximate and variations of a few divisions either way would not alter our plans. They also pressed us for an exact date. While we actually had a tentative date of May 5 at the time, both the British and ourselves were of the opinion that it would be jeopardizing security unnecessarily to inform the Russians so far in advance. They therefore had to be content with being told that the operation would be in the spring and that I would keep the Red Army General Staff informed of the progress of our preparations.

The Soviet delegation appeared to be completely convinced of the sincerity of the Anglo-American intentions and thanked General Ismay and me for the information we had given them. They assured us that the pressure on the Russian front would be continuous and unremitting and that they would do all in their power to help us create the conditions necessary for the invasion.

Taking advantage of the atmosphere of mutual trust and understanding that appeared to exist, I put forward three American proposals as measures for hastening the conclusion of the war: 1) that, in order to effect shuttle bombing of industrial Germany, bases be made available in the Soviet Union on which U.S. aircraft could be refueled, emergency repaired, and rearmed; 2) that more effective mutual interchange of weather information be implemented and, in order to effect this, that U.S. and U.S.S.R. signal communications be improved; and 3) that improved air transport be effected between the U.S. and the U.S.S.R.

These proposals hit the Soviet representatives as a bolt from the blue and as a result of the action taken on them I learned two important lessons for my future dealings with Soviet officials. The first was that no subordinate official in Russia may make a decision on matters in which foreigners are involved without consulting higher authority, and usually this higher authority is Stalin himself, perhaps in consultation with party leaders who move behind the scenes. In most cases subordinate officials will not even discuss proposals made by foreigners for fear of expressing opinions that would not be down the party line. For this reason, if any discussion did take place when a subject was first broached, the Soviet officials would assume a negative attitude and argue against the foreigner's proposal no matter how beneficial it might be to the Soviet Union. I learned, therefore, that it was always better to make a proposal, avoid discussion of it, and indicate that I hoped the proposal would be considered and an answer forthcoming in a few days.

The second lesson was that an "approval in principle" by the Soviet Government means exactly nothing. Two days after I had made the proposals, Molotov announced at a meeting that the Soviet Government had considered them carefully and approved them "in principle." Secretary Hull thanked Molotov and suggested that the details be worked out at once by the Red Army General Staff and the U.S. Military Mission. I, of course, was elated—less than a week in the Soviet Union and three major objectives achieved. Wouldn't the Chiefs of Staff be proud of me! I scarcely left the telephone for days, and each time I did I inquired at once upon my return if any General Staff officers had called me to arrange the details of shuttle bombing. Alas, it was the first of a great many such vigils I was to have in the ensuing two years. It was not until February of 1944 that conversations were started on the proposals, and then only after continuous pressure by the President on Stalin, by Harriman on Molotov, and by me on the General Staff.

Following the disclosure of the Anglo-American invasion plans, Molotov asked Secretary Hull and Mr. Eden for their ideas concerning Turkey and Sweden. Eden indicated that we were all in accord with the idea of the Turks fighting the Germans. The British were then sending supplies to Turkey to enable her to play her part in the war against Germany. The British had promised the Turks twenty-five squadrons of aircraft, which were not then available except at the expense of the Italian operations or the bomber offensive from England. Eden felt that should Turkey meet serious reverses, British or American troops would have to come to her rescue, and this could be done only at the expense of the Italian campaign or the cross-channel build-up. In addition, Eden pointed out that Turkish air bases from which to bomb Balkan oil installations had lost their importance now that bases were available in Italy. Eden did, however, agree that the British would give serious consideration to urging Turkey's entrance into the war if the conferees thought that such a course should be followed.

Secretary Hull felt that the United States would share the opinions expressed by Eden. I knew that the United States Chiefs of Staff would oppose urging Turkey's entrance into the war because it would impose obligations on us far in excess of the gains to be achieved, for they could be fulfilled only at the cost of our Pacific campaign or by a slow-down of the invasion preparations.

With respect to the possibility of obtaining the use of air bases in Sweden, Eden and Hull both felt that such a concession could not be attained without commitments for Sweden's protection that might constitute a serious drain on available resources. The conclusion reached was that final action on both questions would be deferred until all three governments had given them further study.

I did not know how strongly the Soviet representatives felt about getting Turkey into the war until the final day of the Conference. Their displeasure was first evidenced by the refusal to put my proposals concerning shuttle bombing, exchange of weather information, and improved communications, together with their approval "in principle," into the record or Protocol (as they called it) of the Conference. Molotov based his refusal on the contention that the proposals had not been discussed in detail and therefore had no place in the record. We were beginning to learn about approval "in principle." It was finally agreed that I would meet with Vishinsky and attempt to draft something for the record that would be acceptable. At a meeting with Vishinsky which lasted several hours he showed his bitterness about our attitude on Turkey and asked why the Russians should obligate themselves concerning our proposals when we had refused to join them in inducing Turkey to enter the war. He said that the immediate entry of Turkey would take fifteen German divisions from the Russian front, and if this were brought about the Russians would be in Prussia in two months.

I explained our attitude. I emphasized our commitments to Overlord, the Mediterranean, the Pacific, and the delivery of lend-lease supplies to Russia. I pointed out that any new undertakings such as Turkey's entry into the war would create an additional vacuum into which some of our resources would have to be diverted and that such diversion would jeopardize our success in carrying out present commitments.

His response to this was that it was not necessary for us to pour supplies into Turkey; that Turkey, if she were to expect to participate in the peace, would have to suffer during the war as the Russians were suffering. He felt that Turkey should be required to fight with the resources she then had, plus those we could give her without jeopardizing other commitments.

Our meeting ended without agreement. Our proposals and Russia's agreement in principle were finally admitted to the record only as the result of a strong personal letter from Secretary Hull to Molotov, accompanied by another letter indicating generous treatment of Russia in the distribution of Italian naval and merchant vessels.

Agreement on the "Four-Power Declaration" was the outstanding achievement of the Moscow Conference. It has been widely publicized, but briefly it provided for united action against the enemy, unanimity on surrender terms, the necessity to establish an international organization (the inception of the United Nations), agreement not to employ military force within the territories of other states after the war except after joint consultation, and postwar regulation of armaments.

The Declaration was conceived by Secretary Hull and steered through the Conference by the sheer force of his personality. Agreement upon its terms was not difficult, but it was difficult to obtain Soviet consent to include China as a signatory. China's fortunes were then at their lowest ebb, a condition not calculated to induce Soviet respect. On the other hand, China's continued participation in the war against Japan was of extreme importance and her recognition as one of the four big powers would provide a fillip of inestimable value to Chinese morale. Acting on President Roosevelt's instructions, Secretary Hull outplayed and outwaited the Soviet contingent and, with the support of Eden, won the day. It was the crowning achievement of Secretary Hull's career.

I cannot leave the subject of the Moscow Conference without mention of the farewell dinner given for the delegates by Marshal Stalin. It was the first of many such dinners that I attended. It is such dinners as these which have made so many distinguished visitors to Moscow for short periods return to the United States with glowing accounts and spread the gospel of how easy it is to "get along with the Russians," forgetting entirely those public servants whom they leave behind to carry out the agreements made "in principle." Those of us who were in Russia on a more permanent basis characterized such individuals as "vodka visitors."

Stalin's dinner party was held in the Kremlin Palace. The guests entered the front foyer on the ground floor and the first thing that met the eye was the longest, straightest, and most beautiful staircase in the world. The risers were low and it was a pleasure to walk up and down these red-carpeted stairs.

We assembled in a room done in deep red brocade, with exquisite French furniture. The doors, ceilings, and woodwork were of gold, the fixtures of heavy crystal. As usual, everyone shook hands with everyone else, and when all guests were present or accounted for Stalin walked in with Molotov.

It was the first time I had seen him. I was struck by the shortness of his stature, his bristly iron-gray hair, and most of all by the kindly expression on his deeply wrinkled, sallow face. He was dressed in a tan uniform of summer weight and carried the insignia of a Marshal of the Soviet Union on his shoulder tabs. He went around the room shaking hands with each guest, always bent over, seldom looking one in the eye, and saying nothing whatever. When this formality had been completed we filed into the dining-room more or less in order of rank.

The banquet hall and the banquet table were beautiful beyond description. The room was a blaze of light and reflections. The table appointments made those at the luncheon attended earlier in the Conference seem shabby in comparison. The food, however, was much the same as we had had then, and I noticed many familiar faces among the servants—I learned later that they were taken from the Moscow hotels and I encountered them at every official function I attended.

Molotov acted as toastmaster and the usual procession of toasts to British-American-Soviet friendship ensued. I knew that my turn would come sooner or later and I racked my brain for something cute to say. When the time finally arrived I said something to the effect that I felt greatly honored to be assigned to command the American Mission to Russia and that I looked on my little group as the vanguard of the millions of Americans who would serve with their Soviet ally before the war was won. I concluded by drinking a toast to the day when the advance guard of the British and American forces from the west would meet the advance guard of the Red Army from the east in the streets of Berlin. I was probably a little worked up by these lofty sentiments, to say nothing of the vodka consumed in the myriad of preceding toasts—in any event, my effort met with great acclaim. Everyone drank bottoms up and, to my amazement, remained standing. I soon discovered why. Uncle Joe had left his chair and passed around the entire table to drink a separate toast with me. He was shorter than everyone he passed, so his maneuver escaped my notice until I was nudged, turned, and there he was. I had another bottoms up with him. I began to believe that my little toast must have been more original, more inspiring, and cuter than I had thought possible. My ego was deflated the following morning when Averell Harriman telephoned to congratulate me but added that he had given a similar toast on his visit the year before and that it had also been well received. My ego was further deflated during the years that followed when I heard three out of every four distinguished visitors give the same basic toast with minor variations.

After dinner we adjourned to the Red Room for coffee and liqueurs. Then, at a signal, we all followed Stalin to the Palace theater and were shown a picture of the Japanese occupation of Siberia in 1921. It was definitely a propaganda film, and one did not need to understand Russian to understand the theme—it was clear that the Russians did not like the Japanese. Since it was Averell's and my prime objective to induce Soviet participation in the war with Japan, it was delightful to find out how the Russians felt even in such an indirect way. This picture went on and on, and at its conclusion some of us made a move to go. Only Secretary Hull was successful, and he only in deference to his health and age. The rest of us sat back and absorbed a Russian love story that ended in the usual way about three o'clock in the morning.

The Conference was over. It had been a great strain, not the least part of which was the necessity of carrying on small talk through interpreters and sign language at the many social gatherings. Nevertheless, the Conference had taken place in an atmosphere of good will and cordiality. Averell and I were anxious to speed the Secretary and his party on their way and to start to enjoy the many successes which we were sure would come and for which all credit would be ours.

III. The First Days of the Mission

W ITH the conclusion of the Moscow Conference on November 1, 1943, I set about organizing the Military Mission. The next three months were devoted to administration, establishing Soviet contacts, attendance at the Cairo and Teheran Conferences, and attempts to follow up on the agreements in principle that had been reached at the Moscow Conference. The period culminated on February 2, 1944, when Harriman's persistence was rewarded by a faint green light from Stalin which promised some realization of our dreams as far as military collaboration was concerned.

The principal divisions of the Mission were the Army Division, headed by Brigadier General William E. Crist; the Navy Division, headed by Rear Admiral Clarence E. Olsen and later by Rear Admiral Houston L. Maples; and the Supply (Lend-Lease) Division, headed by Major General Sidney P. Spalding. Later, when air matters became of increasing importance, an Air Division was created and headed successively by Major General R. L. Walsh, Major General Edmund W. Hill, and Brigadier General William L. Ritchie. I can deal only in superlatives in praising the work not only of these officers, but of the one hundred and thirty-five Army and Navy officers and enlisted men included in the Mission personnel at the peak of its activity. The organization expanded and contracted as necessity dictated, but it was always our purpose to keep it as small as possible consistent with the tasks to be done.

Much of the energy of the personnel of the Mission was devoted to the simplest problems of living. The larger the size of a foreign group in Moscow, the more difficult do these problems become; and it soon developed that many in our group were engaged solely in obtaining the necessities of life for the group as a whole. The greatest difficulties were in connection with housing, food, and adjusting expenditures in the light of the artificial rate of exchange that exists in Russia.

Prior to the arrival of the Mission the housing available to the American contingent in Moscow was ample. However, during the course of the war the Embassy staff was increased, the Office of War Information established offices, and the Mission increased from a small group of about twenty persons to its maximum strength of one hundred and thirty-five. Most of the enlisted men and many of the officers had to live in hotels. As long as DDT powder was available the hotel rooms were satisfactory, but it was impossible for Americans to survive on the diet available in hotel dining-rooms. We arranged to have those living in hotels mess with those who had apartments elsewhere. In April of 1944 the Moscow Soviet approved the lease of a small hotel to the Military Mission. We moved into it in July 1945. It is only fair to say that while we were crowded in the interim our conditions were not nearly as bad as those of the Russian residents, who were required to crowd large families into single rooms and even the corridors of apartment houses and other dwellings.

Food was strictly rationed in Moscow. We supplemented our Russian rations with American canned goods imported in Russian lend-lease shipments. The extra food not only enabled us to live reasonably well, but it also made employment by us a prize to be sought by Soviet citizens.

The Soviet government had pegged the official rate of exchange at 5.3 rubles to the dollar. Prior to the war, at the insistence of the German Ambassador, the diplomatic corps had been allowed a special rate of 12 rubles to the dollar. We in the Military Mission also enjoyed this, but neither the official rate nor the diplomatic rate reflected the true value of the ruble. Articles purchased on the Russian market, especially those items outside the ration, were fantastically high in price when converted into dollars. An egg cost from sixty to eighty cents and a plain water tumbler as much as ten dollars.

On my way to Russia I had met Brigadier General Joseph A. Michela, who was returning to the United States after having been relieved of his duties as Military Attaché coincident with the creation of the Military Mission. He told me that under the Soviet system all foreign military officers in Moscow came under the aegis of the Foreign Military Liaison Office, commonly referred to by its Russian initials O.V.S. He said that all appointments with Soviet military officials had to be made through this agency, which was headed by Major General V. N. Estigneev, whom he cautioned me to avoid. He said that as a head of a Military Mission I should insist on direct contact with the Red Army General Staff. This sounded like good advice and actually it was. As soon as the Moscow Conference was over I decided to attempt to break down the barrier, presided over by Estigneev, which separated me from those with whom I hoped to do business.

During the Conference I had become quite friendly—especially during the "five o'clock teas" of vodka, caviar, and assorted forms of raw fish that interrupted each daily session—with Marshal Voroshilov and General Gryzlov. I knew that I would have no trouble in seeing such a chum as Voroshilov—but where to find him? We had no telephone books or office directories, and the only legitimate way I could find him was to ask Estigneev, which I had resolved not to do. I solved this dilemma by taking my interpreter, Captain Henry H. Ware, and going to the nearest building that I knew to be occupied by the General Staff. The sentry at the door, who had probably never seen a foreign general before, was aghast when he saw us. He turned pale when I had Captain Ware tell him that we had come to see the Vice Commissar of Defense.

There were several excited phone calls; I was shunted to two other buildings; at the last building I visited I was granted a futile interview in what was called "the adjutant's office" by an officer who said that he would telephone the Marshal to see whether I could be received.

Finally, an officer was sent from General Estigneev's office to tell me that Marshal Voroshilov was not in Moscow and that in the future if I wished to see any Soviet officers I should make the arrangements through O.V.S. Estigneev had me back in his net and thereafter I never completely escaped.

My position as head of a Mission was recognized, however, and a General Staff officer, Lieutenant General N. V. Slavin, was assigned as my contact with the Red Army General Staff. My meetings with him were held in the O.V.S. offices and one of Estigneev's men was always present to make a record of what took place. I shall always believe that it was part of a system whereby Soviet officials watch each other to insure that no one establishes relations with foreigners to the detriment of the Soviet Union. This belief is confirmed by the fact that during my stay I had occasion to deal with a great many branches of the Soviet Government. When I was working with the Air Staff in connection with shuttle bombing, Slavin would always be present representing the General Staff. He accompanied me whenever I consulted the Commissar of Communications, the heads of the Civil Air Administration or the Repatriation Commission. Strangely enough I could visit the highest official in the N.K.V.D. and the Commissariat of Foreign Trade without special chaperons. In the case of the N.K.V.D., the officials were heads of the suspicion department and presumably above suspicion themselves, while in the case of the Foreign Trade group the only business to be transacted was to extract additional resources from the United States, which seemed to be progressing nicely, thank you, and apparently did not require special watching.

In my further efforts to establish initial contacts I committed a rather serious faux pas. Since I could not escape Estigneev I finally called on him. It was at once apparent why Michela had advised me to avoid him. It must have been he or one of his ancestors who first inspired the descriptive appellation "stuffed shirt"—he impressed me as the granddaddy of them all. I have never encountered such dignity and condescension linked up with such stupidity. He queried me as

to my business, and I replied that I had nothing I wished to discuss
with him until after I had seen the Chief of the Red Army General
Staff, at that time Marshal A. M. Vasilievsky. I was a bit of a stuffed
shirt myself in those early days and attached considerable importance
to my position as the senior military representative of the United
States in the Soviet Union. I knew that unless I gained contact with
the Red Army on the highest level very little would come of my
efforts to co-ordinate our military operations. I had resolved not to
become involved on the lower levels until I had seen the Chief of
Staff and had come to an understanding with him. There were times
later when, being given the silent treatment, I would have welcomed
an appointment with a lance corporal.

Estigneev informed me that Marshal Vasilievsky was at the front
but that, if I wished, he could arrange a meeting for me with General
A. E. Antonov, then the Deputy Chief of Staff. I declined this offer,
stating that I would wait until Marshal Vasilievsky returned to Moscow. A week or so later Estigneev sent word to me asking again if I
wished to see General Antonov, and again I declined. As a matter of
fact, although Vasilievsky was designated as Chief of Staff he operated as a co-ordinator of operations among the various front commanders in the field and seldom came to Moscow; Antonov was Chief
of Staff in everything but name. When I discovered this after a month
in Moscow, I realized that I had not been so smart in playing "hard to
get" with Antonov and had to suffer the supercilious grin on Estigneev's face when I finally sought an appointment with Antonov.
Meetings with Voroshilov and Antonov did materialize, and from
them I gained a further insight into the modus operandi of Soviet
officialdom.

When I arrived at Marshal Voroshilov's office the man I met was
not the short round one with the red cherubic face that I had become
so friendly with during the Moscow Conference. He was still short
and round and his face was red, but not cherubic. He knew that I had
come to press for some action on the agreements that had been made
"in principle" regarding shuttle bombing and other matters, and he

assumed a cold demeanor, a scolding attitude, and went at once on the offensive. He complained of the ease with which the Germans were shifting reserve divisions to the Russian front and sharply criticized Anglo-American inability to contain more German divisions on the Italian front. We had a heated argument of considerable length. It was just at the time we had encountered the natural fortress of Cassino and one advance had been stopped considerably south of Rome. The terrain of the Italian front gave every advantage to the defender. Both flanks were secure, making ground maneuver impossible, while frontal attacks, regardless of the strength placed in the main efforts, had to be pushed against mountain defenses and defiles swept by fire from well-concealed and covered enemy positions. The entire front was relatively narrow, enabling the Germans to cut down their defensive reserves through their ability to move quickly to any point of a threatened breakthrough those they did retain. It was to be a long hard campaign which could be expedited only by amphibious landings to the north. And this could be accomplished only at a considerable delay to the preparations for the cross-channel invasion.

Voroshilov's only comment on these conditions was that it was impossible that the forces of two nations with the resources of the British and Americans could not keep more than eight or ten German divisions occupied. As to my difficulties, he was confident that the agreements of the Moscow Conference would be carried out in due time, and he impressed upon me that I would have to conform to the procedure established in the Soviet Union and conduct my negotiations with the Red Army through General Estigneev's office.

A few days later I had my first meeting with General Antonov, with whom I was destined to have a very close association and who eventually became Chief of Staff in name as well as in fact. He was by far the coldest but at the same time the most capable Russian officer with whom I came in contact. I should judge him to be a man in his middle forties, clean cut, with black hair and olive skin. He later met with our Chiefs of Staff at Yalta and Potsdam and certainly gained their respect, if not their affection.

I have never had a reception of more studied coldness. There was not the slightest spark of cordiality as he shook hands and asked me to be seated. I explained that the purpose of the Military Mission was to provide a group through which operational co-ordination could be effected. He seized on this to berate me about our efforts in Italy, reciting in detail the German divisions that had recently appeared on the Russian front from the west. By this time I had become thoroughly chilled except under the collar and recited a few plain truths. I pointed out that we had liquidated Rommel's forces in Africa, forced Italy out of the war, taken on a second front in the Pacific without the help of our great Red Ally, and, at the same time, run the gauntlet of the German submarine menace to deliver supplies to Russia. With that he asked me if I had any further business, indicating that our conference was concluded. This time when we shook hands there were two pairs of eyes which belied any cordiality in the process. My subsequent meetings with General Antonov were extremely pleasant, and I attained the utmost admiration for his intelligence and ability. At the conclusion of the first session, however, I was greatly disheartened and held little hope for success.

At my initial meetings with Voroshilov and Antonov they conformed to a pattern of Russian behavior that should be recognized in future relations with Soviet officials. They illustrated a phase of the cycle that has characterized our military and political relations with the Soviet Union. Periods of accord are invariably followed by periods of dissension. It is difficult to know when or why such periods are to start or end. Moreover, the attitude of the moment is reflected in all agencies of government. At the time that I was being attacked with regard to our Italian efforts, Ambassador Harriman was receiving the same complaints from Molotov, who indicated Stalin's displeasure in the matter. Just as the accord of the Moscow Conference was followed by coolness with regard to our Italian operations, the

Yalta Conference was followed by dissension over Poland and the Potsdam Conference by a complete failure in the Council of Foreign Ministers in London a month or so later.

Harriman and I have often discussed this phenomenon and have attempted to isolate the causes. It may be that there are two schools of thought within the inner circles of Stalin's advisers, one which favors foreign collaboration and one which opposes it. If so, the Soviet attitude toward foreigners might well fluctuate in accordance with which set of advisers is in favor and has caught Stalin's ear. It is more probable that the Soviet Union handles its foreign relations much as a rider handles a spirited horse—giving it its head at times and holding a tight check on the reins at others—always keeping the horse headed toward the predetermined destination and bending its will to that of the rider. At times these periods of dissension or refusal to co-operate are the result of a deliberate and co-ordinated effort on the part of the Soviet leaders to indicate their displeasure of some foreign act or attitude. However, it is always difficult for foreigners to isolate the cause of the trouble.

Another characteristic which was apparent at my meetings with Voroshilov and Antonov was their belief in the value of the offensive. Both knew that the Soviet Government was committed to start making detailed arrangements for shuttle bombing, but they had no intention of doing so until it suited their purposes. They therefore attempted to divert me from my insistence in the matter by berating me concerning Italian operations. This characteristic was to be evidenced time and again in my future dealings with Soviet leaders. For example, every agreement which was made regarding the treatment of American prisoners of war liberated by the Red Army was violated, but when these violations were brought to the attention of the appropriate officials they responded with the most unfounded accusations regarding the treatment of liberated Russian prisoners of war then in British and American hands. To cite a more recent case, the evidence was overwhelmingly against the Russians when the Iranian situation was brought before the Security Council of the

United Nations in January 1946; the first Soviet reaction was to charge Britain with jeopardizing world peace by maintaining troops in Greece and Indonesia. The Russians are prone to meet charges with countercharges that have little or no regard for the facts.

The President and the United States Chiefs of Staff were just leaving for the Cairo and Teheran Conferences when the pressure was put on Harriman and me with regard to our operations in Italy. I reported my conversations to our Chiefs of Staff and urged that they have careful intelligence estimates made of the situation in order that they could meet the Soviet allegations concerning German freedom of action which I felt were exaggerated. I also suggested they might have to be prepared to resist Soviet demands for more active operations in the Mediterranean area designed to draw additional German divisions from the Russian front. I am afraid I caused them considerable unnecessary apprehension, because when they met the Soviet representatives in Teheran the subject of increasing the intensity of our Italian operations or starting new ventures in Southern Europe was scarcely mentioned and certainly not urged by our Soviet friends. The pendulum had swung again and accord was the order of the day.

Averell Harriman, Sir Archibald Clark-Kerr, Chip Bohlen, Lieutenant General G. LeQ. Martel, head of the British Military Mission, and I left Moscow on November 18, 1943, to attend the Cairo and Teheran Conferences. We planned to fly directly from Moscow to Cairo, refueling at Bagdad if necessary. At about noon, as we were passing over Stalingrad, one of our engines acted up and we made an emergency landing in a huge field that served as an airdrome for the city. The impromptu hospitality extended to us in that devastated city during the afternoon and evening was quite different, more spontaneous and heart-warming than anything I had experienced in Moscow.

The airdrome had all the appearance of an open field being prepared for the planting of crops. Here and there were well concealed dug-outs which housed repair shops and offices. The weather was

bitter cold and we were led into the dug-out that housed the operations office. We huddled around a small wood stove while Russian
mechanics turned out to help the engineer of our crew locate the
trouble in the engine. It was discovered that an oil line was clogged
and that repairs would take the remainder of the day, thus delaying
our departure until the following morning. Meanwhile, the officer
on duty had had several animated telephone conversations, and in
no time a caravan of dilapidated automobiles, mostly taken from the
Germans, arrived from the city, which was about five miles distant.
A reception party headed by the mayor had been organized. It included all the city officials and the commandant of the military district. While they were most cordial and made much of us, they were
beside themselves with delight at a visit from Averell Harriman.
Apparently he had been given a great build-up in the press outside
of Moscow as the father of lend-lease aid to Russia, and wherever
he went he was received with acclaim.

The mayor bundled our party into the cars, and all went off to
the city. I remained behind to see that our crew was cared for and
also in the hope of expediting the repairs so that we might depart that
afternoon in spite of the earlier gloomy forecasts. In about an hour the
automobiles returned with instructions that the crew and I were to
come at once to a luncheon that was being prepared. There was no
choice but to stop work, give up hope of departing that day, and
join the messenger.

We were taken over a frozen shell-torn road along both sides of
which, for its entire length, were strewn disabled German and Russian
tanks, trucks, and guns. As we neared the city we could see only one
building that had survived destruction and it proved to be our destination. I was led upstairs to a long narrow room containing a long
table around which were gathered the Stalingrad city fathers and
their unexpected visitors. The table was covered with plates of food,
but not the delicacies we had been served at official functions in
Moscow. There were big chunks of black bread, cheese, sausages, and
cole slaw, and, of course, bottles of vodka. Nor were the table ap-

pointments reminiscent of Moscow. The vodka was served in water tumblers, and I was required to drink one filled to the brim as a penalty for being late. I downed it for the sake of British-American-Soviet friendship and sat back waiting for the blow to fall. Whether it was because I was nearly frozen when I arrived, or because of the large quantity of black bread and cheese that was forced on me, or simply because of my hollow leg, the drink had no ill effects. However, I was soon inveigled into having another, and this was tempting fate too far—a haze hung over me for several hours.

The mayor gave us an eye-witness account of the Battle of Stalingrad that was packed with drama. Every man, woman, and child had participated in the struggle that will become an epic of Russian history. Despite the loss of those dear to them and the hardships they had endured and were still enduring, the survivors were filled with happiness and justifiable pride in the part they had played in turning back the German tide. Stalingrad will rank high with Midway, Leningrad, Remagen, and the Ardennes bulge as local actions which turned the course of the war.

After lunch we were taken to the mayor's office and shown plans for the reconstruction of the city. We were told that no construction would be allowed that did not conform to these plans. Until the war was over and building materials became available, the people were to live in cellars under the ruins or in lean-to's and shacks thrown together with boards covered with tar paper. Fortunately we were soon taken outdoors, where the sub-zero weather helped overcome the effects of the vodka. We toured the city, making frequent stops, where the critical events of the battle were explained to us. We saw a monument that had been constructed on the banks of the Volga in memory of those who had been killed, and we made a detailed inspection of the cellar of a huge building in which Field Marshal von Paulus had had his headquarters and where he ultimately surrendered. The city can only be described as a mass of rubble and ruin from which but a single building escaped. Later in the war I saw many German cities that had been almost completely demolished, but only a few, such as Berlin, Cologne, and one or two others, approached the total destruction of Stalingrad.

We returned to the building where we had had luncheon and where we were to spend the night. We were given an opportunity to freshen up in a washroom that was characteristically Russian. Pails of water were hung on a wall. Attendants in such washrooms were invariably old women who would tip the pails over the hands of those washing and provide towels for drying. I do not know how old the women had to be to qualify for this duty, but they seemed to be entirely uninhibited about presiding over any of the activities that are undertaken in a men's washroom. I had already had some difficulty in Moscow shoving our old cook away from the bathroom when I was bathing. She could never understand how I could get my back clean if she was not allowed to scrub it. Fortunately or unfortunately the younger women seemed to have no interest in such tasks.

The dinner that night started at five-thirty and lasted until well past midnight. Everything edible in Stalingrad was assembled on our table; vodka flowed freely, and from somewhere in the ruins some champagne had been unearthed. The dinner started somewhat stiffly because of the language barrier but, with the help of interpreters supplied by the hosts and the guests, toasts were drunk and stories told. The party soon attained an informality that was delightful—the waitresses all had some specialty known to the city fathers. They would set down their trays and burst into a song or a dance at the slightest hint of invitation. Chip Bohlen, who had spent many years in Russia, revived a great many songs he had learned in his early Russian days, and they were received with thunderous applause. Bohlen's Russian is perfect, but I had a suspicion that his songs were of the bawdy type—no other type ever gets such a reception. Averell had been presented with sabers, pistols, watches, and other trophies taken from the Germans and was in an expansive mood. This was evidenced by his asking me to sing. It was getting late and I was dead tired. I sang "Show Me the Way to Go Home." Sir Archibald Clark-Kerr told me he had never heard the song rendered with such feeling.

We were all given cots in one large room. Most of us had to call on the little old lady who had been master of ceremonies in the washroom to help us solve the mystery of Russian bed-making. The blanket, laid lengthwise and folded to half the width of the bed, is enclosed in an envelope which, when unraveled, proves to be the top sheet. I never did discover how the Russians get fixed for the night, but I always found it necessary to do a complete job of remaking the bed in the American style. The last thing I remember of that night were the two red tabs on the lapels of Martel's blouse peeking out from under the top of his blanket. The party had been too much for him, and he had retired early, fully dressed even to his high leather boots. He looked for all the world like the Chessy Cat of the Chesapeake and Ohio railroad advertisements.

We arrived in Cairo on November 20, 1943, and for the ensuing week participated in the Conference between the British and American Chiefs of Staff that was held in the Mena House located in the shadows of the pyramids. I was called on by the American Chiefs of Staff to give an estimate of the Russian situation. At that time I had been in Moscow a month and was therefore at the peak of my "expertness." (After two years I came to the conclusion that there is no such thing as an expert on that land of contradictions.)

Only a small part of the British and American delegations went from Cairo to Teheran. The British contingent was housed at the British Legation, the Russians at their Legation, while the American group was split up—the President, Admiral Leahy, Harry Hopkins, and Admiral McIntire as house guests of Stalin; the remainder of the civil delegation in the houses of the American Minister, Louis G. Dreyfus, and Major General Donald H. Connolly, commanding the Persian Gulf Command; and the American military contingent, including the Chiefs of Staff, in comfortable quarters in little guest houses at Camp Amirabad, the Teheran Garrison of the Persian Gulf Command.

In the early days of the war Teheran was known to be a hotbed of

Axis agents and the utmost precautions were taken for the safety of the principals at the Conference. Streets were swarming with Iranian, American, and Soviet troops, and unless one was properly documented, to say nothing of the elaborate identification required of cars and chauffeurs, it was impossible to arrive anywhere on time.

The opening speeches of the three heads of state were characteristic of all British-American-Soviet relations. The President spoke first, claiming the privilege because of being the youngest. He expressed his understanding of the purpose of the meeting: winning the war. He likened the group to a "family circle" and hoped that it could achieve constructive accord in order that collaboration would be maintained during and after the war. He suggested that the three General Staffs should conduct military conversations while he, Churchill, and Stalin discussed matters pertaining to postwar conditions. His speech was well delivered through Chip Bohlen, acting as interpreter, and the ball was then passed to Churchill.

The Prime Minister was never one to lose an opportunity to speak. He expounded on the power that was concentrated at the Conference table and the resultant responsibilities that sucn power entailed. He emphasized the effects that Conference decisions might have on the future of mankind and hoped that the conferees might prove worthy of the God-given opportunity.

The President then asked Stalin whether he as the host might wish to say a "few" words. It may have been the President's hint or his own inclination to terseness, but whatever the cause, Stalin's opening remarks were exceedingly brief. He welcomed his guests, agreed that the Conference was important, and then said, "Now let us get down to business."

President Roosevelt started the business of the Conference by reviewing the war from the American point of view, with particular stress on the Pacific operations in our war with Japan. In describing European operations the President emphasized that one of the principal objectives of the Conference was to devise ways and means of assisting the Soviet Union by diverting German divisions from the

Russian front. The Prime Minister indicated his concurrence with the President but reserved further comment until after he had heard from Marshal Stalin.

In those days, and indeed almost until the final collapse of Japan, the President and the Chiefs of Staff attached the greatest importance to Soviet participation in the Pacific war. Marshal Stalin's first words were therefore most heartening to the American delegation since they contained the first hint that Russian help would be forthcoming. Stalin congratulated the President on our successes in the Pacific and regretted that the Russians had been unable to help, that the requirements of the European war precluded Russian participation against Japan at that time. He went on to say that while the Russian forces then in Siberia were sufficient for defensive operations, they would have to be increased threefold before an offensive could be undertaken and that this increase could not be accomplished until after Germany was defeated. Stalin committed the Soviet Union to participation by adding, "*Then* by our common front we shall win."

With the Pacific war disposed of, the remainder of the military discussions centered on the European war. The basic point at issue was whether or not Overlord should be postponed in favor of further Mediterranean operations. The possibilities in the Mediterranean were, first, to hasten the advance in Italy as far as the Po valley by amphibious landings to the north; second, an amphibious landing in the northeast Adriatic aimed at the Danube valley and assisting Tito; third, operation in the Aegean with the Island of Rhodes or the Dodecanese Islands as the objective; and fourth, operations in and from Turkey if she could be induced to enter the war.

Prime Minister Churchill was the only proponent of Mediterranean operations. President Roosevelt was strongly advised by the American Chiefs of Staff against any operations which would result in delay of Overlord. At the same time, he was not immune to Churchill's logical persuasiveness. Stalin knew exactly what he wanted—the second front in France, and the quicker the better.

Churchill based his argument on the disastrous effects of a long period of inactivity that would be necessary for most of the forces in the Mediterranean if they had to remain idle until the invasion took place. He said there were twenty surplus divisions in the Mediterranean which could not be moved to England because of lack of shipping. These could be used to relieve pressure on the Russian front and to create conditions favorable to the cross-channel operations by attracting German divisions to the south. Churchill argued that if the landing craft for two divisions could be diverted from Overlord to the Mediterranean it would delay the invasion date only from six to eight weeks. With these landing craft available, he said, they could be used successively: first, for an amphibious landing in northern Italy; second, to capture Rhodes in conjunction with Turkey's entrance into the war; and third, they would be available in time for a landing in southern France as a diversionary attack to assist Overlord.

Churchill used every trick in his oratorical bag, assisted by illustrative and emphasizing gestures, to put over his point. At times he was smooth and suave, pleasant and humorous, and then he would clamp down on his cigar, growl, and complain. His efforts reached the Russians through his interpreter, an excellent technician but who had none of Churchill's oratorical ability. Heard through the interpreter, Churchill's words lost their force and fell on deaf ears.

Stalin took up the burden of the opposition. His position coincided with that of the American Chiefs of Staff, and every word he said strengthened the support they might expect from President Roosevelt in the ultimate decision. As a matter of fact, Stalin's refutation of Churchill's argument consisted of a few very terse comments which can be summed up in his insistence that Overlord should be the primary operation and that nothing should be undertaken which would delay it. He thought the Mediterranean operations would be merely frittering away the Anglo-American forces and, while helpful, could not be decisive.

The argument covered three sessions at which the Chiefs of State were present and an additional two attended only by the Chiefs of

Staff. The outcome was that a commitment was made to undertake the cross-channel invasion in May of 1944 with the exact day to be determined later and with the understanding that the Red Army would launch an offensive timed to assist Overlord. Stalin attempted to clinch matters further by asking who the Allied Commander would be. When he was told that one had not yet been selected, he urged that the deficiency be corrected at once or the operations could not possibly be launched on the date agreed upon. Stalin's insistence certainly hastened the selection of General Eisenhower.

The Americans at the Conference, with the exception of Averell Harriman and Harry Hopkins, met Stalin there for the first time. They were all considerably and favorably impressed by him, probably because he advocated the American point of view in our differences with the British. Regardless of this, one could not help but recognize qualities of greatness in the man.

Present with him at the Conference table were Molotov, Voroshilov, and Pavlov, his interpreter. As far as we could tell these three completed his entourage. This was quite a contrast to the groups of twenty or thirty each which the British and Americans had brought from Cairo. While Stalin had whispered consultations with Molotov and Voroshilov from time to time, he was the sole Soviet spokesman. There could be no doubt that he was the Soviet supreme authority as there was never the slightest indication that he would have to consult his Government on decisions being reached. He had an advantage over both Roosevelt and Churchill in that he knew he could act without fear of being called to account by Congress, Parliament, or the people.

Stalin appeared to know exactly what he wanted at the Conference. This was also true of Churchill, but not so of Roosevelt. This is not said as a reflection on our President, but his apparent indecision was probably the direct result of our obscure foreign policy. President Roosevelt was thinking of winning the war; the others were thinking of their relative positions when the war was won. Stalin wanted the Anglo-American forces in Western, not Southern Europe; Churchill thought our postwar position would be improved and British interests best served if the Anglo-Americans as well as the Russians participated in the occupation of the Balkans. From the military point of view there can be no doubt of the wisdom of the American Chiefs of Staff in urging the cross-channel invasion as preferable. It meant a short well-protected line of communication, a strong build-up close to the scene of operations in the safety of England, early liberation of France, and the most direct route to the heart of industrial Germany, the Ruhr and the Saar. From the political point of view hindsight on our part points to foresight on Churchill's part. It will always be debatable whether Churchill might not have been right even though the action he proposed put an additional burden on our resources and probably would have prolonged the war.

The Teheran Conference was characterized by the bluntness of Soviet diplomacy. Stalin made no attempt at oratory nor did he search for words that would satisfy diplomatic niceties. His comments were terse and to the point. On one occasion after Churchill had put on an outstanding forensic display, Stalin asked him if the British were only "thinking" of Overlord in order to satisfy the Soviet Union. Again, when the President and Prime Minister urged the creation of an ad hoc committee of the Chiefs of Staff to study the question at issue, Stalin said, "What can such a committee do? We Chiefs of State have more power than a committee and the question can be decided only by us." Once, after a long speech of Churchill's, Stalin asked, "How long is this Conference going to last?" Soviet bluntness is new in diplomatic procedure but at times it is refreshing, and who can say that it has not been successful?

In connection with the Teheran Conference there was also evidence of the tactics which the Russians habitually employ in throwing their opposition off balance. I feel certain that their blasts at Harriman and me concerning the ineffectiveness of our Italian operations were in the nature of a smoke screen thrown up to hide the position they intended taking at the Teheran Conference. They expected both the British and Americans to come to the Conference ready to argue against delaying Overlord in favor of the Mediterranean, which would have played right into Soviet hands. Actually both the British and American delegations were surprised—the British because they met Soviet opposition when they had reason to expect some support, and the Americans because they encountered support when they had expected Soviet opposition.

Before the Conference ended President Roosevelt approached Stalin again on the proposals I had made at the Moscow Conference regarding shuttle bombing and improved weather exchange and communications. He also proposed to Stalin that there be an interchange of intelligence concerning the Japanese. Stalin agreed "in principle" to these proposals. I returned to Moscow with the idea that I would have to augment my staff to help me take care of all the American-Soviet collaboration I envisaged. These hopes were strengthened by General Marshall's calling Voroshilov aside and informing him that I had the complete confidence of the American Chiefs of Staff and was authorized to speak for them. Voroshilov slapped me on the back and assured General Marshall that he and I were old friends and would work closely together in the future. I agreed heartily, but I had already learned enough to have my tongue slightly in the cheek.

IV. Early Objectives of the Mission

I RETURNED to Moscow from the Teheran Conference on December 17. Winter had really set in. The trip from Teheran to Moscow was made at treetop height, and for the last few hundred miles it was a touch-and-go battle; ice formed on our wings and threatened to force us down.

Every foreign airplane flying in Russia must have aboard a Russian navigator and a Russian radio operator. I never could see the necessity of the navigator because he always insisted on contact flying and appeared to be lost when there was no road or railroad to lead the way. He probably had some value in enabling us to avoid areas of strong anti-aircraft defense. At least I always comforted myself with this thought because, despite the fact that the anti-aircraft defenses were presumably informed when friendly foreign planes were in the air, I had my doubts as to the efficiency with which such information was disseminated and would not have been at all surprised had some trigger-happy anti-aircraft gunner taken a pot shot at us. The radio operator was essential because of the difference in language and radio procedure.

Russian navigators and radio operators were never well received by American crews. Their presence resulted in a divided responsibility that was hazardous when flying conditions were bad. The Russians would set the course and the altitude and had revolvers strapped to their sides which added authority to their directions. The American pilots, on the other hand, could not divest themselves of responsibility for the safety of the flights. The biggest point of difference was always the matter of altitude. When weather was bad the American reaction was to get on top of it; the Russian wanted to stay under it even though the fuselage scraped the hilltops. The struggle of wills that went on in the cockpit could be felt back in the passenger cabin and did nothing to promote a feeling of safety—especially as the Russian point of view usually prevailed.

With my return to Moscow it was time to take stock of what the objectives of my Mission were to be and how I was to go about accomplishing them. Harriman and I agreed that our primary long-range objective was to obtain Soviet participation in the war against Japan. Our attitude reflected that of the President and our Chiefs of Staff, whose every thought was to get the war over quickly and thus save American lives. It was felt that Soviet participation against Japan would do much to hasten the end of the war after Germany was defeated.

Our most immediate objective was to effect the maximum co-ordination of effort between Russia and the Western Allies in order to bring about the defeat of Germany. Collaboration with Russia was a virgin field. Prior to the end of 1943 our efforts to collaborate were limited to the Russian supply program under lend-lease. As far as military operations were concerned, co-ordination was almost non-existent. It was true that British and American strategy had been determined largely because of its effects on the Russian situation, but it was difficult to plan intelligently because of our limited knowledge of what the Russian situation really was. There was so much that could be done—free exchange of enemy information, free exchange of operational plans, the timing of the Russian offensives in relation to those of the Western Allies, and use of each other's air bases. These measures held promise of more effective use of our combined power in bringing Germany to her knees—if we could succeed in obtaining Russian co-operation.

Of course there were a great many other fields in which American-Soviet co-operation was possible. Among these were co-ordinating the efforts of the Russian secret intelligence and subversive opera-

tions with those of our Office of Strategic Services; the establishment
of effective signal communications between America and Russia;
a free exchange of weather data; the release of American aviators interned in Russia after forced landings in Siberia following raids on
the Japanese; the repatriation of prisoners of war liberated by one
side or the other; the inauguration of training programs to assist the
Russians in the use of American equipment; and the exchange of
technical data concerning equipment, weapons, and tactical methods.

One of the outstanding characteristics of the Soviet officials with
whom I came in contact was their suspicion of foreign motives.
Perhaps there was some justification for this. Under the Czars, Russia
had had a long history of foreign exploitation because of the weak-
nesses of Russian rulers. The Soviet Union itself had had the experience of seeing foreign technicians, particularly Germans, hired to
assist in carrying out the "five year plans," use their positions to carry
on activities inimical to the Soviet Government. Then, too, the attitude of the Western Allies toward the Soviet Union in the first
twenty-five years of its existence could hardly be characterized as
friendly. Now that one can see the consistency and persistency of
the Soviet foreign policy, which is certainly not friendly to the
western democracies, it is easier to understand why they distrusted
the friendly hand which the Western Allies were extending toward
them. They could not believe that a leopard could change its spots
overnight. Whatever the cause, suspicion existed and was evidenced
by close surveillance of all foreigners, a search for the hidden motive
behind all foreign proposals, and, above all, by maintaining a veil of
secrecy over the means and methods by which the Soviet Union was
waging war against the common enemy.

Until the Military Mission was established, American military representation in Moscow was in the offices of the Military and Naval
Attachés. The function of Attachés, recognized the world over, is
to obtain information concerning the country to which they are
accredited. It is impossible to conceive a more difficult assignment
than that of a Military or Naval Attaché in Russia, nor one that

promises less chance of success. The easiest way for Soviet officials to avoid giving our Attachés information was to avoid seeing them. It was partly to overcome this attitude that the United States withdrew its Attachés and substituted the Military Mission. However, the Russians, again suspicious, were inclined to treat the Mission with the same aloofness with which they had treated the Attachés, convinced that only a change in name had been effected and that our objectives remained the same. Under such circumstances it was difficult to break through suspicion and achieve co-operation.

I had had a long talk with General Marshall before leaving for Russia. He instructed me to avoid seeking information about the Russians. General Marshall took the view that even though the Soviet authorities turned over to us the blueprints of all their weapons, their tables of organization, and their complete tactical doctrine, the information would not change by one iota American production lines, organization, or tactics. He was convinced that a quest for such information was not only unnecessary but would irritate the Russians and make operational collaboration impossible. His attitude made my task in Russia much easier and accounted in large measure for whatever success the Mission enjoyed. Consequently we studiously refrained from seeking information about Soviet equipment, weapons, and tactical methods unless we could present a strong case to show that such information was of value in our fight against Germany. We did ask for and received some information about Russian cold-weather equipment, tactical methods in river crossings, and their organization to discover and handle German agents operating in the rear of the Soviet lines.

In contrast to Soviet secrecy was American openness. We had thousands of Soviet representatives in the United States who were allowed to visit our manufacturing plants, attend our schools, and witness tests of aircraft and other equipment. In Italy and later in France and Germany, Russian representatives were welcomed at our field headquarters and allowed to see anything they desired of our military operations. Our policy was to make any of our new inventions in electronics and other fields available to the Russians once we had used such equipment ourselves, had exploited the element of surprise, and were satisfied that the enemy had probably gained knowledge of the equipment as the result of its having fallen into his hands. Each month I would receive a revised list of secret American equipment about which the Russians could be informed in the hope that, if it could be made available, it might be used on the Russian front. We never lost an opportunity to give the Russians equipment, weapons, or information which we thought might help our combined war effort. This generosity, or at least attitude, was never reciprocated by the Russians except after endless argument, negotiation, and delay.

Toward the end of 1943 we succeeded in starting two projects with the Russians which were to carry on throughout the war. One was a working arrangement with the leaders of the Russian Secret Intelligence and Secret Operations, started by Major General William J. Donovan, head of the Office of Strategic Services. The other concerned the release of American aviators interned in Russia after forced landings on Russian soil. Both projects constitute highlights in our war relations with the Soviet Union and were marked by a degree of collaboration exceeding that attained in other fields.

On November 14, 1943, General Marshall sent me a cable indicating that the President had approved the establishment of a Moscow Mission by the Office of Strategic Services, at the suggestion of General Donovan. At that time the British Secret Operations Executive (S.O.E.) had a Mission in Moscow headed by Brigadier George A. Hill.

I met General Donovan in Cairo and it was arranged that he would come to Moscow and personally try to obtain Soviet agreement to his scheme. He arrived a day or two before Christmas. I was never more pleased to see anyone. We were all feeling a little sorry for ourselves at being in the bleak cold atmosphere of Moscow so far from home. His coming was a breath of fresh air from the outside world, and he was none the less welcome because of the case of Scotch whisky which he brought to brighten my Christmas. We had been old friends in Washington and had fought several battles together against some of the Washington agencies which were jealous of O.S.S. achievement. As Secretary of the Joint Chiefs of Staff, I was well aware of the strength of the organization which Donovan had created and had some appreciation of its capabilities—and apparently the Russians had too.

There can be no doubt that Donovan's reputation had preceded him to Moscow and that a decision to collaborate with him had already been made, for when Harriman took him to Molotov the latter agreed at once to arrange a conference with two N.K.V.D. officials, Lieutenant General P. M. Fitin, head of the Soviet External Intelligence Service, and Major General A. P. Ossipov, head of the section conducting subversive activities in enemy countries, to the end that American and Russian activities might be co-ordinated. Molotov's action must have been prearranged because he apparently took it without the usual necessity of discussing it with Stalin.

On the second night after Christmas, Bill Donovan, Chip Bohlen, who was to act as interpreter, and I made our way to the Commissariat of Internal Affairs, the home of the dreaded N.K.V.D. As we entered we could not help but think of the untold number of Russians whose fate had been sealed within those walls. We were met at the door by members of the police and whisked to the office where our meeting was to be held with an eerie quietness that was a bit chilling.

We found General Fitin and General Ossipov alone in the conference room. Fitin seemed about forty years of age. He was wearing an army uniform that had blue piping to indicate his police status. He was of medium height, smooth-shaven, with long blond hair and blue eyes. He had a pleasing smile and did not impress us at all as a man who would be high in the circles of the secret police. Ossipov was short, smooth-shaven, and had brown eyes, brown wavy hair, and a sallow complexion. He was in civilian clothes, and one could easily picture him as the boon companion of Boris Karloff. He spoke English perfectly and without trace of accent. He was smooth and suave but, personally, after seeing him I was just as glad that Bill and Chip were with me.

Both Russian Generals were extremely cordial. Bill Donovan sat himself down in a seat facing them which had a light so arranged that it shone full in his face—an arrangement obviously intended for those unfortunates who were required to account for their activities to the police. Bill had spied this particular seat when he entered the room and had to go out of his way to reach it. Both Generals were completely disarmed but took it in good grace when Bill announced he was ready for the third degree.

Donovan gave them a complete outline of the O.S.S. organization, specifying the types of his operations and the countries in which they were conducted. Fitin, as the senior of the two, questioned Donovan while Ossipov acted for the most part as an interpreter. They were particularly interested in the methods we used in introducing agents into enemy territory, the types of training and equipment given such agents, and whether they were trained in the United States or elsewhere. Donovan answered their questions fully and frankly and held out additional bait by describing some of the equipment developed by the O.S.S., such as suitcase radios, plastic explosives, and so on.

Donovan said that he had come to Moscow to inform the Soviet authorities of the operations of the O.S.S. and to tell them that the O.S.S. was prepared to co-operate with the equivalent organization of the Soviet Union if the Soviet Government wished to do so. He emphasized that he had no desire to influence their decision in the matter. He then said that if co-operation was agreed upon he was prepared to designate an officer as a member of the United States Military Mission who would work with appropriate Soviet officers and that in turn he would welcome the appointment of a Soviet official in Washington to maintain liaison with the O.S.S.

Fitin said he understood Donovan's proposal and went on to cite some of the ways in which co-operation should be achieved. For example, he thought that if Soviet agents were preparing to sabotage an important industrial establishment or railroad in Germany it would be desirable to have the United States Government informed, and, of course, the reverse held true. He then aroused Donovan's ire by asking if he had come to the Soviet Union solely for the purpose of offering co-operation or whether he had some other intentions. I could not help but snicker at this further evidence of Soviet suspicion, but Donovan simply replied in a cold indignant manner that he had no other intentions.

It was finally agreed that there should be an exchange of representatives and that Colonel John H. F. Haskell would come to Moscow to represent Donovan and Colonel A. G. Grauer would go to Washington to represent Generals Fitin and Ossipov. Each was to have a small staff of assistants.

At this point in the proceedings I assured the Russian Generals of the strong interest of the United States Chiefs of Staff in effecting closer co-ordination with the Soviet Union and said I was sure that their agreement with General Donovan would be happily received in America. I also suggested that during the interim, prior to the exchange of representatives, we should establish a channel of communication through which important information could be exchanged. I not only thought this would be desirable, but secretly I wanted to establish at least one contact that would not have to filter through my old friend General Estigneev. Apparently the secret police were immune to the restrictive activities of Estigneev because, to my great surprise, I was given a telephone number to call when I had business to transact with Fitin or Ossipov. It was my first telephone number in Russia and I felt I had achieved a tremendous victory.

Having accomplished his purpose in Moscow, Donovan was anxious to return to Washington, but getting him away resulted in one of the minor wrangles that characterized all our dealings with Soviet officialdom. Harriman and I had brought to Russia a four-engine transport plane. Harriman had explained to Molotov that he wished to keep the plane in Russia for his use and mine, and Molotov gave at least tacit consent by offering no objections. Using a four-engine plane was most advantageous, especially in winter, because it could fly directly from Moscow to Teheran without refueling. In the smaller two-engine types used by the Russian Civil Air Administration the trip to Teheran had to be broken at least once and frequently twice for refueling, at either Stalingrad, Astrakhan, or Baku. Such stops in themselves required an extra day for the flight because of the limited number of daylight hours, and frequently in winter they delayed the flight for several days because of the necessity of having good weather at both Moscow and the refueling point. Under these circumstances we wanted to send Donovan out of Russia in our four-engine plane.

When Harriman asked Molotov for permission to have our ship make the flight he was flatly refused on the grounds that the American plane was authorized only for use by the Ambassador. Harriman protested vigorously, arguing that Molotov's refusal was not only contrary to his understanding of what use could be made of the plane, but also that to delay unnecessarily the departure of General Donovan, whose duties urgently required his immediate return to the United States, was both unfriendly and to the detriment of the war effort. Molotov was adamant, but he did agree to set up a special Soviet two-engine plane for Donovan's use. There followed a vigil of eleven days, each of which followed the same pattern. Donovan's entire party, Averell and Kathy Harriman, General Spalding, and I would get up at six in the morning and go in sub-zero weather to the airport. Just as the plane was about to take off we would be told that the weather in Stalingrad, Astrakhan, or Baku was bad and there would be no flight that day. We would then return to Spasso House and hold a council of war over breakfast. It was invariably agreed that Averell would see Molotov again, and when he did the result would be the same. Finally, on the eleventh day, Molotov consented to Donovan's using the American plane with the proviso that it would not be returned to Russia until an understanding had been reached as to its use. Donovan left the following day and was in the United States by the time a

Soviet plane which left Moscow at the same time had reached Teheran. Thereafter our plane was kept at Cairo and was brought into Russia only when either Harriman or I was to use it to depart from or return to the Soviet Union.

Throughout the war the Russian authorities consistently refused to allow foreign aircraft in Russia except for the transport of the highest foreign dignitaries such as Churchill, De Gaulle, Eisenhower, and a few others. They said that their position in the matter was taken because of the danger to foreign aircraft which might result from mistakes on the part of their anti-aircraft defenses. I believe the real reason was that the Russians wished to avoid any precedents which would encourage foreign governments to believe that transit rights over the Soviet Union would be forthcoming in the postwar civil aviation scramble. Regardless of the reason for the Russian attitude, it certainly was not that of a friendly ally.

Arrangements for the exchange of Missions between the O.S.S. and intelligence and subversive agencies of the N.K.V.D. seemed to be progressing on both the American and Russian sides when Harriman, on March 16, received a telegram from President Roosevelt indefinitely postponing the exchange.

Harriman and I prepared a long telegram which he sent to the President asking for reconsideration of his decision. We argued that for the first time we had penetrated the most secret intelligence service of the Soviet Union and that the relationship thus established would open the door to greater intimacy with other branches of government. We were then engaged in bringing American troops to Russia in connection with our shuttle-bombing bases and we informed the President of our fears that reneging on Donovan's agreement would adversely affect the shuttle-bombing project.

On March 30 the President replied that the whole subject had received sympathetic consideration at home but that the domestic political consideration in the United States was the predominant factor that prevented him from altering his decision. The President was confident that Marshal Stalin would understand and he hoped we would emphasize that the exchange of Missions was to be postponed only because of timing.

Looking back, I can see that the introduction of representatives of any branch of the N.K.V.D. into the United States would have been a juicy morsel for the columnists in an election year, and from a political point of view it is not difficult to understand the President's apprehensions. However, the Russian representatives were to have been in the United States openly and for the purpose of collaborating with the O.S.S. I believe the association would have been mutually beneficial, and it is hardly possible that they could have conducted activities detrimental to our interests. At that time I still had dreams of being chums with the Russians and I dreaded the task of telling them of the President's decision. Doing so proved to be one of the most amusing experiences I had in Russia.

I called Fitin on the telephone and he agreed to an appointment, saying he would send one of his men to my office at six o'clock that evening to take me to the meeting place. At about six-thirty a typical bomb tosser in a long black overcoat, thick glasses, and a disreputable black hat appeared at my office, saying that Fitin had sent him. When we went outside I proposed taking my car, which was standing at the door, but he declined my offer and pointed to a long black job with dark curtains on all the windows. I turned to my chauffeur, Naum, and told him to follow us. This apparently did not fit in with my escort's plans because when we entered his car he gave some rapid-fire instructions in Russian to his chauffeur and settled back beside me in silence. We were having a thaw that day after a heavy snow, with the result that the streets were a mass of slush. We careened away from my office, up one street and down another, following a zigzag course at a tremendous rate of speed for perhaps twenty minutes. The slushy snow was thrown in a fan-shaped stream far onto the crowded sidewalks, and people attempting to get on streetcars were drenched as we passed them. I realized at once that the driver of our chariot had received instructions to lose Naum in order that I would not know where I had been taken. This struck me as extremely funny as I knew my Buick was faster than any car ever made in Russia and that no one would be more delighted to keep the accelerator on the floor-board than Naum. Sure enough, when we emerged from behind the curtains in front of a dilapidated apartment house in a neighborhood that was strange to me, there was Naum parked in back of us with his motor turned off and looking very bored. My friend must have known what I was laughing at because he did not ask me.

In all my dealings with Fitin and Ossipov I never met them at the same place twice. Apparently they had hide-outs all over town—for what purpose I shall never know. On this occasion we climbed a few flights of stairs, a door was opened cautiously while I was identified and then was thrown open by Ossipov, who invited me in. I found a table set with vodka, cognac, fruit, and chocolates, and they insisted that I indulge. I was a little skeptical about doing any heavy drinking before I delivered my message because I had no idea how it would be received. However, the vodka did whip up my courage, and it apparently had a mellowing effect on them, because as the President had predicted they appeared to "understand perfectly" and agreed that the co-ordination between their secret intelligence and ours could be carried on in Moscow between themselves and me, acting for Donovan. We left it at that, and thus started a relationship that lasted until the war was over.

As usual we gave the Russians, in the field of secret intelligence, much more information than we received. This was probably because the O.S.S. was a much more effective organization than its Russian counterpart. Nevertheless, I think Fitin did his best, and among other things he gave us timely warning of the unreliability of some of the contacts our agents had made in Switzerland and the Balkans, assisted us in ascertaining the fate of a group of agents we had dropped in Czechoslovakia, appointed a Soviet agent to work with the O.S.S. in London, and provided information as to Soviet methods of subversion and the collection of intelligence concerning war industries in Germany. Donovan's organization maintained a constant flow of information to Fitin. This included studies made by the Research and Analysis Branch of the O.S.S. as well as intelligence gained by operatives in the field. Perhaps the most important information Donovan transmitted to the Russians was documentary proof that the Germans had succeeded in breaking certain Russian codes.

I cannot leave the subject of the N.K.V.D. without relating an incident which was in part an aftermath to my wild ride through the streets of Moscow. General Crist and I received an invitation from Fitin and Ossipov to dine with them at the Aragvi, the only restaurant and night club which remained open in Moscow throughout the war. Dinner at this establishment cost forty-five dollars a plate in American money, hence, Crist and I had never been there and, again hence, we were delighted to accept.

We found a beautifully appointed restaurant with deep rugs, soft lights, and enough room for twenty or thirty tables, most of which were empty. There was a balcony at each end of the high-ceilinged room. In one of these was a string orchestra; the other led into a private dining-room where Crist and I were entertained. We left the door to our balcony open and could thus look down on the diners below and at the orchestra in the balcony opposite us. It was a setting such as Crist and I would not have believed existed in Moscow.

Before dinner, over cocktails, I recalled to Fitin and Ossipov the visit I had made them a month or two earlier to deliver the President's decision and described the mad ride through the streets of Moscow, stressing the humor of their chauffeur trying to shake off my Naum who loved nothing better than speed. They both tittered at my delightful story but offered no explanation until dinner was nearly over, when Fitin, who had been thinking as fast as he could, informed me that I was taken to the meeting place in such a roundabout way because his chauffeur knew that he, Fitin, would be late for his appointment and did not want me to be embarrassed by arriving there first. I remarked that we had gone at a tremendous rate of speed in trying to be late and asked why Soviet officials all had their cars fitted out with heavy black curtains. Fitin's reply was that the curtains prevented the occupants from becoming sunburned, and with that I surrendered.

The dinner was a delightful succession of Hungarian dishes for which the restaurant was famous. Throughout I was puzzled as to our hosts' motives in inviting us. I discovered one reason when dinner was over.

Ossipov took me over to a corner and whispered that he had some very important information to give me. It developed that his agents had overheard some American engineers, who were then acting as technical advisers in the construction of an oil refinery in Baku, discussing the forthcoming elections in the United States. One of them had been heard to describe President Roosevelt as a "son of a bitch who should be taken out and shot." They thought I should know about it. I thanked them profusely and said I certainly would see that corrective action was taken. However, I went on to explain that our people get quite wrought up over elections and sometimes are overemphatic in expressing opinions of the rival candidates. I added that as a rule we didn't take such talk at all seriously. Crist and I were tempted to cable the story to President Roosevelt and thank him for being the inspiration of the most delicious dinner we had thus far had in Moscow.

One of the first tasks undertaken by Averell Harriman on his arrival in Moscow was to urge the Soviet Government to release sixty or more American airmen then interned at Tashkent in south-central Russia. Early in December 1943 he succeeded in gaining Molotov's approval for an American doctor, Major John H. Waldron, to make a trip to Tashkent to bring the internees some supplies and to administer such medical treatment as might be necessary.

Waldron found our men comfortably housed in an old school which had been converted into a barracks. He reported that the food was satisfactory and that officers and men were making the best of a bad situation but were naturally depressed at their enforced inactivity. One man was seriously ill with a postoperative condition which made it imperative that he be returned to the United States with the least delay.

As soon as Waldron had submitted his report Harriman went to Molotov and obtained immediate approval for returning the man who was ill to the United States. Molotov arranged to have a special aircraft take the man from Tashkent to Teheran. Molotov also gave Harriman a hint that the remaining men might soon be released or allowed to "escape" by saying, "It is strange that the five crew members whom we picked up after General Doolittle's raid in March of 1942 cannot be found in the Soviet Union."

The release of American internees who had been engaged against the Japanese was a serious undertaking for the Soviet Government and all the Allies as well, since it might provide an incident which would bring on a premature conflict between Japan and the Soviet Union. On the other hand, there was considerable justification for Russia to violate her neutrality with Japan if the interned airmen would be used against the common enemy—Germany. In any event, Marshal Stalin decided to take the chance.

One night, while I was still in bed with an ankle broken as the result of my first skiing attempt, General P. D. Ivanov of the N.K.V.D. and Estigneev came to see me. After insisting that all doors be closed, Ivanov divulged an elaborate scheme which he had devised for the "escape" of our internees.

The plan in brief was that he and I were each to send an officer to the internment camp at Tashkent. Upon arrival there my officer was to deliver an order from me addressed to Major Salter, the senior officer among the internees, directing that, with Soviet approval, the entire group was to be moved to the Caucasus to work on American aircraft being ferried into Russia through the Persian Gulf. The group was then to be put aboard a train which would have a complete crew of N.K.V.D. personnel. When the train approached Ashkhabad, the closest point that the railroad came to the Iranian border, it was to break down. The crew of the train would then get off, tap the wheels with hammers and have a lengthy discussion to add realism to the break-down. At this point my officer was to inform the internees that he and Ivanov's officer would go into Ashkhabad a few miles distant and get some motor trucks to take the internees to Ashkhabad for the night. While waiting for the trucks to arrive the internees were to be locked in their box cars. After a reasonable interval the trucks, all driven by N.K.V.D. drivers, were to arrive at the train. My officer was then to inform the internees that he had succeeded in bribing the truck drivers to make a dash for the Iranian border about ten miles to the south. The internees were to be as quiet as possible and remain concealed under tarpaulins while the trucks were inspected by the border guards, who were also N.K.V.D. men. After that the men were to be pledged to secrecy until the end of the war as to what had occurred.

Everything went exactly as planned. The only element of the plot which was added extemporaneously was the banquet of caviar, fish, cognac, and vodka that the Russian commandant at Ashkhabad insisted on having before turning the trucks over to Colonel Robert E. McCabe, my representative, and his Russian companion.

When the men were safely across the Russian border there followed a forty-eight-hour day-and-night motor trip over mountains and through desert to Teheran. Arriving before daylight, the men were isolated in a special barracks, where General Connolly had arranged for meals of ham and eggs, thick steaks, ice cream, and other dishes that these American boys had been dreaming of the preceding year. Very few people in Teheran knew of the presence of the ex-internees, and they were flown out under cover of darkness to another isolated camp near Cairo. From Cairo they were sent to the United States by steamship. They were interrogated, given furloughs, and eventually returned to duty in the European theater. The men guarded their secret zealously in the fear that a leak would destroy the chances for "escape" of the many who were to be forced to land in Russia in the future.

In a few months another hundred Americans had been accumulated at Tashkent, and their "escape" was an exact replica of that of the first group. By January of 1944 the internment camp at Tashkent had gathered one hundred and ten Americans, and a third "escape" was arranged.

But this was doomed to failure. At first everything went according to plan. The train broke down—wheels were tapped—McCabe (American officer assigned to all three "escapes") and his friend went into Ashkhabad to get the trucks—the Russian Commandant had his banquet—but at this point the plan was changed. McCabe was told that the United States papers had been talking too loud and that the internees would have to remain in Ashkhabad until instructions were received from Moscow. These were forthcoming in a few days and the entire group was sent back to internment in Tashkent.

I had my first inkling of the leak that had occurred in the American press when Henry Shapiro, United Press representative in Moscow, came to my office and told me he had been asked by the United Press for verification of an item which had appeared in an American syndicated news column late in December 1943 or early in January 1944 regarding the escape from Russia of five internees who had made a forced landing two years previously after having participated in the Doolittle raid on Japan. The columnist indicated that the men had actually landed on the Manchurian side of the border but had been seized by a group of Russian soldiers who refused a demand by Japanese troops that the Americans be turned over to them. The Russians argued with the Japanese that the plane had landed on Siberian soil. The Americans were said to have been put into Soviet trucks, and the Russian commander after a considerable ride told the Americans that they were then crossing the border into Siberia. Thereafter the men were said to have been sent west and eventually allowed to escape through Teheran.

I told Shapiro the whole story of what had occurred in the first two escapes and that a third one was under way. He agreed that nothing could be a greater disservice to the United States than to have any further publicity and wired the United Press that the matter was one of the greatest secrecy and should receive no further mention.

The fat was in the fire, and I was not at all surprised when I received word from McCabe a week or so later that the American flyers had been sent back to internment at Tashkent. The American columnist had had his sensational paragraph for which he had probably been amply rewarded, but one hundred and ten American airmen were sent back to the boredom of internment with their hopes dashed. Their specialized training was lost to the war effort and, most serious of all, a Japanese reaction was risked which might have resulted in a premature clash with Russia, who had her hands full on the German front.

While both Stalin and Molotov expressed their indignation concerning the disclosures made in American newspapers, they relented, and the Americans were liberated a few months later. "Escapes" were arranged periodically thereafter and continued until the war was over.

I have written at some length about Donovan's arrangements and the treatment of our internees because both were episodes marked by the utmost cordiality and good will. While the exchange of intelligence between the O.S.S. and Fitin's groups was not particularly productive, I always had the feeling that Fitin and Ossipov at least tried to make it so. In the case of the internees, the Russian attitude was more generous than might reasonably have been expected. In light of the difficulties experienced in our other efforts to collaborate, the Russian attitude in these two cases is difficult to understand—but then in that land of contradictions everything is difficult to understand.

V. Some Minor Projects

E VENTS at the Moscow Conference pointed forcibly to the inadequacy of signal communications between the United States and the Soviet Union. Secretary Hull was almost completely out of touch with the President as far as a timely interchange of communications was concerned. Some of the President's replies to Secretary Hull's many requests for specific instructions did not reach Moscow until after the Conference was concluded and the Secretary had started home; others were so delayed as to cause considerable embarrassment to the Secretary.

At that time communications between Washington and Moscow were almost entirely by commercial radio telegraph operated jointly by the Soviet Commissariat of Communications and commercial radio telegraph companies in the United States. The radio channel followed a great circle path, coming very close to the magnetic pole. Every effort was made to maintain a twenty-four-hour service, but frequent and unexpected delays were caused by electrical disturbances over the North Atlantic. In an emergency the United States companies would attempt to relay traffic to Moscow from London or Bern, Switzerland, both of which enjoyed longer periods of radio operation with Moscow, but such messages were subject to delay by the London and Bern censors.

The United States Army Signal Corps, and particularly the Army Communications Service under Major General Frank E. Stoner, had set up the most widespread and efficient communication net the world had ever seen. Stoner, Harriman, and I knew that the time was coming when instant and reliable communication between the United States and the Soviet Union would be of vital importance, and we knew it could be attained if Moscow could be drawn into the U.S. Army net. The simplest solution was to set up an American radio station in Moscow with a channel to Teheran—that is, it would have been the simplest solution had it not required Soviet approval.

I have already described how my proposal at the Moscow Conference for an improvement in signal communications had received Soviet approval "in principle." On November 14, 1943, I cabled the Chiefs of Staff my recommendation that at the forthcoming Teheran Conference they "put the Soviet authorities on the defensive by having some requests ready to present to them. Use of Pacific bases, co-ordination of the timing of Russian and Allied offensives, use of Russian shuttle-bombing bases, interchange of weather information, and improved signal communications are some of the subjects which you might raise."

Acting on my recommendation, the Chiefs of Staff prepared a memorandum for the President to hand to Stalin, requesting that steps be taken to improve our communications. Stalin told the President that this would be done. Judging from the tempo with which action in the matter was taken after our return to Moscow, I think Stalin's approval must have been a very casual one made between toasts to American-Soviet friendship.

After the Teheran Conference, Harriman maintained pressure on Molotov while I worked on the Red Army General Staff in an effort to substitute action for conversation. The reward for our persistency came in a letter from Molotov on January 31, 1944, two months after the first Soviet approval had been obtained. I was to learn later that this represented a special Russian effort in speed. Molotov informed us that the People's Commissariat of Communications was doing great things to improve radio transmission to the United States. An additional sixty-kilowatt transmitter, four channels for the reception of American traffic during the hours of "stable passage," and special "high-effective" antennae—all would come into being within three or four months.

Well, this was a start, but it was still a far cry from tying Moscow into the U.S. Army net, so we continued the battle. Of course, none of the steps which Molotov indicated were being taken would eliminate the North Atlantic atmospheric conditions, the basic cause of our communication delays. Averell thanked Molotov for what was being done but urged that further consideration be given to the proposal I had made to the General Staff offering the Soviet Union use of U.S. Army Communications to Washington provided we could establish a station in Moscow to communicate with Teheran.

About a week later, early in February 1944, I had a long session with Lieutenant General Slavin of the General Staff in which he indicated that the United States could establish a radio station in Moscow provided the Soviet Union could establish one in Washington or New York. The most serious complication in his proposal in my opinion was that the establishment of foreign radio stations on United States soil was not permissible under United States law.

For my part, I had no hesitancy in recommending that the Russian proposal be accepted, feeling certain that the President, under his wartime powers, could authorize the Russian station in the United States for the duration of the war. I therefore sent Slavin's proposal to our Chiefs of Staff and recommended approval.

On February 12, 1944, I received a reply confirming the fact that the proposal could not be accepted because of legal difficulties, but offering twenty-four-hour circuits by automatic relay via Africa. The United States was willing and ready to provide channels for Soviet Government business with complete Soviet control of its terminal equipment (teletypewriters) in exchange for the privilege of installing a similar channel for our use between Moscow and Washington.

I knew that informing the Russians that American law prevented acceptance of their proposal would require delicate handling. The most efficient way of presenting the American proposition would have been to have had my signal officer, Major Lawrence B. Roy, do it. He was a technical expert and could have readily answered any questions the Russians might have asked. However, had I designated Roy to conduct the negotiations, we would have had no chance of success. Sending a subordinate to talk of making a governmental agreement would not only have been considered as an insult by my rank-conscious Soviet friends, but would also have indicated that I, as head of the Mission, did not consider the matter one of importance. Soviet doubts would have been raised with regard to my determination to see it through. With Roy's help, I learned the details of our proposed arrangement and prepared a layman's presentation, with circuit diagrams of the proposed channels, to give to General Slavin. When I met with Slavin, Roy accompanied me as technical adviser— having an advisory staff at my disposal always added "face" in negotiations with the Russians.

Slavin at once assumed an attitude of hurt dignity when I told him his proposal was impossible for us to accept because of American law. He said that the Soviet proposal to allow us to establish a station in Moscow was contrary to Soviet law, but that Marshal Stalin had waived the restriction in favor of Allied unity. Why could not President Roosevelt do the same? I tried in vain to point out a few of the basic differences between our form of government and theirs, stating that while we might succeed in getting the law changed I was afraid our legislative processes were too slow to accomplish much in this direction in time to be of help in this or the next war.

Apparently the Soviet authorities higher than Slavin were also considerably displeased at our answer, but at the same time they were attracted by the idea of having the United States provide a radio channel between Moscow and Washington which would afford teletypewriter service for Soviet business. In a way peculiarly Russian they expressed both attitudes. On March 11, 1944, Molotov wrote Harriman that because of what I had told Slavin concerning United States law, "the appropriate Soviet authorities consider that the question concerning the establishment of an American station in the U.S.S.R. and a Soviet station in the U.S.A. on the basis of reciprocity should be considered as dropped." However, on March 17, just as we were recovering from the blow, a second letter from the Soviet Foreign Office completely reversed the decision made the previous week. It concluded by saying: "The People's Commissariat for Foreign Affairs communicates that the appropriate Soviet authorities, while agreeing in principle to the establishment of radio communications between the Soviet Union and the United States through the use of teletype machines, nevertheless consider that on a basis of reciprocity a teletype receiver and transmitter should be set up in Moscow on the premises of the appropriate Soviet agency and operated by Soviet personnel."

The letter completely ignored Molotov's previous rejection of the American plan, and thus in a way the Russians succeeded in eating their cake and having it too. The Russians had many more agencies in the United States than we had in Russia. They needed rapid communications, particularly in connection with the Russian lend-lease program. Nevertheless, the phrase "in principle" was still included in the Soviet acquiescence and it still disturbed me. My apprehensions on this score were allowed to intensify for three weeks; not until April 11 was I finally granted an appointment with A. D. Fortushenko, Vice Commissar of Communications, with whom I was to work out the details of our project.

On May 16, 1946, two years after our Russian communications agreement was reached, a famous Washington columnist published an item announcing that the wartime channel between Moscow and Washington was to be discontinued during the week. The article indicated that the Soviet Government had been allowed to set up a radio station in the Pentagon Building during the war and that the portion of the Pentagon in which it was located was guarded by about seventy Russian soldiers. The columnist implied that this had been accomplished in the utmost secrecy because it was in violation of the Communications Act of 1934.

Actually nothing could be further from the truth. The United States provided under lend-lease the equipment for a complete receiving and transmitting station to be set up about fifteen miles from

Moscow by Soviet personnel with American technical assistance, and operated exclusively (after the first month) by Soviet personnel. From this station connections were made to teletypewriter terminals in both American and Russian offices in Moscow. Ours was in my office. Our own coded messages went directly from our teletypewriter to the Soviet-operated radio station, where they were put on the air automatically and followed a channel which relayed through Algiers directly to the American-operated station in the Pentagon. The American terminal was operated by Americans and the Russian terminal by Russians. The terminals were connected with the radio station on alternate hours, thus dividing the use of the channel. Later two channels were provided under the same procedure and gave full-time service to both the Russians and Americans. The terminals could in no sense be considered radio stations. They provided only a simplified method of getting a coded message from our offices to the radio station and onto the air.

This differed considerably from our having a radio station in Moscow under American control. Had we had that, we could have sent messages to any part of the world simply by changing the frequency instead of being limited to the Washington-Moscow channel. The situation was exactly reversed in Washington where we had complete control of the radio station and the Russians had control only of the teletypewriter operations at their terminal. The secrecy which surrounded the project was not because of a violation of American law but because of a desire to keep the enemy in ignorance of the channel so that he would not make attempts to jam it.

My negotiations with Fortushenko proved to be extremely interesting and gave me a further insight into Russian procedure. He was a heavy-set man with the high, widely separated cheekbones which characterize so many Russians. He wore thick-lensed glasses and had the same dead-pan expression as Gromyko. There can be no doubt that he knew the technical aspects of communications backwards and forwards. It was also evident at once that he was not going to be lured into any questionable arrangements with a foreigner. He talked a little English, which he loved to try out on me. The only time I could get a smile out of him was when I tried my Russian on him. He was accompanied at our first meeting by two technical assistants and General Slavin. I had with me Major Roy, who knew much more of the theory of the subject than any of the Russians. Whenever the negotiations would start to bog down I would pass the ball to Roy, who would go into a long theoretical discussion of the point under consideration. He used so many big words that neither the Russians nor I understood him. As a result the Russians would turn back to me with an amiability born of relief.

We decided at the first meeting that a written agreement should be concluded between our two Governments but that in the meanwhile I should have the necessary equipment shipped to Moscow and that the installation should be started. I offered to draw up a draft agreement which we could discuss at our next meeting. I thought I was being helpful, but I could see that Fortushenko accepted my offer with some reluctance. I would have done much better had I let Fortushenko draw up the draft agreement and then negotiated those points with which I was in disagreement. I say this because Fortushenko took exception to almost every word in my draft, and it required weekly meetings from April 11 to June 16 to adjust our differences. The agreement was not signed until June 16, 1944, just one week before the circuit started operating.

During our negotiations one incident nearly wrecked the project. So many corrections were made in my original draft that clean copies had to be made from time to time so that we could start anew. On one occasion we made several pencil changes in the draft and I agreed to have clean copies typed in both Russian and English and to send them to Fortushenko. I rushed back to my office, and in my hurry to get to another appointment I gave my stenographer what I thought was the latest revision, but it was one that had been discussed at a meeting a few weeks earlier. This was sent to Fortushenko's office before I had a chance to check it, and he was furious. I was accused of trying in an underhanded way to reinstate clauses which we had long since agreed to delete and of leaving out clauses which we had agreed to include. My explanations were finally accepted, but only reluctantly, and thereafter I was trusted not at all.

Fortunately during this long period of negotiation the embryo agreement was being carried out actively. When I first received an indication from the Foreign Office that the project would be approved, I took a chance and requested immediate air shipment of the necessary equipment. By the time I had my first discussion with Fortushenko, the equipment was already approaching Teheran. The air shipment included eighty-six boxes of assorted sizes and weighed fourteen thousand pounds. I tried to obtain authority from Fortushenko to let the United States aircraft on which it was loaded come all the way to Moscow in order to avoid transshipment at Teheran. Again Soviet determination not to permit foreign aircraft to fly over the Soviet Union prevented approval of my request. We unloaded our planes in Teheran, and considerable delay in the delivery of the equipment to Moscow resulted from Russian inability or unwillingness to devote cargo space to it for onshipment to Moscow.

General Stoner proposed sending forty American technicians to Moscow to install the radio station and terminals. The Russians finally consented to his sending seven who could act as technical advisers to Soviet installation personnel. Even these seven were not desired, and their arrival was effectively delayed by the Foreign Office's refusal to grant them visas until the station was almost completely installed and certain technical advice was absolutely necessary before it could be put in operation. In fairness to the Soviet communications personnel I should add that Major Raymond B. Jewett, our senior technical adviser, told me that the work as far as it had progressed prior to his arrival had been extremely well done. He thought this was remarkable in view of the fact that the equipment was of a type with which the Russians had had no previous experience.

The importance of weather as a weapon of war came into full focus when a Japanese task force arrived within striking distance of Pearl

Harbor on December 7, 1941, after following bad weather which was moving eastward and which afforded the Japanese complete concealment from observation during their entire journey from Japan. The effectiveness of the Japanese maneuver insured our meteorologists of unlimited support in perfecting the United States military and civil weather services which were to play such a large part in winning the war.

The accuracy of weather predictions, so essential to air and naval operations, increases with the extent of the area under observation. The greatest accuracy is obtained when observations are world-wide. Accuracy decreases materially when there is a large unobserved area in which the build-up and movement of high and low pressure conditions are not known. Prior to the war, weather conditions in Russia, which represents one-sixth of the land mass of the world, were assiduously concealed. The Soviet Union had many broadcasts for their national service, but to insure that these would not become available to the outside world they were in a secret cipher. Weather information from western Russia would do much to improve the effectiveness of our bombing offensive against Germany, while information from Siberia and the Maritime provinces would do much to remove the blackout that existed in Japanese-controlled areas and would thus facilitate our air and naval operations in the Pacific. Obtaining Russian co-operation in this respect was given a high priority in the objectives of my Mission. It seemed like a small concession to ask of an ally, and I anticipated little difficulty in obtaining it.

Some moves toward an exchange of weather information between the United States and the Soviet Union had been made prior to my arrival in Russia and even before our entry into the war. The first representations were made by the Harriman-Beaverbrook Mission in 1941. Their primary purpose had been to start the flow of lend-lease supplies to Russia, and it is not surprising that this had evoked a slight Russian gesture of reciprocation in the form of a weather exchange between San Francisco and Khabarovsk. The data we received from Khabarovsk, collected from fifteen to twenty stations in Siberia, only

scratched the surface of the possibilities, yet were invaluable in connection with our operations in the North Pacific. The next step toward
improving our weather exchange came in July of 1942 in connection
with the establishment of the Alaskan-Siberian air route over which
we were to deliver lend-lease aircraft to Russia. This was negotiated
by Major General Follett Bradley and provided for an exchange of
weather information between Irkutsk near Lake Baikal and Fairbanks,
Alaska.

In February 1943 the Soviet Weather Bureau, which was always
interested in improving the weather exchange, induced the Soviet
Foreign Office, which had considerably less enthusiasm in the matter,
to permit it to send a small Mission to the United States to work out
a complete weather agreement. The Mission was headed by Captain
Konstantin F. Speransky, a Naval officer attached to the Soviet
Weather Bureau. Speransky remained in the United States until July
1943, and during that time the exchange between Khabarovsk and
San Francisco was enlarged to about thirty stations and plans were
prepared for an exchange between Moscow and New York. These
were to become effective after Speransky had returned to Russia and
had obtained the approval of his Government. His efforts in this respect were futile.

Despite the fact that the ground had been broken before the arrival
of the Military Mission in Moscow, the great mass of Siberia and
western Russia was still a blank to the United States weather authorities responsible for the preparation of world weather maps. I have
already mentioned the agreement in principle which Molotov gave
to a free exchange of weather data at the Moscow Conference. This
was followed by a written request on the same subject from President
Roosevelt to Marshal Stalin during the Teheran Conference. Stalin
told the President that arrangements would be made, but it was not
until three months later, on March 21, 1944, that Andrei Vishinsky,
Vice Commissar of Foreign Affairs, in replying to a pressure letter
from Harriman, informed us that the question had been considered
and that "the appropriate Soviet authorities" did not object to the

broadening of the weather information "on the basis of reciprocity." Vishinsky's reply also informed us "that the necessary instructions had been issued to the Chief of the Soviet Weather Service on the matter, directing him to work out the details with the United States Military Mission."

Now that the green light had been flashed, I placed the project in the hands of Rear Admiral Clarence E. Olsen, head of the Naval Division of the Mission. We were informed by both Admiral King and General Arnold that each desired to send a meteorologist to Russia to assist in the negotiations. Admiral King sent Captain Denys W. Knoll, one of the Navy's best technicians, and General Arnold sent Colonel Lewis L. Mundell, also an outstanding meteorologist. It soon developed that Speransky felt he had been snubbed by our Army Air Forces during his visit to the United States, and the Soviet Weather Service was therefore not inclined to play ball with an Air Force representative in Moscow. I do not know whether the slight to Speransky was real or imagined, but we solved the dilemma by having Admiral Olsen and Captain Knoll conduct the negotiations with the Weather Bureau and sent Colonel Mundell to Poltava on the important assignment of handling our own weather service in connection with shuttle bombing from Russian bases which was soon to start.

Olsen and Knoll did a superb job in obtaining the maximum Russian co-operation from that time on. Olsen at once established contact with Lieutenant General Eugene K. Fedorov, Chief of the Russian Weather Service. Fedorov was one of the first four individuals to be made Heroes of the Soviet Union, a reward he received for being a member of Admiral Papanin's expedition to the North Pole. Though holding the rank of Lieutenant General in the Red Army, Fedorov was not essentially a military man. He was a typical scientist and as such was a strong advocate of international co-operation in his particular field. He openly avowed his preference for the United States over other foreign countries and was not hesitant in letting us know his personal desire to effect the maximum co-ordination between his service and ours. However, whenever a foreigner enters the picture

reception was frigid, their freedom of action restricted, and operations made practically impossible by Soviet refusal to agree to radio frequencies on which they could operate. The Soviet Government officially requested that the stations be withdrawn not later than December 15, 1945, and we had no choice but to accede to the request.

Perhaps, though, some hope of future co-operation may be drawn from the visit made to Moscow in July 1945 by Dr. F. W. Reichelderfer, Chief of the United States Weather Bureau. The visit had been suggested by Captain Knoll in May 1944 as potentially helpful to international co-operation in weather matters as well as a courteous gesture, in return for a visit the Soviet Weather Mission had made to the United States in the spring of 1943. Arrangements for this project required fourteen months of negotiation and encountered the usual inner conflicts that exist between different branches of the Soviet Government.

When it finally came about, however, it permitted Reichelderfer and Fedorov to exchange ideas and to discuss the future organization of the international weather service. Fedorov indicated that the Soviet Union would do its utmost to break the dominance of the international weather organization which had previously been exercised by the British and would insist on a completely representative organization. In addition, Fedorov said that it was his intention to continue in peacetime the Soviet weather broadcasts for foreign consumption which had been initiated by the United States and the Soviet Union as a necessity of war. This was the first positive information we had had that the Russians intended to abandon their persistent policy of isolation. It held promise of considerable benefit to postwar commercial aviation. I recently asked Dr. Reichelderfer how Fedorov's promise has been kept in the year which has elapsed since the end of the war. He informed me that the exchange has been continued but the old problem of communications has prevented its full effectiveness. I liked Fedorov and was delighted to hear that he has respected his promise.

Before I left for Russia, General Arnold, who could pound the desk and get things done in the United States, had called me to his office, pounded the desk, and told me what he wanted done in the way of improving air transportation between the United States and Russia. He informed me that I was to obtain Russian approval for American operation of air transport planes to Moscow on any of the following routes in order of priority: one, the Alaskan-Siberian route; two, via the United Kingdom and Stockholm; or three, from Teheran to Moscow. I saluted, said, "Yes, Sir," and tried for two years to carry out his instructions.

Our efforts to effect rapid air transport between the United States and Russia brought out some sharp differences in the characteristics of the Russian and American people. To us, time is of the essence; to the Russians, time means nothing; we plan for future contingencies, the Russians meet them as they arise; yet paradoxically we will compromise the future to take care of the present while the Russians will compromise the present in order to shape a pattern for the future. For example, it was terribly important to us to have ordinary routine business which required sending passengers, mail, or freight to or from Russia accomplished as expeditiously as possible; the Russian attitude was that delay would automatically afford relief from bothersome detail. We always felt that the tempo of the war would increase and reach a climax in its final stages and that we should plan to have the facilities established and available for rapid movement of important personages, vital equipment, or documents from one side to the other; the Russians contended that such emergencies could be handled as special cases. We were willing to meet any Russian terms which would permit the improvement of air transport during the emergency, while the Russians assiduously avoided establishing precedents in war from which it would be difficult to recede in time of peace.

Our interest in the Alaskan-Siberian route was primarily based on our realization of the effect its development might have in the war against Japan. Had we been allowed to operate over it, we would have improved the installations along the route so that they would have been adequate to handle a large redeployment of American air forces from Western Europe to Siberia once Germany had been defeated. The second choice, that is, via England and Stockholm, was operationally feasible in winter when there were long hours of darkness to cover the flight from England to Moscow, but it would have been extremely hazardous in the summer months when part of the flight would have to be over German-controlled territory in daylight hours. The last choice, Teheran to Moscow, was safe enough but extremely circuitous and time consuming.

Admiral Standley had succeeded in 1942 in reaching an agreement with the Russians by which they would handle American traffic from Teheran to Moscow on a reciprocal basis. This was the arrangement that was in effect when Harriman and I arrived. It was extremely unsatisfactory because there was no commitment as to the volume of American traffic that the Russian airlines would carry. There was a continuous backlog of American passengers, mail, and freight piled up in Teheran which delayed delivery in Moscow for from four to six weeks.

Another little item that spurred us to greater effort in obtaining Soviet approval to American air operations in Russia was the peril of flying in Soviet aircraft. The refinements of air travel which we have in the United States are unknown in Russia. Only a few fields have radio beacons, none have control towers to regulate traffic, and the runways are invariably single strips built to conform to the prevailing wind. Pilots warm up their motors as they taxi to the take-off. There is never the slightest pause for "revving-up" nor a final check between taxiing and departure. Landings are made in accordance with which end of the field is closest to the incoming plane, and circling a field is considered a complete waste of time. Landing the aircraft is determined entirely by bulk and never by weight. Finally we Americans were familiar enough with the life span of American aircraft sent to Russia to know that maintenance consisted mainly of substituting new aircraft as the old ones wore out.

One of my outstanding memories of Russia is a trip I made from

Berlin to Moscow. I spent the night in Berlin with Lucius Clay and made arrangements for the flight by telephone from his house. I was to be at the Russian airport in Berlin the following morning at eight o'clock. I arrived on time but could find no one who even knew that a plane was to leave for Moscow, much less that I was to be on it. After half an hour of inquiry I was about to give up, when a Russian colonel came up to me, pointed to an airplane on the field, and told me to take my baggage and stand near it until departure time, which he indefinitely described as "sometime this morning." I waited for perhaps an hour and things began to happen. A lone individual strolled out and unlocked the door. Soon clusters of soldiers, women, and children started to arrive. They were followed by trucks from which furniture, boxes, bicycles, baby carriages, radios, and other German booty were loaded on the aircraft. I marveled at how much one airplane could hold and expected the sides to burst momentarily. When all the passengers were aboard, I was told that a space had been reserved for me toward the front and I climbed in, but not until I had begged the interpreter who was with me to wait until he actually saw the plane leave the ground.

The cabin of the plane was packed with a mass of heterogeneous cargo, none of which was lashed down and all of which was precariously balanced. The passengers were on top of the cargo, and those in front beckoned me to a nice flat box top that had been reserved for me. The pilot taxied to the end of the runway, gave the plane the gun, and our wheels left the ground just as we were about to be fresh out of runway. By that time the perspiration was dropping off of me in hailstones, but the rest of the passengers were not disturbed at all—fatalists!

The trip itself was something out of this world. We dashed along at treetop height, following the roads and railroads and enjoying all the atmospheric bumps that are prevalent just off the ground. The passengers started producing lunch, which they insisted on sharing with me. I had large hunks of black bread, cheese, salami, apples, and frequent swigs from each passenger's bottle of vodka. The *pièce de résistance* was a tumbler full of a synthetic crème de cacao that some enterprising soldier had uncovered in Berlin—after that I could make no further gastronomical sacrifices to American-Soviet friendship. At the same time, I could not help but feel the genuine friendship and hospitality offered by this small representative group of Russian people. As the vodka and crème de cacao took effect, accordions and balalaikas were produced, and the remainder of the trip was spent in singing by the hardier spirits and in sleeping by those of less resistance. It was delightfully informal but impressed me as a little dangerous.

Neither Harriman nor I relented in our efforts to improve air transport between the United States and Russia. We had endless meetings and reams of correspondence on the subject with only moderate success. The Russians, feeling that any extensive American use of the Trans-Siberian route would excite Japanese suspicion, rejected it at once, for at that time they wished to avoid Japanese entanglements at all costs. The route via England was impracticable in the Russians' eyes because of the danger of flying over hostile territory. And so at first we concentrated on American operation of a Teheran-Moscow route. We offered the Russians, through Molotov and Air Marshal Fedor A. Astakhov, Chief of the Soviet Civil Air Fleet, two four-engine planes for their operation of this route in exchange for permitting us to make at least one round trip weekly. Both delayed replying to our proposal for two months and then gave us a definite refusal. As an emergency measure we agreed in August 1944 to provide ten additional Douglas two-engine transports to Russia, over and above our lend-lease commitments, in exchange for a guarantee of five thousand pounds of passenger cargo space per week from Teheran to Moscow. The effect of this agreement was helpful, but the service remained unsatisfactory. In the winter months weather delayed the flight of two-engine aircraft for weeks on end, when the use of four-engine aircraft would have provided sufficient range to eliminate refueling stops which bad weather made impossible.

We finally were convinced that American operation of an airline into Russia was out of the question, and after September 1944 we concentrated on establishing a connecting service. We proposed using four-engine planes on the entire route between the United States and the Soviet Union, with the Russians operating their end of the route. With General Arnold's approval, Harriman and I offered the Russians six four-engine planes to operate a route between Moscow and Stockholm which would connect at Stockholm with American planes from New York or Washington. The Russians liked the idea but countered with a proposal that the connection be made at Cairo to insure greater safety from enemy action and better weather. In addition, they prescribed that the airplanes we were to give them for this operation should be the C-54 type, which they had been trying in vain to obtain through lend-lease.

General Arnold suspected that the Soviet counterproposal was motivated by a political desire to obtain a foothold in the Middle East, but he agreed to it, except for providing the Russians with C-54's, with the understanding that the Soviet Government would take the initiative in obtaining transit rights over Turkey, Syria, the Lebanon, and Egypt. This effectively killed that proposition and nothing more was heard of it. After the defeat of Germany a connecting route was established at Berlin. This is still in existence and provides fairly rapid service between the United States and the Soviet Union.

During the war we were not in a good position to force Soviet co-operation in improving air transportation, although we were granting many privileges to the Russians for which we might have expected reciprocal courtesies. For example, we supported a heavy flow of Russian traffic in and out of Fairbanks, Alaska, where all facilities and shops were available for Soviet use. We flew American aircraft being lend-leased to Russia from the factories to Washington, where they would be loaded with Soviet passengers and freight before being flown to Fairbanks for delivery to the Russians. No request for authority to fly Russian aircraft to the United States via Fairbanks was ever refused. I was frequently asked by General Marshall or General Arnold if we should not deny these courtesies to the Russians until they allowed us to operate our aircraft in Russia. I was always forced to recommend against such action because it might have produced Soviet retaliation in the form of refusing to allow our supply planes to fly between Teheran and our air bases in the Ukraine. This we were being allowed to do as an essential part of the shuttle-bombing project. A Soviet stoppage of these supply planes would have left about two thousand American soldiers more or less stranded and would have made the use of the Russian bases impossible.

I have tried to give a brief sketch of three typical efforts to co-operate with the Russians on matters of moderate importance. Of course, there were a great many projects which I attempted to negotiate other than those of major importance which I shall describe later on. I received all sorts of requests from home and many from our theater commanders abroad. The Air Forces wished to send doctors to study Russian treatment and prevention of diseases peculiar to airmen; the Ordnance Department wished to send experts to examine captured German equipment (Russian equipment if possible); the Ground Forces wished to send observers to learn Russian tactical methods; the Engineers wished to place technicians with front-line Russian units in order that they would be immediately available to examine captured German maps. The list was endless—some requests were sensible, others were silly. For some we obtained Soviet approval, while for others we did not get a reply.

Our American intelligence agencies flooded me with requests for information from the Russians and about the Russians. I decided early to tell General Slavin of the Red Army General Staff that I would submit all the requests I received to him, and he could answer them or not, as he liked. I emphasized that I was in Russia to promote operational co-ordination and not to seek intelligence. Sometimes I would receive the desired information and sometimes there would be no reply—seldom did I receive a direct refusal.

Never in Russia was there the free and easy feeling of partnership which characterized our relations with the British. Every effort to collaborate was a negotiation which had to be bargained out. After I had been in Russia a year I reported my impressions to General Marshall:

2 December 1944

General George C. Marshall,
Chief of Staff, United States Army,
War Department,
Washington, D.C.

Dear General Marshall:

Now that I have been in Russia for some time and am qualified as an "expert," I think it might be of some interest to you to have my general reactions. They may be of value to you since I have served under you long enough to enable you to evaluate them. A report is always more useful if one knows the reporter.

Everyone will agree on the importance of collaboration with Russia—now and in the future. It won't be worth a hoot, however, unless it is based on mutual respect and made to work both ways. I have sat at innumerable Russian banquets and become gradually nauseated by Russian food, vodka, and protestations of friendship. Each person high in public life proposes a toast a little sweeter than the preceding one on Soviet-British-American friendship. It is amazing how these toasts go down past the tongues in the cheeks. After the banquets we send the Soviets another thousand airplanes, and they approve a visa that has been hanging fire for months. We then scratch our heads to see what other gifts we can send, and they scratch theirs to see what else they can ask for.

This picture may be overdrawn, but not much. When the Red Army was back on its heels, it was right for us to give them all possible assistance with no questions asked. It was right to bolster their morale in every way we could. However, they are no longer back on their heels; and, if there is one thing they have plenty of, it's self-confidence. The situation has changed, but our policy has not. We still meet their requests to the limit of our ability, and they meet ours to the minimum that will keep us sweet.

The truth is that they want to have as little to do with foreigners, Americans included, as possible. We never make a request or proposal to the Soviets that is not viewed with suspicion. They simply cannot understand giving without taking, and as a result even our giving is viewed with suspicion. Gratitude cannot be banked in the Soviet Union. Each transaction is complete in itself without regard to past favors. The party of the second part is either a shrewd trader to be admired or a sucker to be despised.

We have obtained some concessions after exerting all the pressure we could assemble. These included the Frantic bases, improved communications, exchange of weather information, trucks to China, exchange of enemy intelligence, some promises regarding the Far East, and some other inconsequential ones. The cost to the Soviet Union for any of these projects has been nil compared to the cost of our efforts in their behalf. Some will say that the Red Army has won the war for us. I can swallow all of this but the last two words. In our dealings with the Soviet authorities, the U.S. Military Mission has made every approach that has been made. Our files are bulging with letters to the Soviets and devoid of letters from them. This situation may be reversed in Washington, but I doubt it. In short, we are in the position of being at the same time the givers and the supplicants. This is neither dignified nor healthy for U.S. prestige.

The picture is not all bad. The individual Russian is a likable person. Their racial characteristics are similar to ours. Individually I think they would be friendly if they dared to be—however, I have yet to see the inside of a Russian home. Officials dare not become too friendly with us, and others are persecuted for this offense. The Soviets have done an amazing job for their own people—both in the war and in the prewar period. One cannot help but admire their war effort and the spirit with which it has been accomplished. We have few conflicting interests, and there is little reason why we should not be friendly now and in the foreseeable future.

In closing, I believe we should revise our present attitude along the following lines:

(1) Continue to assist the Soviet Union, provided they request assistance, and we are satisfied that it contributes to winning the war.

(2) Insist that they justify their needs for assistance in all cases where the need is not apparent to us. If they fail to do so, we should, in such cases, refuse assistance.

(3) In all cases where our assistance does not contribute to the winning of the war, we should insist on a quid pro quo.

(4) We should present proposals for collaboration that would be mutually beneficial, and then leave the next move to them.

(5) When our proposals for collaboration are unanswered after a

reasonable time, we should act as we think best and inform them of our action.

(6) We should stop pushing ourselves on them and make the Soviet authorities come to us. We should be friendly and co-operative when they do so.

I think there is something here worth fighting for, and it is simply a question of the tactics to be employed. If the procedure I suggest above were to be followed, there would be a period in which our interests would suffer. However, I feel certain that we must be tougher if we are to gain their respect and be able to work with them in the future.

VI. The Russian Lend-Lease Program

WHETHER or not our aid to Russia saved her from defeat will always be a matter of speculation. That it was a major element in the Russian and Allied victory is an incontrovertible fact. It may be that Leningrad, Moscow, and Stalingrad could have been saved without American aid, but if the situation was as grave as the Russians say it was, and as I think it was, American supplies, small as they were in those days, were unquestionably a factor in turning the tide. Had Russia been forced to withdraw farther to the east, she would have lost both her northern and Caspian ports as sources of American supplies and would have had to rely on the American supply line across the Pacific. Under such circumstances it is doubtful if Japan would have remained neutral. And if Japan had declared war on Russia at this point, the Pacific route would have been closed too, and Russia might have been eliminated from active participation in the war.

At the Teheran Conference, Stalin told the President and the Prime Minister that his margin of superiority over the Germans was about sixty divisions which could be shifted rapidly from place to place on their extended front in order to provide massed power for a breakthrough in areas of their own choosing. It is impossible to conceive how these divisions could have been moved rapidly, or even at all, had they not had American trucks to ride in, American shoes to march in, and American food to sustain them.

Certainly our aid was prompt. Within one week after Germany launched her attack on Russia, a committee representing all the shipping and supply agencies in the United States had been formed to act under the State Department for the purpose of sending aid to the Soviet Union. This committee was in existence for only four or five weeks, but in that time it approved export licenses for the shipment of $9,000,000 worth of supplies to Russia. In July 1941, one month after Russia was attacked, the President directed the Division of Defense Aid Reports to assume full responsibility for obtaining immediate and substantial shipments to the Soviet Union. A special section of the Division was created to take over the work of the State Department committee. The section was headed by Colonel P. R. Faymonville, the Army's outstanding student of Russian affairs, who had had long service in Russia and who spoke the language fluently. Faymonville's group cleared shipments for Russia in the amount of $145,000,000 during the period of three months which elapsed before the President declared the Soviet Union eligible for lend-lease on November 7, 1941. Only a small part of the supplies cleared were actually shipped, since many of the items requested by the Russians were machine tools and industrial equipment which had to be and were approved for production and given priority ratings.

In September 1941 Averell Harriman and Lord Beaverbrook went to Moscow to learn the needs of the Soviet Union and to prepare a program for fulfilling them. They found that Stalin, Molotov, and Commissar of Foreign Trade Mikoyan, were difficult to deal with and shrewd negotiators. Harriman and Beaverbrook were given a rough time by Stalin when they presented their first list of offerings. He questioned the good faith of the Western Allies and the sincerity of their desire to assist the Soviet Union. Harriman and Beaverbrook, without benefit of advice from their governments, hurriedly revised their list of offerings. When the revision was presented to Stalin the atmosphere changed, the agreement was signed, Harriman and Beaverbrook were given their Kremlin banquet and departed for home.

The Harriman-Beaverbrook agreement, known as the "Moscow Protocol," committed the United States to the delivery of approximately $1,015,000,000 of supplies to Russia in the ensuing year. The President, in declaring the Soviet Union eligible for lend-lease, set up a $1,000,000,000 credit for Russian supplies which was to be interest free, with repayment to start five years after the end of hostilities. It soon developed that this credit would be insufficient to finance the items agreed on in the "Moscow Protocol" and new arrangements had to be made. By that time we had entered the war and Russian success was of more direct and immediate interest to the United States. We therefore concluded the master lend-lease agreement with the Soviet Union which governed our aid program throughout the war.

Because the Russian requirements in some respects cut directly across those of the British and American armed forces, because of the limited availability of shipping, and because of the difficulty in arranging convoys, delivery of supplies to Russia in the latter part of 1941 and the early months of 1942 was disappointingly slow. This prompted the President to send letters on March 7, 1942, to all United States war agencies stating that he wished all material promised to the Soviet Union on Protocol to be released for shipment and shipped at the earliest possible date regardless of the effect of these shipments on any other part of the war program.

I am convinced that the measure taken by the President was one of the most important decisions of the war and one that was vitally essential when it was taken. However, it was the beginning of a policy of appeasement of Russia from which we have never fully recovered and from which we are still suffering.

The effect of the President's dictum was to give the Soviet Union preferential treatment in the allocation of munitions over all other Allies and even over the Armed Forces of the United States. During the war production programs were determined annually by the composite needs of all the Allies. Each country and each service had to adjust its requirements to the capabilities of the production program. Even after the production program had been approved and embarked upon, the timing of deliveries was based on the urgency of need as determined by the Munitions Assignment Boards in Washington and London. It was in this respect that the Soviet Union had preferential treatment; a Protocol or agreement was signed at the beginning of each fiscal year, and thereafter the Soviet Union was subject only to limitations of production and shipping in obtaining deliveries. Those responsible for the Russian program had only to point to the President's instructions to insure assignment of items agreed upon in the Protocol, the needs of other parts of the war program notwithstanding.

On the United States side a group known as the President's Protocol Committee was created to administer the Russian aid program. Harry Hopkins was the chairman of the Committee and Major General James H. Burns was its executive. The Committee included representatives of the Army, Navy, Air Forces, Foreign Economic Administration, the War Shipping Board, and other interested governmental agencies. No one did more for the war effort than Harry Hopkins and few did more than Burns. They were also chairman and executive, respectively, of the Munitions Assignment Board. With respect to Russian aid, however, I always felt that their mission was carried out with a zeal which approached fanaticism. Their enthusiasm became so ingrained that it could not be tempered when conditions indicated that a change in policy was desirable. In the early days of the program their attitude was not only understandable but essential. Russia had her back to the wall, and the news indicated that it was problematical if she could remain in the war. It is not necessary to go into the disastrous effect that Russian capitulation would have had on the Allied effort. And it was right that we should give Russia every material and moral support of which we were capable. However, when the tide finally turned at Stalingrad and a Russian offensive started which ended only at Berlin, a new situation was created. We now had a Red Army which was plenty cocky and which became more so with each successive victory. The Soviet leaders became more and more demanding. The fire in our neighbor's house had been extinguished and we had submitted ourselves to his direction in helping to extinguish it. He assumed that we would continue to submit ourselves to his direction in helping rebuild the house, and unfortunately we did. He allowed us to work on the outside and demanded that we furnish the material for the inside, the exact use of which we were not allowed to see. Now that the house is finished, we have at best only a nodding acquaintance.

At the time the original Moscow Protocol was signed, it was decided that a United States Supply Mission would be established in Moscow under the direction of General Faymonville. Faymonville had had instructions from the President that no strings were to be attached to our aid to Russia and that the program was not to be used as a lever to obtain information about and from the Russians. He carried out the President's instructions almost too literally, and it was over this point that a difficult conflict arose between him and the War and Navy Departments, which, through the Moscow Military and Naval Attachés, attempted to get from him important information as to whether effective use was being made of the supplies we were sending at great sacrifice to ourselves—information which Faymonville did not have. This was one of the considerations which prompted Harriman to propose the creation of a Military Mission which would include all Army, Navy, and lend-lease activities.

Major General Sidney P. Spalding was chosen to head the Supply Division of the Military Mission. He had had his earlier training in the Russian aid program as General Burns's principal assistant in Washington. The first two Russian Protocols had been prepared largely under his direction, and he had come to Russia with Harriman in 1942 in connection with lend-lease matters and to make a survey of Persian Gulf ports before we established the Persian Gulf supply line to Russia.

Sid and I lived together for two years and are still the closest friends, which is a true measure of his character, patience, and generosity. We differed somewhat in our attitude toward the Russian aid program. Sid was inclined to explain and condone Russian delinquencies. I never saw him really angry with our Soviet friends. I, on the other hand, felt that greater co-operation would be obtained if we adopted a tougher attitude which would command respect. I was in a high dudgeon much of the time. Fortunately neither of us was extreme in his views, and it is probable that our recommendations to the authorities at home were more sound as the result of having discussed and composed our differences. Averell was inclined to my point of view, and both of us were glad of Sid's restraining influence, which deterred us from going off the deep end.

The Russian administrator of our aid program was the Commissar of Foreign Trade, A. I. Mikoyan. He is an Armenian by birth, and, like all Armenians, prides himself on his ability as a trader. He gave elaborate luncheons for all foreign representatives who visited Moscow, especially those who had even a remote connection with providing supplies for Russia. These visitors would usually pay some tribute to Mikoyan's shrewdness when responding to his toasts. This always delighted Mikoyan's vanity, but the foreigner was usually dismayed during negotiations to find that the playful jest of his toast was in fact stark reality. Unless one was constantly on guard, Mikoyan would take his shirt.

Mikoyan's principal assistants were Vice Commissar A. D. Krutikov and Major General I. F. Semichastnov. In general, Krutikov handled all matters of industrial and civilian supply as well as shipping matters, while Semichastnov devoted his entire attention to the military supply program.

All three men were cordial and pleasant to deal with, the two assistants more so than Mikoyan. I always felt that Mikoyan was too shrewd, and in one respect at least his shrewdness reacted against the interests of the Soviet Union. In the third Protocol there were items of industrial equipment valued at $300,000,000, while in the fourth Protocol such items were more than tripled, totaling over $1,000,-000,000. Production of most of these items would require over two years. If they were completed and delivered in time to be installed in the Soviet Union for production of war supplies prior to the end of the war, they were proper charges against lend-lease. There seemed to be little likelihood that this would be possible, and the United States could not deliver such equipment to the Soviet Union under lend-lease after the war was over. We therefore offered to negotiate an agreement with the Soviet Union by which we would produce the material for delivery after the conclusion of hostilities if the war ended prior to its delivery. Under these circumstances the proposed agreement provided for repayment over a period of twenty-five to thirty years with interest either at 2⅜ per cent or at an interest rate to be changed annually depending on the current cost of financing our national debt. The agreement was delayed for more than a year and not concluded until after the war ended because Mikoyan insisted on an interest rate of 2 per cent. As a result, much of the industrial equipment was not produced. There can be no doubt that Mikoyan's haggling has delayed Russia's postwar industrial program and will not improve Russia's position in the future should she seek long-term credits from the United States.

I realize that statistics are boring but without their help one cannot appreciate the magnitude of our aid to Russia. In the period from October 1, 1941, to May 31, 1945, there were 2,660 ships sent to Russia carrying a total of 16,529,791 tons of supplies. Of this total, 15,234,791 long tons arrived in Russia, the difference being accounted for by the fact that fifty-two of the ships were diverted to the United Kingdom and seventy-seven ships were lost as the result of enemy action.

It is difficult to evaluate the relative importance of the thousands of items which we sent to Russia, but I believe I am safe in saying that truck transportation and combat vehicles stood first. In these categories we delivered 427,284 trucks, 13,303 combat vehicles, 35,170 motorcycles, and 2,328 ordnance service vehicles.

When Sid Spalding, Bill Crist, and I made a trip to the Russian front in July 1944 we encountered American trucks everywhere. They appeared to be the only sort of vehicles used for convoy work. The roads were jammed with transportation of all descriptions, but except for American trucks there did not appear to be enough of any one kind to set up convoys which could be moved as units. They were easily recognized by the blue "U.S." and the American serial number stenciled on the hood of each. The officers and enlisted men were enthusiastic in their praise of our trucks. Almost universally they favored the Studebaker. They seemed as fascinated with the name as with the truck itself. Their eyes lit up every time they mentioned "Studybachers."

Next in importance, I believe, came petroleum products. In the period from October 1941 through May 1945 we delivered 2,670,371 tons to the Soviet Union. This included not only the gasoline to operate the aircraft we sent to Russia and the oil required for all types of American aircraft, vehicles, and locomotives, but also a large amount of blending agents with which Soviet gasoline could be made usable for aviation purposes. Soviet oil production, mostly in Baku, was considerable. However, their refining processes were poor and the ordinary Russian gasoline was little better than American kerosene. We attempted to use the gasoline allowed us under our ration in the vehicles operated by the Military Mission. It would not work in American high-speed motors. The residue of unburned gasoline soon found its way to the crankcase, which would become filled with a sticky mass the consistency of tar. We overcame this by stealing high octane gas from an occasional American plane arriving in Moscow and mixing it with the Russian gasoline.

In the way of foodstuffs, we sent the Soviet Union 4,478,116 tons. This included canned meats, sugar, flour, salt, and some terrible looking greasy white food called fat-back which the Russians loved to spread on black bread. I saw very little American food on sale in Moscow although there was some. From the amount I saw at the front I concluded that most of it went for Army consumption. I have no doubt that the high development of American packaging was responsible for this. It not only insured against food spoilage but also aided in economizing on precious cargo space. Assuming that the Red Army had an average strength of twelve million men, the food sent to Russia was sufficient to supply each man with more than one-half pound of fairly concentrated food per day.

Another important item of supply was railroad equipment. In the three and one-half year period under consideration we delivered 1,900 steam locomotives, 66 Diesel locomotives, 9,920 flat cars, 1,000 dump cars, 120 tank cars, and 35 heavy machinery cars. This was a tremendous contribution to the Russian effort, since the scarcity of truck transportation forced a maximum use of railroads. All the rail equipment had to be constructed to the special Russian railroad gauge, which is about four and one-half inches wider than ours. This necessitated changes in our production lines. The east-west rail net in Western Russia is fairly good and was used to the maximum. The Germans had changed the gauge of the Russian tracks and these had to be widened after the Germans withdrew before they could be used. The Russians became extremely proficient at accomplishing the reconversion. I was in Minsk five days after it had been captured and Russian trains were already coming in there. Local labor supervised by a few engineers was engaged in this work, and while the reconverted trackage was rather crudely laid, it carried the trains at reduced speed until a better job could be done. Hauling American supplies from Siberian ports placed a heavy burden on the railroads. More than half of our lend-lease shipments used the Pacific route, which meant that over seven million tons of supplies had to be hauled by rail over a route which required twelve days for a passenger train to negotiate.

I have mentioned only a small part of the supplies we sent to Russia. For instance, we sent over one billion dollars worth of machinery and industrial equipment; spare parts for all aircraft, surface vehicles, and weapons; millions of dollars worth of medical supplies; and vast quantities of Quartermaster items, such as cloth, underwear, shoes, and bedding. The money value of our supplies and services amounted to about eleven billion dollars. Our supplies may not have won the war, but they must have been comforting to the Russians.

In the early days of the Russian aid program we could be reasonably sure that the urgency of Russia's needs combined with the limited amount of shipping that could be made available for Russian convoys afforded ample assurance that the Soviet Union would neither over-order, order items for which there was not a pressing need, nor order items more appropriate to postwar reconstruction than to the immediate requirements of the war. We were therefore reasonably safe in responding to Russian requests without too much scrutiny of their validity. In addition, their military situation was so critical that there was no time for haggling. After the Russians had broken the German attack the situation changed. Our shipments increased in volume with our victory over the German submarine, the increased tempo of our production program, and the increased availability of ships and escorts. The critical Russian military situation had been alleviated, and it was time to scan Russian requests more closely to see that fulfilling her needs was not too costly to our own operations in Western Europe and the Pacific.

The danger of sending supplies purely on Soviet declarations of need came to my attention forcibly early in 1944 in connection with Diesel engines for installation in small Naval patrol craft which were being constructed in various shipyards in Russia. These were critical items in the construction of landing craft essential to our cross-channel operations and to our amphibious operations in the Pacific. The Russians were encountering difficulty in the installation of the American engines and called on the Military Mission to provide technical advice in the matter. We arranged to send a Naval officer, Lieutenant Commander Edward W. Yorke, Jr., to several of the Soviet shipyards to assist in overcoming the difficulty. When Yorke returned to Moscow he reported that the Russians had one hundred and twenty-six Diesel engines on hand, only three of which had actually been installed. Hulls were ready for the installation of forty-five of the engines, but the remainder were deteriorating from rust in open storage. Despite the fact that the Soviet Naval authorities had engines on hand in sufficient quantity to meet their hull construction for the following year, they had already placed orders in the United States for fifty more. The engines were a small item in themselves, but their scarcity threatened a deficiency in landing craft which might delay Overlord. Here were about seventy-five precious engines rusting away. How many other critical items were being wasted we had no way of knowing, since we were not permitted to observe the use made of American equipment.

Just at the time I learned of the Diesel engine situation, Mikoyan was asking for sizable increases in the aluminum, nickel, copper wire, and alcohol shipments over those called for in the Protocol, in order to meet circumstances unforeseen when the Protocol was drawn. These items were all in short supply in the United States and were critically needed for our own production. Spalding and I were flooded with requests from the War Production Board and the Foreign Economic Administration to ascertain how badly Russia needed the extra supply of the items requested.

When Sid and I received these requests we took each one to either Mikoyan or Krutikov and asked them to provide us with information which could be used to justify their increased demands. On each such occasion a reply would be promised, but the information was never forthcoming. In connection with the nickel and aluminum I finally wrote to Mikoyan, outlining the number of times we had sought information which we could send to Washington to justify their needs and concluded by saying, "Having had no reply nor any information either from you or Mr. Krutikov on the above subject, I am compelled to cable Washington today that we have not received the necessary information, and that we therefore recommend that no further increases in shipments of aluminum and nickel be made to the U.S.S.R."

My letter to Mikoyan brought a prompt response in that I was asked to come to his office to discuss the matter. I was received coldly, and the chilliness even extended to his interpreter, ordinarily a most affable individual. I was always amazed at the speed with which the attitude of the moment would permeate not only within but among the various branches of the Soviet Government. When it was "Kick-Americans-in-the-pants" week even the charwomen would be sour.

Mikoyan and I had a long discussion. I endeavored to impress on him that when an item was in short supply the limited amount available had to be placed where it would do the most good. This could not be done intelligently unless those responsible for making allocations had the necessary information upon which to base their decisions. He argued that it should not be necessary to go behind a request made by the Soviet Government since it was axiomatic that such a request would not be made unless the need was great. He also implied that his Purchasing Commission in Washington would have no trouble obtaining approval of the Russian requests regardless of what action I might take. The hell of it was, when I reflected on the attitude of the President, I was afraid he was right.

The matter seemed to me to be one of extreme importance not only because of the immediate issue but because I felt it was time to revise our soft attitude toward Russia. Accordingly, on January 16, 1944, I sent a telegram to the Chiefs of Staff recommending that they send letters to the Lend-Lease Administration and the Munitions Assignment Board urging that before allocation of items in short supply were made to the Soviet Government, the United States Military Mission in Moscow be required to obtain information and submit recommendations which would indicate the urgency of Soviet need for the items requested.

I received a reply from General Marshall within a few days approving the recommendations I had made and assuring me of his support in the matter in Washington. Unfortunately Harriman, in reply to a telegram he had sent along the same lines to Harry Hopkins, received what amounted to instructions to attach no strings to our aid to Russia. The Russians on this occasion, as Mikoyan had predicted, received the extra supplies they had requested. However, Harriman, Spalding, and I continued to press our point of view on the authorities at home and our persistence was finally rewarded in the spring of 1945 when we put some backbone into our relations with the Soviet Union.

It always seemed to me that Mikoyan and his crowd, despite their shrewdness as negotiators, were extremely stupid in not being more co-operative with American representatives in Moscow. I believe that they were incapable of producing facts and figures that would justify any of their requests, because their administrative machinery was not geared to do so. No doubt they conserved considerable manpower by refusing to maintain the statistical records to which we devoted so much time and energy. Nor was careful accounting as essential to them as it was to us. They had only a single front to supply, whereas we had to assess carefully not only the needs of many fronts, but those of many countries. Rather than admit that he could not support his requests with facts and figures, Mikoyan took the stand that he need not support them at all. In many cases Averell, Sid, and I would have been prepared to support the Soviet wishes had they been based on nothing more than a sob story, but even this was not forthcoming—only the haughty statement that "the Soviet Union requests 50,000 tons of alcohol; therefore she needs it."

Further, Mikoyan lost a great opportunity by failing to make it possible for Spalding and his assistants to travel freely in the Soviet Union. The authorities in Washington craved firsthand information of Russia's requirements. No one would have been more sympathetic than Spalding in evaluating them, but for the most part he was not allowed to do so. In the few instances in which we were permitted to travel, both Spalding and I saw deficiencies and took action which was of great benefit to the Russian program. For example, on our visit to the front we found field commanders clamoring for amphibious vehicles. When I returned to Washington a week later I obtained an immediate shipment of three hundred of our amphibious trucks, otherwise known as Dukws. Several commanders told Sid of their need for gasoline tank trucks, a change in the last of American shoes, and what types of food were in greatest demand. Spalding took corrective action on these and innumerable other items when he returned to Moscow. Again, when we were planning for Soviet participation in the Far East, I knew from firsthand knowledge that the Russians would have great need for transport planes because of the limitations of their rail net. Despite reluctance in Washington to increase the Russian allocation, I was able to get one hundred and fifty additional C-47's assigned to Russia by presenting a strong case to General Marshall and General Kuter when I met them at the Yalta Conference. Harriman, Spalding, and I were continuously studying Russian needs and made many un-solicited and favorable recommendations which were helpful to Russia's and hence to the entire Allied war effort. We could have done so much more had we been allowed to see the picture, but no, we were dreaded foreigners who must be kept under close surveillance in Moscow.

As the war progressed Soviet requests for American aid included more and more items pointed toward postwar requirements. These included industrial machinery, pipe lines, port installations, oil refineries, and other items, the use of which was extremely questionable in the prosecution of the war. The United States attitude was to approve such requests if at all possible under the requirements of the lend-lease law. As a result, we have already been of great assistance to the Soviet Union in her postwar reconstruction and industrialization programs.

One item typical of many others was a tire plant that was lifted bodily from the United States and transferred to Russia and from which not a single tire was produced during the war. The machinery and equipment were taken from the Ford Company's River Rouge Plant near Detroit. The project was to cost six million dollars, and it was expected to produce one million tires per year from Russian natural and synthetic rubber, thus relieving us of the need to deplete our own critically short supply.

Initial procurement of the plant began in November 1942, and a year later all the machinery at the Ford Company had been dismantled and shipped. Of the equipment needed to supplement the Ford plant, 90 per cent had been shipped to Russia by November 1943, and the remainder, including a power plant, was shipped to Russia by November 1944.

The project was abortive from its conception. Twice during the preliminary negotiations the Soviet representatives changed their plans for the building which was to house the plant, each change necessitating a change in plant design. Requests for additional plant equipment continued to flow to the United States until the original cost was raised from six to a new total of ten million dollars.

In February 1944 General Spalding was allowed to visit the plant in Moscow. He was extremely disappointed at the progress that had been made and arranged to have some American engineers come to Moscow from American Companies which had manufactured various parts of the equipment in order to give advice concerning its installation. Accordingly, in May 1944 J. D. Fitzgerald of the International General Electric Company, E. L. O'Connell of the Farrel-Birmingham Company, Paul Prince of the C. Wilkinson Company, and George Hall and George Atkins of the Bristol Company arrived in Moscow.

The American engineers waited for ten days after arriving before they were given authority to visit the plant. When they did report, they found they were faced with great difficulty because of the changes in building design, lack of blueprints and other technical data. Much of the equipment required in the first stages of construction was not present, and no records were available to show what equipment was or was not there. Hundreds of boxes were piled in a storage yard with no attention paid to markings. Such warnings as "This Side Up" or "For Inside Storage Only" were completely ignored. Boxes were broken, equipment damaged, and everything covered with rust and corrosion.

Although the American engineers were there to help get the plant into operation, the Russians would not tell them their plans, refused to consult them or to accept their advice. When our engineers attempted to anticipate difficulties and take preventive measures, they were rebuffed by the Russians, who told them that the work was progressing according to plan and that the Americans need not concern themselves. Finally, all the Americans save one became disgusted with the lack of progress, their own inactivity and frustration, and returned to the United States.

In June 1945, nearly three years after the project was started and after innumerable postponements of the date for completion, the buildings were finished and most of the equipment installed, but none of the utilities, such as water, steam, compressed air, or electricity, were provided for. When the Military Mission was closed in October 1945 the plant had still not gone into production nor was there any prospect of its doing so. Because of changes made by the Russians, the plant will never operate at more than 70 per cent of designed capacity, as opposed to River Rouge operation of 115 per cent.

Whenever I am asked how long it will take the Russians to produce an atomic bomb, I think first of the vast American plants at Oak Ridge and elsewhere and then of the way the Russians set up a tire plant which was already designed, built, and ready for installation; when I hear how long it is before the first tire rolls out of the Moscow plant I shall have some basis for guessing at an answer.

Americans are always interested in knowing whether or not the Russians were grateful for the aid we sent them during the war. That is a difficult question to answer. If any gratitude was felt by Soviet officialdom, it was not allowed to influence official relations with the United States. Soviet officials from Stalin on down seemed to feel that our aid was prompted by expediency and not by friendliness for the Soviet Union. It is certainly true that basically our contributions to Russia were inspired by the conviction that they were essential to winning the war. However, we Americans had some justification for expecting that the sacrifices in lives and shipping, the diversions from our own requirements, and our unquestioning acquiescence to Russian demands would infuse a spirit of co-operation and friendliness into our efforts which could not help but be reciprocated. In this expectation we were wrong. In succumbing to it we put ourselves under a delusion from which we are only now emerging.

As far as the rank and file of the Russian people are concerned, they knew very little about the supplies and equipment we were sending. It is true they saw trucks with American markings and cases of food with labels written in a foreign language said to be English, but that was not apt to inspire them with gratitude to us any more than a can of pâté de foie gras with a French label inspires us with gratitude to France. For many reasons, the requirements of secrecy being the one usually given, the magnitude of our aid to Russia was scarcely mentioned and certainly not widely publicized in the Soviet press. Finally, the term "lend-lease" implied repayment that no one ever visualized but which gave some basis for looking on our assistance as a business deal rather than as a friendly gesture. The next time we supply the world I hope we shall realize that repayment will be impossible and at least capitalize on the good will that might accrue from generosity.

Among the Russian military forces, especially those outside of Moscow who were using American equipment daily, I believe there was a considerable feeling of gratitude to America. Averell Harriman, who, after President Roosevelt, was looked upon as the father of American aid, was received everywhere outside of Moscow with the acclaim which I have already mentioned was accorded him in Stalingrad. When Sid Spalding, Bill Crist, and I visited the Russian front we felt that the cordiality extended to us was inspired at least in part by a few hundred thousand American trucks which had preceded us there. On the whole, I should say that the story of American generosity will someday percolate to the mass of the Russian people. When it does, it will inspire a friendly feeling in their hearts for America and the American people which party propaganda may repress but will never quite destroy.

PART TWO

Soviet-American Collaboration

in the European War

VII. Shuttle Bombing

"FRANTIC" was the code word selected for shuttle bombing involving the use of Russian bases, and it was a masterpiece of understatement. The difficulties which the United States and the Soviet Union encountered in working toward the same end separately were as nothing compared to those we experienced in working together inside Russia.

General Arnold had always recognized the military advantages which would accrue from our use of Russian bases—and I was to try to obtain them. My talking points were that American use of Russian bases would render all Germany vulnerable to attack by our strategic bombers; Germany would be forced to redistribute and thin out her anti-aircraft and fighter defenses; and the tonnage of bombs on Germany would be increased by our ability to carry out missions on days that weather precluded a return to England or Italy but did permit landings in Russia.

Harriman and I were delighted with General Arnold's attitude and went to Russia feeling certain that sheer logic would enable us to carry out his wishes. We were particularly interested because our major objective was ultimate Soviet-American collaboration in the war against Japan. Bombing bases in western Russia would be a proving ground for the vast American air operations which we visualized would later take place in Siberia. Every difficulty that could be overcome in the European operations would mean time saved in hastening the final pay-off in the Japanese war.

I made my first effort to carry out General Arnold's instructions during the Moscow Conference, with results already described. In November 1943 President Roosevelt raised the question again with Marshal Stalin at the Teheran Conference. However, it was not until February 2, 1944—three months later—that Stalin informed Harriman that our proposals had Soviet approval.

I shall never forget our elation the night that Harriman, after his meeting with Stalin, dropped by to give me the good news. Stalin had displayed a keen interest in the details of our proposed operations. He wished to know the number and types of aircraft we intended using, the octane content of the gasoline they consumed, the length of runway they required, and other data which had little to do with the basic decision. Stalin is a master of detail, and I was to learn later that he has an amazing knowledge of such matters as the characteristics of weapons, the structural features of aircraft, and Soviet methods in even minor tactics. When Harriman had answered his questions he said very simply, "We favor your proposal and I shall have our air staff work out the details with General Deane."

Harriman cabled the news to the President and I informed the Chiefs of Staff. Our messages evoked congratulations from home. We were bursting with pride in our accomplishment and full of optimism for the future. Who said the Russians were not co-operative? Who said we couldn't work together? All that was needed was the frank approach, understanding, and persistence, so well exemplified in Averell and me —or at least so we thought.

A few nights later, on February 5, 1944, Harriman and I had a long meeting with Molotov, who was accompanied by Marshal A. A. Novikov and Colonel General A.V. Nikitin. It was my first contact with officers of the Red Air Force and I found them entirely different from other Soviet officials. Whatever the cause, airmen the world over are a people apart who fail to conform to the accepted pattern of their environment. The Russian airmen were not exceptions. From the night I first met them, I found Novikov and Nikitin, as well as the entire air staff, sympathetic to and understanding of our problems and willing to stick their necks out as far as they dared to help solve them.

Novikov was the General Arnold of the Red Air Force. He looked no older than forty. He was short, clean cut, with closely cropped brown curly hair and blue eyes. A born leader and an able administrator, he was beloved by the entire Air Force, and his presence on any part of the front inspired his men to extraordinary efforts. Nikitin was and is my favorite Russian. He is tall, thin, and stooped. He was in charge of air operations and worked at his job at least fifteen hours each day. He was quiet, courteous, and reserved, and had a good sense of humor. It was he who was put in charge of the Russian end of our combined operations, and had he been free of interference our success would have been tenfold.

Molotov opened the meeting with the statement that Stalin had asked him to have Harriman and me meet with Marshal Novikov to discuss the details of shuttle-bombing operations. I then outlined our conception of the way the operations should be conducted. We hoped that facilities would be made available to accommodate three hundred and sixty heavy four-engine bombers of the Fortress or Liberator types, together with one hundred to one hundred and fifty accompanying fighters. We were willing, however, to start the operations with one-third of this strength. We proposed to send five or six missions each month from either England or Italy. The bombers would strike targets in eastern Germany while en route to Russia, conduct a few raids from Russian bases, and another large raid on the return trip to their home bases. We would expect the Russians to provide gasoline and oil from increased lend-lease shipments and also the bombs with which our planes would be armed on sorties from Russian bases. We proposed that as a principle we would keep the American personnel down to the minimum required for key administrators and technical specialists, relying on the Russians to provide the maximum number of mechanics, housekeepers, and other personnel who did not have to have specialized training. In the hope of making our proposals more attractive, I offered to have our bombers attack strategic targets on the Russian front, such as rail centers or large supply installations, on Soviet request.

Novikov at once produced a map and discussed the various bases which might be made available. To be of value, the bases had to be in areas which the Germans had once occupied. All the airdrome facilities had been completely destroyed by the Germans prior to their retirement, and the Russians had reconstructed only those required by their own Air Force. Even these were too small for our large bombers since the Russians had no aircraft of that type and therefore had not provided accommodations for any. Also, the runways were too short and would have to be reconstructed or lengthened. Novikov advised against selecting any of the sites available in the north because the spring thaws would make it impossible to complete the necessary work in time for use in 1944. He thought the best area would be in the Ukraine just east of Kiev, as the ground there could be expected to dry out in April. He said it was possible to land without runways in this area throughout the summer. Novikov agreed to the proposition of minimizing American personnel and of providing Soviet personnel in any required numbers. In this connection he emphasized that the Soviet authorities believed that defense of the bases should be Russia's responsibility and that they would undertake to arrange for it. Our acquiescence to this was inspired to some extent by a desire "to get along" and to avoid spoiling our budding intimacy. It was a decision we were later to regret.

There followed a period of four months which was the busiest of my stay in Russia. A staff of eleven or twelve young, virile, and vigorous airmen arrived from General Spaatz's headquarters. They had been used to dealing with the British, who were at least approachable. They had been sent to Russia to do a job and couldn't comprehend the delays and frustrations that beset them on every side. They could not get to the Russians to let off steam—but they could get to me. Much of my time was spent in smoothing their feathers. Then, too, General Arnold was not one noted for patience. After his first congratulatory message I received a succession of others in the peculiar jargon affected by our Air Forces, such as, "not understood it is why our operations are to be postponed until May." Meanwhile, in this first real operational venture with the Russians, I was to learn how different from ours are their methods of doing business.

In the first place, centralization of authority is basic in Russia. Nikitin had been placed in charge, so all arrangements had to be made through him. He was an extremely busy man and our project was only one of his many headaches. There was no such thing as our ordnance man meeting with theirs and coming to some decision about using Russian bombs. They might meet but the decision would have to wait for a meeting between Nikitin and me.

Next, the Russians were understaffed almost to the same degree that we were overstaffed. One seldom sees or hears typewriters in Russian offices, and, while they may well be thankful, I doubt if they know the mimeograph has been invented. Records and filing systems are almost nonexistent, and executives must therefore rely on their memories for a mass of detail.

Finally, Russian pride prevents any admission of incapacity or inability. In many cases, where they could not meet our desires they would give any fantastic reason for their refusal that occurred to them except the true one, whereas generally the true reason was perfectly obvious and often reasonable and understandable.

We would have staff meetings with Nikitin and his assistants in which perhaps ten or fifteen questions would come up for decision. Nikitin was quite frank in telling us his views but would always indicate that he would have to refer the questions to his superiors before giving a definite reply. Despite anything we might do, another meeting would not be held until the Russians had reached decisions on all the questions raised at the preceding meeting. During the interim a great many new questions would arise and required immediate answers. It was impossible to pick up a telephone and call the appropriate member of the Russian air staff to ask such questions. I had to wait for the uncertain date of my next meeting with Nikitin. It did

not help General Arnold's blood pressure when he had to wait a week
or two for an answer that should have required but five minutes.

Another lesson I was to learn during this period was that Stalin's
approval of a basic decision does not carry approval for the supporting decisions that are necessary to make it effective. In connection
with the shuttle-bombing project I doubt that Stalin and his advisers
realized at the outset how many timeworn party concepts would have
to be violated before our bombers could really operate from Russian
soil.

Hitherto, foreigners entering the Soviet Union had been thoroughly investigated before being granted entrance visas. After arrival in
Russia they were kept under close surveillance. Now American soldiers were to arrive by the hundreds—not only those who were to be
permanently located at the bases but also those who would swarm in
on our aircraft with each combat mission. It would be difficult to
account for all of them, and there was the dread possibility that capitalistic America would use this means to plant agents in the Soviet Union.
I could not understand this fear on the part of the Foreign Office or
the N.K.V.D., because I would much prefer to risk my chance of
survival on a landing in an African jungle than on a landing in the
Soviet Union when not properly documented. Nevertheless, the question of visas was to be the most troublesome of all.

By the end of March we had worked out a scheme whereby all
Americans who were to be permanently stationed at the Russian bases
would enter the Soviet Union on group visas. When such personnel
arrived in Teheran, General Connolly, our commanding general there,
would present to the Soviet Embassy in Teheran a list of the American crewmen and passengers on each airplane or train which was to
enter the Soviet Union. These lists were to be stamped "approved" by
the Soviet Ambassador and would then constitute group visas. I was
to present duplicates of the lists to the Foreign Office in Moscow.
Upon arrival in the Soviet Union each man would be given an identification card for which he would have to provide two photographs.
The combat crews on each mission were to be listed by airplane, and

these lists were to be checked by the Soviet authorities upon arrival and departure of the aircraft.

The plan seemed all right in theory although a bit complicated as between allies fighting a common enemy. In practice it broke down everywhere. First, there was a long period of delay for our personnel in Teheran because the Soviet Ambassador had not received instructions. It then developed that he would not stamp "approved" on the visa lists until he had had individual approval from Moscow for each list. This meant that our men were further delayed in Persia—the passenger list of each aircraft was cabled to me, I sent it to the Foreign Office, and then the Foreign Office cabled approval to Teheran. By the time this round had been completed it would often be desirable to change the passenger listings for one reason or another, and the process would be repeated. There was also a constant necessity for certain key individuals to return either to Teheran or to England in connection with some administrative aspect of the project. This created great consternation as there was no provision for granting individual exit visas to persons who had entered on group visas. When such individuals had accomplished their tasks outside of the Soviet Union, they would re-enter on another group visa and thus be counted twice in the total of twelve hundred Americans agreed upon as the permanent garrison. These difficulties were eventually ironed out, but not until after Max Hamilton, our Minister Counselor, and I had reduced our life expectancy by at least five years. Eventually the permanent American contingent numbered about thirteen hundred.

Another essential to the success of shuttle bombing which horrified the Russians was American control of communications. This called for another high level decision. Without control of communications we simply could not operate. We had to be able to send last-minute weather reports to England and Italy, have radio direction-finding equipment to guide our combat missions to the Russian bases, send operational and administrative messages to General Spaatz and General Eaker, and have interbase communications within Russia. The lives of hundreds of Americans might depend on effective communications, and because of language and procedural differences they could not be operated and controlled by the Russians.

General Nikitin and the Russian communications experts recognized at once that we would have to control our own communications. The Foreign Office was more difficult to convince. In the end we compromised by agreeing to allow Soviet representatives to be present at all of our communications offices and have access to all messages sent or received. In practice we were able to operate our communications without any apparent Soviet surveillance since the military men with whom we were working did not share Moscow's apprehensions regarding our intentions.

It was also necessary to break down Soviet resistance to having foreign aircraft fly over Soviet territory. This again called for a top level decision. We first obtained permission for thirty American aircraft to fly about three hundred and fifty American specialists to our Russian bases, but the Russians insisted on bringing the supplies we needed in their own planes. Later they agreed to allow two American supply planes a week to make the trip from Teheran to our bases and return.

Within a few days after we had been given the green light on our venture, Brigadier General Alfred A. Kessler, who was to command our forces, and the principal members of his staff were on their way to Moscow. Meanwhile, the Russians had selected Major General A. R. Perminov to command the Russian forces who were to be at our bases. Kessler and Perminov took an immediate liking to each other and proved to be a good team.

After several reconnaissance trips to the Ukraine, the airdromes at Poltava, Mirgorod, and Pyryatin were selected as our bases. These three cities are spaced at intervals of about fifty miles northeast of Kiev on the Kharkov-Kiev railroad. All three had suffered from the scorched-earth policy adopted by the Russians as well as the Germans, and all had been under German occupation for more than a year. There were no hangars, control towers, or other airdrome facilities. Each had a short runway of about one thousand meters constructed of hexagonal concrete blocks about a yard in diameter and six to eight inches thick. The runways were not only too short, but it was doubtful that they could sustain the weight of our heavy bombers. It was therefore decided to lay new runways six thousand feet in length, using the steel mat being sent from England as the surface.

After completing as many of the preliminary arrangements as could be made in Moscow, Kessler and about eleven staff officers moved to his headquarters at Poltava on April 15, 1944. Perminov had preceded him by a few days, and with the arrival of Kessler's group the Americans and Russians joined for the first time in history in undertaking a military operation against a common enemy. They lived with each other under the same conditions, ate the same food, worked at the same tasks, and wooed the same girls—at least they did in the beginning. Their intimacy was subject to the same pitfalls and adjustments which confront two families who decide on joint occupancy of a single house. Certain understandings which should have been reached at once were delayed because of the fear of wounding each other's sensibilities. Initially both sides vied in making concessions to each other, soon little pinpricks, constantly repeated, festered into sores, finally both sides were ready to kill each other and would have if readjustments had not been made with the utmost candor.

I visited Kessler twice during the period our bases were being made ready for operations. My first visit was made about a week after Kessler and his small staff had arrived in Poltava. Little had been accomplished during the short time that Kessler had been there, but he and Perminov had worked out complete plans for the progress of the work that would be done once the American equipment and personnel started to arrive. They went over their plans with me and appeared to have the situation well in hand.

My next visit to the bases was made about three weeks later, in the middle of May, when Major General Fred Anderson, General Spaatz's Deputy, came to Russia to observe the progress of our work. It was amazing what had been accomplished in that short period of time.

Most of our personnel had arrived and the last trains loaded with our supplies were just coming in. The airfields were swarming with Russian women laying down the steel mat that was to make up the runways. They had acquired a rhythm in the process and the work progressed with such speed that the mile-long steel carpet seemed to unfold and approach completion as one watched them. It was apparent that there would be no delays on this score.

The Russian soldiers went into raptures as each piece of American equipment was unloaded from the trains. They could not understand how Americans could be selected at random and told to drive the huge gasoline trucks, shop trucks, or other motor transportation. With the Russians, driving is a specialty that many aspire to but which few have attained. One Russian soldier was put in charge of a wreckage disposal truck. He remained with it day and night and kept it immaculate with cleaning and polishing. Clearly he was the envy of all his comrades, whom he treated thereafter with lofty disdain.

One of the greatest obstacles to be overcome was the language difference. The American and Russian soldiers soon developed a combined vocabulary sufficient to meet their ordinary needs. But the differences of language and customs developed some amusing incidents. The Russians were all eager to learn English and grasped at every opportunity to do so. For instance, there was the Russian sentry who, as the result of G.I. coaching, proudly said "Good morning, you filthy so and so" to each American officer entering headquarters. Then there was the girl in the cafeteria who, when dispensing the meat course, pointed to it and said to each successive patron, "The g. d. so and so K rations again," as the result of having heard one of the early comers make the remark. One Russian entertainment was almost broken up when the G.I.'s resorted to whistling to show their appreciation of a female muscle dancer. In Russia whistling is a sign of disapproval, and the actress left the stage in a huff. The situation was hastily explained to General Perminov, who convinced the girl that her efforts were being highly appreciated. She returned at once and shook more muscles than the G.I.'s knew she had. She was thereupon rewarded with a shrill crescendo of whistles that threw her into ecstasies.

Toward the end of May 1944 the bases were completed and operations were about to start. We thought we had overcome all the difficulties, but two more had to be met. The first concerned the selection of targets and the second was in relation to American and British news correspondents.

On May 27 General Spaatz informed me that he was considering as targets for the first shuttle-bombing mission the principal airfields in the area of Galatz, Rumania, the aircraft manufacture and repair center at Mielic, Poland, and a German aircraft factory at Riga, Latvia. He proposed as first choice the Galatz target but asked me to obtain Russian approval or their suggestions as to suitable targets. Spaatz indicated that he would have to have my reply by May 29 if the mission was to be undertaken on the selected date, June 1.

The Russian Air Staff would have nothing to do with the subject of target selection but informed me that I would have to obtain clearance from the Red Army General Staff. I could see no real reason why any Russian approval was required. However, General Spaatz was asking for it as a matter of courtesy and there was no time for me to argue the matter in an exchange of messages. I approached General Slavin of the General Staff and presented General Spaatz's proposed targets. After a delay of two days Slavin informed me that none were approved. I informed Spaatz of this on May 29 and recommended that he select other objectives and simply inform the Russians of his choice without asking concurrence. He did this, and I believe it was precisely the action that the Soviet General Staff hoped he would take. Slavin would not give me any reason for the disapproval of General Spaatz's original choices, but I suspect it stemmed from the General Staff's desire to deny us any inkling of what the Russians' objectives were to be in the new Red Army offensive about to be launched. The three targets originally selected by Spaatz were distributed at equal distances across the Russian front. The Russian attack when finally launched had its main effort in the north, and for this reason they did not want an American attack on Riga which would attract German fighter aircraft to that area. They could not tell us this without revealing the plans for their offensive. Nor could they approve targets on their central or southern fronts without risking the chance that we would deduce their offensive was to be in the north. They therefore disapproved of all Spaatz's suggestions and were delighted when he selected a target without reference to them.

With regard to the correspondents, I was particularly anxious that they have the advantage of being present to see the first American mission arrive on Russian bases and that they be the ones to break the story to the world under a Moscow dateline. I had taken them into my confidence and they had agreed to avoid any conjecture stories based on the influx of American personnel. Nikitin undertook to obtain permission from the Foreign Office for the British and American correspondents to get to the bases a few days before the first operations. The Foreign Office had given its approval, but when the time arrived only five of some thirty correspondents were told that they could go. The decision that most of the newsmen would be unable to make the trip was not given out by the Foreign Office until about ten o'clock on the morning of June 1, the day they were supposed to leave. Within a few minutes Bill Lawrence of the *New York Times* had me on the telephone. His voice choked with indignation. I immediately called the Chief Censor and protested the Foreign Office decision. After a frantic time spent on the telephone calling Foreign Office officials and answering calls from disappointed correspondents, I succeeded in having the quota raised to ten Americans and ten British correspondents. This was still unsatisfactory, so the British and American Newspaper Guild staged the first labor strike in Soviet Russia and all refused to go. Their action was effective, and at noon all of them were put aboard a Soviet plane and sent to Poltava.

The morning of June 2, 1944, was dark and overcast in the Ukraine. Except for doubtful weather the stage was set. Spaatz had sent word the day before that Debrecin, in Hungary, was to be the initial target. The Russians' anti-aircraft defenses had been informed of the route our bombers would follow from the target to the Russian bases. Everyone was at his post. Radio men were listening for a flash that the mission had left Italy. The hospital was prepared to handle the injured. Wreckage disposal trucks were ready to move battle-damaged aircraft from the runways. Correspondents were everywhere, getting local color to fill out their stories. There was an atmosphere of suppressed excitement—everyone pretending an outward calm to cover the anxiety seething within.

Averell and Kathy Harriman, Major General Robert L. Walsh, who had just arrived to take command of all U.S. Army Air Forces activities in Russia, and I had come to Poltava from Moscow the night before. General Slavin was on hand representing the Red Army General Staff. Nikitin was heartbroken that he could not come to Poltava to see the fruits of his labors. However, he had sent Lieutenant General Grendal and some of his other general officers to represent him. I think that morning was more difficult for the Moscow contingent than it was for those stationed at the bases. They had their jobs on which to concentrate and were busy making last minute preparations; all we could do was wait and fret. The planes were due at Poltava at one o'clock. At noon we had not heard whether they had taken off from Italy.

At half-past twelve we had a flash that the mission was on and had departed from Italy on time! We rushed to the airdrome, where our small group of jeeps and weapons carriers formed in a cluster about one hundred yards from the runway. We dismounted. All eyes were strained to the west.

Within a few minutes the drone of airplanes could be heard, and at precisely one o'clock the first three Fortresses, flying in a V-shaped wedge, came into sight through the overcast. They were followed by seventy more, flying in perfect formation. They circled the field at an elevation of about a thousand feet. The sky was filled with them, and huge as they were, they seemed much bigger with their silver wings silhouetted against the black sky above. For an American standing on the field below it was a thrill beyond description. There in the sky was America at war—these few planes epitomized American power, the skill of American industry and labor, the efficiency of American operations, and the courage of American youth. The scene was the same at Mirgorod and Pyryatin.

The planes dropped out of formation one at a time and landed at one-minute intervals on the steel-covered runway. This was a tense moment for the Russian women who had laid the steel mat. Would it buckle? Had they been careless? Their relief was audible as the first Fortress rolled down its entire length.

We all rushed to the parking area assigned to the leading plane. When it came to a stop the first person to emerge was Lieutenant General Ira C. Eaker. His first act was to decorate General Perminov with the Legion of Merit and a citation expressing the gratitude of the United States for the part Perminov had played in preparing the bases for American use. Perminov responded, giving all credit to Kessler. Color was added to the scene when Kathy Harriman was presented with huge bunches of roses by Perminov and his staff. Movies were taken of this and of my making a speech over a microphone in which I hurled defiance at Hitler which never got further than the disk on which it was recorded some fifteen feet away. It was a festive occasion marred only by the sudden appearance of General Slavin. In the excitement of getting to the airdrome no one had thought to waken Slavin from a nap he was taking. He had been roused from his slumber by the roar of seventy Fortresses passing overhead and, finding himself alone, had run to the field to extend greetings from the great General Staff to Eaker and his men. Unfortunately the field was guarded at its outer edges by American soldiers who had orders not to allow spectators beyond a certain line. The red trimmings of the General Staff inspired none of the fear in our sentries' hearts that it did in those of Red Army soldiers, and Slavin had to view the welcoming ceremonies with the rabble and from afar. When he finally succeeded in breaking through, he attacked Perminov with such heat that I thought he would have apoplexy. I could see that Perminov was worried by the unintentional slight to the Red Army General Staff.

I spent the rest of the day trying to shoulder the blame and pacifying Slavin. That sort of thing is impossible to laugh off in class-conscious Russia.

The day our first landings were made marked the high tide of our military relations with the Soviet Union. The mission had been highly successful and had completely destroyed the German airdrome with all its aircraft, hangars, and shops at Debrecin. Other German targets were successfully attacked in the succeeding days by our operations from the Russian bases. Another target was attacked when our planes returned to Italy. General Eaker had made a great impression on the Russian air leaders by his quiet efficiency, gracious manners, and his evident desire to do everything possible to assist the advance of the Red Army. Averell and Kathy gave a huge party for the Red Army officers who had participated in the shuttle-bombing project, at which Eaker awarded the highest decorations to Novikov and Nikitin. We were sure that the accord thus attained would spread to other fields of military collaboration, but then reaction started to set in.

The first stunning blow was a highly organized German raid on the Poltava base on the night of June 21-22, 1944. A mission arriving from England on the afternoon of June 21 had been followed to the Russian bases by a German reconnaissance plane. At midnight that night one German plane dropped a flare which landed in the exact center of the Poltava airfield, illuminating the whole base area with the brilliance of daylight. An attack lasting for two hours followed immediately. It started with anti-personnel bombs which were dropped by the thousand. They fluttered lightly to the ground and completely covered the airfield. On striking the ground they were armed to go off at the slightest touch, making it almost suicidal for anyone to go on the field. These were followed by incendiary bombs that set fire to fifty of our Flying Fortresses, completely destroying them. There were a few high explosive bombs, one of which killed two American soldiers who were running to get to the cover of trenches which the Russians had provided for just such an emergency. Perminov refused to allow any American soldiers to go onto the field to fight the fires.

Russian soldiers did attempt to extinguish them, and thirty men were killed by the anti-personnel bombs.

The Russian anti-aircraft and fighter defenses failed miserably. Their anti-aircraft batteries fired twenty-eight thousand rounds of medium and heavy shells, assisted by searchlights, without bringing down a single German plane. There were supposed to be forty Yaks on hand as night fighters, but only four or five of them got off the ground. Both their anti-aircraft and night fighters lacked the radar devices which made ours so effective.

Actually the German raid was one of those well-planned concentrations of effort that are almost bound to succeed despite anything the defense can do. There were no recriminations on either side. On the contrary, every effort was made to capitalize on the misfortune by drawing closer together and redoubling our efforts. Nevertheless, the disaster sowed the seed of discontent, the Russians smarting and sensitive because of their failure to provide the protection they had promised, and the Americans forgiving but determined to send their own anti-aircraft defenses as protection for the future.

Meanwhile, we had invaded France and the Russian lines had moved far to the west. The bases in the Ukraine soon were too far to the east to justify the long flights over friendly Soviet territory and we started negotiations with a view to moving them farther west. These negotiations failed completely. I have always felt that we were at least partially responsible for their failure. We wanted much more elaborate installations at the new bases than we had had in the Ukraine. We wished them to include all of the necessary defenses, which meant increased shipment of supplies and personnel. Our chief trouble was in deciding exactly what we did want, and we submitted three rather widely different proposals to the Russians. Before the Russians could act on one they would receive another. Approaching winter weather combined with Russian procrastination finally forced abandonment of a move. It was then agreed that Poltava would be retained over the winter months and that shuttle bombing would be resumed in the spring of 1945 if conditions justified. When spring arrived, the end of the war was in sight and Hitler's domain had so contracted as the result of British and American advances from the west and Russian advances from the east as to make shuttle bombing unnecessary.

Poltava continued to be used to salvage American aircraft which had been forced to land behind the Russian lines and to care for American airmen injured in forced landings.

The conclusion of active operations started a sharp decline in the relations between the Russian and American soldiers remaining at the Poltava base. This was aggravated to a considerable degree by deterioration of the political relations between the United States and the Soviet Union, particularly in the differences which arose between them with regard to Poland. When the Polish dispute occurred, Soviet displeasure was reflected in all branches of government and many restrictions were placed on American activities in Poltava. Our aircraft were unnecessarily grounded, rescue crews were refused permission to service American planes known to have force-landed in Poland, seriously injured American airmen were not allowed to be moved from Poltava to our general hospital at Teheran and Russian women were not allowed to associate with American men. Russian airmen, who were undoubtedly simply carrying out instructions from Moscow in applying restrictions, incurred the resentment of the American soldiers. Morale and friendliness waned rapidly. Russians began to loot American warehouses.

In fairness it must be said that the situation was not improved by the irresponsible acts of a few Americans. For example, one crew attempted to smuggle a discontented Polish citizen out of Poland by disguising him in American uniform. This was used as evidence that our Air Forces were carrying on subversive activities against the Red Army. A discontented Russian sergeant major was taken to Italy as a stowaway on an American plane which we had salvaged in Poland. He was returned at once, but the incident was held against us. There were two cases of American reckless driving in Poltava, each of which resulted in the death of a Russian woman.

The truth was that the presence of Americans in the Soviet Union, and particularly the Ukraine, which is an area of questionable loyalty, was no longer desired. The true attitude of the Communist Party leaders toward foreigners could no longer be concealed, especially since there was no operational necessity for their presence. The Russians were no more relieved than I was when it was decided in April 1945 to remove the last American soldier from the Ukraine.

In retrospect I feel that our shuttle-bombing venture was of immeasurable value to the United States. As a military operation it made possible eighteen strong attacks on important strategic targets in Germany which would otherwise have been immune. More important than that, it must have had a shattering effect on the morale of the Germans. They knew better than anyone of the Soviet leaders' antipathy to foreigners. To see Russia let down the bars and permit American operations on her soil must have destroyed the last hope the Germans may have had of dividing her enemies and concluding a separate peace with one or another.

As far as our future relations with Russia are concerned, I feel that the shuttle-bombing venture will be of value in pointing to the vast difference in the attitude toward Americans that exists between the rank and file of the Russian people and their leaders. Starting with Novikov, Nikitin, the entire air staff, and extending down to the women who laid the steel mat for our runways, we encountered nothing but a spirit of friendliness and co-operation. We lived, planned, worked, and played together—the only discordant notes being those struck from above which perforce reverberated below. Starting in the other direction and working on up through the General Staff, the N.K.V.D., the Foreign Office, and the party leaders who lurk behind the scenes as Stalin's closest advisers, we found nothing but a desire to sabotage the venture which they had reluctantly approved. Everything was made difficult, including approval of visas, control of communications, selection of targets, and clearances for landings and departures, and in the end we were literally forced out of Russia by restrictions which had become unbearable. The attitude of the people may be changed by one-sided propaganda emanating from above—the attitude of the present leaders never has changed and probably never will.

VIII. Co-ordination
of European Air Operations

WHEN two great Air Forces such as the British and Americans had in the west and the Russians had in the east are bent on destruction of a common enemy that lies between them, there is always a chance that they will have head-on collisions and destroy each other or at least destroy any good will that may have existed between them. Unless an effective system of co-ordination is established, clashes are unavoidable because of the difficulty of identifying friend from enemy in fast moving air situations. More important than avoiding clashes are the operational advantages which accrue from the co-ordinated action of friendly Air Forces. But what constitutes an effective system of co-ordination? It was on this question that we differed violently with our Russian friends.

Fortunately the Russians had only a tactical Air Force, which meant that its operations were confined to supporting the advance of the Red Army. Russian planes were therefore seldom found more than one hundred miles in advance of their ground forces. I shudder to think of what might have happened had the Russians had a strategic air force which penetrated to all parts of Germany as ours did.

Early in the war co-ordination was unnecessary. The British were immune from clashing with the Russians because their bombing operations were carried on at night when Russian planes were on the ground. The Americans were also safe so long as the Russian front was beyond the range of our heavy bombers. As the war progressed, however, it became evident that this would soon cease to be the case, and I was directed to establish a method of co-ordination with the Russians.

The American concept was simple. We wanted an exchange of liaison officers between American and Russian field headquarters. We proposed that the Red Air Force send a few officers and enlisted men to General Spaatz's headquarters in England and a similar group to General Eaker's headquarters in Italy, as these two commanders had complete control of American operations that might interfere with the Russians. In exchange, we would send small groups to the Russian headquarters that had direct control of the operations of the Red Air Force, presumably the headquarters of the various front commanders. We were ready to establish teletypewriter communications between all the headquarters involved. The plan would work this way: assume that General Spaatz decided to attack an installation in Warsaw which was, say, forty miles in front of Marshal Zhukov's lines. Spaatz would radio his intentions to his liaison officer at Zhukov's headquarters, who would inform the Marshal of our intentions. If, then, Zhukov had already planned to have the Red Air Force attack some German target near Warsaw on the same day, he could either have informed Spaatz that his plan was disapproved or he could have adjusted the timing so that both the Russian and American attacks could have been made. Our system was the normal one used in insuring liaison between military commanders.

The Red Army General Staff would have none of our plan. They desired that all liaison and co-ordination be effected in Moscow. The reason given was that the strategic operations of the Red Air Force were controlled by the General Staff in Moscow and hence must be co-ordinated there. Like most reasons given by the Russians when refusing to meet foreign requests, this one was absurd. The Russians had no strategic air force with which to conduct strategic operations.

Using the same example as before, the inefficiency of the Soviet plan is at once apparent. Under their system, Spaatz would have informed me of his desire to attack Warsaw. I would then have had to call General Estigneev, whose job was to keep me out of the

128 The Strange Alliance

Russians' hair, and arrange an appointment with General Slavin. Slavin would have had no authority to approve Spaatz's plan but would have had to consult the Deputy Chief of Staff, General Antonov. Antonov would have had to send a message to Marshal Zhukov to see if Spaatz's proposal interfered with his plans. Zhukov would then have replied to Antonov, Antonov to Slavin, Slavin to me, and I to Spaatz. It would have worked—except for the two small items of time and weather. The time lag alone might have caused Spaatz either to give up in disgust or to risk making the attack without Soviet concurrence. Even more likely, the time lag would have seen a change of weather which would have made the attack impossible. Of course the Russian system was not acceptable to us.

The situation became acute early in April 1944 when the Red Army was driving through the Carpathians into Rumania. At the same time our Strategic Air Forces were attacking the Rumanian oil fields and refineries, then Germany's principal source of petroleum products. The American Chiefs of Staff could see trouble brewing and sent me a message stating that the rapid advance of the Russian forces into Rumania, together with the developing situation in the Crimea, suggested the possibility that there might be some unfortunate contacts between the U.S. Strategic Air Forces and Russian Air Forces. Recognizing the primary interest of the Russians in all that pertained to the conduct of the campaign in Rumania, the U.S. Chief of Staff directed me to inquire of the appropriate Russian officials if they desired to impose any restrictions on the operations of American Air Forces in this area.

On the same day I received a radio from General Arnold in which he directed me to congratulate Marshal Vasilievsky on the Red Army advance and to inform him that the 15th Air Force had been directed to assist the Red Army whenever weather conditions made it impossible to carry out its primary mission of participating in the combined bomber offensive against Germany. I was also to inform Vasilievsky that to assist the Red Army the 15th Air Force was attacking the Bucharest, Ploesti, Budapest, and Sofia railroad yards. I was to inquire if there were any other targets Vasilievsky wanted struck. Vasilievsky was not in Moscow, so I sent both messages to the Deputy Chief of Staff, General Antonov. I failed to receive replies to either.

It was only after considerable pressure on my part that I received a reluctant admission that the Russians had "no objections" to our Air Forces continuing their attacks on the railroad yards. There were no requests for additional assistance despite the fact that Russian reconnaissance must have revealed an untold number of lucrative targets. Throughout the war the Russians, except in a very few instances, not only refrained from asking for, but frequently refused to accept, assistance from our Air Forces. Their attitude clearly revealed their regard for us as an ally. We should fight the same enemy but each in our own way. When victory came there could then be no false claims concerning the part the Americans had played in defeating the Germans on the Russian front.

A week or so after I had delivered the messages from the Joint Chiefs of Staff and General Arnold to General Antonov and while I was still waiting for a reply, General Sir Henry Maitland Wilson, who commanded the British and American forces in the Mediterranean Theater, became alarmed at the situation. He asked the Combined Chiefs of Staff to negotiate an agreement with the Russians whereby he would be allowed to send liaison officers to the headquarters of the Southern Group of Russian Armies to effect co-ordination between his air forces and theirs. But our proposal met the same adamant insistence that air activities in the Balkans would have to be co-ordinated in Moscow.

Finally, in desperation, I suggested that we establish a bomb line restricting British and American operations to the west and Russian operations to the east. This proposal was accepted by Antonov, and a line through Constanţa, Bucharest, Ploesti, and Budapest was agreed upon. It was understood that neither side was to cross the line without prior concurrence from the other. It was also agreed that the line was

an interim measure pending further consideration of the whole problem and that it could be adjusted from time to time as the military
situation changed.

In connection with this first effort to establish co-ordination between our Air Forces an incident occurred that was revealing of
Russian suspicion of foreigners and which was the result of my own
stupidity. I had the bright idea that it would be demoralizing to the
Germans to know that we were now to co-ordinate our air operations
with those of the Russians. I proposed that we prepare a brief press
release concerning the accord that had been reached. The Soviet General Staff and the Foreign Office both agreed that the idea had merit
and suggested that I submit a short statement for their approval.
I started out by saying, "Now that the Red Army has penetrated the
borders of Poland and Rumania the time has come when the operations of the Red Air Force must be co-ordinated with those of the
Western Allies." I went on to say what had been done, painting the
agreement in much more glowing terms than I felt it deserved. At
that time the Red Army had passed the recognized prewar boundary
of Poland but was only just then approaching the so-called Curzon
line, which Stalin maintained was rightfully the eastern Polish border.
There I was in the middle of the most violent political dispute. The
Russians wanted to change the statement to read "Now that the Red
Army is approaching the eastern borders of Poland and has entered
Rumania. . . ." Since the point had been raised, I could not agree to
the change without infuriating the London Poles and the British and
Americans who were supporting them. I was accused by the Russians
of trying to use an innocuous press release to trick them into admitting the validity of the territorial claims of the London Poles. After
much self-abnegation and a great display of unfelt contrition, I induced them to approve the press release without reference to the Red
Army's location in or out of Poland. However, I doubt if I succeeded
in even partially dispelling Russian suspicion of my motives.

Our fears about the efficacy of a bomb line as a means of co-ordination were soon confirmed. Time and again a German troop or trans-

portation concentration known to exist somewhere east of the line
would offer an attractive target for our Mediterranean Air Forces.
But by the time we had gone through the cumbersome procedure of
obtaining Moscow's approval of an American attack, the Germans
would have disappeared. The Russians must have realized that the
bomb line gave the Germans considerable immunity, because on June
10, 1944, they agreed to abolish it. At the same time we agreed to try
to effect liaison in Moscow. General Eaker sent one of his ablest staff
officers, Colonel Samuel J. Gormley, to Moscow to represent him,
and I succeeded in getting the Russians to promise that they would
have a General Staff representative meet with Gormley daily and
adjust air operations so as to make the best use of our combined air
power and to avoid clashes between our Air Forces. We struggled
along with this procedure until November 1944. It was never quite
satisfactory. General Eaker was extremely reluctant to keep Gormley
informed of his plans because of the danger to our aviators if the
Germans succeeded in breaking our radio codes. He therefore sent
only periodic messages when he thought there was real danger of his
operations conflicting with those of the Russians. Thus there were
many days on which Gormley had nothing to discuss, so the practice
of holding daily meetings was soon abandoned. After that, when a
truly important situation was about to develop, considerable time was
lost before Gormley was able to re-establish his contact. Nevertheless,
the Russians were informed in advance of American operations which
might interfere with theirs even though there was frequently not
sufficient time for them to do much about it.

The clash we had always feared occurred on November 7, 1944.
The Red Army had swept across Rumania to the Yugoslav border
and had turned north in the direction of Vienna. The Yugoslav partisans under Tito had been considerably strengthened by supplies
from both the Western Allies and Russia. The Germans, caught between the Red Army and the Yugoslavs, were hurriedly moving
north in an effort to withdraw from the Balkans. The entire road net
in eastern Yugoslavia, all the way from Greece to the Austro-Hun-

garian border, swarmed with German troops and transports. If they were allowed to escape, they would appear on either the eastern or western fronts of Germany to fight another day. They presented perfect targets, especially to the light bombers and long-range fighters of the 15th Air Force operating from Italy. However, the targets were dangerously close to the west flank of the almost static Red Army in Yugoslavia, then engaged only in covering the Russians' movement to the north.

The 15th Air Force attacked the retreating Germans every day. As part of the program of November 7, one squadron of about thirty Lightnings was given the mission of strafing German columns on the road from Novi Pazar to a little town named Kaska about fifteen miles to the northeast. At Kaska they were to turn southeast, strafe the road to Mitrovica, a distance of about thirty-five miles, and return to Italy. The pilots were given maps, and the terrain features surrounding their target were carefully noted. Unfortunately about sixty miles, or fifteen minutes' flight, farther to the east there was another set of terrain features almost identical with those of the area in which our squadron was to attack. There, too, a road ran northeast from one village to another—in this case from Kruševac to the little village of Cicevac—where it joined with another running southeast to a town called Niš. The distances between the villages were the same, the size of the villages were the same, and in both cases the road running southeast paralleled small rivers of the same size. The similarity of the two areas was an almost unbelievable freak of nature, and on the map they appeared to be identical.

Long before our squadron commander reached the area of his objective he had come under heavy anti-aircraft fire which caused him to change his course. His planes were traveling at about two hundred and fifty miles an hour and were at treetop height so as to gain the element of surprise against the Germans. Under these conditions it is not surprising that the squadron leader passed the area he was supposed to attack and thought he was over his objective when he reached the one identical in appearance sixty miles farther east. There was the village, there was the stream, there was the road junction and the road leading southeast—filled with troops—but the troops were Russian.

I first heard of the disastrous results of our mistake on November 10, 1944, when General Antonov called me to his office and handed me the following letter:

Dear General Deane:

This is to bring to your attention that at 1250 hours, 7 November 1944, between Niš and Aleksinac in Yugoslavia an automobile column of Red Army troops was attacked by a group of American fighters composed of twenty-seven Lightning planes. A protecting group of nine Soviet planes were attacked while they were gaining altitude in spite of the fact that they were clearly marked as planes of the Red Army Air Force. Nevertheless, for fifteen minutes the American Lightning planes continued attacking the Soviet fighters, forcing them to defend themselves.

The attack of the Lightnings was stopped only after the leader of the group of Soviet fighters, Captain Kolchunov, at the risk of being shot down, took position under the leader of the group of American fighters and showed him the markings of his plane.

As a result of the attack of the American planes on the Soviet automobile column, Lieutenant General Kotov, the Commander of the Corps, was killed, also two officers and three men. Twenty automobiles with equipment were set on fire. Of the group of Soviet fighters, three planes were shot down. Two pilots were killed. In addition to this, in the region of the airdrome, four people were killed by fire from the American planes.

This unwarranted instance of an attack by American planes on a column of troops and the group of Red Army planes completely perplexes us, since the attack was fifty kilometers behind the front lines, between the towns of Niš and Aleksinac. On the 14th and 16th of October information was given in the Soviet communiqué that these two towns had been captured by the Red Army. The clearly visible markings on the Soviet planes also removes the possibility that there might have been mistakes in determining to whom these planes belonged. There is also no justification for these operations of American Air Forces not having been co-ordinated with the General Staff of the Red Army.

Please inform the Combined Chiefs of Staff of the altogether deplorable facts stated above and ask them to carry out an immediate investigation of this incident and to punish severely those responsible for this unexplainable attack on Soviet units. Ask them also that henceforth they not allow flights of Allied aviation into the zone of activity of Soviet troops without preliminary agreement with the General Staff of the Red Army.

Please let me know the results of the investigation and the measures being taken.

Sincerely yours,

Antonov

The atmosphere was chilly while the letter was being translated. I at once expressed the regrets that I knew our Chiefs of Staff would feel and assured Antonov that we would take the action he suggested. I took advantage of the opportunity to point out to him that we had taken the initiative and had been endeavoring for the past eight months to establish a system of co-ordination which would make such incidents impossible. I suggested that we agree right there and then on a method of improving our co-ordination—my proposal, of course, was the exchange of liaison officers between field headquarters, and his reply was the old one about co-ordinating our Balkan air efforts in Moscow. I then proposed that we revert to a bomb line or boundary between our forces with the understanding that it could be changed daily if necessary. He seemed to favor this and promised to take the matter up with his superiors.

It is probable that the error on the part of our squadron leader would have occurred regardless of what system of co-ordination had been in effect. It was the result of a human error caused by an unusual combination of circumstances that could not be foreseen. However, the chances of its occurrence would have been minimized had we had representatives with each of the Red Army front commanders who would have kept our Air Forces informed of Russian dispositions and troop movements.

The statement in Antonov's letter that our attack could not possibly have been a mistake was in fact an accusation that we had intentionally attacked our Soviet ally. As a matter of fact, our investigation revealed that when our planes were over Niš they were still at treetop height and were themselves attacked from above by Russian Yaks which succeeded in shooting down two of our planes. The Yaks were justified in attacking our squadron to drive them away from the Russian columns on the road below. Our planes were justified in defending themselves because in the heat of battle they thought the Russian planes were German. As soon as the Russians were recognized our squadron leader broke away from them as quickly as possible. It was an unfortunate accident, but only that. Antonov's attitude was not reflected by Russian officers in the field. When a few British and American officers attended General Kotov's funeral in Sofia they were warmly received and assured that the Russians recognized the incident as an unavoidable accident. Our Chiefs of Staff sent the Red Army General Staff their sincere apologies and satisfied Antonov's desire for disciplinary action by relieving the squadron leader of his command.

Unlike the General Staff in Moscow, Russian commanders in the field clearly saw the value of our having American air representatives at their headquarters. Shortly before the time that our Lightnings had attacked the Russian column, General Donovan's O.S.S. representatives in the Mediterranean Theater had succeeded in sending a small group into Rumania to locate American prisoners of war who had been liberated as a result of the advance of the Red Army. On September 16, 1944, the senior air officer, Colonel P. M. Barr, was sent for by a Russian general in Bucharest whose name had best not be mentioned. The Russian general expressed the opinion that direct liaison was definitely necessary because of the situation resulting from the advance of the Second Ukrainian Army into the area where the 15th Air Force had been operating for some months. Barr agreed to report the Russian general's views to General Eaker, and it was understood that the Russian general would seek concurrence from Moscow.

A second meeting held a few days later was attended by Brigadier

General C. P. Cabell, who was then in Rumania to assess our bomb damage to Ploesti, and two key staff officers of the Second Ukrainian Army. It was agreed that an American officer would consult with the staff of the Second Ukrainian Army daily to co-ordinate air operations. The Americans stated that they had General Eaker's approval to the plan and the Russians said that Moscow had approved.

Colonel John F. Batjer, our representative, set up a small headquarters close to that of the Second Ukrainian Army and had conferences with senior Russian commanders or staff officers once or twice a day. He was in direct communication with the headquarters of the 15th Air Force at Bari and a courier plane made a daily round trip to Italy. The arrangement was a great success: there was a rapid exchange of weather information and Russian troop movements and air operations were reported to Eaker, who kept Colonel Batjer fully informed of his intentions. The only difficulty was that the coverage was not broad enough. There were two other Russian armies in the Balkans, the Third and Fourth Ukrainian Armies, and with them co-ordination was still effected through Moscow.

General Eaker kept me informed as to what was going on and asked my advice as to whether he should continue to make arrangements with local Russian commanders. I replied by all means yes, as I was fearful that the entire plan would be upset once it came to the attention of the General Staff. The local Russian commanders who had approved the arrangement had already expressed their opinion of their General Staff when they said, "Now the matter is in the hands of soldiers. Let us go ahead."

By the middle of October the results were so successful that Eaker was convinced the liaison group should be expanded to cover the remaining two Russian armies. His efforts to accomplish this locally were unsuccessful, so he asked me to take the matter up with the General Staff in Moscow. I was reluctant to do this, but when Antonov gave me his complaint about our attack against Russian units I took a chance and told him how well our unofficial liaison was working with the Second Ukrainian Army and asked his approval of

extending it to the other two. The results were just what I had feared
—the arrangement had been made without referral to Moscow, and
its existence came as a great shock. Not only was my proposal disapproved, but the existing procedure at the headquarters of the Second
Ukrainian Army was immediately discontinued.

The Combined Chiefs of Staff were greatly concerned over the protest Antonov had made as well as about the incident. They directed
Admiral E. R. Archer, then acting head of the British Military Mission,
and me to re-establish a bomb line suitable to the Russians and ordered
a discontinuance of air operations in Yugoslavia until a line was agreed
upon. Archer and I met with Slavin at once and agreed on a boundary
that was entirely unacceptable to General Eaker. When he heard of
it he immediately complained to the Combined Chiefs of Staff and
to Archer and me. We attempted to readjust the bomb line and move
it farther to the east. It was essential that we do so as the Germans,
taking advantage of our inactivity, were making good their escape
to the north.

After several weeks of negotiation General Eaker took the bit in
his teeth and sent Archer and me a message in which he asked us to
inform the Russians that effective at two o'clock in the morning, Sunday, December 3, 1944, the Mediterranean Air Forces would confine
their activities to the west of a line which he designated. The line
was sufficiently far to the west to give full protection to Russian Air
and Ground Forces but far enough to the east to include the principal
roads over which the Germans were retreating.

Archer and I informed General Slavin orally and in writing of the
action General Eaker was taking. Surprisingly enough, Slavin and
his chief, General Antonov, took Eaker's pronouncement very well.
As a matter of fact, there was little they could do about it. They had
been given advance notice of just where American Air Forces were
to operate, and the burden was on them to make the Red Air Force
conform if accidental clashes were to be avoided.

The Russians' acquiescence to Eaker's arbitrary action confirmed
the suspicion that had long been growing in my mind that relations

with Soviet authorities would be improved if they were characterized by a tougher attitude on our part. Thereafter we had little difficulty as far as our Balkan co-ordination was concerned because we adopted a firm policy of simply informing the Russians of our intentions and putting the responsibility on them of avoiding conflicts. Minor clashes did occur, but Soviet recriminations were not violent, usually because of the weakness of their position.

As the war approached its climax in the winter of 1944–45, it became necessary to extend the co-ordination to operations in northern Europe as well as the Balkans. While the Russians were still well within the western boundary of Poland, in the vicinity of the Vistula, they proposed that the British and Americans should limit their air activities to a north and south line through Stettin and Berlin. The proposal amazed us since the suggested boundary was then from four to five hundred miles west of the Russian front lines. Acceptance of the Russian proposal would have meant that all of eastern Germany, western Poland, and the greater part of Czechoslovakia would have been free from attack by our heavy bombers. The area contained many of the oil refineries that were included as targets in the combined British-American bomber offensive which was then concentrating on German oil. General Slavin proposed the adoption of this line to Archer and me on December 10, 1944. We informed him at once that it would be unacceptable and countered with a proposal that we establish a line which we would not cross from seventy-five to one hundred miles in front of the Russian advance. In the course of our argument Slavin revealed that his proposed line was placed so far to the west in order to stop the British practice of dropping weapons, ammunition, and food to Polish partisans loyal to the London Polish government-in-exile. He claimed that the supplies were being used to retard the advance of the Red Army, which was being forced to "disarm bandit-type opposition armed with British weapons and equipped with British radio stations." While it was true that the Western Allies had been dropping supplies to Polish partisans, they were for the purpose of helping them to harass and resist the Germans. In view of the political issue involved, the question of co-ordination in the north remained dormant until the British, Russian, and American Chiefs of Staff met at Yalta in January 1945.

At the Yalta Conference a formula was worked out whereby the British and American Air Forces would not enter the zone that lay two hundred miles west of the Red Army's front lines without giving the Russians twenty-four hours' notice of our intentions. Russian silence was to be taken as consent. The formula was worked out by Air Chief Marshal Portal, Marshal Khudyakov, and General Kuter. We all thought it was an agreement until the last day of the Conference when General Antonov said that Russian silence should not be taken as consent but rather as disapproval. The Conference therefore adjourned without agreement having been reached and General Spaatz continued to operate at will, being careful to give the Russians ample notice of operations which might interfere with theirs.

Fortunately for me, Major General Edmund W. Hill arrived in Russia in December 1944 as the senior air member of my Mission and commander of Army Air Forces activities in Russia. I was delighted to turn the whole question of air liaison over to him. He worked around the clock, meeting with and sending letters to the General Staff in an effort to keep them fully informed of American air activities on the Russian front. Frequently notice of an American attack would be delayed until after it had been made, and Hill was kept busy explaining such incidents to the Russians. Clashes between our Air Forces occurred with increasing frequency as the Allies converged on the Germans, and Hill had to bear the brunt of Soviet displeasure as if he alone were to blame. Finally, in March 1945, Hill succeeded in obtaining Russian agreement to the arrangement worked out at Yalta, and this was the method of co-ordination used until the end of the war.

The whole story of collaboration in the air operations of the United States and the Soviet Union is one of American initiative and Russian resistance. The American Chiefs of Staff foresaw the possibility of conflicts, and the bitterness and recriminations which such conflicts would engender, and made early and continuous efforts to avoid them. The amazing thing is that the Soviet General Staff, which put every obstacle in the way of effective co-ordination, were the most acrimonious when the inevitable conflicts occurred. Red Army General Staff protests were invariably so phrased as not only to decry the event, but also to imply that American attacks on Soviet aircraft were deliberate and directed. In contrast to the Soviet attitude, we never protested a Soviet attack on our aircraft without acknowledging it as an accident and suggesting ways and means for the prevention of recurrences.

While Soviet requests for American assistance were few, those which were made were invariably granted. In one instance we were requested to bomb the Citadel, the headquarters of the German General Staff about thirty miles south of Berlin. It was thirty-four feet underground and heavily constructed of concrete and steel. We had known of its existence for two years before its location became known to the Russians. We had always refrained from attacking it because we felt it was really bomb-proof. Upon Soviet request we attacked it heavily, purely as a gesture of collaboration. On another occasion we were asked to launch an attack against Swinemünde, where the Russians reported a huge concentration of German shipping. We launched a particularly violent attack on the harbor through heavy clouds with the help of radar. We could not observe the results and asked the Red Air Force to photograph them for us so that the attack could be repeated if necessary. It took us three weeks to obtain a reply to our request, and then we were not given photographs but simply a terse report deprecating the value of our attack.

Aside from the shuttle-bombing bases we were allowed to have in the Ukraine, which were reduced in effectiveness because of Soviet restrictions, none of our requests for assistance to our Air Forces was approved. We sought bases at which our disabled aircraft could land when forced to come down behind the Russian lines. We were told they could land anywhere, which was not much help to a disabled pilot looking for a runway. A considerable number of our planes which did land behind the Soviet lines in fairly good condition were not returned to us, and when I left Russia it was not at all unusual to see an American Flying Fortress or Liberator with a red star on it parked on a Soviet airdrome. Late in the war we developed a radar device whereby our aircraft could accurately locate their position within an area of four hundred yards by triangulation with base stations within a few hundred miles. We also wanted to set up six base stations in Soviet Russia to provide navigational assistance to our huge bomber formations over Germany. Having these bases would have added considerably to the accuracy of our bombing when the target area was invisible. We were not allowed to establish them—the silly reason given for refusal of our request was that they would have caused interference to Red Army radio communications. While we could have disproved this fear by scientific evidence, we knew that the real reason was that the stations would require one American officer and twenty American enlisted men to operate them.

I think the most outstanding lesson that came out of our efforts to co-ordinate air operations with the Red Army was the effectiveness of positive action as opposed to negotiation when dealing with Soviet officials. Eaker's arbitrary action in setting his own bomb line in December 1944 was a forceful example of what I mean. We had been attempting for eight months to negotiate an agreement through which we could be of mutual assistance and avoid unfortunate incidents. On our part it was purely a co-operative effort. It was defeated by the Russians in their search for our hidden motive. They had much more respect for us and acquiesced more readily when we simply informed them that "This is what we are going to do—take it or leave it." There is merit in considering adherence to similar procedure in the future.

IX. Co-ordinating
the European Land Battle

As I look back over the pattern of Russia's collaboration with the Western Allies, there emerges constantly evidence of Russia's desire to avoid any entanglements from which she would have difficulty in extricating herself in the postwar world. Russia wanted to fight and end the war with none of the heterogeneous mixture of troops, divided responsibilities, and mutual obligations which the British and Americans were prepared to accept with regard to each other. Russia's position at the end of the war was to be that which she herself had won—a position which Russia would control free of obligations to and interference from her allies. True, she was ready to conduct her military operations so as to assist the western powers if this would hasten the defeat of Germany, but she would conduct them alone and with the minimum conversation with her British and American friends.

In the early days of the war close collaboration was unnecessary. The Russians and the Anglo-Americans were far removed, and all strategic requirements would be satisfied if the Allies on both fronts would fight like hell against the Germans. All that was needed was a western front, and Lord knows the Russians cried loudly enough for that.

The American Chiefs of Staff were convinced that the day would come when Germany would be caught between the jaws of a vise closing in on them from the east and west. It seemed evident that when that time came, the final destruction of Germany would be hastened if the operations of Eisenhower's armies and the Red armies could be brought into tune on a day-to-day basis. We would then be close enough to the Russians so that our actions could dislocate the Germans to the Red Army's advantage, and, similarly, the Red Army could do much to assist us. It was one of the primary objectives of my Mission to set up the machinery through which close co-ordination could be effected once it became apparent that it would be mutually advantageous.

There can be no doubt that the Soviet Union alone absorbed the fury of the German attack in the period of nearly a year and a half that elapsed between the fall of France and our invasion of Africa. I say this in full recognition of the suffering endured and the courage displayed by the British in the Battle of Britain and of the gallant battles fought by the British Empire in the Middle East. Western Russia was Russia, and it was completely destroyed. By her valor and suffering Russia blunted the edge of the German sword, and when she finally turned the tide at Stalingrad the outcome of the war was no longer in doubt. Let us give the Soviet Union full credit and all honor for what she did in those perilous days. At the same time, we should vehemently deny the oft-repeated implication of the Soviet leaders that the Soviet Union won the war for us. Russia fought bravely and she fought well, but she did it to save her own skin and for no other purpose. On the other hand, we should be honest with ourselves and admit that our most compelling motive in sending supplies to Russia was to save our skins. We were prone to look for gratitude from the Soviet Union when we thought of the needed equipment our own troops were obliged to forego, and of the dangers of running the German submarine blockade which cost us the crews and cargoes of the seventy-seven merchant ships that were sunk. As far as Russia's leaders are concerned, there never was gratitude and there never will be.

It may be said then that in the early part of the war collaboration with Russia consisted of our sending her supplies with which she could fight. As time went on we made several endeavors to come closer together. For example, we organized an air raid against Ploesti that was to be undertaken from the Middle East in the early part of 1942. Because of Turkey's neutrality, our planes had to avoid flying over her territory, which made it questionable whether they would have sufficient fuel for the return flight to their home bases. Stalin was approached by the President with a request to permit emergency landings in southern Russia. Reluctant approval of the President's request was received one week after an abortive attack had been made in which almost all of our planes were either lost or interned after forced landings in Turkey.

About the time of the siege of Stalingrad we offered to send a group of heavy bombers to Russian bases in the Caucasus for the sole purpose of assisting the defensive operations of the Red Army. Despite the critical situation which existed, Stalin replied that he would accept the planes but not the American personnel to fly them. Since it was manifestly impossible to train Soviet personnel in the use of such aircraft in time to be of help, Stalin's proposal was rejected.

At the time of the Casablanca Conference, President Roosevelt was anxious to have General Marshall go to Moscow after the Conference was over to get a true picture of the Russian situation, so that our strategic operations could be adjusted to be of the maximum assistance to Russia and so that our supply program could be made more effective. Stalin could not see that a visit by General Marshall to Moscow would serve any useful purpose. This slight to our Chief of Staff was keenly felt by all Americans who knew about it except General Marshall himself. The Russian leaders could see only another American effort to pry into their affairs and thereby lost the advantages of allowing the most influential American, aside from the President himself, a firsthand and sympathetic knowledge of the problems confronting the Russian war machine.

One of the great determining factors in British-American strategy was the necessity to do everything possible to relieve German pressure against the Red Army. It was one of the compelling considerations that led to our decision to invade Africa. The need to assist Russia was emphasized at each of the British-American Conferences from Casablanca on. Our Combined Chiefs of Staff always expressed their over-all objective as being "In conjunction with Russia and other Allies to bring about at the earliest possible moment the unconditional surrender of the Axis powers."

I have already described how General Ismay and I revealed our plans for the cross-channel operations to Molotov and Voroshilov at the Moscow Conference in October 1943. This was purely a one-sided exchange of information; we were told nothing of the Russians' plans. It was not until the first meeting of the Big Three at Teheran in November 1943 that the veil of secrecy was even partially lifted with regard to the Red Army's operations. There for the first time we had a mutual exchange of information. There for the first time the operations of the British and American forces in the west and the Red Army in the east were planned so as to be mutually supporting.

At Teheran, Stalin described the Red Army's operations in considerable detail. Prior to this time we had had a fair idea of the German strength and dispositions on the Russian front as the result of our own intelligence as well as by an exchange of information that General Michela had started with the Red Army prior to my arrival in Moscow. Stalin confirmed our estimate that the Germans had two hundred and sixty divisions, but for the first time revealed that there were three hundred and thirty Red Army divisions opposing them. This gave the Russians a margin of seventy divisions with which to maneuver, retain the initiative, and continue the offensive. Stalin was fearful that the strength of the German defense would succeed in reducing his margin of superiority unless the Western Allies succeeded in attracting more German divisions from the Russian front.

I have already mentioned the controversy that took place at Teheran in which Churchill advocated delaying Overlord in favor of more extended operations in the Mediterranean, while Stalin insisted that we should launch our cross-channel invasion at the earliest practicable date. The argument over the main issue brought out a full discussion of all the factors involved, and for the first time the Western Allies and Russia were sufficiently informed of each other's problems. The

principal military conclusions of the heads of state at Teheran were
(1) that Overlord would be launched in May 1944 in conjunction
with an operation against southern France, and the Red Army would
launch an offensive on the eastern front at about the same time to
prevent the Germans from withdrawing forces with which to oppose
Overlord; and (2) that the staffs of the three powers would henceforth
keep in close touch with each other in regard to European operations.
It was also agreed that a cover plan to mystify and mislead the enemy
with regard to Overlord should be developed jointly by the three
staffs.

The most important decision was that concerning the timing of
Overlord and the agreement concerning the Red Army offensive
which would support Overlord. However, from my point of view,
the decision which was of most interest was the agreement concerning
staff co-ordination and the development of a cover plan. Because of
the distance separating the Combined British and American Chiefs
of Staff in Washington from the Russian Chiefs of Staff in Moscow,
I knew that my Mission would become a clearing house for whatever
co-ordination was effected.

When Churchill finally surrendered to the pressure from Stalin
and the President and agreed on a May date for Overlord, he did it
with all good grace. For the moment at least he outshone the others
in his enthusiasm to carry through the invasion. It was he who suggested the necessity of preparing a cover and deception plan which
would keep "that man Hitler" in ignorance of our preparations and
intentions. Stalin picked up the ball and described some of the Red
Army's deceptive measures. He stated that at times the Russians constructed as many as five thousand false tanks and two thousand false
aircraft to mislead the German Intelligence. By this time Soviet-
British accord had reached a new high, and Churchill remarked in
his puckish way that "Truth deserves a bodyguard of lies." It was
thus that the code word "Bodyguard" was selected for the cover and
deception plan that was to be agreed on with the Red Army General
Staff a month or so later in Moscow.

The British had developed the art of cover and deception during the war to a degree that was far more advanced than that attained by either the Russians or the Americans. Colonel J. H. Bevan was in charge of the preparation of such plans in the British War Office. It was he who developed "Plan Bodyguard," which was to include Russian participation in our efforts to deceive the Germans concerning Overlord. Bevan developed his plans with such subtlety and skill that it was difficult for his own people to know what parts of the plan were to be carried out and what parts were simply to appear as though they were being carried out.

Bevan came to Moscow toward the end of January 1944 and was accompanied by Lieutenant Colonel William H. Baumer, an American expert on cover plans. I had been designated to represent the United States in the discussion of the plan with British and Soviet representatives, and Baumer was to be my principal adviser. It took Bevan and Baumer several hours to explain the plan to me despite the fact that it was fairly simple once I saw the light. I could foresee the difficulty we were going to have in making the Soviet representatives understand it through the medium of interpreters.

Bevan, Baumer, and I met with Colonel General Fedor F. Kuznetzov of the Red Army General Staff on February 10, 1944. He had an interpreter with him who insisted on his prerogative of translating everything that Kuznetzov said to us and was equally insistent that our interpreter translate everything we said to Kuznetzov. He started every translation with "General, he says," and then would proceed with a jumbled mass of English construction which revealed nothing that anyone could possibly have said. To his great displeasure, our interpreter would then whisper to us the gist of Kuznetzov's remarks. I thought Kuznetzov a mental giant when, in spite of the difficulties, he appeared in a very short time to have mastered the intricacies of Bevan's plan.

Plan Bodyguard recognized that we could not conceal the build-up for cross-channel operations from the Germans, but it provided ways and means of deceiving them with regard to the time that the operations would be started. It was designed to lead the Germans to believe that other operations were to be undertaken by the Allies and thus cause them to have faulty troop dispositions at the time the invasion was actually launched. Under the plan we were to try to make the enemy believe that we could not possibly invade the Continent until July and that the Russian summer offensive could not be started until about the same time. Once that idea was planted, we were to attempt to make the Germans believe that operations would be started in the early summer at several places in the Mediterranean area and also in Scandinavia. It was through this means that we hoped to dissuade the Germans from strongly reinforcing northern France until it was too late.

Russian participation in the plan was to allow information to leak out that they could not start an offensive until July. The Russians were asked to make the Germans believe that a joint Allied attack on Norway would occur in the late spring. They were also to give the impression of preparing a landing against the Bulgarian and Rumanian coasts during the month of May or early June.

We had three meetings with Kuznetzov and he became very enthusiastic over Bevan's plan. He and his colleagues proposed a great many changes, many of which were accepted by us after an exchange of cables with our Chiefs of Staff. Representatives of the Soviet Foreign Office were called in to discuss the diplomatic aspects of the matter with representatives of the British and American Embassies. Finally, the Russians went into seclusion for two weeks. During this time Bevan, Baumer, and I were unable to contact them to see what was wrong. On March 5, 1944, Kuznetzov called another meeting to which he brought a "Protocol," nicely bound with silk ribbons, in which the Russians agreed to the original plan as presented without any of the changes we had so thoroughly argued and agreed upon.

In carrying out the plan some of the information leakages which appeared in the Soviet press were just as startling to Russia's allies as they were to the Germans. Only those who knew of Plan Bodyguard realized that these revelations were for deception purposes. In

May 1944 I was informed by General Kuznetzov that the Soviet Union was simulating a sea-borne attack on Petsamo by an actual concentration of ships, troops, and equipment in the Kola inlet, by air and sea reconnaissance of the Norwegian coast line, and by increasing their interservice radio communications in that area, thus carrying out its part of Bodyguard in Scandinavia. Information had been allowed to reach the Germans that Soviet Army and Navy officers had gone to Scotland to co-ordinate the Soviet attack with that of the British and Americans. With regard to their inability to launch a summer offensive until July, the Germans had been led to believe that the Soviet High Command was forming a new army of selected troops on the central front and that it had been ordered to complete its organization by the end of June; also that new Russian reserves were being trained for employment in July. Kuznetzov said he felt that the Soviet threat to the Rumanian coast had been accomplished by the unexpectedly rapid advance of the Red Army into that country. The Russians gave us full co-operation in the development and execution of our cover plan. It was one of those co-operative ventures that promised results of mutual advantage and in which the Russian part of the operation could be carried out without British or American assistance. When these conditions existed, the Russians were usually co-operative.

At Teheran it had been agreed that the Red Army would launch an offensive timed to assist Overlord. However, the actual date of Overlord was indefinitely fixed as "during the month of May" and nothing was agreed regarding the scale and character of the Red Army offensive. In the early part of 1944 the Red Army launched a general attack over its entire front. The main effort was in the south across the Carpathians and into Rumania. The Russian advance progressed with unexpected rapidity, and I became fearful that it would outrun its communications sometime in the spring and that there would not be sufficient time for the Red Army to regroup, shorten its supply line, and be ready for the summer attack that was to help us across the channel. With the Red Army bogged down, the Germans would be able to take troops from the Russian front to oppose our landings in France. I therefore sent a message on February 27, 1944, to the Chiefs of Staff urging that the head of the British Mission and I be instructed to inform the Red Army General Staff of the exact date of our invasion so that they could plan accordingly, at the same time seeking information with regard to the promised Russian supporting offensive. We received the necessary instructions on April 7, 1944, the date for Overlord being given as May 31, "with two or three days margin on either side to allow for weather and tide."

When Lieutenant General M. B. Burrows, who succeeded General Martel as head of the British Military Mission in March 1944, and I gave General Antonov this information he thanked us and promised a reply within a day or two. On April 23, 1944, he wrote me a terse letter of three paragraphs. The first said the Red Army General Staff was satisfied with the date selected; the second stated that the Red Army would attack on the same date, but gave no intimation of where or how; and the third paragraph asked me to inform the Combined Chiefs of Staff of the first two.

As the time of our invasion drew near, I was given several changes of date to impart to Antonov. As I recall, the first was June 2, then June 5, and finally June 6. Even then, for a while, weather threatened to delay the operation for from two to three weeks after June 6. Each time I announced a postponement of even a day my stock reached a new low. The General Staff had never been convinced that the May date agreed upon in Teheran was not part of a deception plan that the western powers were using against their Russian ally. To convince them of our sincerity, I had bet General Slavin twelve bottles of vodka in February that our invasion would take place in May. I think this did more to convince the General Staff of the firmness of our plans than did the promises of Churchill and Roosevelt. In any event, producing the vodka to pay my debt enabled me to relieve the strained atmosphere when I called to announce one of the postponements.

When June 6, 1944, did arrive and the invasion was actually launched, I felt certain that it would mark the beginning of a period of close co-operative effort between the three big allies. I was so confident of this that I put on my cap and walked a mile or two through the busiest section of Moscow to Spasso House for the sole purpose of receiving kudos from the crowd. When I started out I thought the appearance of an American officer on the streets would be received with such acclaim that I would have difficulty avoiding the cheers of the men and the embraces of the women. Actually I covered the entire distance without being noticed by anyone. The news had been broadcast over the public radio and it received due notice in the press. There was a general feeling of relief that the British and Americans were on the Continent, but there was no demonstrative outburst of enthusiasm. A week after the invasion Anatole Litvak, an American Army colonel who in civil life had been one of Hollywood's best producers, arrived in Moscow with moving pictures of the crossing. I invited the Red Army General Staff and other military and political leaders to see the pictures. Their eyes were on their cheeks with amazement at the magnitude of the invasion. It was a phase of war with which the Russians were totally unfamiliar. The pictures definitely changed their previous attitude that crossing the English Channel was only a little more difficult than crossing the Volga or the Dnieper or the Vistula.

On the day following the Allied landings a letter from General Antonov informed me that a new Red Army offensive had been organized in accordance with the agreements reached at Teheran. It was to start on "one of the important sectors of the front in the middle of June and would develop into a general offensive by the middle of July." The information was meager, but it must have been heartening to General Eisenhower, who was then engaged in the early and most critical stages of securing a toehold on the beaches of northern France.

Now that we were both fighting on the same continent against the same enemy, it seemed to us that we should set up machinery for daily liaison between British, American, and Russian field commanders. We advocated an exchange of liaison officers between field headquar-

ters just as we had in connection with the co-ordination of air operations. All the Soviet leaders, from Stalin on down, admitted that when
our forces came close enough to each other an exchange of liaison
officers would be desirable. Meanwhile, they advocated co-ordinating
our combined effort through the Red Army General Staff and the
British and American Military Missions in Moscow.

Since my arrival in Moscow in October 1943, we had been furnish-
ing the Red Army General Staff and Marshal Stalin personally with
a daily summary of our operations not only in Italy but also in the
Pacific, as a gesture of co-operation, without asking anything in return
but in the hope that they would be reciprocated when it became
necessary for us to know the day-to-day actions of the Red Army.
We felt that that time had now come.

I approached the General Staff and offered to broaden the scope of
our daily reports to include not only what had happened but also the
actions envisaged for the immediate future provided they would do
the same. The Russians agreed to this in principle but failed to carry
out their part of the agreement in fact. Each night about ten o'clock
we would get a three- or four-page message from Eisenhower outlining in detail his operations for the day and when necessary his plans
for the future. These messages would be translated into Russian, carefully plotted on maps, and sent to the General Staff and to Stalin. In
return, my representative would be called to General Estigneev's
office about one to two hours before the time of release of the Soviet
communiqué and be given an advance copy of it. By the time we had
these translated and had dispatched them to General Eisenhower and
our Chiefs of Staff, the same information had been disseminated all
over the world by the British and American press correspondents in
Moscow. My messages may have reached their destinations a few
hours before the morning papers were published, but that was the
only advantage gained from this co-operative venture with our Soviet
ally.

On June 28, 1944, Harriman had an interesting meeting with
Marshal Stalin. The purpose of the meeting was to enable Averell to

deliver some scrolls that the President was sending to Stalin as mementos of the Teheran Conference. After the scrolls had been presented and received, Stalin commented on Overlord. He described our crossing and landings as "an unheard of achievement, the magnitude of which had never been undertaken in the history of warfare." He, too, had seen the pictures. He was particularly impressed by the fact that 650,000 men had been landed in so short a time.

Stalin then surprised Harriman by suggesting that rather than depend on messages for exchanging important information, a combined military staff should be set up. Harriman told the Marshal that I was leaving for a short visit to the United States and would present his proposal to the American Chiefs of Staff and to General Eisenhower whom I would visit en route.

When I saw the American Chiefs of Staff in Washington and General Eisenhower in Reims, they all agreed that while they would prefer an exchange of liaison officers between field headquarters, Stalin's proposal of a combined staff would be well worth trying. Accordingly, after I returned to Moscow I received instructions from the U.S. Chiefs of Staff to take the matter up with the appropriate Soviet officials. They suggested that a Tripartite Committee be established in Moscow to deal with strategical and operational matters. They emphasized that the committee should be consultative and advisory in character and that it would have no power to make decisions but would refer matters requiring decision to their respective chiefs of staff.

Harriman and Sir Archibald Clark-Kerr met with Stalin on September 23, 1944. Harriman referred to the proposal Stalin had made at their June meeting and outlined the ideas of our Chiefs of Staff concerning the establishment of a consultative committee. Stalin liked the idea but did not like the word "committee," as it implied power of decision. It was tentatively decided that the "committee" would be established but that it would be called a "commission." I was to be the American representative. The actual formation of the commission was held in abeyance pending the arrival of a new permanent Chief of the

British Military Mission, as Stalin indicated he would not be satisfied with Lieutenant General Burrows as the British representative.

General Burrows, an outstanding British officer, had become persona non grata in Soviet officialdom. The British Ambassador was informed by the Russians that Burrows was arrogant and difficult to deal with, and there was little choice but to change his assignment. He was replaced in October 1944 by Admiral E. R. Archer, who served as acting chief of the British Mission until March of the following year. Actually Burrows had had every desire to co-operate but was somewhat discouraged by the failure of his efforts. When the British Military Mission was disbanded at the end of the war, Burrows' office was found to be infested with well-concealed dictaphones, and it was evident that everything he had said in the privacy of his office was a matter of record in the N.K.V.D. I can well understand why he was unpopular—I could have been hanged for many of my comments about Soviet officials in some of my moments of frustration—there could not have been any dictaphones in my office.

Burrows was not replaced in Moscow until March of 1945, and as a result the consultative commission never materialized. The question was raised again at the Yalta Conference in February 1945, but everyone seemed to be satisfied to continue the liaison that had been established between the British and American Military Missions and the Soviet General Staff in Moscow. It was again agreed that when our forces came closer together, an exchange of liaison officers between field headquarters would be desirable.

Another effort to bring the Allied Armies into closer harmony had been made by Prime Minister Churchill when he and Anthony Eden, accompanied by Lord Alanbrooke, Chief of the Imperial General Staff, and General Ismay, visited Moscow in October 1944. Churchill invited Harriman and me to attend his military conferences with Stalin and his military staff, and agreed that as the American representatives we should handle the British-American side of any discussion concerning operations in the Pacific. We made great strides in our collaboration with Russia in the Pacific war during this conference, and these shall be described later.

It was amusing to listen to the British and Soviet discussions of the European war. Lord Alanbrooke gave an excellent presentation of General Eisenhower's situation, but he was subject to constant interruptions by the Prime Minister, who would leap from his seat and stride to the map in order to emphasize the magnitude or difficulties of certain phases of the British-American operations. General Antonov described the Red Army's operations, and he was subject to constant interruptions from Stalin, who wished to impress Churchill with the tremendous accomplishments of the Red Army. Antonov displayed his usual caution in revealing the Red Army's plans and this seemed to irritate Stalin, who took over the pointer from Antonov and outlined on the map in considerable detail the Red Army's proposed operations. The only agreement that was reached was that both sides would continue unrelenting pressure through the winter in order to make it impossible for any large movement of German troops from one front to the other.

Of course there was the usual round of entertainment for Churchill and his party. A special performance was held at the Bolshoi Theater, which included one act of ballet, one act of opera, and several concert numbers. The official party was in the state box. I had a very inconspicuous seat in the rear of the box and could see nothing of the performance. However, to see the ovation that Churchill received from the audience was well worth the boredom of looking at the back of his head for several hours. Between the first and second acts he received an ovation from a standing, cheering audience which lasted for fifteen minutes. Churchill loved it and revived the applause whenever it seemed to lag by well-timed finger signals of the V for Victory. Stalin retired from the box as soon as the lights had gone on but returned after about ten minutes to take the applause with Churchill.

Air Chief Marshal Sir Arthur Tedder, Deputy Supreme Commander to General Eisenhower, came to Moscow on January 14, 1945, for a military meeting with Stalin. He was accompanied by Major General H. R. Bull and Brigadier General T. J. Betts, Americans who represented the planning and intelligence sections of Eisenhower's staff. A meeting was arranged with Stalin at the Kremlin on the following night. Admiral Archer, acting head of the British Military Mission, and I also attended.

The Red Army had started a large-scale offensive just three days before Stalin's meeting with Tedder. In describing the offensive to Tedder, Stalin emphasized that it had been started on January 12 because he knew of President Roosevelt's and Prime Minister Churchill's worry over the situation on the western front, particularly with regard to the Ardennes bulge. Stalin said that the present offensive would last for about two and one half months and its ultimate objective was the line of the Oder River.

The big question that confronted Eisenhower at that time was what the Russians would be doing during the latter half of March, which would be the earliest time that the spring floods would permit an attempted crossing of the Rhine. Obtaining an answer to the question was the principal objective of Tedder's visit. If the Russian offensive were bogged down by the spring thaws just at the time the Anglo-Americans were crossing the Rhine, the Germans would be able to shift troops from the Russian front to oppose our effort.

Tedder presented our plans and worries with the utmost clarity and made a great impression on Stalin by his blunt sincerity. Stalin responded at once and promised that the Red Army would prevent any withdrawal of Germans from the Russian front by means of local actions and general pressure over the entire front from the time the present Red Army offensive was halted until another could be launched about the end of May. All in all, Tedder's meeting with Stalin was highly successful, and Eisenhower at least had the comfort of Stalin's promise that he would prevent German withdrawal from his front during our Rhine crossing. He was not informed how Stalin proposed to carry out his promises. As events worked out, the spring thaws failed to stop the advance of the Red Army and the offensive which had begun on January 12, 1945, continued until Germany's surrender.

During the Yalta Conference held about a month after Tedder's visit to Moscow, our Chiefs of Staff succeeded in obtaining many Soviet promises. One was that our scientists would be allowed to visit the German submarine experimental station in Gdynia as soon as the Russians had taken it. Another was that the United States would be allowed to establish air bases in the vicinity of Budapest in order to extend the perimeter of our air attack against Germany. Other Soviet commitments were made with regard to the Pacific war. As the result of Soviet displeasure over our later differences with the Soviet Union concerning the organization of a Polish Government, none of these promises was fulfilled.

While at Yalta I had an opportunity to get a complete radiotele-type transmitting and receiving station that had been used aboard the U.S.S. *Catoctin* to connect Yalta with Washington. I had the equipment shipped to Moscow and tried to get Antonov either to have the Red Army set it up to establish a direct channel with General Eisenhower's headquarters for our joint use or allow us to do so. This would have meant that Eisenhower or his staff officers could have had instantaneous teletype conferences with the Soviet High Command in Moscow. Such a service would have been of immeasurable value in the final and critical stages of the war. But the Foreign Office's displeasure over the Polish situation had spread to the General Staff and my proposed radio circuit was disapproved.

After the Yalta Conference and until Germany was defeated co-ordination between the Allies was accomplished through the British and American Military Missions in Moscow. On March 28, 1945, General Eisenhower sent me a message to deliver to Marshal Stalin. He requested me to do everything I could to obtain a full reply. Eisenhower said that the immediate objective of his northern and southern armies was to circle the Ruhr and pocket the Germans in that area. He expected his two forces to join at Kassel, Germany, at about the end of April. With the Ruhr encirclement completed, his next move would be to split Germany by joining hands with the Russians. He said to accomplish this he would make his main effort along the Erfurt-Leipzig-Dresden line. He proposed making a secondary effort to the south in the hope of joining forces with the Russians in the Regensburg-Linz area in Austria. Eisenhower asked Stalin if his plans conformed with the probable action of the Red Army.

Admiral Archer and I accompanied our Ambassadors to a meeting with Stalin to deliver Eisenhower's message. He immediately approved of Eisenhower's tactical plan and gave us a message to send to him stating that Eisenhower's plan fitted in with those of the Red Army. He said that henceforth the main effort of the Red Army would be in the direction of Dresden to form a junction with our forces. With regard to the secondary attack, Stalin stated that the Red Army was already attacking in the direction of Linz and hoped to join with the Western Allies in that area. It was thus that the final offensive which was to crush Germany's last hopes was formulated.

In the middle of April 1945 the war with Germany was in its final stages. General Eisenhower sent me a message asking that I call the General Staff's attention to the necessity of arranging for recognition signals so that there would be no unfortunate incidents when our troops came together. He offered to send Air Chief Marshal Tedder to Moscow to discuss the matter with General Antonov. This suggestion elicited a prompt response from Antonov, who must have had his staff work overtime in preparing a suggested set of signals which he could propose to Eisenhower and thus avoid the necessity of having Tedder, another foreigner, visit Moscow. The system he proposed was accepted by Eisenhower with minor variations. Eisenhower also proposed that while hostilities continued both sides should be free to advance until contact was imminent, and that thereafter a division of responsibility should be defined by boundary lines agreed upon between our respective Armies. This suggestion alarmed Antonov, who saw in it a desire on our part to advance into the Russian occupation zone already agreed upon by the three governments. I had to ask General Eisenhower to send Antonov confirmation of our assurance that we would withdraw to the agreed occupation areas once Germany had surrendered.

Our final efforts at co-ordination in the European war were, first, to reach an agreement on a press release announcing the junction of the American 69th Division with the 58th Russian Guards Division at Torgau, about twenty miles northeast of Leipzig, on the 26th of April 1945; and second, to reach an agreement limiting the advance of the Western Allies and that of the Red Army. The press release presented no difficulty and a simultaneous announcement of our junction with the Red Army was made at seven o'clock in the evening, Moscow time, on April 27, 1945. The agreement as to the limits of advance of the two converging forces was less easily achieved.

On May 1, 1945, General Eisenhower sent a message to my Mission asking us to inform the Red Army General Staff of his plans. He proposed to halt the British-American advance generally along the west bank of the Elbe River in Germany and along the 1937 boundary of Czechoslovakia south of Germany. If the situation warranted, he proposed advancing into Czechoslovakia to a general line—Karlsbad-Pilsen-Budejovice. Within a day or two after we had sent General Eisenhower's plan to Antonov, he gave his full concurrence. On May 4 General Eisenhower sent us another message for transmission to Antonov, saying that if the situation made it possible he proposed to advance farther into Czechoslovakia, to the west banks of the Elbe and Vitava Rivers. This brought a violent protest from Antonov since Eisenhower's proposed advance might have meant that American rather than Soviet forces might liberate the Czechoslovakian capital of Prague. The fine hand of the Soviet Foreign Office could be seen in Antonov's attitude—Czechoslovakia was to be in the orbit of the Soviet Union and Czech gratitude to America for the liberation of her capital was not part of the program.

Eisenhower was confronted with a difficult decision. On the one hand, he had already agreed to limit his advance to the Karlsbad-Pilsen line and yet he would probably be able to liberate the capital of our brave Czech ally much sooner than the Russians could if he continued his advance. Eisenhower informed the Russians that he would adhere to his original plan of advancing only to the Karlsbad-Pilsen-Budejovice line. Had he had a crystal ball he might well have made a different decision, but it was his job to get along with the Russians and he still had hopes of doing so. It is interesting to speculate on the advantages we may have lost in failing to seize the opportunity to obtain the lasting gratitude of the Czechoslovakian people.

When General Eisenhower visited Moscow after the war, he held a press conference at which he stated that after January 1945 he was kept fully informed at all times of the essentials of the Red Army's plans, particularly the timing of their offensives, their objectives, and the direction of their main efforts. This was true, but his possession of such information was a far cry from the co-operative action that might normally be expected between allies. All the information Eisenhower had concerning the Red Army's plans was the result of our initiative in seeking to obtain it, and then it was only obtained after continuous pressure at the highest levels. Not once during the war did Stalin or his subordinates seek a meeting with British or American authorities in order to present proposals for improving our co-operative effort. It was either the President or the Prime Minister who proposed Teheran, Yalta, and Potsdam. No single event of the war irritated me more than seeing the President of the United States lifted from wheel chair to automobile, to ship, to shore, and to aircraft, in order to go halfway around the world as the only possible means of meeting J. V. Stalin.

There were innumerable little ways in which our joint war effort could have been made more effective. We might have learned something of immeasurable value in defeating the German submarines had we been allowed to see Gdynia as soon as it was taken; we might have brought Germany to her knees quicker had we been allowed to establish radar triangulation stations in Russia as navigational aids to our bomber formations in eastern Germany. We might have defeated

Germany more quickly had we shared our operational experience by having observers on each other's fronts. We might have, we might have—on and on. No! In Soviet Russia each such venture would have meant a closer association with capitalistic foreigners. Well, perhaps we were among friends, but it was difficult to believe it.

X. The German Surrender

PRESIDENT ROOSEVELT's "Unconditional Surrender" slogan, coined at a Casablanca press conference, established a policy which was unanimously adopted by the Allies. The policy which it reflected will provide a fertile field for evaluation by historians for centuries to come. We are still too close to the event to appraise it accurately. The policy certainly relieved the Allied powers from endless negotiations as to what the conditions for an enemy surrender should be, but at the same time it strengthened the propaganda statements of enemy leaders that they must continue the war to the bitter end as their only chance of survival. It was a policy that the Soviet Union accepted with alacrity, probably because a completely destroyed Germany would facilitate Russia's postwar expansion program. The idea of unconditional surrender, together with an agreement to refuse a separate peace, was reiterated in the Four Power Declaration at the Moscow Conference in October 1943.

In Moscow our first hint that the German war machine was beginning to crumble came from Italy on March 11, 1945, in a message that was sent by Field Marshal Sir Harold Alexander to the Combined Chiefs of Staff. The message was forwarded to us for transmission to the Soviet Government. Bill Donovan's O.S.S. representatives in Switzerland had reported to Field Marshal Alexander that certain key German staff officers were to come to Lugano, Switzerland, in order to discuss the surrender of German forces in Italy. Alexander said that if the German approach materialized and if it appeared to be sincere and authentic, he proposed to send General Lyman L. Lemnitzer, his

Deputy Chief of Staff, to Bern to make the necessary arrangements. He said that his instructions to Lemnitzer would be to tell the German representatives (1) that only a surrender on a purely military basis would be considered and not on a governmental or political basis; (2) that for detailed military discussions they must come to Allied Force Headquarters at Caserta; and (3) that a method of communication with the German commander must be arranged by them. The Combined Chiefs of Staff had given their approval to the action proposed by Alexander but directed him not to send his representatives to Bern until the Soviet Government had been informed through our State Department and the British Foreign Office.

Averell Harriman sent the complete text of Field Marshal Alexander's message to Molotov. As a matter of courtesy he asked for any comments the Soviet Government might have. Molotov replied that he considered the matter one of importance and had no objections to conversations between British and American officers and the German representatives. He added that his Government wished to designate three Red Army general officers, then in France, to participate in the discussions. He asked that we arrange for their transportation to Bern since the Soviet Government did not have diplomatic relations with Switzerland.

I was greatly concerned about Molotov's desire for Soviet participation. In the first place, arranging for the entry of Red Army officers into Switzerland meant delay; but more important, I was afraid that the success of the project might be jeopardized if Soviet representatives participated. Nor was there any requirement, either of military necessity or courtesy, which dictated that Russia should participate in a surrender of German forces in the Italian theater, where Allied military operations had been conducted entirely under Anglo-American command. It was as though the United States had requested permission to attend the possible future surrender of twenty or thirty divisions of the German army in Latvia to the Soviets—a request which would most certainly have been refused. Such a surrender, being local and of a purely military nature, did not come within the purview of our agreement not to conclude a separate peace. I sent my views in a personal message to General Marshall and recommended refusal of the Soviet request.

Things were not going so well at that time in any of my co-operative efforts with the Russians, and there may have been an underlying note of vindictiveness in my recommendation to General Marshall. In any event, the Combined Chiefs of Staff reached a decision which tempered firmness with recognition of some justification of the Soviet demands. They directed that the Soviet Government be informed that nothing would be done in Bern save to arrange for a meeting at Field Marshal Alexander's headquarters, where all matters concerning surrender would be discussed. Further, Alexander was to make all the necessary arrangements for the presence of Soviet representatives at any discussions which might take place at his headquarters. They also wished to inform the Red Army General Staff that as the Germans' proposal was for the surrender of a military force on a British-American front, Field Marshal Alexander, as Supreme Commander in the Theater, would alone be responsible for conducting negotiations and reaching decisions.

The Soviet reaction to the message sent by the Combined Chiefs of Staff was contained in a letter from General Antonov which I received on March 18, 1945. Antonov said that in view of our refusal to allow Soviet representatives to participate in the discussions at Bern, the Soviet Government had informed the British and American Governments that it "insists" upon the negotiations being broken off. He added that his generals had been directed not to go to Caserta.

At the direction of the Combined Chiefs of Staff, Alexander continued his efforts to arrange for a German capitulation at his headquarters. Stalin, Molotov, and the General Staff were seething, and I think we only added fuel to the flames by keeping them fully informed of everything that went on. The tenseness of the situation was ameliorated somewhat when we captured Franz von Papen on April 10, 1945, and asked the Soviet General Staff to assign officers to participate in his interrogation. The Soviet officers who were to have gone to Caserta were designated to question von Papen.

The tension was further relieved when the Combined Chiefs of Staff sent a message to General Antonov in which they stated that the present stage of the war indicated the possibility of the surrender of large-scale German forces on all fronts in the immediate future. They proposed that each of the three big Allies be allowed to observe the negotiations for such surrenders, but emphasized that surrenders could not be refused because of the non-presence of representatives of any of the Allies. They recommended that there be an immediate exchange of representatives between the headquarters of all fronts and nominated Admiral Archer to represent the British and me to represent the United States at any surrender negotiations which the Russians might conduct. The Red Army General Staff accepted this proposal and named General Ivan A. Suslaparov to represent them at General Eisenhower's headquarters and General Alexei P. Kislenko to represent them at Field Marshal Alexander's headquarters. It was thus that Soviet representation re-entered the picture in the negotiations that Alexander was attempting to conclude.

Meanwhile, the discussions at Bern and Caserta were having their ups and downs. On April 21, 1945, we were asked by Alexander to inform the Russians that the project had definitely broken down and that the whole matter should be considered as closed. However, a new approach was made by the Germans on April 24, and this time the negotiations were concluded by the capitulation of all German forces in Italy on May 2, 1945. Fortunately General Kislenko and an assistant were present during all the discussions.

While the Bern incident caused a severe strain in our relations with the Soviet Union for more than a month and a half, I believe that it did serve a useful purpose. Regardless of the merits of the case, it marked a distinct turn in the attitude of the United States toward the Soviet Union and gave notice that we were not to be pushed around. Soviet use of the word "insists" in demanding that Alexander's negotiations be broken off brought out into the open a domineering attitude which we had hitherto only suspected. The Soviet officials were told just where they could "get off," and as a result the remainder of the surrender negotiations were conducted in a more friendly atmosphere.

During the period of Alexander's discussions there were indications that the whole German Army was disintegrating. Several approaches were made to General Eisenhower, and he kept the Soviet High Command informed of all of them.

On April 22, 1945, Eisenhower asked me to inform the Russians that the Freedom Council in Denmark had been approached with an offer that the Wehrmacht in Denmark would lay down its arms. Eisenhower sent word to the Freedom Council to obtain further details of the offer. Nothing came of this, but at least the Red Army General Staff was informed that the approach had been made.

On April 24, 1945, Eisenhower sent word of a proposed truce with the German forces in Holland for the purpose of introducing supplies into that country to prevent civilian starvation. He asked that the Red Army General Staff designate a Soviet officer, already at his headquarters, to participate in the discussions.

On April 26, 1945, the Soviet Foreign Office was informed that Himmler had approached the Swedish Government with an offer to surrender all German forces on the western front, including those in Norway, Denmark, and Holland. At the same time, the Soviet Foreign Office was informed that President Truman had sent word to our Minister in Sweden that the only acceptable surrender by Germany was unconditional surrender to the Soviet Government, Great Britain, and the United States on all fronts.

These German approaches were but preliminary feelers to the ultimate surrender that was to take place within a few days. General Eisenhower's efforts to keep the Soviet Government meticulously informed did much to facilitate agreement with the Soviet Union on the final surrender terms.

On May 4, 1945, Eisenhower sent a message to Antonov in which he said that the forces in northwest Germany and Denmark had just surrendered to Field Marshal Montgomery. He said that he had been told by Montgomery that a representative of Admiral Doenitz was proceeding to his headquarters on the following day, the 5th, to arrange for further surrenders, the implication being that all remaining forces of the enemy wished to surrender. Eisenhower added that he intended to inform this representative that Admiral Doenitz should arrange to communicate with the Russian High Command and to surrender to Russia all forces then facing the Red Army, while he took the surrender of those facing the Western Allies, including Norway. He asked, as a matter of urgency, whether this arrangement was satisfactory to the Russian High Command and that he be informed as soon as possible.

The surrender General Eisenhower proposed to accept was to be purely military, and it was to be made clear that it would be entirely independent of political and economic terms to be imposed later upon Germany by the political heads of the Allied nations.

General Eisenhower said he thought that it would be highly desirable for the surrender on the Russian front and the surrender on his front to be arranged so that all hostilities would cease at the same time. He thought this day and hour should be as soon as possible in the interest of saving lives.

Eisenhower asked that he be given a reply from the Russians before Doenitz's representative left headquarters the following day so that he could inform him definitely on these points. He said that General Suslaparov would be invited to attend the negotiations.

Alternately to the above suggestion and in the interests of speed, Eisenhower suggested that if the Russians should like to send representatives to his headquarters fully empowered to act for them, he would be most happy to receive them, provide accommodations, and meet with them jointly in arranging a single and complete military surrender. In this event, he said, basic terms would still be as above suggested, namely, all forces facing the Red Army to surrender locally to the Russians and those on the western front to him.

Eisenhower's proposals were delivered to Antonov orally and in writing. Antonov replied sometime after midnight on the morning of May 5 that Eisenhower's plan was acceptable. He added that should Doenitz refuse to accept the condition of simultaneous surrender on the Russian front, the negotiations should be broken off. He also authorized General Suslaparov to participate in the surrender negotiations, since there would not be time to send additional representatives as suggested in Eisenhower's alternate proposal.

Early in the evening of May 5 I was able to inform General Antonov that Admiral Friedeburg, representing Doenitz, had arrived at General Eisenhower's headquarters at five o'clock that afternoon and had attempted to surrender the remaining German forces on the western front. Further, that General Eisenhower had flatly rejected Friedeburg's offer and had informed him that the Germans would either surrender simultaneously to the Soviet High Command or there would be no cessation of hostilities. Eisenhower wanted Antonov to know that Friedeburg had asked Doenitz for instructions.

On May 6, 1945, we sent General Antonov two documents that were to be signed by the German representatives at General Eisenhower's headquarters provided Doenitz approved a surrender to the Russians. One was entitled "An agreement between the Allied High Commands and certain German Emissaries." In this document the Germans were to agree to appear at a time and place to be designated to sign an unconditional surrender. The other document was entitled "Act of Military Surrender" and provided for simultaneous surrender on both the eastern and western fronts.

Early on the morning of May 7 I received a letter from Antonov in which he had some minor comments to make on these two documents. His suggestions were embodied in the formal act of surrender later signed at Berlin. Antonov also expressed his fear that the Germans had no intention of surrendering on the Russian front. To support this view he called attention to broadcasts that had been made from the German headquarters, calling for continued resistance to the Red Army. These broadcasts were not surprising as they were made on May 5, and it will be recalled that at that time Friedeburg was authorized to surrender only to the Western Allies. Antonov's final demand came in the nature of a bombshell when he stated that the Soviet Government would wish the signing of the "Act of Military Surrender" to take place in Berlin, with Marshal Zhukov representing the Soviet Government.

At about the same time I received Antonov's letter I received word from General Eisenhower announcing that General Jodl, representing the German High Command, had signed the unconditional surrender of all German land, sea, and air forces to the Allied Expeditionary Forces and simultaneously to the Soviet High Command at 1:41 A.M., Central European Time, on the morning of May 7. The message said that General Suslaparov had signed for the Russians. The surrender was to be effective at 11:01 P.M., Central European Time, May 8. My message to Eisenhower saying that the Russians wanted the surrender to take place in Berlin had crossed his to me saying that it had already taken place at Reims.

While General Eisenhower and his staff believed that another signing would be anticlimactic, they had prepared for such an eventuality by having the German emissaries sign an undertaking in which they agreed to appear later at any place designated to execute a formal ratification, on behalf of the German High Command, of the unconditional surrender already signed.

General Eisenhower was deeply concerned when he received General Antonov's message questioning the sincerity of the German surrender and stating that the Soviet High Command desired the surrender to be accomplished in Berlin. He immediately sent Antonov a reply saying that he felt that Antonov would understand that he had scrupulously adhered to the engagement of no separate truce on the western front and that he (Eisenhower) would be very happy to come to Berlin on the following day at an hour to be specified by Marshal Zhukov. Eisenhower added that in the event that weather prevented his arrival at the specified time, he would be entirely satisfied to have the British and American heads of the Military Missions in Moscow sign for him in his absence.

Eisenhower's message reached me at 9:30 P.M. on the night of May 7, and he proposed a full-dress meeting be held in Berlin at noon the following day! During the remainder of that night I was to have ample evidence that the Russians can work fast if the spirit moves them. Messages kept coming in from Eisenhower which I had to take to Antonov and interpret orally to avoid the necessity of written translations. At 9:45 P.M. I received word that eleven members of the press would accompany Eisenhower's party to Berlin. At 10:00 P.M. I received a message asking me to obtain Soviet approval for General Suslaparov to accompany Eisenhower; one received at midnight informed me that Eisenhower would not come but would send Air Chief Marshal Tedder as his representative, together with ten other officers; one at 3:25 A.M. on May 8 gave the types and serial numbers of our party's aircraft and the routes they would follow; finally, one arrived at 9:00 A.M. stating that General de Lattre de Tassigny would be included in the party to represent the French. I also received a number of messages from Antonov to send to Eisenhower. The most important of these was Soviet approval of the Berlin meeting which was handed to me at 11:30 P.M., two hours after I had submitted General Eisenhower's proposal. It must have been a busy night for the Red Army General Staff, because they had to send directions to Zhukov and answer the many questions he must have had to ask. I can well imagine that Antonov that night regretted that he had refused to allow a radioteletype channel to be set up between Moscow and General Eisenhower's headquarters—I know that I longed for it many times.

In Eisenhower's message to Antonov he said that he would be perfectly satisfied to have Admiral Archer and me sign for him in Berlin if weather prevented the arrival of his party. This meant that we had to be in Berlin by the following noon! Normally it required a week or two to arrange for the exit of foreigners from the Soviet Union.

In this case, however, the Soviet Foreign Office responded promptly, and that was the only occasion on which I escaped without the formality of an exit visa. A C-54 four-engine plane was scheduled to depart from Moscow for the United States on the morning of May 8 at eight o'clock. I cancelled that at once and had the plane stand by to take Archer and me to Berlin at five o'clock in the morning. We offered to take any Soviet officials who cared to accompany us, but the only ones who accepted were the inevitable navigator and radio operator.

Before describing that unforgettable day in Berlin I shall digress for a moment and outline some of the difficulties which attended our joint efforts to make a simultaneous announcement of the German capitulation to the waiting world.

Shortly after Jodl had signed the surrender at Reims on the morning of May 7, General Eisenhower sent the Combined Chiefs of Staff in Washington his ideas on how the public announcement should be handled. He sent me an information copy of this message. He said that if it was deemed necessary to time the announcement with the cessation of hostilities, it should be made at 1:00 P.M., Greenwich Mean Time, on Tuesday, May 8. Eisenhower was fearful, however, that the news would leak out earlier because of the orders to cease hostilities that were being broadcast in the clear. He therefore suggested that the three Governments try, if possible, to arrange for a release later in the day on May 7. I sent General Eisenhower's proposals to General Antonov so that the Soviet Government would have time to consider the question before they were approached by the British and American Governments.

On the evening of May 7, George Kennan, our Chargé d'Affaires, transmitted a message to Marshal Stalin from President Truman. The President said he assumed that General Eisenhower's suggestion that the news release be made at 1:00 P.M., May 8, Greenwich Mean Time, was acceptable to all and that he would therefore make the announcement at the corresponding Washington time, which would be 9:00 A.M., May 8.

At about the same time that President Truman's message was being delivered to Marshal Stalin, I received a reply from General Antonov concerning Eisenhower's proposals for the announcement. Antonov said that in the Soviet High Command there was no conviction that the Germans would surrender on the Russian front. He was afraid that the announcement might put the Soviet High Command in an embarrassing position and mislead Soviet public opinion. He said that despite the surrender that had been signed at Reims, radio intercepts indicated that a significant group of German troops had openly stated that they would refuse to obey Doenitz's order to surrender. Antonov proposed that the announcement be postponed until after the formal signing in Berlin and suggested that it be made at 7:00 P.M., Moscow time, on May 9. He said by that time we would know if the surrender was actually to be made.

I sent Antonov's views to the Combined Chiefs of Staff in Washington and to General Eisenhower. While they no doubt reflected the attitude of Stalin, the burden was on Stalin to inform the President personally if he disagreed with the procedure the President had proposed. This Stalin did not do.

The situation was further complicated by the enthusiasm of Prime Minister Churchill, who was eager to let his people know that victory had come. On the afternoon of May 7 he sent word to the President that he felt an announcement was inevitable and inferred that he intended to go ahead and make one at 6:00 P.M., British time, May 7, which was noon in Washington and 8:00 P. M. in Moscow. Washington was in a turmoil. The President felt he had made a commitment to Stalin not to make an announcement before 9:00 A.M., May 8, Washington time. He was willing to move the time forward, however, if Stalin's concurrence could be obtained.

At 6:00 P.M., Moscow time, which was only two hours before Churchill's threatened time of announcement, I was called to our radio station for a radioteletype conference with Colonel Frank McCarthy, Secretary of the War Department General Staff. He told me the situation and asked if I could obtain Stalin's concurrence to making the announcement in just two hours. Frank agreed to stand by at the radio station in Washington and I agreed to do my best to get him the desired information. Of course the idea was preposterous—things are simply not done in Russia on two hours' notice, particularly when they involve a complicated national radio hook-up and the preparation of a speech by the head of state. Nevertheless, I asked George Kennan to tackle the Foreign Office while I arranged a meeting with the General Staff through the office of my old brush-off friend General Estigneev. George was much more successful than I and at 7:00 P.M. I was able to inform Frank McCarthy that Vishinsky had answered officially that they could not agree to advancing the hour of the announcement. The reason given was that the Soviet Government had not yet heard officially from General Suslaparov that the surrender had actually been signed.

In the end, both the President and the Prime Minister made their announcements at the hour on May 8 that had been proposed originally by General Eisenhower. I heard the President's announcement over a radio in Berlin. The Russian announcement was not made until thirteen hours later, at 2:00 A.M. on the morning of May 9, following the formal signing in Berlin. Nothing could provide better evidence of the isolation of the Russian people than the fact that the whole world had been celebrating the peace for twelve hours and had accumulated millions of headaches and hangovers before Russians in Russia even knew that the war was over.

Admiral Archer and I left Moscow for Berlin at five o'clock on the morning of May 8. I was dead tired, as I had had no sleep since May 5. When I boarded our plane, the crew insisted that I come up to the forward compartment and sleep on one of their bunks. The crew was in seventh heaven at the prospect of going to Berlin, and as I was responsible for it, nothing was too good for me. There was some element of danger connected with flying into Berlin in a foreign plane, since it was possible that not all of the Soviet anti-aircraft defenses had been informed of our arrival, but I was too tired to think of that. I don't think I had turned over once before I was wakened and told that we were about to land on Tempelhof airdrome. The flight required six hours, but because of a time difference of one hour, we landed in Berlin at ten.

When Archer and I got out of our plane we found Zhukov's entire staff, headed by Marshal Vasili D. Sokolovsky, on hand to greet us. They were there early to be sure they would be in time to greet General Eisenhower. When they saw Archer and me their jaws dropped as though at a command. They recovered quickly, however, and were most gracious to us. They were disappointed again when I told them that General Eisenhower would not be able to come himself but would be represented by Air Chief Marshal Tedder.

The Russians had a guard of honor of about one battalion with a band and the massed Allied colors waiting on the airdrome to greet Air Chief Marshal Tedder. Their greatest immediate concern was to see that the German emissaries who were included in Tedder's party should not be allowed to leave their airplanes until the guard of honor had completed its ceremony. They asked if we could help them arrange this. I said I thought we could and went back to my plane to have the radio operator send word to the planes in Tedder's group not to let any Germans disembark upon arrival at Tempelhof. I found the crew of my plane stretched out on the grass in the shade of the wings of our big C-54. They were busily congratulating themselves on their "firsts"—"the first Americans in Berlin," "the first C-54 in Berlin," "the first navigator in Berlin," and so on. They were having such fun I hated to break it up, but I detailed one man to meet each of Tedder's five planes to see that the Germans stayed aboard.

Tempelhof was the largest airdrome I have ever seen. Oddly enough, it had no hard metal runways, but the whole tremendous field was circled by a wide concrete taxiing strip. From the air it looked like a huge doughnut. On the outer edge of a ninety-degree arc stood four-story concrete and steel buildings that were concave to conform to the curve. Most of them were completely gutted as the result of our strategic bombing. The first two stories were hangars and some could still be used as such once the debris had been removed.

Underground, beneath the airdrome, were several stories of an airplane assembly plant. This had suffered very little damage.

Tedder and his party arrived about an hour after we did. He was accompanied by General "Tooey" Spaatz, an old classmate of mine from Leavenworth days, Admiral Sir Bertram Ramsay, Major General H. R. ("Pinky") Bull, who had been one of my instructors years ago at Fort Benning, Major General Ken Strong, the British Intelligence officer on Eisenhower's Staff, and General de Lattre de Tassigny, the French representative. Captain Harry C. Butcher, Eisenhower's Naval aide, was on hand to take care of the British-American press, and he was assisted by Colonel R. Ernest Depuy, Colonel John ("Tex") O'Reilly, and Lieutenant Colonel James Gault. Three women were included in the party, Lieutenant Kay Summersby, General Eisenhower's WAC aide; Major Sally Bagby, General Spaatz's WAC aide, and Warrant Officer Nana Rae, General Eisenhower's secretary.

As soon as the guard of honor had finished its ceremony, the Germans were allowed to leave the planes. The principal German emissaries who were to sign the surrender were Field Marshal Wilhelm Keitel, Admiral Hans von Friedeburg and General P. F. Stumpf of the German Luftwaffe. Keitel was the embodiment of all things Prussian. He carried his marshal's baton, wore a monocle, and was covered with decorations, including the blue ribbon, the most cherished German award. The Germans were aloof and disdainful but militarily correct.

The entire party was taken to Karlhorst, a little suburb east of Berlin, in a caravan of captured German motor vehicles. The automobiles must have been specially selected, as they were most luxurious. Mine was a long convertible job with deep soft red leather seats. I could not help but think of what the Russian reaction must have been to such automobiles, considering the old and rickety cars one saw in the streets of Moscow.

Our trip to Karlhorst was made at lightning speed along a route around the southern edge of Berlin. Off to our left we could see the city in ruins. The Russian guide in my car explained that it had been impossible to find sufficient housing in Berlin proper to take care of the group attending the surrender ceremony. They had been forced to select a small military engineering college in Karlhorst which was about fifteen miles from the center of the city.

When we arrived at Karlhorst we were divided into groups of two or three persons each and assigned to cottages. The neighborhood must have been occupied normally by persons of modest circumstances. The houses were of the small cracker-box type, all very much the same. However, each one had a garden, the rooms were neat, and the furniture and fixtures included such luxuries and conveniences as tiled bathrooms and combination radio-phonographs.

The house to which I was assigned had a small library and the most handsomely bound book was a copy of *Mein Kampf* which the Russians had not yet seen and destroyed. I examined it with great interest, and when I returned to Moscow and described it to my friends they were surprised that I had not pocketed it as a souvenir. When I thought of it, I was surprised myself, and I am sure I would have taken it had it occurred to me to do so.

The British and American delegation soon assembled in the largest of the cottages, which had been assigned to Tedder. He was anxious to sign the instrument of surrender at once and return to Paris. But he had reckoned without the Russians. We all sat around waiting for something to happen and soon some Red Army women appeared with caviar, both black and red, raw salmon on bread, wine and vodka— invariable Russian preliminaries to any important event. We ate while we listened to President Truman's announcement of the peace to the people of the United States.

Presently an orderly appeared who informed Tedder that Marshal Zhukov would be pleased to meet him at his headquarters at four o'clock that afternoon. The chances of Tedder's returning to Paris that day began to fade. We learned later that Zhukov had to wait for the arrival of Vishinsky from Moscow before he could make a move.

When the four o'clock meeting did materialize, the French representative, De Tassigny, complicated the proceedings by producing a letter from De Gaulle stating that he should sign the instrument of surrender on behalf of the French High Command. This was objectionable to Tedder, whose instructions authorized him to sign the surrender as General Eisenhower's representative on behalf of all the Western Allies. If the French were to be specially represented, then the Americans, Canadians, Brazilians, and innumerable other Allies should also participate as separate entities. This issue was argued back and forth for several hours and was finally settled by preparing the document for the signatures of Zhukov and Tedder as principals, and De Tassigny and Spaatz as witnesses. The argument developed some heated discussions, with Zhukov, probably at Vishinsky's instigation, taking sides with De Tassigny. It was the first strong Soviet bid for a closer postwar relationship with France, and this became more pronounced as the day wore on.

It was arranged that the ceremony would take place in the assembly hall of the small engineering college across the street from the quarters we occupied. We all went there at about eight o'clock in the evening and sat around in anterooms until about a half-hour past midnight, when the surrender document was ready in its final form. Vishinsky had a great many changes in language to suggest. None were radical departures from the document that had been signed at Reims the day before, but each one had to be thoroughly explored to determine its implications. Each change necessitated a complete rewrite of the surrender document in Russian and English, and each rewrite had to be carefully compared by interpreters to see that the meaning was the same in both languages. The lights in the anteroom we were in did not work, and so Warrant Officer Nana Rae wrote and rewrote the document in English time and again on her portable typewriter by candlelight.

It was a long and trying wait for all of us, and occasionally we would slip across the street to our cottages and have a nip of Scotch which some of our people had thoughtfully brought along. Meanwhile, the German emissaries were closeted in a closely guarded room where they must have been wondering why the Allies could not make up their minds and get the agony over with.

When we gathered in the assembly hall for the surrender we found a long table at the end of the room at which the principal Allied representatives were to sit. Zhukov took his place at the center, as master of ceremonies. Tedder was not sure that he liked this and thought for a while that the seats should be moved a bit so that he could share the central place with Zhukov. He let the arrangement stand, however, on the grounds that Berlin was a Russian bailiwick at the moment, which justified Zhukov, as the representative of the host nation, in acting as chairman. Tedder sat on Zhukov's right and Spaatz on his left. Vishinsky sat on Tedder's right, which considerably irritated Admiral Ramsay. Vishinsky might just as well have remained standing as he was constantly bobbing up to whisper instructions in Zhukov's ear. The table was completed with Admiral Ramsay on Vishinsky's right and De Tassigny on Spaatz's left. The whole table was under the glare of klieg lights, and the Allied colors were arranged in a stand in back of it.

Three long tables extended at right angles from the head table. The one on the right was for the press; that in the center for Soviet, British, and American officers; and that on the left was left vacant and reserved for the Germans.

I think that all the cameramen in the Soviet Union must have been present that night. Comparing them with the few whom Tedder had brought, I concluded that news photographers must be the same the world over. They were on chairs, tables, and each other's shoulders, and Archer and I soon gave up trying to brush them off so that we could see what was going on.

Zhukov called the meeting to order and directed a Russian general to bring the Germans in. They entered the room led by Keitel, arrogant and dignified. Tedder rose and asked them in a thin but harsh voice if they were ready to sign the instrument of surrender. Keitel nodded his acquiescence. The three German principals then took seats at the head table, with the assistants grouped in rear, and all copies of the document were signed in silence—except for the explosion of hundreds of flash bulbs. As soon as the signing was concluded, the Germans filed out, and Zhukov announced that the delegation would assemble again in the same room in about one hour for a banquet of celebration.

The banquet was one never to be forgottten. The food must have been specially imported from Moscow. It was the usual Moscow spread, but the linen, china, and silverware must have been gathered from the cottages in the neighborhood. The tablecloth was made up of overlapping unbleached linen bedsheets, and the napkins were small squares of material torn from the sheets. It was a somewhat crude setting, but the festive mood of the participants more than made up for any shortcomings.

As usual, the toasts were continuous and endless. British-American-Soviet friendship was at its peak. Zhukov paid a glowing tribute to Eisenhower, characterizing him as "the greatest military strategist of our time." Vishinsky talked for nearly an hour and pretty well covered the history of the Soviet Union in coming to his point, whatever it may have been. Even this did not relieve the pressure of heavy drinking, because he interrupted his speech several times to drink bottoms up to some aspect of our joint friendship. Zhukov at once resorted to drinking his toasts in a light white wine. Tedder saw him and followed suit. "Tooey" Spaatz, on Zhukov's left, must have been blind in his right eye or else he overestimated his staying powers, for he matched Zhukov's white wine with tumblers of vodka. I have never been prouder of "Tooey" than when I later saw him walk out of the banquet hall on his own two feet. The Russians had an interpreter who soon lost his voice, leaving the entire burden of translating the glowing sentiments that were being bandied about to Captain Henry Ware, whom I had brought with me from Moscow. Ware has a flair for the dramatic and he translated the toasts in a loud falsetto voice which carried even more feeling than the person making the toast had intended. We were almost overcome with emotion, vodka, or both.

The banquet lasted until six o'clock in the morning, when we formed our motor caravan again for the return trip to Templehof. On the way the Russians took us on a tour of Berlin that started at the Opera House at the head of Unter den Linden and carried us past the tomb of the unknown soldier, the Adlon, the Reichstag, the monument commemorating the Franco-Prussian war, and the Reichs-chancellory. We made stops at all the points of interest but they were unnecessary. Everything looked the same—a mass of rubble and debris. It was still too soon for the streets to have been cleared, and the caravan raised a cloud of dust that was nearly blinding as we threaded our way along the lanes that had been cut through the bricks and masonry.

The guard of honor was at Tempelhof to salute Tedder and his delegation. Most of his party missed the ceremony, however, and dashed to their aircraft, where they dropped into their seats and into unconsciousness as a result of fatigue from the day before and the vodka at the party which followed. Archer and I were old hands at Russian parties and hence were still able to navigate. We finally justified our presence in Berlin by acting as Tedder's staff as he took the review of the Templehof guard of honor.

Archer and I reached Moscow about two o'clock in the afternoon and found the city in the midst of a celebration that had started twelve hours earlier. General Spalding and my aide, Major Howard R. Taylor, met me at the airport and cautioned me to lock the doors of my car as it approached the American Embassy. The square in front of the Embassy, which is about as large as four of our square city blocks, was jammed with people. They were there to show their friendship for the United States. Their efforts to open the doors of my car and pull Spalding, Taylor, and me out were futile. However, they did seize every American who emerged from our Embassy and tossed him like a cork on water on their upraised hands over the heads of the crowd. Whenever an American appeared at the Embassy windows, there were prolonged cheers and calls for him to come out.

I finally succeeded in reaching my quarters and went immediately to bed. I dropped off to sleep at once despite the riotous celebration that continued outdoors. The day was cold in Moscow, but my heart was warmed by the spontaneous spirit of friendship being shown by the thousands of Russian people in the square outside my window. I had great hopes for the future.

XI. Repatriation of Prisoners of War

M Y DARKEST days in Russia were in the winter of 1944-45 when
I was trying to arrange for the best possible care and speedy
repatriation of American prisoners of war liberated by the
advance of the Red Army. Of all the casualties of war, none elicit
more sympathy from the American people than those known to be in
the hands of the enemy. I felt a great personal responsibility in the
matter. As the senior military officer in Russia it was up to me to see
that American war prisoners liberated on the eastern front received
the sympathetic treatment and warm reception which they had earned
by their valor and suffering. Thousands of American families were
looking to me to see that their loved ones were returned to them
quickly. I knew that General Marshall would not be one to condone
any failure on my part in caring for our liberated soldiers. From a
broader viewpoint, there was an opportunity to build up good will
between our two countries by the solicitude we displayed for each
other's liberated prisoners. Despite all this, none of my negotiations
with Soviet officialdom met with less success. The story is not a pleasant one. It is marked by broken agreements, vindictiveness, recriminations, and stupidity on the part of the Soviet leaders.

Germany had millions of Allied prisoners of war. There were more
Russians among them than any other nationality. There were a great
many categories of Russians, including those captured in military action, those who voluntarily or involuntarily went over to the German
side to fight, and those taken from Russia for forced labor. In all,
they totaled from three to five million. Aside from the few interned

at the beginning of the war, there was only one category of Americans in Germany—those captured in military action. In the winter of 1944-45 these totaled about seventy-five thousand. One would have thought that the Russians had everything to gain through close adherence to reciprocal agreements concerning the treatment to be afforded liberated persons as there were so many more Russians involved. Instead, the Soviet leaders tried to eat their cake and have it too. Their interpretation of agreements reached coincided with ours concerning the treatment of Russians liberated by us, but they made a different interpretation with regard to the treatment of Americans liberated by them.

The problems that would arise from the liberation of Allied nationals could be foreseen with more certainty than victory itself. Generally speaking, Germany kept her war prisoners as far from the countries of which they were nationals as possible. This meant that most of the Americans were in prisoner-of-war camps in eastern Germany, Poland, or the Balkans. Through the International Red Cross we had a fairly accurate idea of where the American camps were situated and of the numbers in each. By the middle of 1944 the Red Army began to arrive within striking distance of many of these camps, and there appeared to be a good chance of some of them being overrun if the Red Army made some unusually long and rapid advances.

Since the British and the Americans were acting as a combined force on the western front, Lieutenant General Burrows, head of the British Military Mission, and I approached the problem of repatriating liberated prisoners on a joint basis. We made our first approach to the Red Army General Staff on June 11, 1944. We called attention to the quick advance of the Red Army into Rumania and presented the Russians with a list of British and American prisoner-of-war camps known to be in its path. We requested the General Staff to inform us without delay of any of our camps which might be taken so that we could arrange for a prompt return of our men to Britain and the United States. At the same time, I gave General Slavin, my General

Staff contact, a full list of the names of all Americans known to be in Rumania and Hungary.

Slavin reassured us that instructions would be issued which would make certain that any British or American nationals whom the Red Army might liberate would be well cared for. We could see that the problem was one that had not occurred to the General Staff and that they had made no plans to meet it.

The first large-scale release of American prisoners of war came with Rumania's collapse and withdrawal from the Axis toward the end of August 1944. I first heard of their liberation on August 29 in a message from General Ben Giles, who was commanding the American forces in the Middle East. He said his Air Force representative in Rumania had reported that all British and American prisoners of war were being concentrated in Bucharest and that King Michael had personally guaranteed their safety. The following day I had word from our Military Attaché in Ankara that the Rumanian Military Attaché to Turkey had told him that Americans liberated in Rumania would be released promptly. There were about one thousand officers and enlisted men involved, and the Rumanian Attaché suggested that they be evacuated by air.

Giles worked out a plan with General Eaker, commanding our Mediterranean Air Force, whereby American planes were flown to designated fields in Rumania on September 1, 2, and 3 to pick up our ex-prisoners. This mass evacuation by air was accomplished through arrangements made with the Rumanian military authorities before the Russians had complete control of the country. It was successful through a fortunate combination of circumstances, which included the presence of a few Americans who seized the initiative and put the project over before the Russian regime had become fully established. However, in certain areas the local Russian commanders did assist us without prior reference to Moscow.

Meanwhile, the Red Army was approaching some of the American prisoner-of-war camps in western Poland and eastern Prussia. In the north we would have to rely completely on Russian co-operation, so it was imperative that we reach some preliminary agreements and prepare for the event by advance planning.

On August 30, 1944, I prepared a letter which I asked Averell Harriman to send to Molotov, and at the same time I sent a similar one to General Antonov. I proposed that our two Governments agree, first, that when the liberation of American or Soviet prisoners of war could be foreseen through the imminent recapture of territory where prisoner-of-war camps were known to exist, plans should be worked out as far in advance as possible for the prompt return of such prisoners to their respective homelands; second, that there should be a prompt and continued exchange of information regarding the location of prisoner-of-war camps in hostile territory and that Soviet and American officers should always be available to go to those which came under the control of each other's armies for the purpose of establishing the nationality of the prisoners who were liberated and assuming control of them until they were repatriated; and, third, that individuals or small groups claiming Soviet or American nationality should be promptly reported by name to the authorities of the nation in which they claimed citizenship so that their claims could be substantiated and they could be repatriated promptly.

Neither Harriman nor I had replies to our letters for several months although we each kept pressing for one. While we were waiting I appointed a board of officers to prepare a plan for handling ex-prisoners once they were liberated in sizable numbers. We sent to England for medical supplies, new clothing, and a few luxury items such as candy and tobacco. We arranged for the Persian Gulf Command to set aside a reserve of supplies for delivery by air to such points as we might designate. Arrangements were made to increase the hospital accommodations of our air base at Poltava, as we hoped to fly those seriously ill from Poland or eastern Germany to Poltava for medical attention. Finally, we arranged to have a group of officers and enlisted men who had had special training sent from England to Russia to make contact with any Americans who might be liberated. Our arrangements were closely co-ordinated with those of the British, and it was agreed that we would double our coverage by sharing our supplies and facilities.

General Eisenhower's staff became concerned about Russia's unwillingness to make any commitments concerning the treatment of American prisoners liberated by the Red Army. They wrote me a letter in which they stated that there was a group of Russians at General Eisenhower's headquarters in connection with the repatriation of displaced Russian and Red Army prisoners of war which was being afforded every facility for its work. There was the possibility of curtailing their activities if the Russians did not show some disposition to reciprocate. I did not favor doing this because there was no chance whatever of our winning in a competition of discourtesy with Soviet officials. On the other hand, something had to be done.

Harriman was away, so on November 6 I asked our Chargé, George Kennan, to write to Molotov again, asking for a Foreign Office reply to the proposals Averell had made in his letter of August 30. In addition, I tackled Slavin in an attempt to get an answer to the letter I had written Antonov. The only satisfaction I could get was that the Red Army was doing and would continue to do everything possible for the well-being of Americans whom they might liberate. He then gave me the first of a series of complaints about how we were handling Russians liberated on the western front. It was an attack typical of the Russians when they fully realized the insecurity of their own position. He was unable to tell me just what his complaints were but promised to do so in a few days. I told him if there was any basis for his accusations there was all the more reason why we should reach an agreement on the measures to be taken in looking after each other's ex-prisoners of war.

I received a full statement of the situation on the western front from General Eisenhower's headquarters after I had informed him of Slavin's complaints. Prior to the invasion the Russians had been asked to advise General Eisenhower as to the disposition they desired made of Russian nationals found serving in the German forces. The Russian representatives at Eisenhower's headquarters replied that the question would not arise since there were no Russians so serving. About four months after the invasion we had accumulated twenty-eight thousand Russians in German uniform, but, in view of what the Russian representatives had said, they were treated as German prisoners of war. General Vasiliev, the senior Russian representative at Eisenhower's headquarters, became alarmed at this and asked that the Russian nationals be segregated and given preferential treatment. This was being done, but the administrative problem of segregating the Russians from more than half a million Germans who had been captured was tremendous. It was admitted that conditions were unsatisfactory but remedial action was being taken as fast as possible.

Actually, of course, this was one of the most troublesome of all the problems which arose in connection with liberated persons. In the first place, it took some time to determine the nationality of Russians in the process of interrogating thousands upon thousands of German prisoners. In the second, those taken in German uniforms objected, almost without exception, to being returned to Russian custody for fear of the retribution which would await them. A large number of these prisoners stood on their rights, claimed German citizenship as a result of their inclusion in the German Armed Forces, and insisted on being treated as German prisoners of war under the provisions of the Geneva Convention. To avoid reprisals by Germany against our own men held as prisoners of war by the Germans, we took the position that we would have to hold those Russians found in German uniform until the end of the war, when the danger of reprisals had been removed by victory.

The Government-controlled Soviet press, never as concerned with maintaining Allied unity as were we in the United States, began to voice Soviet displeasure. Slavin's protest to me was expanded upon by Colonel General Filip Golikov in the November 9 issue of *Pravda*. He spoke of the millions of Russians who had been taken to Germany and France as forced laborers. He said that many of them had escaped to assist the French Partisans. Then he pointed to the countless Russians who had been forced into German uniform but who had deserted at the first opportunity to fight on the side of the Allies. Golikov complained that despite these heroic feats by Soviet citizens, they had been put into prisoner-of-war camps with Germans and that the latter were being given preferential treatment by the Western Allies.

On November 25, 1944, Molotov, in a letter addressed to George Kennan, finally replied to the proposals and looked toward reciprocal treatment of liberated prisoners. Molotov accepted our proposals "in principle" and said that Soviet representatives would meet with me to work out the details. However, he also registered a complaint about the way Russian citizens were being detained by the Allies in German prisoner-of-war camps in both Western Europe and the United States. It was the old question of Russians captured in German uniforms while in the act of shooting at American soldiers. We could hardly be expected to put them up at the Ritz in Paris or the Mayflower in Washington—at least not until we found out that they were really our friends.

Nothing happened for a month, and so, on December 28, Harriman wrote Molotov again asking that the discussions be arranged. On the same day we received a reply saying that Lieutenant General K. D. Golubev and Major General Slavin had been selected to meet with me to work out "questions connected with the plan for mutual repatriation of Soviet and American prisoners of war and civilians." I had my first meeting with Golubev on January 19, 1945, just a little over six months after my first approach to the General Staff on the subject.

General Golubev was the deputy administrator of the newly formed Repatriation Commission, which was headed by Colonel General Golikov. Physically he was the most tremendous human being I have ever seen. He must have been seven feet tall and was almost as wide. Unfortunately his mental stature did not conform to the size of his body. I don't think there was anything vicious in his make-up and I believe he tried to do his best to live up to the agreements we finally reached. He was unable to do so because of restrictions placed on him as a result of our strained relations with Russia over the Polish political situation and the resultant Soviet displeasure which was reflected in all branches of government.

I found him in his office surrounded by his satellites. They seemed to be as necessary to him as food and drink. When he made a statement they would nod in agreement; when he was humorous they would laugh; when he was angry they would frown. He was the sort of boss who looked at each of his assistants in turn to see that they were reacting properly, and I had the impression that they had damned well better.

Golubev had followed the usual Soviet procedure of avoiding arguments that might arise in working out a joint plan with a foreigner by having one ready to hand to me. It was a reasonable plan and with a few minor amendments was exactly what we wanted. Since it involved the treatment to be afforded Soviet ex-prisoners of war on the western front, I said I would have to send it to General Eisenhower in France and to General McNarney in Italy for comment before negotiating further. This was satisfactory to Golubev, and we adjourned to an outer office where a banquet was spread to celebrate our first meeting. After a few rounds of vodka we parted on a note of cordiality that was never again to be attained. The agreement was signed a few weeks later at the Yalta Conference. I signed for us and Lieutenant General Gryzlov, my old General Staff friend from Moscow Conference days, signed for the Soviet Union. The agreement was a good one, but, so far as the Russians were concerned, it turned out to be just another piece of paper.

Article One of the agreement provided that all Soviet citizens liberated by the United States and all United States citizens liberated by the Soviet Union would be segregated from enemy prisoners of war and maintained in separate camps until they had been handed over to their respective military authorities at places to be mutually agreed upon. By agreeing that each army would protect camps so established from enemy bombing and artillery fire, we implied that the initial concentrations of liberated prisoners were to be as close to the point of liberation as possible. This point was made clear to the Soviet representatives when we were negotiating the agreement at Yalta. We pointed out our desire to meet liberated American prisoners of war at once with medical aid, clean clothing, telegraph blanks, money, and other necessities.

As the agreement was actually carried out by the Russians, we were not allowed to meet our men until they had made their way on their own and as best they could all the way across Poland and had come onto Russian soil. The reason for this probably was that the Soviet leaders did not want American or British officers within Poland where they could observe the methods being used to bring Poland under the domination of the Soviet Union. The world was to be led to believe that the Poles were so enthusiastically happy at their deliverance from the Germans that they wanted nothing more than to embrace their Russian liberators, including their ideology. It was true that the Poles were grateful for their deliverance from Nazi domination, but from the reports of our liberated prisoners who made their way through Poland, one cannot but believe that the Polish people soon began to wonder if they had not jumped from the frying pan into the fire.

Article Two of our agreement provided that our respective military authorities would inform each other without delay regarding American or Soviet citizens found or liberated, and that the repatriation representatives of each nation would have the right of immediate access to the camps or concentration points in which their citizens were located, where they would take over the internal administration and discipline of the camps. The article stipulated that facilities would be given for the dispatch of contact officers to camps containing ex-prisoners of their own nationality. It was in the implementation of this article that we met with our most miserable failure.

The first sizable group of Americans to be liberated by the Red Army were those from the American officers' prisoner-of-war camp at Szubin in northwestern Poland. The Germans, forced to leave Szubin in a hurry on January 21, 1945, because of the unusually rapid advance of the Red Army, left behind them about one hundred Americans, some of them quite seriously ill. Those able to travel were taken westward by the Germans. Daily thereafter, American prisoners of war either escaped from the Germans or were liberated by the Russians, but my first information concerning them came from the Polish Minister in Moscow on February 14, 1945, who sent word to me that there were about one thousand Americans in various Polish cities. Three days later three American officers arrived in Moscow after hitch-hiking across Poland and western Russia. This was almost a month after they had escaped from the Germans, and yet I had had no notification from Golubev concerning their release. The officers who arrived in Moscow were Captain Ernest M. Gruenberg, a medical officer from New York City, who had been captured while serving with the 317th Parachute Battalion on June 8, 1944, near Monteburg, France; Second Lieutenant Frank H. Colley from Washington, Georgia, captured while serving with the 17th Field Artillery on February 17, 1943, in Tunisia; and Second Lieutenant John N. Dimmling, Jr., from Winston-Salem, North Carolina, captured while serving with the 30th Infantry on February 1, 1944, at the Anzio beachhead.

The fact that these three officers could have made their way across Poland and Russia without being taken into custody by the N.K.V.D. was one of the freakish incidents of war that defy explanation. Their story was packed with drama. They had been in the American camp at Szubin and were among those whom the Germans attempted to evacuate to the west. They left Szubin on January 21, 1945, and made long daily forced marches toward the interior of Germany in order to avoid capture by the Red Army, which was close on the heels of the retreating Germans. At night they would be allowed to sleep in stables or whatever shelter might be available. On the second morning these three officers hid themselves in some hay in the stables at which they had spent the night, and when their German guards formed the columns to resume the march they simply failed to appear. The Russians were so close that the Germans did not take time to search for them.

That afternoon they were behind the lines of the Red Army. The

Russians paid little attention to them except to tell them to go to the east. This started their trek that was to end in Moscow. Captain Gruenberg spent some days assisting the Russians in the care of their wounded. He worked with a woman major who was the surgeon of one of the Russian field hospitals. The three officers made their way to Wegheim, near Exin in Poland, where they found a small concentration of American ex-prisoners in a camp under Russian control. They remained at this camp for a few days; they tried to find out what disposition was to be made of them but obtained no satisfaction from the camp commander. They escaped from the Wegheim camp on February 3, 1945, and started east. During the day they would get rides on Russian supply vehicles going to the rear for replenishment, and at night they would seek shelter from Polish farmers and peasants. They met other small groups of Americans, all seeking some American in authority. They avoided forming large groups for fear of being taken to the Russian repatriation camp at Rembertow on the outskirts of Warsaw; they had all been warned of the hardships they would encounter there. Finally, they found a troop train on its way to Moscow. When they got off the train at the Moscow station, a Russian soldier told them how they could get to the American Military Mission. The N.K.V.D. had fallen down. Other Americans who arrived in Moscow later were seized by the Secret Police as soon as they left their trains and taken to a barracks outside the city where they were thoroughly interrogated for a few days before being turned over to my custody.

I don't think any officers ever had a more sincere welcome than those first three bedraggled ex-prisoners did when they came into our headquarters. To us they represented the thousands of Americans who we expected would be liberated and for whom we were prepared to do so much if only allowed the opportunity. At last I could get firsthand information. It would no longer be necessary to theorize in my negotiations with the Russians. They were taken to one of our officers' messes and given hot baths, clean clothes, insignia of rank, American food, and whisky. I dropped in at the mess later in the evening and found that my officers had promoted a huge party in their honor. Our guests were the center of attraction, and all their hardships seemed to have been forgotten. Certainly by that time a complete metamorphosis in their appearance had been accomplished, and once again they looked like officers of the American Army.

I learned from them that about two hundred Americans had either been left behind by the Germans at Szubin or had escaped from the German column before they themselves had left it. They told me of about thirty Americans who were in a Russian hospital at Wegheim. Hundreds of American families were relieved of considerable anxiety when we were able to send word to the War Department of those who Gruenberg, Colley, and Dimmling knew had escaped from the Germans. Among these was First Lieutenant Craig Campbell, one of General Eisenhower's personal aides. We were also able to let General Patton know that his son-in-law, Colonel J. K. Waters, was in the best of health but was still in German custody, being moved to a camp in the interior. One story they told which was of considerable interest to me concerned a lifelong friend, Colonel Paul R. Goode, who was the senior American officer at Szubin. He had remained with the column being marched west by the Germans despite his opportunities to escape. He felt a responsibility to look after the welfare of those Americans who were unable to get away from their German guards. I learned that after Goode had been captured in France he was put in a boxcar train with hundreds of other Americans and sent across France to a prisoner-of-war camp in Germany. During the trip some enterprising prisoners had cut a hole in the boxcar through which they hoped to escape before the train passed the German border. Several of them did, but Colonel Goode, who weighs well over two hundred pounds, got stuck in the escape hole and was in this position when the German guards discovered what was going on. He had to do some fast talking to avoid being executed on the spot for the part he had played in the plot.

Gruenberg and his companions told me that they had had the kindest treatment from the civilian population of Poland. The people were more than willing to share their meager food supply with the liberated Americans. The officers said that the Red Army was indifferent to them—a few cases were reported in which Americans had had their wrist watches confiscated at the point of a gun by Red Army soldiers but these were the acts of irresponsible individuals more or less out of control in the confusion which characterized the Russians' pursuit of the Germans. Apparently the Red Army took no responsibility for caring for liberated Americans and no other Russian agency was interested. Gruenberg reported that liberated American prisoners were being concentrated at Wegheim, Rembertow, and Brest-Litovsk. I learned later that others had seen signs in Poland directing liberated prisoners to report to Wreznia, Lodz, Rembertow, and Lublin.

I interrogated the three American officers on February 18, 1945, and sought an immediate appointment with Golubev, which I obtained the following day. Armed with the data I had received, I tried to obtain his approval to the plan we had been formulating for six months. I asked for authority to send small contact teams of from three to five Americans to each of several key localities as close behind the Russian lines in Poland as possible and to dispatch American aircraft which could carry emergency supplies in and the seriously ill or wounded out to the American hospital at Poltava. I suggested the cities which the Russian field commanders had already designated as concentration points, arguing that every American was searching for some American official to report to and the news would soon get around as to where American officials might be found. They would thus act as magnets to attract concentrations of Americans. The liberated prisoners could then be evacuated to a port of debarkation as transportation became available.

Golubev told me that so far only four hundred and fifty Americans had been liberated and that these were being assembled and sent to a prisoner-of-war transit camp at Odessa. He proposed that we send an American contact team there and suggested the possibility of establishing another transit camp at the northern port of Murmansk if later releases of Americans justified another camp. Meanwhile, he said, the

Foreign Office had approved a request I had made on February 14, five days earlier, that a small group of American officers be allowed to go to Lublin to contact Americans in Poland.

Golubev's statement that four hundred and fifty Americans had already been liberated came as something of a surprise to me because I knew positively of only the two hundred that had escaped from Szubin. However, I doubted the accuracy of his figures because of the report that I had received from the Poles that a thousand Americans were in various Polish cities and because of the indications I had received from Gruenberg that most of the Americans were avoiding Russian concentration centers because of the poor conditions known to exist at them. As it turned out, Golubev revised his figures upward every few days until an eventual figure of about three thousand Americans was reached. Golubev's continued uncertainty as to how many Americans had been liberated at any time offered ample evidence of the ineffectiveness of his organization and the lack of foresight which had been displayed in planning to meet a problem which was certain to arise.

His proposal that our contact should be only at Odessa and possibly Murmansk was a shock to me and I felt it to be a serious violation of our agreement. It meant that we could not give aid to our liberated soldiers until they had traveled nearly two thousand miles from the points of their liberation under the most difficult conditions. I was delighted to hear, however, that I would be allowed to send a small group to Lublin. I selected Lieutenant Colonel J. D. Wilmeth, and he was to be accompanied by Lieutenant Colonel C. B. Kingsbury, a medical officer, and Corporal Paul Kisil, an excellent Russian interpreter. I had already sent them to Poltava on February 14 in order that they would be ready to proceed by air into Poland as soon as permission was granted. I was further cheered when Vishinsky assured Harriman that Wilmeth would be allowed to go anywhere in Poland where there were American prisoners of war provided the Polish Government approved and the places were not too close to the Russian front.

My delight did not last long. In the first place, Wilmeth was not allowed to leave Poltava until February 28. This was maddening because the situation was one that called for immediate action. When he finally obtained permission to go, he was not allowed to use an American airplane to make the trip. This was also disappointing as I had planned not only to have an American plane take his party to Lublin but to have it remain there for him to use in going to other parts of Poland where he or one of his assistants might be needed, and also to obtain supplies of the necessities we proposed to distribute to our men.

When Wilmeth and his party arrived in Lublin he was promptly informed that he would be allowed to remain only ten days. This, despite the fact that there were then about one hundred Americans in Lublin who were awaiting train transportation to Odessa. Further, he was not allowed to leave the city because of Soviet rather than Polish restrictions. His operations within Lublin were also restricted. Initially he was refused access to the American ex-prisoners of war then in the city. Restrictions even ran to a point-blank refusal by the Russian commandant to allow Colonel Kingsbury, the American medical officer, to visit two seriously wounded Americans known to be within a few miles of Lublin. Permission was even refused for any messages or supplies to be sent to the two sick men.

Wilmeth was invited to leave Lublin and return to Moscow on six different occasions. I could get word from and to him occasionally through Polish channels, and I directed him to remain in Lublin as long as there were any Americans whom he could assist unless he was forcibly removed by the Russians. When the last Americans were entrained at Lublin for Odessa, the Russian commander in Warsaw sent word to Wilmeth in writing that he should leave Lublin. Wilmeth's group was in Poland for about three weeks, and his was the only contact team that reached a point within five hundred miles of the localities at which American prisoners were liberated.

I took advantage of Golubev's offer and sent a contact team to Odessa. Major Paul S. Hall was in command, assisted by Major Earl D.

Cramer, a medical officer, and Sergeant Emil W. Doktor, an interpreter. They arrived in Odessa on February 26, 1945, one day prior to the arrival of the first group of our liberated prisoners. They were the first Americans the ex-prisoners had seen and they were regarded as angels from heaven when they produced the supplies they had brought. Hall and his party remained in Odessa for about two months, and during that time they sent three thousand Americans through the port. Our men were sent home on British transports which had brought liberated Russians home from the western front. The British authorities, under the direction of Admiral Archer, did everything possible for the welfare of our men, even to granting them loans of one hundred dollars apiece on no more security than Hall's say-so.

The facilities provided by the Soviet Repatriation Commission at Odessa were as good as might have been expected. They were hastily improvised but improved steadily during the period in which our soldiers were passing through. Food was meager but it was well prepared, and the Soviet ration was amply supplemented by American food. Medical attention was almost nonexistent except for that provided by Major Cramer. Our men were confined to the buildings in which they were housed from the time of their arrival in Odessa until they were placed aboard ships for the trip home. Hall and Cramer were allowed to visit them at certain hours each day. The trains on which they arrived at Odessa were made up of boxcars without heat or sanitary arrangements. The conditions were bad and the journey difficult, but the transportation facilities were the same as those provided for soldiers of the Red Army. Those of our men who retained their health during their hitch-hiking journey across Poland and on the train trip from eastern Poland to Odessa had few complaints concerning their hardships. In fact, most of them emerged from the ordeal hard as nuts and in the pink of condition. However, each group that arrived in Odessa told Hall of sick and injured Americans scattered throughout Poland. These were the men about whom Harriman and I were most concerned.

Of course, the situation was extremely fluid. By the time a report was received in Odessa concerning American boys who were sick in Poland, several weeks had elapsed since they had been seen. Golubev continued to assure me that all our men were being evacuated, but I could not be sure that this was the case until the men who had been reported as being ill actually arrived in Odessa. I was eager to go to Poland and see the situation for myself. I asked Golubev for authority to make such a trip, offering to take one of his officers with me so that we could work out joint plans to overcome whatever situation we might find. He told me that I would have to obtain permission from the Foreign Office. Averell went to see Vishinsky, who said that I might go if I could obtain approval of the Polish Government. Considering the degree of independence exercised by the Polish Government, the condition imposed of requiring its approval of my trip was ridiculous. Averell then radioed to President Roosevelt and asked him to send a message to Stalin requesting that I be given permission to visit Poland for the purpose of locating Americans who might be ill or hospitalized there.

The President sent a message to Stalin on March 18, 1945, in which he said he understood that I had not been allowed to survey the United States prisoner-of-war situation in Poland. The President referred to a previous request which he had made of Stalin, at Harriman's instigation, asking that American aircraft be allowed to fly supplies to Poland and evacuate the sick. He pointed out that Stalin had refused his previous request on the grounds that all of our ex-prisoners had already been sent to Odessa—a statement not borne out by subsequent events. The President told Stalin he could not understand his reluctance to permit American contact officers to assist their own people in Poland and asked that Stalin accede to his desire to have me go to Poland at once.

On March 23 Stalin replied to President Roosevelt stating that all Americans, except seventeen who were then ill in Poland, had been sent to Odessa. The remaining seventeen were to be sent within a few days. As far as my visit was concerned, Stalin said that his personal inclination was to accede to the President's request but that he could not burden his front commanders by having superfluous foreign officers around them who would require special communication facilities and protection from German agents. Stalin concluded his message by saying that all Americans were being well cared for in Soviet camps, in contrast to former Soviet prisoners of war in American camps who were housed with German prisoners and had suffered unjust treatment.

Stalin's reply effectively killed any hope of satisfying my desire to get to Poland. The efforts of the President and Harriman were not entirely wasted, however, as they served to maintain a constant pressure on the Soviet authorities which resulted in their evacuating all our men to Odessa much more expeditiously than might otherwise have been the case.

When it appeared that all our men had finally been sent to Odessa, I had one of them, Captain Richard Rossback, come to Moscow to give Golubev a narrative account of what he, as a typical case, had gone through from the time of his liberation to the time of his arrival at Odessa. Rossback did not spare the horses and must have left Golubev wondering if his Repatriation Commission was actually as high-powered as he had previously considered it to be.

Article Three of our agreement stated that the United States and the Soviet Union would provide liberated citizens with adequate food, clothing, housing, and medical attention, and with transportation until they were handed over to United States or Soviet authorities at places agreed upon between those authorities. In this connection it has already been pointed out that our liberated men had to depend on the generosity of the Polish people for their food and on the generosity of individual Russian or Polish truck drivers for transportation during the four hundred to five hundred mile journey from their points of liberation to the places where the Soviet Government provided boxcars to carry them to their destination at Odessa.

Article Four provided that each of the contracting governments would be free to use such of its own means of transportation as might be available for repatriating its own citizens and bringing supplies to them. In anticipation of the need, we had accumulated thousands of tons of supplies in Russia to distribute to our men. But, in spite of the agreement, we were never allowed to use our own aircraft, and I was unable to give our men American supplies until after they had arrived at Odessa.

The remaining five articles covered such matters as the advance of money loans to liberated citizens, the conditions under which they might be employed as laborers, arrangements for the most rapid means of evacuating them to their homelands, and a saving clause that the execution of the entire agreement would be subject to the limitations existing in each theater in the availability of supply and transport. None of these articles occasioned us any difficulty in their implementation.

During the entire course of the reciprocal repatriation program the Soviet authorities, including Stalin, Molotov, and others, poured forth a continuous stream of accusations regarding the treatment which Soviet citizens were receiving at the hands of the United States forces which had liberated them. In almost all cases these accusations were proved false and were admitted to be unfounded by Soviet representatives at American field headquarters. On one occasion we were charged with attempting to poison Soviet nationals by giving them methyl alcohol in their food. Investigation revealed that there was a tank car containing methyl alcohol at one of our camps in France occupied by liberated Soviet citizens. The car was looted by the Russians, and many of them died from the alcohol they had stolen despite all our doctors could do to save them. We immediately placed guards over the tank car, posted signs of warning, and destroyed every bottle found in the camp containing methyl alcohol which had been taken from the car.

The Russians had none of the administrative problems which confronted General Eisenhower in the care of liberated nationals of Allied countries. Where the Russians liberated hundreds, we liberated thousands. General Eisenhower created a special section of his staff to handle the problem and their plans had been made well in advance.

He had over one hundred and fifty Russians at his headquarters who were given every facility to assist in caring for their own people.

No one has ever had more support from his own people in carrying out a mission than I had in endeavoring to obtain reasonably good treatment for the American prisoners of war liberated by the Red Army. On two occasions the President attempted to help through personal appeals to Stalin. Averell Harriman was relentless in his pressure on the Soviet Foreign Office. The Army Air Forces made eight four-engine transports available to me. The United States Navy sent a special shipload of supplies from Italy to Odessa to provide medicines, clothing, and food for our men. Extra supplies were received from the United States, England, and the Persian Gulf Command. Colonel Wilmeth's and Major Hall's parties accomplished the impossible in caring for those Americans who came under their control. With a little co-operation from the Soviet authorities my problem would have been relatively simple.

XII. It Was Not All Bad

IF, IN my sketchy account of the prisoner-of-war episode, I have given the impression that I plumbed the depths of discouragement and despair, I can only say that that impression is correct. Thank God, there were other episodes that presented a brighter outlook. In the hope of retaining some semblance of objectivity in this narrative, I shall attempt to describe two of them. The first concerns the visit I made to the Russian front in July 1944, and the second, General Eisenhower's visit to Moscow in August 1945.

From the day I arrived in Moscow I had the most compelling desire to see the Russian front and to witness the Red Army in action. I tried to make myself believe that it would be of tremendous value in the training of our own Army if I could send home a full description of what made the Red Army tick and perhaps a few lessons concerning German tactics on the Russian front. I knew in my heart, however, that I was motivated mainly by a desire to satisfy my own curiosity.

Admittedly, I dropped a few well-timed hints to Antonov, Slavin, and Estigneev that I should be allowed to visit the front, but I soon found that hints were not enough. I would have to make an issue of going or there would be no chance. I restrained myself for many reasons. In the first place, I had had General Marshall's injunction to play down the intelligence aspect. Next, there were the preparations for shuttle bombing and other projects of operational collaboration which kept me at the grindstone in Moscow and required occasional visits to our bases in the Ukraine. The most restraining factor, however, was the burden a trip to the front would add to an already overburdened war machine. The Soviet penchant for secrecy and security would require that such a trip be carefully chaperoned. This would mean taking senior officers from their duties in Moscow. The Russian fear for the safety of foreigners went to such extremes as to give the impression that they felt that accidents would be charged against them as being deliberately planned. I therefore knew that my visit to the front would mean a special fighter escort both going and returning, to say nothing of the many guards who would be responsible for my safety while there. Finally, I knew that Russian pride would never allow me to drop in on their field headquarters and take pot-luck with officers of the Red Army. It was certain that special servants, food, and bedding would be sent from Moscow and set up for me wherever I went. I felt that this was asking too much even for one of my exalted position.

Lieutenant General Burrows of the British Military Mission had none of these inhibitions. He did not want the Russians to go to any extremes in making arrangements for his safety and comfort, but their insistence upon doing so bothered him not at all. After all, he was the senior military officer in Russia of the British Empire and it was imperative that he visit the front if for no other reason than to call on Marshal Vasilievsky, then Chief of Staff—at least so he argued. By a combination of charm and persistence Burrows succeeded in arranging his visit for the early part of July. When I heard of his success, I put on a great show of hurt feelings and was rewarded by being asked to make a similar trip immediately following Burrows' return.

In making the arrangements for my jaunt some amusing incidents occurred which served to highlight certain Russian characteristics. For example, I was told on July 10 that Marshal Vasilievsky would have kidney trouble until July 20 and therefore we should not leave Moscow until after that date. Undoubtedly there was some excellent and logical reason for a delay in my departure—probably Marshal Vasilievsky's schedule. It was typically Russian, and reminiscent of the years I had spent in China, to have some fantastic reason put forth with a perfectly straight face in preference to the real one. Another incident concerned the composition of the party. Burrows had taken his personal aide-de-camp, a batman, and an interpreter. In my efforts to be as little trouble as possible I suggested to General Slavin that I take only an interpreter. I could see that this worried him when he tried to induce me to take an aide and a batman just as Burrows had done. I said that I had no batman and thought it would be better if I could include General Spalding instead of an aide. He brightened at this but was still not satisfied. It dawned on me that he had had instructions that my trip was to be a replica of Burrows' and I would have to take three people or Slavin would be in trouble. He was all smiles when I finally arranged my party to include General Spalding, General Crist, Captain Ware, and myself. Slavin told me that he and his principal assistant, Colonel Dyakanov, would accompany us.

Our party left Moscow about three o'clock on the afternoon of July 20 in a very plush American C-47 transport which was reserved for the use of the General Staff. Slavin was not allowed to tell us our destination until the plane had taken off. He then unfolded his map and revealed our plans. We were to go to General Chernyakovsky's headquarters of the First Baltic front at Vilna. We would stop at Minsk and pick up a fighter escort which would accompany us to our destination. Slavin was in a holiday mood despite his responsibility, and he had his assistants pass out refreshments. He was a different man from the shrewd negotiator I had known in Moscow. Both he and Dyakanov proved to be charming traveling companions.

We picked up eight fighters at Minsk and they cut capers over us during the one-hour run to Vilna. We thought we had flown close to the ground on the trip to Minsk, but it was nothing compared to the hedgehopping we did after leaving there. The idea was to seek concealment from enemy aircraft, but all of us would have preferred the risks of an enemy encounter to those involved in just clearing roofs, treetops, and slight ground elevations.

We found the arrangements at Vilna even more elaborate than we had anticipated. We were taken to a group of *dachas*, or cottages, in a little forest just outside the city. Through the windows of the *dacha* assigned to us we could see some women busily making up our beds and putting the finishing decorative touches on a rather primitive interior. When we entered the building I was given an office which connected with my bedroom. The office was pure swank, as I had no use for it. Sid Spalding and Bill Crist shared a room across from the office, and Ware was put in his place as a lowly captain by being assigned a bunk in a small cubbyhole just off the kitchen. The walls had been completely covered with green cardboard and flowers were on all tables. All in all it did not promise to be a heavy battle.

A Colonel Moise of General Chernyakovsky's staff acted as our host, and presently we assembled for dinner at another *dacha* about one hundred yards from ours. In the dining-room a table was set with delicacies which could have come only from Moscow. There were five waitresses who had been brought there for the occasion. We fell to and had a typical Moscow banquet—speeches and all.

The following morning we were up at the crack of dawn and after another banquet started on our tour of the front, except that instead of going to the front we went to the rear. It developed that we were to be shown the battleground at Minsk where twelve German divisions had been annihilated in the woods just outside the city. It would have been much more sensible to have left Moscow earlier on the preceding day and to have seen this when we stopped at Minsk on our way to Vilna. As it was, we had to ride back there in automobiles, a distance of about seventy-five miles, over roads crowded with refugee and supply vehicles.

The trip proved to be extremely interesting. There was about the same density of destroyed German transport that I had seen on some of the roads in Italy. One striking thing in this connection was the Red Army's efforts to salvage every bit of transportation that was not completely destroyed by fire. Salvage crews roamed the roads, taking something here and something there until they had enough parts accumulated to repair the German vehicles that had suffered the least damage. These were then put back in the service of supply.

We were also struck by the crude repair jobs done on the bridges.

The Germans destroyed everything as they withdrew. Bridges were repaired by partisans and civilians remaining in the area under the supervision of a very few Red Army engineers. The timber used consisted of trees cut from the nearest forest. We were told that bridges so reconstructed would sustain any army loads during the immediate advance and that they would be properly rebuilt later. Certainly they were not as good as the bridges thrown up by American Army engineers, but they seemed to answer their purpose and there was a considerable saving of manpower and transportation.

We saw thousands of American trucks on the road. They were the only vehicles which appeared to be organized into transportation units. Many of them carried troops, and seldom did we see a troop carrier that did not have at least one or two women aboard. They were used for all sorts of combat assignments. Many were expert rifle shots and were used as snipers, many manned the anti-aircraft batteries, but the majority were employed as cooks and for work at supply installations.

The battlefield at Minsk was all that we were promised it would be. Apparently twelve German divisions had been completely surrounded and annihilated. There were thousands of dead German soldiers lying on the ground, and the area was a veritable museum of German equipment. Burrows had been shown the same sight a week or so earlier and the condition of the German bodies had not improved any since then. I had a suspicion that the battlefield had been left in its unsavory condition as an exhibit for Burrows and me. However, the next night when I met Marshal Vasilievsky he expressed great indignation that it had not yet been cleared and ordered Chernyakovsky to see to it at once.

After our tour of the battlefield we were led to an area that was free of deceased Germans, and the waitresses from our mess at Vilna appeared with the identical spread of food that had been on the dining-room table the night before. Tablecloths were laid on the grass and we had a picnic supper which was much the same as one might have on a summer evening in the United States. We were pestered by flies and ants and sat in the same uncomfortable positions. The outstanding difference was a lavish supply of vodka, which did much to overcome the petty annoyances that I usually experience on picnics.

The trip back was made at night and without lights. It seemed endless and there were frequent stops caused by German planes flying over us. Each time they would appear Slavin would insist that we get out of the cars and move well off the road. We could see bombs exploding in Vilna. Certainly they had no interest in the few motor vehicles the Russians had on the road that night, but Slavin took his responsibility for our safety quite seriously. I was so tired it would have taken a bomb really to arouse me. We arrived at our *dacha* at three o'clock the following morning.

Our next day was spent in the city of Vilna, and the battle that had taken place there was explained to us. The story of Vilna was typical of all the fighting on the Russian front. From one news account during the war, one gained the impression that two long lines of Russians and Germans faced each other on a front extending from the Baltic through the Balkans. It was not that sort of thing at all. Almost all the fighting was along the east-west roads, with the cities and villages fortified by the Germans as centers of resistance. During the Russian advance there was practically no fighting between cities. For example, the Russians had had to fight for two to three weeks to capture Minsk, but then they were practically unimpeded until they had gone seventy-five miles farther and had to fight for Vilna. They succeeded in reducing that city in about one week.

I shall not go into the tactics employed by the Russians in overcoming the defense of the city. However, from the account given to us, it was apparent that the Russian victories were won by superior mobility. The combined bomber offensive of the Western Allies was taking its toll of German oil, and the German artillery and much of the transport we saw was mostly horse-drawn. The Russians with their preponderance of motorized and mechanized equipment were thus able to outmaneuver the Germans. Here again one could see the results of American assistance. Besides the motor trucks already referred to, there were scattered through the city innumerable American Sherman tanks which had been disabled by German artillery fire.

The most important event of our entire trip was to take place the evening of the day we went over the Vilna campaign. I was to be taken to meet the Chief of the Red Army General Staff, Marshal Vasilievsky. I had been communicating with him for nearly a year through his deputy in Moscow, General Antonov, and at last I was to see him. During our tour of Vilna, Slavin had word that Vasilievsky would receive us that night. Slavin at once became jittery, and it was evident that an audience with the Chief of Staff was something in his life too. I could not help but think of the jitters I had seen in my office on the part of officers waiting to see General Marshall when I was Secretary of our General Staff—in fact I could remember a number of occasions when I was on the nervous side myself.

Sid Spalding, Bill Crist, and I spruced ourselves as best we could. At about seven o'clock in the evening we were driven to the little cottage which was General Chernyakovsky's headquarters. As we came within a mile of the place we found sentries spaced at about fifty yards on each side of the road who snapped to attention and saluted as our cars passed them.

Our party was received in a small room in which there was a conference table large enough to seat twelve. The walls were covered with maps, particularly those of the Baltic front. Vasilievsky came forward to greet me as I entered and I succumbed to his charm at once. He was tall and heavy set with sunburned leathery skin, blue eyes, and brown hair. He and the other officers with him wore their white flannel blouses, which slip over the head, extend almost to the knees, and are bloused at the waist with a belt. Their shoulder tabs were bright gold and their chests covered with medals. The uniforms looked cool and comfortable, but I was surprised to find anything quite so dressy in the field. Among the other officers present was Colonel General Kuznetzov, with whom I had worked on the Bodyguard plan.

We sat around the conference table with Vasilievsky at its head, Chernyakovsky on his left, and me on his right. Vasilievsky apologized for not having seen me earlier but explained that he seldom visited Moscow. I think I tickled his vanity by remarking that the success of the Red Army under his leadership ruled out the necessity for him to apologize to anyone, much less to me. At the same time I was happy to bring him greetings from the American Chiefs of Staff and also to have the privilege of meeting him.

The most striking part of the conference was the devotion and mutual respect that Vasilievsky and Chernyakovsky appeared to have for each other. Chernyakovsky wanted to give his chief all credit for the Red Army's victories and told us that everyone referred to Vasilievsky as the "Papa of all generals." Vasilievsky was equally anxious to let us know of the accomplishments of Chernyakovsky. It seemed to be a good partnership, and all of us were quite impressed with the quality of the Red Army's top-flight leaders. Unfortunately Chernyakovsky was later killed in action.

Vasilievsky asked Slavin what our plans were for the following day. Slavin turned white at being addressed personally by the Chief of Staff but jumped to his feet and reported that we were to go out to the front lines of the Fifth Army. Vasilievsky told him we were to be allowed to see anything we wished but took all the promise out of his instructions by cautioning Slavin that we should not be exposed to any unnecessary hazards. He then said that General Chernyakovsky had invited us to his mess for tea.

The tea turned out to be the usual Russian spread. The table held all the standard equipment for such occasions and included the ever present profusion of bottles. Chernyakovsky started the party off by proposing a toast to the great and only "Marshala Stalina," and that accounted for my first water tumbler full of vodka, there being no vodka glasses available. Courtesy demanded that "Presidenta Roosevelta" receive an equal honor, and that was tumbler number two. They were still drinking to "Churchilla" in those days and he accounted for number three—then the lights went out for me. I can

vaguely remember Vasilievsky giving one of the waiters a dressing
down for filling our glasses too full and my grateful acquiescence to
the thought he expressed. Sid Spalding and Bill Crist afterward assured me that I arose a little abruptly but very courteously and
thanked them all for a very nice party and led the procession outdoors
to our waiting automobiles—I will never know exactly what happened. I saw Kuznetzov in Moscow a great many times after that and
he never failed to tell me that I had made a great impression on
Vasilievsky—what he did not tell me was whether it was good or bad.

On the following day we were first driven to the headquarters of
the Fifth Army, which was about fifteen miles west of Vilna. Colonel
General Krylov was in command and he received us with his entire
staff. It was certainly a far cry from the American conception of an
Army headquarters. The entire staff consisted of fifteen to twenty
officers who lived and worked in a few small trailers scattered through
the woods. There was one huge hospital tent, well camouflaged,
which served both as a conference room and as a headquarters mess.
Some offices had stenographers at work, but most of them did not.
We could not help but think of the enormous installation and all the
office space and facilities found at an American Army headquarters.
It highlighted some very different concepts in our methods of operating. The Russian system had the advantage of almost eliminating
overhead, but it also confirmed our growing belief that advance planning was neglected; that statistical, personnel, and supply records
were not kept; and that the co-ordination of subordinate units and
liaison with adjacent units was pretty much hit or miss.

Of course the Russian problem was considerably different from
ours. In the matter of supply they had only one theater to consider
as opposed to the many all over the world in which we were fighting.
Their supply lines were confined to an east and west rail and road net,
whereas ours extended back across the ocean. To them a supply deficiency meant a few days' delay, whereas we had to wait for the
availability of convoys. In the matter of personnel all Russia's manpower was close at hand, and her willingness to accept losses allowed

the Red Army to rely on sheer force of numbers rather than careful planning in order to achieve objectives with the least loss of life. In the matter of training Russia had the advantage of an agrarian population already hardened and for whom the rigors of battle were little more severe than the rigors of peace. Post Exchanges, United Service Organizations, doughnut wagons, and other morale agencies which call for overhead were unheard of. The incentive of driving the enemy from Russian soil and seeking revenge for atrocities endured provided all the necessary stimulus to morale. In short, the Russian methods were satisfactory for the conditions under which she was fighting—unlimited manpower, relatively simple administrative problems, and great incentive. As long as she was fighting on her own or contiguous soil she did quite well; I don't believe, however, that she could create the machinery nor develop the administrative capacity to support an expeditionary force such as ours.

Krylov, his staff, and our small party gathered round the conference table, and Sid Spalding quizzed them on the use and effectiveness of American equipment. As was the case with all the field commanders, they were enthusiastic about the supplies that were being sent from America. The meeting was a fruitful one, and Sid and I were able to get firsthand evidence of how some of our equipment should be altered to meet their needs. The corrective action we were able to take after we returned to Moscow more than repaid the Red Army for any inconvenience that accrued from our visit to the front. If we could only have gone more freely and without such elaborate preparations, we could have done much more.

After leaving Krylov we went forward to the divisions occupying the front of the Fifth Army. We were given a chance to examine their heavy and light artillery positions. We could hear sporadic rifle fire a few hundred yards to the front, but we could not induce Slavin to let us go farther forward. It was perhaps just as well because the situation was relatively static and the Russians had about reached the limit of their advance until such time as their supply lines could be shortened and the offensive resumed.

We had luncheon with Krylov and were presented with German pistols, swords, and other battlefield souvenirs. During the luncheon a young major arrived from Moscow and a place was made for him on General Krylov's left. He had brought decorations for several members of the staff and proceeded with the ceremony of presentation. The major seemed to be a much more important individual than his rank justified and we Americans were puzzled regarding his status. It developed that he was the political commissar on Krylov's staff and as such commanded almost as much respect as the commanding general. Political commissars could, and I believe as a rule did, help the commanders to whom they were attached through the direct relationships which they had with the government in Moscow. The system of having commissars with the Army certainly serves to insure that no disaffection will develop, but they must have a deterring effect on the initiative of commanders who are conscious that their every act is being reported favorably or unfavorably to their government, depending on the mood of the commissar who accompanies them.

Our party returned to Moscow the following day and thus ended one of my most pleasant interludes in Russia. We felt we had seen an army which by the power of its mass and the mobility of its equipment would relentlessly push back an enemy already approaching total defeat through the lack of fuel needed for mobility on the ground and in the air. We had seen an army supplied, pushed forward, and actually reinforced by a liberated friendly civil population in the area in which it was operating. We had seen an army that had few of the refinements of technique which characterized the armies of the Western Allies but one which was second to none in its valor and its will to win.

Following the surrender of Germany, the Allies were confronted with problems that required even more co-ordination of effort than those which confronted them during the war. Eisenhower and Zhukov soon established a fine personal relationship as members of the Allied Control Council in Berlin. They paid visits to each other's headquarters, exchanged the highest Soviet and American decorations, and, following Russian custom, each expressed his admiration for the other in innumerable toasts. Had Zhukov been given the freedom of action which our government allowed Eisenhower, I believe all the Soviet-American occupational problems could have been solved easily. But suspicion of American motives which emanated from Moscow resulted in restrictions which seriously hampered our work. American vehicles coming into Berlin were restricted to certain roads; our aircraft had to follow certain lanes when over the Soviet occupation zone; and nothing was done toward the joint occupation of Vienna until the European Advisory Council formally ratified the assignment of zones that had long since been agreed upon.

Thinking that a much greater degree of co-operation would be attained if Eisenhower were to come to Moscow, meet the Soviet leaders, and win their confidence as he had Zhukov's, and if Zhukov would visit the United States in return, Averell Harriman suggested the two visits. President Truman and Eisenhower approved. Stalin fell in with the plan at once and invited Eisenhower to come as soon as he could. He arrived in Moscow on August 11, 1945.

Marshal Zhukov was to have visited the United States in October 1945. Plans were prepared for his reception in New York and he was to have been taken to many of the principal cities and military installations in the country. Unfortunately his scheduled departure coincided with the breakdown of the meeting of Foreign Ministers in London and word was received that Marshal Zhukov was too ill to make the journey.

I have never been happier to see anyone come nor happier to see anyone go than Eisenhower. His arrival in Moscow coincided with negotiations for the surrender of Japan. I not only had to participate in the strenuous program that was laid out for him, but also had to act as the liaison officer between MacArthur and the Soviet High Command in obtaining agreements concerning the Japanese surrender. It took me weeks to recover from the strain.

Zhukov accompanied Eisenhower to Moscow from Berlin and they arrived late on a Saturday afternoon. The American officers in the party included Lieutenant General Lucius Clay, Brigadier General T. J. Davis, and Lieutenant John Eisenhower, the General's son. It was apparent as soon as they got off the plane that Eisenhower and Zhukov had developed a real personal affection for each other.

After the formalities at the airport, including an exceptionally good ceremony by the guard of honor, it was arranged that Eisenhower would pay a call on Zhukov and Chief of Staff Antonov that evening, at which time we would agree on the itinerary for the following days. We Americans then adjourned to Spasso House, where Eisenhower was to stay, and relaxed over a highball or two in preparation for the strenuous time to come.

At General Staff headquarters that night Eisenhower presented Antonov with the order of Chief Commander of the Legion of Merit, an American decoration which had been created during the war. Four degrees were established for presentation to foreigners—Legionnaire, Officer, Commander, and Chief Commander.

I believe we bungled our handling of the award of decorations, particularly with regard to foreigners. Rather late in the war we decided that the highest decoration we could give them was that of Chief Commander of the Legion of Merit. This decision was not made until after we had presented several British officers with the Distinguished Service Medal, which to Americans is a much higher award than the Legion of Merit. The Russians set much store on decorations in general and are the greatest students in the world on the relative importance of each. They had presented Eisenhower with the "Order of Victory," their super-super award, and I suspect they were a little hurt when their leaders such as Zhukov, Konev, Rokossovsky, and Antonov were awarded something that was not considered by Americans to be the best they had in the bag.

In the Sunday morning paper for August 12, the day after Eisenhower's arrival, there was only the barest announcement of his presence in Moscow. This was in strange contrast to the headlines and pictures which we knew would herald Zhukov's arrival in the United States. Nevertheless, when we left our cars about two blocks from Red Square on that Sunday morning, having come at Stalin's invitation to see the annual sports parade, Eisenhower was recognized and wildly cheered by the Russian people who were lined up to participate in the parade or who were hurrying to try and get places from which to see it. As he walked to the reviewing stand the cheers of the people preceded and followed him the entire distance. It was apparently the party line not to place too much emphasis on Eisenhower's importance, but upon seeing him the people reacted with spontaneous and unrestrained admiration. It takes some sort of spontaneous combustion to highlight the differences between the party line and the will of the people, and it is only occasionally that one is aware that differences do exist.

As soon as our party was seated in the space reserved for us, Antonov arrived to say that Marshal Stalin wished General Eisenhower, together with Harriman and me, to come to the top of Lenin's Tomb and join him on the reviewing stand. We were the first foreigners who had ever been invited to witness a Soviet ceremony from atop Lenin's Tomb, and I was fully conscious of the honor even though I had attained it by sliding in on Eisenhower's coattails.

Stalin's party included all those whom the world reads about— Molotov, Vishinsky, Mikoyan, Zhukov, and others. There were also eight or ten—doubtless party leaders—whom one never sees or hears of except on occasions such as this. Many of them were dressed in the loose gray flannel coats, trousers, and caps which used to be worn by all Communist leaders and which impress Westerners as suitable prison garb.

It was Eisenhower's first meeting with Stalin and I know he made a great impression on the Russian leader by saying very little and refraining from any of the flattering remarks that Stalin was accustomed to receive from foreigners. They stood together for the next five hours, but because of the language difference they did not get into any lively conversations. Even had they spoken the same language,

I doubt if the result would have been different, because Stalin is, as a rule, rather oblivious to his surroundings and is not one to indulge in superfluous chatter. I could not help but sympathize with Eisenhower; it was an extremely warm day and he had to stand almost at attention for the entire ceremony. He had to match Stalin, who did not sit down once or even lean on the balustrade during the whole period. It was shortly afterward that people began to wonder about Stalin's health. After witnessing his stamina on that occasion I could never become greatly concerned. I was at the extreme end of the line, and while I could not sit down, I did sink onto my elbows from time to time. I also succeeded in sneaking a cigarette or two. Eisenhower had to pay the price of fame and just stand and take it.

The sports parade was most colorful but also extremely boring. Every Republic in the Soviet Union was represented by both men and women. The parade opened with all participants in a mass formation in the Red Square facing Lenin's Tomb. Each Republic tried to outdo all others in the beauty of its costumes, and the result was a kaleidoscope of color. After the national anthem and a salute to Stalin the participants passed in review. Each delegation was headed by a banner on which was Stalin's picture—all large enough to require being carried by six to eight men. The parade lasted for over an hour and the salute was held as each banner passed the reviewing stand. It was followed by a drill or gymnastic performance by the participants from each Republic. Each group began and ended its special show by obeisance to Stalin in one form or another. It was endless and repugnant to me because of the regimentation it connoted even in the recreation of the people. I have never been averse to the beauty of the female figure but even that palled after the first few hours. Another thing that struck me was the relatively few people who were able to witness this tremendous spectacle. Red Square is huge, but all its space except a small strip on one side to the right and left of the Tomb was required by the participants. There could not have been more than five thousand in a city of five million who were privileged to see it. I suppose the morale factor is in the nation-wide competition for selection to make the trip to Moscow and take part in the performance.

We barely had time to return to Spasso House and get a bite to eat before we were to set out again—this time to a football game. It was to be a soccer game, which at best is pretty much of a last gasp to Americans. Eisenhower was a bit weary by that time and asked me to notify our hosts that we would remain for only the first half. This was agreeable, but it did not work out that way. The stadium in Moscow seats seventy thousand people and it was packed. Zhukov and his staff met Eisenhower in a reception room that opened out onto the state box at the top and center of the stands. He and Eisenhower led our party into the box and at their appearance the entire audience rose and cheered.

The weather had turned cool and the game was a close one and far more interesting than we had anticipated. When the first half ended, nothing was said about leaving. Instead we were taken back to the reception room where *zakouskas* and vodka were served, which brought on the inevitable toasts. After that we went back to see the second half of the game.

When the game ended and Eisenhower and Zhukov rose to leave, the crowd gave them an ovation that grew larger and larger in volume. Finally Eisenhower, in a gesture of friendliness, threw his arm over Zhukov's shoulder, and Zhukov responded by embracing Eisenhower. With that, pandemonium broke loose. Eisenhower and Zhukov waved to the crowd, and the only way they could bring the demonstration to an end was by leaving the box, which they did after it had gone on for about ten minutes. There was nothing rehearsed about this and it had nothing to do with ideologies or political aspirations. It was a sincere demonstration by a representative cross-section of the Russian people of their affection for the American people as embodied in Eisenhower. It was heart-warming and reassuring to us Americans who were there.

On the two remaining days of Eisenhower's visit I saw more of Moscow than I had in the preceding two years. On Monday we started off with an art gallery and ended the morning with a tour of the Moscow subway. I am certain that this is by far the most beautiful thing of its kind in the world. There is no construction above the ground in Moscow that compares with it in either utility or beauty. The subway stations are done in marble with mosaic ceilings and floors. People are taken down to and up from the cars in modern escalators. The decorations of the waiting platforms below are on the same elaborate scale as the station entrances above. It was my first trip on a Moscow subway and I was amazed at what I saw after living for two years amid the disrepair and neglect that characterizes the city. In America I am certain we shall never attempt anything like that subway, for we shall always think of subway stations and tubes as places of utility rather than beauty. I think the Russian leaders must have selected this one project which was certain to be seen daily by millions of its citizens to illustrate what Russian engineers could accomplish if given the means. It is probably an incentive to the masses to work harder so that some day the grandeur now planted underground will spring up and flourish all over Russia as the fruits of their labors.

That afternoon Eisenhower was taken on a tour of the Kremlin. We used Eisenhower's invitation to include all the members of my Mission. Eisenhower had given them a little talk earlier in the afternoon and had met each one of them, so it was a memorable day for the personnel of the Mission in their otherwise drab existence in Moscow.

The following morning we visited a collective farm. Eisenhower made a great hit there with both Zhukov and the farmers because his Kansas background enabled him to show an intelligent interest. This particular farm was operated by about fifty families. During the war it had been run—as all collective farms were—almost entirely by women, and records were produced to show us how production had increased. The men were slowly returning from the Army and were confronted with the added incentive of maintaining or improving the records established by the women.

When we left the collective farm Eisenhower and Zhukov were in the same car, and when they arrived at Spasso House, Eisenhower invited the Marshal in to lunch. It was an embarrassing situation. No Soviet official is allowed to accept invitations to the homes of foreigners without prior reference to higher authority. As a rule, however, the invitation is not extended on the spur of the moment nor on the doorsteps of the foreigner's home. Zhukov was not fast enough to think of an excuse and he certainly could not say that he would have to get permission—so in he came. Eisenhower has never achieved a greater victory and I hope he fully appreciates it.

We had a delicious cold luncheon that was whipped up on a minute's notice. Following it, Eisenhower and Zhukov got into a friendly argument concerning the freedom of the press. This was quite revealing of fundamental differences in our thinking. Eisenhower stated our position extremely well but made no impression whatever on Zhukov. He was the product of generations that had never known individual freedom of any sort, and to him no argument could justify an individual expressing sentiments or thoughts either in writing or orally that were opposed to the interests of the state.

Averell gave a tremendous party in Eisenhower's honor on his last night in Moscow. Our military and diplomatic acquaintances were all invited. After a buffet supper some movies were shown, and during this time Averell was called to the communications office for a teletype conference with the Secretary of State. He returned about the time the movies were over and was able to announce to the assemblage that the Japanese had sued for peace. This touched off a celebration that lasted the rest of the night. The last thing I recall was little Marshal Budenny, an old ex-cavalry enlisted man with a long handlebar mustache, trying to kiss Eisenhower on both cheeks. The purpose of Eisenhower's visit had, we hoped, been accomplished.

In recounting the two episodes covered in this chapter I have endeavored to give an impression of the atmosphere of friendliness I encountered in the Soviet Union when not dealing with Soviet officials on official business. On our trip to the front we enjoyed the most generous hospitality, and our interest and curiosity were satisfied by a frank response that denied suspicion of our motives. During Eisenhower's visit we encountered huge masses of people and small groups of people. We could almost physically feel the attitude of kindliness with which they regarded us. I realize that in our normal relations with the Soviet Union it is difficult to reach the masses. I am convinced, however, that we should make every effort to break through the wall which surrounds them and seize every opportunity of nourishing the spirit of friendship already existing between the rank and file of our two peoples.

PART THREE

Soviet-American Collaboration
in the Pacific War

XIII. Early Negotiations

THE gods of war must have been on the side of the Western Allies when at the time of Leningrad, Moscow, and Stalingrad, Japan was restrained from violating her neutrality pact and did not attack Russia in the Far East. The Red Army had seriously depleted its Siberian forces for the battle of Stalingrad and had left the eastern provinces dangling as ripe plums for the Japanese. Had Japan attacked Russia, the Pacific supply route from America over which more than 50 per cent of our supplies were being delivered would have been eliminated. Germany could have let Africa and everything else go in favor of concentrating to drive the Red Army farther to the east. Russia might then have been deprived of access to her northern ports and to those of the Persian Gulf. Had such a situation developed, the Soviet Union would no longer have been a major factor in the war. Instead, Japan elected to secure her rear by her neutrality pact with Russia—supplemented by her strong Kwantung Army in Manchuria—and launch an attack against the United States at Pearl Harbor.

Time and timing were the essential elements of the situation with regard to Russia's participation in the Pacific war. Let us use the hourglass to illustrate my point and assume that all the sand was in the upper half on December 7, 1941. At that time continued Japanese-Russian neutrality was vital to the Allied cause. Japan's Kwantung Army, with close to a million men organized into eighteen divisions and a number of independent brigades, was considerably stronger than the Red Siberian Army. It had been in Manchuria since 1932, where it had been stockpiling, training, and maneuvering in preparation for the day when it would be turned loose on Russia. It controlled the greatest industrial area of the Asiatic mainland and might be said to have been a self-contained unit, especially so for a relatively brief campaign. It could have gone into action against Russia without causing any serious drain on the resources Japan required for the conduct of the Pacific war.

On December 7, 1941, the sand in the hourglass began to trickle slowly to the lower half. As it descended the importance of continued Russian-Japanese neutrality lessened. With the tide turned at Stalingrad, the Red Army gradually reconstituted its Siberian forces so that toward the end of 1943 Russia felt reasonably sure of her defensive capabilities in the Far East. The Japanese lost the offensive to us at the Battle of Midway in June 1942, and from then on they became increasingly aware that sometime, somehow, the Kwantung Army and its Manchurian resources might be needed in the defense of the Japanese mainland, and the practicability of using the Kwantung Army against Russia thus diminished correspondingly.

The sand continued to pour down and the Americans continued to roll on. It was difficult to say just how full the lower half of the glass would have to be before Russia could disregard the threat of the Japanese forces in Manchuria. Stalin and his advisers thought the time would be when Germany collapsed; we thought it would be considerably sooner. Both sides knew that the day when the lower half of the hourglass would be filled would come. If we could have our plans laid in advance to co-ordinate the efforts of Russia and the United States against Japan the instant continued Soviet-Japanese neutrality ceased to be necessary, the lives of Allied soldiers would be saved. Harriman and I considered that our primary and ultimate mission in Russia was not only to obtain Russian aid in the defeat of Japan, but also to insure that the Russian efforts would be co-ordinated with ours.

Broadly speaking, we thought our combined action would be most effective if the Red Army would launch an offensive against the Japanese in Manchuria and Korea designed to eliminate the Kwantung Army, and if we would establish air bases in the Maritime Provinces from which to bomb the Japanese islands and soften them for the final American invasion.

In the early days of the war we could not foresee that the Japanese forces on the Asiatic mainland would respond to the Emperor's instructions to capitulate as readily as proved to be the case. Nor were we sure that the atomic bomb would be a success. Even though the Japanese islands would be conquered, we could not be certain that the Kwantung Army, a powerful and almost completely self-sustained force, would not continue to fight, perhaps joining with Japanese forces in China in attempting to set up a new Japanese state. Victory would not be complete while this Army was still in existence, and it was certain that our Army could not accomplish its defeat with anything like the facility with which the task could be accomplished by the Red Army already facing it. It therefore seemed extremely important that Russia be induced to accept this as her mission.

American use of air bases in the Maritime Provinces would make it possible for us to redeploy quickly much of our European Air Force once Germany was defeated. In the early days we could not foresee the scale of the successes that General MacArthur, Admiral Nimitz, and General Kenney were to have. Nor could we foresee that their air attacks would have the Japanese mainland pretty well softened by the time Russian bases were available to us. We did not realize the results that were to be attained from our B-29 bombing program. For these reasons Harriman and I exerted every effort to insure that Russian bases would be available at the earliest date possible.

I do not think that any responsible American ever doubted that Russia would eventually come into the war against Japan. The Soviet Union had too many interests in the Far East to have allowed the affairs of that part of the world to be settled without her participating voice, and she could hardly have claimed a place at the peace table without having been one of the victorious belligerents. It was always evident that at the proper time Russia should declare war on Japan—but would she?

Harriman was the first American to receive an inkling of Stalin's intentions. In August 1942 he accompanied Churchill to Moscow to represent President Roosevelt when the Prime Minister broke the news to Stalin of another postponement of our invasion of the Continent. Harriman took the opportunity to explain to the Marshal the current American efforts against Japan. Stalin recognized the importance of the American operations in preventing a Japanese attack against the Soviet Union in Siberia and urged that we continue the strongest possible effort for that reason. Stalin told Harriman then that Japan was the historic enemy of Russia and that her eventual defeat was essential to Russia's interests. He implied that while the Soviet Union's military position at that time would not permit participation, eventually she would come in.

I have already mentioned the Teheran Conference at which Stalin made his first positive statement to Roosevelt and Churchill that Russia would some day fight Japan. He explained why this was impossible until after Germany had been defeated, but added, "Then, by our common front, we shall win." I was present when Stalin made this announcement and I could hardly wait to get back to Moscow to start planning for "the day." Upon my return I found, however, that it was to take considerable time for Stalin's intentions to be translated into action.

Before the Teheran Conference ended, Harriman persuaded the President to go into the matter of Soviet-American collaboration with Stalin in more detail. On November 29, 1943, the President handed Stalin a memorandum in which he said that he would like to arrange for the exchange of such information concerning the Japanese and for such preliminary planning as might be appropriate for eventual operations against Japan. He added that he thought it imperative that planning begin at once, and asked these specific questions:

1) Would Stalin agree to provide the United States with combat intelligence concerning the Japanese?

2) Was it desired that the United States should expand its Alaskan and Aleutian base facilities to take care of Soviet destroyers and submarines which might be threatened in Soviet ports by Japanese attack?

3) Would the Soviet Union be able to provide any direct or indirect assistance in case of an American attack against the northern Kuriles?

4) Would Stalin agree to furnish us with data concerning Siberian ports which our forces might use?

5) Would Stalin agree to furnish us with data concerning air bases which we might use in the Maritime Provinces to accommodate up to a thousand heavy bombers?

Harriman was given a response to the President's memorandum by Molotov on Christmas night, 1943. Molotov said the Soviet Government was prepared to give us such information about the Japanese as could be obtained by their existing facilities. In respect to the remaining questions, the Soviet Government considered some of them would require further study, while others, for reasons which the President would understand (meaning Soviet-Japanese neutrality), could not be answered "at the present time." The emphasis that he put on the words in quotes at least held promise for favorable action in the future.

For some time I had been worried about transportation problems which would inevitably arise within Russia in connection with our use of Russian bases, if we were given the opportunity to use them. The Trans-Siberian railroad constitutes the bottleneck in the support of military operations in Siberia. It is now double-tracked for most of its ten thousand miles, but there are still enough stretches of single track to reduce its capacity considerably. On its eastern end the roadbed is within a few miles of the northern and eastern borders of Manchuria, and it was therefore quite vulnerable to Japanese land and air attack. It has a number of bridges and tunnels the destruction of which would have indefinitely interrupted traffic between western Russia and the Maritime Provinces. The only other source of supply was from across the Pacific, and it was reasonable to suppose that Japan would be able to blockade that route.

Even though Russia might be able to defend the Trans-Siberian railroad, I felt certain that in a war with Japan she would require its entire capacity. If this proved to be the case, I could not foresee any way of introducing the large stocks of supplies that would be required by an American strategic air force unless they could be accumulated in advance.

Now, encouraged by Stalin's announcement at Teheran and by Molotov's reply to the questions raised by President Roosevelt, I prepared a proposal on December 26, 1943, which I presented to the Chief of the Red Army General Staff both orally and in writing. I argued that the westbound traffic of the railroad was then being utilized fully in delivering American supplies to western Russia. The eastbound traffic was at that time practically nil. I proposed that the United States be allowed to send a stock of steel mat for runways, repair machinery, portable housing, aircraft spare parts, weapons, ammunition, and fuel to Russia via the Atlantic and to utilize the eastbound traffic of the Trans-Siberian railroad to build up a supply depot in the Irkutsk-Chita area just east of Lake Baikal. I felt that this could be accomplished quietly and that the purpose of the project could be covered by leading the Japanese to believe that the depot was designed to service aircraft being ferried from Alaska to western Russia.

Antonov and Slavin were shocked by my proposal and literally turned white when I mentioned the word "Japan." Apparently the Soviet leaders still attached such importance to their continued neutrality that subordinate officials were prohibited from even discussing the possibility that some day it would end. I was greatly depressed by this because I was certain that each day lost reduced the possibility of ever operating American air forces in eastern Russia. With General

Arnold's approval, I tried to make my proposal more attractive by offering to stockpile concurrently, supplies for a Russian strategic air force made up of United States aircraft which would work in conjunction with ours. It was still too early, however, and the Russians would have none of it. Nevertheless, I am sure that my proposal was given serious consideration in the inner councils of the General Staff.

February 2, 1944, was a red-letter day for Harriman and me. He had a conference with Stalin in which we were not only given permission to have American air bases in the Ukraine but, more important, we were informed for the first time and in response to the request made by the President at Teheran that we would be allowed to operate American aircraft from Siberia after the Soviet Union declared war on Japan. Stalin said he had understood from the President that we would like to operate one thousand heavy bombers from Siberian bases. He told Harriman that facilities for more than three hundred would have to be constructed and that the matter would be given consideration. At the same time he said he was sending for high-ranking air officers to come from the Far East, and upon their arrival in Moscow they would be authorized to discuss plans with me for the establishment of an American strategic air force.

Either the train broke down or Stalin forgot to tell the Far Eastern air officers to come to Moscow. We waited for a month and my meeting with them did not materialize. Harriman went to see Stalin again early in March and was again promised that the air officers would meet with me "soon."

Toward the end of April 1944 I learned that the Soviet Union had requested delivery of three hundred Liberators and two hundred and forty Flying Fortresses as part of the Fourth Protocol which was then being formulated. We had never given Russia any four-engine bombers for the excellent reason that we never had any to spare after filling our own needs in the Pacific and Europe. In addition, a strategic air force takes a long time to create. It was a new arm of the service and required not only heavy bombers, but also the most elaborate ground organization and equipment to maintain them, as well as the development of a new technique and very specialized training. The Russians had always more or less decried the value of strategic bombing, preferring to use their air power in direct support of their ground forces. They had asked us before to give them some four-engine bombers, but we had consistently refused, both because we believed that their special characteristics would be wasted in Russian hands and because we had such great need for them ourselves.

When I heard of the Soviet request for over five hundred of these planes, I felt that it was too late for Russia to create a strategic air force for use in the war against Germany but that it was not too late for its use against Japan. Giving four-engine planes to Russia offered the additional prospect of our sending in big stocks of maintenance equipment for our own later use without exciting the suspicions of the Japanese. In view of these considerations, I recommended to the Chiefs of Staff that approval of the Soviet request be conditioned on the immediate preparation of plans looking toward the establishment of both Soviet and American strategic air forces in Siberia. My recommendation was approved, and I was thus provided with a weapon with which to attempt to force Soviet co-operation in preparing for joint action in the Pacific war.

Despite the promise made by Stalin in February and again in March, June 1944 arrived and my meeting with representatives of the Soviet Far Eastern Air Forces had not materialized. On June 10, Harriman, who had just returned from the United States, approached Stalin again and told him of the President's anxiety to have agreements concluded and plans started for the establishment of an American air force in Siberia.

From Stalin's attitude at this meeting it was apparent to us that the time we had spent in waiting had not been entirely wasted. I frequently found this to be the case in Russia. Time and again I would submit some proposal or other and hear nothing more of it. Just as I was about to discount my proposition as another failure, I would be asked to a meeting and be amazed to find that the Soviet authorities had gone as far as they could on their own in carrying out the suggested action. They preferred to operate independently rather than in conjunction with us.

Stalin told Harriman that he had been giving the whole question of our collaboration in the Far East serious consideration and that we should arrange for joint co-operation in waging the war on land and sea as well as in the air. Stalin said he had talked with his Far Eastern air commanders and had already arranged to have twelve airdromes, suitable for heavy bombers, constructed in the Vladivostok-Soviet-skaya Gavan area. He said that six or seven of these fields would be available for United States use. At the same time he asked that the Soviet Union receive several hundred heavy bombers for operations in the Far East. Harriman replied at once that the President and our Chiefs of Staff were most anxious to provide the means for creating a Soviet strategic air force which would co-ordinate its operations with ours and that four-engine planes would be sent to Russia just as soon as a joint program had been agreed upon, emphasizing the fact that it took us at least six months to train our heavy bomber personnel. Stalin laughed this off, saying that the Red Air Force would use only trained pilots and navigators for such a project and could therefore build up its force in much less time. It was plainly evident that neither he nor any of his military advisers had any conception of the specialized technique required to insure target coverage, formation control, or defense against hostile fighters. Stalin suggested that a few American instructors come to the Soviet Union to advise his Air Force on these matters.

Harriman then pointed out the supply difficulties which would be encountered in laying down in Siberia the tremendous tonnages that would be required by both the Russian and American air forces. He told Stalin that this would involve the development of a naval strategy which would keep a Pacific supply route open, careful allocation of the Trans-Siberian railroad capacity, and the establishment of an air route from Alaska or the Aleutians to Siberia. These were all matters, he said, that my Military Mission wished to thrash out with appropriate Russian Army, Navy, and Air officials. Stalin would not commit himself as to when our discussions should start except to say "no time should be lost and the sooner the discussions start the better."

Nothing was done toward eventual Soviet-American collaboration in Siberia for another six weeks. While I was at the front, Slavin woke me one night to tell me that he had had a message from Moscow saying that I was to meet Deputy Chief of Staff Antonov on the night of our return to discuss "a matter of great secrecy." I was thrilled—perhaps the gate was opening!

When I arrived at Antonov's office, he was his usual chilly self. He said that he had been directed by Marshal Stalin to meet with me and that he understood I had some proposals to make. If so, what were they? As the result of previous experience I had anticipated his attitude and I was ready to present a complete program which I had already cleared with General Arnold.

I proposed that we set up a small joint staff at once which would be charged with planning for our co-operative efforts in the war against Japan. I went over the agenda of subjects to be studied by such a joint staff, giving Antonov our ideas on each. One subject was the size of the American and Soviet air forces to be operated in Siberia. We suggested an initial force of ten heavy bomber groups and ten fighter groups, with the Americans operating six of each and the Russians four. The reason for the difference was that we would have the groups already in being, whereas the Russians would have to build theirs from scratch. We suggested that they accept the lower figure initially with the understanding that our forces could be of equal strength if time and the availability of aircraft permitted. This was a mistake, and Antonov was convinced that we wanted to relegate the Soviet Air Forces to a secondary position on their own territory. I think this was the chief reason for the long period of several months which the General Staff required for deliberation before taking action on the propositions I had made.

On the day following my meeting with Antonov I left Moscow with Admiral Olsen and Major Taylor for a hurried trip to General

Eisenhower's headquarters in London and then on to Washington to report on our co-operative ventures with Russia to the American Chiefs of Staff. In Washington I was surprised to learn that General Arnold had had a meeting on August 8, 1944, which Lieutenant General Leonid G. Rudenko, head of the Soviet Purchasing Commission, during which he had become bighearted and had told Rudenko that two hundred Liberators (B-24's) could be made available to the Soviet Union for delivery at the rate of fifty per month. In addition, General Arnold had agreed that we would send a group of American specialists to Russia to train Soviet crews and that we would undertake to train Soviet maintenance personnel in the United States. It had also been more or less settled that the aircraft would be ferried to Russia through Abadan and the Persian Gulf.

This was all contrary to the understanding that I had had about using the allocation of four-engine bombers to Russia as a bargaining point in securing American air bases in Siberia. I went to see General Arnold and persuaded him to inform Rudenko that while the bombers were available, their actual delivery would be held up pending the outcome of my negotiations with General Antonov. Also, I felt very strongly that if we did send four-engine planes to Russia, they should be sent via Alaska and Siberia in order to force the development of installations along that route so that they could handle heavy bombers. This would be of assistance if we were later allowed to ferry aircraft from England across Russia to Siberia. General Arnold agreed and informed Rudenko that when we sent Liberators to the Soviet Union we would be able to do so only over the Alaskan-Siberian route.

Admiral Olsen, Major Taylor, and I returned to Moscow over this route. It was a memorable experience. In the first place, we found that our air base at Fairbanks was at least half under Soviet control. Officers' quarters, office space, hangars, and shops had been turned over to the Red Air Force. Russian and American officers ate at a central mess. There were no restrictions whatsoever on Soviet personnel. They were free to use all the facilities of the station and to travel at will. It presented a great contrast to the conditions under which Olsen and I lived in Moscow.

The trip from Fairbanks to Moscow required three and one-half days. It could have been made much faster except for the fact that only one pilot was assigned to the plane, which was one of our C-47 transports being delivered under lend-lease, and he, of course, required his rest at night. In addition, Oley, Taylor, and I were invited to have a cup of tea wherever we stopped. This meant driving in to the nearest town where we would be confronted with huge meals that could not be refused without jeopardizing international relations. Our stops were frequent, and we found it impossible to do justice to the hospitality extended to us. Before the first day was over Oley came out of the plane at each stop shouting, *"Tolko chai, pajolista,"* which meant "Only tea, please." His pronunciation must have been poor, however, as his earnest plea never had the desired effect.

Before my departure from the United States the Army Air Forces had started to gather a training cadre of one hundred specialists to go to Russia and train Soviet crews in the handling of American Liberators and the technique of long-range strategic bombing. They had selected a number of used Liberators which they were to bring with them for training purposes.

As soon as I got back to Moscow I went to see General I. F. Semichastnov in the Commissariat of Foreign Trade to make arrangements for our training cadre to come to Russia. He told me that the Soviet authorities could not see the necessity of having one hundred Americans come to Russia to give this training and suggested that the number be reduced to twenty. These, he said, could train a cadre of Russian instructors who could then take over the mass training that would later be required. We did not agree that the best results would be obtained in this manner and we were extremely anxious that a really effective Soviet strategic air force be created. Nevertheless, we acquiesced to Soviet wishes and reduced our group to twenty-six highly selected specialists taken from key positions in our own Air Force. This group, together with six Liberators they were to take with them, were assembled at Topeka, Kansas, where they waited a month for entrance visas to the Soviet Union.

On September 29, 1944, two months after agreement had been reached that a training program would be undertaken, Semichastnov informed Spalding that the Soviet Government had decided not to go on with the training project in view of the uncertainty regarding the delivery schedule of Liberator aircraft.

Before communicating this decision to Washington I called again on General Antonov and assured him that we could start the delivery of Liberators to Russia at once, provided we could come to some agreement on the proposals I had submitted to him. Apparently, however, the General Staff had decided that it would forego the advantages of creating a strategic air force rather than be forced into making any commitment to the United States until they were ready to do so. I had lost my weapon and was forced to recommend to General Arnold that the training group be disbanded.

This really ended all efforts on both sides to provide the Red Air Force with long-range bombers. Stalin did suggest the possibility a month or so later and even proposed that we send a small number of Liberators for training purposes. His suggestion was not greeted with much warmth on our part, and the project eventually died. We still had his promise, however, that we would be allowed at the proper time to operate our bombers from Siberia and we continued to plan on this basis.

It was just as difficult to deal with Soviet officials in undertakings of which they were to be the sole beneficiaries as in matters in which we had a joint interest. Soviet use of the Norden bombsight was a striking example.

During the early stages of the negotiations for our use of air bases in the Ukraine, Colonel General Repin, chief of the engineer and matériel section of the Red Air Staff, asked me if I could let the Soviet Union have a Norden bombsight. Up until that time this sight had been one of our most closely guarded secrets. We knew, however, that many of them had been recovered by the Germans from American planes that had been shot down and that so far as the enemy was concerned the necessity for secrecy no longer existed. General Arnold therefore approved the Soviet request but told me to inform the Russians that our production would not permit making the sight available to them in quantity.

By the middle of 1944 production had improved, and at the request of the Soviet Purchasing Commission we agreed to install the Norden sight on the medium bombers which were to be sent to the Soviet Union starting in the fall of 1944. We were glad to do this because we felt the Norden sight would increase the effectiveness of Russian bombing in the war against Japan. In mid-July 1944 General Rudenko asked General Arnold to send some American instructors to Russia to train the Red Air Force in the use of the new sight.

General Arnold selected four of his outstanding experts for the assignment and designated the senior, Major Warren C. Williams, to be in charge of the project. Williams and his three assistants applied for visas to enter Russia and then awaited results. At the end of three weeks I recommended to General Arnold that if Soviet visas were not forthcoming by August 17, he should send his specialists back to their duties in the United States. I informed General Semichastnov of the recommendation I had made, and on the morning of August 17 he asked me to have the group held together and assured me that their visas would be issued immediately. On August 24, a week later, as nothing had been done, I informed Semichastnov that the project was off. He replied that the Soviet authorities had decided that the training would not be necessary. He said this, I believe, in order to cover up his failure to have the Foreign Office act more quickly, because on September 10 the visas arrived in Washington. General Arnold forgave all, reassembled his specialists, and they arrived in Moscow on October 15.

Major Williams started a class of twenty-five officers in Moscow on October 25. They were all engineers and more than half of them had studied the bombsight I had obtained for them the preceding March. Williams was impressed by the caliber of his students but was surprised to learn that they could remain with him for a course of only seventy-two hours, which by our standards was totally inadequate. This meant that individual instruction would have to be minimized in favor of group training. Because of the limited passenger capacity of a light bomber, Williams asked General Arnold to send him one Liberator to use for that part of the course requiring instruction in the air. General Arnold immediately ordered a heavy bomber to proceed to Russia. On November 2 we were told that it would not be allowed to enter the Soviet Union. The reason given was that the urgent need to put the light bombers, then on hand, into combat made it undesirable to waste time on preliminary instruction in a heavy bomber. Williams thereupon decided to confine the air training to those of his students who could speak English and to rely on them to impart the training to the others after the course was concluded. As the program worked out, the allotted time of seventy-two hours expired before weather would permit any training in the air. The school ended with the class fairly proficient in the theory of operating the sight, but with no practical experience, yet this was the group that was to train all Red Air Force bombardiers in the use of this highly complex device. General Arnold considered the training a failure. He asked me to express his disappointment to the Soviet authorities and to caution them against any unwarranted criticism of American equipment, training personnel, and methods of training in the almost certain event that Soviet bombing technique proved to be inadequate.

In our exchange of combat intelligence concerning the Japanese, we met with a little more success. Molotov had informed Harriman on December 25, 1943, that Stalin had approved the President's request for an exchange of information. However, it took a long while for the news to percolate down to the working levels.

On February 29, 1944, the Soviet Navy agreed to start an exchange of Japanese naval intelligence with Admiral Olsen. It is noteworthy that the Soviet Naval Staff was much more approachable and co-operative than the Red Army General Staff. This was due in part to the tact and skill with which Olsen handled his relations with the Naval officials, but mostly, I believe, it was because the Navy had not yet reached the proud estate of the Army and was therefore eager to acquire knowledge through contacts with American Naval officers. We soon found that because of the limited facilities available the Navy was unable to add anything to our knowledge concerning Japanese naval matters.

In the case of the Army, we felt certain that we could obtain valuable information, particularly with regard to the location of Japanese units, known in military parlance as the "order of battle." Our intelligence experts had developed a system of perfecting our knowledge of Japanese order of battle to a degree that has never been attained elsewhere. Our system was based on a 1942 edition of the Japanese register, captured in the South Pacific, which included the names, assignments, and location of her regular and volunteer officers. It furnished the basic pattern, and the movement of all units could be carefully followed by information gained from orders and other documents found on Japanese casualties and by the interception of Japanese radio communications. Because of the isolation and independence of the Kwantung Army from the remainder of their military establishments, we felt that information on the Japanese forces in Manchuria, including Manchurian puppet troops, was the dimmest part of an otherwise complete picture. It was in this respect that we thought we could obtain most assistance from the Russians.

Colonel Moses W. Pettigrew was in charge of the Japanese order of battle section of the Military Intelligence Department of our General Staff and was our outstanding expert on the subject. We decided to send him to Russia. He arrived on April 6, 1944, after waiting two months for a visa. Despite the fact that the purpose of his coming was known to the Red Army General Staff, I did not succeed in arranging a meeting between Pettigrew and the Soviet Far Eastern Intelligence experts until June 9, 1944.

Pettigrew's first meeting was chaperoned by Slavin, and I attended as evidence that I considered the exchange to be important. At first it was understood that there would be a series of only four meetings at which would be discussed those questions which we had raised in our correspondence with the General Staff. Pettigrew, however, had his material so carefully arranged and his information so well documented that he convinced the Russians at the first meeting that they had much more to gain than they had to lose by continuing them. As a result, the relationship thus established continued until the end of the war. The quality and importance of the intelligence exchanged improved steadily until, at the end, Pettigrew had a daily teletype conference with Washington to make sure that every bit of Japanese intelligence received by us was turned over promptly to the Red Army. In turn, the Russians provided firsthand information of Japanese troop movements and dispositions in Manchuria which they obtained by actual contact and by the infiltration of intelligence agents.

I can hardly describe my first year in Russia as a productive one in the matter of preparation for Soviet-American collaboration in the war against Japan. Considering the neutrality pact the Soviet Union had signed with Japan, she was perfectly within her rights in avoiding any action which might be construed as a violation of neutrality. But in my opinion the Soviet leaders can be criticized for their timidity long after the need for caution had disappeared; for their skepticism of American security after our demonstrated ability in this respect in connection with the North African and European invasions; and for their broken promises made as far back as February 1944 that Soviet-American planning should be undertaken. Fortunately the nightmare was to last only a year. In the autumn of 1944 the situation improved.

XIV. Churchill's Visit
and the Yalta Conference

AVERELL HARRIMAN and Sir Archibald Clark-Kerr called on Stalin on September 23, 1944, to give him a report of the proceedings of the second Quebec Conference. Such reports had become an habitual aftermath of all British-American meetings. They were entirely voluntary and contained only a broad outline of the conclusions that had been reached. Stalin was probably skeptical concerning them, particularly with regard to the frankness with which the plans of the Western Allies were revealed. Despite the fact that his vanity seemed somewhat appeased by the thought that the President and Prime Minister considered it necessary to report their activities to him, Stalin was inclined to read between the lines rather than take the written document at its face value.

On this occasion Stalin noted that the report from Roosevelt and Churchill said nothing concerning Russian participation when speaking of contemplated operations in the Pacific. He asked Harriman if the President still considered it essential that Russia should join the war against Japan. He appeared to be somewhat surprised that after the assurances he had given the President at Teheran, we had not taken Soviet participation into account in our planning. Stalin said that there had been no change in the Russian attitude, but if the United States and Great Britain preferred to bring Japan to her knees without Russian participation, he was ready to agree.

Harriman and Clark-Kerr assured Stalin that both the President and the Prime Minister were counting on Russia's help in the Far

East, but they pointed out that we had to rely on fulfilling the task by ourselves until Stalin was ready to participate in joint planning for the best use of our combined resources. Harriman pressed the point by saying that at the direction of the President he and I had been trying for a year to initiate planning for Soviet-American collaboration. He again emphasized the importance of starting preparations at once in order that the United States could plan the redeployment of forces following the defeat of Germany.

Stalin agreed, but added that on their part it was essential that the Russians should be informed of the operations the Western Allies had in mind and particularly of the role they wished the Soviet Union to play. He said that he was ready to have his military leaders meet with me. He promised to issue the necessary instructions and set a time so that the discussions could start in a few days.

Harriman was convinced that this time Stalin meant business. He was filled with enthusiasm when he told me about the meeting. I was a bit more pessimistic. Nevertheless, I had to be prepared to discuss Stalin's query as to what role the United States would like Russia to play. Fearing that I would not be able to receive instructions from Washington before my first meeting with the Russians, I sent the Chiefs of Staff a message in which I said I would suggest the following missions for Russia, in order of priority, unless they had in the meantime directed me differently:

1) Securing the Trans-Siberian railroad and the Vladivostok peninsula. (This was placed first because supply would be impossible unless it was accomplished.)

2) Setting up Soviet and American strategic air forces for operations against Japan from the Maritime Provinces. (It was still not too late for this.)

3) Securing the Pacific supply route in which Russian participation would include:
   a) Making Petropavlovsk available to the United States as a naval base.

b) Neutralization by air of southern Sakhalin and Hokkaido.

c) Improvement of port facilities of the Amur River.

d) Military occupation of southern Sakhalin.

e) Soviet-American naval co-operation as the situation dictated.

4) Defeat of the Japanese Army in Manchuria. (This was to be the Soviet Union's principal role, but the others were necessary preliminaries.)

On September 29 I received word from the Chiefs of Staff that they approved the missions I had proposed for the Soviet Union with minor amendments. They added a mission, which they assigned third priority, of Soviet interdiction or interruption of Japanese shipping and air traffic between Japan proper and the Asiatic mainland. They also moved securing of a Pacific supply route to last priority in the belief that the Russian operations could be supported if necessary by the Trans-Siberian railroad and by stockpiles laid down in Russia before the Pacific route was closed.

Now that I was armed with the authentic views of the Chiefs of Staff it was time to needle the Russians again in order to get our discussions started. Harriman made two attempts to do this. On September 29 he informed Molotov that I had been officially designated by the President to represent the United States in the conferences that Stalin had promised and asked when they might be expected to begin. No reply was received to this query. On October 4 Harriman called on Stalin to present him with a bronze bust of President Roosevelt, but he took advantage of the opportunity to raise again the question that was nearest our hearts. Stalin told Harriman that he had sent for General Shevchenko, the commanding general of the Siberian Ground Forces, and General Zhegelev, commander of the Siberian Air Forces, to come to Moscow to discuss Far Eastern matters. Stalin said that he himself desired to be brought up to date on this constantly changing situation and that thereafter he would have these officers meet with me. This implied that some delay could be expected. Meanwhile, we had heard that Churchill was coming to Moscow in the middle of

October, so Harriman and I began plotting to take advantage of his visit to bring the question of Soviet participation in the Japanese war to a head.

Churchill arrived in Moscow on October 11, 1944. He was accompanied by Anthony Eden, Lord Alanbrooke, then Chief of the Imperial General Staff, General Sir Hastings Ismay, the Prime Minister's Chief of Staff, and Major General E. I. C. Jacob, a member of the War Cabinet Secretariat. Harriman immediately solicited Churchill's aid in impressing on Stalin the importance of starting preparations for Russia's part in the Pacific war. Both Harriman and I met with Churchill's military advisers to work out ways and means by which our purpose could be accomplished.

The situation was a bit ticklish for us. We knew how zealously our chiefs in Washington guarded the United States' position of leadership in the conduct of the Pacific war. We knew that our efforts would not be appreciated at home if it were made to appear in Moscow that the British were seizing the initiative in obtaining Soviet participation. As a matter of fact, I had already received instructions from the American Chiefs of Staff that the United States' conception as to how Soviet forces could be best employed should be presented by me if this could possibly be arranged. On the other hand, the President had informed Churchill that upon his arrival in Moscow I would show him the instructions I had received from our Chiefs of Staff regarding the part we hoped the Russians would play.

Despite our apprehensions Churchill and his advisers could not have been more co-operative. They agreed at once and wholeheartedly that since the direction of the Pacific war was being carried out by the United States, Harriman should attend the military conferences to be held with Stalin as President Roosevelt's representative, and I should present any military views that might be expressed at the conferences concerning the conduct of the war against Japan and the part we hoped the Soviet Union would undertake. Churchill agreed to back our play to the limit but would otherwise leave the matter in our hands.

We all assembled in the conference room outside Stalin's office at about nine o'clock in the evening on October 14, 1944. The room was typical of all the other Soviet conference rooms I had visited: a long conference table covered with green felt and surrounded by chairs, a few deep leather armchairs, a small plain flat-top desk in one corner, and a little stand holding a pitcher of water and some glasses which stood against one of the walls. The floors were of polished hardwood and covered with a few scatter rugs. The lighting was that thrown out from a green-top porcelain shade in the center of the ceiling— it was satisfactory but certainly not brilliant. I have no idea what Stalin's personal office or his living quarters might be like, but I gained the impression from the bare simplicity of his conference room that he has not made use of his power to enhance his personal comforts.

Both the British and American delegations had brought a number of maps, and our first problem was to find some place to hang them. Stalin took a lively interest in this and soon we had them hanging by strings attached to window catches and other protrusions from one of the walls. The easy chairs were arranged in front of the maps, Churchill lit up a cigar that was ten inches long, and the party settled down for the discussions. Churchill and Stalin sat together in the center of the front and the rest of us were grouped around them.

As a matter of procedure Churchill suggested that the conference start with presentations of the military situation of the Western Allies, first in Europe and then in the Pacific. He proposed that these be followed by a description of the Russian situation in the war with Germany and whatever Stalin cared to say in relation to the Pacific war. Lord Alanbrooke was to present our case regarding the European war and I was to follow with a discussion of the Japanese situation.

Lord Alanbrooke outlined Eisenhower's operations and future plans in the greatest detail. He made an excellent presentation, and I remember being particularly grateful for the tributes he paid to the American armies and the emphasis he placed on our successes. I must confess, however, that I missed much of what he said and that I broke out in a cold perspiration every time I realized that I would be at bat in just a few minutes.

I had arranged to have Pavlov, the little blond-headed interpreter who accompanies Molotov everywhere, interpret for me. As soon as I started, I realized that nothing is easier than to speak through an interpreter—especially one as good as Pavlov. While sentences are being translated, one can arrange one's thoughts about what is to come next and at the same time observe the audience to see the impression made by the thought just expressed.

One incident of my presentation that struck me as amusing was in connection with Churchill. In preparing my talk I had thought of introducing a merry quip about the Japanese whom we had by-passed on some of the Pacific Islands as being "forced to subsist on coconuts and fish until the rising sun sets." I was afraid, however, that the subtlety of such humor might be lost in the translation and in any event it was a bit too flip for the occasion. As I was speaking, Churchill followed me intently. He was slumped down in his chair, chewing on his cigar and scowling. His hands were characteristically clasped across his spacious stomach and one leg was bobbing up and down as the result of a well-developed toe action. Suddenly he waved his cigar at me and said, "Tell them about the Japanese we have left on those islands." This gave me my opening and I reinserted the bright remark previously discarded. Churchill only snorted at this but apparently it stuck in his mind. After I had progressed far beyond the islands in question and was on an entirely different subject, he jumped up, shook his cigar at Stalin, and shouted, "They'll rot, they'll rot." The same question came to everyone's mind but only Stalin had the temerity to ask, "Who will rot?" Churchill reddened a little when he answered, "The Japs on those islands." With that he subsided and allowed me to continue without interruption.

In presenting our case to Stalin I first reviewed the Pacific war from the time of Pearl Harbor, covering the build-up of our communications, the battles of the Coral Sea and Midway, and the approaches of our double offensive from the South Pacific and through the Central Pacific. I discussed the operations then in progress and those envisaged until Japan had been invaded. In this connection I recall saying that we intended "seizing a position in the central Philippines in the near future." I did not know it, but at the moment I was speaking Mac-Arthur's expedition was already on its way, and two days later he made good my statement by landing his forces on Leyte.

I concluded my talk by answering the question Stalin had asked concerning our conception of the role the Soviet Union should play. I then said that the American Chiefs of Staff considered it essential to their planning to have answers to the following questions:

1) How long after the defeat of Germany may we expect Soviet-Japanese hostilities to commence?
2) How much time will be required to build up the Soviet forces in the Far East to the point where they can initiate an offensive?
3) How much of the capacity of the Trans-Siberian railroad can be devoted to the build-up and support of an American strategic air force?

When I had finished speaking, Stalin asked only one question—"How many divisions do the Japanese have?" I had the answer in my papers but not in my mind. The only excuse for such ignorance was that I had been concentrating all my thought on the small part of the Japanese war in which Russia might become involved. When I hesitated, Stalin looked a bit annoyed, and the day went to the British when Lord Alanbrooke quickly thumbed through his papers and came up with the right answer.

The first meeting then adjourned with the understanding that we would meet the following night to hear a description of the Red Army's operations. As we were going out Churchill said to me, "Young man, I admired your nerve in asking Stalin those last three questions. I have no idea that you will get an answer, but there was certainly no harm in asking."

On the following night, when Stalin took the floor, he gave answers to most of the questions I had asked the night before. The Red Army would have to have sixty divisions in the Far East before it could take the offensive—thirty more than those already there—and the movement would require three months after Germany was defeated. Since the Trans-Siberian railroad would not be able to supply sixty divisions despite its capacity of thirty-six trains a day, a reserve of two to three months' supplies would have to be stockpiled in Siberia before the start of operations. In reply to a direct question from Harriman, Stalin said the Soviet Union would take the offensive against Japan three months after Germany's defeat provided the United States would assist in building up the necessary reserve supplies and provided the political aspects of Russia's participation had been clarified. His latter proviso referred to the recognition by China of Russian claims against the Japanese in the Far East. Stalin further agreed that air bases would be made available to the American Air Forces in the Maritime Provinces but implied that we would have to rely on the Pacific route for our supply since all the Trans-Siberian rail capacity would be otherwise utilized. In addition, he assured us the use of Petropavlovsk as a naval base. We adjourned with the conviction that progress was being made even though the immediate action was to consist, as usual, of sending more American equipment abroad.

The first two meetings had resulted in certain definite conclusions with regard to Russia's participation in the Pacific war. Eden thought it would be well if he and Harriman would put their understanding of these conclusions in writing and submit a paper to Molotov for his stamp of approval. Harriman was a little apprehensive about the propriety of doing this as it would carry the implication that we did not have complete faith in the sincerity of Stalin's spoken word. However, Eden felt strongly that for purposes of clarity a written agreement was desirable, and Harriman reluctantly agreed. Stalin was highly indignant when he received the paper and pointed to it as another example of the Western Allies' disregard for secrecy. At our next meeting he berated Harriman for being a party to the preparation of the paper and said that any leakage concerning the discussions in progress would almost certainly bring on a Japanese attack which might result in the loss of the vital Vladivostok area. He said, "Stenographers and secretaries are eager to exaggerate their own importance by telling news to their friends, and thus military secrets no longer remain military secrets." He added, "I am a cautious old man." There was some validity to his argument, but at the same time he and his advisers were the leading proponents of written agreements when there was any Soviet doubt about their fulfillment. This was amply illustrated at the beginning of our third meeting when he followed his objection to the paper prepared by Eden and Harriman by handing us a seven-page typewritten document listing the supplies needed from the United States for a two months' reserve in Siberia. I am certain that Stalin did not type this document himself!

The British, at their own suggestion, did not attend the third meeting, on October 17, at which we were given a list of the needs of the Soviet Union for a two months' supply of food, fuel, transport equipment, and other supplies, calculated on the requirements of a force of 1,500,000 men, 3,000 tanks, 75,000 motor vehicles, and 5,000 airplanes. The total tonnage involved was 860,410 tons of dry cargo and 206,000 tons of liquid cargo. It was considered necessary to have the deliveries completed by June 30, 1945, and it was all in addition to the program under the current Fourth Protocol. It was a neat little chore which the Soviet Union presented to the United States. In view of the time limit imposed, I could not help feeling resentful of the time that had been wasted the preceding year.

We went over the list item by item and found that while many of them, such as those required for port improvements and rail transportation, had a marked postwar significance, all of them would benefit Russia's attack on the Japanese if they could be delivered in time.

During the remainder of the meeting we discussed the operations the Red Army contemplated in their war with Japan. Stalin reiterated that the Russian attack would be launched three months after Germany's surrender. He accepted the missions that the United States Chiefs of Staff proposed and which I had presented at the first meeting. Stalin illustrated on a map the strategy that had been planned for the Red Army's offensive. In general, he proposed to exert direct pressure on the Japanese along the northern and eastern borders of Manchuria while making his main effort with a highly mobile force that would sweep down from the Lake Baikal area through Outer and Inner Mongolia to Kalgan, Peiping, and Tientsin. The purpose of this wide movement was to separate the Japanese forces in Manchuria from those in China. This was precisely the strategy that was followed in the few days that Russia was at war with Japan.

When presenting us with his bill of goods, Stalin was agreeable to the counterproposals we made. We could have air bases; we could count on the same priority in the build-up of our air force as was given to that of the Red Army; we could have Petropavlovsk as a naval base; we could send small parties to make secret physical surveys of the air bases in the Maritime Provinces and of the Petropavlovsk area; and, most important, we could proceed at once with joint and detailed planning. But, despite these promises, the end result was that the Russians got their supplies and the United States got nothing except a belated and last minute Russian attack against the Japanese.

The United States succeeded in delivering 80 per cent of the promised supplies by June 30, 1945. We could have done better had we had more co-operation from the Russians themselves. There were difficulties in nomenclature and endless delays while the Russians tried to clarify what was actually wanted; shipping problems created a bottleneck; and the Commissariat of Foreign Trade objected to every suggested change in priorities as we attempted to make adjustments between the needs of the Siberian program and those of the Fourth Protocol, with the result that both programs suffered.

Finally, there was the matter of substitutes offered by the United States when items on the Soviet list were not available. Such offers were either rejected entirely or their acceptance was delayed so long as to make delivery within the time prescribed impossible. For instance, the Russian list requested delivery of 25,000 tons of canned meat. On December 21, 1944, Spalding informed General Semichastnov that canned meat was not available but offered to substitute meat and vegetable hash or stew. This offer was flatly rejected, and we dismissed the matter from further consideration in the belief that the Soviet need could not have been very great in the first place. Three months later, however, we were thrown into considerable consternation when Semichastnov announced that upon reconsideration the Soviet Government had decided to accept the substitution. By that time it was impossible to assemble 25,000 tons of canned hash or stew in time to deliver it by the date set for the completion of the program. Shoes were another item that caused difficulty. The Soviet list requested delivery of 2,000,000 pairs. We could send them only rebuilt shoes, and these were not accepted. The remarkable thing is that the Russians seemed to get along quite well without the items for which they refused to accept substitutes.

Following our meeting with Stalin on October 17, in spite of former disillusionment, I looked forward to immediate and continued meetings with the Soviet General Staff. As usual, the days passed and nothing happened. On October 27 I did succeed in obtaining a meeting with Antonov, to which I brought General Spalding and Admiral Olsen. We outlined our conception of the problem involved in respect to land, sea, and air. We found, however, that Antonov was interested only in our report that the Siberian supply program was approved and that deliveries would begin at once. He listened courteously to all the other problems which we raised, but brushed them aside by saying they were all under consideration by the General Staff. He promised to name Army, Navy, and Air representatives in the near future with whom we could discuss these matters.

By this time I was pretty well discouraged about the prospects of ever establishing an American air force in Russia. For one thing, weather was against us. Winter weather and Russian obstructionism were combining to make it impossible for us to get our air force established in time to be of use. Therefore, when I returned from our unfruitful meeting with Antonov, I sent a message to Washington recommending that we give up the idea of building a force of our own. I suggested, however, that if we thought strategic bombing of Japan from the Maritime Provinces was necessary, we should renew our efforts to build up a Soviet strategic air force. General Arnold disapproved my recommendation and we continued to seek co-operative action in Moscow.

The Yalta Conference was held during the first ten days of February 1945. It was the Soviet Union's first experience as host on such an occasion and the preparations for the Conference caused them considerable anguish. The Crimea is a flat peninsula that tilts upward from north to south. The flat plateau rises as it nears the Black Sea and suddenly breaks off into a precipitous slope that leads down to the southern shore. It was on this steep slope that the Russian nobility had established a winter resort long before the revolution. The slope from the shore line to the top of the plateau is heavily wooded, and the woods are studded with the country estates of the old Russian aristocracy. The setting closely resembles that of the Riviera in southern France.

The American delegation to the Conference was given the Livadia Palace formerly owned by the Czar. Like all other buildings in the area, it had been completely stripped of its furniture and fixtures during the German occupation. It had been used as a convalescent home for Soviet soldiers after the Germans had been driven out. Every bit of furniture needed to make the place habitable for the President had to be brought from Moscow. My Mission had been given the task of co-ordinating with the Soviet authorities in making suitable arrangements for the American delegation. The Soviet Navy had been put in charge on the Russian side, so I designated Admiral Olsen to work with them.

Since we had learned (both from Russian statements and independent studies of our own) that the Vladivostok area could not accommodate American heavy bombers, I had sent Brigadier General William L. Ritchie to Washington to convince the Chiefs of Staff that they should concentrate their efforts at the Conference on obtaining Russian bases for our longer range B-29's. Ritchie succeeded in his mission.

Soon after their arrival at Yalta the American Chiefs of Staff induced the President to press Stalin for his attitude on the questions of bomber bases and the Pacific supply route. As a result, he said that our long-range bombers could operate in the Komsomolsk-Nikolaevsk area along the lower reaches of the Amur River, and that it would be necessary to keep the Pacific supply route open after Russo-Japanese hostilities commenced, mainly for the delivery of petroleum products.

Using Stalin's statements as a basis, I proposed a list of seven questions for the American Chiefs of Staff to ask Antonov. His replies to these questions were as follows:

1) There would be no change in the Soviet operational plans as outlined at the Churchill conference.

2) United States' assistance in the defense of Kamchatka would be desirable.

3) The Soviet Union would undertake the preliminary construction necessary for an American air force in the Komsomolsk-Nikolaevsk area.

4) American survey parties would be authorized to visit Kamchatka and the Amur River district. The Kamchatka survey should be delayed as long as possible for reasons of secrecy but the Amur survey could be made at once.

5) In order to open La Perouse Strait, the Red Army would take the southern half of Sakhalin Island as one of its first operations.

6) Planning between American and Soviet teams in Moscow would be pursued vigorously.

7) Additional weather stations would be opened in the Far East to give greater coverage.

The Kamchatka survey was a project which had been approved both by the United States and the Soviets early in December. At that time we had been told by Antonov that it would have to be conducted with the greatest secrecy, and that for that reason our party would have to wear Russian uniforms which the Russian Government would furnish if we would supply the measurements of the men who were to wear them. The survey party had been assembled in Washington and had sent their measurements by the end of December, but in mid-January I had been told that the survey would have to be indefinitely delayed because Japanese fishermen who usually left Kamchatka before the beginning of the New Year had unexplainably remained there and could not be forced out without exciting suspicion.

The Yalta Conference thus ended with generalized answers to a number of questions which had been troubling us. It remained only to work out the details necessary for the implementation of the decisions that had been reached. But there were decisions taken at Yalta other than those pertaining to the Japanese war which affected adversely our efforts to secure Russian co-operation. One of these concerned the future of Poland. I have mentioned elsewhere how our different interpretation of the agreement regarding Poland placed a considerable strain on Soviet-American relations in Europe during the spring of 1945. The accord reached concerning the Japanese war was likewise to suffer from this strain.

As soon as General Marshall returned to the United States he sent a message to Antonov in which he recognized the need to maintain secrecy with regard to proposed American use of Kamchatka and suggested that instead of our sending an American survey party, a group of Soviet officers should come to the United States and provide us with such information as we had to have in planning for American installations in the Kamchatka peninsula. I was unsuccessful in my efforts to obtain a reply to General Marshall's proposal.

With regard to the American survey of the Amur River area, I was told by General Slavin on March 14, 1945, to have our party arrive at Fairbanks, Alaska, in two days. I asked Slavin if it would be necessary for the three officers in the party to obtain Soviet visas before their departure from the United States. He promised that the necessary instructions concerning entrance documents would be cabled that night to the Soviet authorities in Fairbanks.

Our party arrived in Fairbanks at the appointed time, March 16. They had made a hurried attempt to obtain visas in Washington, but because of the short notice they did not have time to wait for them. Upon arriving in Fairbanks, they reported to General Obraskov in accordance with instructions given me by Slavin. Obraskov knew nothing of their proposed visit and refused to approve their entry. The party remained at Fairbanks until April 6, a period of twenty-one days, hoping from day to day to receive clearance. Meanwhile Harriman and I were doing our best in Moscow to break the impasse. First we were told that the delay had been caused by the failure of our party to obtain visas—later the delay was attributed to weather. On the twenty-first day I sent word to Washington that I was convinced that the delay resulted from Soviet displeasure over the Polish situation, the Bern peace negotiations, and incidents resulting from air clashes in Europe. I said I thought it was undignified to have our party sitting in Fairbanks awaiting Soviet pleasure and recommended that it be returned to the United States. My recommendation was approved, and the prospect of B-29's being based in the Amur River district receded still further.

During the whole period in which the Soviet Union was either violating or failing to carry out its agreements concerning Soviet-American collaboration in the Pacific war, we continued to exert unusual efforts to deliver supplies for her Siberian reserve. There were many times when I had the greatest desire to recommend that our flow of supplies to Russia be shut off until the Soviet Union showed some more tangible evidence of the co-operation it had promised. I was always restrained from doing so by the thought that a strong Soviet attack on the Japanese would hasten the end of the war. I also had considerable pride in representing a nation that lives up to its obligations and fulfills its commitments.

XV. Soviet-American Planning
for the Pacific War

SOVIET-AMERICAN planning for combined operations in the Pacific war was impossible because of the different concept each country had of the way our military alliance should function. The Americans thought that there would be some operations which we should carry out together and which would have to be closely coordinated if we were to bring our maximum weight to bear against the enemy. The Russians believed that we should simply agree on the tasks each nation should perform and then proceed to carry them out independently of each other. I think this accounts for the difficulty Harriman and I encountered in our efforts to initiate detailed planning.

By September 1944 I had become pretty much discouraged about the prospect of doing anything toward collaboration in the Far East, but I felt certain that the day would come when we would be forced into some sort of co-operative effort and that then our plans would have to be concerted in the utmost haste. In order to be prepared for that eventuality I resolved to do some advance planning of my own. Colonel James C. Crockett was a member of the Mission and a friend of long standing whom I remembered as an expert in conducting war games during the days we had been instructors at Fort Leavenworth. I suggested to Crockett that he take all fifty of the officers assigned to the Mission and hold a series of war games designed to point up the problems that would arise in connection with Soviet and Soviet-American operations in Siberia. We decided to divide the games into five problems; first, an immediate Japanese attack on the Trans-Siberian railroad and the Vladivostok area; second, the establishment of an American strategic air force in the Maritime Provinces; third, the establishment and defense of American air and naval bases on Kamchatka; fourth, keeping the Pacific supply route open after Russo-Japanese hostilities commenced; and fifth, a Russian offensive against the Kwantung Army. All phases of each operation were to be played with particular emphasis on the supply problems in each. It was necessary for us to make certain assumptions concerning strengths, dispositions, and other matters, but wherever we could we took the conditions as we actually knew them to be. Regardless of the correctness of our assumptions, I believed that the major problems inherent in each situation would stand out in bold relief as the games progressed.

Crockett set to work at once, and soon my Mission was divided into two camps, one Japanese and the other Russian. I recall that Colonel Pettigrew, our expert on Japanese affairs, was named as the supreme commander of the Japanese forces and was thereafter known as Tojo. I doubt if any more incongruous situation developed during the war than that of the American military and naval representation in Moscow resorting to schoolroom war games in order to get some conception of the situation which might confront the Soviet forces.

Harriman let us have the ballroom of Spasso House for our workshop. It was soon divided into compartments for the various staff sections of both forces. The walls were covered with maps on which our hypothetical situations were staked out. We guarded the security of the ballroom as best we could. However, some Soviet employees were needed to translate documents from Russian to English and others were required for housekeeping purposes. It is inconceivable that the N.K.V.D. was not fully aware of what was going on, and I have no doubt that our activities created considerable curiosity in the Red Army General Staff when news of them reached its ears.

Crockett and his assistants did a remarkable job. Every American who traveled over the Trans-Siberian railroad was given a list of items about which he should attempt to obtain information. Before long we knew the locations of all the vulnerable bridges and tunnels, the character of the terrain, the locations of spurs and sidings, and the number of trains being run each day. Personal observation supplemented by research in Moscow libraries and information pieced together from news items soon reduced our unknowns to the barest minimum. Each problem in the series of games was played before Harriman, Admiral Olsen, Generals Spalding and Crist, and me. Artificial as these problems were, they proved to be of immeasurable value. We became fairly well convinced that we could not expect to set up a strategic air force in the Maritime Provinces, that there was considerable doubt as to the necessity of keeping the Pacific supply route open, that a reserve stockpile of supplies would have to be on hand in Siberia, and, perhaps most important of all, we obtained some basis for answering queries constantly being received from Washington as to the validity of some of the Soviet supply requests.

When Stalin announced at the end of Churchill's visit that we should start to plan jointly, I asked the Chiefs of Staff to send a planning team to Moscow. They sent the four best qualified officers they could find, at a considerable sacrifice to the American High Command in Washington. Brigadier General Frank N. Roberts was placed in charge of the group. He had been the senior Army member of the Joint Staff Planners, the group that directly served the Joint Chiefs of Staff. Brigadier General William L. Ritchie was chosen from the Army Air Forces. He had been the liaison officer between MacArthur and the War Department during the early part of the war and was then serving as General Roberts' deputy in the Planning Division of the War Department General Staff. Rear Admiral Houston L. Maples, then Captain, was to be our Naval representative. He had been engaged in naval logistical planning in Washington. The fourth member of the group was Colonel Frank A. Bogart, who then was in the Planning Division of General Somervell's staff.

These officers, thoroughly familiar with the American operations planned for the Pacific, and extremely well qualified to co-ordinate

Soviet and American plans, arrived in Moscow on December 6, 1944; their work was doomed to failure from the start. The Russians met us reluctantly, coming to the discussions under all of the handicaps of the Soviet system of centralized authority, and with the conviction that it was all a waste of time. They knew full well that they had not the power to make any firm agreements with the American group. In fact, it was necessary for them to get clearance from above before talking about each new subject as it was raised. They were so inhibited in their freedom of thought and expression that they could not answer even the most inconsequential questions at the meetings in which the questions were asked. Further, joint planning was a new experience for the Russians, and they did not have the vaguest idea of how to go about it or what it implied. At least in this respect we could appreciate their difficulty.

Joint planning as between nations and to some extent as between the armed services within a nation was a development of the war. We were forced to learn the technique of planning between nations by reason of our close alliance and combined operations with the British, and that of planning between our separate services because of the amphibious character of our Pacific operations. We were new at the game in the early stages of the war, and as a result plans were delayed and were characterized by ineffective compromises. The most difficult part of the procedure was to be able to organize a group of planners who could and would study their problems objectively and endeavor to reach the best solution without regard to national or service interests. They could do this only when their respective superiors allowed them to approach the problem with open minds and unhampered by prior instructions from which they could not depart. Planning was best when it was accomplished with complete objectivity and when it was left to those responsible for approval of the plan to adjust the demands of special interests. Throughout the war our own American planning suffered because of deadlocks on the planning level that resulted from attempts to protect some national or service interest or because of the rigidity of instructions previously given individual planners. It seems almost ridiculous to have expected objective planning for Soviet-American operations in the light of the known Soviet penchant for centralized control.

I succeeded in getting a meeting with Antonov on December 16 to introduce General Roberts, the senior officer of the planning team. It was at this meeting that Antonov announced: "After careful calculation we have determined that the Soviet forces will need all the air and naval bases in the Maritime Provinces and therefore American air and naval forces will be unable to operate from there." I staggered a bit under the blow but recovered in time to point out that his announcement was in direct contradiction to promises that Stalin had given us on six separate occasions. I called his attention to the fact that the United States was carrying out its part of the commitments made at the Churchill-Stalin conference on the assumption that the Soviet Union would do likewise. Antonov replied that in view of the fact that I had raised the matter of promises made by Stalin, he would take the matter up with him and let me have a decision in a few days. Three days later he sent word to me that the decision against the project would stand. I was amazed at Antonov's bland renunciation of a firm agreement, and especially at the way in which the decision had been withheld until our Siberian supply program had gained a momentum which would be difficult if not impossible to stop.

The United States Chiefs of Staff sent a protest which I delivered to Antonov, and Harriman protested to Stalin, but the decision remained the same. There was a ray of light, however. We were just then reaching full production of our B-29 bombers and were searching for places to base them. These could, because of their long range, operate from bases far north of Vladivostok, perhaps near the mouth of the Amur River. Bases that far north could not possibly interfere with any Soviet installations. We decided to accept the decision on the Maritime Provinces and demand bases farther to the north for our B-29's when we met at the Yalta Conference, then just a few weeks off, and did so, as I have related in the preceding chapter.

At our December 16 meeting Antonov promised to name at once

four Soviet officers to meet with our planning team. Six weeks passed before their first meeting took place on January 26, 1945, just two days before we departed for Yalta.

The first planning meeting turned out pretty much as we had anticipated. General Slavin appeared as the representative of the Soviet General Staff and as the Russian expert on ground forces. I was disappointed at seeing him because I had been attempting to do business with him for over a year and was convinced that he was little more than a messenger boy with no authority in his own right. The Soviet Air Force was represented by Marshal Khudyakov, who was Chief of Staff to Novikov, head of the Soviet Air Force. Rear Admiral Kucherov was the representative of the Soviet Navy, and General Semichastnov was selected as the Soviet supply expert.

When the meeting opened General Roberts suggested that the Soviet delegation, as representatives of the host nation, name a permanent chairman of the group. We thought that without question Marshal Khudyakov as the senior would be given the honor. We were surprised when the Russians informed us that Slavin, as a representative of the General Staff, should occupy the chair. Since Slavin was junior in rank to all the others, this was evidence that the Red Army General Staff occupies a position of power comparable to that which the General Staff did in Germany.

The Russian officers appeared to be disappointed and somewhat condescending when they found that their American opposite numbers were of such relatively low rank. Slavin was a Major General, Roberts a Brigadier; Kucherov was a Rear Admiral, Maples a Captain; Khudyakov was a Marshal and Ritchie was then a Colonel; Semichastnov was a Major General, Bogart a Colonel. The disparity in rank was greatest between Khudyakov and Ritchie, and so Khudyakov let it be known that the Soviet representatives would each appoint a deputy to represent them at future meetings. I tried to narrow the difference by recommending both Ritchie and Maples for well-deserved promotions. One would expect the Russians with their Communistic ideology to be the least rank-conscious people in the world, but the fact is just the opposite. One might also expect that in a highly developed capitalistic state such as ours where emphasis is placed on individual achievement, considerable importance would be attached to rank. On the contrary, Americans were outranked country for country and job for job throughout the war. Because of the handicap this entails in dealing with the Russians, the point is one worthy of consideration in the future.

As soon as he had been installed as chairman Slavin announced that the first meeting should be devoted solely to the organization of the group and on reaching agreements concerning rules of procedure. In spite of Roberts' vigorous attempts to get down to business—at least to the extent of formulating an outline of the problems with which the group would be confronted—nothing was accomplished at that meeting but an agreement to begin to begin. As soon as the details of organization were completed Slavin invited us all to an adjoining room where we had the usual banquet that the Russians indulge in to mark their first meeting with a group of foreigners or the start of a new enterprise.

Despite the Soviet promise at Yalta that joint planning in Moscow would be "pursued vigorously," our group met with little success when we returned. Two meetings were held, but they consisted for the most part in the Soviet delegation making notes of American proposals and questions and promising that the matters would be studied and the answers forthcoming. There was no discussion or joint examination of any of the problems involved. At one of the meetings it was agreed that opposite numbers should pair off and have separate meetings to discuss problems of particular interest to them but not of general interest to the group. We tried that without success. The only Soviet planner who was interested at all was Semichastnov, and his sole concern was to see that the United States rushed the build-up of the Siberian reserve. When Roberts, Ritchie, or Maples approached their opposite numbers of the Russian ground, air, or sea forces, they could succeed only in discussing the specialized supply requests of the different services.

By the end of February 1945 it was plainly evident that our planning team was wasting its time, and I became convinced that we would have to re-examine our whole position and reach some conclusions of our own concerning the possibilities of operating in co-operation with Soviet forces in the Far East.

Throughout my first year in Moscow we had been continuously engaged in some co-operative venture, large or small, that required Russian good will for its successful accomplishment. First there had been our shuttle-bombing bases in the Ukraine, then the establishment of teletype communications, then the exchange of weather information, then the co-ordination of operations against Germany, and finally the hope of setting up an air force close to Japan in the Maritime Provinces. As long as we attached importance to these ventures, we hesitated to take a firm tough attitude toward Russia for fear that we would lose whatever concessions had been granted.

In the spring of 1945 I began to suspect that the importance of the concessions we were receiving or hoped to receive from the Soviet Union was being reduced to practically nothing. If my suspicion was correct, our attitude could be revised. I determined to find out.

Roberts and his group were thorough investigators and by this time they were relatively idle between their occasional meeting with their Russian counterparts. I asked Roberts to have his group make two studies, the first to determine the over-all increase in the tonnage of bombs that could be dropped on Japan prior to our invasion of the Japanese islands by reason of having American air bases in the Amur River area; and the second to determine the necessity of keeping the Pacific supply route open after the start of Russo-Japanese hostilities. It was a tall order, but within six weeks, on about April 1, his group had produced both studies and arrived at such convincing conclusions that I was able to persuade our Chiefs of Staff that our military policy in relation to Russia should be revised.

With regard to setting up B-29 bomber bases in the Komsomolsk-Nikolaevsk district, our planners' study revealed that tremendous shipments of personnel and supplies would have to be completed from the United States to Siberia by October 31, 1945, if the force was to operate at all before the scheduled American invasion of Japan. The personnel would total about 52,000, and it would be necessary to ship 572,000 long tons of dry cargo and over 2,000,000 barrels of petroleum products. The shipments would have to be complete by October 31 because of ice in the mouth of the Amur River after that date. Shipments could not start until Russia and Japan were at war, which meant that unless hostilities started by mid-July our shipments could not be completed by the end of October.

Most important of all was the necessity for complete Soviet co-operation in meeting the tight schedule. Experience had shown that it would not be realistic to count on such co-operation. At best we could expect only reluctant Soviet assistance, but more probably we would encounter only their expert resistance because of the introduction of 50,000 foreigners to the Soviet Union and because the tonnages involved might detract from the volume of supply being sent from the United States to build up the Siberian reserve.

Meanwhile, American successes in the Pacific had been greater than had been anticipated and bases had already been established to care for all the B-29 groups we were organizing. It was found that the net increase that would result from putting four groups of B-29's in the Amur River district would be 1.39 per cent of the total bomb tonnage we could place on Japan without using Russian bases. This was convincing proof that the slight increase in our bombing effort and the advantage of an added direction of approach for our bomber formations were not at all commensurate with the logistical effort involved in establishing our forces in Siberia. In addition, it was evident that we could not carry out the project without prompt, continued, and wholehearted Soviet co-operation—this in itself was sufficient proof that the venture should not be tried.

In considering the necessity of keeping the Pacific supply route open, our planners based their study on the number of forces involved that had been given to us by Stalin at the time of the Churchill meeting. They applied supply and maintenance figures that are used to meet American standards. Since there is no army in the world that is better or more generously supplied and equipped than ours, it was almost certain that our planners' calculations would overestimate rather than underestimate Soviet requirements. Assuming that the delivery of reserve supplies requested from the United States would have been completed by the time hostilities started and that a reserve of supplies would have been brought from western Russia, we estimated that there would be a total reserve of about 2,000,000 long tons available in Siberia. We calculated that the Trans-Siberian railroad would fall short of the capacity needed to maintain the Soviet Far Eastern forces by about 200,000 tons per month. This then would be the amount that would have to be taken from the reserve each month, and the reserve would therefore last from nine to ten months. This seemed to be ample, as Stalin had indicated that he did not expect the Russian campaign to last more than two and one-half to three months. The progress of American forces in the Pacific also indicated that the Russians would not be called on for extended operations before the final defeat of Japan. Of course there was the possibility that the Japanese would succeed in cutting the Trans-Siberian railroad, in which case the Russian forces east of the interruption would have to be maintained entirely by reserves available in their area. It was reasonable to suppose, however, that the bulk of the reserves would be located east of where interruptions to the railroad were most apt to occur. Even in this eventuality it appeared certain that forces which might be cut off from supply from the west could be maintained by the reserves for a period of from three to six months.

The conclusion reached by Roberts' group was that a Pacific supply route would not be vital to the success of the Soviet offensive, but that it would provide insurance against initial reverses and an unexpectedly long duration of the war.

These studies were completed at the time that our military relations with the Soviet Union were at their lowest ebb. I have already mentioned the strain which existed in our relations and which had resulted in the main from our political differences. I shall go into the subject in more detail later. Suffice it to say at this time that in an effort to restore our relations to a workable basis, I thought it would be wise to withdraw from all co-operative ventures that were not essential to winning the war and to stop pushing our proposals on the Russians and force them to come to us. The results of Roberts' studies fitted into the program I had in mind, so I took them to Washington to help sell my ideas to the Chiefs of Staff.

When I arrived in Washington I found that the Chiefs were more disturbed about the situation than I. After considering Roberts' studies, they at once directed me to inform Antonov that since the operation of long-range bombers from the Komsomolsk-Nikolaevsk area within the limited time available would not contribute sufficiently to the war against Japan to warrant the expenditure of resources and effort for its accomplishment, the United States had decided to cancel the project.

In connection with the Pacific supply route, it was decided to ask Admiral Nimitz if he considered it necessary to have bases on Kamchatka in order to force convoys through the Kurile Islands. If his reply was in the affirmative, the Chiefs of Staff intended to inform the Russians what our requirements would be on Kamchatka and then leave it to them to initiate the fulfillment of our needs. If, on the other hand, Admiral Nimitz replied that he could force the Kurile Islands without bases on Kamchatka, they proposed to do nothing further toward keeping a Pacific supply route open except in response to Soviet request. Admiral Nimitz said he did not need Kamchatka, and the latter course was adopted.

I was elated by these decisions. As far as military collaboration was concerned, they cleared the decks of any dependence we were placing on Russian generosity and for the first time put the United States in the position of being able to comply or to refuse to comply with Soviet requests purely on the merits of the case. The fear of a separate peace had long since been removed by Russian military successes, and now the fear of jeopardizing some co-operative venture with Russia was removed because there were no longer any in which we were interested. We continued to do our utmost to build up the Russian supply reserve in Siberia because we still felt that a Russian offensive against the Japanese would shorten the war and because we had committed ourselves to the project. However, we could now tell the Russians that new shoes were not available without fear of their retaliating by saying that bases in the Maritime Provinces would not be available to us.

When Antonov was informed of the decision of the Chiefs of Staff concerning the Amur River bases he made no comment whatsoever. I think, however, the adoption of our new attitude was rewarded by much more co-operation on the part of the Soviet military authorities when they met our Chiefs of Staff at Potsdam in the following July. The agreements reached at that time were scrupulously observed.

Our efforts to effect joint planning were ended with the decisions reached by the Chiefs of Staff. In view of the rapidity of Japan's final collapse, it is questionable if any of the joint plans which we might have made with the Russians would ever have been put into operation. We might have set up an air force in Siberia if the Russians had been more co-operative. However, had we succeeded in doing so, the result would have been effort wasted because of the short time it would have had to operate. By the time Russia did enter the war, a Pacific supply route offered no problem because we had virtually eliminated Japanese naval power. The gods of war plus the American Army, Navy, and Air Forces saved us from what might have been a costly blunder in failing to have joint plans prepared to meet the worst possible contingencies.

XVI. The Potsdam Conference and the End of the Japanese War

THE Potsdam Conference was approached by the United States Chiefs of Staff with greater hopes for Soviet-American military collaboration than they had felt at their previous meetings with Russian military leaders. Germany had been defeated, the Allied Control Council had been set up in Berlin, our troops were occupying their part of the capital and had completed the withdrawal to the American occupation zone in Germany. There were problems to be sure, but they were at least quasi-political in nature and at that time such problems aroused no undue concern in the minds of American military authorities.

In the Far East we had reached positions from which we could effectively blockade Japan; our Air Force was blanketing the Japanese islands with high explosive and incendiary bombs, and while we were at Potsdam word was received that the atomic bomb had passed its experimental test. We were all set for the kill. But we wanted Russian participation; although the Kwantung Army had been depleted, it was still in existence. If the Red Army could account for the Japanese on the mainland, it would not be necessary for American forces to land there in order to assist the Chinese in overcoming the last remnants of Japanese resistance.

And, although it was believed that Russia's entry into the war would shorten it, even this was becoming a debatable point. Certainly, Soviet participation was no longer an essential ingredient of victory. Best of all, as a result of the decisions which the Chiefs of Staff had taken in the spring during my trip to Washington, we were no longer involved in any enterprises with the Soviet Union which would be jeopardized if we incurred the displeasure of its leaders. We were in a position to be tough and indifferent. As a result the Conference marked the high point of Soviet-American military collaboration.

The preliminary arrangements for the Potsdam Conference were not accomplished without the usual petty annoyances. Major General Floyd L. Parks, representing General Eisenhower, had been put in charge of making arrangements for the American delegation. The first snag developed when the Russians refused to allow Parks to go to Berlin for a preliminary survey of the situation. The reason given was that nothing could be done in the absence of Marshal Zhukov who was then in Moscow and who would not return to Berlin until June 28. Harriman had to see Molotov personally to overcome this difficulty. When Parks did arrive in Berlin, he was put in touch with Colonel General Sergei N. Kruglov, who was in charge of arrangements for the Russians. Kruglov was cordial and went over the plans for the Conference accommodations. The residential section of Babelsberg, fronting on the Griebnitz See, had been evacuated of all Germans and was being renovated by the Red Army for use by the conferees. Parks was shown the house selected for President Truman and the area that was to be set aside for American use. However, Kruglov said it was beyond his authority to permit Parks to reconnoiter another small suburb for a camp site for American soldiers who were to be employed at the Conference or to authorize operation of American supply vehicles over the Halle-Berlin autobahn without special permission in each case. Parks was forced to ask me to obtain Moscow approval for these and other matters of similar importance. Fortunately Moscow was in an agreeable mood and gave us favorable decisions without too much deliberation.

I arrived in Berlin with Harriman on July 13, and I was amazed to see the changes that had taken place in the city since my previous visit on May 9. The streets had been cleared of rubble, broken-down streetcars and motor transportation had been removed, and Stalin's picture was prominently displayed on big red banners wherever one looked. The city was still in ruins, but withal there was a trace of tidiness in its appearance. Red Army girls had been given new uniforms and clean bright red and yellow flags with which they directed traffic all through the Russian zone. They developed a little ritual in handling these flags which though difficult to describe was smart and effective. When an officer's car approached, they would go through quick gyrations which would end with the red flag held vertical to stop cross traffic and with the yellow flag pointing in the direction the officer's car was to go. The final touch occurred as the car passed, when they would be found with both flags tucked under their arms and standing at the hand salute. It was a drill that would have done credit to Radio City's Rockettes.

As we approached the little suburb of Babelsberg just outside of Potsdam, the women traffic directors gave way to men of the Red Army. They lined both sides of all the streets approaching the Conference area and each soldier saluted as he was passed. The soldiers' uniforms were immaculate and all wore white gloves. Salutes were given with a snap and precision which demanded that each salute be returned separately. I envied Harriman his civilian clothes.

Babelsberg was far enough from Berlin to have escaped the full fury of Allied bombing, and only an occasional dwelling had been destroyed. It was divided into Russian, British, and American areas for the duration of the Conference, each area containing about seventy houses. I was assigned to one of these, which I shared with Admiral Maples and General Ritchie who had also come from Moscow, and with Lieutenant General J. E. Hull and a few members of his staff, all of whom were old friends from Washington. It was a quiet country village. The houses were spacious and were surrounded by beautiful gardens. These were beginning to show signs of neglect, but they still gave evidence of the thought with which they had been laid out and the care with which they had been tended. More than in any place I have ever been, this little spot in Germany seemed like a ghost city. One could almost feel the presence of its former occupants in these surroundings which they had created for pleasant living. Having just come from the rigors of life in Moscow, I think I could appreciate more than most people the stupidity of Hitler and the German people in risking the loss of what must have been such a peaceful and happy existence.

Early in July and just before our departure from Moscow, the Chinese Foreign Minister, T. V. Soong, had come to see Stalin to work out an agreement with regard to the concessions Russia would receive in Manchuria as the result of her participation in the war against Japan. Stalin drove a hard bargain with Soong, and his demands to some extent exceeded the program that Roosevelt and Churchill had agreed to support during the Yalta Conference. While Soong had not been able to reach a final agreement with Stalin and considered it necessary to report Stalin's proposals to Chiang Kai-shek, it was a foregone conclusion that a satisfactory adjustment would be reached. The way was thus paved for Russia's entry into the war. The two conditions that Stalin had placed on Soviet participation had been met. The United States had virtually completed the build-up of the necessary Siberian supply reserve and the political considerations in which China was involved were almost certain to be satisfactorily arranged. More than that, over two months had elapsed since the defeat of Germany, and Stalin had promised that the Soviet Union would enter the war three months after Germany's surrender. It seemed certain that Russia would enter the war in a matter of weeks.

The first military meeting at the Potsdam Conference was held on July 26 and was attended by the British, Soviet, and American Chiefs of Staff. It was held in the Cecilienhof Palace in Babelsburg, which was beautifully furnished and had the outward appearance of an American estate that one might see in Newport, Grosse Point, or Burlingame.

Admiral Leahy was selected as chairman for the first meeting. Without any unnecessary beating about the bush, he asked Antonov to outline Russia's plans and intentions concerning the Japanese.

Antonov stated briefly that the Red Army would begin offensive operations in the latter half of August, with the exact date dependent on the conclusion of negotiations then being held with the Chinese. There was a thinly veiled invitation to the United States to needle Chiang into prompt acceptance of Stalin's proposals. Antonov described the build-up of the Soviet forces in the Far East, putting particular emphasis on Russia's dependence on the limited capacity of the Trans-Siberian railroad in the supply of her troops. This was a belated attempt to start discussions on the necessity of keeping American supplies flowing across the Pacific. Antonov gave further evidence of his apprehension in this regard by asking Admiral King if the Americans intended to occupy the northern Kurile Islands.

It will be recalled that the preceding April the American Chiefs of Staff had decided they would not take any further action toward maintaining a supply route across the Pacific unless the Russians took the initiative in the matter. In reply to Antonov's question, Admiral King said that we had no intention of occupying the Kuriles, but that if necessary we could maintain a line of communication with Russia without them. Admiral King's manner left a definite impression that we would force a passage through the Kuriles only if the Soviet authorities convinced us of a sufficiently urgent need for American supplies and also that the burden of proof was on the Russians. It was refreshing to hear an American take such a firm and independent stand in dealing with our Soviet friends.

General Marshall then outlined the American military situation in the Japanese war. He was followed by General Arnold, who described our air operations. My heart was in my mouth when I heard him say that we had been unable to find places to put all the bombers we had left over from the European war. I fully expected the Russians to ask him to give them some, and I had visions of starting the old squabbles concerning deliveries and training programs all over again. Fortunately the Russians realized it was too late for them to create a strategic air force, so General Arnold's remark passed without comment. In any case, our reliance on Russian aid had diminished to such a degree that General Arnold would have had no hesitancy in refusing a Russian request for American bombers had he felt it best to do so. It was comforting to be in that position too.

After my experience in trying to act as a go-between in the co-ordination of Russian operations with those of the Western Allies in the European war, I was convinced that some better system should be worked out with regard to co-ordination in the Far East. I was pretty certain that the Russians would want to retain operational control in Moscow, but I did not believe it would be possible. The distance to the Far East would be too great to permit Moscow to pull the strings as it had done in the war against Germany.

With the approval of the Chiefs of Staff, on June 26, 1945, I proposed to Antonov that there be an exchange of liaison officers and a system of radio teletype communications between Marshal Vasilievsky's headquarters and the headquarters of both General MacArthur and Admiral Nimitz. I suggested that these arrangements be made in time so that they could be put in operation on the day that Japanese-Soviet hostilities commenced. Each liaison group was to include about fifteen officers and thirty enlisted men. The United States offered to provide the necessary communications equipment. I suggested to Antonov that he make no attempt to reply to my proposal until he met our Chiefs of Staff at Potsdam. I thought he would find it more difficult to refuse them than to refuse me.

When the American Chiefs of Staff arrived at Potsdam, I prepared a list of five requests which I recommended that they hand to the Soviet Chiefs of Staff. The first asked that the United States Navy be permitted to establish two weather stations on Soviet territory, one at Khabarovsk and the other at Petropavlovsk. These were desired by both Admiral King and General Arnold to improve weather forecasts in connection with naval and air operations. The second and third requests were for Soviet comments (without asking for their approval) on lines which the United States would recognize as the northern boundary for its naval and air operations. The fourth request was for an answer to the proposal I had made for liaison arrangements. The fifth asked for an agreement to use each other's naval and air bases for safe haven and the repair of battle-damaged ships or aircraft. At the conclusion of the first meeting Admiral Leahy handed General Antonov the list of requests, and it was agreed that the United States and Soviet Chiefs of Staff would have another meeting at which answers would be received.

Meanwhile, on the political level the Soviet Government had informed the Western Allies of an approach which the Japanese had made to the Soviet Union asking it to act as intermediary in arranging for the cessation of hostilities. The Japanese offer failed to go into the conditions under which the war should be ended, but it stressed the futility of continuing the struggle and suggested that it be ended for humanitarian reasons. The response was the Potsdam Declaration, which called for unconditional surrender but did offer Japan the prospect of retaining its sovereignty as a nation. While the Soviet Union was not a party to the Declaration, it was promulgated with Stalin's concurrence.

The second military meeting of the Potsdam Conference did not include the British Chiefs of Staff. Antonov opened the meeting by stating that Marshal Stalin had that day handed President Truman the answers to the five requests which had been submitted by the United States Chiefs of Staff. Our Chiefs had not seen them as yet so Antonov proceeded to read the answers aloud. In reply to the first he said that the Soviet Union was agreeable to the installation of weather stations at Khabarovsk and Petropavlovsk to serve American air and naval forces, but felt that they should be manned by Soviet personnel. A deep red flush appeared above Admiral King's collar and soon spread to his face and head. I could see that he was a bit irate, but he restrained himself admirably and simply expressed his disappointment. He requested reconsideration, pointing out that the whole value of the proposed stations was in having them operated by American weather and communications personnel who were not only familiar with the sort of information our forces required, but who could communicate it rapidly by using American codes and radio procedure. Antonov must have known in advance how his proposal would be received, because he reversed himself at once and agreed to allow American personnel to operate the stations.

Antonov suggested minor changes in the operational boundaries that we had set between American and Soviet naval and air operations in our second and third requests. The changes Antonov proposed were agreeable to Admiral King and General Arnold, and so those questions were settled.

We were quite surprised when in answering our fourth request Antonov announced that Marshal Vasilievsky would have complete control, without supervision from Moscow, of all Soviet operations in the Far East. He agreed that there should be an exchange of liaison detachments and that a system of communications between Soviet and American headquarters should be established at once so as to be ready to operate when Russo-Japanese hostilities began. He went us one better by suggesting that there should be an American detachment at the Soviet naval headquarters at Vladivostok as well as at Vasilievsky's headquarters in Khabarovsk. This was of course acceptable to us. In response to our last question Antonov not only agreed to the use of each other's naval and air bases for safe haven and the repair of damaged naval vessels and aircraft, but gave our Chiefs of Staff maps showing where these bases were located and the facilities available at them.

Antonov again gave evidence of his apprehension about continued supplies from America by asking when we thought we would be able to convoy ships through Tsushima Strait between the southern tips of Japan and Korea. He said that if this could be done by October, it would insure supply through the winter when ice conditions prevented a passage north of Japan. In reply Admiral King said that Tsushima would have to be cleared of mines while under fire from Japanese suicide planes and that this could not be started until the southern island of Kyushu had been taken. He said he thought it would be possible to count on using the Strait by December, and this seemed to satisfy the Russians.

The military meetings at Potsdam thus ended in complete accord. Not only were the Russian military leaders amenable to our proposals, but for the first time they were punctilious in carrying them out.

It took considerable time to assemble the personnel and equipment for the weather stations and for the liaison detachments we were to establish, but when the Japanese surrendered on August 14 our parties were ready to leave Seattle. When hostilities ceased both General MacArthur and Admiral Nimitz decided it would not be necessary to send liaison detachments to Russian headquarters, and so on our initiative that project was canceled. The cancellation did not occur, however, until after the Russians had lived up to their promise and had made all arrangements for the reception and housing of the American groups. In the case of the weather detachments, our Naval authorities considered that they would be of value in the period of occupation. The Red Army General Staff suggested that this project be canceled also, but on our insistence allowed the American stations to be set up in Khabarovsk and Petropavlovsk. While the Soviet authorities carried out their Potsdam commitment in allowing the two weather stations to be established, they completely destroyed their effectiveness by the restrictions they imposed on operations. When it was suggested that they be closed on December 15, we were glad to acquiesce. During the few days that the Russians were at war with the Japanese, the Soviets carefully observed the boundaries which separated their naval and air operations from ours.

Following the Potsdam Conference, events cascaded with amazing rapidity toward the end of the war. Stalin had told the President, and Antonov had told the Chiefs of Staff, that Russia would begin hostilities in the latter half of August. When the atomic bomb fell on Hiroshima shortly after our return from Potsdam it received scant notice in the Soviet press, but it must have received the greatest attention in the inner councils of the Soviet Government. Russia had to buy her ticket to the Pacific peace conference, but she had to hurry or the show would have started and the seats would all be taken.

On the afternoon of August 8 Antonov sent word that he would like to see the head of the British Military Mission and me at five o'clock. As soon as we were seated in his office he handed us each a copy of the note that had been sent to the Japanese Government. It stated in brief that Japan was the only great power still holding out for continuance of the war. It rebuked Japan for failure to accept the terms of the Potsdam Declaration to which the Soviet Union adhered and said that, as the only means open to the Soviet Union to avoid further bloodshed and to save the Japanese people from destruction, Russia had joined forces with the Allied powers. In view of all this the Soviet Union declared that as of midnight August 8-9, it would consider itself to be in a state of war with Japan.

Both Molotov, who informed Harriman of Russo-Japanese hostilities, and Antonov put particular emphasis on the fact that Russia was entering the war almost three months to the minute after Germany's surrender had been accepted in Berlin. This was held up as evidence of the sanctity with which Stalin regarded his agreements. I could not help but feel that the atomic bomb had provided an urge that was somewhat more impelling. It was not the proper time to say so, however.

I was considerably surprised at the apathy with which the Russian people received the news that they were at war with Japan. Even more surprising was their indifference less than a week later when they heard the war had ended. In the case of the Germans the bulk of the Russian population had been directly affected by the war. Nearly every Russian had some relative and many friends who had either been killed by the Germans or who had been taken into Germany for slave labor. The property destruction and vandalism carried on by the Germans was there to see. A hatred for the German people was thus engendered which required little of the anti-Fascist propaganda that filled the Soviet press.

On the other hand, only those few Russians who inhabited Siberia close to the Manchurian border had had any contact with the Japanese. Because of the necessity to maintain Japanese neutrality during four years of war, little mention had been made of Japan in the Soviet press. It was impossible to arouse any great hatred against a nation as remote as Japan, and perhaps that is why even in the last few weeks the party propaganda machine made no effort to do so.

The situation was one in which several elements stood out in striking relief. There was evidence that the Government was so certain of its power as to be able to lead the people into a war in which they had no apparent interest and without making an effort to arouse an interest. On the other hand, the apathy and silence on the part of the people was indicative of a cohesiveness and solidarity of opinion which, though repressed, constituted a considerable force. It seemed apparent that if Russia had needed the spirit of her people in a war against Japan as she had needed it in her fight with Germany, it would not have been forthcoming, at least not to the same degree. It would appear then that Russia will always have difficulty in inducing her peacefully inclined people to support a war that has to be carried to an enemy far removed from her borders.

The night of August 10-11 was a hectic one for the American delegation in Moscow. In my opinion, it marked Harriman's most important victory in Russia. The evening started out quietly enough. I had invited Averell and Kathy Harriman, George and Analise Kennan, and Ed and Barbara Pauley to my house for dinner. After dinner we had some movies, and at about midnight Averell was called to the Kremlin by Molotov.

When Harriman arrived, Clark-Kerr, the British Ambassador, was already there. Molotov told them that when the Soviet Ambassador had handed the Japanese Foreign Minister the Soviet Declaration of War, the Foreign Minister had informed him the Japanese Government was prepared to accept the conditions of the Potsdam Declaration subject only to certain reservations about retaining the Emperor as the sovereign ruler of Japan. Molotov said he understood that a similar message had been sent to the British and Americans through the Swiss Government. He was anxious to know our attitude, saying at the same time that he was skeptical with regard to accepting the offer inasmuch as the reservations concerning the Emperor were not in accord with unconditional surrender.

Meanwhile, George Kennan had been called from my party to receive an urgent message from Washington giving the proposed American reply to the Japanese offer. George hurried to the Kremlin and arrived just as Molotov had finished stating the Soviet views with regard to Japan's proposal. The American reply, to which Soviet concurrence was requested, simply informed the Japanese in effect that surrender would have to be unconditional, that the Emperor would be required to assist in its implementation, and that the ultimate form of the Japanese Government would be a matter for decision by the free will of the Japanese people.

Molotov's reaction was noncommittal, but he told Harriman that the Soviet Government would give its answer the following day. Harriman replied that that would be unsatisfactory as he had to send an answer to Washington that night. Molotov said he would do his best.

At two o'clock on the morning of August 11 Molotov again called Harriman and Clark-Kerr to his office. He informed them that the Soviet Government agreed to the reply the United States proposed sending to Japan. He added, however, that in case the Japanese decided to surrender, the Allied powers should reach an agreement on the candidacy or candidacies of the Allied High Command to which the Japanese Emperor and the Japanese Government were to be subordinated.

Harriman quizzed Molotov a bit to make sure he had the true sense of his remarks about the Allied High Command before he went through the roof. He asked Molotov if MacArthur would be acceptable, to which Molotov replied that he thought so but would have to consult his Government. Molotov then said it was conceivable that there might be two Supreme Commanders, MacArthur and Vasilievsky. Harriman pointed out that the United States had carried the main burden of the Pacific war for four years and had kept the Japanese off Russia's back. He said the Soviet Union had been in the war but two days and that it was only just that an American should be the Supreme Commander—any other solution was unthinkable. Molotov said heatedly that he did not wish to make a reply as he would have to refer to the European war. He said he would consult with Stalin and send us an answer.

Harriman came back to my office fighting mad, but he had no sooner arrived than a telephone call came from Pavlov, Molotov's interpreter, who said that there had been a misunderstanding. The Soviet reply to the United States was changed to suggest that there should be consultation as to who was to be the Supreme Commander rather than agreement. The word "candidacies" was removed from the Soviet reply, and with its removal the implication that there might be more than one Supreme Commander.

The firm attitude taken by Harriman successfully repelled the first postwar bid on the part of the Soviet Government to extend its influence over the future of Japan. The effort had been made and the Soviet Government had been met with a firm and definite "no." I think a victory must be credited to Harriman because any vacillation at the start would have been the opening wedge to some unfortunate compromise. The following day President Truman proposed to Stalin that General MacArthur be named Supreme Allied Commander with powers to accept and co-ordinate the Japanese surrender. The President asked whom the Soviet Government wished to designate as its representative in the negotiations. Stalin replied at once, concurring in the choice of MacArthur and appointing Lieutenant General Kuzma Derevyanko to represent the Soviet Union. On August 14, 1945, I was informed by the Joint Chiefs of Staff of Japan's capitulation.

The day after Japan's surrender I received a message from General MacArthur which was an information copy of one he was sending to all commanders under his control. The message was a directive to cease all offensive operations consistent with the safety of our troops pending the complete cessation of hostilities. I was asked to pass the message on to the Russian High Command, which I did. However, in reading the address I had missed the fact that my copy of the message was for information only and passed it on to Antonov with a statement that, in carrying out his duties of arranging and co-ordinating the surrender, General MacArthur wished to have similar instructions issued to Soviet field commanders. It was a stupid blunder on my part, and the reaction was not long in forthcoming. Antonov asked me to inform MacArthur that the Supreme Commander of the Soviet forces was the sole judge of when offensive operations should cease in his theater. I sent Antonov's reply to General MacArthur but went to Antonov at once, explained my error, and assured him that General MacArthur's only desire was to keep the Soviet High Command fully informed of the action he was taking. In a day or two I had a reply from General MacArthur addressed to General Antonov which verified the statement I had made in my apology. Fortunately all was forgiven, but for a time I was certain that I had created an irreparable international rift.

The period from August 14, when the Japanese capitulated, until September 2, when the surrender ceremonies took place aboard the U.S.S. *Missouri*, was one of considerable confusion and mutual suspicion in our military relations with the Soviet Union. For the greater part of the period there were no Soviet representatives at General MacArthur's headquarters, and all his communications with the Soviet High Command had to come through my office in an exchange of messages relayed almost completely around the world. Frequently, important messages were delayed, and the Russians would get their first information of events about which they should have been informed through press reports that were highly colored and only partially true. This led to an atmosphere of suspicion which was dispelled in the end by the thoroughness with which General MacArthur kept the Soviet High Command informed of his activities despite the delay in some of his communications.

Most of the Japanese arrangements for the surrender, including the cessation of hostilities, the first visit of Japanese emissaries to Manila, and the orders to be issued by the Emperor, were made by means of broadcasts in the clear from certain Japanese radio stations which were carefully monitored by us. Each Japanese communication was numbered, and upon its receipt General MacArthur would transmit it to me to be passed on to the Russians. The Japanese sent these messages at all hours of the day and night and they reached a considerable volume. Some were important and others concerned details that were of no importance at all. American reception of the messages depended on continuous monitoring of the Japanese stations and on the existence of suitable conditions for radio reception. As a result there were frequently gaps in the numbered messages which I passed on to the Russians. I am certain that the Red Army in the Far East was monitoring the Japanese stations and knew pretty well what was going on, but in Moscow the High Command became suspicious of our motives when the Japanese broadcasts were not given to them in their proper sequence. It was therefore necessary for me to have even the unimportant ones translated into Russian and to deliver them to Antonov. In addition, I had to send tracers to General MacArthur's headquarters to obtain copies of the missing numbers.

Some of the Japanese broadcasts were inaccurate. For example, one said that Russian forces were landing on Hokkaido. Stalin had previously suggested that the Red Army accept the surrender of Japanese forces on Hokkaido and he had been refused on the grounds that the United States forces had earned the right to accept the surrender on the main Japanese islands. The message emanating from Japan made it appear as though the Russians were landing on Hokkaido without our concurrence. I took the matter up with Antonov as soon as I heard of ʻit, and he assured me that no Soviet forces had landed on Hokkaido and that none would. Thus our suspicions and apprehensions were dispelled. On another occasion there was a Japanese report that Allied troops were landing on Shimushiri, the most northern of the Kurile Islands. This was an area of Soviet responsibility, and we assumed that if landings were being made the Russians were making them. The Russians, on the other hand, suspected that we had gone back on our promise that the Kuriles would go to Russia, and on the basis of the Japanese report the Soviet leaders were certain that American troops were landing on Shimushiri. General MacArthur succeeded in convincing the Russians that this was not so, and suspicion was again overcome.

Another controversy arose in connection with General Order Number One that was to be issued by the Japanese Emperor to effect the surrender. In the original document which we passed on to the Soviet Government for approval nothing was said about Japanese forces on the Kurile Islands surrendering to Soviet commanders. At Stalin's request the document was amended to take care of the discrepancy, and I gave General Slavin a copy of the amended order, calling attention to the correction that had been made. Meanwhile, President Truman had informed Stalin that the proposed amendment was acceptable. For some reason the General Staff failed to show the Foreign Office the corrected copy, and Molotov sent a formal protest to Harriman that this document had not been amended as agreed to by the President. I went to see Antonov about it and pointed out the correction that had been made on the copy I had given Slavin five days previously. Antonov was taken by surprise, and I could see that Slavin was about to die of mortification. I tried to cover him with his chief by suggesting that in view of the mass of material that was being translated I could easily understand how this correction had escaped their notice. In any event, Soviet suspicion of American motives proved to be unfounded.

On August 19 I received word that we had succeeded in dropping a prisoner-of-war contact team in Mukden, which was still under Japanese control. The Japanese were agreeable to the immediate release of General Wainwright but insisted that they could do nothing in the matter without Soviet consent. I was requested to ask the Russians to issue the necessary instructions.

I went to see Antonov and explained that Wainwright and all other Americans who had fought on Bataan and Corregidor were national heroes, and I emphasized the gratitude the American people would have for Soviet assistance in effecting their immediate release. A few hours later Antonov informed me that instructions had been sent to Vasilievsky to do everything he could to further the prompt release of General Wainwright and other American prisoners of war in the Mukden area. He was also authorized to allow our planes to bring supplies to the Americans until all had been evacuated from Manchuria.

Vasilievsky's action was prompt and effective. He sent a group of Russian officers to Mukden, and their first query upon arrival was concerning the location of General Wainwright. When they were told that Wainwright was in a camp at Hsian about one hundred miles north of Mukden, a special Soviet train was sent there to get the American prisoners of war and bring them out. By the time the train arrived at Hsian, a group of Russians had already taken General Wainwright from Hsian to Mukden in a Soviet motor convoy. He and a number of other American officers departed from Mukden in American aircraft on August 27. The assistance given by the Russians in effecting the prompt release of General Wainwright recalled their co-operative attitude in allowing American internees to escape from Tashkent. It was further evidence that Soviet officials are inclined to be co-operative when they are convinced that the Americans involved in a given situation are not actuated by any ulterior motives. Unfortunately there are few instances where the innocence of American intentions are so plainly evident as they were with regard to the release of internees and of American prisoners of war in Manchuria.

Marshal Stalin had told the President that General Derevyanko would represent the Soviet Union in the surrender negotiations at General MacArthur's headquarters. I knew that the Red Army had no aircraft with sufficient range to go from Siberia to Manila, so I suggested to General MacArthur that he offer to send a B-29 or one of our four-engine transports to get Derevyanko. MacArthur responded with a cordial invitation and at the same time gave me all the data concerning the flight of the aircraft he intended to send. Careful co-ordination was required at the Russian end, including the selection of an airfield large enough to accommodate one of our big airplanes and data concerning approaches and identification signals to insure its safety from Red Army anti-aircraft batteries. The arrangements were all completed and it was agreed that the plane would arrive in Russia on August 19. Meanwhile, a typhoon developed off the southern coast of Japan and the American plane was postponed daily for a period of ten days because of bad weather. Due to poor communications, I was unable to tell the Russians that the plane would be delayed until long after it had failed to arrive at its destination at the appointed hour.

Getting Derevyanko to Manila was one of my last co-operative ventures with the Red Army General Staff. It was one in which I had a great personal interest, not only because I had proposed sending him to Manila in an American plane, but because when he arrived there Soviet-American liaison would be carried out on the spot instead of through my office on the other side of the world. His safe arrival would be a superdose of aspirin for my many headaches. Despite my interest I was viewed with extreme suspicion each time I announced that our plane had been delayed. It was intimated that the use of an American plane had been proposed so that Derevyanko's departure could be delayed until it was too late for him to participate in the surrender ceremonies. Finally the Russians decided to send their party to Manila in an American Catalina which we had sent them under the lend-lease program. Before it could be made ready the weather lifted, and General MacArthur's plane arrived in Siberia in ample time to take Derevyanko back before the Allied party left for Tokyo. I have never felt more relieved.

The last Soviet request for which I was to obtain American approval was for permission to send a group of correspondents and movie men to Tokyo to record the surrender proceedings. Before I left Moscow movies were shown of the surrender ceremonies aboard the *Missouri*. Pictures were taken from a small boat as the camera men approached the "Mighty Mo," and by some freak of photography it appeared to be colossal. The bow looked as high as the Empire State Building, and the ship tapered off to a point at the stern which appeared as though it were a mile away. Had we been endeavoring to intimidate the Soviet Union with a display of American might, we could not have done better. We Americans realized that the picture was a distortion, but we were delighted at the gasps of amazement that came from the Russians—in that picture the "Mighty Mo" more than lived up to its name.

With the end of the Japanese war the reasons that prompted the establishment of the United States Military Mission no longer existed. Shortly after hostilities ended the British received an intimation from the Russians that their Mission should be withdrawn; and I recommended that ours should depart from the Soviet Union before it was invited to do so. Accordingly we closed our offices on October 31, 1945, and American representation in Moscow was restored to our Military and Naval Attachés.

It can scarcely be said that the Mission was an outstanding success. We had barely scratched the surface of the possibilities that existed for a full Soviet-American partnership in the prosecution of the war. In our efforts we had the full support of all Americans, from the President and the Chiefs of Staff on down. Our moderate successes were applauded and our many failures accepted with sympathetic understanding. In the Ambassador the Mission had a champion and an adviser who spared himself nothing in his endeavors to help us achieve our purpose. It is unfortunate that our successes could not have been more.

I left Russia with a deep affection for her people but with high skepticism about the possibility of future American collaboration with her leaders.

PART FOUR

Can We Get Along
with Russia?

XVII. The Soviet Leaders
and Their Policy

I APPROACH this part of my book with the deepest humility. From my experience I would like to draw a pattern of the behavior that might be expected from Soviet leaders. I would like to leave the thought that the great mass of the Russian people are peace-loving and kindly disposed toward us. Finally, I would like to present an accurate diagnosis and prescribe a cure for the ills which may beset the world, and the United States in particular, if present Soviet policy continues unhampered. To accomplish these objectives fully I should be an "expert" on Russia—and there is no such thing. I should be one who understands Russia, when in fact she is beyond understanding Nevertheless, as an American who has lived in Russia for two years under circumstances which forced a closer contact with the Soviet Government than is afforded to most foreigners, I shall present, with no particular brief for their validity, the conclusions I have drawn about this land of contradictions.

I am ready to accept as fact the theory that the Russian leaders are inspired by sincere motives rather than by desire for personal power and self-aggrandizement. They truly believe that Communism offers salvation to mankind, and they seek to impose their ideology on a world that would be receptive were it not for the ugly power emanating from capitalism. To them, Communism is the medicine that will cure all evils. Its beneficial effects have been demonstrated in Russia where, in the short span of twenty-five years, a nation has risen from chaos to become, in their minds, the strongest power in the world. However, Russia will not be safe from reinfection until the same dosage has immunized the rest of the world from the scourge of capitalism. The medicine may be difficult to administer and bitter for the patient to take. The cure may be applied by force or it may be necessary to resort to deception and guile. Soviet leaders justify any means that will accomplish the end.

Let us pause for a moment and look objectively at the Russian leaders before examining the methods by which they work. Starting with Stalin, who is the leader of an unlimited autocracy with power as absolute as that of Ivan the Terrible or Peter the Great, we are struck at once by his isolation both from Russia and the rest of the world. Only on rare occasions is he seen outside the Kremlin. During my stay in Russia I saw him twice at parades when he stood on Lenin's Tomb beneath the Kremlin walls, and once at the theater on the occasion of Churchill's visit. None of us in the foreign delegations knew exactly where or with whom he lived—presumably he has living quarters somewhere within the Kremlin. He has a *dacha* that lies hidden behind a high fence on the outskirts of Moscow, but I know of no one who has seen him going to or from it. He has been in power for twenty-two years, and during that time I doubt if he has ever walked the streets of Moscow, certainly not unattended.

Stalin's only direct contacts with the outside world—at least so far as I have been able to learn—consist of a brief visit to Stockholm in his youth, his conferences with British and American leaders at Teheran, Yalta, and Potsdam, and the interviews he grants to foreigners. For his knowledge of the world beyond Russian borders, and even of Russia beyond the walls of the Kremlin, he must rely on news dispatches and the reports of his subordinates. I think it is important to appreciate the isolation which Stalin's position imposes on him as it emphasizes his dependence on his assistants and advisers. As may be expected in any totalitarian state, there is evidence of considerable jockeying for Stalin's favor and for influence in forming his policies among those closest to him. This accounts for the contradictions that appear repeatedly in Stalin's conduct of foreign relations.

In appearance Stalin is unprepossessing. He is short and colorless. One gets the impression that a physical toughness of early days is giving way to a pallid paunchiness developed by the sedentary habits of later years. He shows the marks of his sixty-seven years in the deep wrinkles of his skin and the gray thinness of what must once have been thick black hair. He betrays little emotion, and his manner is neither pleasant nor unpleasant. I have seen him smile, but I have not heard him laugh. I have seen him frown, and occasionally his words impart quick scathing anger, but I have never seen him appear particularly agitated. He has all the attributes of a good poker player.

As to his character, I should say Stalin was courageous but cautious. He can act quickly and decisively or wait with infinite patience. He can be kind or merciless as the spirit moves him. He has a keen intellect evidenced from time to time by his application of historical lessons to present events and by his understanding of the characteristics and use of weapons. His intelligence is demonstrated by a quick grasp of the essential elements of any situation with which he is confronted. Stalin has the typical politician's psychology. His picture is prominently displayed on all the buildings of Russia on the slightest provocation—the people are not allowed to forget his position of leadership. I have seen him fawn over children before the multitude with the same political acumen that prompts similar public displays by American politicians. At official banquets he pays a special tribute to each and every subordinate leader present. His blind spots result from the narrow confines of ideological fanaticism in which his life has run.

It is generally conceded that the Politburo is the advisory and to some extent the policy-making body which exerts the greatest influence on Stalin. It is composed of thirteen members, almost equally divided among those who are public figures and those who appear only behind the scenes. This is really a Communist party organization rather than a governmental agency. Those best known to the world among this group are Molotov, Mikoyan, Voroshilov, and possibly Zhdanov. Almost without question, one of the thirteen members of the Politburo has already been selected as Stalin's successor but probably no one save Stalin himself—and perhaps the man he has chosen—knows who he may be. Prominent mention is given to Molotov as heir-apparent. Mikoyan is sometimes spoken of, but it is probable that as head of the Commissariat of Foreign Trade he has become too immersed in the economic aspects of government to have developed the political qualifications that the party leadership will require. Others who are suggested are Zhdanov, the party leader in Leningrad, who established a national reputation in conducting the defense of that city, and Marshal Zhukov, who is the most publicized military hero. Whoever it is, we may expect him to continue the policies established by Stalin.

In several places in this narrative I have mentioned the strain that occurred in Soviet-American relations following Yalta. The difficulty stemmed from a difference in the interpretation the United States and the Soviet Union placed on the procedure that should be followed in reconstituting the Polish Government. It was our understanding that Molotov, Sir Archibald Clark-Kerr, and Harriman were to comprise an Allied Committee to consult with the Polish leaders of all factions and to create a Provisional Government in which all parties would be represented and which would carry on until conditions permitted holding elections at which the people could select a government of their own choice. The Russians took the view that the Polish Government already established under Soviet auspices should be expanded to include representatives of other Polish parties. However, Molotov would not consent to interview any Polish representatives other than those acceptable to the Soviet-sponsored Polish Government, which meant in reality those acceptable to the Soviet Union.

The differences which arose over the Polish question were aggravated by our refusal to give way to the Soviet demand that Field Marshal Alexander's negotiations for the surrender of German forces in Italy be broken off. This resulted in an acrimonious exchange of telegrams between President Roosevelt and Stalin which must have made the President question just before his death the wisdom of his beneficent policy toward the Soviet Union.

On top of the Bern situation three incidents occurred as the result of irresponsible acts by young American aviators. In one case, a plane was forced down in Poland because of insufficient fuel to return to Italy. It was undamaged, and the crew was hospitably received at the airfield where they landed. The Russian commandant refueled the plane but told the crew they could not depart until clearance had been obtained from Moscow. The pilot asked for permission for himself and his crew to go to the plane to get some clothes. This was granted, and when they were aboard they slammed the doors, started the engine, and departed. In another case, a Pole friendly to the London regime was dressed in an American uniform and taken from one part of Poland to another on an American plane then on its way out of the country. Needless to say, the N.K.V.D. was waiting to apprehend him when the plane made its last stop on Polish territory. In the third case, a Red Army major, who claimed to have been born in America, was a stowaway on an American plane leaving Poland for Italy. Our authorities in Italy returned him to Russia and almost certain execution as soon as he landed. As a result of these acts of thoughtless individuals, Stalin, at a meeting with Harriman, accused the United States Army Air Forces of indulging in subversive activities in Poland aimed at interference with the operations of the Red Army.

The Russian reaction to our differences over Poland, Alexander's surrender negotiations, and the air incidents referred to above followed a pattern of behavior that we had experienced in the past and which we may confidently expect to experience in the future whenever Stalin's displeasure is incurred. A complete stop was put to all American activities within the Soviet Union. The methods employed in clamping down on us were characteristically Russian.

Word seemed to have been passed to all agencies of the Government to suspend action in all ventures in which Americans were involved. We were hardest hit in connection with the evacuation of prisoners of war. I have described elsewhere how we were denied the right, granted to us under the Yalta agreement, to meet our prisoners close to the point of their release, and how we felt the effects of Soviet displeasure at our air base in Poltava.

The blackout on Americans extended elsewhere. We had been promised that we would be permitted to study the German submarine experimental station at Gdynia as soon as it was captured. We were not allowed to do so on the grounds that the city was unsafe until it had been cleared of mines. We were promised air bases at Budapest, but after permitting one reconnaissance trip by General Hill the Russians refused to issue the necessary instructions to implement the plan. The American group that was to be allowed to survey the Amur River valley was delayed at Fairbanks for twenty-one days before we gave up in disgust. The Civil Air Administration refused to continue discussions concerning the establishment of a connecting air route between the United States and the Soviet Union.

On the political side the situation was perhaps even worse. The importance of the United Nations Conference was depreciated by Molotov's refusal to appear at San Francisco. It took President Roosevelt's death and prompt action by Averell Harriman to induce Stalin finally to allow Molotov to go. Settlement of the Polish problem went by default because of Molotov's refusal to act except on his own terms. Equipment from the Rumanian oil fields, some of it American owned, was transported to Russia, thus cutting off a prospective increase in the Allied oil supply and losing an opportunity to save shipping space by getting Rumanian oil into production quickly.

In only one field were our relations at all amicable. That was in connection with the delivery of American supplies to Russia. Even here the American task was not made easier by any marked degree of Soviet co-operation. For example, we could have effected a considerable saving of American shipping by prompt use of Black Sea ports as soon as it was safe to do so. Instead, there was a delay of several months in clearing mine fields and rehabilitating ports. We were refused the privilege of having an American representative at Constanţa in Rumania, one of the ports of call for our ships.

From the situation that existed in the spring of 1945 it seems that certain definite conclusions stand out as irrefutable. First, we may expect prompt reprisals whenever we incur Soviet displeasure by refusing to play the game exactly in accordance with their rules. Second, we can expect reprisals to extend to all activities in which contact with the Soviet Union is involved regardless of the remoteness of such activities from the field in which the original difference of opinion occurred. Third, Soviet reprisals will be resorted to even though they adversely affect the immediate interests of the Soviet Union.

Throughout my stay in Moscow I was constantly impressed by evidence that Soviet leaders were determined to defeat any joint enterprise that involved close contact with foreigners. There were probably several reasons for this. The foremost was suspicion of foreign motives. In view of the historical background of Russian experience with foreigners, it was the most understandable reason. In Russian eyes, the war with Germany and Japan was only the first phase in the ultimate struggle between Communism and Capitalism. The long-range objectives of the Communist leaders were clear, and it was logical to them to take for granted that Capitalist leaders had equal vision. They suspected that Allied probing for closer contacts with Russia was for the purpose of obtaining intelligence that would be useful in the struggle between ideologies that would eventually come.

Another reason for Russian aloofness, in my opinion, was her desire to achieve a complete Russian victory in her own theater of operations. Allied participation in any degree would dilute a Russian victory by just that much. In addition, Russia's postwar prestige would be weakened in the eyes of those countries she hoped to dominate by threat rather than use of strength. Soviet leaders were determined to have a Russian victory that was untainted by Allied participation on Russia's battlefield. It was to be a victory that could be held up before the world as evidence of the might of the Red Army—it was to be decorated with no other banners. True, she would accept munitions from her allies, but this only emphasized their weakness in having to call on Russia to fight with weapons the allies could not man themselves. This is the type of dissembling argument that has reached perfection in Russia through force of circumstance.

Finally, it seems obvious to me that Russia remained aloof from her allies for fear of contaminating her own people by contact with the representatives of effete capitalism. Poltava offered an example of what could happen. When the Americans came, they brought with them refinements of maintenance equipment about which the Red Air Force had not even dreamed. They paraded their shiny monstrous refueling trucks, their snow plows, their fire-fighting apparatus, and their wreckage disposal trucks. In the infirmary were surgical instruments, sterilizing machines, dental chairs, and other equipment on a scale hitherto unknown in Russia. Then there was the American soldier with his chocolate bars, cigarettes, and other attractions for the Russian girls which lured them away from their own men. This experience made it seem certain that contacts with foreigners could only sow the seed of discontent which would weaken the cohesiveness of the Soviet nation during the war and in the future.

Whatever the reasons, the fact that Russia desired, insofar as possible, to play a lone hand was proved by undeniable evidence. In her darkest days she refused to allow a group of Allied bombers to base in the Caucasus in order to assist her at Stalingrad. Our well-meant voluntary efforts to support her advance in the Balkans with our Air Force operating from Italy brought forth protests rather than gratitude. No single American was allowed to enter the Soviet Union without pressure from the Ambassador or me, and then a visa was granted only after an exhaustive study of the background of the individual involved. Under these circumstances it was clear that nothing much could come of a partnership in which one of the principals was not only reluctant, but proficient in sabotaging its effectiveness.

There has been considerable discussion among United States authorities and in the editorial pages of the American press as to the advisability of dealing with Russia on a quid pro quo basis. From my experience, it is the only basis upon which we can establish reasonably good relations with present Soviet leadership. However, such a policy must be intelligently applied. It would be unwise, for example, for the United States to refuse a reasonable request made by the Soviet Government for the sole reason that the Russians had previously refused a reasonable but unrelated request made by us. Such procedure would soon develop a competition of discourtesy in which our chances of winning would be nil. Far better to adopt a positive attitude and make concessions to the Soviet leaders provided that they agree at the same time to make related concessions to us. In short, a quid pro quo policy should be adopted for reaching agreement rather than as a means of retaliation.

There are several reasons for advocating this policy. It was my experience that Soviet officials are intelligent and shrewd traders. They do not permit sentiment to play a part in negotiations in which the interests of the Soviet Union are involved. There is no such thing as banking good will in Russia. Each proposition is negotiated on its merits without regard to past favors.

Unfortunately in the early part of the war the United States was in a position where it had to meet all Soviet demands without question in order to keep Russia in the war. It might have been expected that our attitude of helpfulness and generosity would arouse a feeling of friendliness or gratitude on the part of the Soviet authorities which would influence them favorably toward the United States in subsequent negotiations. On the contrary, American generosity was taken as a sign of weakness, and the Soviet leaders became increasingly overbearing and demanding. They persisted in this attitude long after the urgent need for American aid ceased to exist. We continued our appeasement policy long after it was necessary to do so. Whenever we did take a firm stand during the war, our relations took a turn for the better. I believe it can be said with some degree of certainty that Soviet officials are much happier, more amenable, and less suspicious when an adversary drives a hard bargain than when he succumbs easily to Soviet demands.

An ideal opportunity for applying the quid pro quo policy arose during the war when our inspection of the German submarine experimental station at Gdynia, promised to us at Yalta, fell under the blight of the post-Yalta blackout. This was a perfect chance to force the Soviet hand. We had been running the German submarine blockade with convoys of Russian supplies for four years. In doing so we had lost seventy-seven ships with their crews and cargoes. Yet we were denied access to Gdynia because the Russians were displeased over an entirely unrelated matter. We should have gone to the Soviet leaders and said that we could not justify sending our men, supplies, and ships through submarine-infested waters until we had satisfied ourselves that no stone had been left unturned to insure their maximum safety. Further, that if we were not to be allowed to examine the submarine experimental station, convoys to Russia would cease at once. This would have been a blow that the Soviet leaders could not have taken. They would either have met our demand or they would have been forced to admit that American supplies were no longer urgently needed. I recommended that we take such action, but my recommendation was disapproved. There were still some people in Washington who lived in dire fear of risking Soviet displeasure.

Another instance in which the quid pro quo policy might have been applied was in the case of Rumanian oil. When Rumania was occupied much of the production machinery was shipped to the Soviet Union over the protest of the Western Allies. We should have told the Russians that either the Rumanian oil fields would be restored to maximum production with the least practicable delay or American oil shipments to the Soviet Union would stop.

Still a third case arose when American aircraft were grounded in Russia for a period of over a month. We should simply have grounded Soviet aircraft at Fairbanks, Alaska, until the ban imposed on us was lifted.

I have cited these cases to illustrate what I mean by bargaining on a quid pro quo basis. The important aspect of such a policy is that bargaining be on the basis of reciprocal action in connection with related matters.

Another difficulty I had in my relations with Soviet leaders was in deciding whether or not to approach them on projects that were desirable but not of primary importance to the United States. In this connection our American system of decentralized authority worked to our disadvantage in the Soviet Union. Almost every American agency was anxious to know how its particular problems were being met in Russia. Each one assumed that it had a Russian counterpart with which it might co-operate. Hardly a day passed that I did not receive a request to make some proposal for Soviet co-operation on the most inconsequential matters. One group wished to have representatives with the forward headquarters of units of the Red Army so that prompt investigation could be made of German topographical maps stored in the public buildings of German cities captured by the Red Army. Another agency wished to have representatives on hand to conduct joint studies of over three hundred German industrial sites and experimental stations as soon as they were occupied by the Russians. Such requests were viewed with the utmost suspicion by the Soviet leaders and had no chance of winning their approval. They succeeded only in helping to build up a habit of saying "no" to American requests that carried over to proposals we made that were of real importance. In many instances the Soviet Union had no counterpart to the American agency which submitted the requests, but, if it did, it was idle to have expected that it could co-operate freely with Americans. All foreign contacts are closely scrutinized and carefully directed by the highest Soviet authority. For this reason we should resign ourselves to seeking Soviet co-operation only on the broad aspects of any joint enterprise and refrain from seeking it at all unless the results expected are essential to our interests.

After encountering almost unfailing Soviet opposition to American proposals I recommended to our Chiefs of Staff that we keep the

Soviet military authorities informed of action we intended to take but ask for their comment or concurrence only when the necessity to do so was plainly indicated. This suggestion was motivated by my conviction that Soviet leaders have respect only for strength. The wisdom of this proposed policy had been illustrated time and again. We had very little difficulty in co-ordinating air operations in southern Europe after General Eaker's blunt announcement that effective at such and such time his air force would operate to a bomb line he had selected himself. There was also the case in the Far East when we arbitrarily announced the northern limits of our naval and air operations. Soviet concurrence was not requested; hence it was forthcoming at once. On the other hand, we unfailingly ran into difficulties when we asked for prior Soviet concurrence for some action we proposed to take. Illustrative of this was the difficulty we had in obtaining Soviet approval in the selection of targets for the first shuttle-bombing mission. Another case was when we requested Soviet comment on the negotiations Field Marshal Alexander was carrying on for the surrender of German forces in Italy. I believe there is no question but that Soviet approval of our actions, not requiring concurrent Soviet action, will be given more freely if we proceed to act independently and as we think best without seeking prior agreement.

Much of the difficulty encountered in attempting to collaborate with the Soviet Union stems from differences in basic concepts and methods. If we recognize these differences we shall have some tolerance for the Soviet point of view, but at the same time we are entitled to expect that Soviet leaders will have some tolerance for ours.

In Russia authority is centralized in one man; in America we decentralize to many. The effect of this difference is that agreement can be reached in the first instance only when Stalin is present to make it. In all other cases and in all negotiations below the highest level, Soviet representatives cannot make decisions and are usually afraid to discuss the matter. A proposition being considered by the American and Soviet Governments is seldom explored thoroughly and agreed upon objectively. In no case was I able to meet the Soviet Chief of

Staff, thrash out a problem, and arrive at a solution acceptable to both. The same restrictions apply to our relations with Gromyko in the United Nations and with Molotov in the Council of Foreign Ministers. They can only advocate a predetermined point of view and can never recognize any validity in an adversary's argument. When we meet with any Soviet official we are meeting with a specialized messenger. His freedom of action is only in the method used to support his master's point of view. He can reach no agreement until he has carried our arguments back to his master and has received instructions as to what compromises may be made. This applies not only to basic decisions, but also to the numberless supporting decisions which might be called for in carrying them out. It is a system that is not conducive to close collaboration.

We differ in our beliefs concerning the four freedoms, and each of us is amazed at those of the other. We differ in our interpretation of the meaning of words. We lay stress on the spirit of agreements; the Russians recognize only the written word. These are only some of our basic differences in which both sides are not only sincere but irreconcilable.

Some of our differences with the Russians spring from the language difficulty. Russian is a more precise language than English. In Russian there is more apt to be a word to express each different shade of meaning. In English the same word not only has different meanings, but inflections on words and their relations to other words in the context connote different thoughts. Thus a Russian translation into English often appears blunt and unnecessarily offensive, while an English translation into Russian is likely to result in an interpretation not intended. I recall one case in which a joint Russian-American committee was to be organized which we thought should remain in continuous session. To the Russians this meant that members could not leave the committee room to eat, to sleep, or for any other purpose. After arguing the point with mounting suspicion on both sides for half an hour, it was settled by agreeing that the committee should always be available to meet immediately upon call of the chairman.

Another deterrent to close collaboration is the impossibility of establishing close personal relations with the Soviet officials with whom we deal. In the two years I was in Russia I had close contacts with officials of a great many branches of the Government. I was not invited to the home of any one of them. In self-defense I must hasten to add that my experience in this respect was identical with that of all foreigners. At meetings with officials with whom I had business there was usually a third person present from some other branch of the Government who took copious notes on everything. I remember one such individual who took notes of a risqué story I was attempting to tell after the conclusion of the business of the meeting. I stopped in the middle and asked him if his notes would not ruin my reputation when he turned them in to whoever received them. He was a bit embarrassed and allowed the rest of my story to go unrecorded.

I did succeed in inducing some of my contacts to dine with me. I soon learned that in each case it was necessary for that Soviet official to obtain approval from higher authority before accepting. It was embarrassing to see them squirm for an excuse when I invited them orally, so I usually sent invitations in writing. I frequently asked them to bring their wives with them, but that was apparently expecting too much. I think that those who did dine with me enjoyed themselves while they were there. I made it a point to avoid "shop talk" and did my best to fill them with American whisky in revenge for the vodka I had to consume at official Soviet functions. I definitely gained the impression, however, that my friends much preferred not to be invited to my house, as any association with foreigners subjected them to the risk of becoming suspect among their own people.

The greatest deterrent to full collaboration lies in Soviet distrust of foreigners. I believe that this can be overcome to a limited degree by complete frankness. I was fortunate in being directed by General Marshall to be entirely open in all my dealings with Soviet officials. I can honestly say that not once in my two years in Russia did I tell a Soviet official one thing and mean or intend something else. Because of the support I had from home I was able to make good on every statement or promise that I made. If I did not like something, I made no bones about saying so. I am convinced that this is the best policy to follow. It was adopted by every member of the Mission, and while our success was not great, it was relatively so.

The Soviet leaders pride themselves on living up to their agreements. I really believe that they think they do. However, they are past masters at rationalizing and dissembling, and they have no difficulty whatsoever in concluding that the other party to an agreement has done something which relieves them from their obligations. In addition, their suspicion of foreigners is so inbred that it is inconceivable to them that a foreigner can enter into an agreement in good faith. This in itself is a rational reason for Soviet repudiation of almost any commitment. I can think offhand of ten agreements that were violated in their entirety by the Soviet Government during my stay in Russia, but I am sure that if confronted by charges to that effect, Soviet officialdom would present reasons which they would consider sufficient to justify their action in each case. When Soviet leaders are unable to rationalize sufficiently to void an agreement which they regret, they are particularly adept at creating conditions which make it impossible of fulfillment. Anything can happen in such cases—key officials will get sick, others will be out of town, boats will sink, and so on and so on—with the result that the agreement might just as well not have been made.

In summary, a thumbnail sketch reveals a Soviet leadership sincerely inspired by the urge to spread Communism throughout the world. It is unscrupulous in accomplishing its ideological purpose. It is centered in one man to whom all must bend their wills. By force of circumstance the leader must remain secluded. He can lay out the master plan but must rely on advisers who differ among themselves as to the methods of carrying it out. The enemies of Soviet leadership are the leaders of the capitalist world. Since this is so, every act of the capitalistic leaders must be viewed with suspicion. Until their followers are cleansed of the taint of capitalism, they must be kept from contacting the Russian people, whose thought is being fitted to the Communistic mold. Soviet leadership will meet with an enemy when it is expedient to do so in progressing to the ultimate objective. It will bargain shrewdly; it will bluff at every opportunity; it will stop and wait whenever and wherever the enemy is stronger; its objective is not one to be reached in a day, a year, a generation; attainment will come through patient and unremitting pressure and by taking full advantage of the soft spots in the enemy's armor.

And so, with respect to her leaders, we come to the question "Can we get along with Russia?" My answer is "Yes" despite the gloomy picture I have painted. We can get along with the present Russian leaders if we recognize them for what they are. We can, if we are stronger, smarter, and at least as certain of our objectives as they are of theirs. We must appreciate that we are dealing with individuals who are motivated by realism and not by sentiment. We must be shrewd enough to get value received for concessions we make. We must be certain that our own hands are clean in our relations with Soviet leaders. We must be motivated by principles in which we believe rather than by retaliation against principles which we abhor. Above all, we must abandon the hopes that go with the weakness of appeasement. We are dealing with people who respond only to strength. It may not be a happy relationship, but it can be a workable one. Leadership is a transient thing, and beneath the oppression of the present Soviet regime is a people with whom we shall someday be proud to march into a happier future.

XVIII. The Russian People

M Y ADMIRATION and affection for the Russian people may inspire hopes for the future that cannot be fulfilled. Nevertheless, I believe that in the last analysis they represent the power and strength of the Soviet Union—power and strength that may be temporarily diverted to sinister purposes but which in the long run will be exerted toward the peace and happiness of mankind. Considering the effectiveness with which foreigners are isolated from the people of Russia, it is no doubt presumptuous on my part to attempt to reach conclusions concerning them. However, my position on the sidelines of Russian life may have given me a better perspective in viewing her people than would have been the case in a more intimate association in which it might have been difficult to see the woods because of the trees.

My task would be simplified if I could place the leaders and the people in separate compartments. An attempt to do so could result only in a distorted picture of both. They are inextricably bound together and mutually dependent on each other. Difficult as it is for Americans to understand, I believe it can be said that on the whole the leaders in Russia today have the support, confidence, and acclaim of the people. To us it seems impossible that any people could support a government which denies them the personal freedoms that we have struggled to win and preserve, a government that reaches down into family life and banishes those dearest to them on the slightest suspicion of disloyalty, or a government that regiments their lives down to the most minute detail. But we should remember that the mass of the Russian people have never experienced personal freedom, that a secret police with its arbitrary power has been an accepted part of Russian life for centuries, and that to the people of Russia regimentation has always been normal to existence.

Nothing succeeds like success, and it is difficult for the masses to believe that the present leaders have failed. The doubts that may have been raised through the years by the hardships and sacrifices the people have been forced to endure, or by the purge of those whose doubts became known, have been dispelled by ultimate victory in a war that drew Government and people together in pursuit of a righteous cause. National self-confidence has made its first appearance in Russia. No longer is it felt that failure must attend every Russian undertaking. The people have accepted as fact that Russian achievement in defeating the common enemy far outshone that of the western powers. They have reason to believe that achievement will shine still more brightly and that Russia's position will be universally recognized once her untapped resources have been put to their proper uses. The way was hard and mistakes were made, but much of the past has been forgiven in the bright light of the future. Unfortunately the Russian people are not allowed to see that the pattern being cut by their leaders is much the same as that which was followed in Germany. If they could only know the truth about their German neighbors, they might realize that a nation which is led to dizzy heights by unscrupulous leaders can expect a disastrous fall.

Life within Russia holds greater promise than ever before. The full pay-off is always just around the corner, but the threat of disaster is easily obscured by government propaganda. Though the domestic achievements of Russian leadership may seem to us to be only those which ought to be taken for granted in the modern world, they loom large in the eyes of the Russian people. In the short span of twenty-seven years illiteracy, once prevalent, has almost disappeared; education, once impossible to the average Russian, has now become universal. The capabilities of the individual, once suppressed, are now nurtured and developed primarily for the good of the state but incidentally to the benefit of the individual. Culture and the arts, once reserved for the few, are now enjoyed by the many. Despite regimentation the individual is made to feel that he is a contributing member of society—a feeling that adds purpose and happiness to life. Except for the ban that has now been partially lifted on religion, there has been a marked increase in the intellectual if not in the material advantages of Russian life. Even material advantages have been increased somewhat and with fair consistency, however gradual. The smallest rise in living standards, such as that represented by a few additional grams of bread, has meant more to the Russian people than refrigerators, television, or frequency modulation would mean to us. The suffering endured by the people in making these slight advantages possible has no doubt made them more appreciative. These are all additional reasons for the confidence the people give to their leaders. Confidence will continue only so long as the Government can successfully keep the people in ignorance of the way the rest of the world lives.

When I first went to Russia I had a language teacher, a woman then thirty-five years of age. She lived in a dingy, unheated single room with her bedridden mother. There was scarcely enough to eat for either of them. She was charming and well educated—a woman of culture—and I confess I was more interested in learning her background and something of her outlook on life than I was in the language she was trying to teach me. Her story came out in snatches and somewhat reluctantly. She was born eleven years before the revolution, of a family that must have been one of considerable wealth. Her perfect English was learned from an English governess, her French from a French governess. She spoke of her grandmother's estate with its tremendous house, horses, and cattle. Her breeding and background were plainly evident in her dignity, her carriage, her speech, the care of her hands, and the well-dressed effect she achieved with her limited wardrobe.

I frequently went to the theater because I thought the perfect diction of the actors would help me get an ear for the language. I asked my teacher to go with me one night to see a play called *Kremlin*

Chimes. Like all Russian drama in a modern setting, this play was obviously a medium of propaganda designed to make the people content with their lot. The theme was so obvious that a knowledge of the language was not required to understand it. The actors were made up to resemble the characters they portrayed, and the central figures were Lenin and Stalin. The story concerned an outstanding engineer who had abandoned his profession rather than make his talents available to the Bolshevik regime. In one scene the secret police came to the engineer's house late at night, and, to the despair of his family, he was taken away from his home. Instead of being taken to Siberia he was brought before Lenin, succumbed to his charm, became a party member, worked at his profession, and everyone was happy ever after.

Frequently I would look at my teacher, and whenever I did she was completely absorbed in the play, which she had already seen seven times. When the N.K.V.D. came for the engineer she wept at the scene and told me that it was a very real portrayal of what had happened in so many Russian homes. However, there was reverence in her eyes whenever Lenin or Stalin appeared on the stage. From the way she looked at them and from what she said, it was apparent that she was firmly convinced that despite the injustices and suffering, the end result of the revolution had been the greatest good for the greatest number. Her attitude was amazing in view of the background of her early life which she still vividly remembered, and in view of her present circumstances in comparison to what they might have been. She felt she was participating in a great experiment and seemed to have no regrets.

I realize that it is easy to exonerate a people from the sins of its leaders. We made that mistake with the German people after World War I, and there are those who would repeat the same mistake today. There is a considerable difference, however, between the Germans and the Russians. The Germans have enjoyed centuries of literacy and culture, whereas the mass of the Russian people have become literate only in the last generation or two. The Germans had liberty and freedom within their grasp but voluntarily stood by when losing them. The Russians have never known freedom. Some thought they were winning it in the revolution, only to emerge with a leadership at least as ruthless as any they had had before. Thousands upon thousands of Russians have paid with their lives for opposition to the present regime. It should be remembered also that there was a long period in which the German people could plot their own course unhampered by a secret police or government propaganda. The Russian people have never been free from either. These are factors which should be considered before holding the Russian people responsible for the acts of their leaders.

Yet the strength of Russia is in the mass of her people. This is the force that Soviet leadership must control if it is to continue on the course which it has laid out for itself. The impression I gained of the characteristics of the people leads me to believe that they will surrender much of their freedom but never freedom of thought, that they will remain docile to a point but if sufficiently provoked will fight and die for their ideals, and that on the whole they are intensely nationalistic in their devotion to Mother Russia.

What, then, are the ingredients we may expect to find in the composite Russian character?

I saw a people's war in Russia which through force of necessity more nearly approached a total effort than was the case in the western democracies. Every man, woman, and child contributed to the limit of his or her capabilities. Because of the lesser degree of industrialization which exists in Russia, great reliance was placed on manpower. Even the sick, the very old, and the very young contributed by enduring hunger and cold in order that able-bodied workers could be sustained. Wherever one turned, the essential tasks were being performed by manpower that could have been conserved by machines had the machines been available. In the Stormovik factory was a production line made up of single operation machines; we would have combined many operations in one machine. In the field, bridges were reconstructed with timber cut from the forest and carried by hand;

we would have used prefabricated steel. Supplies of all sorts were man-handled; we would have had cranes and hoists. The waste of man-power was enormous viewed by our standards, but backs were bent and the job was done. Women carried on the work of the collective farms, drove trucks, repaired wire lines, laid rails, and even held combat assignments in the Army. Everyone had the barest minimum of food and shelter, and those who received more because of the requirements of their work tightened their belts and shared with loved ones whose allowances were less. It was a bedrock total effort under the most severe circumstances—after seeing it, I can never be convinced that the Russian people are unwilling to work.

Except in a very few cases, those with whom I came in contact religiously abstained from discussing government or politics, and yet as a whole I think the people are politically minded. Government exerts too great an influence to allow the individual to remain indifferent. It is probable that these subjects are discussed only in the greatest confidence and secrecy among Russians themselves, yet there is outward evidence that a public opinion exists. It would not be surprising if the one-sided political propaganda of Russia is evaluated and accepted or rejected with more thought on the part of the Russian people than the pro and con presentation of political subjects receives from the American people. When government is the master, it is much more likely to inspire interest than when it is the servant—it is also likely to be viewed with more skepticism. I think that those in control of the propaganda machinery of the Soviet Union underestimate the intelligence of the people. On all the busy street corners of Moscow were outlets from a public address system which harangued the passers-by throughout the day on the progress of the war and with political propaganda. It was surprising how few would stop to listen. The press never presents two sides of a question whether it is a domestic or an international issue. Only the party line is expressed, and as a rule it is supported by reasons that are so fantastic as to cause doubt rather than conviction. I doubt that the people are as gullible as they are believed to be. Nor do I think that they can take the quick and sudden reversals of policy that characterize government propaganda. It is illogical that America can be a friend today, an enemy tomorrow, and a friend the day after. Many of the blasts that appear in *Pravda* and *Izvestia* are designed for foreign consumption, but they must cause a slight lift of the eyebrows at home. Evidence that at times there are thoughts not in accordance with those which the Government seeks to instill came out in the popular apathy to the Japanese war, in the enthusiastic reception accorded Eisenhower during his unpublicized visit, and in the wholehearted recognition of the part America played in the war as evidenced by the mass demonstration in front of the American Embassy on V-E day.

The Kremlin has already given ground in its fight to mold the character of the people. It has abandoned its effort to disinherit them from the spiritual values handed down by their forefathers. The Orthodox Church has returned from exile, and even the generation bombarded from its youth with anti-religious propaganda is unconcerned by the sight of its elders filling the temples and permits its own children to be baptized. After years of suppression Leo Tolstoy has emerged from the past as the most widely read Russian author. In the theater, propaganda themes have somewhat given way to the revival of such classics as *The Three Sisters*, *The Cherry Orchard*, and *Anna Karenina*. Certainly these are victories of a silent but forceful public opinion.

On the lighter side the Russian people have a tremendous capacity for pleasure and enjoyment. Their tastes are simple and easily satisfied. Formal entertainment centers in the ballet, in the theater, and to a limited extent in sports. Even more enjoyment is derived from local talent. The presence of an accordion or balalaika is sufficient to provide hours of hilarious fun. The strains of these instruments induce mass singing of old Russian songs or set the tempo for strenuous Russian dances. With the Russians, old songs and old dances are always best—new ones must stand the test of time before they are universally accepted. It is this characteristic in so many phases of Russian social life that makes relaxation enjoyable and complete.

The ballet, for example, will seldom introduce more than one new performance in a single season. There are certain ones that are repeated year after year. These include *Swan Lake*, *The Nutcracker Suite*, *Don Quixote*, and *Giselle*. The Russians argue the merits of their ballet favorites as we do those of our baseball players. Each prominent ballerina has her loyal supporters who can present endless arguments in support of her supremacy. Ballet enthusiasts can detect differences in performance of the same ballet that will throw them either into raptures or despair.

The drama is much the same. Seldom does a new play appear, and it must be something extraordinary to survive. If it does survive, it may go on forever. I was told for example that *The Three Sisters* has been played once a week since 1896. The pleasure which the people derive from repeated attendance lies in the search for perfection of performance. They much prefer this to the quest for something new.

In no case does the desire for pleasure require the artificial stimulus of novelty for its fulfillment. It is completely satisfied through media that have been handed down for generations. This is perhaps less exhilarating but certainly more relaxing and allows more time for dreams.

I was amazed at the craving for culture and knowledge which seems to grip all the people. They appear to need something more than the technical education and specialization for industry or agriculture that is provided by the state. Every third person I met was studying English, and the gift of an American novel or periodical won undying gratitude. During the time I was there we were allowed to publish a magazine in the Russian language known as *America*. The number of copies was limited, but each one was read by hundreds. A copy will bring its owner a huge price in rubles.

Even the manners of foreigners are studied and copied closely. I remember having some Russians to dinner one night. Everything I did was repeated after me. I soon became the self-conscious principal in a game of follow the leader. When I selected a spoon, they took the same one; when I broke a piece of bread, they did likewise. The game broke up when a topic of conversation attracted more interest than the matter of etiquette and one of my guests leaped from his chair, reached across the table, and speared a piece of bread with his fork. I was glad when they gave up following my lead because I am no Emily Post myself.

It was not necessary for me to go farther than my own apartment in Russia to discover that the people as a whole have many lovable traits of character. Within the apartment were Proskovia, Ganya, and Naum—my cook, maid, and chauffeur—while from the window I could see the ebb and flow of Russian life passing in the busy street below.

Proskovia was old, a *babushka* or grandmother, and she was treated by the others with the tolerance and respect which old age commands. Her life had narrowed down to her kitchen, the church, and ministering to the needs of the small group around her. In the latter respect Spalding and I stood first and Ganya and Naum a close second. She was something of a dictator herself, and we seldom dared to cross her. If I failed to eat enough I did not fail to hear about it. She was on hand to see that I was warmly bundled up whenever I went outdoors. Urgent messages would come from Washington at all hours of the night, but Proskovia would fight like a mother hen to prevent the duty officer from wakening me to deliver them. Like most Russians I met, she was reticent about her past. She had been born in Tiflis, had spent the greater part of her life in Leningrad, and had finally come to Moscow. I should say that she was one of the millions who went along with the tide, interested only in her immediate family and adjusting herself philosophically to its changing fortunes. At the time of which I write we were her family, and her only interest was in our welfare.

Ganya, the maid, lived a double life. From eight in the morning until eight at night she worked for Spalding and me. At night and on Sunday she had perhaps a harder job in caring for her own family. Her husband had gone to the front at the beginning of the war and that was the last she had heard of him. His silence led her to believe that he had been killed, but she could not be sure. This situation was a usual one in wartime Russia, where the absence of administrative paper work precluded the carefully prepared casualty lists and notifications to the next of kin to which we pay so much attention. She had no congressman to whom she could go for aid when the Army's administrative machinery broke down. Ganya's contribution to the war was to refrain from bothering the authorities; she did not seek to learn the fate of her husband and carried on cheerfully day and night in order to provide for her daughter and her mother. She was the exact opposite of Proskovia in many ways. Ganya was young and Proskovia old; Ganya was neat and orderly, Proskovia a perfectionist in disorder; Ganya patient and serene, Proskovia irritable and moody. However, one complemented the other and they made a harmonious team. Neither of them would ask favors for herself but only for the other.

Naum, the chauffeur, was a lovable harum-scarum type. He had a wife to whom I suspect he was none too faithful. He had a myriad of minor faults but also a charm which it was impossible to resist. He was available day and night, but the car was frequently broken down. Naum was confident he could fix anything, but his attempts to do so only aggravated the trouble. Withal he was intensely willing and loyal. The night before I left he found his way to the kitchen and the source of the punch at a farewell party that was given for me. When I came out I found him in tears over my departure from Russia, but he wrecked the car on the way home. There was never a dull moment riding with him. I have mentioned these people before, and I mention them again because I believe that while they were three entirely different personalities, together they were representative of the mass of Russians not actively interested in politics or the party.

Looking from my window, I was impressed by the difference between the outward appearance of the people and that of those one would see on the streets of America. I was even more impressed, however, by the similarity between what might be described as the composite character of the people in Russia and America. In a material sense the difference was marked. There were no new clothes and, especially in winter, people had the appearance of drab shabbiness. Women had no cosmetics to make them more attractive. There was a dull monotony in the appearance of all as compared with the contrasts that stand out in an American crowd.

On the other hand, there was the same joy in meeting friends, the same good-natured humor, the same devotion and care for children and the aged, the same pairing off of the young, and the same courtesies and respect for the rights and comforts of one another. Put in American clothes and in an American setting, the Russian people could not be distinguished from our own.

The Soviet Union, exclusive of the countries which have come under its control as a result of the war, has a population of from one hundred and seventy-five to two hundred million people. Of these only about six million are members of the Communist party. Party membership affords increased opportunity, but it can hardly be said to promise security. It is almost impossible for the individual who is not a party member to reach a high position in Soviet life unless he is endowed with some particular talent as an accident of birth. Artists, actors, dancers, and musicians can remain aloof and still attain a measure of success. However, their activities are subject to the direction of the state and are invariably utilized to further the aims of the party.

The outstanding painter in the Soviet Union is Gerasimov. He was anxious to make a group picture of the delegates to the Moscow Conference and had all their photographs from which he could copy except mine. He therefore wanted me to come to his studio for a sitting so that he could complete the work. I postponed the ordeal for nearly two years, but shortly before I left the country I agreed to go.

I had great difficulty finding Gerasimov's house. It was a dilapidated little cottage far out in the country. His studio was a high-ceilinged room in the front half of the building. Living quarters for himself and his family were in the other half. The light was fair but came in only through the front windows, which gave him little choice in arranging lights and shadows. The room had the appearance of an unfinished garret. It was littered with paintings which must have represented a lifetime of work—some of them were hung but most were stacked three and four deep against the walls and on the floor. The workshop of the outstanding Soviet artist had little resemblance to studios as we know them in America.

Gerasimov is a roly-poly little man with a bright, cheerful personality. When I arrived he had me sit down while he lit his pipe and talked for fifteen or twenty minutes. Suddenly he announced that he had an appointment and asked me to return the following week. I had not wanted to go to his studio at all and had no intention of going more than once. When I told him this he accepted my ultimatum calmly and settled back for more smoking and conversation. After this had gone on for another fifteen minutes he jumped up and with feverish activity arranged my pose and his easel and started to work. All the while he kept up a constant chatter, and before I left he had won my affection. I agreed to return for five or six sittings. The completed portrait was to be mine after he had copied my likeness into the group picture that had prompted the whole thing.

Having my portrait done by Gerasimov was an experience I shall never forget. I was posed standing behind a chair, looking off to the left. Unfortunately there was a group picture of Russian women at the bath which I could see by looking off to the right—he corrected me constantly. It was also difficult to keep from watching him. The floor in front of his easel was littered with all sorts of obstacles—rumpled rugs, chairs, pictures, and little tables on which stood bottles of oil and turpentine. Gerasimov was constantly backing away from the portrait into the midst of these obstacles. He would invariably trip or knock something over, but always either good fortune or years of experience enabled him to make miraculous recoveries.

During rest periods Gerasimov and I had long talks. He was eager to hear about America and especially American art. He was violently opposed to modern art and looked on the efforts of futuristic painters with a disdain with which I fully sympathized. This type of art has little chance of making headway in the Soviet Union as long as Gerasimov is the dean of Russian artists and exercises control over what appears in galleries and exhibitions. I could never lead him into any discussion which had the remotest bearing on government or politics. I wanted to purchase the portrait he was doing of me but he would not hear of it. He said the price he would have to charge me in rubles would be fantastic when converted into dollars and in any event there was little he could do with money. Without telling me in so many words, I gathered that though his services were at the command of the Government, he could also work on his own. As a matter of fact, my sittings were interrupted when he was required to go to Budapest to do a portrait of Marshal Tolbukhin. It was quite evident that Gerasimov was not inspired by the profit motive. His reward came with the power he exerted over Russian art because of his recognized position of leadership, from the acclaim his work received from the people, and the pleasure and satisfaction he had in his work. Incidentally, I have never received the promised portrait.

The question of whether or not to aspire to party membership must be a difficult one for the average Soviet citizen. If he is at all ambitious, it offers the only chance of having his ambitions realized, since leadership in most fields is limited to the members of the party. There must also be the hope in the hearts of some that by joining the party they may some day contribute to improving the lot of the people. Yet there must also be the knowledge that in joining the party they subject themselves to a life of intrigue and jealousies in which their every act is scrutinized by the secret police and its net of informers. They must thereafter support the program of the party leader no matter how revolting it may be. The slightest appearance or suggestion of noncompliance may result in punishment far more drastic than that meted out to non-party members. There must be many well qualified for leadership who prefer to sacrifice their ambitions and opportunities in order to retain the security of mediocrity which is theirs while they are outside the privileged fold. The result is a society in which leadership is confined to about 4 per cent of its members, who, no matter how well intentioned, must live in continuous compromise with their principles. The remainder, which almost constitutes the whole, must forego ambition either because they are unable to meet the requirements of admission to the party or because they prefer the relative security that goes with nonentity and resignation to the scheme of life directed by the party leaders.

From my observation I believe that the average Russian of today is a strong virile individual inured to hardship that has been the heritage of centuries; an individual who is generous, sympathetic, and full of human understanding as the result of generations of common suffering and oppression, and who can get satisfaction from life through the simplest material advantages and the capacity for spiritual fulfillment and lighter pleasures which is within himself. The average Russian is just a youth in his national self-consciousness. He has all the unsophistication and naïveté that goes with youth. He is capable of tremendous accomplishment if the spirit moves him, but he can be a silent and subtle obstructionist when it does not. He is docile to authority, but intensely curious and thoughtful. Intellectually he is growing with the increased opportunity for education. In the war he has just fought he was inspired first by the urge of self-preservation and later by revenge. In his invasion of foreign soil he has had a glimpse of how the rest of the world lives. The comparison has perhaps bred discontent.

So far Soviet leadership has succeeded in bending to its will the good-natured giant that is the average Russian. Whether it can continue to do so time alone will tell. With education, youth will become more sophisticated and inquiring. With continued physical and spiritual growth, he may become too big for chastisement. With added knowledge of the outside world, he may develop an unconquerable urge to copy rather than conquer. He may discover that his masters have feet of clay and insist on restoration of his lost illusions. His basic traits of character are sound and he may refuse to participate in a national program which violates his principles. Herein lies the greatest hope for peace in our time and in the future. Soviet leadership may someday learn the wisdom of Lincoln's philosophy "that you may fool all the people some of the time; you can even fool some of the people all the time; but you can't fool all of the people all the time."

XIX. The Situation

IN MY opinion there can no longer be any doubt that Soviet leadership has always been motivated by the belief that Communism and Capitalism cannot coexist. Nor is there any doubt in my mind that present-day Soviet leaders have determined upon a program pointed toward imposing Communism on those countries under their control and, elsewhere, creating conditions favorable to the triumph of Communism in the war against Capitalism which they consider to be inevitable. Going back to the birth of Soviet ideology, to the doctrine of Karl Marx, we find that one of its basic tenets is the abolition of private ownership. Lenin, the father of the Soviet Union, reiterated this thesis and predicted that a series of conflicts with imperialist states would come to pass before Communism could emerge victorious. Despite the domestic problems that have confronted its leaders since the creation of the Soviet Union, the growth of Moscow-controlled Communist parties throughout the world gives ample evidence that the international objective has never been neglected. World War II has resulted in long strides along the path that Soviet leadership has chosen. The inner concentric ring of capitalistic encirclement has been obliterated. The number of people under Soviet control has nearly doubled, and the security in depth needed by the Soviet Union while it masses its strength for the next phase of its offensive has been provided. Best of all from the Russian point of view, this initial victory was accomplished with the help of those imperialist states which were forced to join the Soviet Union in wiping out another ideology which threatened the western democracies as well as Russia. It was a marriage of expediency, and the Russian leaders gave us little reason to believe otherwise. If the record up until the end of the war was not sufficient to clarify Soviet intentions, certainly all doubt should have been dispelled on February 9, 1946, when Stalin reaffirmed the doctrine of Marx and Lenin and exhorted his people to extraordinary efforts in preparation for the inevitable wars which must be expected so long as the capitalist system exists.

In a sense we are fortunate that the issue is so clearly drawn. Never before in our history have we had so much advance warning of the peril which confronts us. Never has it been more important to take preventive measures to avoid the dangers which lie ahead and to prepare to overcome them if they prove to be unavoidable. This is going to require American leadership which is crystal clear as to our own objectives and which is supported in pursuit of them by a unified public opinion. The pattern of the Soviet program should be carefully studied in order that we may recognize its manifestations. We should examine the factors which favor its success and those which will contribute to its defeat. Most important, we must adopt a program which is designed not to defend our American way of life passively but offensively to counteract constructively those forces which threaten it.

The program of the Soviet leaders is being carried out with equal aggressiveness in two ways: first, by the introduction and compulsory acceptance of Communism in those countries which the Soviet Union controls either by force or by the threat of force; and second, by the infiltration of Communistic ideology into those countries which, for the moment, are beyond the orbit of Soviet control. In between are some nations that are subject both to Soviet threat of force and ideological infiltration. Among these are Greece, Turkey, Iraq, and to some extent China. It is safe to predict that these countries will be subjected to a war of nerves which they will be able to resist only by the firm support of the western democracies.

In Soviet-controlled countries a definite pattern has been set. The people are subjected to the terrors of a secret police and the intellectual starvation of controlled propaganda. Those who are vocal in their

doubts disappear. Economic dependence on Soviet Russia is assured
by the removal or destruction of capital goods claimed by Russians
either as war booty or as reparations. In most of them survival has
been made difficult by the added burden of supporting armies of occupation of far greater strength than the situation demands. Elections
have been held which were farcical in the certainty of their outcome.
In some of these countries, notably Hungary, Rumania, and Bulgaria,
the Soviet program has been carried out with the stamp of American
approval, at least technically so in the eyes of the world. In each of
them our representatives have been members of so-called Allied Control Councils supposed to act collectively in the direction of government. Under the guise of military necessity the Russian members of
these Councils have invariably acted unilaterally without prior consultation with British and American colleagues and seldom have notified
them of actions taken. Our representatives have been totally ineffective so far as the real purpose of their presence is concerned. However, they performed a useful service in voicing American opposition
to the methods which were employed, in indicating to the people of
these countries that the United States had not lost all interest in them
prior to the peace conference, and in learning at first hand the tactics
of Soviet leadership in bending a conquered people to its will.

It is probable that Soviet leaders give even more thought to the infiltration of Communist ideology into countries not subject to the
threat of force than they do to fostering its development in those
countries in which their objectives have been more or less achieved.
For example, there is the rapid rise of the Communist party in France
which carries the threat that Spain, dominating the Strait of Gibraltar,
will be brought into the Russian orbit. A more recent example was
Russia's diplomatic approach to the Argentine, an adroit political maneuver which did nothing to strengthen United States prestige in the
eyes of Latin America. It was a perfect example of how the Soviet
theme changes with expediency. Less than a year ago all those who did
not agree with Soviet policy were denounced as "Fascist beasts." It
might reasonably have been expected that Argentina would be the

last to be forgiven, and this would probably have been so were it not
expedient to drive in every wedge that would serve to destroy western
hemispheric solidarity. The program of infiltration is world-wide. It is
evident throughout Latin America, Canada, the British Empire, Asia,
and not least—the United States.

What are the factors favoring the success of the Soviet program
and what are those against it? First let us consider the former.

I believe that first among these is the certainty of Soviet leaders as
to their objectives and the singleness of purpose with which they can
pursue them. I believe that their strategic aim is world Communism to
be directed from Moscow. The tactics to be employed will vary with
circumstances. If the end can be reached without resort to force, so
much the better; if not, force will be used when it is safe to do so.
Where the adversary is strong the advance will be delayed until a
soft spot is found which will permit a further move forward. Whether
the advance is accomplished by force of arms, by diplomatic maneuvering, or by psychological methods, it will always have the advantage of the unity of command that comes with centralization of
authority in one individual. This means that the struggle will be
directed without the diversionary influence of public opinion or the
necessity of composing conflicting views regarding the tactics to be
employed. Public opinion will be kept in hand through controlled
propaganda, and public support will be enforced by the secret police.

A second factor in favor of the success of the Soviet program is the
relatively strong position in which the Soviet Union found itself upon
conclusion of the war as compared with that of the western democracies. Her immediate war objectives had been attained without waiting
for settlement at the peace table. Russia accomplished her purpose in
the countries contiguous to her western borders. British and American
troops left Iran, thus allowing the Soviet Union a clear field for political and economic if not military penetration of that country. In
the Far East the southern half of Sakhalin Island and the Kuriles had
already reverted to Soviet sovereignty. In addition, Russia had obtained a thirty-year lease on Port Arthur and had arranged for joint

operation with the Chinese of Manchurian railroads. She had attained joint administrative control with the Chinese of the free port of Dairen and recognition of the independence of Communistic Outer Mongolia. The western democracies, on the other hand, emerged from the war with full accomplishment of their primary purpose—the defeat of Germany and Japan—but with no assurance of being able to establish conditions which would promote their long-range and perhaps more important objective of making future wars improbable. Aside from the victory which came with the enemy's capitulation, the western democracies must wait for the final peace treaties for realization of their further objectives. At the time this is written the Paris peace conference has begun and it appears that the Soviet Union will have a strong voice in the proceedings which will be used to obtain further concessions to strengthen its cause. It appears also that Soviet leaders will do everything possible to delay final peace settlements. With Russia's own position already consolidated, it is to her advantage to keep the western democracies in the state of confusion that comes from unsettled world conditions; every hour of delay will be added time for the development of Soviet strength. The effects of this policy are evident in the United States: world trade cannot be resumed; resources must be devoted to the maintenance of unsettled European and Asiatic peoples; labor troubles have reached a new peak; the military policy of the country cannot be settled; and as a result of the unrest which prevails we are letting the greatest opportunity for development and prosperity slip through our fingers. Russia, on the other hand, free from debt, free from labor difficulties, with unlimited natural resources, and industrializing with capital goods obtained as trophies of war, is busily engaged strengthening her position.

Still another factor favoring the success of the Soviet program is the maintenance of a strong military establishment at a time when those of the western democracies are disintegrating. This is a factor of particular importance in Europe, which is after all the current arena of the conflicting ideologies. The most immediate phase of the over-all

Soviet plan is the spread of Communism in Europe. The Red Army is a much more potent argument to those Europeans who may hesitate than the potential but always belated military capabilities of the United States. It may be taken as certain that the Soviet leaders watched with amazement and considerable satisfaction the rapidity with which the United States responded to the cry of "Bring the boys home." Soviet leaders would probably have used the threat of the Red Army with much greater abandon were it not that they know that we still have a strategic air force whereas they have none, that we still have naval superiority despite the number of our ships that are inactive, and, above all, that we alone have the atomic bomb. Nevertheless, Red Army strength will be used as a threat to enforce the Soviet will—witness its use in Iran, its massing on the eastern and western borders of Turkey, and the number of Soviet troops maintained in occupied countries.

Not the least important factor favorable to the Soviet success is in the Communist organization planted throughout the world. It is dangerous because it bores from within. Its membership is drawn from intellectual idealists who are inspired by the Utopian promises of Communist ideology and from the malcontents to be found among the people of any country. The organization is a creature of Moscow and follows the "party line" emanating from there. It is unscrupulous in its attempts to bring about fulfillment of its dreams and is protected in a democratic state by the very freedoms it seeks to destroy. It attempts to divide and conquer and will never lose an opportunity to foster unrest or civil conflict. It creeps insidiously into every walk of life and makes unwitting tools of those whom it can deceive with the sugar-coating of the bitter pill it hopes to administer. It can draw on Moscow for funds needed in its program and for the propaganda used in spreading its influence. It creates a divided public opinion that makes democratic people susceptible to propaganda from Moscow. A good illustration of this was in connection with the Iranian case that assumed such prominence during and after the London meeting of the United Nations. Soviet behavior in Iran had reached a point where the people of the United States were overwhelmingly in favor of taking whatever action was necessary to defeat the Soviet cause. Because of the tension that existed, Eddy Gilmore, the Associated Press correspondent in Moscow, addressed a series of questions to Stalin concerning his attitude toward the United Nations. Stalin established an unheard-of precedent in answering all of Gilmore's questions. He took advantage of the opportunity to reaffirm his belief in the ideals of the United Nations Charter and to assure continued Soviet support. The tension in the United States was relieved overnight. Public opinion, instead of being, say ten to one against the Soviet Union, was equally divided. Yet there was not the slightest tangible evidence of a change in Russia's attitude then or at any time since. It was amazing that Stalin's voice could have such an electric effect on American public opinion and could eliminate it as a deterrent to continuing a policy naturally abhorrent to the average American.

Consider now the factors that are working toward the defeat of the Soviet program. To my mind they are far more potent than those working toward its success—so much so that the program is doomed to failure unless the democracies completely close their eyes to its danger and facilitate its fulfillment through appeasement or apathetic indifference.

I believe that foremost among the factors negative to the success of the Soviet program is the basic character of the Russian people. Herein lies the power that is Russia. At the moment it is repressed and carefully controlled. However, for fulfillment of the world-wide program envisaged by Soviet leadership this power must be unleashed. When it is, its explosive force may not follow the expected lines; for I personally believe that the elemental traits of Russian character are not compatible with the aims and methods of present Soviet leaders.

In the early conversational or diplomatic phases of the Soviet expansion program the people will remain docile. They will bend their efforts to strengthening the Soviet Union internally under the inspiration of their love for Mother Russia. They will be indifferent to the international activities of their leaders because of the remote bearing which they have on the daily struggle for existence or because of the propaganda to which they are subjected. However, as expansion continues it will require the full moral as well as physical support of the Russian people. The moral force within the people will then no longer be susceptible to suppression. Long before this comes to pass the masses will have become more sophisticated and inquiring; they will have passed beyond the iron curtain which hides the outside world; the fallacies of Soviet propaganda will have been exposed. It may well be that the people will then demand and install a leadership more compatible with their own basic moral concepts.

Another factor which will work against the Soviet cause is the enormousness of the task of building up the physical strength needed for its fulfillment. In this respect I believe that the democracies of the world have let their attitudes and actions be influenced by a gross overestimation of the Soviet Union's present and potential strength.

It is true that Russia has almost unlimited natural resources, but industrially she is an infant. Even her natural resources are limited in their importance by a lack of communications which renders them inaccessible. She has begun an industrialization program which so far is restricted and specialized. Her industry is dependent on foreign machine tools, and unless assisted by foreign technical advice it is stumbling and inefficient. My experience and observations convince me that the Russian people simply do not have industrial "know how" comparable to ours and that they will not attain it until it becomes inbred through several generations of industrial life. I base my conclusions on my observations of the tire plant they attempted to construct in Moscow, on the oil refineries they tried to build in several localities while I was in Russia, on the reports of our engineers regarding the maintenance of American equipment, on the visits I made to their factories, and on the writings of foreigners and Russians alike who have worked in Soviet industry.

Foremost is the difficulty the Soviet leaders will have in establishing a heavy industry. Even though Russia can accomplish this she will then be confronted with the necessity of creating specialized industries. None should be able to appreciate the magnitude of the task of creating naval power better than the American people. In this respect, Russia must start from scratch. A strategic air force calls for far greater industrial effort than is evident in the few aircraft that may comprise it at any one time. It requires an industry in which production can scarcely keep pace with the rate of obsolescence. This is another field in which Russia has barely started. The creation of modern naval and air forces calls for subsidiary industries in the fields of ordnance, electronics, and communications, to mention only a few.

Then there is the matter of atomic energy. Until the Soviet Union has atomic bombs of her own, she will be restrained from crossing swords with those who have. It is true that her quest for this weapon has been facilitated by the knowledge that it is possible of attainment, but without our help she will not only have to discover the formula but devote the resources, develop the ingenuity, and have the luck to translate it from theory to reality. Our scientists say the Soviet Union can do this, but it will most certainly add to the immensity of her over-all "must" program.

Adding to the problems inherent in industrialization is the necessity for improved communications. Fairly good road and rail nets exist in western Russia, but they were completely neglected during the war. Rail roadbeds hastily repaired for wartime traffic will have to be torn up and relaid to handle the peacetime loads required in an industrialized nation. Motor roads almost without exception require widening, grading, and hard metal surfaces. For security reasons industry will no doubt follow the wartime pattern of centralization east of the Urals, which again will call for the construction of numberless miles of roads and railroads.

I think I have said enough to indicate the size of the task which confronts the Soviet Union, although I have only scratched the surface. It is a task not made easier by the inroads which war casualties made on the cream of Russian manhood or by the drain on manpower that will result from maintaining the military establishment that is contemplated.

I have already indicated the possibility that the Soviet program may be defeated by a moral awakening of the Russian people. It may be defeated even sooner by revolt against more material abuses which the people are forced to endure. In attempting to give reality to Soviet strength, which so far is only potential, the burden will fall on the masses. They have now lived for nearly thirty years on the barest minimum required to sustain life. Their sacrifices have been made bearable by promises which must by now be somewhat threadbare. Five-year plan succeeded five-year plan, and just as the promised land appeared in sight greater sacrifices had to be endured because of the war. Now the propagandists have substituted the western democracies for Germany, Italy, and Japan, spreading the fear of capitalist encirclement in order to make the people amenable to continued and indefinitely prolonged sacrifice and suffering. The indignity of this is made more acute by the knowledge, certain to be spread by returning soldiers, that the lowliest of their conquered enemies enjoyed living standards far better than those enjoyed by the rank and file of the Russian people. The discontent thus engendered may not result in open revolt, but it cannot help but have a dampening effect on the inspiration required for superhuman effort on an empty stomach. The demand for improved living standards will be manifested by a decrease in human output, and Soviet leadership may of necessity be diverted from its primary purpose by requirements at home. Only those who have lived and traveled in Russia can appreciate what the cost would be to bring the Russian living standards up to what Americans would consider an irreducible minimum.

Still another factor working against the success of the Soviet program is the organization through which it is administered. Centralized authority has its drawbacks as well as its advantages. This is especially so when subordinates are answerable with their lives for their mistakes. Nowhere is individual initiative and willingness to assume responsibility more necessary than in the forward areas of an expansion program. Representatives on the spot are apt to resort to the mediocrity of safety and refer all problems that are questionable to the supreme authority whom they represent. As expansion progresses such problems will become more varied and complex. They will soon reach proportions far beyond the capabilities of one man or even a small group of men, and the administrative system is almost certain to break down.

Even within Russia the Soviet administrative system results in waste and inefficiency. The watchful eye of the secret police promotes a feeling of personal insecurity which stifles initiative. Industry is hampered by outside interference. Charges of sabotage result from failure to meet the prescribed norms of production or from overburdening and destroying machinery in attempts to meet or exceed them. Continuity of management is lost in the upheaval of political purges, and the full effectiveness of labor is lost by overtaxing its power. The urge to curry favor with those in authority and the fear of punishment induces padded reports of accomplishment and deception in covering mistakes. Immediate results are all that count, so the future suffers from lack of planning and foresight.

Uncertainty as to who will succeed to Stalin's power is another factor which may work toward the defeat of Soviet plans for world domination. Regardless of how well a plan is prepared for the installation of Stalin's successor, its execution will be dependent on the voluntary co-operation of those who control the power to insure its success. Among these will be political, military, and police leaders. Any of them may have secret aspirations which will emerge when Stalin dies and thus inaugurate a period of internal dissension that will indefinitely postpone if not entirely defeat Russia's expansion program.

All the factors I have mentioned thus far as working against the success of the Soviet program of ideological domination are independent of the action the democracies of the world may take themselves to prevent its spread. In the latter respect circumstances force leadership upon the United States, and it is within our power to devise a positive counterprogram which will eliminate the necessity for wishful thinking. With considerably more temerity than is justified I shall outline briefly what I believe our program should be.

It should have as its basis a clearly defined objective in our relations with the Soviet Union which has the united support of the American people. The obstacles to be overcome in reaching our objective must be thoroughly analyzed and an integrated positive plan prepared for overcoming those which can be foreseen. The objective might well be stated succinctly as "maintaining the security of the United States." Attainment of this objective would require a definite plan to prevent anywhere and at any time Soviet action which threatens our security. It would require plans to prevent Soviet action aimed at other democracies whose preservation and well-being contribute to our security. It would require winning the friendship and good will of those nations susceptible to being drawn within the Soviet orbit and withholding assistance to those already there.

In preparing our counterprogram, plans should be worked out in advance regarding the action we should take in meeting a conflict of interests with the Soviet Union in each of the sore spots of the world. We should avoid settlement of such conflicts on an opportunistic basis without regard to the effect which action taken "here" may have later in protecting American interests "there." I believe we can foresee now with considerable accuracy where the Soviet program and our counterprogram may clash. To mention only a few, there are the questions of the future of Germany, control of the Mediterranean, the future of Japan and Korea, American bases in the Pacific, and the control of atomic energy. If the action we plan in connection with these and similar questions is to be effective, it must have the support of American public opinion. This will be forthcoming if the people are authoritatively informed concerning the American interests involved in each case. Planning of this sort represents a colossal task. Passage of time and changing conditions will call for continuous revision. In many respects plans will be obsolete before they are completed and new ones will have to be prepared. However, since the preservation of the democratic way of life is at stake, we should certainly not balk at exerting extraordinary efforts.

We should be motivated at all times by the strongest urge to maintain our position by peaceful means. At the same time, we should be fully prepared to meet force with force if that becomes necessary. As an immediate objective in our counterprogram we should seek to halt Soviet expansion by all means short of war in order to gain time: first, to convince Soviet leadership of the fallacy of its conception that Capitalism and Communism cannot coexist; second, to break through the iron curtain and acquaint the Russian people with the disaster into which they are being led; and third, to become fully prepared in case war is forced upon us.

I doubt if we would meet with any great success in changing the basic lines of Communist policy, but at least we should try. Our counterprogram should provide for such an effort and give full recognition to Soviet interests. It should envisage efforts to compose our differences with the Soviet Union on a fair and equitable basis. While such a program may not change the Soviet point of view, it will certainly muster world opinion in support of ours. Breaking through to the Russian people will be even more difficult, but again it should be tried. Small advances have already been made in this direction. Radio broadcasts beamed to Russia will filter through to some extent; contacts between American and Russian occupational forces are certain to increase Russian knowledge of the American way of life; and American literature which reaches the Soviet Union will be avidly devoured by the people.

The chances of attaining our objective by peaceful means will be enhanced immeasurably if we are prepared to defend our position by force at any point where it is threatened. Nothing induces greater restraint on the part of Soviet leaders than a display of strength by their adversaries. In this connection I believe our military program should be designed to meet the specialized situation which war with Russia would entail. In such a war it seems evident that we should avoid being drawn into a land battle on the continents of Europe and Asia.

This would be the type of battle for which Russia, with her huge Red Army, would be best prepared. I believe we should have naval forces which will guarantee us control of the seas, ground forces both airborne and amphibiously trained that can operate with naval and air support to seize and hold areas from which to base air operations, and that we should concentrate on air power for the delivery of our offensive blows. In the initial stages of such a war the Red Army could occupy any part or all of the Eurasian continent. But such conquest would be empty if its warmaking capacity was being systematically reduced by attack from the air.

Unqualified support of the United Nations Charter offers the best medium for winning our struggle with the Soviet Union without resort to war. The Charter expresses precisely the American people's concept of what our foreign policy should be, and therefore adherence to its principles is certain to have their support. In addition, the provisions of the Charter are so diametrically opposed to the program upon which Soviet leadership has embarked as to make a unified world opinion against the Soviet Union inevitable if her program is pursued. Soviet leaders are not impervious to the adverse effects of world opinion; they are just as anxious to gain their objectives by peaceful means as we are. To do so, Russia must have the friendship of some and at least the respect of others. Continued violation of the principles of the United Nations Charter is certain to result in the loss of both.

Another medium for combating the Soviet program is the economic power of the United States. This power must be used judiciously; it may be the means by which we can convince Soviet leaders that it is possible for our respective ideologies to live peacefully alongside each other. This possibility should be kept in mind and legitimate trade between our two countries should be fostered. Our economic power should be used to strengthen the democratic countries of the world and to win nations to our side that might otherwise fall within the sphere of Soviet influence. We should make certain, above all, that our economic power is not used to strengthen

Russia's ability to wage war against us. We should remember the scrap iron we sent to Japan which she returned to us in the form of bullets.

And so my answer to the question "Can we get along with Russia?" is "Yes." Once the policies of present Soviet leadership are modified, there will be nothing to prevent an enduring friendship between the Soviet Union and the United States which will insure a lasting peace. There is some prospect that their program can be changed; it has already undergone considerable alteration within Russia. Necessity has forced recognition of individual worth, private enterprise is allowed on a small scale, and the military has adopted a caste system which makes ours look socialistic by comparison. Necessity may require a change of Soviet aims in foreign affairs just as it has in domestic affairs. It is our job to make such modification necessary. We can do it if we know our objective, if we make plans to achieve it, and if, in adhering to our program, we are tougher than the Russians could ever be. We have the moral and physical power to stop the Soviet leaders cold, and we should not hesitate to use it. We can check any future aggression if we are alive to the danger that confronts us. If we emulate the ostrich and bury our head in the sand, we shall get the resounding kick from a Russian boot that such an undignified posture invites.

Index

Abadan, 233
Adriatic operations, 41
Aegean operations, 41
Africa, invasion of, 16–17, 143, 144
Aims, Soviet *vs.* British, at Teheran, 43–44
Air bases: emergency, 140–41; Siberian, 228–29, 230, 233, 241, 247, 249, 256; Ukrainian, 83, 110, 114ff., 124, 229, 235, 262
Aircraft; and Russian navigators, 46–47; diplomatic, 53–55; Russian treatment of, 79–81
Air Force, Soviet, 108ff.. 232
Airmen, release of interned, 59ff.
Air rights, Soviet protection of, 55, 71, 114
Air Staff, Soviet, and shuttle bombing, 117–18
Air transport problems, 78–83
Alanbrooke, Lord, 154, 155; at Moscow, 243, 244, 246
Alaskan bases, for Soviet use, 227; *see also* Fairbanks
Alaskan-Siberian air route, 73, 78–79, 231, 233
Aleksinac, 133
Aleutian: air route, 231; bases for Soviet vessels, 227
Alexander, Field Marshal Sir Harold, 162, 163, 164, 165, 166; and German surrender, 292, 293, 300
Allied Committee, on Poland, 292
Allied Control Council, 212, 267, 321
America, 312
Amur River, 252, 253, 254, 259, 262, 263, 266, 294; port facilities, 242
Anderson, Maj. Gen. Fred, 115

Antiaircraft, at Poltava, 122
Antonov, Gen. A. E., 31, 32, 33, 34, 128, 208; and air co-ordination, 129, 139; and communications, 157; and Eisenhower, 214; and German surrender, 164, 165, 168ff.; and intelligence exchange, 272; and invasion support, 150, 151; and Japanese surrender, 280, 281; and Japanese war, 228, 252, 270–71; and joint operations, 259, 265, 266; and junction of forces, 158–59; and Kamchatka survey, 252–53; and liaison, 136–37, 155; and note to Japan, 276; and Siberian bases, 232, 233; and strategic air force, 235; and supplies, 250; and visit to front, 202; and war prisoners, 185, 186, 282–83; and weather data, 76; at Potsdam, 273, 274; letter quoted, 133–34; on U.S.-S.R. *vs.* Japan, 275
Archer, Adm. E. R., 137, 154, 156, 158, 165, 173, 174, 178, 180, 197; at German surrender, 170–71
Argentina, U.S.S.R. and, 321
Army Communications Service, 64, 66
Arnold, Gen. H. H., 74, 75, 78, 129, 228–29, 232, 233, 235, 250, 272, 274; and air force co-ordination, 128–29; and air routes, 82; and Norden bombsight, 236–37; and shuttle bombing, 107, 109, 110; at Potsdam, 271, 272
Ashkhabad, 60, 61, 62
Astakhov, Air Marshal Fedor A., 81
Atkins, George, 101
Atomic bomb, 267, 275, 276, 324, 330; possible Soviet, 102, 327
Attitude toward Japanese war, public, 276–77
Austria, tactical plans for, 158